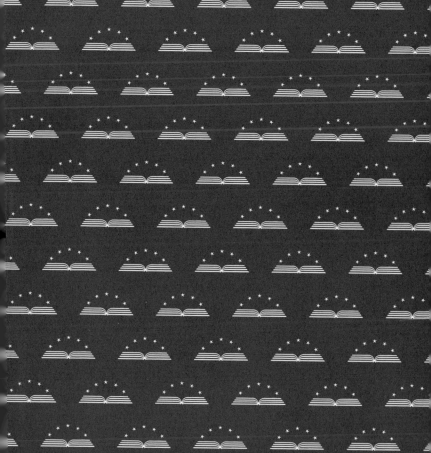

AMBROSE BIERCE

AMBROSE BIERCE

THE DEVIL'S DICTIONARY, TALES, & MEMOIRS

S. T. Joshi, *editor*

THE LIBRARY OF AMERICA

The paper used in this publication meets the
minimum requirements of the American National Standard for
Information Sciences–Permanence of Paper for Printed
Library Materials, ANSI z39.48–1984.

Distributed to the trade in the United States
by Penguin Group (USA) Inc.
and in Canada by Penguin Group Canada Ltd.

Library of Congress Control Number: 2010942020
ISBN 978-1-59853-102-2

———

Second Printing
The Library of America—219

Manufactured in the United States of America

Contents

IN THE MIDST OF LIFE
(TALES OF SOLDIERS AND CIVILIANS)

SOLDIERS

A Horseman in the Sky

I

ONE sunny afternoon in the autumn of the year 1861 a soldier lay in a clump of laurel by the side of a road in western Virginia. He lay at full length upon his stomach, his feet resting upon the toes, his head upon the left forearm. His extended right hand loosely grasped his rifle. But for the somewhat methodical disposition of his limbs and a slight rhythmic movement of the cartridge-box at the back of his belt he might have been thought to be dead. He was asleep at his post of duty. But if detected he would be dead shortly afterward, death being the just and legal penalty of his crime.

The clump of laurel in which the criminal lay was in the angle of a road which after ascending southward a steep acclivity to that point turned sharply to the west, running along the summit for perhaps one hundred yards. There it turned southward again and went zigzagging downward through the forest. At the salient of that second angle was a large flat rock, jutting out northward, overlooking the deep valley from which the road ascended. The rock capped a high cliff; a stone dropped from its outer edge would have fallen sheer downward one thousand feet to the tops of the pines. The angle where the soldier lay was on another spur of the same cliff. Had he been awake he would have commanded a view, not only of the short arm of the road and the jutting rock, but of the entire profile of the cliff below it. It might well have made him giddy to look.

The country was wooded everywhere except at the bottom of the valley to the northward, where there was a small natural meadow, through which flowed a stream scarcely visible from the valley's rim. This open ground looked hardly larger than an ordinary dooryard, but was really several acres in extent. Its green was more vivid than that of the inclosing forest. Away beyond it rose a line of giant cliffs similar to those upon which we are supposed to stand in our survey of the savage scene,

3

and through which the road had somehow made its climb to the summit. The configuration of the valley, indeed, was such that from this point of observation it seemed entirely shut in, and one could but have wondered how the road which found a way out of it had found a way into it, and whence came and whither went the waters of the stream that parted the meadow more than a thousand feet below.

No country is so wild and difficult but men will make it a theatre of war; concealed in the forest at the bottom of that military rat-trap, in which half a hundred men in possession of the exits might have starved an army to submission, lay five regiments of Federal infantry. They had marched all the previous day and night, and were resting. At nightfall they would take to the road again, climb to the place where their unfaithful sentinel now slept, and descending the other slope of the ridge fall upon a camp of the enemy at about midnight. Their hope was to surprise it, for the road led to the rear of it. In case of failure, their position would be perilous in the extreme; and fail they surely would should accident or vigilance apprise the enemy of the movement.

II

The sleeping sentinel in the clump of laurel was a young Virginian named Carter Druse. He was the son of wealthy parents, an only child, and had known such ease and cultivation and high living as wealth and taste were able to command in the mountain country of western Virginia. His home was but a few miles from where he now lay. One morning he had risen from the breakfast-table and said, quietly but gravely: "Father, a Union regiment has arrived at Grafton. I am going to join it."

The father lifted his leonine head, looked at the son a moment in silence, and replied: "Well, go, sir, and whatever may occur, do what you conceive to be your duty. Virginia, to which you are a traitor, must get on without you. Should we both live to the end of the war, we will speak further of the matter. Your mother, as the physician has informed you, is in a most critical condition; at the best, she cannot be with us longer than a few weeks, but that time is precious. It would be better not to disturb her."

So Carter Druse, bowing reverently to his father, who returned the salute with a stately courtesy that masked a breaking heart, left the home of his childhood to go soldiering. By conscience and courage, by deeds of devotion and daring, he soon commended himself to his fellows and his officers; and it was to these qualities and to some knowledge of the country that he owed his selection for his present perilous duty at the extreme outpost. Nevertheless, fatigue had been stronger than resolution, and he had fallen asleep. What good or bad angel came in a dream to rouse him from his state of crime, who shall say? Without a movement, without a sound, in the profound silence and the languor of the late afternoon, some invisible messenger of fate touched with unsealing finger the eyes of his consciousness—whispered into the ear of his spirit the mysterious awakening word which no human lips ever have spoken, no human memory ever has recalled. He quietly raised his forehead from his arm and looked between the masking stems of the laurels, instinctively closing his right hand about the stock of his rifle.

His first feeling was a keen artistic delight. On a colossal pedestal, the cliff,—motionless at the extreme edge of the capping rock and sharply outlined against the sky,—was an equestrian statue of impressive dignity. The figure of the man sat the figure of the horse, straight and soldierly, but with the repose of a Grecian god carved in the marble which limits the suggestion of activity. The gray costume harmonized with its aërial background; the metal of accoutrement and caparison was softened and subdued by the shadow; the animal's skin had no points of high light. A carbine strikingly foreshortened lay across the pommel of the saddle, kept in place by the right hand grasping it at the "grip"; the left hand, holding the bridle rein, was invisible. In silhouette against the sky the profile of the horse was cut with the sharpness of a cameo; it looked across the heights of air to the confronting cliffs beyond. The face of the rider, turned slightly away, showed only an outline of temple and beard; he was looking downward to the bottom of the valley. Magnified by its lift against the sky and by the soldier's testifying sense of the formidableness of a near enemy the group appeared of heroic, almost colossal, size.

For an instant Druse had a strange, half-defined feeling that he had slept to the end of the war and was looking upon a noble work of art reared upon that commanding eminence to commemorate the deeds of an heroic past of which he had been an inglorious part. The feeling was dispelled by a slight movement of the group: the horse, without moving its feet, had drawn its body slightly backward from the verge; the man remained immobile as before. Broad awake and keenly alive to the significance of the situation, Druse now brought the butt of his rifle against his cheek by cautiously pushing the barrel forward through the bushes, cocked the piece, and glancing through the sights, covered a vital spot of the horseman's breast. A touch upon the trigger and all would have been well with Carter Druse. At that instant the horseman turned his head and looked in the direction of his concealed foeman—seemed to look into his very face, into his eyes, into his brave, compassionate heart.

Is it then so terrible to kill an enemy in war—an enemy who has surprised a secret vital to the safety of one's self and comrades—an enemy more formidable for his knowledge than all his army for its numbers? Carter Druse grew pale; he shook in every limb, turned faint, and saw the statuesque group before him as black figures, rising, falling, moving unsteadily in arcs of circles in a fiery sky. His hand fell away from his weapon, his head slowly dropped until his face rested on the leaves in which he lay. This courageous gentleman and hardy soldier was near swooning from intensity of emotion.

It was not for long; in another moment his face was raised from earth, his hands resumed their places on the rifle, his forefinger sought the trigger; mind, heart and eyes were clear, conscience and reason sound. He could not hope to capture that enemy; to alarm him would but send him dashing to his camp with his fatal news. The duty of the soldier was plain: the man must be shot dead from ambush—without warning, without a moment's spiritual preparation, with never so much as an unspoken prayer, he must be sent to his account. But no—there is a hope; he may have discovered nothing—perhaps he is but admiring the sublimity of the landscape. If permitted, he may turn and ride carelessly away in the direction whence he came. Surely it will be possible to judge at the instant of his withdrawing whether he knows. It may well be that his fixity of attention—Druse turned his head and looked through the deeps of air downward, as from the surface to the bottom of a translucent sea. He saw creeping across the green meadow a sinuous line of figures of men and horses—some foolish commander was permitting the soldiers of his escort to water their beasts in the open, in plain view from a dozen summits!

Druse withdrew his eyes from the valley and fixed them again upon the group of man and horse in the sky, and again it was through the sights of his rifle. But this time his aim was at the horse. In his memory, as if they were a divine mandate, rang the words of his father at their parting: "Whatever may occur, do what you conceive to be your duty." He was calm now. His teeth were firmly but not rigidly closed; his nerves were as tranquil as a sleeping babe's—not a tremor affected any muscle of his body; his breathing, until suspended in the act of taking aim, was regular and slow. Duty had conquered; the spirit had said to the body: "Peace, be still." He fired.

III

An officer of the Federal force, who in a spirit of adventure or in quest of knowledge, had left the hidden *bivouac* in the valley, and with aimless feet had made his way to the lower edge of a small open space near the foot of the cliff, was considering what he had to gain by pushing his exploration further. At a distance of a quarter-mile before him, but apparently at a stone's throw, rose from its fringe of pines the gigantic face of rock, towering to so great a height above him that it made him giddy to look up to where its edge cut a sharp, rugged line against the sky. It presented a clean, vertical profile against a background of blue sky to a point half the way down, and of distant hills hardly less blue, thence to the tops of the trees at its base. Lifting his eyes to the dizzy altitude of its summit the officer saw an astonishing sight—a man on horseback riding down into the valley through the air!

Straight upright sat the rider, in military fashion, with a firm seat in the saddle, a strong clutch upon the rein to hold his charger from too impetuous a plunge. From his bare head his long hair streamed upward, waving like a plume. His hands were concealed in the cloud of the horse's lifted mane. The animal's body was as level as if every hoof-stroke encountered the resistant earth. Its motions were those of a wild gallop, but even as the officer looked they ceased, with all the legs thrown sharply forward as in the act of alighting from a leap. But this was a flight!

Filled with amazement and terror by this apparition of a horseman in the sky—half believing himself the chosen scribe of some new Apocalypse, the officer was overcome by the intensity of his emotions; his legs failed him and he fell. Almost at the same instant he heard a crashing sound in the trees—a sound that died without an echo—and all was still.

The officer rose to his feet, trembling. The familiar sensation of an abraded shin recalled his dazed faculties. Pulling himself together he ran obliquely away from the cliff to a point distant from its foot; thereabout he expected to find his man; and thereabout he naturally failed. In the fleeting instant of his vision his imagination had been so wrought upon by the apparent grace and ease and intention of the marvelous performance that it did not occur to him that the line of march of aërial cavalry is directly downward, and that he could find the objects of his search at the very foot of the cliff. A half-hour later he returned to camp.

This officer was a wise man; he knew better than to tell an incredible truth. He said nothing of what he had seen. But when the commander asked him if in his scout he had learned anything of advantage to the expedition, he answered:

"Yes, sir; there is no road leading down into this valley from the southward."

The commander, knowing better, smiled.

IV

After firing his shot, Private Carter Druse reloaded his rifle and resumed his watch. Ten minutes had hardly passed when a Federal sergeant crept cautiously to him on hands and knees. Druse neither turned his head nor looked at him, but lay without motion or sign of recognition.

"Did you fire?" the sergeant whispered.

"Yes."

"At what?"

"A horse. It was standing on yonder rock—pretty far out. You see it is no longer there. It went over the cliff."

The man's face was white, but he showed no other sign of emotion. Having answered, he turned away his eyes and said no more. The sergeant did not understand.

"See here, Druse," he said, after a moment's silence, "it's no use making a mystery. I order you to report. Was there anybody on the horse?"

"Yes."

"Well?"

"My father."

The sergeant rose to his feet and walked away. "Good God!" he said.

An Occurrence at Owl Creek Bridge

A MAN stood upon a railroad bridge in northern Alabama, looking down into the swift water twenty feet below. The man's hands were behind his back, the wrists bound with a cord. A rope closely encircled his neck. It was attached to a stout cross-timber above his head and the slack fell to the level of his knees. Some loose boards laid upon the sleepers supporting the metals of the railway supplied a footing for him and his executioners—two private soldiers of the Federal army, directed by a sergeant who in civil life may have been a deputy sheriff. At a short remove upon the same temporary platform was an officer in the uniform of his rank, armed. He was a captain. A sentinel at each end of the bridge stood with his rifle in the position known as "support," that is to say, vertical in front of the left shoulder, the hammer resting on the forearm thrown straight across the chest—a formal and unnatural position, enforcing an erect carriage of the body. It did not appear to be the duty of these two men to know what was occurring at the center of the bridge; they merely blockaded the two ends of the foot planking that traversed it.

Beyond one of the sentinels nobody was in sight; the railroad ran straight away into a forest for a hundred yards, then, curving, was lost to view. Doubtless there was an outpost farther along. The other bank of the stream was open ground—a gentle acclivity topped with a stockade of vertical tree trunks, loopholed for rifles, with a single embrasure through which protruded the muzzle of a brass cannon commanding the bridge. Midway of the slope between the bridge and fort were the spectators—a single company of infantry in line, at "parade rest," the butts of their rifles on the ground, the barrels inclining slightly backward against the right shoulder, the hands crossed upon the stock. A lieutenant stood at the right of the line, the point of his sword upon the ground, his left hand resting upon his right. Excepting the group of four at the center of the bridge, not a man moved. The company faced the bridge, staring stonily, motionless. The sentinels, facing the banks of the stream, might have been statues to adorn the bridge. The captain stood with folded arms, silent, observing the work of his subordinates, but making no sign. Death is a dignitary who when he comes announced is to be received with formal manifestations of respect, even by those most familiar with him. In the code of military etiquette silence and fixity are forms of deference.

The man who was engaged in being hanged was apparently about thirty-five years of age. He was a civilian, if one might judge from his habit, which was that of a planter. His features were good—a straight nose, firm mouth, broad forehead, from which his long, dark hair was combed straight back, falling behind his ears to the collar of his well-fitting frock-coat. He wore a mustache and pointed beard, but no whiskers; his eyes were large and dark gray, and had a kindly expression which one would hardly have expected in one whose neck was in the hemp. Evidently this was no vulgar assassin. The liberal military code makes provision for hanging many kinds of persons, and gentlemen are not excluded.

The preparations being complete, the two private soldiers stepped aside and each drew away the plank upon which he had been standing. The sergeant turned to the captain, saluted and placed himself immediately behind that officer, who in turn moved apart one pace. These movements left the condemned man and the sergeant standing on the two ends of the same plank, which spanned three of the cross-ties of the bridge. The end upon which the civilian stood almost, but not quite, reached a fourth. This plank had been held in place by the weight of the captain; it was now held by that of the sergeant. At a signal from the former the latter would step aside, the plank would tilt and the condemned man go down between two ties. The arrangement commended itself to his judgement as simple and effective. His face had not been covered nor his eyes bandaged. He looked a moment at his "unsteadfast footing," then let his gaze wander to the swirling water of the stream racing madly beneath his feet. A piece of dancing driftwood caught his attention and his eyes followed it down the current. How slowly it appeared to move! What a sluggish stream!

He closed his eyes in order to fix his last thoughts upon his wife and children. The water, touched to gold by the early sun, the brooding mists under the banks at some distance down the stream, the fort, the soldiers, the piece of drift—all had distracted him. And now he became conscious of a new disturbance. Striking through the thought of his dear ones was a sound which he could neither ignore nor understand, a sharp, distinct, metallic percussion like the stroke of a blacksmith's hammer upon the anvil; it had the same ringing quality. He wondered what it was, and whether immeasurably distant or near by—it seemed both. Its recurrence was regular, but as slow as the tolling of a death knell. He awaited each new stroke with impatience and—he knew not why—apprehension. The intervals of silence grew progressively longer; the delays became maddening. With their greater infrequency the sounds increased in strength and sharpness. They hurt his ear like the trust of a knife; he feared he would shriek. What he heard was the ticking of his watch.

He unclosed his eyes and saw again the water below him. "If I could free my hands," he thought, "I might throw off the noose and spring into the stream. By diving I could evade the bullets and, swimming vigorously, reach the bank, take to the woods and get away home. My home, thank God, is as yet outside their lines; my wife and little ones are still beyond the invader's farthest advance."

As these thoughts, which have here to be set down in words, were flashed into the doomed man's brain rather than evolved from it the captain nodded to the sergeant. The sergeant stepped aside.

II

Peyton Fahrquhar was a well-to-do planter, of an old and highly respected Alabama family. Being a slave owner and like other slave owners a politician he was naturally an original secessionist and ardently devoted to the Southern cause. Circumstances of an imperious nature, which it is unnecessary to relate here, had prevented him from taking service with the gallant army which had fought the disastrous campaigns ending with the fall of Corinth, and he chafed under the inglorious restraint, longing for the release of his energies, the larger life of the soldier, the opportunity for distinction. That opportunity, he felt, would come, as it comes to all in war time. Meanwhile he did what he could. No service was too humble for him to perform in the aid of the South, no adventure too perilous for him to undertake if consistent with the character of a civilian who was at heart a soldier, and who in good faith and without too much qualification assented to at least a part of the frankly villainous dictum that all is fair in love and war.

One evening while Fahrquhar and his wife were sitting on a rustic bench near the entrance to his grounds, a gray-clad soldier rode up to the gate and asked for a drink of water. Mrs. Fahrquhar was only too happy to serve him with her own white hands. While she was fetching the water her husband approached the dusty horseman and inquired eagerly for news from the front.

"The Yanks are repairing the railroads," said the man, "and are getting ready for another advance. They have reached the Owl Creek bridge, put it in order and built a stockade on the north bank. The commandant has issued an order, which is posted everywhere, declaring that any civilian caught interfering with the railroad, its bridges, tunnels, or trains will be summarily hanged. I saw the order."

"How far is it to the Owl Creek bridge?" Fahrquhar asked.

"About thirty miles."

"Is there no force on this side the creek?"

"Only a picket post half a mile out, on the railroad, and a single sentinel at this end of the bridge."

"Suppose a man—a civilian and student of hanging—should elude the picket post and perhaps get the better of the sentinel," said Fahrquhar, smiling, "what could he accomplish?"

The soldier reflected. "I was there a month ago," he replied. "I observed that the flood of last winter had lodged a great quantity of driftwood against the wooden pier at this end of the bridge. It is now dry and would burn like tow."

The lady had now brought the water, which the soldier drank. He thanked her ceremoniously, bowed to her husband and rode away. An hour later, after nightfall, he repassed the plantation, going northward in the direction from which he had come. He was a Federal scout.

III

As Peyton Fahrquhar fell straight downward through the bridge he lost consciousness and was as one already dead. From this state he was awakened—ages later, it seemed to him—by the pain of a sharp pressure upon his throat, followed by a sense of suffocation. Keen, poignant agonies seemed to shoot from his neck downward through every fiber of his body and limbs. These pains appeared to flash along well defined lines of ramification and to beat with an inconceivably rapid periodicity. They seemed like streams of pulsating fire heating him to an intolerable temperature. As to his head, he was conscious of nothing but a feeling of fullness—of congestion. These sensations were unaccompanied by thought. The intellectual part of his nature was already effaced; he had power only to feel, and feeling was torment. He was conscious of motion. Encompassed in a luminous cloud, of which he was now merely the fiery heart, without material substance, he swung through unthinkable arcs of oscillation, like a vast pendulum. Then all at once, with terrible suddenness, the light about him shot upward with the noise of a loud plash; a frightful roaring was in his ears, and all was cold and dark. The power of thought was restored; he knew that the rope had broken and he had fallen into the stream. There was no additional strangulation; the noose about his neck was already suffocating him and kept the water from his lungs. To die of hanging at the bottom of a river!—the idea seemed to him ludicrous. He opened his eyes in the darkness and saw above him a gleam of light, but how distant, how inaccessible! He was still sinking, for the light became fainter and fainter until it was a mere glimmer. Then it began to grow and brighten, and he knew that he was rising toward the surface—knew it with reluctance, for he was now very comfortable. "To be hanged and drowned," he thought, "that is not so bad; but I do not wish to be shot. No; I will not be shot; that is not fair."

He was not conscious of an effort, but a sharp pain in his wrist apprised him that he was trying to free his hands. He gave the struggle his attention, as an idler might observe the feat of a juggler, without interest in the outcome. What splendid effort!—what magnificent, what superhuman strength! Ah, that was a fine endeavor! Bravo! The cord fell away; his arms parted and floated upward, the hands dimly seen on each side in the growing light. He watched them with a new interest as first one and then the other pounced upon the noose at his neck. They tore it away and thrust it fiercely aside, its undulations resembling those of a water snake. "Put it back, put it back!" He thought he shouted these words to his hands, for the undoing of the noose had been succeeded by the direst pang that he had yet experienced. His neck ached horribly; his brain was on fire, his heart, which had been fluttering faintly, gave a great leap, trying to force itself out at his mouth. His whole body was racked and wrenched with an insupportable anguish! But his disobedient hands gave no heed to the command. They beat the water vigorously with quick, downward strokes, forcing him to the surface. He felt his head emerge; his eyes were blinded by the sunlight; his chest expanded convulsively, and with a supreme and crowning agony his lungs engulfed a great draught of air, which instantly he expelled in a shriek!

He was now in full possession of his physical senses. They were, indeed, preternaturally keen and alert. Something in the awful disturbance of his organic system had so exalted and refined them that they made record of things never before perceived. He felt the ripples upon his face and heard their separate sounds as they struck. He looked at the forest on the bank of the stream, saw the individual trees, the leaves and the veining of each leaf—he saw the very insects upon them: the locusts, the brilliant-bodied flies, the gray spiders stretching their webs from twig to twig. He noted the prismatic colors in all the dewdrops upon a million blades of grass. The humming of the gnats that danced above the eddies of the stream, the beating of the dragon-flies' wings, the strokes of the water spiders' legs, like oars which had lifted their boat—all these made audible music. A fish slid along beneath his eyes and he heard the rush of its body parting the water.

He had come to the surface facing down the stream; in a moment the visible world seemed to wheel slowly round, himself the pivotal point, and he saw the bridge, the fort, the soldiers upon the bridge, the captain, the sergeant, the two privates, his executioners. They were in silhouette against the blue sky. They shouted and gesticulated, pointing at him. The captain had drawn his pistol, but did not fire; the others were unarmed. Their movements were grotesque and horrible, their forms gigantic.

Suddenly he heard a sharp report and something struck the water smartly within a few inches of his head, spattering his face with spray. He heard a second report, and saw one of the sentinels with his rifle at his shoulder, a light cloud of blue smoke rising from the muzzle. The man in the water saw the eye of the man on the bridge gazing into his own through the sights of the rifle. He observed that it was a gray eye and remembered having read that gray eyes were keenest, and that all famous marksmen had them. Nevertheless, this one had missed.

A counter-swirl had caught Fahrquhar and turned him half round; he was again looking into the forest on the bank opposite the fort. The sound of a clear, high voice in a monotonous singsong now rang out behind him and came across the water with a distinctness that pierced and subdued all other sounds, even the beating of the ripples in his ears. Although no soldier, he had frequented camps enough to know the dread significance of that deliberate, drawling, aspirated chant; the lieutenant on shore was taking a part in the morning's work. How coldly and pitilessly—with what an even, calm intonation, presaging, and enforcing tranquility in the men—with what accurately measured interval fell those cruel words:

"Attention, company! . . . Shoulder arms! . . . Ready! . . . Aim! . . . Fire!"

Fahrquhar dived—dived as deeply as he could. The water roared in his ears like the voice of Niagara, yet he heard the dulled thunder of the volley and, rising again toward the surface, met shining bits of metal, singularly flattened, oscillating slowly downward. Some of them touched him on the face and hands, then fell away, continuing their descent. One lodged between his collar and neck; it was uncomfortably warm and he snatched it out.

As he rose to the surface, gasping for breath, he saw that he had been a long time under water; he was perceptibly farther downstream—nearer to safety. The soldiers had almost finished reloading; the metal ramrods flashed all at once in the sunshine as they were drawn from the barrels, turned in the air, and thrust into their sockets. The two sentinels fired again, independently and ineffectually.

The hunted man saw all this over his shoulder; he was now swimming vigorously with the current. His brain was as energetic as his arms and legs; he thought with the rapidity of lightning.

"The officer," he reasoned, "will not make that martinet's error a second time. It is as easy to dodge a volley as a single shot. He has probably already given the command to fire at will. God help me, I cannot dodge them all!"

An appalling plash within two yards of him was followed by a loud, rushing sound, *diminuendo*, which seemed to travel back through the air to the fort and died in an explosion which stirred the very river to its deeps! A rising sheet of water curved over him, fell down upon him, blinded him, strangled him! The cannon had taken a hand in the game. As he shook his head free from the commotion of the smitten water he heard the deflected shot humming through the air ahead, and in an instant it was cracking and smashing the branches in the forest beyond.

"They will not do that again," he thought; "the next time they will use a charge of grape. I must keep my eye upon the gun; the smoke will apprise me—the report arrives too late; it lags behind the missile. That is a good gun."

Suddenly he felt himself whirled round and round—spinning like a top. The water, the banks, the forests, the now distant bridge, fort and men—all were commingled and blurred. Objects were represented by their colors only; circular horizontal streaks of color—that was all he saw. He had been caught in a vortex and was being whirled on with a velocity of advance and gyration that made him giddy and sick. In a few moments he was flung upon the gravel at the foot of the left bank of the stream—the southern bank—and behind a projecting point which concealed him from his enemies. The sudden arrest of his motion, the abrasion of one of his hands on the gravel, restored him, and he wept with delight. He dug his fingers into the sand, threw it over himself in handfuls and audibly blessed it. It looked like diamonds, rubies, emeralds; he could think of nothing beautiful which it did not resemble. The trees upon the bank were giant garden plants; he noted a definite order in their arrangement, inhaled the fragrance of their blooms. A strange roseate light shone through the spaces among their trunks and the wind made in their branches the music of æolian harps. He had no wish to perfect his escape—was content to remain in that enchanting spot until retaken.

A whiz and rattle of grapeshot among the branches high above his head roused him from his dream. The baffled cannoneer had fired him a random farewell. He sprang to his feet, rushed up the sloping bank, and plunged into the forest.

All that day he traveled, laying his course by the rounding sun. The forest seemed interminable; nowhere did he discover a break in it, not even a woodman's road. He had not known that he lived in so wild a region. There was something uncanny in the revelation.

By nightfall he was fatigued, footsore, famishing. The thought of his wife and children urged him on. At last he found a road which led him in what he knew to be the right direction. It was as wide and straight as a city street, yet it seemed untraveled. No fields bordered it, no dwelling anywhere. Not so much as the barking of a dog suggested human habitation. The black bodies of the trees formed a straight wall on both sides, terminating on the horizon in a point, like a diagram in a lesson in perspective. Overhead, as he looked up through this rift in the wood, shone great golden stars looking unfamiliar and grouped in strange constellations. He was sure they were arranged in some order which had a secret and malign significance. The wood on either side was full of singular noises, among which— once, twice, and again—he distinctly heard whispers in an unknown tongue.

His neck was in pain and lifting his hand to it found it horribly swollen. He knew that it had a circle of black where the rope had bruised it. His eyes felt congested; he could no longer close them. His tongue was swollen with thirst; he relieved its fever by thrusting it forward from between his teeth into the cold air. How softly the turf had carpeted the untraveled avenue—he could no longer feel the roadway beneath his feet!

Doubtless, despite his suffering, he had fallen asleep while walking, for now he sees another scene—perhaps he has merely recovered from a delirium. He stands at the gate of his own home. All is as he left it, and all bright and beautiful in the morning sunshine. He must have traveled the entire night. As he pushes open the gate and passes up the wide white walk, he sees a flutter of female garments; his wife, looking fresh and cool and sweet, steps down from the veranda to meet him. At the bottom of the steps she stands waiting, with a smile of ineffable joy, an attitude of matchless grace and dignity. Ah, how beautiful she is! He springs forwards with extended arms. As he is about to clasp her he feels a stunning blow upon the back of the neck; a blinding white light blazes all about him with a sound like the shock of a cannon—then all is darkness and silence!

Peyton Fahrquhar was dead; his body, with a broken neck, swung gently from side to side beneath the timbers of the Owl Creek bridge.

Chickamauga

O NE sunny autumn afternoon a child strayed away from its rude home in a small field and entered a forest unobserved. It was happy in a new sense of freedom from control, happy in the opportunity of exploration and adventure; for this child's spirit, in bodies of its ancestors, had for thousands of years been trained to memorable feats of discovery and conquest—victories in battles whose critical moments were centuries, whose victors' camps were cities of hewn stone. From the cradle of its race it had conquered its way through two continents and passing a great sea had penetrated a third, there to be born to war and dominion as a heritage.

The child was a boy aged about six years, the son of a poor planter. In his younger manhood the father had been a soldier, had fought against naked savages and followed the flag of his country into the capital of a civilized race to the far South. In the peaceful life of a planter the warrior-fire survived; once kindled, it is never extinguished. The man loved military books and pictures and the boy had understood enough to make himself a wooden sword, though even the eye of his father would hardly have known it for what it was. This weapon he now bore bravely, as became the son of an heroic race, and pausing now and again in the sunny space of the forest assumed, with some exaggeration, the postures of aggression and defense that he had been taught by the engraver's art. Made reckless by the ease with which he overcame invisible foes attempting to stay his advance, he committed the common enough military error of pushing the pursuit to a dangerous extreme, until he found himself upon the margin of a wide but shallow brook, whose rapid waters barred his direct advance against the flying foe that had crossed with illogical ease. But the intrepid victor was not to be baffled; the spirit of the race which had passed the great sea burned unconquerable in that small breast and would not be denied. Finding a place where some bowlders in the bed of the stream lay but a step or a leap apart, he made his way across and fell again upon the rear-guard of his imaginary foe, putting all to the sword.

Now that the battle had been won, prudence required that he withdraw to his base of operations. Alas; like many a mightier conqueror, and like one, the mightiest, he could not

> curb the lust for war,
> Nor learn that tempted Fate will leave the loftiest star.

Advancing from the bank of the creek he suddenly found himself confronted with a new and more formidable enemy: in the path that he was following, sat, bolt upright, with ears erect and paws suspended before it, a rabbit! With a startled cry the child turned and fled, he knew not in what direction, calling with inarticulate cries for his mother, weeping, stumbling, his tender skin cruelly torn by brambles, his little heart beating hard with terror—breathless, blind with tears—lost in the forest! Then, for more than an hour, he wandered with erring feet through the tangled undergrowth, till at last, overcome by fatigue, he lay down in a narrow space between two rocks, within a few yards of the stream and still grasping his toy sword, no longer a weapon but a companion, sobbed himself to sleep. The wood birds sang merrily above his head; the squirrels, whisking their bravery of tail, ran barking from tree to tree, unconscious of the pity of it, and somewhere far away was a strange, muffled thunder, as if the partridges were drumming in celebration of nature's victory over the son of her immemorial enslavers. And back at the little plantation, where white men and black were hastily searching the fields and hedges in alarm, a mother's heart was breaking for her missing child.

Hours passed, and then the little sleeper rose to his feet. The chill of the evening was in his limbs, the fear of the gloom in his heart. But he had rested, and he no longer wept. With some blind instinct which impelled to action he struggled through the undergrowth about him and came to a more open ground —on his right the brook, to the left a gentle acclivity studded with infrequent trees; over all, the gathering gloom of twilight. A thin, ghostly mist rose along the water. It frightened and repelled him; instead of recrossing, in the direction whence he had come, he turned his back upon it, and went forward toward the dark inclosing wood. Suddenly he saw before him a strange moving object which he took to be some large animal —a dog, a pig—he could not name it; perhaps it was a bear.

IIe had seen pictures of bears, but knew of nothing to their discredit and had vaguely wished to meet one. But something in form or movement of this object—something in the awkwardness of its approach—told him that it was not a bear, and curiosity was stayed by fear. He stood still and as it came slowly on gained courage every moment, for he saw that at least it had not the long menacing ears of the rabbit. Possibly his impressionable mind was half conscious of something familiar in its shambling, awkward gait. Before it had approached near enough to resolve his doubts he saw that it was followed by another and another. To right and to left were many more; the whole open space about him were alive with them—all moving toward the brook.

They were men. They crept upon their hands and knees. They used their hands only, dragging their legs. They used their knees only, their arms hanging idle at their sides. They strove to rise to their feet, but fell prone in the attempt. They did nothing naturally, and nothing alike, save only to advance foot by foot in the same direction. Singly, in pairs and in little groups, they came on through the gloom, some halting now and again while others crept slowly past them, then resuming their movement. They came by dozens and by hundreds; as far on either hand as one could see in the deepening gloom they extended and the black wood behind them appeared to be inexhaustible. The very ground seemed in motion toward the creek. Occasionally one who had paused did not again go on, but lay motionless. He was dead. Some, pausing, made strange gestures with their hands, erected their arms and lowered them again, clasped their heads; spread their palms upward, as men are sometimes seen to do in public prayer.

Not all of this did the child note; it is what would have been noted by an elder observer; he saw little but that these were men, yet crept like babes. Being men, they were not terrible, though unfamiliarly clad. He moved among them freely, going from one to another and peering into their faces with childish curiosity. All their faces were singularly white and many were streaked and gouted with red. Something in this—something too, perhaps, in their grotesque attitudes and movements—reminded him of the painted clown whom he had seen last summer in the circus, and he laughed as he watched them. But on and ever on they crept, these maimed and bleeding men, as heedless as he of the dramatic contrast between his laughter and their own ghastly gravity. To him it was a merry spectacle. He had seen his father's negroes creep upon their hands and knees for his amusement—had ridden them so, "making believe" they were his horses. He now approached one of these crawling figures from behind and with an agile movement mounted it astride. The man sank upon his breast, recovered, flung the small boy fiercely to the ground as an unbroken colt might have done, then turned upon him a face that lacked a lower jaw—from the upper teeth to the throat was a great red gap fringed with hanging shreds of flesh and splinters of bone. The unnatural prominence of nose, the absence of chin, the fierce eyes, gave this man the appearance of a great bird of prey crimsoned in throat and breast by the blood of its quarry. The man rose to his knees, the child to his feet. The man shook his fist at the child; the child, terrified at last, ran to a tree near by, got upon the farther side of it and took a more serious view of the situation. And so the clumsy multitude dragged itself slowly and painfully along in hideous pantomime—moved forward down the slope like a swarm of great black beetles, with never a sound of going—in silence profound, absolute.

Instead of darkening, the haunted landscape began to brighten. Through the belt of trees beyond the brook shone a strange red light, the trunks and branches of the trees making a black lacework against it. It struck the creeping figures and gave them monstrous shadows, which caricatured their movements on the lit grass. It fell upon their faces, touching their whiteness with a ruddy tinge, accentuating the stains with which so many of them were freaked and maculated. It sparkled on buttons and bits of metal in their clothing. Instinctively the child turned toward the growing splendor and moved down the slope with his horrible companions; in a few moments had passed the foremost of the throng—not much of a feat, considering his advantages. He placed himself in the lead, his wooden sword still in hand, and solemnly directed the march, conforming his pace to theirs and occasionally turning as if to see that his forces did not straggle. Surely such a leader never before had such a following.

Scattered about upon the ground now slowly narrowing by

the encroachment of this awful march to water, were certain articles to which, in the leader's mind, were coupled no significant associations: an occasional blanket, tightly rolled lengthwise, doubled and the ends bound together with a string; a heavy knapsack here, and there a broken rifle—such things, in short, as are found in the rear of retreating troops, the "spoor" of men flying from their hunters. Everywhere near the creek, which here had a margin of lowland, the earth was trodden into mud by the feet of men and horses. An observer of better experience in the use of his eyes would have noticed that these footprints pointed in both directions; the ground had been twice passed over—in advance and in retreat. A few hours before, these desperate, stricken men, with their more fortunate and now distant comrades, had penetrated the forest in thousands. Their successive battalions, breaking into swarms and re-forming in lines, had passed the child on every side—had almost trodden on him as he slept. The rustle and murmur of their march had not awakened him. Almost within a stone's throw of where he lay they had fought a battle; but all unheard by him were the roar of the musketry, the shock of the cannon, "the thunder of the captains and the shouting." He had slept through it all, grasping his little wooden sword with perhaps a tighter clutch in unconscious sympathy with his martial environment, but as heedless of the grandeur of the struggle as the dead who had died to make the glory.

The fire beyond the belt of woods on the farther side of the creek, reflected to earth from the canopy of its own smoke, was now suffusing the whole landscape. It transformed the sinuous line of mist to the vapor of gold. The water gleamed with dashes of red, and red, too, were many of the stones protruding above the surface. But that was blood; the less desperately wounded had stained them in crossing. On them, too, the child now crossed with eager steps; he was going to the fire. As he stood upon the farther bank he turned about to look at the companions of his march. The advance was arriving at the creek. The stronger had already drawn themselves to the brink and plunged their faces into the flood. Three or four who lay without motion appeared to have no heads. At this the child's eyes expanded with wonder; even his hospitable understanding could not accept a phenomenon implying such vitality as that. After slaking their thirst these men had not had the strength to back away from the water, nor to keep their heads above it. They were drowned. In rear of these, the open spaces of the forest showed the leader as many formless figures of his grim command as at first; but not nearly so many were in motion. He waved his cap for their encouragement and smilingly pointed with his weapon in the direction of the guiding light—a pillar of fire to this strange exodus.

Confident of the fidelity of his forces, he now entered the belt of woods, passed through it easily in the red illumination, climbed a fence, ran across a field, turning now and again to coquet with his responsive shadow, and so approached the blazing ruin of a dwelling. Desolation everywhere! In all the wide glare not a living thing was visible. He cared nothing for that; the spectacle pleased, and he danced with glee in imitation of the wavering flames. He ran about, collecting fuel, but every object that he found was too heavy for him to cast in from the distance to which the heat limited his approach. In despair he flung in his sword—a surrender to the superior forces of nature. His military career was at an end.

Shifting his position, his eyes fell upon some outbuildings which had an oddly familiar appearance, as if he had dreamed of them. He stood considering them with wonder, when suddenly the entire plantation, with its inclosing forest, seemed to turn as if upon a pivot. His little world swung half around; the points of the compass were reversed. He recognized the blazing building as his own home!

For a moment he stood stupefied by the power of the revelation, then ran with stumbling feet, making a half-circuit of the ruin. There, conspicuous in the light of the conflagration, lay the dead body of a woman—the white face turned upward, the hands thrown out and clutched full of grass, the clothing deranged, the long dark hair in tangles and full of clotted blood. The greater part of the forehead was torn away, and from the jagged hole the brain protruded, overflowing the temple, a frothy mass of gray, crowned with clusters of crimson bubbles—the work of a shell.

The child moved his little hands, making wild, uncertain

gestures. He uttered a series of inarticulate and indescribable cries—something between the chattering of an ape and the gobbling of a turkey—a startling, soulless, unholy sound, the language of a devil. The child was a deaf mute.

Then he stood motionless, with quivering lips, looking down upon the wreck.

A Son of the Gods

A BREEZY day and a sunny landscape. An open country to right and left and forward; behind, a wood. In the edge of this wood, facing the open but not venturing into it, long lines of troops, halted. The wood is alive with them, and full of confused noises—the occasional rattle of wheels as a battery of artillery goes into position to cover the advance; the hum and murmur of the soldiers talking; a sound of innumerable feet in the dry leaves that strew the interspaces among the trees; hoarse commands of officers. Detached groups of horsemen are well in front—not altogether exposed—many of them intently regarding the crest of a hill a mile away in the direction of the interrupted advance. For this powerful army, moving in battle order through a forest, has met with a formidable obstacle—the open country. The crest of that gentle hill a mile away has a sinister look; it says, Beware! Along it runs a stone wall extending to left and right a great distance. Behind the wall is a hedge; behind the hedge are seen the tops of trees in rather straggling order. Among the trees—what? It is necessary to know.

Yesterday, and for many days and nights previously, we were fighting somewhere; always there was cannonading, with occasional keen rattlings of musketry, mingled with cheers, our own or the enemy's, we seldom knew, attesting some temporary advantage. This morning at daybreak the enemy was gone. We have moved forward across his earthworks, across which we have so often vainly attempted to move before, through the debris of his abandoned camps, among the graves of his fallen, into the woods beyond.

How curiously we had regarded everything! how odd it all had seemed! Nothing had appeared quite familiar; the most commonplace objects—an old saddle, a splintered wheel, a forgotten canteen—everything had related something of the mysterious personality of those strange men who had been killing us. The soldier never becomes wholly familiar with the

27

conception of his foes as men like himself; he cannot divest himself of the feeling that they are another order of beings, differently conditioned, in an environment not altogether of the earth. The smallest vestiges of them rivet his attention and engage his interest. He thinks of them as inaccessible; and, catching an unexpected glimpse of them, they appear farther away, and therefore larger, than they really are—like objects in a fog. He is somewhat in awe of them.

From the edge of the wood leading up the acclivity are the tracks of horses and wheels—the wheels of cannon. The yellow grass is beaten down by the feet of infantry. Clearly they have passed this way in thousands; they have not withdrawn by the country roads. This is significant—it is the difference between retiring and retreating.

That group of horsemen is our commander, his staff and escort. He is facing the distant crest, holding his field-glass against his eyes with both hands, his elbows needlessly elevated. It is a fashion; it seems to dignify the act; we are all addicted to it. Suddenly he lowers the glass and says a few words to those about him. Two or three aides detach themselves from the group and canter away into the woods, along the lines in each direction. We did not hear his words, but we know them: "Tell General X. to send forward the skirmish line." Those of us who have been out of place resume our positions; the men resting at ease straighten themselves and the ranks are re-formed without a command. Some of us staff officers dismount and look at our saddle girths; those already on the ground remount.

Galloping rapidly along in the edge of the open ground comes a young officer on a snow-white horse. His saddle blanket is scarlet. What a fool! No one who has ever been in action but remembers how naturally every rifle turns toward the man on a white horse; no one but has observed how a bit of red enrages the bull of battle. That such colors are fashionable in military life must be accepted as the most astonishing of all the phenomena of human vanity. They would seem to have been devised to increase the death-rate.

This young officer is in full uniform, as if on parade. He is all agleam with bullion—a blue-and-gold edition of the Poetry of War. A wave of derisive laughter runs abreast of him all along the line. But how handsome he is!—with what careless grace he sits his horse!

He reins up within a respectful distance of the corps commander and salutes. The old soldier nods familiarly; he evidently knows him. A brief colloquy between them is going on; the young man seems to be preferring some request which the elder one is indisposed to grant. Let us ride a little nearer. Ah! too late—it is ended. The young officer salutes again, wheels his horse, and rides straight toward the crest of the hill!

A thin line of skirmishers, the men deployed at six paces or so apart, now pushes from the wood into the open. The commander speaks to his bugler, who claps his instrument to his lips. *Tra-la-la! Tra-la-la!* The skirmishers halt in their tracks.

Meantime the young horseman has advanced a hundred yards. He is riding at a walk, straight up the long slope, with never a turn of the head. How glorious! Gods! what would we not give to be in his place—with his soul! He does not draw a sabre; his right hand hangs easily at his side. The breeze catches the plume in his hat and flutters it smartly. The sunshine rests upon his shoulder-straps, lovingly, like a visible benediction. Straight on he rides. Ten thousand pairs of eyes are fixed upon him with an intensity that he can hardly fail to feel; ten thousand hearts keep quick time to the inaudible hoof-beats of his snowy steed. He is not alone—he draws all souls after him. But we remember that we laughed! On and on, straight for the hedge-lined wall, he rides. Not a look backward. O, if he would but turn—if he could but see the love, the adoration, the atonement!

Not a word is spoken; the populous depths of the forest still murmur with their unseen and unseeing swarm, but all along the fringe is silence. The burly commander is an equestrian statue of himself. The mounted staff officers, their field glasses up, are motionless all. The line of battle in the edge of the wood stands at a new kind of "attention," each man in the attitude in which he was caught by the consciousness of what is going on. All these hardened and impenitent man-killers, to whom death in its awfulest forms is a fact familiar to their every-day observation; who sleep on hills trembling with the thunder of great guns, dine in the midst of streaming missiles, and play cards among the dead faces of their dearest friends—all

are watching with suspended breath and beating hearts the
outcome of an act involving the life of one man. Such is the
magnetism of courage and devotion.

If now you should turn your head you would see a simultaneous movement among the spectators—a start, as if they had
received an electric shock—and looking forward again to the
now distant horseman you would see that he has in that instant
altered his direction and is riding at an angle to his former
course. The spectators suppose the sudden deflection to be
caused by a shot, perhaps a wound; but take this field-glass and
you will observe that he is riding toward a break in the wall
and hedge. He means, if not killed, to ride through and overlook the country beyond.

You are not to forget the nature of this man's act; it is not
permitted to you to think of it as an instance of bravado, nor,
on the other hand, a needless sacrifice of self. If the enemy has
not retreated he is in force on that ridge. The investigator will
encounter nothing less than a line-of-battle; there is no need
of pickets, videttes, skirmishers, to give warning of our approach; our attacking lines will be visible, conspicuous, exposed
to an artillery fire that will shave the ground the moment they
break from cover, and for half the distance to a sheet of rifle
bullets in which nothing can live. In short, if the enemy is
there, it would be madness to attack him in front; he must be
manœuvred out by the immemorial plan of threatening his
line of communication, as necessary to his existence as to the
diver at the bottom of the sea his air tube. But how ascertain if
the enemy is there? There is but one way,—somebody must go
and see. The natural and customary thing to do is to send
forward a line of skirmishers. But in this case they will answer
in the affirmative with all their lives; the enemy, crouching in
double ranks behind the stone wall and in cover of the hedge,
will wait until it is possible to count each assailant's teeth. At
the first volley a half of the questioning line will fall, the other
half before it can accomplish the predestined retreat. What a
price to pay for gratified curiosity! At what a dear rate an army
must sometimes purchase knowledge! "Let me pay all," says
this gallant man—this military Christ!

There is no hope except the hope against hope that the crest
is clear. True, he might prefer capture to death. So long as he

advances, the lines will not fire—why should it? He can safely ride into the hostile ranks and become a prisoner of war. But this would defeat his object. It would not answer our question; it is necessary either that he return unharmed or be shot to death before our eyes. Only so shall we know how to act. If captured—why, that might have been done by a half-dozen stragglers.

Now begins an extraordinary contest of intellect between a man and an army. Our horseman, now within a quarter of a mile of the crest, suddenly wheels to the left and gallops in a direction parallel to it. He has caught sight of his antagonist; he knows all. Some slight advantage of ground has enabled him to overlook a part of the line. If he were here he could tell us in words. But that is now hopeless; he must make the best use of the few minutes of life remaining to him, by compelling the enemy himself to tell us as much and as plainly as possible —which, naturally, that discreet power is reluctant to do. Not a rifleman in those crouching ranks, not a cannoneer at those masked and shotted guns, but knows the needs of the situation, the imperative duty for forbearance. Besides, there has been time enough to forbid them all to fire. True, a single rifle-shot might drop him and be no great disclosure. But firing is infectious—and see how rapidly he moves, with never a pause except as he whirls his horse about to take a new direction, never directly backward toward us, never directly forward toward his executioners. All this is visible through the glass; it seems occurring within pistol-shot; we see all but the enemy, whose presence, whose thoughts, whose motives we infer. To the unaided eye there is nothing but a black figure on a white horse, tracing slow zigzags against the slope of a distant hill—so slowly they seem almost to creep.

Now—the glass again—he has tired of his failure, or sees his error, or has gone mad; he is dashing directly forward at the wall, as if to take it at a leap, hedge and all! One moment only and he wheels right about and is speeding like the wind straight down the slope—toward his friends, toward his death! Instantly the wall is topped with a fierce roll of smoke for a distance of hundreds of yards to right and left. This is as instantly dissipated by the wind, and before the rattle of the rifles reaches us he is down. No, he recovers his seat; he has but pulled his horse upon its haunches. They are up and away! A tremendous cheer bursts from our ranks, relieving the insupportable tension of our feelings. And the horse and its rider? Yes, they are up and away. Away, indeed—they are making directly to our left, parallel to the now steadily blazing and smoking wall. The rattle of the musketry is continuous, and every bullet's target is that courageous heart.

Suddenly a great bank of white smoke pushes upward from behind the wall. Another and another—a dozen roll up before the thunder of the explosions and the humming of the missiles reach our ears and the missiles themselves come bounding through clouds of dust into our covert, knocking over here and there a man and causing a temporary distraction, a passing thought of self.

The dust drifts away. Incredible!—that enchanted horse and rider have passed a ravine and are climbing another slope to unveil another conspiracy of silence, to thwart the will of another armed host. Another moment and that crest too is in eruption. The horse rears and strikes the air with its forefeet. They are down at last. But look again—the man has detached himself from the dead animal. He stands erect, motionless, holding his sabre in his right hand straight above his head. His face is toward us. Now he lowers his hand to a level with his face and moves it outward, the blade of the sabre describing a downward curve. It is a sign to us, to the world, to posterity. It is a hero's salute to death and history.

Again the spell is broken; our men attempt to cheer; they are choking with emotion; they utter hoarse, discordant cries; they clutch their weapons and press tumultuously forward into the open. The skirmishers, without orders, against orders, are going forward at a keen run, like hounds unleashed. Our cannon speak and the enemy's now open in full chorus; to right and left as far as we can see, the distant crest, seeming now so near, erects its towers of cloud and the great shot pitch roaring down among our moving masses. Flag after flag of ours emerges from the wood, line after line sweeps forth, catching the sunlight on its burnished arms. The rear battalions alone are in obedience; they preserve their proper distance from the insurgent front.

The commander has not moved. He now removes his field-glass from his eyes and glances to the right and left. He sees the human current flowing on either side of him and his huddled escort, like tide waves parted by a rock. Not a sign of feeling in his face; he is thinking. Again he directs his eyes forward; they slowly traverse that malign and awful crest. He addresses a calm word to his bugler. *Tra-la-la! Tra-la-la!* The injunction has an imperiousness which enforces it. It is repeated by all the bugles of all the subordinate commanders; the sharp metallic notes assert themselves above the hum of the advance and penetrate the sound of the cannon. To halt is to withdraw. The colors move slowly back; the lines face about and sullenly follow, bearing their wounded; the skirmishers return, gathering up the dead.

Ah, those many, many needless dead! That great soul whose beautiful body is lying over yonder, so conspicuous against the sere hillside—could it not have been spared the bitter consciousness of a vain devotion? Would one exception have marred too much the pitiless perfection of the divine, eternal plan?

One of the Missing

JEROME SEARING, a private soldier of General Sherman's army, then confronting the enemy at and about Kennesaw Mountain, Georgia, turned his back upon a small group of officers with whom he had been talking in low tones, stepped across a light line of earthworks, and disappeared in a forest. None of the men in line behind the work had said a word to him, nor had he so much as nodded to them in passing, but all who saw understood that this brave man had been intrusted with some perilous duty. Jerome Searing, though a private, did not serve in the ranks; he was detailed for service at division headquarters, being borne upon the rolls as an orderly. "Orderly" is a word covering a multitude of duties. An orderly may be a messenger, a clerk, an officer's servant—anything. He may perform services for which no provision is made in orders and army regulations. Their nature may depend upon his aptitude, upon favor, upon accident. Private Searing, an incomparable marksman, young, hardy, intelligent and insensible to fear, was a scout. The general commanding his division was not content to obey orders blindly without knowing what was in his front, even when his command was not on detached service, but formed a fraction of the line of the army; nor was he satisfied to receive his knowledge of his *vis-à-vis* through the customary channels; he wanted to know more than he was apprised of by the corps commander and the collisions of pickets and skirmishers. Hence Jerome Searing, with his extraordinary daring, his woodcraft, his sharp eyes, and truthful tongue. On this occasion his instructions were simple: to get as near the enemy's lines as possible and learn all that he could.

In a few moments he had arrived at the picket-line, the men on duty there lying in groups of two and four behind little banks of earth scooped out of the slight depression in which they lay, their rifles protruding from the green boughs with which they had masked their small defenses. The forest extended without a break toward the front, so solemn and silent that only by an effort of the imagination could it be conceived as populous with armed men, alert and vigilant—a

34

forest formidable with possibilities of battle. Pausing a moment in one of these rifle-pits to apprise the men of his intention Searing crept stealthily forward on his hands and knees and was soon lost to view in a dense thicket of underbrush.

"That is the last of him," said one of the men; "I wish I had his rifle; those fellows will hurt some of us with it."

Searing crept on, taking advantage of every accident of ground and growth to give himself better cover. His eyes penetrated everywhere, his ears took note of every sound. He stilled his breathing, and at the cracking of a twig beneath his knee stopped his progress and hugged the earth. It was slow work, but not tedious; the danger made it exciting, but by no physical signs was the excitement manifest. His pulse was as regular, his nerves were as steady as if he were trying to trap a sparrow.

"It seems a long time," he thought, "but I cannot have come very far; I am still alive."

He smiled at his own method of estimating distance, and crept forward. A moment later he suddenly flattened himself upon the earth and lay motionless, minute after minute. Through a narrow opening in the bushes he had caught sight of a small mound of yellow clay—one of the enemy's rifle-pits. After some little time he cautiously raised his head, inch by inch, then his body upon his hands, spread out on each side of him, all the while intently regarding the hillock of clay. In another moment he was upon his feet, rifle in hand, striding rapidly forward with little attempt at concealment. He had rightly interpreted the signs, whatever they were; the enemy was gone.

To assure himself beyond a doubt before going back to report upon so important a matter, Searing pushed forward across the line of abandoned pits, running from cover to cover in the more open forest, his eyes vigilant to discover possible stragglers. He came to the edge of a plantation—one of those forlorn, deserted homesteads of the last years of the war, upgrown with brambles, ugly with broken fences and desolate with vacant buildings having blank apertures in place of doors and windows. After a keen reconnaissance from the safe seclusion of a clump of young pines Searing ran lightly across a field and through an orchard to a small structure which stood apart from the other farm buildings, on a slight elevation. This he thought would enable him to overlook a large scope of country in the direction that he supposed the enemy to have taken in withdrawing. This building, which had originally consisted of a single room elevated upon four posts about ten feet high, was now little more than a roof; the floor had fallen away, the joists and planks loosely piled on the ground below or resting on end at various angles, not wholly torn from their fastenings above. The supporting posts were themselves no longer vertical. It looked as if the whole edifice would go down at the touch of a finger.

Concealing himself in the débris of joists and flooring Searing looked across the open ground between his point of view and a spur of Kennesaw Mountain, a half-mile away. A road leading up and across this spur was crowded with troops—the rear-guard of the retiring enemy, their gun-barrels gleaming in the morning sunlight.

Searing had now learned all that he could hope to know. It was his duty to return to his own command with all possible speed and report his discovery. But the gray column of Confederates toiling up the mountain road was singularly tempting. His rifle—an ordinary "Springfield," but fitted with a globe sight and hair-trigger—would easily send its ounce and a quarter of lead hissing into their midst. That would probably not affect the duration and result of the war, but it is the business of a soldier to kill. It is also his habit if he is a good soldier. Searing cocked his rifle and "set" the trigger.

But it was decreed from the beginning of time that Private Searing was not to murder anybody that bright summer morning, nor was the Confederate retreat to be announced by him. For countless ages events had been so matching themselves together in that wondrous mosaic to some parts of which, dimly discernible, we give the name of history, that the acts which he had in will would have marred the harmony of the pattern. Some twenty-five years previously the Power charged with the execution of the work according to the design had provided against that mischance by causing the birth of a certain male child in a little village at the foot of the Carpathian Mountains, had carefully reared it, supervised its education, directed its desires into a military channel, and in due time made it an officer of artillery. By the concurrence of an infinite number of

favoring influences and their preponderance over an infinite
number of opposing ones, this officer of artillery had been made
to commit a breach of discipline and flee from his native country to avoid punishment. He had been directed to New Orleans
(instead of New York), where a recruiting officer awaited him
on the wharf. He was enlisted and promoted, and things were
so ordered that he now commanded a Confederate battery
some two miles along the line from where Jerome Searing,
the Federal scout, stood cocking his rifle. Nothing had been
neglected—at every step in the progress of both these men's
lives, and in the lives of their contemporaries and ancestors,
and in the lives of the contemporaries of their ancestors, the
right thing had been done to bring about the desired result.
Had anything in all this vast concatenation been overlooked
Private Searing might have fired on the retreating Confederates that morning, and would perhaps have missed. As it fell
out, a Confederate captain of artillery, having nothing better
to do while awaiting his turn to pull out and be off, amused
himself by sighting a field-piece obliquely to his right at what
he mistook for some Federal officers on the crest of a hill, and
discharged it. The shot flew high of its mark.

As Jerome Searing drew back the hammer of his rifle and
with his eyes upon the distant Confederates considered where
he could plant his shot with the best hope of making a widow
or an orphan or a childless mother,—perhaps all three, for Private Searing, although he had repeatedly refused promotion,
was not without a certain kind of ambition,—he heard a rushing sound in the air, like that made by the wings of a great bird
swooping down upon its prey. More quickly than he could
apprehend the gradation, it increased to a hoarse and horrible
roar, as the missile that made it sprang at him out of the sky,
striking with a deafening impact one of the posts supporting
the confusion of timbers above him, smashing it into matchwood, and bringing down the crazy edifice with a loud clatter,
in clouds of blinding dust!

When Jerome Searing recovered consciousness he did not at
once understand what had occurred. It was, indeed, some time
before he opened his eyes. For a while he believed that he had
died and been buried, and he tried to recall some portions of
the burial service. He thought that his wife was kneeling upon

his grave, adding her weight to that of the earth upon his breast. The two of them, widow and earth, had crushed his coffin. Unless the children should persuade her to go home he would not much longer be able to breathe. He felt a sense of wrong. "I cannot speak to her," he thought; "the dead have no voice; and if I open my eyes I shall get them full of earth."

He opened his eyes. A great expanse of blue sky, rising from a fringe of the tops of trees. In the foreground, shutting out some of the trees, a high, dun mound, angular in outline and crossed by an intricate, patternless system of straight lines; the whole an immeasurable distance away—a distance so inconceivably great that it fatigued him, and he closed his eyes. The moment that he did so he was conscious of an insufferable light. A sound was in his ears like the low, rhythmic thunder of a distant sea breaking in successive waves upon the beach, and out of this noise, seeming a part of it, or possibly coming from beyond it, and intermingled with its ceaseless undertone, came the articulate words: "Jerome Searing, you are caught like a rat in a trap—in a trap, trap, trap."

Suddenly there fell a great silence, a black darkness, an infinite tranquillity, and Jerome Searing, perfectly conscious of his rathood, and well assured of the trap that he was in, remembering all and nowise alarmed, again opened his eyes to reconnoitre, to note the strength of his enemy, to plan his defense.

He was caught in a reclining posture, his back firmly supported by a solid beam. Another lay across his breast, but he had been able to shrink a little away from it so that it no longer oppressed him, though it was immovable. A brace joining it at an angle had wedged him against a pile of boards on his left, fastening the arm on that side. His legs, slightly parted and straight along the ground, were covered upward to the knees with a mass of débris which towered above his narrow horizon. His head was as rigidly fixed as in a vise; he could move his eyes, his chin—no more. Only his right arm was partly free. "You must help us out of this," he said to it. But he could not get it from under the heavy timber athwart his chest, nor move it outward more than six inches at the elbow.

Searing was not seriously injured, nor did he suffer pain. A smart rap on the head from a flying fragment of the splintered post, incurred simultaneously with the frightfully sudden shock to the nervous system, had momentarily dazed him. His term of unconsciousness, including the period of recovery, during which he had had the strange fancies, had probably not exceeded a few seconds, for the dust of the wreck had not wholly cleared away as he began an intelligent survey of the situation.

With his partly free right hand he now tried to get hold of the beam that lay across, but not quite against, his breast. In no way could he do so. He was unable to depress the shoulder so as to push the elbow beyond that edge of the timber which was nearest his knees; failing in that, he could not raise the forearm and hand to grasp the beam. The brace that made an angle with it downward and backward prevented him from doing anything in that direction, and between it and his body the space was not half so wide as the length of his forearm. Obviously he could not get his hand under the beam nor over it; the hand could not, in fact, touch it at all. Having demonstrated his inability, he desisted, and began to think whether he could reach any of the débris piled upon his legs.

In surveying the mass with a view to determining that point, his attention was arrested by what seemed to be a ring of shining metal immediately in front of his eyes. It appeared to him at first to surround some perfectly black substance, and it was somewhat more than a half-inch in diameter. It suddenly occurred to his mind that the blackness was simply shadow and that the ring was in fact the muzzle of his rifle protruding from the pile of débris. He was not long in satisfying himself that this was so—if it was a satisfaction. By closing either eye he could look a little way along the barrel—to the point where it was hidden by the rubbish that held it. He could see the one side, with the corresponding eye, at apparently the same angle as the other side with the other eye. Looking with the right eye, the weapon seemed to be directed at a point to the left of his head, and *vice versa*. He was unable to see the upper surface of the barrel, but could see the under surface of the stock at a slight angle. The piece was, in fact, aimed at the exact centre of his forehead.

In the perception of this circumstance, in the recollection that just previously to the mischance of which this uncomfortable situation was the result he had cocked the rifle and set the trigger so that a touch would discharge it, Private Searing was affected with a feeling of uneasiness. But that was as far as possible from fear; he was a brave man, somewhat familiar with the aspect of rifles from that point of view, and of cannon too. And now he recalled, with something like amusement, an incident of his experience at the storming of Missionary Ridge, where, walking up to one of the enemy's embrasures from which he had seen a heavy gun throw charge after charge of grape among the assailants he had thought for a moment that the piece had been withdrawn; he could see nothing in the opening but a brazen circle. What that was he had understood just in time to step aside as it pitched another peck of iron down that swarming slope. To face firearms is one of the commonest incidents in a soldier's life—firearms, too, with malevolent eyes blazing behind them. That is what a soldier is for. Still, Private Searing did not altogether relish the situation, and turned away his eyes.

After groping, aimless, with his right hand for a time he made an ineffectual attempt to release his left. Then he tried to disengage his head, the fixity of which was the more annoying from his ignorance of what held it. Next he tried to free his feet, but while exerting the powerful muscles of his legs for that purpose it occurred to him that a disturbance of the rubbish which held them might discharge the rifle; how it could have endured what had already befallen it he could not understand, although memory assisted him with several instances in point. One in particular he recalled, in which in a moment of mental abstraction he had clubbed his rifle and beaten out another gentleman's brains, observing afterward that the weapon which he had been diligently swinging by the muzzle was loaded, capped, and at full clock—knowledge of which circumstance would doubtless have cheered his antagonist to longer endurance. He had always smiled in recalling that blunder of his "green and salad days" as a soldier, but now he did not smile. He turned his eyes again to the muzzle of the rifle and for a moment fancied that it had moved; it seemed somewhat nearer.

Again he looked away. The tops of the distant trees beyond the bounds of the plantation interested him: he had not before observed how light and feathery they were, nor how darkly blue the sky was, even among their branches, where they somewhat paled it with their green; above him it appeared almost black. "It will be uncomfortably hot here," he thought, "as the day advances. I wonder which way I am looking."

Judging by such shadows as he could see, he decided that his face was due north; he would at least not have the sun in his eyes, and north—well, that was toward his wife and children.

"Bah!" he exclaimed aloud, "what have they to do with it?"

He closed his eyes. "As I can't get out I may as well go to sleep. The rebels are gone and some of our fellows are sure to stray out here foraging. They'll find me."

But he did not sleep. Gradually he became sensible of a pain in his forehead—a dull ache, hardly perceptible at first, but growing more and more uncomfortable. He opened his eyes and it was gone—closed them and it returned. "The devil!" he said, irrelevantly, and stared again at the sky. He heard the singing of birds, the strange metallic note of the meadow lark, suggesting the clash of vibrant blades. He fell into pleasant memories of his childhood, played again with his brother and sister, raced across the fields, shouting to alarm the sedentary larks, entered the sombre forest beyond and with timid steps followed the faint path to Ghost Rock, standing at last with audible heart-throbs before the Dead Man's Cave and seeking to penetrate its awful mystery. For the first time he observed that the opening of the haunted cavern was encircled by a ring of metal. Then all else vanished and left him gazing into the barrel of his rifle as before. But whereas before it had seemed near, it now seemed an inconceivable distance away, and all the more sinister for that. He cried out and, startled by something in his own voice—the note of fear—lied to himself in denial: "If I don't sing out I may stay here till I die."

He now made no further attempt to evade the menacing stare of the gun barrel. If he turned away his eyes an instant it was to look for assistance (although he could not see the ground on either side the ruin), and he permitted them to return, obedient to the imperative fascination. If he closed them it was from weariness, and instantly the poignant pain in his forehead—the prophecy and menace of the bullet—forced him to reopen them.

The tension of nerve and brain was too severe; nature came

to his relief with intervals of unconsciousness. Reviving from one of these he became sensible of a sharp, smarting pain in his right hand, and when he worked his fingers together, or rubbed his palm with them, he could feel that they were wet and slippery. He could not see the hand, but he knew the sensation; it was running blood. In his delirium he had beaten it against the jagged fragments of the wreck, had clutched it full of splinters. He resolved that he would meet his fate more manly. He was a plain, common soldier, had no religion and not much philosophy; he could not die like a hero, with great and wise last words, even if there had been some one to hear them, but he could die "game," and he would. But if he could only know when to expect the shot!

Some rats which had probably inhabited the shed came sneaking and scampering about. One of them mounted the pile of debris that held the rifle; another followed and another. Searing regarded them at first with indifference, then with friendly interest; then, as the thought flashed into his bewildered mind that they might touch the trigger of his rifle, he cursed them and ordered them to go away. "It is no business of yours," he cried.

The creatures went away; they would return later, attack his face, gnaw away his nose, cut his throat—he knew that, but he hoped by that time to be dead.

Nothing could now unfix his gaze from the little ring of metal with its black interior. The pain in his forehead was fierce and incessant. He felt it gradually penetrating the brain more and more deeply, until at last its progress was arrested by the wood at the back of his head. It grew momentarily more insufferable: he began wantonly beating his lacerated hand against the splinters again to counteract that horrible ache. It seemed to throb with a slow, regular recurrence, each pulsation sharper than the preceding, and sometimes he cried out, thinking he felt the fatal bullet. No thoughts of home, of wife and children, of country, of glory. The whole record of memory was effaced. The world had passed away—not a vestige remained. Here in this confusion of timbers and boards is the sole universe. Here is immortality in time—each pain an everlasting life. The throbs tick off eternities.

Jerome Searing, the man of courage, the formidable enemy, the strong, resolute warrior, was as pale as a ghost. His jaw was fallen; his eyes protruded; he trembled in every fibre; a cold sweat bathed his entire body; he screamed with fear. He was not insane—he was terrified.

In groping about with his torn and bleeding hand he seized at last a strip of board, and, pulling, felt it give way. It lay parallel with his body, and by bending his elbow as much as the contracted space would permit, he could draw it a few inches at a time. Finally it was altogether loosened from the wreckage covering his legs; he could lift it clear of the ground its whole length. A great hope came into his mind: perhaps he could work it upward, that is to say backward, far enough to lift the end and push aside the rifle; or, if that were too tightly wedged, so place the strip of board as to deflect the bullet. With this object he passed it backward inch by inch, hardly daring to breathe lest that act somehow defeat his intent, and more than ever unable to remove his eyes from the rifle, which might perhaps now hasten to improve its waning opportunity. Something at least had been gained: in the occupation of his mind in this attempt at self-defense he was less sensible of the pain in his head and had ceased to wince. But he was still dreadfully frightened and his teeth rattled like castanets.

The strip of board ceased to move to the suasion of his hand. He tugged at it with all his strength, changed the direction of its length all he could, but it had met some extended obstruction behind him and the end in front was still too far away to clear the pile of debris and reach the muzzle of the gun. It extended, indeed, nearly as far as the trigger guard, which, uncovered by the rubbish, he could imperfectly see with his right eye. He tried to break the strip with his hand, but had no leverage. In his defeat, all his terror returned, augmented tenfold. The black aperture of the rifle appeared to threaten a sharper and more imminent death in punishment of his rebellion. The track of the bullet through his head ached with an intenser anguish. He began to tremble again.

Suddenly he became composed. His tremor subsided. He clenched his teeth and drew down his eyebrows. He had not exhausted his means of defense; a new design had shaped itself in his mind—another plan of battle. Raising the front end of the strip of board, he carefully pushed it forward through the wreckage at the side of the rifle until it pressed against the trigger guard. Then he moved the end slowly outward until he could feel that it had cleared it, then, closing his eyes, thrust it against the trigger with all his strength! There was no explosion; the rifle had been discharged as it dropped from his hand when the building fell. But it did its work.

Lieutenant Adrian Searing, in command of the picket-guard on that part of the line through which his brother Jerome had passed on his mission, sat with attentive ears in his breastwork behind the line. Not the faintest sound escaped him; the cry of a bird, the barking of a squirrel, the noise of the wind among the pines—all were anxiously noted by his overstrained sense. Suddenly, directly in front of his line, he heard a faint, confused rumble, like the clatter of a falling building translated by distance. The lieutenant mechanically looked at his watch. Six o'clock and eighteen minutes. At the same moment an officer approached him on foot from the rear and saluted.

"Lieutenant," said the officer, "the colonel directs you to move forward your line and feel the enemy if you find him. If not, continue the advance until directed to halt. There is reason to think that the enemy has retreated."

The lieutenant nodded and said nothing; the other officer retired. In a moment the men, apprised of their duty by the non-commissioned officers in low tones, had deployed from their rifle-pits and were moving forward in skirmishing order, with set teeth and beating hearts.

This line of skirmishers sweeps across the plantation toward the mountain. They pass on both sides of the wrecked building, observing nothing. At a short distance in their rear their commander comes. He casts his eyes curiously upon the ruin and sees a dead body half buried in board and timbers. It is so covered with dust that its clothing is Confederate gray. Its face is yellowish white; the cheeks are fallen in, the temples sunken, too, with sharp ridges about them, making the forehead forbiddingly narrow; the upper lip, slightly lifted, shows the white teeth, rigidly clenched. The hair is heavy with moisture, the face as wet as the dewy grass all about. From his point of view the officer does not observe the rifle; the man was apparently killed by the fall of the building.

"Dead a week," said the officer curtly, moving on and absently pulling out his watch as if to verify his estimate of time. Six o'clock and forty minutes.

Killed at Resaca

THE best soldier of our staff was Lieutenant Herman Brayle, one of the two aides-de-camp. I don't remember where the general picked him up; from some Ohio regiment, I think; none of us had previously known him, and it would have been strange if we had, for no two of us came from the same State, nor even from adjoining States. The general seemed to think that a position on his staff was a distinction that should be so judiciously conferred as not to beget any sectional jealousies and imperil the integrity of that part of the country which was still an integer. He would not even choose officers from his own command, but by some jugglery at department headquarters obtained them from other brigades. Under such circumstances, a man's services had to be very distinguished indeed to be heard of by his family and the friends of his youth; and "the speaking trump of fame" was a trifle hoarse from loquacity, anyhow.

Lieutenant Brayle was more than six feet in height and of splendid proportions, with the light hair and gray-blue eyes which men so gifted usually find associated with a high order of courage. As he was commonly in full uniform, especially in action, when most officers are content to be less flamboyantly attired, he was a very striking and conspicuous figure. As to the rest, he had a gentleman's manners, a scholar's head, and a lion's heart. His age was about thirty.

We all soon came to like Brayle as much as we admired him, and it was with sincere concern that in the engagement at Stone's River—our first action after he joined us—we observed that he had one most objectionable and unsoldierly quality: he was vain of his courage. During all the vicissitudes and mutations of that hideous encounter, whether our troops were fighting in the open cotton fields, in the cedar thickets, or behind the railway embankment, he did not once take cover, except when sternly commanded to do so by the general, who usually had other things to think of than the lives of his staff officers—or those of his men, for that matter.

In every later engagement while Brayle was with us it was

the same way. He would sit his horse like an equestrian statue, in a storm of bullets and grape, in the most exposed places—wherever, in fact, duty, requiring him to go, permitted him to remain—when, without trouble and with distinct advantage to his reputation for common sense, he might have been in such security as is possible on a battlefield in the brief intervals of personal inaction.

On foot, from necessity or in deference to his dismounted commander or associates, his conduct was the same. He would stand like a rock in the open when officers and men alike had taken to cover; while men older in service and years, higher in rank and of unquestionable intrepidity, were loyally preserving behind the crest of a hill lives infinitely precious to their country, this fellow would stand, equally idle, on the ridge, facing in the direction of the sharpest fire.

When battles are going on in open ground it frequently occurs that the opposing lines, confronting each other within a stone's throw for hours, hug the earth as closely as if they loved it. The line officers in their proper places flatten themselves no less, and the field officers, their horses all killed or sent to the rear, crouch beneath the infernal canopy of hissing lead and screaming iron without a thought of personal dignity.

In such circumstances the life of a staff officer of a brigade is distinctly "not a happy one," mainly because of its precarious tenure and the unnerving alternations of emotion to which he is exposed. From a position of that comparative security from which a civilian would ascribe his escape to a "miracle," he may be despatched with an order to some commander of a prone regiment in the front line—a person for the moment inconspicuous and not always easy to find without a deal of search among men somewhat preoccupied, and in a din in which question and answer alike must be imparted in the sign language. It is customary in such cases to duck the head and scuttle away on a keen run, an object of lively interest to some thousands of admiring marksmen. In returning—well, it is not customary to return.

Brayle's practice was different. He would consign his horse to the care of an orderly,—he loved his horse,—and walk quietly away on his perilous errand with never a stoop of the back, his splendid figure, accentuated by his uniform, holding the eye with a strange fascination. We watched him with suspended breath, our hearts in our mouths. On one occasion of this kind, indeed, one of our number, an impetuous stammerer, was so possessed by his emotion that he shouted at me:

"I'll b-b-bet you t-two d-d-dollars they d-drop him b-b-before he g-gets to that d-d-ditch!"

I did not accept the brutal wager; I thought they would.

Let me do justice to a brave man's memory; in all these needless exposures of life there was no visible bravado nor subsequent narration. In the few instances when some of us had ventured to remonstrate, Brayle had smiled pleasantly and made some light reply, which, however, had not encouraged a further pursuit of the subject. Once he said:

"Captain, if ever I come to grief by forgetting your advice, I hope my last moments will be cheered by the sound of your beloved voice breathing into my ear the blessed words, 'I told you so.'"

We laughed at the captain—just why we could probably not have explained—and that afternoon when he was shot to rags from an ambuscade Brayle remained by the body for some time, adjusting the limbs with needless care—there in the middle of a road swept by gusts of grape and canister! It is easy to condemn this kind of thing, and not very difficult to refrain from imitation, but it is impossible not to respect, and Brayle was liked none the less for the weakness which had so heroic an expression. We wished he were not a fool, but he went on that way to the end, sometimes hard hit, but always returning to duty about as good as new.

Of course, it came at last; he who ignores the law of probabilities challenges an adversary that is seldom beaten. It was at Resaca, in Georgia, during the movement that resulted in the taking of Atlanta. In front of our brigade the enemy's line of earthworks ran through open fields along a slight crest. At each end of this open ground we were close up to him in the woods, but the clear ground we could not hope to occupy until night, when darkness would enable us to burrow like moles and throw up earth. At this point our line was a quarter-mile away in the edge of a wood. Roughly, we formed a semicircle, the enemy's fortified line being the chord of the arc.

"Lieutenant, go tell Colonel Ward to work up as close as he

can get cover, and not to waste much ammunition in unnecessary firing. You may leave your horse."

When the general gave this direction we were in the fringe
of the forest, near the right extremity of the arc. Colonel Ward
was at the left. The suggestion to leave the horse obviously
enough meant that Brayle was to take the longer line, through
the woods and among the men. Indeed, the suggestion was
needless; to go by the short route meant absolutely certain failure to deliver the message. Before anybody could interpose,
Brayle had cantered lightly into the field and the enemy's works
were in crackling conflagration.

"Stop that damned fool!" shouted the general.

A private of the escort, with more ambition than brains,
spurred forward to obey, and within ten yards left himself and
his horse dead on the field of honor.

Brayle was beyond recall, galloping easily along, parallel to
the enemy and less than two hundred yards distant. He was a
picture to see! His hat had been blown or shot from his head,
and his long, blond hair rose and fell with the motion of his
horse. He sat erect in the saddle, holding the reins lightly in his
left hand, his right hanging carelessly at his side. An occasional
glimpse of his handsome profile as he turned his head one way
or the other proved that the interest which he took in what
was going on was natural and without affectation.

The picture was intensely dramatic, but in no degree theatrical. Successive scores of rifles spat at him viciously as he came
within range, and our line in the edge of the timber broke out
in visible and audible defense. No longer regardful of themselves or their orders, our fellows sprang to their feet, and
swarming into the open sent broad sheets of bullets against the
blazing crest of the offending works, which poured an answering fire into their unprotected groups with deadly effect. The
artillery on both sides joined the battle, punctuating the rattle
and roar with deep, earth-shaking explosions and tearing the
air with storms of screaming grape, which from the enemy's
side splintered the trees and spattered them with blood, and
from ours defiled the smoke of his arms with banks and clouds
of dust from his parapet.

My attention had been for a moment drawn to the general
combat, but now, glancing down the unobscured avenue between

these two thunderclouds, I saw Brayle, the cause of the carnage. Invisible now from either side, and equally doomed by friend and foe, he stood in the shot-swept space, motionless, his face toward the enemy. At some little distance lay his horse. I instantly saw what had stopped him.

As topographical engineer I had, early in the day, made a hasty examination of the ground, and now remembered that at that point was a deep and sinuous gully, crossing half the field from the enemy's line, its general course at right angles to it. From where we now were it was invisible, and Brayle had evidently not known about it. Clearly, it was impassable. Its salient angles would have afforded him absolute security if he had chosen to be satisfied with the miracle already wrought in his favor and leapt into it. He could not go forward, he would not turn back; he stood awaiting death. It did not keep him long waiting.

By some mysterious coincidence, almost instantaneously as he fell, the firing ceased, a few desultory shots at long intervals serving rather to accentuate than break the silence. It was as if both sides had suddenly repented of their profitless crime. Four stretcher-bearers of ours, following a sergeant with a white flag, soon afterward moved unmolested into the field, and made straight for Brayle's body. Several Confederate officers and men came out to meet them, and with uncovered heads assisted them to take up their sacred burden. As it was borne toward us we heard beyond the hostile works fifes and a muffled drum—a dirge. A generous enemy honored the fallen brave.

Amongst the dead man's effects was a soiled Russia-leather pocketbook. In the distribution of mementoes of our friend, which the general, as administrator, decreed, this fell to me.

A year after the close of the war, on my way to California, I opened and idly inspected it. Out of an overlooked compartment fell a letter without envelope or address. It was in a woman's handwriting, and began with words of endearment, but no name.

It had the following date line: "San Francisco, Cal., July 9, 1862." The signature was "Darling," in marks of quotation. Incidentally, in the body of the text, the writer's full name was given—Marian Mendenhall.

The letter showed evidence of cultivation and good breeding, but it was an ordinary love letter, if a love letter can be ordinary. There was not much in it, but there was something. It was this:

"Mr. Winters, whom I shall always hate for it, has been telling that at some battle in Virginia, where he got his hurt, you were seen crouching behind a tree. I think he wants to injure you in my regard, which he knows the story would do if I believed it. I could bear to hear of my soldier lover's death, but not of his cowardice."

These were the words which on that sunny afternoon, in a distant region, had slain a hundred men. Is woman weak?

One evening I called on Miss Mendenhall to return the letter to her. I intended, also, to tell her what she had done—but not that she did it. I found her in a handsome dwelling on Rincon Hill. She was beautiful, well bred—in a word, charming.

"You knew Lieutenant Herman Brayle," I said, rather abruptly. "You know, doubtless, that he fell in battle. Among his effects was found this letter from you. My errand here is to place it in your hands."

She mechanically took the letter, glanced through it with deepening color, and then, looking at me with a smile, said:

"It is very good of you, though I am sure it was hardly worth while." She started suddenly and changed color. "This stain," she said, "is it—surely it is not——"

"Madam," I said, "pardon me, but that is the blood of the truest and bravest heart that ever beat."

She hastily flung the letter on the blazing coals. "Uh! I cannot bear the sight of blood!" she said. "How did he die?"

I had involuntarily risen to rescue that scrap of paper, sacred even to me, and now stood partly behind her. As she asked the question she turned her face about and slightly upward. The light of the burning letter was reflected in her eyes and touched her cheek with a tinge of crimson like the stain upon its page. I had never seen anything so beautiful as this detestable creature.

"He was bitten by a snake," I replied.

The Affair at Coulter's Notch

"D o you think, Colonel, that your brave Coulter would like to put one of his guns in here?" the general asked.

He was apparently not altogether serious; it certainly did not seem a place where any artillerist, however brave, would like to put a gun. The colonel thought that possibly his division commander meant good-humouredly to intimate that in a recent conversation between them Captain Coulter's courage had been too highly extolled.

"General," he replied warmly, "Coulter would like to put a gun anywhere within reach of those people," with a motion of his hand in the direction of the enemy.

"It is the only place," said the general. He was serious, then.

The place was a depression, a "notch," in the sharp crest of a hill. It was a pass, and through it ran a turnpike, which reaching this highest point in its course by a sinuous ascent through a thin forest made a similar, though less steep, descent toward the enemy. For a mile to the left and a mile to the right, the ridge, though occupied by Federal infantry lying close behind the sharp crest and appearing as if held in place by atmospheric pressure, was inaccessible to artillery. There was no place but the bottom of the notch, and that was barely wide enough for the roadbed. From the Confederate side this point was commanded by two batteries posted on a slightly lower elevation beyond a creek, and a half-mile away. All the guns but one were masked by the trees of an orchard; that one—it seemed a bit of impudence—was on an open lawn directly in front of a rather grandiose building, the planter's dwelling. The gun was safe enough in its exposure—but only because the Federal infantry had been forbidden to fire. Coulter's Notch—it came to be called so—was not, that pleasant summer afternoon, a place where one would "like to put a gun."

Three or four dead horses lay there sprawling in the road, three or four dead men in a trim row at one side of it, and a little back, down the hill. All but one were cavalrymen belonging to the Federal advance. One was a quartermaster. The general commanding the division and the colonel commanding the brigade, with their staffs and escorts, had ridden into the notch to have a look at the enemy's guns—which had straightway obscured themselves in towering clouds of smoke. It was hardly profitable to be curious about guns which had the trick of the cuttlefish, and the season of observation had been brief. At its conclusion—a short remove backward from where it began—occurred the conversation already partly reported. "It is the only place," the general repeated thoughtfully, "to get at them."

The colonel looked at him gravely. "There is room for only one gun, General—one against twelve."

"That is true—for only one at a time," said the commander with something like, yet not altogether like, a smile. "But then, your brave Coulter—a whole battery in himself."

The tone of irony was now unmistakable. It angered the colonel, but he did not know what to say. The spirit of military subordination is not favourable to retort, nor even deprecation.

At this moment a young officer of artillery came riding slowly up the road attended by his bugler. It was Captain Coulter. He could not have been more than twenty-three years of age. He was of medium height, but very slender and lithe, and sat his horse with something of the air of a civilian. In face he was of a type singularly unlike the men about him; thin, high-nosed, grey-eyed, with a slight blonde mustache, and long, rather straggling hair of the same color. There was an apparent negligence in his attire. His cap was worn with the visor a trifle askew; his coat was buttoned only at the sword belt, showing a considerable expanse of white shirt, tolerably clean for that stage of the campaign. But the negligence was all in his dress and bearing; in his face was a look of intense interest in his surroundings. His gray eyes, which seemed occasionally to strike right and left across the landscape, like search-lights, were for the most part fixed upon the sky beyond the Notch; until he should arrive at the summit of the road there was nothing else in that direction to see. As he came opposite his division and brigade commanders at the roadside he saluted mechanically and was about to pass on. The colonel signed him to halt.

"Captain Coulter," he said, "the enemy has twelve pieces over there on the next ridge. If I rightly understand the general, he directs that you bring up a gun and engage them."

There was a blank silence; the general looked stolidly at a distant regiment swarming slowly up the hill through rough undergrowth, like a torn and draggled cloud of blue smoke; the captain appeared not to have observed him. Presently the captain spoke, slowly and with apparent effort:

"On the next ridge, did you say, sir? Are the guns near the house?"

"Ah, you have been over this road before. Directly at the house."

"And it is—necessary—to engage them? The order is imperative?"

His voice was husky and broken. He was visibly paler. The colonel was astonished and mortified. He stole a glance at the commander. In that set, immobile face was no sign; it was as hard as bronze. A moment later the general rode away, followed by his staff and escort. The colonel, humiliated and indignant, was about to order Captain Coulter in arrest, when the latter spoke a few words in a low tone to his bugler, saluted, and rode straight forward into the Notch, where, presently, at the summit of the road, his field-glass at his eyes, he showed against the sky, he and his horse, sharply defined and statuesque. The bugler had dashed down the road in the opposite direction at headlong speed and disappeared behind a wood. Presently his bugle was heard singing in the cedars, and in an incredibly short time a single gun with its caisson, each drawn by six horses and manned by its full complement of gunners, came bounding and banging up the grade in a storm of dust, unlimbered under cover, and was run forward by hand to the fatal crest among the dead horses. A gesture of the captain's arm, some strangely agile movements of the men in loading, and almost before the troops along the way had ceased to hear the rattle of the wheels, a great white cloud sprang forward down the slope, and with a deafening report the affair at Coulter's Notch had begun.

It is not intended to relate in detail the progress and incidents of that ghastly contest—a contest without vicissitudes, its alternations only different degrees of despair. Almost at the instant when Captain Coulter's gun blew its challenging cloud twelve answering clouds rolled upward from among the trees about the plantation house, a deep multiple report roared back like a broken echo, and thenceforth to the end the Federal cannoneers fought their hopeless battle in an atmosphere of living iron whose thoughts were lightnings and whose deeds were death.

Unwilling to see the efforts which he could not aid and the slaughter which he could not stay, the colonel ascended the ridge at a point a quarter of a mile to the left, whence the Notch, itself invisible, but pushing up successive masses of smoke, seemed the crater of a volcano in thundering eruption. With his glass he watched the enemy's guns, noting as he could the effects of Coulter's fire—if Coulter still lived to direct it. He saw that the Federal gunners, ignoring those of the enemy's pieces whose position could be determined by their smoke only, gave their whole attention to the one that maintained its place in the open—the lawn in front of the house. Over and about that hardy piece the shells exploded at intervals of a few seconds. Some exploded in the house, as could be seen by thin ascensions of smoke from the breached roof. Figures of prostrate men and horses were plainly visible.

"If our fellows are doing such good work with a single gun," said the colonel to an aide who happened to be nearest, "they must be suffering like the devil from twelve. Go down and present the commander of that piece with my congratulations on the accuracy of his fire."

Turning to his adjutant-general he said, "Did you observe Coulter's damned reluctance to obey orders?"

"Yes, sir, I did."

"Well say nothing about it, please. I don't think the general will care to make any accusations. He will probably have enough to do in explaining his own connection with this uncommon way of amusing the rearguard of a retreating enemy."

A young officer approached from below, climbing breathless up the acclivity. Almost before he had saluted he gasped out:

"Colonel, I am directed by Colonel Harmon to say that the enemy's guns are within easy reach of our rifles, and most of them visible from various points along the ridge."

The brigade commander looked at him without a trace of interest in his expression. "I know it," he said quietly.

The young adjutant was visibly embarrassed. "Colonel Harmon would like to have permission to silence those guns," he stammered.

"So should I," the colonel said in the same tone. "Present my compliments to Colonel Harmon and say to him that the general's orders not to fire are still in force."

The adjutant saluted and retired. The colonel ground his heel into the earth and turned to look again at the enemy's guns.

"Colonel," said the adjutant-general, "I don't know that I ought to say anything, but there is something wrong in all this. Do you happen to know that Captain Coulter is from the South?"

"No; *was* he, indeed?"

"I heard that last summer the division which the general then commanded was in the vicinity of Coulter's home—camped there for weeks, and——"

"Listen!" said the colonel, interrupting with an upward gesture. "Do you hear *that?*"

"That" was the silence of the Federal gun. The staff, the orderlies, the lines of infantry behind the crest—all had "heard," and were looking curiously in the direction of the crater, whence no smoke now ascended except desultory cloudlets from the enemy's shells. Then came the blare of a bugle, a faint rattle of wheels; a minute later the sharp reports recommenced with double activity. The demolished gun had been replaced with a sound one.

"Yes," said the adjutant-general, resuming his narrative, "the general made the acquaintance of Coulter's family. There was trouble—I don't know the exact nature of it—something about Coulter's wife. She is a red-hot Secessionist, as they all are, except Coulter himself, but she is a good wife and high-bred lady. There was a complaint to army headquarters. The general was transferred to this division. It is odd that Coulter's battery should afterward have been assigned to it."

The colonel had risen from the rock upon which they had been sitting. His eyes were blazing with a generous indignation.

"See here, Morrison," said he, looking his gossiping staff officer straight in the face, "did you get that story from a gentleman or a liar?"

"I don't want to say how I got it, Colonel, unless it is necessary"—he was blushing a trifle—"but I'll stake my life upon its truth in the main."

The colonel turned toward a small knot of officers some distance away. "Lieutenant Williams!" he shouted.

One of the officers detached himself from the group and coming forward saluted, saying: "Pardon me, Colonel, I thought you had been informed. Williams is dead down there by the gun. What can I do, sir?"

Lieutenant Williams was the aide who had had the pleasure of conveying to the officer in charge of the gun his brigade commander's congratulations.

"Go," said the colonel, "and direct the withdrawal of that gun instantly. No—I'll go myself."

He strode down the declivity toward the rear of the Notch at a break-neck pace, over rocks and through brambles, followed by his little retinue in tumultuous disorder. At the foot of the declivity they mounted their waiting animals and took to the road at a lively trot, round a bend and into the Notch. The spectacle which they encountered there was appalling!

Within that defile, barely broad enough for a single gun, were piled the wrecks of no fewer than four. They had noted the silencing of only the last one disabled—there had been a lack of men to replace it quickly with another. The débris lay on both sides of the road; the men had managed to keep an open way between, through which the fifth piece was now firing. The men?—they looked like demons of the pit! All were hatless, all stripped to the waist, their reeking skins black with blotches of powder and spattered with gouts of blood. They worked like madmen, with rammer and cartridge, lever and lanyard. They set their swollen shoulders and bleeding hands against the wheels at each recoil and heaved the heavy gun back to its place. There were no commands; in that awful environment of whooping shot, exploding shells, shrieking fragments of iron, and flying splinters of wood, none could have been heard. Officers, if officers there were, were indistinguishable; all worked together—each while he lasted—governed by the eye. When the gun was sponged, it was loaded; when loaded, aimed and fired. The colonel observed something new to his military experience—something horrible and unnatural: the gun was bleeding at the mouth! In temporary default of water, the man sponging had dipped his sponge in a pool of his comrades' blood. In all this work there was no clashing; the duty of the instant was obvious. When one fell, another, looking a trifle cleaner, seemed to rise from the earth in the dead man's tracks, to fall in his turn.

With the ruined guns lay the ruined men—alongside the wreckage, under it and atop of it; and back down the road—a ghastly procession!—crept on hands and knees such of the wounded as were able to move. The colonel—he had compassionately sent his cavalcade to the right about—had to ride over those who were entirely dead in order not to crush those who were partly alive. Into that hell he tranquilly held his way, rode up alongside the gun, and, in the obscurity of the last discharge, tapped upon the cheek the man holding the rammer —who straightway fell, thinking himself killed. A fiend seven times damned sprang out of the smoke to take his place, but paused and gazed up at the mounted officer with an unearthly regard, his teeth flashing between his black lips, his eyes, fierce and expanded, burning like coals beneath his bloody brow. The colonel made an authoritative gesture and pointed to the rear. The fiend bowed in token of obedience. It was Captain Coulter.

Simultaneously with the colonel's arresting sign silence fell upon the whole field of action. The procession of missiles no longer streamed into that defile of death; the enemy also had ceased firing. His army had been gone for hours, and the commander of his rear-guard, who had held his position perilously long in hope to silence the Federal fire, at that strange moment had silenced his own. "I was not aware of the breadth of my authority," said the colonel to anybody, riding forward to the crest to see what had really happened.

An hour later his brigade was in bivouac on the enemy's ground, and its idlers were examining, with something of awe, as the faithful inspect a saint's relics, a score of straddling dead horses and three disabled guns, all spiked. The fallen men had been carried away; their torn and broken bodies would have given too great satisfaction.

Naturally, the colonel established himself and his military family in the plantation house. It was somewhat shattered, but it was better than the open air. The furniture was greatly deranged and broken. Walls and ceilings were knocked away here and there, and a lingering odor of powder smoke was everywhere. The beds, the closets of women's clothing, the cupboards were not greatly damaged. The new tenants for a night made themselves comfortable, and the virtual effacement of Coulter's battery supplied them with an interesting topic.

During supper an orderly of the escort showed himself into the dining-room, and asked permission to speak to the colonel.

"What is it, Barbour?" said that officer pleasantly, having overheard the request.

"Colonel, there is something wrong in the cellar; I don't know what—somebody there. I was down there rummaging about."

"I will go down and see," said a staff officer, rising.

"So will I," the colonel said; "let the others remain. Lead on orderly."

They took a candle from the table and descended the cellar stairs, the orderly in visible trepidation. The candle made but a feeble light, but presently, as they advanced, its narrow circle of illumination revealed a human figure seated on the ground against the black stone wall which they were skirting, its knees elevated, its head bowed sharply forward. The face, which should have been seen in profile, was invisible, for the man was bent so far forward that his long hair concealed it; and, strange to relate, the beard, of a much darker hue, fell in a great tangled mass and lay along the ground at his side. They involuntarily paused; then the colonel, taking the candle from the orderly's shaking hand, approached the man and attentively considered him. The long dark beard was the hair of a woman—dead. The dead woman clasped in her arms a dead babe. Both were clasped in the arms of the man, pressed against his breast, against his lips. There was blood in the hair of the woman; there was blood in the hair of the man. A yard away, near an irregular depression in the beaten earth which formed the cellar's floor—a fresh excavation with a convex bit of iron, having jagged edges, visible in one of the sides—lay an infant's foot. The colonel held the light as high as he could. The floor of the room above was broken through, the splinters pointing at all angles downward. "This casemate is not bomb-proof," said the colonel gravely; it did not occur to him that his summing up of the matter had any levity in it.

They stood about the group awhile in silence; the staff officer was thinking of his unfinished supper, the orderly of what might possibly be in one of the casks on the other side of the cellar. Suddenly the man whom they had thought dead raised his head and gazed tranquilly into their faces. His complexion was coal black; the cheeks were apparently tattooed in irregular sinuous lines from the eyes downward. The lips, too, were white, like those of a stage negro. There was blood upon his forehead.

The staff officer drew back a pace, the orderly two paces.

"What are you doing here, my man?" said the colonel, unmoved.

"This house belongs to me, sir," was the reply, civilly delivered.

"To you? Ah, I see! And these?"

"My wife and child. I am Captain Coulter."

The Coup de Grâce

THE fighting had been hard and continuous; that was attested by all the senses. The very taste of battle was in the air. All was now over; it remained only to succor the wounded and bury the dead—to "tidy up a bit," as the humorist of a burial squad put it. A good deal of "tidying up" was required. As far as one could see through the forests, among the splintered trees, lay wrecks of men and horses. Among them moved the stretcher-bearers, gathering and carrying away the few who showed signs of life. Most of the wounded had died of neglect while the right to minister to their wants was in dispute. It is an army regulation that the wounded must wait; the best way to care for them is to win the battle. It must be confessed that victory is a distinct advantage to a man requiring attention, but many do not live to avail themselves of it.

The dead were collected in groups of a dozen or a score and laid side by side in rows while the trenches were dug to receive them. Some, found at too great a distance from these rallying points, were buried where they lay. There was little attempt at identification, though in most cases, the burial parties being detailed to glean the same ground which they had assisted to reap, the names of the victorious dead were known and listed. The enemy's fallen had to be content with counting. But of that they got enough: many of them were counted several times, and the total, as given afterward in the official report of the victorious commander, denoted rather a hope than a result.

At some little distance from the spot where one of the burial parties had established its "bivouac of the dead," a man in the uniform of a Federal officer stood leaning against a tree. From his feet upward to his neck his attitude was that of weariness reposing; but he turned his head uneasily from side to side; his mind was apparently not at rest. He was perhaps uncertain in which direction to go; he was not likely to remain long where he was, for already the level rays of the setting sun straggled redly through the open spaces of the wood and the weary soldiers were quitting their task for the day. He would hardly make a night of it alone there among the dead. Nine men in ten whom you meet after a battle inquire the way to some fraction of the army—as if any one could know. Doubtless this officer was lost. After resting himself a moment he would presumably follow one of the retiring burial squads.

When all were gone he walked straight away into the forest toward the red west, its light staining his face like blood. The air of confidence with which he now strode along showed that he was on familiar ground; he had recovered his bearings. The dead on his right and on his left were unregarded as he passed. An occasional low moan from some sorely-stricken wretch whom the relief-parties had not reached, and who would have to pass a comfortless night beneath the stars with his thirst to keep him company, was equally unheeded. What, indeed, could the officer have done, being no surgeon and having no water?

At the head of a shallow ravine, a mere depression of the ground, lay a small group of bodies. He saw, and swerving suddenly from his course walked rapidly toward them. Scanning each one sharply as he passed, he stopped at last above one which lay at a slight remove from the others, near a clump of small trees. He looked at it narrowly. It seemed to stir. He stooped and laid his hand upon its face. It screamed.

The officer was Captain Downing Madwell, of a Massachusetts regiment of infantry, a daring and intelligent soldier, an honorable man.

In the regiment were two brothers named Halcrow—Caffal and Creede Halcrow. Caffal Halcrow was a sergeant in Captain Madwell's company, and these two men, the sergeant and the captain, were devoted friends. In so far as disparity of rank, difference in duties and considerations of military discipline would permit they were commonly together. They had, indeed, grown up together from childhood. A habit of the heart is not easily broken off. Caffal Halcrow had nothing military in his taste nor disposition, but the thought of separation from his friend was disgreeable; he enlisted in the company in which Madwell was second-lieutenant. Each had taken two steps upward in rank, but between the highest noncommissioned and the lowest commissioned officer the gulf is deep and wide and the old relation was maintained with difficulty and a difference.

Creede Halcrow, the brother of Caffal, was the major of the

regiment—a cynical, saturnine man, between whom and Captain Madwell there was a natural antipathy which circumstances had nourished and strengthened to an active animosity. But for the restraining influence of their mutual relation to Caffal these two patriots would doubtless have endeavored to deprive their country of each other's services.

At the opening of the battle that morning the regiment was performing outpost duty a mile away from the main army. It was attacked and nearly surrounded in the forest, but stubbornly held its ground. During a lull in the fighting, Major Halcrow came to Captain Madwell. The two exchanged formal salutes, and the major said: "Captain, the colonel directs that you push your company to the head of this ravine and hold your place there until recalled. I need hardly apprise you of the dangerous character of the movement, but if you wish, you can, I suppose, turn over the command to your first-lieutenant. I was not, however, directed to authorize the substitution; it is merely a suggestion of my own, unofficially made."

To this deadly insult Captain Madwell coolly replied:

"Sir, I invite you to accompany the movement. A mounted officer would be a conspicuous mark, and I have long held the opinion that it would be better if you were dead."

The art of repartee was cultivated in military circles as early as 1862.

A half-hour later Captain Madwell's company was driven from its position at the head of the ravine, with a loss of one-third its number. Among the fallen was Sergeant Halcrow. The regiment was soon afterward forced back to the main line, and at the close of the battle was miles away. The captain was now standing at the side of his subordinate and friend.

Sergeant Halcrow was mortally hurt. His clothing was deranged; it seemed to have been violently torn apart, exposing the abdomen. Some of the buttons of his jacket had been pulled off and lay on the ground beside him and fragments of his other garments were strewn about. His leather belt was parted and had apparently been dragged from beneath him as he lay. There had been no great effusion of blood. The only visible wound was a wide, ragged opening in the abdomen. It was defiled with earth and dead leaves. Protruding from it was a loop of small intestine. In all his experience Captain Madwell had not seen a wound like this. He could neither conjecture how it was made nor explain the attendant circumstances—the strangely torn clothing, the parted belt, the besmirching of the white skin. He knelt and made a closer examination. When he rose to his feet, he turned his eyes in different directions as if looking for an enemy. Fifty yards away, on the crest of a low, thinly wooded hill, he saw several dark objects moving about among the fallen men—a herd of swine. One stood with its back to him, its shoulders sharply elevated. Its forefeet were upon a human body, its head was depressed and invisible. The bristly ridge of its chine showed black against the red west. Captain Madwell drew away his eyes and fixed them again upon the thing which had been his friend.

The man who had suffered these monstrous mutilations was alive. At intervals he moved his limbs; he moaned at every breath. He stared blankly into the face of his friend and if touched screamed. In his giant agony he had torn up the ground on which he lay; his clenched hands were full of leaves and twigs and earth. Articulate speech was beyond his power; it was impossible to know if he were sensible to anything but pain. The expression of his face was an appeal; his eyes were full of prayer. For what?

There was no misreading that look; the captain had too frequently seen it in eyes of those whose lips had still the power to formulate it by an entreaty for death. Consciously or unconsciously, this writhing fragment of humanity, this type and example of acute sensation, this handiwork of man and beast, this humble, unheroic Prometheus, was imploring everything, all, the whole non-ego, for the boon of oblivion. To the earth and the sky alike, to the trees, to the man, to whatever took form in sense or consciousness, this incarnate suffering addressed that silent plea.

For what, indeed? For that which we accord to even the meanest creature without sense to demand it, denying it only to the wretched of our own race: for the blessed release, the rite of uttermost compassion, the *coup de grâce*.

Captain Madwell spoke the name of his friend. He repeated it over and over without effect until emotion choked his utterance. His tears plashed upon the livid face beneath his own and blinded himself. He saw nothing but a blurred and moving object, but the moans were more distinct than ever, interrupted at briefer intervals by sharper shrieks. He turned away, struck his hand upon his forehead, and strode from the spot. The swine, catching sight of him, threw up their crimson muzzles, regarding him suspiciously a second, and then with a gruff, concerted grunt, raced away out of sight. A horse, its foreleg splintered by a cannon-shot, lifted its head sidewise from the ground and neighed piteously. Madwell stepped forward, drew his revolver and shot the poor beast between its eyes, narrowly observing its death-struggle, which, contrary to his expectation, was violent and long; but at last it lay still. The tense muscles of its lips, which had uncovered the teeth in a horrible grin, relaxed; the sharp, clean-cut profile took on a look of profound peace and rest.

Along the distant, thinly wooded crest to westward the fringe of sunset fire had now nearly burned itself out. The light upon the trunks of the trees had faded to a tender gray; shadows were in their tops, like great dark birds aperch. Night was coming and there were miles of haunted forest between Captain Madwell and camp. Yet he stood there at the side of the dead animal, apparently lost to all sense of his surroundings. His eyes were bent upon the earth at his feet; his left hand hung loosely at his side, his right still held the pistol. Presently he lifted his face, turned it toward his dying friend and walked rapidly back to his side. He knelt upon one knee, cocked the weapon, placed the muzzle against the man's forehead, and turning away his eyes pulled the trigger. There was no report. He had used his last cartridge for the horse.

The sufferer moaned and his lips moved convulsively. The froth that ran from them had a tinge of blood.

Captain Madwell rose to his feet and drew his sword from the scabbard. He passed the fingers of his left hand along the edge from hilt to point. He held it out straight before him, as if to test his nerve. There was no visible tremor of the blade; the ray of bleak skylight that it reflected was steady and true. He stooped and with his left hand tore away the dying man's shirt, rose and placed the point of the sword just over the heart. This time he did not withdraw his eyes. Grasping the hilt with both hands, he thrust downward with all his strength and weight. The blade sank into the man's body—through his body into the earth; Captain Madwell came near falling forward upon his work. The dying man drew up his knees and at the same time threw his right arm across his breast and grasped the steel so tightly that the knuckles of the hand visibly whitened. By a violent but vain effort to withdraw the blade the wound was enlarged; a rill of blood escaped, running sinuously down into the deranged clothing. At that moment three men stepped silently forward from behind the clump of young trees which had concealed their approach. Two were hospital attendants and carried a stretcher.

The third was Major Creede Halcrow.

Parker Adderson, Philosopher

"PRISONER, what is your name?"

"As I am to lose it at daylight tomorrow morning it is hardly worth while concealing it. Parker Adderson."

"Your rank?"

"A somewhat humble one; commissioned officers are too precious to be risked in the perilous business of a spy. I am a sergeant."

"Of what regiment?"

"You must excuse me; my answer might, for anything I know, give you an idea of whose forces are in your front. Such knowledge as that is what I came into your lines to obtain, not to impart."

"You are not without wit."

"If you have the patience to wait you will find me dull enough to-morrow."

"How do you know that you are to die to-morrow morning?"

"Among spies captured by night that is the custom. It is one of the nice observances of the profession."

The general so far laid aside the dignity appropriate to a Confederate officer of high rank and wide renown as to smile. But no one in his power and out of his favor would have drawn any happy augury from that outward and visible sign of approval. It was neither genial nor infectious; it did not communicate itself to the other persons exposed to it—the caught spy who had provoked it and the armed guard who had brought him into the tent and now stood a little apart, watching his prisoner in the yellow candle-light. It was no part of that warrior's duty to smile; he had been detailed for another purpose. The conversation was resumed; it was in character a trial for a captial offense.

"You admit, then, that you are a spy—that you came into my camp, disguised as you are in the uniform of a Confederate soldier, to obtain information secretly regarding the numbers and disposition of my troops."

"Regarding, particularly, their numbers. Their disposition I already knew. It is morose."

The general brightened again; the guard, with a severer sense of his responsibility, accentuated the austerity of his expression and stood a trifle more erect than before. Twirling his gray slouch hat round and round upon his forefinger, the spy took a leisurely survey of his surroundings. They were simple enough. The tent was a common "wall tent," about eight feet by ten in dimensions, lighted by a single tallow candle stuck into the haft of a bayonet, which was itself stuck into a pine table at which the general sat, now busily writing and apparently forgetful of his unwilling guest. An old rag carpet covered the earthen floor; an older leather trunk, a second chair and a roll of blankets were about all else that the tent contained; in General Clavering's command Confederate simplicity and penury of "pomp and circumstance" had attained their highest development. On a large nail driven into the tent pole at the entrance was suspended a sword-belt supporting a long sabre, a pistol in its holster and, absurdly enough, a bowie-knife. Of that most unmilitary weapon it was the general's habit to explain that it was a souvenir of the peaceful days when he was a civilian.

It was a stormy night. The rain cascaded upon the canvas in torrents, with the dull, drum-like sound familiar to dwellers in tents. As the whooping blasts charged upon it the frail structure shook and swayed and strained at its confining stakes and ropes.

The general finished writing, folded the half-sheet of paper and spoke to the soldier guarding Adderson: "Here, Tassman, take that to the adjutant-general; then return."

"And the prisoner, General?" said the soldier, saluting, with an inquiring glance in the direction of that unfortunate.

"Do as I said," replied the officer, curtly.

The soldier took the note and ducked himself out of the tent. General Clavering turned his handsome face toward the Federal spy, looked him in the eyes, not unkindly, and said: "It is a bad night, my man."

"For me, yes."

"Do you guess what I have written?"

"Something worth reading, I dare say. And—perhaps it is my vanity—I venture to suppose that I am mentioned in it."

"Yes; it is a memorandum for an order to be read to the

troops at *reveille* concerning your execution. Also some notes for the guidance of the provost-marshal in arranging the details of that event."

"I hope, General, the spectacle will be intelligently arranged, for I shall attend it myself."

"Have you any arrangements of your own that you wish to make? Do you wish to see a chaplain, for example?"

"I could hardly secure a longer rest for myself by depriving him of some of his."

"Good God, man! do you mean to go to your death with nothing but jokes upon your lips? Do you know that this is a serious matter?"

"How can I know that? I have never been dead in all my life. I have heard that death is a serious matter, but never from any of those who have experienced it."

The general was silent for a moment; the man interested, perhaps amused him—a type not previously encountered.

"Death," he said, "is at least a loss—a loss of such happiness as we have, and of opportunities for more."

"A loss of which we shall never be conscious can be borne with composure and therefore expected without apprehension. You must have observed, General, that of all the dead men with whom it is your soldierly pleasure to strew your path none shows signs of regret."

"If the being dead is not a regrettable condition, yet the becoming so—the act of dying—appears to be distinctly disagreeable to one who has not lost the power to feel."

"Pain is disagreeable, no doubt. I never suffer it without more or less discomfort. But he who lives longest is most exposed to it. What you call dying is simply the last pain—there is really no such thing as dying. Suppose, for illustration, that I attempt to escape. You lift the revolver that you are courteously concealing in your lap, and——"

The general blushed like a girl, then laughed softly, disclosing his brilliant teeth, made a slight inclination of his handsome head and said nothing. The spy continued: "You fire, and I have in my stomach what I did not swallow. I fall, but am not dead. After a half-hour of agony I am dead. But at any given instant of that half-hour I was either alive or dead. There is no transition period.

"When I am hanged to-morrow morning it will be quite the same; while conscious I shall be living; when dead, unconscious. Nature appears to have ordered the matter quite in my interest—the way that I should have ordered it myself. It is so simple," he added with a smile, "that it seems hardly worth while to be hanged at all."

At the finish of his remarks there was a long silence. The general sat impassive, looking into the man's face, but apparently not attentive to what had been said. It was as if his eyes had mounted guard over the prisoner while his mind concerned itself with other matters. Presently he drew a long, deep breath, shuddered, as one awakened from a dreadful dream, and exclaimed almost inaudibly: "Death is horrible!"—this man of death.

"It was horrible to our savage ancestors," said the spy, gravely, "because they had not enough intelligence to dissociate the idea of consciousness from the idea of the physical forms in which it is manifested—as an even lower order of intelligence, that of the monkey, for example, may be unable to imagine a house without inhabitants, and seeing a ruined hut fancies a suffering occupant. To us it is horrible because we have inherited the tendency to think it so, accounting for the notion by wild and fanciful theories of another world—as names of places give rise to legends explaining them and reasonless conduct to philosophies in justification. You can hang me, General, but there your power of evil ends; you cannot condemn me to heaven."

The general appeared not to have heard; the spy's talk had merely turned his thoughts into an unfamiliar channel, but there they pursued their will independently to conclusions of their own. The storm had ceased, and something of the solemn spirit of the night had imparted itself to his reflections, giving them the sombre tinge of a supernatural dread. Perhaps there was an element of prescience in it. "I should not like to die," he said—"not to-night."

He was interrupted—if, indeed, he had intended to speak further—by the entrance of an officer of his staff, Captain Hasterlick, the provost-marshal. This recalled him to himself; the absent look passed away from his face.

"Captain," he said, acknowledging the officer's salute, "this

man is a Yankee spy captured inside our lines with incriminating papers on him. He has confessed. How is the weather?"

"The storm is over, sir, and the moon shining."

"Good; take a file of men, conduct him at once to the parade
ground, and shoot him."

A sharp cry broke from the spy's lips. He threw himself forward, thrust out his neck, expanded his eyes, clenched his hands.

"Good God!" he cried hoarsely, almost inarticulately; "you
do not mean that! You forget—I am not to die until morning."

"I have said nothing of morning," replied the general, coldly;
"that was an assumption of your own. You die now."

"But, General, I beg—I implore you to remember; I am to
hang! It will take some time to erect the gallows—two hours
—an hour. Spies are hanged; I have rights under military law.
For Heaven's sake, General, consider how short——"

"Captain, observe my directions."

The officer drew his sword and fixing his eyes upon the
prisoner pointed silently to the opening of the tent. The prisoner hesitated; the officer grasped him by the collar and pushed
him gently forward. As he approached the tent pole the frantic
man sprang to it and with cat-like agility seized the handle of
the bowie-knife, plucked the weapon from the scabbard and
thrusting the captain aside leaped upon the general with the
fury of a madman, hurling him to the ground and falling headlong upon him as he lay. The table was overturned, the candle
extinguished and they fought blindly in the darkness. The
provost-marshal sprang to the assistance of his superior officer
and was himself prostrated upon the struggling forms. Curses
and inarticulate cries of rage and pain came from the welter of
limbs and bodies; the tent came down upon them and beneath
its hampering and enveloping folds the struggle went on. Private Tassman, returning from his errand and dimly conjectur-
ing the situation, threw down his rifle and laying hold of the
flouncing canvas at random vainly tried to drag it off the men
under it; and the sentinel who paced up and down in front,
not daring to leave his beat though the skies should fall, discharged his rifle. The report alarmed the camp; drums beat the
long roll and bugles sounded the assembly, bringing swarms of
half-clad men into the moonlight, dressing as they ran, and
falling into line at the sharp commands of their officers. This

was well; being in line the men were under control; they stood at arms while the general's staff and the men of his escort brought order out of confusion by lifting off the fallen tent and pulling apart the breathless and bleeding actors in that strange contention.

Breathless, indeed, was one: the captain was dead; the handle of the bowie-knife, protruding from his throat, was pressed back beneath his chin until the end had caught in the angle of the jaw and the hand that delivered the blow had been unable to remove the weapon. In the dead man's hand was his sword, clenched with a grip that defied the strength of the living. Its blade was streaked with red to the hilt.

Lifted to his feet, the general sank back to the earth with a moan and fainted. Besides his bruises he had two sword-thrusts —one through the thigh, the other through the shoulder.

The spy had suffered the least damage. Apart from a broken right arm, his wounds were such only as might have been incurred in an ordinary combat with nature's weapons. But he was dazed and seemed hardly to know what had occurred. He shrank away from those attending him, cowered upon the ground and uttered unintelligible remonstrances. His face, swollen by blows and stained with gouts of blood, nevertheless showed white beneath his disheveled hair—as white as that of a corpse.

"The man is not insane," said the surgeon, preparing bandages and replying to a question; "he is suffering from fright. Who and what is he?"

Private Tassman began to explain. It was the opportunity of his life; he omitted nothing that could in any way accentuate the importance of his own relation to the night's events. When he had finished his story and was ready to begin it again nobody gave him any attention.

The general had now recovered consciousness. He raised himself upon his elbow, looked about him, and, seeing the spy crouching by a camp-fire, guarded, said simply:

"Take that man to the parade ground and shoot him."

"The general's mind wanders," said an officer standing near.

"His mind does *not* wander," the adjutant-general said. "I have a memorandum from him about this business; he had given that same order to Hasterlick"—with a motion of the hand toward the dead provost-marshal—"and, by God! it shall be executed."

Ten minutes later Sergeant Parker Adderson, of the Federal army, philosopher and wit, kneeling in the moonlight and begging incoherently for his life, was shot to death by twenty men. As the volley rang out upon the keen air of the midnight, General Clavering, lying white and still in the red glow of the camp-fire, opened his big blue eyes, looked pleasantly upon those about him and said: "How silent it all is!"

The surgeon looked at the adjutant-general, gravely and significantly. The patient's eyes slowly closed, and thus he lay for a few moments; then, his face suffused with a smile of ineffable sweetness, he said, faintly: "I suppose this must be death," and so passed away.

An Affair of Outposts

CONCERNING THE WISH TO BE DEAD

TWO men sat in conversation. One was the Governor of the State. The year was 1861; the war was on and the Governor already famous for the intelligence and zeal with which he directed all the powers and resources of his State to the service of the Union.

"What! *you*?" the Governor was saying in evident surprise—"you too want a military commission? Really, the fifing and drumming must have effected a profound alteration in your convictions. In my character of recruiting sergeant I suppose I ought not to be fastidious, but"—there was a touch of irony in his manner—"well, have you forgotten that an oath of allegiance is required?"

"I have altered neither my convictions nor my sympathies," said the other, tranquilly. "While my sympathies are with the South, as you do me the honor to recollect, I have never doubted that the North was in the right. I am a Southerner in fact and in feeling, but it is my habit in matters of importance to act as I think, not as I feel."

The Governor was absently tapping his desk with a pencil; he did not immediately reply. After a while he said: "I have heard that there are all kinds of men in the world, so I suppose there are some like that, and doubtless you think yourself one. I've known you a long time and—pardon me—I don't think so."

"Then I am to understand that my application is denied?"

"Unless you can remove my belief that your Southern sympathies are in some degree a disqualification, yes. I do not doubt your good faith, and I know you to be abundantly fitted by intelligence and special training for the duties of an officer. Your convictions, you say, favor the Union cause, but I prefer a man with his heart in it. The heart is what men fight with."

"Look here, Governor," said the younger man, with a smile that had more light than warmth: "I have something up my sleeve —a qualification which I had hoped it would not be necessary to mention. A great military authority has given a simple recipe for being a good soldier: 'Try always to get yourself killed.' It is with that purpose that I wish to enter the service. I am not, perhaps, much of a patriot, but I wish to be dead."

The Governor looked at him rather sharply, then a little coldly. "There is a simpler and franker way," he said.

"In my family, sir," was the reply, "we do not do that—no Armisted has ever done that."

A long silence ensued and neither man looked at the other. Presently the Governor lifted his eyes from the pencil, which had resumed its tapping, and said:

"Who is she?"

"My wife."

The Governor tossed the pencil into the desk, rose and walked two or three times across the room. Then he turned to Armisted, who also had risen, looked at him more coldly than before and said: "But the man—would it not be better that he —could not the country spare him better than it can spare you? Or are the Armisteds opposed to 'the unwritten law'?"

The Armisteds, apparently, could feel an insult: the face of the younger man flushed, then paled, but he subdued himself to the service of his purpose.

"The man's identity is unknown to me," he said, calmly enough.

"Pardon me," said the Governor, with even less of visible contrition than commonly underlies those words. After a moment's reflection he added: "I shall send you to-morrow a captain's commission in the Tenth Infantry, now at Nashville, Tennessee. Good night."

"Good night, sir. I thank you."

Left alone, the Governor remained for a time motionless, leaning against his desk. Presently he shrugged his shoulders as if throwing off a burden. "This is a bad business," he said.

Seating himself at a reading-table before the fire, he took up the book nearest his hand, absently opening it. His eyes fell upon this sentence:

"When God made it necessary for an unfaithful wife to lie about her husband in justification of her own sins He had the tenderness to endow men with the folly to believe her."

He looked at the title of the book; it was, *His Excellency the Fool.*

He flung the volume into the fire.

II
HOW TO SAY WHAT IS WORTH HEARING

The enemy, defeated in two days of battle at Pittsburg Landing, had sullenly retired to Corinth, whence he had come. For manifest incompetence Grant, whose beaten army had been saved from destruction and capture by Buell's soldierly activity and skill, had been relieved of his command, which neverthless had not been given to Buell, but to Halleck, a man of unproved powers, a theorist, sluggish, irresolute. Foot by foot his troops, always deployed in line-of-battle to resist the enemy's bickering skirmishers, always entrenching against the columns that never came, advanced across the thirty miles of forest and swamp toward an antagonist prepared to vanish at contact, like a ghost at cock-crow. It was a campaign of "excursions and alarums," of reconnoissances and counter-marches, of cross-purposes and countermanded orders. For weeks the solemn farce held attention, luring distinguished civilians from fields of political ambition to see what they safely could of the horrors of war. Among these was our friend the Governor. At the headquarters of the army and in the camps of the troops from his State he was a familiar figure, attended by the several members of his personal staff, showily horsed, faultlessly betailored and bravely silk-hatted. Things of charm they were, rich in suggestions of peaceful lands beyond a sea of strife. The bedraggled soldier looked up from his trench as they passed, leaned upon his spade and audibly damned them to signify his sense of their ornamental irrelevance to the austerities of his trade.

"I think, Governor," said General Masterson one day, going into informal session atop of his horse and throwing one leg across the pommel of his saddle, his favorite posture—"I think I would not ride any farther in that direction if I were you. We've nothing out there but a line of skirmishers. That, I presume, is why I was directed to put these siege guns here: if the skirmishers are driven in the enemy will die of dejection at being unable to haul them away—they're a trifle heavy."

There is reason to fear that the unstrained quality of this military humor dropped not as the gentle rain from heaven upon the place beneath the civilian's silk hat. Anyhow he abated none of his dignity in recognition.

"I understand," he said, gravely, "that some of my men are out there—a company of the Tenth, commanded by Captain Armisted. I should like to meet him if you do not mind."

"He is worth meeting. But there's a bad bit of jungle out there, and I should advise that you leave your horse and"—with a look at the Governor's retinue—"your other impedimenta."

The Governor went forward alone and on foot. In a half-hour he had pushed through a tangled undergrowth covering a boggy soil and entered upon firm and more open ground. Here he found a half-company of infantry lounging behind a line of stacked rifles. The men wore their accoutrements—their belts, cartridge-boxes, haversacks and canteens. Some lying at full length on the dry leaves were fast asleep: others in small groups gossiped idly of this and that; a few played at cards; none was far from the line of stacked arms. To the civilian's eye the scene was one of carelessness, confusion, indifference; a soldier would have observed expectancy and readiness.

At a little distance apart an officer in fatigue uniform, armed, sat on a fallen tree noting the approach of the visitor, to whom a sergeant, rising from one of the groups, now came forward.

"I wish to see Captain Armisted," said the Governor.

The sergeant eyed him narrowly, saying nothing, pointed to the officer, and taking a rifle from one of the stacks, accompanied him.

"This man wants to see you, sir," said the sergeant, saluting. The officer rose.

It would have been a sharp eye that would have recognized him. His hair, which but a few months before had been brown, was streaked with gray. His face, tanned by exposure, was seamed as with age. A long livid scar across the forehead marked the stroke of a sabre; one cheek was drawn and puckered by the work of a bullet. Only a woman of the loyal North would have thought the man handsome.

"Armisted—Captain," said the Governor, extending his hand, "do you not know me?"

"I know you, sir, and I salute you—as the Governor of my State."

Lifting his right hand to the level of his eyes he threw it outward and downward. In the code of military etiquette there is no provision for shaking hands. That of the civilian was withdrawn. If he felt either surprise or chagrin his face did not betray it.

"It is the hand that signed your commission," he said.

"And it is the hand——"

The sentence remains unfinished. The sharp report of a rifle came from the front, followed by another and another. A bullet hissed through the forest and struck a tree near by. The men sprang from the ground and even before the captain's high, clear voice was done intoning the command "At-tention!" had fallen into line in rear of the stacked arms. Again—and now through the din of a crackling fusillade—sounded the strong, deliberate sing-song of authority: "Take . . . arms!" followed by the rattle of unlocking bayonets.

Bullets from the unseen enemy were now flying thick and fast, though mostly well spent and emitting the humming sound which signified interference by twigs and rotation in the plane of flight. Two or three of the men in the line were already struck and down. A few wounded men came limping awkwardly out of the undergrowth from the skirmish line in front; most of them did not pause, but held their way with white faces and set teeth to the rear.

Suddenly there was a deep, jarring report in front, followed by the startling rush of a shell, which passing overhead exploded in the edge of a thicket, setting afire the fallen leaves. Penetrating the din—seeming to float above it like the melody of a soaring bird—rang the slow, aspirated monotones of the captain's several commands, without emphasis, without accent, musical and restful as an evensong under the harvest moon. Familiar with this tranquilizing chant in moments of imminent peril, these raw soldiers of less than a year's training yielded themselves to the spell, executing its mandates with the composure and precision of veterans. Even the distinguished civilian behind his tree, hesitating between pride and terror, was accessible to its charm and suasion. He was conscious of a fortified resolution and ran away only when the skirmishers, under orders to rally on the reserve, came out of the woods like hunted hares and formed on the left of the stiff little line, breathing hard and thankful for the boon of breath.

III

THE FIGHTING OF ONE WHOSE HEART WAS NOT IN THE QUARREL

Guided in his retreat by that of the fugitive wounded, the Governor struggled bravely to the rear through the "bad bit of jungle." He was well winded and a trifle confused. Excepting a single rifle-shot now and again, there was no sound of strife behind him; the enemy was pulling himself together for a new onset against an antagonist of whose numbers and tactical disposition he was in doubt. The fugitive felt that he would probably be spared to his country, and only commended the arrangements of Providence to that end, but in leaping a small brook in more open ground one of the arrangements incurred the mischance of a disabling sprain at the ankle. He was unable to continue his flight, for he was too fat to hop, and after several vain attempts, causing intolerable pain, seated himself on the earth to nurse his ignoble disability and deprecate the military situation.

A brisk renewal of the firing broke out and stray bullets came flitting and droning by. Then came the crash of two clean, definite volleys, followed by a continuous rattle, through which he heard the yells and cheers of the combatants, punctuated by thunderclaps of cannon. All this told him that Armisted's little command was bitterly beset and fighting at close quarters. The wounded men whom he had distanced began to straggle by on either hand, their numbers visibly augmented by new levies from the line. Singly and by twos and threes, some supporting comrades more desperately hurt than themselves, but all deaf to his appeals for assistance, they sifted through the underbrush and disappeared. The firing was increasingly louder and more distinct, and presently the ailing fugitives were succeeded by men who strode with a firmer tread, occasionally facing about and discharging their pieces, then doggedly resuming their retreat, reloading as they walked. Two or three fell as he looked, and lay motionless. One had enough of life left in him to make a pitiful attempt to drag himself to cover. A passing comrade paused beside him long enough to fire, appraised the poor devil's disability with a look and moved sullenly on, inserting a cartridge in his weapon.

In all this was none of the pomp of war—no hint of glory. Even in his distress and peril the helpless civilian could not forbear to contrast it with the gorgeous parades and reviews held in honor of himself—with the brilliant uniforms, the music, the banners, and the marching. It was an ugly and sickening business: to all that was artistic in his nature, revolting, brutal, in bad taste.

"Ugh!" he grunted, shuddering—"this is beastly! Where is the charm of it all? Where are the elevated sentiments, the devotion, the heroism, the——"

From a point somewhere near, in the direction of the pursuing enemy, rose the clear, deliberate sing-song of Captain Armisted.

"Stead-y, men—stead-y. Halt! Commence fir-ing."

The rattle of fewer than a score of rifles could be distinguished through the general uproar, and again that penetrating falsetto:

"Cease fir-ing. In re-treat . . . . maaarch!"

In a few moments this remnant had drifted slowly past the Governor, all to the right of him as they faced in retiring, the men deployed at intervals of a half-dozen paces. At the extreme left and a few yards behind came the captain. The civilian called out his name, but he did not hear. A swarm of men in gray now broke out of cover in pursuit, making directly for the spot where the Governor lay—some accident of the ground had caused them to converge upon that point: their line had become a crowd. In a last struggle for life and liberty the Governor attempted to rise, and looking back the captain saw him. Promptly, but with the same slow precision as before, he sang his commands:

"Skirm-ish-ers, halt!" The men stopped and according to rule turned to face the enemy.

"Ral-ly on the right!"—and they came in at a run, fixing bayonets and forming loosely on the man at that end of the line.

"Forward . . to save the Gov-ern-or of your State . . doub-le quick . . . maaarch!"

Only one man disobeyed this astonishing command! He was dead. With a cheer they sprang forward over the twenty or thirty paces between them and their task. The captain having a shorter distance to go arrived first—simultaneously with the enemy. A half-dozen hasty shots were fired at him, and the foremost man—a fellow of heroic stature, hatless and bare-breasted—made a vicious sweep at his head with a clubbed rifle. The officer parried the blow at the cost of a broken arm and drove his sword to the hilt into the giant's breast. As the body fell the weapon was wrenched from his hand and before he could pluck his revolver from the scabbard at his belt another man leaped upon him like a tiger, fastening both hands upon his throat and bearing him backward upon the prostrate Governor, still struggling to rise. This man was promptly spitted upon the bayonet of a Federal sergeant and his death-gripe on the captain's throat loosened by a kick upon each wrist. When the captain had risen he was at the rear of his men, who had all passed over and around him and were thrusting fiercely at their more numerous but less coherent antagonists. Nearly all the rifles on both sides were empty and in the crush there was neither time nor room to reload. The Confederates were at a disadvantage in that most of them lacked bayonets; they fought by bludgeoning—and a clubbed rifle is a formidable arm. The sound of the conflict was a clatter like that of the interlocking horns of battling bulls—now and then the pash of a crushed skull, an oath, or a grunt caused by the impact of a rifle's muzzle against the abdomen transfixed by its bayonet. Through an opening made by the fall of one of his men Captain Armisted sprang, with his dangling left arm; in his right hand a full-charged revolver, which he fired with rapidity and terrible effect into the thick of the gray crowd: but across the bodies of the slain the survivors in the front were pushed forward by their comrades in the rear till again they breasted the tireless bayonets. There were fewer bayonets now to breast—a beggarly half-dozen, all told. A few minutes more of this rough work—a little fighting back to back—and all would be over.

Suddenly a lively firing was heard on the right and the left: a fresh line of Federal skirmishers came forward at a run, driving before them those parts of the Confederate line that had been separated by staying the advance of the centre. And behind these new and noisy combatants, at a distance of two or three hundred yards, could be seen, indistinct among the trees a line-of-battle!

Instinctively before retiring, the crowd in gray made a tremendous rush upon its handful of antagonists, overwhelming them by mere momentum and, unable to use weapons in the crush, trampled them, stamped savagely on their limbs, their bodies, their necks, their faces; then retiring with bloody feet across its own dead it joined the general rout and the incident was at an end.

IV

THE GREAT HONOR THE GREAT

The Governor, who had been unconscious, opened his eyes and stared about him, slowly recalling the day's events. A man in the uniform of a major was kneeling beside him; he was a surgeon. Grouped about were the civilian members of the Governor's staff, their faces expressing a natural solicitude regarding their offices. A little apart stood General Masterson addressing another officer and gesticulating with a cigar. He was saying: "It was the beautifulest fight ever made—by God, sir, it was great!"

The beauty and greatness were attested by a row of dead, trimly disposed, and another of wounded, less formally placed, restless, half-naked, but bravely bebandaged.

"How do you feel, sir?" said the surgeon. "I find no wound."

"I think I am all right," the patient replied, sitting up. "It is that ankle."

The surgeon transferred his attention to the ankle, cutting away the boot. All eyes followed the knife.

In moving the leg a folded paper was uncovered. The patient picked it up and carelessly opened it. It was a letter three months old, signed "Julia." Catching sight of his name in it he read it. It was nothing very remarkable—merely a weak woman's confession of unprofitable sin—the penitence of a faithless wife deserted by her betrayer. The letter had fallen from the pocket of Captain Armisted; the reader quietly transferred it to his own.

An aide-de-camp rode up and dismounted. Advancing to the Governor he saluted.

"Sir," he said, "I am sorry to find you wounded—the Commanding General has not been informed. He presents his compliments and I am directed to say that he has ordered for to-morrow a grand review of the reserve corps in your honor. I venture to add that the General's carriage is at your service if you are able to attend."

"Be pleased to say to the Commanding General that I am deeply touched by his kindness. If you have the patience to wait a few moments you shall convey a more definite reply."

He smiled brightly and glancing at the surgeon and his assistants added: "At present—if you will permit an allusion to the horrors of peace—I am 'in the hands of my friends.'"

The humor of the great is infectious; all laughed who heard.

"Where is Captain Armisted?" the Governor asked, not altogether carelessly.

The surgeon looked up from his work, pointing silently to the nearest body in the row of dead, the features discreetly covered with a handkerchief. It was so near that the great man could have laid his hand upon it, but he did not. He may have feared that it would bleed.

The Story of a Conscience

CAPTAIN PARROL HARTROY stood at the advanced post of his picket-guard, talking in low tones with the sentinel. This post was on a turnpike which bisected the captain's camp, a half-mile in rear, though the camp was not in sight from that point. The officer was apparently giving the soldier certain instructions—was perhaps merely inquiring if all were quiet in front. As the two stood talking a man approached them from the direction of the camp, carelessly whistling, and was promptly halted by the soldier. He was evidently a civilian—a tall person, coarsely clad in the home-made stuff of yellow gray, called "butternut," which was men's only wear in the latter days of the Confederacy. On his head was a slouch felt hat, once white, from beneath which hung masses of uneven hair, seemingly unacquainted with either scissors or comb. The man's face was rather striking; a broad forehead, high nose, and thin cheeks, the mouth invisible in the full dark beard, which seemed as neglected as the hair. The eyes were large and had that steadiness and fixity of attention which so frequently mark a considering intelligence and a will not easily turned from its purpose—so say those physiognomists who have that kind of eyes. On the whole, this was a man whom one would be likely to observe and be observed by. He carried a walking-stick freshly cut from the forest and his ailing cowskin boots were white with dust.

"Show your pass," said the Federal soldier, a trifle more imperiously perhaps than he would have thought necessary if he had not been under the eye of his commander, who with folded arms looked on from the roadside.

" 'Lowed you'd rec'lect me, Gineral," said the wayfarer tranquilly, while producing the paper from the pocket of his coat. There was something in his tone—perhaps a faint suggestion of irony—which made his elevation of his obstructor to exalted rank less agreeable to that worthy warrior than promotion is commonly found to be. "You-all have to be purty pertickler, I reckon," he added, in a more conciliatory tone, as if in half-apology for being halted.

Having read the pass, with his rifle resting on the ground, the soldier handed the document back without a word, shouldered his weapon, and returned to his commander. The civilian passed on in the middle of the road, and when he had penetrated the circumjacent Confederacy a few yards resumed his whistling and was soon out of sight beyond an angle in the road, which at that point entered a thin forest. Suddenly the officer undid his arms from his breast, drew a revolver from his belt and sprang forward at a run in the same direction, leaving his sentinel in gaping astonishment at his post. After making to the various visible forms of nature a solemn promise to be damned, that gentleman resumed the air of stolidity which is supposed to be appropriate to a state of alert military attention.

II

Captain Hartroy held an independent command. His force consisted of a company of infantry, a squadron of cavalry, and a section of artillery, detached from the army to which they belonged, to defend an important defile in the Cumberland Mountains in Tennessee. It was a field officer's command held by a line officer promoted from the ranks, where he had quietly served until "discovered." His post was one of exceptional peril; its defense entailed a heavy responsibility and he had wisely been given corresponding discretionary powers, all the more necessary because of his distance from the main army, the precarious nature of his communications and the lawless character of the enemy's irregular troops infesting that region. He had strongly fortified his little camp, which embraced a village of a half-dozen dwellings and a country store, and had collected a considerable quantity of supplies. To a few resident civilians of known loyalty, with whom it was desirable to trade, and of whose services in various ways he sometimes availed himself, he had given written passes admitting them within his lines. It is easy to understand that an abuse of this privilege in the interest of the enemy might entail serious consequences.

Captain Hartroy had made an order to the effect that any one so abusing it would be summarily shot.

While the sentinel had been examining the civilian's pass the captain had eyed the latter narrowly. He thought his appearance familiar and had at first no doubt of having given him the pass which had satisfied the sentinel. It was not until the man had got out of sight and hearing that his identity was disclosed by a revealing light from memory. With soldierly promptness of decision the officer had acted on the revelation.

III

To any but a singularly self-possessed man the apparition of an officer of the military forces, formidably clad, bearing in one hand a sheathed sword and in the other a cocked revolver, and rushing in furious pursuit, is no doubt disquieting to a high degree; upon the man to whom the pursuit was in this instance directed it appeared to have no other effect than somewhat to intensify his tranquillity. He might easily enough have escaped into the forest to the right or the left, but chose another course of action—turned and quietly faced the captain, saying as he came up: "I reckon ye must have something to say to me, which ye disremembered. What mout it be, neighbor?"

But the "neighbor" did not answer, being engaged in the unneighborly act of covering him with a cocked pistol.

"Surrender," said the captain as calmly as a slight breathlessness from exertion would permit, "or you die."

There was no menace in the manner of his demand; that was all in the matter and in the means of enforcing it. There was, too, something not altogether reassuring in the cold gray eyes that glanced along the barrel of the weapon. For a moment the two men stood looking at each other in silence; then the civilian, with no appearance of fear—with as great apparent unconcern as when complying with the less austere demand of the sentinel—slowly pulled from his pocket the paper which had satisfied that humble functionary and held it out, saying:

"I reckon this 'ere parss from Mister Hartroy is——"

"The pass is a forgery," the officer said, interrupting. "I am Captain Hartroy—and you are Dramer Brune."

It would have required a sharp eye to observe the slight pallor of the civilian's face at these words, and the only other manifestation attesting their significance was a voluntary relaxation of the thumb and fingers holding the dishonored paper, which, falling to the road, unheeded, was rolled by a gentle wind and then lay still, with a coating of dust, as in humiliation for the lie that it bore. A moment later the civilian, still looking unmoved into the barrel of the pistol, said:

"Yes, I am Dramer Brune, a Confederate spy, and your prisoner. I have on my person, as you will soon discover, a plan of your fort and its armament, a statement of the distribution of your men and their number, a map of the approaches, showing the positions of all your outposts. My life is fairly yours, but if you wish it taken in a more formal way than by your own hand, and if you are willing to spare me the indignity of marching into camp at the muzzle of your pistol, I promise you that I will neither resist, escape, nor remonstrate, but will submit to whatever penalty may be imposed."

The officer lowered his pistol, uncocked it, and thrust it into its place in his belt. Brune advanced a step, extending his right hand.

"It is the hand of a traitor and a spy," said the officer coldly, and did not take it. The other bowed.

"Come," said the captain, "let us go to camp; you shall not die until to-morrow morning."

He turned his back upon his prisoner, and these two enigmatical men retraced their steps and soon passed the sentinel, who expressed his general sense of things by a needless and exaggerated salute to his commander.

IV

Early on the morning after these events the two men, captor and captive, sat in the tent of the former. A table was between them on which lay, among a number of letters, official and private, which the captain had written during the night, the incriminating papers found upon the spy. That gentleman had slept through the night in an adjoining tent, unguarded. Both, having breakfasted, were now smoking.

"Mr. Brune," said Captain Hartroy, "you probably do not understand why I recognized you in your disguise, nor how I was aware of your name."

"I have not sought to learn, Captain," the prisoner said with quiet dignity.

"Nevertheless I should like you to know—if the story will not offend. You will perceive that my knowledge of you goes back to the autumn of 1861. At that time you were a private in an Ohio regiment—a brave and trusted soldier. To the surprise and grief of your officers and comrades you deserted and went over to the enemy. Soon afterward you were captured in a skirmish, recognized, tried by court-martial and sentenced to be shot. Awaiting the execution of the sentence you were confined, unfettered, in a freight car standing on a side track of a railway."

"At Grafton, Virginia," said Brune, pushing the ashes from his cigar with the little finger of the hand holding it, and without looking up.

"At Grafton, Virginia," the captain repeated. "One dark and stormy night a soldier who had just returned from a long, fatiguing march was put on guard over you. He sat on a cracker box inside the car, near the door, his rifle loaded and the bayonet fixed. You sat in a corner and his orders were to kill you if you attempted to rise."

"But if I *asked* to rise he might call the corporal of the guard."

"Yes. As the long silent hours wore away the soldier yielded to the demands of nature: he himself incurred the death penalty by sleeping at his post of duty."

"You did."

"What! you recognize me? you have known me all along?"

The captain had risen and was walking the floor of his tent, visibly excited. His face was flushed, the grey eyes had lost the cold, pitiless look which they had shown when Brune had seen them over the pistol barrel; they had softened wonderfully.

"I knew you," said the spy, with his customary tranquility, "the moment you faced me, demanding my surrender. In the circumstances it would have been hardly becoming in me to recall these matters. I am perhaps a traitor, certainly a spy; but I should not wish to seem a suppliant."

The captain had paused in his walk and was facing his

prisoner. There was a singular huskiness in his voice as he spoke again.

"Mr. Brune, whatever your conscience may permit you to be, you saved my life at what you must have believed the cost of your own. Until I saw you yesterday when halted by my sentinel I believed you dead—thought that you had suffered the fate which through my own crime you might easily have escaped. You had only to step from the car and leave me to take your place before the firing-squad. You had a divine compassion. You pitied my fatigue. You let me sleep, watched over me, and as the time drew near for the relief-guard to come and detect me in my crime, you gently waked me. Ah, Brune, Brune, that was well done—that was great—that——"

The captain's voice failed him; the tears were running down his face and sparkled upon his beard and his breast. Resuming his seat at the table, he buried his face in his arms and sobbed. All else was silence.

Suddenly the clear warble of a bugle was heard sounding the "assembly." The captain started and raised his wet face from his arms; it had turned ghastly pale. Outside, in the sunlight, were heard the stir of the men falling into line; the voices of the sergeants calling the roll; the tapping of the drummers as they braced their drums. The captain spoke again:

"I ought to have confessed my fault in order to relate the story of your magnanimity; it might have procured you a pardon. A hundred times I resolved to do so, but shame prevented. Besides, your sentence was just and righteous. Well, Heaven forgive me! I said nothing, and my regiment was soon afterward ordered to Tennessee and I never heard about you."

"It was all right, sir," said Brune, without visible emotion; "I escaped and returned to my colors—the Confederate colors. I should like to add that before deserting from the Federal service I had earnestly asked a discharge, on the ground of altered convictions. I was answered by punishment."

"Ah, but if I had suffered the penalty of my crime—if you had not generously given me the life that I accepted without gratitude you would not be again in the shadow and imminence of death."

The prisoner started slightly and a look of anxiety came into his face. One would have said, too, that he was surprised. At that moment a lieutenant, the adjutant, appeared at the opening of the tent and saluted. "Captain," he said, "the battalion is formed."

Captain Hartroy had recovered his composure. He turned to the officer and said: "Lieutenant, go to Captain Graham and say that I direct him to assume command of the battalion and parade it outside the parapet. This gentleman is a deserter and a spy; he is to be shot to death in the presence of the troops. He will accompany you, unbound and unguarded."

While the adjutant waited at the door the two men inside the tent rose and exchanged ceremonious bows, Brune immediately retiring.

Half an hour later an old negro cook, the only person left in camp except the commander, was so startled by the sound of a volley of musketry that he dropped the kettle that he was lifting from a fire. But for his consternation and the hissing which the contents of the kettle made among the embers, he might also have heard, nearer at hand, the single pistol shot with which Captain Hartroy renounced the life which in conscience he could no longer keep.

In compliance with the terms of a note that he left for the officer who succeeded him in command, he was buried, like the deserter and spy, without military honors; and in the solemn shadow of the mountain which knows no more of war the two sleep well in long-forgotten graves.

One Kind of Officer

OF THE USES OF CIVILITY

CAPTAIN RANSOME, it is not permitted to you to know *anything*. It is sufficient that you obey my order—which permit me to repeat. If you perceive any movement of troops in your front you are to open fire, and if attacked hold this position as long as you can. Do I make myself understood, sir?"

"Nothing could be plainer. Lieutenant Price,"—this to an officer of his own battery, who had ridden up in time to hear the order—"the general's meaning is clear, is it not?"

"Perfectly."

The lieutenant passed on to his post. For a moment General Cameron and the commander of the battery sat in their saddles, looking at each other in silence. There was no more to say; apparently too much had already been said. Then the superior officer nodded coldly and turned his horse to ride away. The artillerist saluted slowly, gravely, and with extreme formality. One acquainted with the niceties of military etiquette would have said that by his manner he attested a sense of the rebuke that he had incurred. It is one of the important uses of civility to signify resentment.

When the general had joined his staff and escort, awaiting him at a little distance, the whole cavalcade moved off toward the right of the guns and vanished in the fog. Captain Ransome was alone, silent, motionless as an equestrian statue. The gray fog, thickening every moment, closed in about him like a visible doom.

II

UNDER WHAT CIRCUMSTANCES MEN DO NOT WISH TO BE SHOT

The fighting of the day before had been desultory and indecisive. At the points of collision the smoke of battle had hung in blue sheets among the branches of the trees till beaten into nothing by the falling rain. In the softened earth the wheels of cannon and ammunition wagons cut deep, ragged furrows, and movements of infantry seemed impeded by the mud that clung to the soldiers' feet as, with soaken garments and rifles imperfectly protected by capes of overcoats they went dragging in sinuous lines hither and thither through dripping forest and flooded field. Mounted officers, their heads protruding from rubber ponchos that glittered like black armor, picked their way, singly and in loose groups, among the men, coming and going with apparent aimlessness and commanding attention from nobody but one another. Here and there a dead man, his clothing defiled with earth, his face covered with a blanket or showing yellow and claylike in the rain, added his dispiriting influence to that of the other dismal features of the scene and augmented the general discomfort with a particular dejection. Very repulsive these wrecks looked—not at all heroic, and nobody was accessible to the infection of their patriotic example. Dead upon the field of honor, yes; but the field of honor was so very wet! It makes a difference.

The general engagement that all expected did not occur, none of the small advantages accruing, now to this side and now to that, in isolated and accidental collisions being followed up. Half-hearted attacks provoked a sullen resistance which was satisfied with mere repulse. Orders were obeyed with mechanical fidelity; no one did any more than his duty.

"The army is cowardly to-day," said General Cameron, the commander of a Federal brigade, to his adjutant-general.

"The army is cold," replied the officer addressed, "and—yes, it doesn't wish to be like that."

He pointed to one of the dead bodies, lying in a thin pool of yellow water, its face and clothing bespattered with mud from hoof and wheel.

The army's weapons seemed to share its military delinquency. The rattle of rifles sounded flat and contemptible. It had no meaning and scarcely roused to attention and expectancy the unengaged parts of the line-of-battle and the waiting reserves. Heard at a little distance, the reports of cannon were feeble in volume and *timbre*: they lacked sting and resonance. The guns seemed to be fired with light charges, unshotted. And so the futile day wore on to its dreary close, and then to a night of discomfort succeeded a day of apprehension.

An army has a personality. Beneath the individual thoughts and emotions of its component parts it thinks and feels as a unit. And in this large, inclusive sense of things lies a wiser wisdom than the mere sum of all that it knows. On that dismal morning this great brute force, groping at the bottom of a white ocean of fog among trees that seemed as sea weeds, had a dumb consciousness that all was not well; that a day's manœuvring had resulted in a faulty disposition of its parts, a blind diffusion of its strength. The men felt insecure and talked among themselves of such tactical errors as with their meager military vocabulary they were able to name. Field and line officers gathered in groups and spoke more learnedly of what they apprehended with no greater clearness. Commanders of brigades and divisions looked anxiously to their connections on the right and on the left, sent staff officers on errands of inquiry and pushed skirmish lines silently and cautiously forward into the dubious region between the known and the unknown. At some points on the line the troops, apparently of their own volition, constructed such defenses as they could without the silent spade and the noisy ax.

One of these points was held by Captain Ransome's battery of six guns. Provided always with intrenching tools, his men had labored with diligence during the night, and now his guns thrust their black muzzles through the embrasures of a really formidable earthwork. It crowned a slight acclivity devoid of undergrowth and providing an unobstructed fire that would sweep the ground for an unknown distance in front. The position could hardly have been better chosen. It had this peculiarity, which Captain Ransome, who was greatly addicted to the use of the compass, had not failed to observe: it faced northward, whereas he knew that the general line of the army must face eastward. In fact, that part of the line was "refused"—that is to say, bent backward, away from the enemy. This implied that Captain Ransome's battery was somewhere near the left flank of the army; for an army in line of battle retires its flanks if the nature of the ground will permit, they being its vulnerable points. Actually, Captain Ransome appeared to hold the extreme left of the line, no troops being visible in that direction beyond his own. Immediately in rear of his guns occurred that conversation between him and his brigade commander, the concluding and more picturesque part of which is reported above.

III

HOW TO PLAY THE CANNON WITHOUT NOTES

Captain Ransome sat motionless and silent on horseback. A few yards away his men were standing at their guns. Somewhere —everywhere within a few miles—were a hundred thousand men, friends and enemies. Yet he was alone. The mist had isolated him as completely as if he had been in the heart of a desert. His world was a few square yards of wet and trampled earth about the feet of his horse. His comrades in that ghostly domain were invisible and inaudible. These were conditions favorable to thought, and he was thinking. Of the nature of his thoughts his clear-cut handsome features yielded no attesting sign. His face was as inscrutable as that of the sphinx. Why should it have made a record which there was none to observe? At the sound of a footstep he merely turned his eyes in the direction whence it came; one of his sergeants, looking a giant in stature in the false perspective of the fog, approached, and when clearly defined and reduced to his true dimensions by propinquity, saluted and stood at attention.

"Well, Morris," said the officer, returning his subordinate's salute.

"Lieutenant Price directed me to tell you, sir, that most of the infantry has been withdrawn. We have not sufficient support."

"Yes, I know."

"I am to say that some of our men have been out over the works a hundred yards and report that our front is not picketed."

"Yes."

"They were so far forward that they heard the enemy."

"Yes."

"They heard the rattle of the wheels of artillery and the commands of officers."

"Yes."

"The enemy is moving toward our works."

Captain Ransome, who had been facing to the rear of his line—toward the point where the brigade commander and his cavalcade had been swallowed up by the fog—reined his horse about and faced the other way. Then he sat motionless as before.

"Who are the men who made that statement?" he inquired, without looking at the sergeant; his eyes were directed straight into the fog over the head of his horse.

"Corporal Hassman and Gunner Manning."

Captain Ransome was a moment silent. A slight pallor came into his face, a slight compression affected the lines of his lips, but it would have required a closer observer than Sergeant Morris to note the change. There was none in the voice.

"Sergeant, present my compliments to Lieutenant Price and direct him to open fire with all the guns. Grape."

The sergeant saluted and vanished in the fog.

IV

TO INTRODUCE GENERAL MASTERSON

Searching for his division commander, General Cameron and his escort had followed the line of battle for nearly a mile to the right of Ransome's battery, and there learned that the division commander had gone in search of the corps commander. It seemed that everybody was looking for his immediate superior—an ominous circumstance. It meant that nobody was quite at ease. So General Cameron rode on for another half-mile, where by good luck he met General Masterson, the division commander, returning.

"Ah, Cameron," said the higher officer, reining up, and throwing his right leg across the pommel of his saddle in a most unmilitary way—"anything up? Found a good position for your battery, I hope—if one place is better than another in a fog."

"Yes, general," said the other, with the greater dignity appropriate to his less exalted rank, "my battery is very well placed. I wish I could say that it is as well commanded."

"Eh, what's that? Ransome? I think him a fine fellow. In the army we should be proud of him."

It was customary for officers of the regular army to speak of it as "the army." As the greatest cities are most provincial, so the self-complacency of aristocracies is most frankly plebeian.

"He is too fond of his opinion. By the way, in order to occupy the hill that he holds I had to extend my line dangerously. The hill is on my left—that is to say the left flank of the army."

"Oh, no, Hart's brigade is beyond. It was ordered up from Drytown during the night and directed to hook on to you. Better go and——"

The sentence was unfinished: a lively cannonade had broken out on the left, and both officers, followed by their retinues of aides and orderlies making a great jingle and clank, rode rapidly toward the spot. But they were soon impeded, for they were compelled by the fog to keep within sight of the line-of-battle, behind which were swarms of men, all in motion across their way. Everywhere the line was assuming a sharper and harder definition, as the men sprang to arms and the officers, with drawn swords, "dressed" the ranks. Color-bearers unfurled the flags, buglers blew the "assembly," hospital attendants appeared with stretchers. Field officers mounted and sent their impedimenta to the rear in care of negro servants. Back in the ghostly spaces of the forest could be heard the rustle and murmur of the reserves, pulling themselves together.

Nor was all this preparation vain, for scarcely five minutes had passed since Captain Ransome's guns had broken the truce of doubt before the whole region was aroar: the enemy had attacked nearly everywhere.

V

HOW SOUNDS CAN FIGHT SHADOWS

Captain Ransome walked up and down behind his guns, which were firing rapidly but with steadiness. The gunners worked alertly, but without haste or apparent excitement. There was really no reason for excitement; it is not much to point a cannon into a fog and fire it. Anybody can do as much as that.

The men smiled at their noisy work, performing it with a lessening alacrity. They cast curious regards upon their captain, who had now mounted the banquette of the fortification and was looking across the parapet as if observing the effect of his fire. But the only visible effect was the substitution of wide, low-lying sheets of smoke for their bulk of fog. Suddenly out of the obscurity burst a great sound of cheering, which filled the intervals between the reports of the guns with startling distinctness! To the few with leisure and opportunity to observe, the sound was inexpressibly strange– so loud, so near, so menacing, yet nothing seen! The men who had smiled at their work smiled no more, but performed it with a serious and feverish activity.

From his station at the parapet Captain Ransome now saw a great multitude of dim gray figures taking shape in the mist below him and swarming up the slope. But the work of the guns was now fast and furious. They swept the populous declivity with gusts of grape and canister, the whirring of which could be heard through the thunder of the explosions. In this awful tempest of iron the assailants struggled forward foot by foot across their dead, firing into the embrasures, reloading, firing again, and at last falling in their turn, a little in advance of those who had fallen before. Soon the smoke was dense enough to cover all. It settled down upon the attack and, drifting back, involved the defense. The gunners could hardly see to serve their pieces, and when occasional figures of the enemy appeared upon the parapet—having had the good luck to get near enough to it, between two embrasures, to be protected from the guns—they looked so unsubstantial that it seemed hardly worth while for the few infantrymen to go to work upon them with the bayonet and tumble them back into the ditch.

As the commander of a battery in action can find something better to do than cracking individual skulls, Captain Ransome had retired from the parapet to his proper post in rear of his guns, where he stood with folded arms, his bugler beside him. Here, during the hottest of the fight, he was approached by Lieutenant Price, who had just sabred a daring assailant inside the work. A spirited coloquy ensued between the two officers —spirited, at least, on the part of the lieutenant, who gesticulated with energy and shouted again and again into his commander's ear in the attempt to make himself heard above the infernal din of the guns. His gestures, if cooly noted by an

actor, would have been pronounced to be those of protesta-
tion: one would have said that he was opposed to the proceedings. Did he wish to surrender?

Captain Ransome listened without a change of countenance
or attitude, and when the other man had finished his harangue,
looked him coldly in the eyes and during a seasonable abatement of the uproar said:

"Lieutenant Price, it is not permitted to you to know *anything*. It is sufficient that you obey my orders."

The lieutenant went to his post, and the parapet being now
apparently clear Captain Ransome returned to it to have a look
over. As he mounted the banquette a man sprang upon the
crest, waving a great brilliant flag. The captain drew a pistol
from his belt and shot him dead. The body, pitching forward,
hung over the inner edge of the embankment, the arms straight
downward, both hands still grasping the flag. The man's few
followers turned and fled down the slope. Looking over the
parapet, the captain saw no living thing. He observed also that
no bullets were coming into the work.

He made a sign to the bugler, who sounded the command
to cease firing. At all other points the action had already ended
with a repulse of the Confederate attack; with the cessation of
this cannonade the silence was absolute.

VI

WHY, BEING AFFRONTED BY A, IT IS NOT BEST
TO AFFRONT B

General Masterson rode into the redoubt. The men, gathered in groups, were talking loudly and gesticulating. They
pointed at the dead, running from one body to another. They
neglected their foul and heated guns and forgot to resume
their outer clothing. They ran to the parapet and looked over,
some of them leaping down into the ditch. A score were gathered about a flag rigidly held by a dead man.

"Well, my men," said the general cheerily, "you have had a
pretty fight of it."

They stared; nobody replied; the presence of the great man
seemed to embarrass and alarm.

Getting no response to his pleasant condescension, the easy-mannered officer whistled a bar or two of a popular air, and riding forward to the parapet, looked over at the dead. In an instant he had whirled his horse about and was spurring along in rear of the guns, his eyes everywhere at once. An officer sat on the trail of one of the guns, smoking a cigar. As the general dashed up he rose and tranquilly saluted.

"Captain Ransome!"—the words fell sharp and harsh, like the clash of steel blades—"you have been fighting our own men—our own men, sir; do you hear? Hart's brigade!"

"General, I know that."

"You know it—you know that, and you sit here smoking? Oh, damn it, Hamilton, I'm losing my temper,"—this to his provost-marshal. "Sir—Captain Ransome, be good enough to say—to say why you fought our own men."

"That I am unable to say. In my orders that information was withheld."

Apparently the general did not comprehend.

"Who was the aggressor in this affair, you or General Hart?" he asked.

"I was."

"And could you not have known—could you not see, sir, that you were attacking our own men?"

The reply was astounding!

"I knew that, general. It appeared to be none of my business."

Then, breaking the dead silence that followed his answer, he said:

"I must refer you to General Cameron."

"General Cameron is dead, sir—as dead as he can be—as dead as any man in this army. He lies back yonder under a tree. Do you mean to say that he had anything to do with this horrible business?"

Captain Ransome did not reply. Observing the altercation his men had gathered about to watch the outcome. They were greatly excited. The fog, which had been partly dissipated by the firing, had again closed in so darkly about them that they drew more closely together till the judge on horseback and the accused standing calmly before him had but a narrow space free from intrusion. It was the most informal of courts-martial, but all felt that the formal one to follow would but affirm its judgment. It had no jurisdiction, but it had the significance of prophecy.

"Captain Ransome," the general cried impetuously, but with something in his voice that was almost entreaty, "if you can say anything to put a better light upon your incomprehensible conduct I beg you will do so."

Having recovered his temper this generous soldier sought for something to justify his naturally sympathetic attitude toward a brave man in the imminence of a dishonorable death.

"Where is Lieutenant Price?" the captain said.

That officer stood forward, his dark saturnine face looking somewhat forbidding under a bloody hand-kerchief bound about his brow. He understood the summons and needed no invitation to speak. He did not look at the captain, but addressed the general:

"During the engagement I discovered the state of affairs, and apprised the commander of the battery. I ventured to urge that the firing cease. I was insulted and ordered to my post."

"Do you know anything of the orders under which I was acting?" asked the captain.

"Of any orders under which the commander of the battery was acting," the lieutenant continued, still addressing the general, "I know nothing."

Captain Ransome felt his world sink away from his feet. In those cruel words he heard the murmur of the centuries breaking upon the shore of eternity. He heard the voice of doom; it said, in cold, mechanical, and measure tones: "Ready, aim, fire!" and he felt the bullets tear his heart to shreds. He heard the sound of the earth upon his coffin and (if the good God was so merciful) the song of a bird above his forgotten grave. Quietly detaching his sabre from its supports, he handed it up to the provost-marshal.

One Officer, One Man

CAPTAIN GRAFFENREID stood at the head of his company. The regiment was not engaged. It formed a part of the front line-of-battle, which stretched away to the right with a visible length of nearly two miles through the open ground. The left flank was veiled by woods; to the right also the line was lost to sight, but it extended many miles. A hundred yards in rear was a second line; behind this, the reserve brigades and division in column. Batteries of artillery occupied the spaces between and crowned the low hills. Groups of horsemen—generals with their staffs and escorts, and field officers of regiments behind the colors—broke the regularity of the line and columns. Numbers of these figures of interest had field-glasses at their eyes and sat motionless, stolidly scanning the country in front; others came and went at a slow canter, bearing orders. There were squads of stretcher-bearers, ambulances, wagon-trains with ammunition, and officers' servants in rear of all—of all that was visible—for still in rear of these, along the roads, extended for many miles all that vast multitude of non-combatants who with their various *impedimenta* are assigned to the inglorious but important duty of supplying the fighters' many needs.

An army in line-of-battle awaiting attack, or prepared to deliver it, presents strange contrasts. At the front are precision, formality, fixity, and silence. Toward the rear these characteristics are less and less conspicuous, and finally, in point of space, are lost altogether in confusion, motion and noise. The homogeneous becomes heterogeneous. Definition is lacking; repose is replaced by an apparently purposeless activity; harmony vanishes in hubbub, form in disorder. Commotion everywhere and ceaseless unrest. The men who do not fight are never ready.

From this position at the right of his company in the front rank, Captain Graffenreid had an unobstructed outlook toward the enemy. A half-mile of open and nearly level ground lay before him and beyond it an irregular wood, covering a slight acclivity; not a human being anywhere visible. He could imagine nothing more peaceful than the appearance of that pleasant landscape with its long stretches of brown fields over which the atmosphere was beginning to quiver in the heat of the morning sun. Not a sound came from forest or field—not even the barking of a dog or the crowing of a cock at the half-seen plantation house on the crest among the trees. Yet every man in those miles of men knew that he and death were face to face.

Captain Graffenreid had never in his life seen an armed enemy, and the war in which his regiment was one of the first to take the field was two years old. He had had the rare advantage of a military education, and when his comrades had marched to the front he had been detached for administrative service at the capital of his State, where it was thought that he could be most useful. Like a bad soldier he protested, and like a good one obeyed. In close official and personal relations with the governor of his State, and enjoying his confidence and favor, he had firmly refused promotion and seen his juniors elevated above him. Death had been busy in his distant regiment; vacancies among the field officers had occurred again and again; but from a chivalrous feeling that war's rewards belonged of right to those who bore the storm and stress of battle he had held his humble rank and generously advanced the fortunes of others. His silent devotion to principle had conquered at last: he had been relieved of his hateful duties and ordered to the front, and now, untried by fire, stood in the van of battle in command of a company of hardy veterans, to whom he had been only a name, and that name a by-word. By none—not even by those of his brother officers in whose favor he had wavied his rights—was his devotion to duty understood. They were too busy to be just; he was looked upon as one who had shirked his duty, until forced unwillingly into the field. Too proud to explain, yet not too insensible to feel, he could only endure and hope.

Of all the Federal Army on that summer morning none had accepted battle more joyously than Anderton Graffenreid. His spirit was buoyant, his faculties were riotous. He was in a state of mental exaltation and scarcely could endure the enemy's tardiness in advancing to the attack. To him this was opportunity —for the result cared nothing. Victory or defeat, as God might will; in one or in the other he should prove himself a soldier and a hero; he should vindicate his right to the respect to his men and the companionship of his brother officers—to the consideration of his superiors. How his heart leaped in his breast as the bugle sounded the stirring notes of the "assembly"! With what a light tread, scarcely conscious of the earth beneath his feet, he strode forward at the head of his company, and how exultingly he noted the tactical disposition which placed his regiment in the front line! And if perchance some memory came to him of a pair of dark eyes that might take on a tenderer light in reading the account of that day's doings, who shall blame him for the unmartial thought or count it a debasement of soldierly ardor?

Suddenly, from the forest a half-mile in front—apparently from among the upper branches of the trees, but really from the ride beyond—rose a tall column of white smoke. A moment later came a deep, jarring explosion, followed—almost attended—by a hideous rushing sound that seemed to leap forward across the intervening space with inconceivable rapidity, rising from whisper to roar with too quick a gradation for attention to note the successive stages of its horrible progression! A visible tremor ran along the lines of men; all were startled into motion. Captain Graffenreid dodged and threw up his hands to one side of his head, palms outward. As he did so he heard a keen, ringing report, and saw on a hillside behind the line a fierce roll of smoke and dust—the shell's explosion. It had passed a hundred feet to his left! He heard, or fancied he heard, a low, mocking laugh and turning in the direction whence it came saw the eyes of his first lieutenant fixed upon him with an unmistakable look of amusement. He looked along the line of faces in the front ranks. The men were laughing. At him? The thought restored the color to his bloodless face—restored too much of it. His cheeks burned with a fever of shame.

The enemy's shot was not answered: the officer in command at that exposed part of the line had evidently no desire to provoke a cannonade. For the forbearance Captain Graffenreid was conscious of a sense of gratitude. He had not known that the flight of a projectile was a phenomenon of so appalling character. His conception of war had already undergone a profound change, and he was conscious that his new feeling was manifesting itself in visible perturbation. His blood was boiling in his veins; he had a choking sensation and felt that if he had a command to give it would be inaudible, or at least unintelligible. The hand in which he held his sword trembled; the other moved automatically, clutching at various parts of his clothing. He found a difficulty in standing still and fancied that his men observed it. Was it fear? He feared it was.

From somewhere away to the right came, as the wind served, a low, intermittent murmur like that of ocean in a storm—like that of a distant railway train—like that of wind among the pines—three sounds so nearly alike that the ear, unaided by the judgment, cannot distinguish them one from another. The eyes of the troops were drawn in that direction; the mounted officers turned their field-glasses that way. Mingled with the sound was an irregular throbbing. He thought it, at first, the beating of his fevered blood in his ears; next, the distant tapping of a bass drum.

"The ball is opened on the right flank," said an officer.

Captain Graffenreid understood: the sounds were musketry and artillery. He nodded and tried to smile. There was apparently nothing infectious in the smile.

Presently a light line of blue smoke-puffs broke out along the edge of the wood in front, succeeded by a crackle of rifles. There were keen, sharp hissings in the air, terminating abruptly with a thump near by. The man at Captain Graffenreid's side dropped his rifle; his knees gave way and he pitched awkwardly forward, falling upon his face. Somebody shouted "Lie down!" and the dead man was hardly distinguishable from the living. It looked as if those few rifle-shots had slain ten thousand men. Only the field officers remained erect; their concession to the emergency consisted in dismounting and sending their horses to the shelter of the low hills immediately in rear.

Captain Graffenreid lay alongside the dead man, from beneath whose breast flowed a little rill of blood. It had a faint, sweetish odor that sickened him. The face was crushed into the earth and flattened. It looked yellow already, and was repulsive. Nothing suggested the glory of a soldier's death nor mitigated the loathsomeness of the incident. He could not turn his back upon the body without facing away from his company.

He fixed his eyes upon the forest, where all again was silent. He tried to imagine what was going on there—the lines of troops forming to attack, the guns being pushed forward by hand to the edge of the open. He fancied he could see their black muzzles protruding from the undergrowth, ready to deliver their storm of missles—such missiles as the one whose shriek had so unsettled his nerves. The distension of his eyes became painful; a mist seemed to gather before them; he could no longer see across the field, yet would not withdraw his gaze lest he see the dead man at his side.

The fire of battle was not now burning very brightly in this warrior's soul. From inaction had come introspection. He sought rather to analyze his feelings than distinguish himself by courage and devotion. The result was profoundly disappointing. He covered his face with his hands and groaned aloud.

The hoarse murmur of battle grew more and more distinct upon the right; the murmur had, indeed, become a roar, the throbbing, a thunder. The sounds had worked round obliquely to the front; evidently the enemy's left was being driven back, and the propitious moment to move against the salient angle of his line would soon arrive. The silence and mystery in front were ominous; all felt that they boded evil to the assailants.

Behind the prostrate lines sounded the hoofbeats of galloping horses; the men turned to look. A dozen staff officers were riding to the various brigade and regimental commanders, who had remounted. A moment more and there was a chorus of voices, all uttering out of time the same words—"Attention, battalion!" The men sprang to their feet and were aligned by the company commanders. They awaited the word "forward" —awaited, too, with beating hearts and set teeth the gusts of lead and iron that were to smite them at their first movement in obedience to that word. The word was not given; the tempest did not break out. The delay was hideous, maddening! It unnerved like a respite at the guillotine.

Captain Graffenreid stood at the head of his company, the dead man at his feet. He heard the battle on the right—rattle and crash of musketry, ceaseless thunder of cannon, desultory cheers of invisible combatants. He marked ascending clouds of smoke from distant forests. He noted the sinister silence of the forest in front. These contrasting extremes affected the whole range of his sensibilities. The strain upon his nervous organization was insupportable. He grew hot and cold by turns. He panted like a dog, and then forgot to breathe until reminded by vertigo.

Suddenly he grew calm. Glancing downward, his eyes had fallen upon his naked sword, as he held it, point to earth. Foreshortened to his view, it resembled somewhat, he thought, the short heavy blade of the ancient Roman. The fancy was full of suggestion, malign, fateful, heroic!

The sergeant in the rear rank, immediately behind Captain Graffenreid, now observed a strange sight. His attention drawn by an uncommon movement made by the captain—a sudden reaching forward of the hands and their energetic withdrawal, throwing the elbows out, as in pulling an oar—he saw spring from between the officer's shoulders a bright point of metal which prolonged itself outward, nearly a half-arm's length—a blade! It was faintly streaked with crimson, and its point approached so near to the sergeant's breast, and with so quick a movement, that he shrank backward in alarm. That moment Captain Graffenreid pitched heavily forward upon the dead man and died.

A week later the major-general commanding the left corps of the Federal Army submitted the following official report:

"Sir: I have the honor to report, with regard to the action of the 19th inst., that owing to the enemy's withdrawal from my front to reinforce his beaten left, my command was not seriously engaged. My loss was as follows: Killed, one officer, one man."

George Thurston

THREE INCIDENTS IN THE LIFE OF A MAN

GEORGE THURSTON was a first lieutenant and aide-de-camp on the staff of Colonel Brough, commanding a Federal brigade. Colonel Brough was only temporarily in command, as senior colonel, the brigadier-general having been severely wounded and granted a leave of absence to recover. Lieutenant Thurston was, I believe, of Colonel Brough's regiment, to which, with his chief, he would naturally have been relegated had he lived till our brigade commander's recovery. The aide whose place Thurston took had been killed in battle; Thurston's advent among us was the only change in the *personnel* of our staff consequent upon the change in commanders. We did not like him; he was unsocial. This, however, was more observed by others than by me. Whether in camp or on the march, in barracks, in tents, or *en bivouac*, my duties as topographical engineer kept me working like a beaver—all day in the saddle and half the night at my drawing-table, platting my surveys. It was hazardous work; the nearer to the enemy's lines I could penetrate, the more valuable were my field notes and the resulting maps. It was a business in which the lives of men counted as nothing against the chance of defining a road or sketching a bridge. Whole squadrons of cavalry escort had sometimes to be sent thundering against a powerful infantry outpost in order that the brief time between the charge and the inevitable retreat might be utilized in sounding a ford or determining the point of intersection of two roads.

In some of the dark corners of England and Wales they have an immemorial custom of "beating the bounds" of the parish. On a certain day of the year the whole population turns out and travels in procession from one landmark to another on the boundary line. At the most important points lads are soundly beaten with rods to make them remember the place in after life. They become authorities. Our frequent engagements with the Confederate outposts, patrols, and scouting parties had, incidentally, the same educating value; they fixed in my memory a vivid and apparently imperishable picture of the locality—a picture serving instead of accurate field notes, which, indeed, it was not always convenient to take, with carbines cracking, sabers clashing, and horses plunging all about. These spirited encounters were observations entered in red.

One morning as I set out at the head of my escort on an expedition of more than the usual hazard Lieutenant Thurston rode up alongside and asked if I had any objection to his accompanying me, the colonel commanding having given him permission.

"None whatever," I replied rather gruffly; "but in what capacity will you go? You are not a topographical engineer, and Captain Burling commands my escort."

"I will go as a spectator," he said. Removing his sword-belt and taking the pistols from his holsters he handed them to his servant, who took them back to headquarters. I realized the brutality of my remark, but not clearly seeing my way to an apology, said nothing.

That afternoon we encountered a whole regiment of the enemy's cavalry in line and a field-piece that dominated a straight mile of the turnpike by which we had approached. My escort fought deployed in the woods on both sides, but Thurston remained in the center of the road, which at intervals of a few seconds was swept by gusts of grape and canister that tore the air wide open as they passed. He had dropped the rein on the neck of his horse and sat bolt upright in the saddle, with folded arms. Soon he was down, his horse torn to pieces. From the side of the road, my pencil and field book idle, my duty forgotten, I watched him slowly disengaging himself from the wreck and rising. At that instant, the cannon having ceased firing, a burly Confederate trooper on a spirited horse dashed like a thunderbolt down the road with drawn saber. Thurston saw him coming, drew himself up to his full height, and again folded his arms. He was too brave to retreat before the word, and my uncivil words had disarmed him. He was a spectator. Another moment and he would have been split like a mackerel, but a blessed bullet tumbled his assailant into the dusty road so near that the impetus sent the body rolling to Thurston's feet. That evening, while platting my hasty survey, I found time to frame an apology, which I think took the rude, primitive form of a confession that I had spoken like a malicious idiot.

A few weeks later a part of our army made an assault upon the enemy's left. The attack, which was made upon an unknown position and across unfamiliar ground, was led by our brigade. The ground was so broken and the underbrush so thick that all mounted officers and men were compelled to fight on foot—the brigade commander and his staff included. In the *mêlée* Thurston was parted from the rest of us, and we found him, horribly wounded, only when we had taken the enemy's last defense. He was some months in hospital at Nashville, Tennessee, but finally rejoined us. He said little about his misadventure, except that he had been bewildered and had strayed into the enemy's lines and been shot down; but from one of his captors, whom we in turn had captured, we learned the particulars. "He came walking right upon us as we lay in line," said the man. "A whole company of us instantly sprang up and leveled our rifles at his breast, some of them almost touching him. 'Throw down that sword and surrender, you damned Yank!' shouted some one in authority. The fellow ran his eyes along the line of rifle barrels, folded his arms across his breast, his right hand still clutching his sword, and deliberately replied, 'I will not.' If we had all fired he would have been torn to shreds. Some of us didn't. I didn't, for one; nothing could have induced me."

When one is tranquilly looking death in the eye and refusing him any concession one naturally has a good opinion of one's self. I don't know if it was this feeling that in Thurston found expression in a stiffish attitude and folded arms; at the mess table one day, in his absence, another explanation was suggested by our quartermaster, an irreclaimable stammerer when the wine was in: "It's h—is w—ay of m-m-mastering a c-c-consti-t-tutional t-tendency to r—un aw—ay."

"What!" I flamed out, indignantly rising; "you intimate that Thurston is a coward—and in his absence?"

"If he w—ere a cow—wow-ard h—e w—wouldn't t-try to m-m-master it; and if he w—ere p-present I w—wouldn't d-d-dare to d-d-discuss it," was the mollifying reply.

This intrepid man, George Thurston, died an ignoble death.

The brigade was in camp, with headquarters in a grove of immense trees. To an upper branch of one of these a venturesome
climber had attached the two ends of a long rope and made a
swing with a length of not less than one hundred feet. Plunging downward from a height of fifty feet, along the arc of a
circle with such a radius, soaring to an equal altitude, pausing
for one breathless instant, then sweeping dizzily backward—no
one who has not tried it can conceive the terrors of such sport
to the novice. Thurston came out of his tent one day and asked
for instruction in the mystery of propelling the swing—the art
of rising and sitting, which every boy has mastered. In a few
moments he had acquired the trick and was swinging higher
than the most experienced of us had dared. We shuddered to
look at his fearful flights.

"St-t-top him," said the quartermaster, snailing lazily along
from the mess-tent, where he had been lunching; "h—e d-
doesn't know that if h—e g-g-goes c-clear over h—e'll w—ind
up the sw—ing."

With such energy was that strong man cannonading himself
through the air that at each extremity of his increasing arc his
body, standing in the swing, was almost horizontal. Should he
once pass above the level of the rope's attachment he would
be lost; the rope would slacken and he would fall vertically to
a point as far below as he had gone above, and then the sudden
tension of the rope would wrest it from his hands. All saw the
peril—all cried out to him to desist, and gesticulated at him as,
indistinct and with a noise like the rush of a cannon shot in
flight, he swept past us through the lower reaches of his hideous oscillation. A woman standing at a little distance away
fainted and fell unobserved. Men from the camp of a regiment
near by ran in crowds to see, all shouting. Suddenly, as Thurston was on his upward curve, the shouts all ceased.

Thurston and the swing had parted—that is all that can be
known; both hands at once had released the rope. The impetus
of the light swing exhausted, it was falling back; the man's
momentum was carrying him, almost erect, upward and forward, no longer in his arc, but with an outward curve. It could
have been but an instant, yet it seemed an age. I cried out, or
thought I cried out: "My God! will he never stop going up?"
He passed close to the branch of a tree. I remember a feeling

of delight as I thought he would clutch it and save himself. I speculated on the possibility of it sustaining his weight. He passed above it, and from my point of view was sharply outlined against the blue. At this distance of many years I can distinctly recall that image of a man in the sky, its head erect, its feet close together, its hands—I do not see its hands. All at once, with astonishing suddenness and rapidity, it turns clear over and pitches downward. There is another cry from the crowd, which has rushed instinctively forward. The man has become merely a whirling object, mostly legs. Then there is an indescribable sound—the sound of an impact that shakes the earth, and these men, familiar with death in its most awful aspects, turn sick. Many walk unsteadily away from the spot; others support themselves against the trunks of trees or sit at the roots. Death has taken an unfair advantage; he has struck with an unfamiliar weapon; he has executed a new and disquieting stratagem. We did not know that he had so ghastly resources, possibilities of terror so dismal.

Thurston's body lay on its back. One leg, bent beneath, was broken above the knee and the bone driven into the earth. The abdomen had burst; the bowels protruded. The neck was broken.

The arms were folded tightly across the breast.

The Mocking-Bird

THE time, a pleasant Sunday afternoon in the early autumn of 1861. The place, a forest's heart in the mountain region of southwestern Virginia. Private Grayrock of the Federal Army is discovered seated comfortably at the root of a great pine tree, against which he leans, his legs extended straight along the ground, his rifle lying across his thighs, his hands (clasped in order that they may not fall away to his sides) resting upon the barrel of the weapon. The contact of the back of his head with the tree has pushed his cap downward over his eyes, almost concealing them; one seeing him would say that he slept.

Private Grayrock did not sleep; to have done so would have imperiled the interests of the United States, for he was a long way outside the lines and subject to capture or death at the hands of the enemy. Moreover, he was in a frame of mind unfavorable to repose. The cause of his perturbation of spirit was this: during the previous night he had served on the picket-guard, and had been posted as a sentinel in this very forest. The night was clear, though moonless, but in the gloom of the wood the darkness was deep. Grayrock's post was at a considerable distance from those to right and left, for the pickets had been thrown out a needless distance from the camp, making the line too long for the force detailed to occupy it. The war was young, and military camps entertained the error that while sleeping they were better protected by thin lines a long way toward the enemy than by thicker ones close in. And surely they needed as long notice as possible of an enemy's approach, for they were at that time addicted to the practice of undressing—than which nothing could be more unsoldierly. On the morning of the memorable 6th of April, at Shiloh, many of Grant's men when spitted on Confederate bayonets were as naked as civilians; but it should be allowed that this was not because of any defect in their picket line. Their error was of another sort: they had no pickets. This is perhaps a vain digression. I should not care to undertake to interest the reader in the fate of an army; what we have here to consider is that of Private Gray-rock.

For two hours after he had been left at his lonely post that Saturday night he stood stock-still, leaning against the trunk of a large tree, staring into the darkness in his front and trying to recognize known objects; for he had been posted at the same spot during the day. But all was now different; he saw nothing in detail, but only groups of things, whose shapes, not observed when there was something more of them to observe, were now unfamiliar. They seemed not to have been there before. A landscape that is all trees and undergrowth, moreover, lacks definition, is confused and without accentuated points upon which attention can gain a foothold. Add the gloom of a moonless night, and something more than great natural intelligence and a city education is required to preserve one's knowledge of direction. And that is how it occurred that Private Grayrock, after vigilantly watching the spaces in his front and then imprudently executing a circumspection of his whole dimly visible environment (silently walking around his tree to accomplish it) lost his bearings and seriously impaired his usefulness as a sentinel. Lost at his post—unable to say in which direction to look for an enemy's approach, and in which lay the sleeping camp for whose security he was accountable with his life—conscious, too, of many another awkward feature of the situation and of considerations affecting his own safety, Private Grayrock was profoundly disquieted. Nor was he given time to recover his tranquillity, for almost at the moment that he realized his awkward predicament he heard a stir of leaves and a snap of fallen twigs, and turning with a stilled heart in the direction whence it came, saw in the gloom the indistinct outlines of a human figure.

"Halt!" shouted Private Grayrock, peremptorily as in duty bound, backing up the command with the sharp metallic snap of his cocking rifle—"who goes there?"

There was no answer; at least there was an instant's hesitation, and the answer, if it came, was lost in the report of the sentinel's rifle. In the silence of the night and the forest the sound was deafening, and hardly had it died away when it was repeated by the pieces of the pickets to right and left, a

sympathetic fusillade. For two hours every unconverted civilian of them had been evolving enemies from his imagination,
and peopling the woods in his front with them, and Grayrock's
shot had started the whole encroaching host into visible existence. Having fired, all retreated, breathless, to the reserves—all
but Grayrock, who did not know in what direction to retreat.
When, no enemy appearing, the roused camp two miles away
had undressed and got itself into bed again, and the picket line
was cautiously re-established, he was discovered bravely holding his ground, and was complimented by the officer of the
guard as the one soldier of that devoted band who could rightly
be considered the moral equivalent of that uncommon unit of
value, "a whoop in hell."

In the mean time, however, Grayrock had made a close but
unavailing search for the mortal part of the intruder at whom
he had fired, and whom he had a marksman's intuitive sense of
having hit; for he was one of those born experts who shoot
without aim by an instinctive sense of direction, and are nearly
as dangerous by night as by day. During a full half of his
twenty-four years he had been a terror to the targets of all the
shooting-galleries in three cities. Unable now to produce his
dead game he had the discretion to hold his tongue, and was
glad to observe in his officer and comrades the natural assumption that not having run away he had seen nothing hostile. His
"honorable mention" had been earned by not running away
anyhow.

Nevertheless, Private Grayrock was far from satisfied with
the night's adventure, and when the next day he made some
fair enough pretext to apply for a pass to go outside the lines,
and the general commanding promptly granted it in recognition of his bravery the night before, he passed out at the point
where that had been displayed. Telling the sentinel then on
duty there that he had lost something,—which was true
enough—he renewed the search for the person whom he supposed himself to have shot, and whom if only wounded he
hoped to trail by the blood. He was no more successful by
daylight than he had been in the darkness, and after covering a
wide area and boldly penetrating a long distance into "the
Confederacy" he gave up the search, somewhat fatigued, seated

himself at the root of the great pine tree, where we have seen him, and indulged his disappointment.

It is not to be inferred that Grayrock's was the chagrin of a cruel nature balked of its bloody deed. In the clear large eyes, finely wrought lips, and broad forehead of that young man one could read quite another story, and in point of fact his character was a singularly felicitous compound of boldness and sensibility, courage and conscience.

"I find myself disappointed," he said to himself, sitting there at the bottom of the golden haze submerging the forest like a subtler sea—"disappointed in failing to discover a fellow-man dead by my hand! Do I then really wish that I had taken life in the performance of a duty as well performed without? What more could I wish? If any danger threatened, my shot averted it; that is what I was there to do. No, I am glad indeed if no human life was needlessly extinguished by me. But I am in a false position. I have suffered myself to be complimented by my officers and envied by my comrades. The camp is ringing with praise of my courage. That is not just; I know myself courageous, but this praise is for specific acts which I did not perform, or performed—otherwise. It is believed that I remained at my post bravely, without firing, whereas it was I who began the fusillade, and I did not retreat in the general alarm because bewildered. What, then, shall I do? Explain that I saw an enemy and fired? They have all said that of themselves, yet none believes it. Shall I tell a truth which, discrediting my courage, will have the effect of a lie? Ugh! it is an ugly business altogether. I wish to God I could find my man!"

And so wishing, Private Grayrock, overcome at last by the languor of the afternoon and lulled by the stilly sounds of insects droning and prosing in certain fragrant shrubs, so far forgot the interests of the United States as to fall asleep and expose himself to capture. And sleeping he dreamed.

He thought himself a boy, living in a far, fair land by the border of a great river upon which the tall steamboats moved grandly up and down beneath their towering evolutions of black smoke, which announced them along before they had rounded the bends and marked their movements when miles out of sight. With him always, at his side as he watched them, was one to whom he gave his heart and soul in love—a twin brother. Together they strolled along the banks of the stream; together explored the fields lying farther away from it, and gathered pungent mints and sticks of fragrant sassafras in the hills overlooking all—beyond which lay the Realm of Conjecture, and from which, looking southward across the great river, they caught glimpses of the Enchanted Land. Hand in hand and heart in heart they two, the only children of a widowed mother, walked in paths of light through valleys of peace, seeing new things under a new sun. And through all the golden days floated one unceasing sound—the rich, thrilling melody of a mocking-bird in a cage by the cottage door. It pervaded and possessed all the spiritual intervals of the dream, like a musical benediction. The joyous bird was always in song; its infinitely various notes seemed to flow from its throat, effortless, in bubbles and rills at each heart-beat, like the waters of a pulsing spring. That fresh, clear melody seemed, indeed, the spirit of the scene, the meaning and interpretation to sense of the mysteries of life and love.

But there came a time when the days of the dream grew dark with sorrow in a rain of tears. The good mother was dead, the meadowside home by the great river was broken up, and the brothers were parted between two of their kinsmen. William (the dreamer) went to live in a populous city in the Realm of Conjecture, and John, crossing the river into the Enchanted Land, was taken to a distant region whose people in their lives and ways were said to be strange and wicked. To him, in the distribution of the dead mother's estate, had fallen all that they deemed of value—the mocking-bird. They could be divided, but it could not, so it was carried away into the strange country, and the world of William knew it no more forever. Yet still through the aftertime of his loneliness its song filled all the dream, and seemed always sounding in his ear and in his heart.

The kinsmen who had adopted the boys were enemies, holding no communication. For a time letters full of boyish bravado and boastful narratives of the new and larger experience—grotesque descriptions of their widening lives and the new worlds they had conquered—passed between them; but these gradually became less frequent, and with William's removal to another and greater city ceased altogether. But ever through it all ran the song of the mocking-bird, and when the dreamer opened his eyes and stared through the vistas of the pine forest the cessation of its music first apprised him that he was awake.

The sun was low and red in the west; the level rays projected from the trunk of each giant pine a wall of shadow traversing the golden haze to eastward until light and shade were blended in undistinguishable blue.

Private Grayrock rose to his feet, looked cautiously about him, shouldered his rifle and set off toward camp. He had gone perhaps a half-mile, and was passing a thicket of laurel, when a bird rose from the midst of it and perching on the branch of a tree above, poured from its joyous breast so inexhaustible floods of song as but one of all God's creatures can utter in His praise. There was little in that—it was only to open the bill and breathe; yet the man stopped as it struck—stopped and let fall his rifle, looked upward at the bird, covered his eyes with his hands and wept like a child! For the moment he was, indeed, a child, in spirit and in memory, dwelling again by the great river, over-against the Enchanted Land! Then with an effort of the will he pulled himself together, picked up his weapon and audibly damning himself for an idiot strode on. Passing an opening that reached into the heart of the little thicket he looked in, and there, supine upon the earth, its arms all abroad, its gray uniform stained with a single spot of blood upon the breast, its white face turned sharply upward and backward, lay the image of himself!—the body of John Grayrock, dead of a gunshot wound, and still warm! He had found his man.

As the unfortunate soldier knelt beside that masterwork of civil war the shrilling bird upon the bough overhead stilled her song and, flushed with sunset's crimson glory, glided silently away through the solemn spaces of the wood. At roll-call that evening in the Federal camp the name William Grayrock brought no response, nor ever again thereafter.

CIVILIANS

The Man Out of the Nose

A T the intersection of two certain streets in that part of San Francisco known by the rather loosely applied name of North Beach, is a vacant lot, which is rather more nearly level than is usually the case with lots, vacant or otherwise, in that region. Immediately at the back of it, to the south, however, the ground slopes steeply upward, the acclivity broken by three terraces cut into the soft rock. It is a place for goats and poor persons, several families of each class having occupied it jointly and amicably "from the foundation of the city." One of the humble habitations of the lowest terrace is noticeable for its rude resemblance to the human face, or rather to such a simulacrum of it as a boy might cut out of a hollowed pumpkin, meaning no offense to his race. The eyes are two circular windows, the nose is a door, the mouth an aperture caused by removal of a board below. There are no doorsteps. As a face, this house is too large; as a dwelling, too small. The blank, unmeaning stare of its lidless and browless eyes is uncanny.

Sometimes a man steps out of the nose, turns, passes the place where the right ear should be and making his way through the throng of children and goats obstructing the narrow walk between his neighbors' doors and the edge of the terrace gains the street by descending a flight of rickety stairs. Here he pauses to consult his watch and the stranger who happens to pass wonders why such a man as that can care what is the hour. Longer observations would show that the time of day is an important element in the man's movements, for it is at precisely two o'clock in the afternoon that he comes forth 365 times in every year.

Having satisfied himself that he has made no mistake in the hour he replaces the watch and walks rapidly southward up the street two squares, turns to the right and as he approaches the next corner fixes his eyes on an upper window in a three-story building across the way. This is a somewhat dingy structure, originally of red brick and now gray. It shows the touch of age and dust. Built for a dwelling, it is now a factory. I do not know what is made there; the things that are commonly made in a factory, I suppose. I only know that at two o'clock in the afternoon of every day but Sunday it is full of activity and clatter; pulsations of some great engine shake it and there are recurrent screams of wood tormented by the saw. At the window on which the man fixes an intensely expectant gaze nothing ever appears; the glass, in truth, has such a coating of dust that it has long ceased to be transparent. The man looks at it without stopping; he merely keeps turning his head more and more backward as he leaves the building behind. Passing along to the next corner, he turns to the left, goes round the block, and comes back till he reaches the point diagonally across the street from the factory—a point on his former course, which he then retraces, looking frequently backward over his right shoulder at the window while it is in sight. For many years he has not been known to vary his route nor to introduce a single innovation into his action. In a quarter of an hour he is again at the mouth of his dwelling, and a woman, who has for some time been standing in the nose, assists him to enter. He is seen no more until two o'clock the next day.

The woman is his wife. She supports herself and him by washing for the poor people among whom they live, at rates which destroy Chinese and domestic competition.

This man is about fifty-seven years of age, though he looks greatly older. His hair is dead white. He wears no beard, and is always newly shaven. His hands are clean, his nails well kept. In the matter of dress he is distinctly superior to his position, as indicated by his surroundings and the business of his wife. He is, indeed, very neatly, if not quite fashionably, clad. His silk hat has a date no earlier than the year before the last, and his boots, scrupulously polished, are innocent of patches. I am told that the suit which he wears during his daily excursions of fifteen minutes is not the one that he wears at home. Like everything else that he has, this is provided and kept in repair by the wife, and is renewed as frequently as her scanty means permit.

Thirty years ago John Hardshaw and his wife lived on Rincon Hill in one of the finest residences of that once aristocratic quarter. He had once been a physician, but having inherited a considerable estate from his father concerned himself no more about the ailments of his fellow-creatures and found as much work as he cared for in managing his own affairs. Both he and his wife were highly cultivated persons, and their house was frequented by a small set of such men and women as persons of their tastes would think worth knowing. So far as these knew, Mr. and Mrs. Hardshaw lived happily together; certainly the wife was devoted to her handsome and accomplished husband and exceedingly proud of him.

Among their acquaintances were the Barwells—man, wife and two young children—of Sacramento. Mr. Barwell was a civil and mining engineer, whose duties took him much from home and frequently to San Francisco. On these occasions his wife commonly accompanied him and passed much of her time at the house of her friend, Mrs. Hardshaw, always with her two children, of whom Mrs. Hardshaw, childless herself, grew fond. Unluckily, her husband grew equally fond of their mother—a good deal fonder. Still more unluckily, that attractive lady was less wise than weak.

At about three o'clock one autumn morning Officer No. 13 of the Sacramento police saw a man stealthily leaving the rear entrance of a gentleman's residence and promptly arrested him. The man—who wore a slouch hat and shaggy overcoat —offered the policeman one hundred, then five hundred, then one thousand dollars to be released. As he had less than the first mentioned sum on his person the officer treated his proposal with virtuous contempt. Before reaching the station the prisoner agreed to give him a check for ten thousand dollars and remain ironed in the willows along the river bank until it should be paid. As this only provoked new derision he would say no more, merely giving an obviously fictitious name. When he was searched at the station nothing of value was found on him but a miniature portrait of Mrs. Barwell—the lady of the house at which he was caught. The case was set with costly diamonds; and something in the quality of the man's linen sent a pang of unavailing regret through the severely incorruptible bosom of Officer No. 13. There was nothing about the prisoner's clothing nor person to identify him and he was booked for burglary under the name that he had given, the honorable name of John K. Smith. The K. was an inspiration upon which, doubtless, he greatly prided himself.

In the mean time the mysterious disappearance of John Hardshaw was agitating the gossips of Rincon Hill in San Francisco, and was even mentioned in one of the newspapers. It did not occur to the lady whom that journal considerately described as his "widow," to look for him in the city prison at Sacramento—a town which he was not known ever to have visited. As John K. Smith he was arraigned and, waiving examination, committed for trial.

About two weeks before the trial, Mrs. Hardshaw, accidentally learning that her husband was held in Sacramento under an assumed name on a charge of burglary, hastened to that city without daring to mention the matter to any one and presented herself at the prison, asking for an interview with her husband, John K. Smith. Haggard and ill with anxiety, wearing a plain traveling wrap which covered her from neck to foot, and in which she had passed the night on the steamboat, too anxious to sleep, she hardly showed for what she was, but her manner pleaded for her more strongly than anything that she chose to say in evidence of her right to admittance. She was permitted to see him alone.

What occurred during that distressing interview has never transpired; but later events prove that Hardshaw had found means to subdue her will to his own. She left the prison, a broken-hearted woman, refusing to answer a single question, and returning to her desolate home renewed, in a half-hearted way, her inquiries for her missing husband. A week later she was herself missing: she had "gone back to the States"—nobody knew any more than that.

On his trial the prisoner pleaded guilty—"by advice of his counsel," so his counsel said. Nevertheless, the judge, in whose mind several unusual circumstances had created a doubt, insisted on the district attorney placing Officer No. 13 on the stand, and the deposition of Mrs. Barwell, who was too ill to attend, was read to the jury. It was very brief: she knew nothing of the matter except that the likeness of herself was her property, and had, she thought, been left on the parlor table when she had retired on the night of the arrest. She had intended it as a present to her husband, then and still absent in Europe on business for a mining company.

This witness's manner when making the deposition at her residence was afterward described by the district attorney as most extraordinary. Twice she had refused to testify, and once, when the deposition lacked nothing but her signature, she had caught it from the clerk's hands and torn it in pieces. She had called her children to the bedside and embraced them with streaming eyes, then suddenly sending them from the room, she verified her statement by oath and signature, and fainted— "slick away," said the district attorney. It was at that time that her physician, arriving upon the scene, took in the situation at a glance and grasping the representative of the law by the collar chucked him into the street and kicked his assistant after him. The insulted majesty of the law was not vindicated; the victim of the indignity did not even mention anything of all this in court. He was ambitious to win his case, and the circumstances of the taking of that deposition were not such as would give it weight if related; and after all, the man on trial had committed an offense against the law's majesty only less heinous than that of the irascible physician.

By suggestion of the judge the jury rendered a verdict of guilty; there was nothing else to do, and the prisoner was sentenced to the penitentiary for three years. His counsel, who had objected to nothing and had made no plea for lenity—had, in fact, hardly said a word—wrung his client's hand and left the room. It was obvious to the whole bar that he had been engaged only to prevent the court from appointing counsel who might possibly insist on making a defense.

John Hardshaw served out his term at San Quentin, and when discharged was met at the prison gates by his wife, who had returned from "the States" to receive him. It is thought they went straight to Europe; anyhow, a general power-of-attorney to a lawyer still living among us—from whom I have many of the facts of this simple history—was executed in Paris. This lawyer in a short time sold everything that Hardshaw owned in California, and for years nothing was heard of the unfortunate couple; though many to whose ears had come vague and inaccurate intimations of their strange story, and who had known them, recalled their personality with tenderness and their misfortunes with compassion.

Some years later they returned, both broken in fortune and spirits and he in health. The purpose of their return I have not been able to ascertain. For some time they lived, under the name of Johnson, in a respectable enough quarter south of Market Street, pretty well out, and were never seen away from the vicinity of their dwelling. They must have had a little money left, for it is not known that the man had any occupation, the state of his health probably not permitting. The woman's devotion to her invalid husband was matter of remark among their neighbors; she seemed never absent from his side and always supporting and cheering him. They would sit for hours on one of the benches in a little public park, she reading to him, his hand in hers, her light touch occasionally visiting his pale brow, her still beautiful eyes frequently lifted from the book to look into his as she made some comment on the text, or closed the volume to beguile his mood with talk of—what? Nobody ever overheard a conversation between these two. The reader who has had the patience to follow their history to this point may possibly find a pleasure in conjecture: there was probably something to be avoided. The bearing of the man was one of profound dejection; indeed, the unsympathetic youth of the neighborhood, with that keen sense for visible characteristics which ever distinguishes the young male of our species, sometimes mentioned him among themselves by the name of Spoony Glum.

It occurred one day that John Hardshaw was possessed by the spirit of unrest. God knows what led him whither he went, but he crossed Market Street and held his way northward over the hills, and downward into the region known as North Beach. Turning aimlessly to the left he followed his toes along an unfamiliar street until he was opposite what for that period was a rather grand dwelling, and for this is a rather shabby factory. Casting his eyes casually upward he saw at an open window what it had been better that he had not seen—the face and figure of Elvira Barwell. Their eyes met. With a sharp exclamation, like the cry of a startled bird, the lady sprang to her feet and thrust her body half out of the window, clutching the casing on each side. Arrested by the cry, the people in the street below looked up. Hardshaw stood motionless, speechless, his eyes two flames. "Take care!" shouted some one in the crowd, as the woman strained further and further forward, defying the silent, implacable law of gravitation, as once she had defied that other law which God thundered from Sinai. The suddenness of her movements had tumbled a torrent of dark hair down her shoulders, and now it was blown about her cheeks, almost concealing her face. A moment so, and then—! A fearful cry rang through the street, as, losing her balance, she pitched headlong from the window, a confused and whirling mass of skirts, limbs, hair, and white face, and struck the pavement with a horrible sound and a force of impact that was felt a hundred feet away. For a moment all eyes refused their office and turned from the sickening spectacle on the sidewalk. Drawn again to that horror, they saw it strangely augmented. A man, hatless, seated flat upon the paving stones, held the broken, bleeding body against his breast, kissing the mangled cheeks and streaming mouth through tangles of wet hair, his own features indistinguishably crimson with the blood that half-strangled him and ran in rills from his soaken beard.

The reporter's task is nearly finished. The Barwells had that very morning returned from a two years' absence in Peru. A week later the widower, now doubly desolate, since there could be no missing the significance of Hardshaw's horrible demonstration, had sailed for I know not what distant port; he has never come back to stay. Hardshaw—as Johnson no longer—passed a year in the Stockton asylum for the insane, where also, through the influence of pitying friends, his wife was admitted to care for him. When he was discharged, not cured but harmless, they returned to the city; it would seem ever to have had some dreadful fascination for them. For a time they lived near the Mission Dolores, in poverty only less abject than that which is their present lot; but it was too far away from the objective point of the man's daily pilgrimage. They could not afford car fare. So that poor devil of an angel from Heaven—wife to this convict and lunatic—obtained, at a fair enough rental, the blank-faced shanty on the lower terrace of Goat Hill. Thence to the structure that was a dwelling and is a factory the distance is not so great; it is, in fact, an agreeable walk, judging from the man's eager and cheerful look as he takes it. The return journey appears to be a trifle wearisome.

An Adventure at Brownville*

I TAUGHT a little country school near Brownville, which, as every one knows who has had the good luck to live there, is the capital of a considerable expanse of the finest scenery in California. The town is somewhat frequented in summer by a class of persons whom it is the habit of the local journal to call "pleasure seekers," but who by a juster classification would be known as "the sick and those in adversity." Brownville itself might rightly enough be described, indeed, as a summer place of last resort. It is fairly well endowed with boarding-houses, at the least pernicious of which I performed twice a day (lunching at the schoolhouse) the humble rite of cementing the alliance between soul and body. From this "hostelry" (as the local journal preferred to call it when it did not call it a "caravanserai") to the schoolhouse the distance by the wagon road was about a mile and a half; but there was a trail, very little used, which led over an intervening range of low, heavily wooded hills, considerably shortening the distance. By this trail I was returning one evening later than usual. It was the last day of the term and I had been detained at the schoolhouse until almost dark, preparing an account of my stewardship for the trustees—two of whom, I proudly reflected, would be able to read it, and the third (an instance of the dominion of mind over matter) would be overruled in his customary antagonism to the schoolmaster of his own creation.

I had gone not more than a quarter of the way when, finding an interest in the antics of a family of lizards which dwelt thereabout and seemed full of reptilian joy for their immunity from the ills incident to life at the Brownville House, I sat upon a fallen tree to observe them. As I leaned wearily against a branch of the gnarled old trunk the twilight deepened in the somber woods and the faint new moon began casting visible shadows and gilding the leaves of the trees with a tender but ghostly light.

I heard the sound of voices—a woman's, angry, impetuous,

*This story was written in collaboration with Miss Ina Lillian Peterson, to whom is rightly due the credit for whatever merit it may have.

rising against deep masculine tones, rich and musical. I strained my eyes, peering through the dusky shadows of the wood, hoping to get a view of the intruders on my solitude, but could see no one. For some yards in each direction I had an uninterrupted view of the trail, and knowing of no other within a half mile thought the persons heard must be approaching from the wood at one side. There was no sound but that of the voices, which were now so distinct that I could catch the words. That of the man gave me an impression of anger, abundantly confirmed by the matter spoken.

"I will have no threats; you are powerless, as you very well know. Let things remain as they are or, by God! you shall both suffer for it."

"What do you mean?"—this was the voice of the woman, a cultivated voice, the voice of a lady. "You would not— murder us."

There was no reply, at least none that was audible to me. During the silence I peered into the wood in hope to get a glimpse of the speakers, for I felt sure that this was an affair of gravity in which ordinary scruples ought not to count. It seemed to me that the woman was in peril; at any rate the man had not disavowed a willingness to murder. When a man is enacting the rôle of potential assassin he has not the right to choose his audience.

After some little time I saw them, indistinct in the moonlight among the trees. The man, tall and slender, seemed clothed in black; the woman wore, as nearly as I could make out, a gown of gray stuff. Evidently they were still unaware of my presence in the shadow, though for some reason when they renewed their conversation they spoke in lower tones and I could no longer understand. As I looked the woman seemed to sink to the ground and raise her hands in supplication, as is frequently done on the stage and never, so far as I knew, anywhere else, and I am now not altogether sure that it was done in this instance. The man fixed his eyes upon her; they seemed to glitter bleakly in the moonlight with an expression that made me apprehensive that he would turn them upon me. I do not know by what impulse I was moved, but I sprang to my feet out of the shadow. At that instant the figures vanished. I peered in vain through the spaces among the trees and clumps of undergrowth. The night wind rustled the leaves; the lizards had retired early, reptiles of exemplary habits. The little moon was already slipping behind a black hill in the west.

I went home, somewhat disturbed in mind, half doubting that I had heard or seen any living thing excepting the lizards. It all seemed a trifle odd and uncanny. It was as if among the several phenomena, objective and subjective, that made the sum total of the incident there had been an uncertain element which had diffused its dubious character over all—had leavened the whole mass with unreality. I did not like it.

At the breakfast table the next morning there was a new face; opposite me sat a young woman at whom I merely glanced as I took my seat. In speaking to the high and mighty female personage who condescended to seem to wait upon us, this girl soon invited my attention by the sound of her voice, which was like, yet not altogether like, the one still murmuring in my memory of the previous evening's adventure. A moment later another girl, a few years older, entered the room and sat at the left of the other, speaking to her a gentle "good morning." By *her* voice I was startled: it was without doubt the one of which the first girl's had reminded me. Here was the lady of the sylvan incident sitting bodily before me, "in her habit as she lived."

Evidently enough the two were sisters. With a nebulous kind of apprehension that I might be recognized as the mute inglorious hero of an adventure which had in my consciousness and conscience something of the character of eavesdropping, I allowed myself only a hasty cup of the lukewarm coffee thoughtfully provided by the prescient waitress for the emergency, and left the table. As I passed out of the house into the grounds I heard a rich, strong male voice singing an aria from "Rigoletto." I am bound to say that it was exquisitely sung, too, but there was something in the performance that displeased me, I could say neither what nor why, and I walked rapidly away.

Returning later in the day I saw the elder of the two young women standing on the porch and near her a tall man in black clothing—the man whom I had expected to see. All day the desire to know something of these persons had been uppermost in my mind and I now resolved to learn what I could of them in any way that was neither dishonorable nor low.

The man was talking easily and affably to his companion, but at the sound of my footsteps on the gravel walk he ceased, and turning about looked me full in the face. He was apparently of middle age, dark and uncommonly handsome. His attire was faultless, his bearing easy and graceful, the look which he turned upon me open, free, and devoid of any suggestion of rudeness. Nevertheless it affected me with a distinct emotion which on subsequent analysis in memory appeared to be compounded of hatred and dread—I am unwilling to call it fear. A second later the man and woman had disappeared. They seemed to have a trick of disappearing. On entering the house, however, I saw them through the open doorway of the parlor as I passed; they had merely stepped through a window which opened down to the floor.

Cautiously "approached" on the subject of her new guests my landlady proved not ungracious. Restated with, I hope, some small reverence for English grammar the facts were these: the two girls were Pauline and Eva Maynard of San Francisco; the elder was Pauline. The man was Richard Benning, their guardian, who had been the most intimate friend of their father, now deceased. Mr. Benning had brought them to Brownville in the hope that the mountain climate might benefit Eva, who was thought to be in danger of consumption.

Upon these short and simple annals the landlady wrought an embroidery of eulogium which abundantly attested her faith in Mr. Benning's will and ability to pay for the best that her house afforded. That he had a good heart was evident to her from his devotion to his two beautiful wards and his really touching solicitude for their comfort. The evidence impressed me as insufficient and I silently found the Scotch verdict, "Not proven."

Certainly Mr. Benning was most attentive to his wards. In my strolls about the country I frequently encountered them—sometimes in company with other guests of the hotel—exploring the gulches, fishing, rifle shooting, and otherwise wiling away the monotony of country life; and although I watched them as closely as good manners would permit I saw nothing that would in any way explain the strange words that I had overheard in the wood. I had grown tolerably well acquainted with the young ladies and could exchange looks and even greetings with their guardian without actual repugnance.

A month went by and I had almost ceased to interest myself in their affairs when one night our entire little community was thrown into excitement by an event which vividly recalled my experience in the forest.

This was the death of the elder girl, Pauline.

The sisters had occupied the same bedroom on the third floor of the house. Waking in the gray of the morning Eva had found Pauline dead beside her. Later, when the poor girl was weeping beside the body amid a throng of sympathetic if not very considerate persons, Mr. Benning entered the room and appeared to be about to take her hand. She drew away from the side of the dead and moved slowly toward the door.

"It is you," she said—"you who have done this. You—you—you!"

"She is raving," he said in a low voice. He followed her, step by step, as she retreated, his eyes fixed upon hers with a steady gaze in which there was nothing of tenderness nor of compassion. She stopped; the hand that she had raised in accusation fell to her side, her dilated eyes contracted visibly, the lids slowly dropped over them, veiling their strange wild beauty, and she stood motionless and almost as white as the dead girl lying near. The man took her hand and put his arm gently about her shoulders, as if to support her. Suddenly she burst into a passion of tears and clung to him as a child to its mother. He smiled with a smile that affected me most disagreeably—perhaps any kind of smile would have done so—and led her silently out of the room.

There was an inquest—and the customary verdict: the deceased, it appeared, came to her death through "heart disease." It was before the invention of heart *failure*, though the heart of poor Pauline had indubitably failed. The body was embalmed and taken to San Francisco by some one summoned thence for the purpose, neither Eva nor Benning accompanying it. Some of the hotel gossips ventured to think that very strange, and a few hardy spirits went so far as to think it very strange indeed; but the good landlady generously threw herself into the breach, saying it was owing to the precarious nature of the girl's health. It is not of record that either of the two persons most affected and apparently least concerned made any explanation.

One evening about a week after the death I went out upon the veranda of the hotel to get a book that I had left there. Under some vines shutting out the moonlight from a part of the space I saw Richard Benning, for whose apparition I was prepared by having previously heard the low, sweet voice of Eva Maynard, whom also I now discerned, standing before him with one hand raised to his shoulder and her eyes, as nearly as I could judge, gazing upward into his. He held her disengaged hand and his head was bent with a singular dignity and grace. Their attitude was that of lovers, and as I stood in deep shadow to observe I felt even guiltier than on that memorable night in the wood. I was about to retire, when the girl spoke, and the contrast between her words and her attitude was so surprising that I remained, because I had merely forgotten to go away.

"You will take my life," she said, "as you did Pauline's. I know your intention as well as I know your power, and I ask nothing, only that you finish your work without needless delay and let me be at peace."

He made no reply—merely let go the hand that he was holding, removed the other from his shoulder, and turning away descended the steps leading to the garden and disappeared in the shrubbery. But a moment later I heard, seemingly from a great distance, his fine clear voice in a barbaric chant, which as I listened brought before some inner spiritual sense a consciousness of some far, strange land peopled with beings having forbidden powers. The song held me in a kind of spell, but when it had died away I recovered and instantly perceived what I thought an opportunity. I walked out of my shadow to where the girl stood. She turned and stared at me with something of the look, it seemed to me, of a hunted hare. Possibly my intrusion had frightened her.

"Miss Maynard," I said, "I beg you to tell me who that man is and the nature of his power over you. Perhaps this is rude in me, but it is not a matter for idle civilities. When a woman is in danger any man has a right to act."

She listened without visible emotion—almost I thought without interest, and when I had finished she closed her big blue eyes as if unspeakably weary.

"You can do nothing," she said.

I took hold of her arm, gently shaking her as one shakes a person falling into a dangerous sleep.

"You must rouse yourself," I said; "something must be done and you must give me leave to act. You have said that that man killed your sister, and I believe it—that he will kill you, and I believe that."

She merely raised her eyes to mine.

"Will you not tell me all?" I added.

"There is nothing to be done, I tell you—nothing. And if I could do anything I would not. It does not matter in the least. We shall be here only two days more; we go away then, oh, so far! If you have observed anything, I beg you to be silent."

"But this is madness, girl." I was trying by rough speech to break the deadly repose of her manner. "You have accused him of murder. Unless you explain these things to me I shall lay the matter before the authorities."

This roused her, but in a way that I did not like. She lifted her head proudly and said: "Do not meddle, sir, in what does not concern you. This is my affair, Mr. Moran, not yours."

"It concerns every person in the country—in the world," I answered, with equal coldness. "If you had no love for your sister I, at least, am concerned for you."

"Listen," she interrupted, leaning toward me. "I loved her, yes, God knows! But more than that—beyond all, beyond expression, I love *him*. You have overheard a secret, but you shall not make use of it to harm him. I shall deny all. Your word against mine—it will be that. Do you think your 'authorities' will believe you?"

She was now smiling like an angel and, God help me! I was heels over head in love with her! Did she, by some of the many methods of divination known to her sex, read my feelings? Her whole manner had altered.

"Come," she said, almost coaxingly, "promise that you will not be impolite again." She took my arm in the most friendly way. "Come, I will walk with you. He will not know—he will remain away all night."

Up and down the veranda we paced in the moonlight, she seemingly forgetting her recent bereavement, cooing and murmuring girl-wise of every kind of nothing in all Brownville; I silent, consciously awkward and with something of the feeling of being concerned in an intrigue. It was a revelation—this most charming and apparently blameless creature coolly and confessedly deceiving the man for whom a moment before she had acknowledged and shown the supreme love which finds even death an acceptable endearment.

"Truly," I thought in my inexperience, "here is something new under the moon."

And the moon must have smiled.

Before we parted I had exacted a promise that she would walk with me the next afternoon—before going away forever —to the Old Mill, one of Brownville's revered antiquities, erected in 1860.

"If he is not about," she added gravely, as I let go the hand she had given me at parting, and of which, may the good saints forgive me, I strove vainly to repossess myself when she had said it—so charming, as the wise Frenchman has pointed out, do we find woman's infidelity when we are its objects, not its victims. In apportioning his benefactions that night the Angel of Sleep overlooked me.

The Brownville House dined early, and after dinner the next day Miss Maynard, who had not been at table, came to me on the veranda, attired in the demurest of walking costumes, saying not a word. "He" was evidently "not about." We went slowly up the road that led to the Old Mill. She was apparently not strong and at times took my arm, relinquishing it and taking it again rather capriciously, I thought. Her mood, or rather her succession of moods, was as mutable as skylight in a rippling sea. She jested as if she had never heard of such a thing as death, and laughed on the lightest incitement, and directly afterward would sing a few bars of some grave melody with such tenderness of expression that I had to turn away my eyes lest she should see the evidence of her success in art, if art it was, not artlessness, as then I was compelled to think it. And she said the oddest things in the most unconventional way, skirting sometimes unfathomable abysms of thought, where I had hardly the courage to set foot. In short, she was fascinating in a thousand and fifty different ways, and at every step I executed a new and profounder emotional folly, a hardier spiritual indiscretion, incurring fresh liability to arrest by the constabulary of conscience for infractions of my own peace.

Arriving at the mill, she made no pretense of stopping, but turned into a trail leading through a field of stubble toward a creek. Crossing by a rustic bridge we continued on the trail, which now led uphill to one of the most picturesque spots in the country. The Eagle's Nest, it was called—the summit of a cliff that rose sheer into the air to a height of hundreds of feet above the forest at its base. From this elevated point we had a noble view of another valley and of the opposite hills flushed with the last rays of the setting sun. As we watched the light escaping to higher and higher planes from the encroaching flood of shadow filling the valley we heard footsteps, and in another moment were joined by Richard Benning.

"I saw you from the road," he said carelessly; "so I came up."

Being a fool, I neglected to take him by the throat and pitch him into the treetops below, but muttered some polite lie instead. On the girl the effect of his coming was immediate and unmistakable. Her face was suffused with the glory of love's transfiguration: the red light of the sunset had not been more obvious in her eyes than was now the lovelight that replaced it.

"I am so glad you came!" she said, giving him both her hands; and, God help me! it was manifestly true.

Seating himself upon the ground he began a lively dissertation upon the wild flowers of the region, a number of which he had with him. In the middle of a facetious sentence he suddenly ceased speaking and fixed his eyes upon Eva, who leaned against the stump of a tree, absently plaiting grasses. She lifted her eyes in a startled way to his, as if she had *felt* his look. She then rose, cast away her grasses, and moved slowly away from him. He also rose, continuing to look at her. He had still in his hand the bunch of flowers. The girl turned, as if to speak, but said nothing. I recall clearly now something of which I was but half-conscious then—the dreadful contrast between the smile upon her lips and the terrified expression in her eyes as she met his steady and imperative gaze. I know nothing of how it happened, nor how it was that I did not sooner understand; I only know that with the smile of an angel upon her lips and that look of terror in her beautiful eyes Eva Maynard sprang from the cliff and shot crashing into the tops of the pines below!

How and how long afterward I reached the place I cannot say, but Richard Benning was already there, kneeling beside the dreadful thing that had been a woman.

"She is dead—quite dead," he said coldly. "I will go to town for assistance. Please do me the favor to remain."

He rose to his feet and moved away, but in a moment had stopped and turned about.

"You have doubtless observed, my friend," he said, "that this was entirely her own act. I did not rise in time to prevent it, and you, not knowing her mental condition—you could not, of course, have suspected."

His manner maddened me.

"You are as much her assassin," I said, "as if your damnable hands had cut her throat." He shrugged his shoulders without reply and, turning, walked away. A moment later I heard, through the deepening shadows of the wood into which he had disappeared, a rich, strong, baritone voice singing "*La donna e mobile*," from "Rigoletto."

The Famous Gilson Bequest

IT was rough on Gilson. Such was the terse, cold, but not altogether unsympathetic judgment of the better public opinion at Mammon Hill—the dictum of respectability. The verdict of the opposite, or rather the opposing, element—the element that lurked red-eyed and restless about Moll Gurney's "deadfall," while respectability took it with sugar at Mr. Jo. Bentley's gorgeous "saloon"—was to pretty much the same general effect, though somewhat more ornately expressed by the use of picturesque expletives, which it is needless to quote. Virtually, Mammon Hill was a unit on the Gilson question. And it must be confessed that in a merely temporal sense all was not well with Mr. Gilson. He had that morning been led into town by Mr. Brentshaw and publicly charged with horse stealing; the sheriff meantime busying himself about The Tree with a new manila rope and Carpenter Pete being actively employed between drinks upon a pine box about the length and breadth of Mr. Gilson. Society having rendered its verdict, there remained between Gilson and eternity only the decent formality of a trial.

These are the short and simple annals of the prisoner: He had recently been a resident of New Jerusalem, on the north fork of the Little Stony, but had come to the newly discovered placers of Mammon Hill immediately before the "rush" by which the former place was depopulated. The discovery of the new diggings had occurred opportunely for Mr. Gilson, for it had only just before been intimated to him by a New Jerusalem vigilance committee that it would better his prospects in, and for, life to go somewhere; and the list of places to which he could safely go did not include any of the older camps; so he naturally established himself at Mammon Hill. Being eventually followed thither by all his judges, he ordered his conduct with considerable circumspection, but as he had never been known to do an honest day's work at any industry sanctioned by the stern local code of morality except draw poker he was still an object of suspicion. Indeed, it was conjectured that he was the author of the many daring depredations that had recently been committed with pan and brush on the sluice boxes.

Prominent among those in whom this suspicion had ripened into a steadfast conviction was Mr. Brentshaw. At all seasonable and unseasonable times Mr. Brentshaw avowed his belief in Mr. Gilson's connection with these unholy midnight enterprises, and his own willingness to prepare a way for the solar beams through the body of any one who might think it expedient to utter a different opinion—which, in his presence, no one was more careful not to do than the peace-loving person most concerned. Whatever may have been the truth of the matter, it is certain that Gilson frequently lost more "clean dust" at Jo. Bentley's faro table than it was recorded in local history that he had ever honestly earned at draw poker in all the days of the camp's existence. But at last Mr. Bentley—fearing, it may be, to lose the more profitable patronage of Mr. Brentshaw—peremptorily refused to let Gilson copper the queen, intimating at the same time, in his frank, forthright way, that the privilege of losing money at "this bank" was a blessing appertaining to, proceeding logically from, and coterminous with, a condition of notorious commercial righteousness and social good repute.

The Hill thought it high time to look after a person whom its most honored citizen had felt it his duty to rebuke at a considerable personal sacrifice. The New Jerusalem contingent, particularly, began to abate something of the toleration begotten of amusement at their own blunder in exiling an objectionable neighbor from the place which they had left to the place whither they had come. Mammon Hill was at last of one mind. Not much was said, but that Gilson must hang was "in the air." But at this critical juncture in his affairs he showed signs of an altered life if not a changed heart. Perhaps it was only that "the bank" being closed against him he had no further use for gold dust. Anyhow the sluice boxes were molested no more forever. But it was impossible to repress the abounding energies of such a nature as his, and he continued, possibly from habit, the tortuous courses which he had pursued for profit of Mr. Bentley. After a few tentative and resultless undertakings in the way of highway robbery—if one may venture to designate road-agency by so harsh a name—he made one or two

modest essays in horse-herding, and it was in the midst of a
promising enterprise of this character, and just as he had taken
the tide in his affairs at its flood, that he made shipwreck. For
on a misty, moonlight night Mr. Brentshaw rode up alongside
a person who was evidently leaving that part of the country,
laid a hand upon the halter connecting Mr. Gilson's wrist with
Mr. Harper's bay mare, tapped him familiarly on the cheek
with the barrel of a navy revolver and requested the pleasure of
his company in a direction opposite to that in which he was
traveling.

It was indeed rough on Gilson.

On the morning after his arrest he was tried, convicted, and
sentenced. It only remains, so far as concerns his earthly career,
to hang him, reserving for more particular mention his last will
and testament, which, with great labor, he contrived in prison,
and in which, probably from some confused and imperfect
notion of the rights of captors, he bequeathed everything he
owned to his "lawfle execketer," Mr. Brentshaw. The bequest,
however, was made conditional on the legatee taking the testator's body from The Tree and "planting it white."

So Mr. Gilson was—I was about to say "swung off," but I
fear there has been already something too much of slang in
this straightforward statement of facts; besides, the manner
in which the law took its course is more accurately described in
the terms employed by the judge in passing sentence: Mr.
Gilson was "strung up."

In due season Mr. Brentshaw, somewhat touched, it may
well be, by the empty compliment of the bequest, repaired to
The Tree to pluck the fruit thereof. When taken down the
body was found to have in its waistcoat pocket a duly attested
codicil to the will already noted. The nature of its provisions
accounted for the manner in which it had been withheld, for
had Mr. Brentshaw previously been made aware of the conditions under which he was to succeed to the Gilson estate he
would indubitably have declined the responsibility. Briefly
stated, the purport of the codicil was as follows:

Whereas, at divers times and in sundry places, certain persons had asserted that during his life the testator had robbed
their sluice boxes; therefore, if during the five years next succeeding the date of this instrument any one should make proof

of such assertion before a court of law, such person was to receive as reparation the entire personal and real estate of which the testator died seized and possessed, minus the expenses of court and a stated compensation to the executor, Henry Clay Brentshaw; provided, that if more than one person made such proof the estate was to be equally divided between or among them. But in case none should succeed in so establishing the testator's guilt, then the whole property, minus court expenses, as aforesaid, should go to the said Henry Clay Brentshaw for his own use, as stated in the will.

The syntax of this remarkable document was perhaps open to critical objection, but that was clearly enough the meaning of it. The orthography conformed to no recognized system, but being mainly phonetic it was not ambiguous. As the probate judge remarked, it would take five aces to beat it. Mr. Brentshaw smiled good-humoredly, and after performing the last sad rites with amusing ostentation, had himself duly sworn as executor and conditional legatee under the provisions of a law hastily passed (at the instance of the member from the Mammon Hill district) by a facetious legislature; which law was afterward discovered to have created also three or four lucrative offices and authorized the expenditure of a considerable sum of public money for the construction of a certain railway bridge that with greater advantage might perhaps have been erected on the line of some actual railway.

Of course Mr. Brentshaw expected neither profit from the will nor litigation in consequence of its unusual provisions; Gilson, although frequently "flush," had been a man whom assessors and tax collectors were well satisfied to lose no money by. But a careless and merely formal search among his papers revealed title deeds to valuable estates in the East and certificates of deposit for incredible sums in banks less severely scrupulous than that of Mr. Jo. Bentley.

The astounding news got abroad directly, throwing the Hill into a fever of excitement. The Mammon Hill *Patriot*, whose editor had been a leading spirit in the proceedings that resulted in Gilson's departure from New Jerusalem, published a most complimentary obituary notice of the deceased, and was good enough to call attention to the fact that his degraded contemporary, the Squaw Gulch *Clarion*, was bringing virtue into contempt by beslavering with flattery the memory of one who in life had spurned the vile sheet as a nuisance from his door. Undeterred by the press, however, claimants under the will were not slow in presenting themselves with their evidence; and great as was the Gilson estate it appeared conspicuously paltry considering the vast number of sluice boxes from which it was averred to have been obtained. The country rose as one man!

Mr. Brentshaw was equal to the emergency. With a shrewd application of humble auxiliary devices, he at once erected above the bones of his benefactor a costly monument, over-topping every rough headboard in the cemetery, and on this he judiciously caused to be inscribed an epitaph of his own composing, eulogizing the honesty, public spirit and cognate virtues of him who slept beneath, "a victim to the unjust asper-sions of Slander's viper brood."

Moreover, he employed the best legal talent in the Territory to defend the memory of his departed friend, and for five long years the Territorial courts were occupied with litigation grow-ing out of the Gilson bequest. To fine forensic abilities Mr. Brentshaw opposed abilities more finely forensic; in bidding for purchasable favors he offered prices which utterly deranged the market; the judges found at his hospitable board entertain-ment for man and beast, the like of which had never been spread in the Territory; with mendacious witnesses he con-fronted witnesses of superior mendacity.

Nor was the battle confined to the temple of the blind goddess—it invaded the press, the pulpit, the drawing-room. It raged in the mart, the exchange, the school; in the gulches, and on the street corners. And upon the last day of the memo-rable period to which legal action under the Gilson will was limited, the sun went down upon a region in which the moral sense was dead, the social conscience callous, the intellectual capacity dwarfed, enfeebled, and confused! But Mr. Brentshaw was victorious all along the line.

On that night it so happened that the cemetery in one cor-ner of which lay the now honored ashes of the late Milton Gilson, Esq., was partly under water. Swollen by incessant rains, Cat Creek had spilled over its banks an angry flood which, after scooping out unsightly hollows wherever the soil had been disturbed, had partly subsided, as if ashamed of the sacrilege, leaving exposed much that had been piously concealed. Even the famous Gilson monument, the pride and glory of Mammon Hill, was no longer a standing rebuke to the "viper brood"; succumbing to the sapping current it had toppled prone to earth. The ghoulish flood had exhumed the poor, decayed pine coffin, which now lay half-exposed, in pitiful contrast to the pompous monolith which, like a giant note of admiration, emphasized the disclosure.

To this depressing spot, drawn by some subtle influence he had sought neither to resist nor analyze, came Mr. Brentshaw. An altered man was Mr. Brentshaw. Five years of toil, anxiety, and wakefulness had dashed his black locks with streaks and patches of gray, bowed his fine figure, drawn sharp and angular his face, and debased his walk to a doddering shuffle. Nor had this lustrum of fierce contention wrought less upon his heart and intellect. The careless good humor that had prompted him to accept the trust of the dead man had given place to a fixed habit of melancholy. The firm, vigorous intellect had overripened into the mental mellowness of second childhood. His broad understanding had narrowed to the accommodation of a single idea; and in place of the quiet, cynical incredulity of former days, there was in him a haunting faith in the supernatural, that flitted and fluttered about his soul, shadowy, batlike, ominous of insanity. Unsettled in all else, his understanding clung to one conviction with the tenacity of a wrecked intellect. That was an unshaken belief in the entire blamelessness of the dead Gilson. He had so often sworn to this in court and asserted it in private conversation—had so frequently and so triumphantly established it by testimony that had come expensive to him (for that very day he had paid the last dollar of the Gilson estate to Mr. Jo. Bentley, the last witness to the Gilson good character)—that it had become to him a sort of religious faith. It seemed to him the one great central and basic truth of life—the sole serene verity in a world of lies.

On that night, as he seated himself pensively upon the prostrate monument, trying by the uncertain moonlight to spell out the epitaph which five years before he had composed with a chuckle that memory had not recorded, tears of remorse came into his eyes as he remembered that he had been mainly instrumental in compassing by a false accusation this good man's death; for during some of the legal proceedings, Mr. Harper, for a consideration (forgotten) had come forward and sworn that in the little transaction with his bay mare the deceased had acted in strict accordance with the Harperian wishes, confidentially communicated to the deceased and by him faithfully concealed at the cost of his life. All that Mr. Brentshaw had since done for the dead man's memory seemed pitifully inadequate—most mean, paltry, and debased with selfishness!

As he sat there, torturing himself with futile regrets, a faint shadow fell across his eyes. Looking toward the moon, hanging low in the west, he saw what seemed a vague, watery cloud obscuring her; but as it moved so that her beams lit up one side of it he perceived the clear, sharp outline of a human figure. The apparition became momentarily more distinct, and grew, visibly; it was drawing near. Dazed as were his senses, half locked up with terror and confounded with dreadful imaginings, Mr. Brentshaw yet could but perceive, or think he perceived, in this unearthly shape a strange similitude to the mortal part of the late Milton Gilson, as that person had looked when taken from The Tree five years before. The likeness was indeed complete, even to the full, stony eyes, and a certain shadowy circle about the neck. It was without coat or hat, precisely as Gilson had been when laid in his poor, cheap casket by the not ungentle hands of Carpenter Pete—for whom some one had long since performed the same neighborly office. The spectre, if such it was, seemed to bear something in its hands which Mr. Brentshaw could not clearly make out. It drew nearer, and paused at last beside the coffin containing the ashes of the late Mr. Gilson, the lid of which was awry, half disclosing the uncertain interior. Bending over this, the phantom seemed to shake into it from a basin some dark substance of dubious consistency, then glided stealthily back to the lowest part of the cemetery. Here the retiring flood had stranded a number of open coffins, about and among which it gurgled with low sobbings and stilly whispers. Stooping over one of these, the apparition carefully brushed its contents into the basin, then returning to its own casket, emptied the vessel into that, as before. This mysterious operation was repeated at every exposed coffin, the ghost sometimes dipping its laden basin into the running water, and gently agitating it to free it of the baser clay, always hoarding the residuum in its own private box. In short, the immortal part of the late Milton Gilson was cleaning up the dust of its neighbors and providently adding the same to its own.

Perhaps it was a phantasm of a disordered mind in a fevered body. Perhaps it was a solemn farce enacted by pranking existences that throng the shadows lying along the border of another world. God knows; to us is permitted only the knowledge that when the sun of another day touched with a grace of gold the ruined cemetery of Mammon Hill his kindliest beam fell upon the white, still face of Henry Brentshaw, dead among the dead.

The Applicant

PUSHING his adventurous shins through the deep snow that had fallen overnight, and encouraged by the glee of his little sister, following in the open way that he made, a sturdy small boy, the son of Grayville's most distinguished citizen, struck his foot against something of which there was no visible sign on the surface of the snow. It is the purpose of this narrative to explain how it came to be there.

No one who has had the advantage of passing through Grayville by day can have failed to observe the large stone building crowning the low hill to the north of the railway station—that is to say, to the right in going toward Great Mowbray. It is a somewhat dull-looking edifice, of the Early Comatose order, and appears to have been designed by an architect who shrank from publicity, and although unable to conceal his work—even compelled, in this instance, to set it on an eminence in the sight of men—did what he honestly could to insure it against a second look. So far as concerns its outer and visible aspect, the Abersush Home for Old Men is unquestionably inhospitable to human attention. But it is a building of great magnitude, and cost its benevolent founder the profit of many a cargo of the teas and silks and spices that his ships brought up from the under-world when he was in trade in Boston; though the main expense was its endowment. Altogether, this reckless person had robbed his heirs-at-law of no less a sum than half a million dollars and flung it away in riotous giving. Possibly it was with a view to get out of sight of the silent big witness to his extravagance that he shortly afterward disposed of all his Grayville property that remained to him, turned his back upon the scene of his prodigality and went off across the sea in one of his own ships. But the gossips who got their inspiration most directly from Heaven declared that he went in search of a wife—a theory not easily reconciled with that of the village humorist, who solemnly averred that the bachelor philanthropist had departed this life (left Grayville, to wit) because the marriageable maidens had made it too hot to hold him. However this may have been, he had not returned, and although at long intervals there had come to Grayville, in a desultory way, vague rumors of his wanderings in strange lands, no one seemed certainly to know about him, and to the new generation he was no more than a name. But from above the portal of the Home for Old Men the name shouted in stone.

Despite its unpromising exterior, the Home is a fairly commodious place of retreat from the ills that its inmates have incurred by being poor and old and men. At the time embraced in this brief chronicle they were in number about a score, but in acerbity, querulousness, and general ingratitude they could hardly be reckoned at fewer than a hundred; at least that was the estimate of the superintendent, Mr. Silas Tilbody. It was Mr. Tilbody's steadfast conviction that always, in admitting new old men to replace those who had gone to another and a better Home, the trustees had distinctly in will the infraction of his peace, and the trial of his patience. In truth, the longer the institution was connected with him, the stronger was his feeling that the founder's scheme of benevolence was sadly impaired by providing any inmates at all. He had not much imagination, but with what he had he was addicted to the reconstruction of the Home for Old Men into a kind of "castle in Spain," with himself as castellan, hospitably entertaining about a score of sleek and prosperous middle-aged gentlemen, consummately good-humored and civilly willing to pay for their board and lodging. In this revised project of philanthropy the trustees, to whom he was indebted for his office and responsible for his conduct, had not the happiness to appear. As to them, it was held by the village humorist aforementioned that in their management of the great charity Providence had thoughtfully supplied an incentive to thrift. With the inference which he expected to be drawn from that view we have nothing to do; it had neither support nor denial from the inmates, who certainly were most concerned. They lived out their little remnant of life, crept into graves neatly numbered, and were succeeded by other old men as like them as could be desired by the Adversary of Peace. If the Home was a place of punishment for the sin of unthrift the veteran offenders sought justice with a persistence that attested the sincerity of their penitence. It is to one of these that the reader's attention is now invited.

In the matter of attire this person was not altogether

engaging. But for this season, which was midwinter, a careless observer might have looked upon him as a clever device of the husbandman indisposed to share the fruits of his toil with the crows that toil not, neither spin—an error that might not have been dispelled without longer and closer observation than he seemed to court; for his progress up Abersush Street, toward the Home in the gloom of the winter evening, was not visibly faster than what might have been expected of a scare-crow blessed with youth, health, and discontent. The man was indisputably ill-clad, yet not without a certain fitness and good taste, withal; for he was obviously an applicant for admittance to the Home, where poverty was a qualification. In the army of indigence the uniform is rags; they serve to distinguish the rank and file from the recruiting officers.

As the old man, entering the gate of the grounds, shuffled up the broad walk, already white with the fast-falling snow, which from time to time he feebly shook from its various coigns of vantage on his person, he came under inspection of the large globe lamp that burned always by night over the great door of the building. As if unwilling to incur its revealing beams, he turned to the left and, passing a considerable distance along the face of the building, rang at a smaller door emitting a dimmer ray that came from within, through the fanlight, and expended itself incuriously overhead. The door was opened by no less a personage than the great Mr. Tilbody himself. Observing his visitor, who at once uncovered, and somewhat shortened the radius of the permanent curvature of his back, the great man gave visible token of neither surprise nor displeasure. Mr. Tilbody was, indeed, in an uncommonly good humor, a phenomenon ascribable doubtless to the cheerful influence of the season; for this was Christmas Eve, and the morrow would be that blessed 365th part of the year that all Christian souls set apart for mighty feats of goodness and joy. Mr. Tilbody was so full of the spirit of the season that his fat face and pale blue eyes, whose ineffectual fire served to distinguish it from an untimely summer squash, effused so genial a glow that it seemed a pity that he could not have lain down in it, basking in the consciousness of his own identity. He was hatted, booted, overcoated, and umbrellaed, as became a person who was about to expose himself to the night and the storm on an errand of charity; for Mr. Tilbody had just parted from his wife and children to go "down town" and purchase the wherewithal to confirm the annual falsehood about the hunch-bellied saint who frequents the chimneys to reward little boys and girls who are good, and especially truthful. So he did not invite the old man in, but saluted him cheerily:

"Hello! just in time; a moment later and you would have missed me. Come, I have no time to waste; we'll walk a little way together."

"Thank you," said the old man, upon whose thin and white but not ignoble face the light from the open door showed an expression that was perhaps disappointment; "but if the trustees—if my application——"

"The trustees," Mr. Tilbody said, closing more doors than one, and cutting off two kinds of light, "have agreed that your application disagrees with them."

Certain sentiments are inappropriate to Christmastide, but Humor, like Death, has all seasons for his own.

"Oh, my God!" cried the old man, in so thin and husky a tone that the invocation was anything but impressive, and to at least one of his two auditors sounded, indeed, somewhat ludicrous. To the Other—but that is a matter which laymen are devoid of the light to expound.

"Yes," continued Mr. Tilbody, accommodating his gait to that of his companion, who was mechanically, and not very successfully, retracing the track that he had made through the snow; "they have decided that, under the circumstances—under the very peculiar circumstances, you understand—it would be inexpedient to admit you. As superintendent and *ex officio* secretary of the honorable board"—as Mr. Tilbody "read his title clear" the magnitude of the big building, seen through its veil of falling snow, appeared to suffer somewhat in comparison—"it is my duty to inform you that, in the words of Deacon Byram, the chairman, your presence in the Home would—under the circumstances—be peculiarly embarrassing. I felt it my duty to submit to the honorable board the statement that you made to me yesterday of your needs, your physical condition, and the trials which it has pleased Providence to send upon you in your very proper effort to present your claims in person; but, after careful, and I may say prayerful, consideration of your case—with something too, I trust, of the large charitableness appropriate to the season—it was decided that we would not be justified in doing anything likely to impair the usefulness of the institution intrusted (under Providence) to our care."

They had now passed out of the grounds; the street lamp opposite the gate was dimly visible through the snow. Already the old man's former track was obliterated, and he seemed uncertain as to which way he should go. Mr. Tilbody had drawn a little away from him, but paused and turned half toward him, apparently reluctant to forego the continuing opportunity.

"Under the circumstances," he resumed, "the decision——"

But the old man was inaccessible to the suasion of his verbosity; he had crossed the street into a vacant lot and was going forward, rather deviously toward nowhere in particular —which, he having nowhere in particular to go to, was not so reasonless a proceeding as it looked.

And that is how it happened that the next morning, when the church bells of all Grayville were ringing with an added unction appropriate to the day, the sturdy little son of Deacon Byram, breaking a way through the snow to the place of worship, struck his foot against the body of Amasa Abersush, philanthropist.

A Watcher by the Dead

IN an upper room of an unoccupied dwelling in the part of
San Francisco known as North Beach lay the body of a
man, under a sheet. The hour was near nine in the evening; the
room was dimly lighted by a single candle. Although the
weather was warm, the two windows, contrary to the custom
which gives the dead plenty of air, were closed and the blinds
drawn down. The furniture of the room consisted of but three
pieces—an arm-chair, a small reading-stand supporting the
candle, and a long kitchen table, supporting the body of
the man. All these, as also the corpse, seemed to have been
recently brought in, for an observer, had there been one,
would have seen that all were free from dust, whereas everything else in the room was pretty thickly coated with it, and
there were cobwebs in the angles of the walls.

Under the sheet the outlines of the body could be traced,
even the features, these having that unnaturally sharp definition which seems to belong to faces of the dead, but is really
characteristic of those only that have been wasted by disease.
From the silence of the room one would rightly have inferred
that it was not in the front of the house, facing a street. It really faced nothing but a high breast of rock, the rear of the
building being set into a hill.

As a neighboring church clock was striking nine with an indolence which seemed to imply such an indifference to the
flight of time that one could hardly help wondering why it
took the trouble to strike at all, the single door of the room
was opened and a man entered, advancing toward the body. As
he did so the door closed, apparently of its own volition; there
was a grating, as of a key turned with difficulty, and the snap of
the lock bolt as it shot into its socket. A sound of retiring
footsteps in the passage outside ensued, and the man was to all
appearance a prisoner. Advancing to the table, he stood a moment looking down at the body; then with a slight shrug of
the shoulders walked over to one of the windows and hoisted
the blind. The darkness outside was absolute, the panes were

covered with dust, but by wiping this away he could see that the window was fortified with strong iron bars crossing it within a few inches of the glass and imbedded in the masonry on each side. He examined the other window. It was the same. He manifested no great curiosity in the matter, did not even so much as raise the sash. If he was a prisoner he was apparently a tractable one. Having completed his examination of the room, he seated himself in the arm-chair, took a book from his pocket, drew the stand with its candle alongside and began to read.

The man was young—not more than thirty—dark in complexion, smooth-shaven, with brown hair. His face was thin and high-nosed, with a broad forehead and a "firmness" of the chin and jaw which is said by those having it to denote resolution. The eyes were gray and steadfast, not moving except with definitive purpose. They were now for the greater part of the time fixed upon his book, but he occasionally withdrew them and turned them to the body on the table, not, apparently, from any dismal fascination which under such circumstances it might be supposed to exercise upon even a courageous person, nor with a conscious rebellion against the contrary influence which might dominate a timid one. He looked at it as if in his reading he had come upon something recalling him to a sense of his surroundings. Clearly this watcher by the dead was discharging his trust with intelligence and composure, as became him.

After reading for perhaps a half-hour he seemed to come to the end of a chapter and quietly laid away the book. He then rose and taking the reading-stand from the floor carried it into a corner of the room near one of the windows, lifted the candle from it and returned to the empty fireplace before which he had been sitting.

A moment later he walked over to the body on the table, lifted the sheet and turned it back from the head, exposing a mass of dark hair and a thin face-cloth, beneath which the features showed with even sharper definition than before. Shading his eyes by interposing his free hand between them and the candle, he stood looking at his motionless companion with a serious and tranquil regard. Satisfied with his inspection, he pulled the sheet over the face again and returning to the chair, took some matches off the candlestick, put them in the side pocket of his sack-coat and sat down. He then lifted the candle from its socket and looked at it critically, as if calculating how long it would last. It was barely two inches long; in another hour he would be in darkness. He replaced it in the candlestick and blew it out.

II

In a physician's office in Kearny Street three men sat about a table, drinking punch and smoking. It was late in the evening, almost midnight, indeed, and there had been no lack of punch. The gravest of the three, Dr. Helberson, was the host—it was in his rooms they sat. He was about thirty years of age; the others were even younger; all were physicians.

"The superstitious awe with which the living regard the dead," said Dr. Helberson, "is hereditary and incurable. One needs no more be ashamed of it than of the fact that he inherits, for example, an incapacity for mathematics, or a tendency to lie."

The others laughed. "Oughtn't a man to be ashamed to lie?" asked the youngest of the three, who was in fact a medical student not yet graduated.

"My dear Harper, I said nothing about that. The tendency to lie is one thing; lying is another."

"But do you think," said the third man, "that this superstitious feeling, this fear of the dead, reasonless as we know it to be, is universal? I am myself not conscious of it."

"Oh, but it is 'in your system' for all that," replied Helberson; "it needs only the right conditions—what Shakespeare calls the 'confederate season'—to manifest itself in some very disagreeable way that will open your eyes. Physicians and soldiers are of course more nearly free from it than others."

"Physicians and soldiers!—why don't you add hangmen and headsmen? Let us have in all the assassin classes."

"No, my dear Mancher; the juries will not let the public executioners acquire sufficient familiarity with death to be altogether unmoved by it."

Young Harper, who had been helping himself to a fresh

cigar at the sideboard, resumed his seat. "What would you consider conditions under which any man of woman born would become insupportably conscious of his share of our common weakness in this regard?" he asked, rather verbosely.

"Well, I should say that if a man were locked up all night with a corpse—alone—in a dark room—of a vacant house— with no bed covers to pull over his head—and lived through it without going altogether mad, he might justly boast himself not of woman born, nor yet, like Macduff, a product of Cæsarean section."

"I thought you never would finish piling up conditions," said Harper, "but I know a man who is neither a physician nor a soldier who will accept them all, for any stake you like to name."

"Who is he?"

"His name is Jarette—a stranger here; comes from my town in New York. I have no money to back him, but he will back himself with loads of it."

"How do you know that?"

"He would rather bet than eat. As for fear—I dare say he thinks it some cutaneous disorder, or possibly a particular kind of religious heresy."

"What does he look like?" Helberson was evidently becoming interested.

"Like Mancher, here—might be his twin brother."

"I accept the challenge," said Helberson, promptly.

"Awfully obliged to you for the compliment, I'm sure," drawled Mancher, who was growing sleepy. "Can't I get into this?"

"Not against me," Helberson said. "I don't want *your* money."

"All right," said Mancher; "I'll be the corpse."

The others laughed.

The outcome of this crazy conversation we have seen.

III

In extinguishing his meagre allowance of candle Mr. Jarette's object was to preserve it against some unforeseen need. He may have thought, too, or half thought, that the darkness would be no worse at one time than another, and if the situation became insupportable it would be better to have a means of relief, or even release. At any rate it was wise to have a little reserve of light, even if only to enable him to look at his watch.

No sooner had he blown out the candle and set it on the floor at his side than he settled himself comfortably in the arm-chair, leaned back and closed his eyes, hoping and expecting to sleep. In this he was disappointed; he had never in his life felt less sleepy, and in a few minutes he gave up the attempt. But what could he do? He could not go groping about in absolute darkness at the risk of bruising himself—at the risk, too, of blundering against the table and rudely disturbing the dead. We all recognize their right to lie at rest, with immunity from all that is harsh and violent. Jarette almost succeeded in making himself believe that considerations of this kind restrained him from risking the collision and fixed him to the chair.

While thinking of this matter he fancied that he heard a faint sound in the direction of the table—what kind of sound he could hardly have explained. He did not turn his head. Why should he—in the darkness? But he listened—why should he not? And listening he grew giddy and grasped the arms of the chair for support. There was a strange ringing in his ears; his head seemed bursting; his chest was oppressed by the constric-tion of his clothing. He wondered why it was so, and whether these were symptoms of fear. Then, with a long and strong expiration, his chest appeared to collapse, and with the great gasp with which he refilled his exhausted lungs the vertigo left him and he knew that so intently had he listened that he had held his breath almost to suffocation. The revelation was vexa-tious; he arose, pushed away the chair with his foot and strode to the centre of the room. But one does not stride far in dark-ness; he began to grope, and finding the wall followed it to an angle, turned, followed it past the two windows and there in another corner came into violent contact with the reading-stand, overturning it. It made a clatter that startled him. He was annoyed. "How the devil could I have forgotten where it was?" he muttered, and groped his way along the third wall to the fireplace. "I must put things to rights," said he, feeling the floor for the candle.

Having recovered that, he lighted it and instantly turned his eyes to the table, where, naturally, nothing had undergone any change. The reading-stand lay unobserved upon the floor: he had forgotten to "put it to rights." He looked all about the room, dispersing the deeper shadows by movements of the candle in his hand, and crossing over to the door tested it by turning and pulling the knob with all his strength. It did not yield and this seemed to afford him a certain satisfaction; indeed, he secured it more firmly by a bolt which he had not before observed. Returning to his chair, he looked at his watch; it was half-past nine. With a start of surprise he held the watch at his ear. It had not stopped. The candle was now visibly shorter. He again extinguished it, placing it on the floor at his side as before.

Mr. Jarette was not at his ease; he was distinctly dissatisfied with his surroundings, and with himself for being so. "What have I to fear?" he thought. "This is ridiculous and disgraceful; I will not be so great a fool." But courage does not come of saying, "I will be courageous," nor of recognizing its appropriateness to the occasion. The more Jarette condemned himself, the more reason he gave himself for condemnation; the greater the number of variations which he played upon the simple theme of the harmlessness of the dead, the more insupportable grew the discord of his emotions. "What!" he cried aloud in the anguish of his spirit, "what! shall I, who have not a shade of superstition in my nature—I, who have no belief in immortality—I, who know (and never more clearly than now) that the after-life is the dream of a desire—shall I lose at once my bet, my honor and my self-respect, perhaps my reason, because certain savage ancestors dwelling in caves and burrows conceived the monstrous notion that the dead walk by night? —that——" Distinctly, unmistakably, Mr. Jarette heard behind him a light, soft sound of footfalls, deliberate, regular, successively nearer!

IV

Just before daybreak the next morning Dr. Helberson and his young friend Harper were driving slowly through the streets of North Beach in the doctor's coupé.

"Have you still the confidence of youth in the courage or

stolidity of your friend?" said the elder man. "Do you believe that I have lost this wager?"

"I *know* you have," replied the other, with enfeebling emphasis.

"Well, upon my soul, I hope so."

It was spoken earnestly, almost solemnly. There was a silence for a few moments.

"Harper," the doctor resumed, looking very serious in the shifting half-lights that entered the carriage as they passed the street lamps, "I don't feel altogether comfortable about this business. If your friend had not irritated me by the contemptuous manner in which he treated my doubt of his endurance—a purely physical quality—and by the cool incivility of his suggestion that the corpse be that of a physician, I should not have gone on with it. If anything should happen we are ruined, as I fear we deserve to be."

"What can happen? Even if the matter should be taking a serious turn, of which I am not at all afraid, Mancher has only to 'resurrect' himself and explain matters. With a genuine 'subject' from the dissecting-room, or one of your late patients, it might be different."

Dr. Mancher, then, had been as good as his promise; he was the "corpse."

Dr. Helberson was silent for a long time, as the carriage, at a snail's pace, crept along the same street it had traveled two or three times already. Presently he spoke: "Well, let us hope that Mancher, if he has had to rise from the dead, has been discreet about it. A mistake in that might make matters worse instead of better."

"Yes," said Harper, "Jarette would kill him. But, Doctor"—looking at his watch as the carriage passed a gas lamp—"it is nearly four o'clock at last."

A moment later the two had quitted the vehicle and were walking briskly toward the long-unoccupied house belonging to the doctor in which they had immured Mr. Jarette in accordance with the terms of the mad wager. As they neared it they met a man running. "Can you tell me," he cried, suddenly checking his speed, "where I can find a doctor?"

"What's the matter?" Helberson asked, non-committal.

"Go and see for yourself," said the man, resuming his running.

They hastened on. Arrived at the house, they saw several persons entering in haste and excitement. In some of the dwellings near by and across the way the chamber windows were thrown up, showing a protrusion of heads. All heads were asking questions, none heeding the questions of the others. A few of the windows with closed blinds were illuminated; the inmates of those rooms were dressing to come down. Exactly opposite the door of the house that they sought a street lamp threw a yellow, insufficient light upon the scene, seeming to say that it could disclose a good deal more if it wished. Harper paused at the door and laid a hand upon his companion's arm. "It is all up with us, Doctor," he said in extreme agitation, which contrasted strangely with his free-and-easy words; "the game has gone against us all. Let's not go in there; I'm for lying low."

"I'm a physician," said Dr. Helberson, calmly; "there may be need of one."

They mounted the doorsteps and were about to enter. The door was open; the street lamp opposite lighted the passage into which it opened. It was full of men. Some had ascended the stairs at the farther end, and, denied admittance above, waited for better fortune. All were talking, none listening. Suddenly, on the upper landing there was a great commotion; a man had sprung out of a door and was breaking away from those endeavoring to detain him. Down through the mass of affrighted idlers he came, pushing them aside, flattening them against the wall on one side, or compelling them to cling to the rail on the other, clutching them by the throat, striking them savagely, thrusting them back down the stairs and walking over the fallen. His clothing was in disorder, he was without a hat. His eyes, wild and restless, had in them something more terrifying than his apparently superhuman strength. His face, smooth-shaven, was bloodless, his hair frost-white.

As the crowd at the foot of the stairs, having more freedom, fell away to let him pass Harper sprang forward. "Jarette! Jarette!" he cried.

Dr. Helberson seized Harper by the collar and dragged him

back. The man looked into their faces without seeming to see them and sprang through the door, down the steps, into the street, and away. A stout policeman, who had had inferior success in conquering his way down the stairway, followed a moment later and started in pursuit, all the heads in the windows —those of women and children now—screaming in guidance.

The stairway being now partly cleared, most of the crowd having rushed down to the street to observe the flight and pursuit, Dr. Helberson mounted to the landing, followed by Harper. At a door in the upper passage an officer denied them admittance. "We are physicians," said the doctor, and they passed in. The room was full of men, dimly seen, crowded about a table. The newcomers edged their way forward and looked over the shoulders of those in the front rank. Upon the table, the lower limbs covered with a sheet, lay the body of a man, brilliantly illuminated by the beam of a bull's-eye lantern held by a policeman standing at the feet. The others, excepting those near the head—the officer himself—all were in darkness. The face of the body showed yellow, repulsive, horrible! The eyes were partly open and upturned and the jaw fallen; traces of froth defiled the lips, the chin, the cheeks. A tall man, evidently a doctor, bent over the body with his hand thrust under the shirt front. He withdrew it and placed two fingers in the open mouth. "This man has been about six hours dead," said he. "It is a case for the coroner."

He drew a card from his pocket, handed it to the officer and made his way toward the door.

"Clear the room—out, all!" said the officer, sharply, and the body disappeared as if it had been snatched away, as shifting the lantern he flashed its beam of light here and there against the faces of the crowd. The effect was amazing! The men, blinded, confused, almost terrified, made a tumultuous rush for the door, pushing, crowding, and tumbling over one another as they fled, like the hosts of Night before the shafts of Apollo. Upon the struggling, trampling mass the officer poured his light without pity and without cessation. Caught in the current, Helberson and Harper were swept out of the room and cascaded down the stairs into the street.

"Good God, Doctor! did I not tell you that Jarette would

kill him?" said Harper, as soon as they were clear of the crowd.

"I believe you did," replied the other, without apparent emotion.

They walked on in silence, block after block. Against the graying east the dwellings of the hill tribes showed in silhouette. The familiar milk wagon was already astir in the streets; the baker's man would soon come upon the scene; the newspaper carrier was abroad in the land.

"It strikes me, youngster," said Helberson, "that you and I have been having too much of the morning air lately. It is unwholesome; we need a change. What do you say to a tour in Europe?"

"When?"

"I'm not particular. I should suppose that four o'clock this afternoon would be early enough."

"I'll meet you at the boat," said Harper.

V

Seven years afterward these two men sat upon a bench in Madison Square, New York, in familiar conversation. Another man, who had been observing them for some time, himself unobserved, approached and, courteously lifting his hat from locks as white as frost, said: "I beg your pardon, gentlemen, but when you have killed a man by coming to life, it is best to change clothes with him, and at the first opportunity make a break for liberty."

Helberson and Harper exchanged significant glances. They were obviously amused. The former then looked the stranger kindly in the eye and replied:

"That has always been my plan. I entirely agree with you as to its advant——"

He stopped suddenly, rose and went white. He stared at the man, open-mouthed; he trembled visibly.

"Ah!" said the stranger, "I see that you are indisposed, Doctor. If you cannot treat yourself Dr. Harper can do something for you, I am sure."

"Who the devil are you?" said Harper, bluntly.

The stranger came nearer and, bending toward them, said in

a whisper: "I call myself Jarette sometimes, but I don't mind telling you, for old friendship, that I am Dr. William Mancher."

The revelation brought Harper to his feet. "Mancher!" he cried; and Helberson added: "It is true, by God!"

"Yes," said the stranger, smiling vaguely, "it is true enough, no doubt."

He hesitated and seemed to be trying to recall something, then began humming a popular air. He had apparently forgotten their presence.

"Look here, Mancher," said the elder of the two, "tell us just what occurred that night—to Jarette, you know."

"Oh, yes, about Jarette," said the other. "It's odd I should have neglected to tell you—I tell it so often. You see I knew, by over-hearing him talking to himself, that he was pretty badly frightened. So I couldn't resist the temptation to come to life and have a bit of fun out of him—I couldn't really. That was all right, though certainly I did not think he would take it so seriously; I did not, truly. And afterward—well, it was a tough job changing places with him, and then—damn you! you didn't let me out!"

Nothing could exceed the ferocity with which these last words were delivered. Both men stepped back in alarm.

"We?—why—why," Helberson stammered, losing his self-possession utterly, "we had nothing to do with it."

"Didn't I say you were Drs. Hell-born and Sharper?" inquired the man, laughing.

"My name is Helberson, yes; and this gentleman is Mr. Harper," replied the former, reassured by the laugh. "But we are not physicians now; we are—well, hang it, old man, we are gamblers."

And that was the truth.

"A very good profession—very good, indeed; and, by the way, I hope Sharper here paid over Jarette's money like an honest stakeholder. A very good and honorable profession," he repeated, thoughtfully, moving carelessly away; "but I stick to the old one. I am High Supreme Medical Officer of the Bloomingdale Asylum; it is my duty to cure the superintendent."

The Man and the Snake

It is of veritabyll report, and attested of so many that there be nowe of wyse and learned none to gaynsaye it, that ye serpente hys eye hath a magnetick propertie that whosoe falleth into its svasion is drawn forwards in despyte of his wille, and perisheth miserabyll by ye creature hys byte.

STRETCHED at ease upon a sofa, in gown and slippers, Harker Brayton smiled as he read the foregoing sentence in old Morryster's *Marvells of Science*. "The only marvel in the matter," he said to himself, "is that the wise and learned in Morryster's day should have believed such nonsense as is rejected by most of even the ignorant in ours."

A train of reflections followed—for Brayton was a man of thought—and he unconsciously lowered his book without altering the direction of his eyes. As soon as the volume had gone below the line of sight, something in an obscure corner of the room recalled his attention to his surroundings. What he saw, in the shadow under his bed, was two small points of light, apparently about an inch apart. They might have been reflections of the gas jet above him, in metal nail heads; he gave them but little thought and resumed his reading. A moment later something—some impulse which it did not occur to him to analyze—impelled him to lower the book again and seek for what he saw before. The points of light were still there. They seemed to have become brighter than before, shining with a greenish luster which he had not at first observed. He thought, too, that they might have moved a trifle—were somewhat nearer. They were still too much in the shadow, however, to reveal their nature and origin to an indolent attention, and again he resumed his reading. Suddenly something in the text suggested a thought that made him start and drop the book for the third time to the side of the sofa, whence, escaping from his hand, it fell sprawling to the floor, back upward. Brayton, half-risen, was staring intently into the obscurity beneath the bed, where the points of light shone with, it seemed to him, an added fire. His attention was now fully aroused, his gaze eager and imperative. It disclosed, almost directly under the foot-rail of the bed, the coils of a large serpent—the points of light were its eyes! Its horrible head, thrust flatly forth from the innermost coil and resting upon the outermost, was directed straight toward him, the definition of the wide, brutal jaw and the idiot-like forehead serving to show the direction of its malevolent gaze. The eyes were no longer merely luminous points; they looked into his own with a meaning, a malign significance.

II

A snake in a bedroom of a modern city dwelling of the better sort is, happily, not so common a phenomenon as to make explanation altogether needless. Harker Brayton, a bachelor of thirty-five, a scholar, idler, and something of an athlete, rich, popular, and of sound health, had returned to San Francisco from all manner of remote and unfamiliar countries. His tastes, always a trifle luxurious, had taken on an added exuberance from long privation; and the resources of even the Castle Hotel being inadequate for their perfect gratification, he had gladly accepted the hospitality of his friend, Dr. Druring, the distinguished scientist. Dr. Druring's house, a large, old-fashioned one in what is now an obscure quarter of the city, had an outer and visible aspect of reserve. It plainly would not associate with the contiguous elements of its altered environment, and appeared to have developed some of the eccentricities which come of isolation. One of these was a "wing," conspicuously irrelevant in point of architecture, and no less rebellious in the matter of purpose; for it was a combination of laboratory, menagerie, and museum. It was here that the doctor indulged the scientific side of his nature in the study of such forms of animal life as engaged his interest and comforted his taste—which, it must be confessed, ran rather to the lower types. For one of the higher nimbly and sweetly to recommend itself unto his gentle senses, it had at least to retain certain rudimentary characteristics allying it to such "dragons of the prime" as toads and snakes. His scientific sympathies were distinctly reptilian; he loved nature's vulgarians and described himself as the Zola of zoölogy. His wife and daughters, not having the advantage to share his enlightened curiosity regarding the works and ways of our ill-starred fellow-creatures, were with needless austerity excluded from what he called the Snakery and doomed to companionship with their own kind, though, to soften the rigors of their lot he had permitted them out of his great wealth to outdo the reptiles in the gorgeousness of their surroundings and to shine with a superior splendor.

Architecturally and in point of "furnishing," the Snakery had a severe simplicity befitting the humble circumstances of its occupants, many of whom, indeed, could not safely have been intrusted with the liberty which is necessary to the full enjoyment of luxury, for they had the troublesome peculiarity of being alive. In their own apartments, however, they were under as little personal restraint as was compatible with their protection from the baneful habit of swallowing one another; and, as Brayton had thoughtfully been apprised, it was more than a tradition that some of them had at divers times been found in parts of the premises where it would have embarrassed them to explain their presence. Despite the Snakery and its uncanny associations—to which, indeed, he gave little attention —Brayton found life at the Druring mansion very much to his mind.

III

Beyond a smart shock of surprise and a shudder of mere loathing, Mr. Brayton was not greatly affected. His first thought was to ring the call bell and bring a servant; but, although the bell cord dangled within easy reach, he made no movement toward it; it had occurred to his mind that the act might subject him to the suspicion of fear, which he certainly did not feel. He was more keenly conscious of the incongruous nature of the situation than affected by its perils; it was revolting, but absurd.

The reptile was of a species with which Brayton was unfamiliar. Its length he could only conjecture; the body at the largest visible part seemed about as thick as his forearm. In what way was it dangerous, if in any way? Was it venomous? Was it a constrictor? His knowledge of nature's danger signals did not enable him to say; he had never deciphered the code.

If not dangerous, the creature was at least offensive. It was *de trop*—"matter out of place"—an impertinence. The gem was unworthy of the setting. Even the barbarous taste of our time and country, which had loaded the walls of the room with pictures, the floor with furniture, and the furniture with bric-a-brac, had not quite fitted the place for this bit of the savage life of the jungle. Besides—insupportable thought!—the exhalations of its breath mingled with the atmosphere which he himself was breathing!

These thoughts shaped themselves with greater or less definition in Brayton's mind, and begot action. The process is what we call consideration and decision. It is thus that we are wise and unwise. It is thus that the withered leaf in an autumn breeze shows greater or less intelligence than its fellows, falling upon the land or upon the lake. The secret of human action is an open one: something contracts our muscles. Does it matter if we give to the preparatory molecular changes the name of will?

Brayton rose to his feet and prepared to back softly away from the snake, without disturbing it if possible, and through the door. Men retire so from the presence of the great, for greatness is power and power is a menace. He knew that he could walk backward without error. Should the monster follow, the taste which had plastered the walls with paintings had consistently supplied a rack of murderous Oriental weapons from which he could snatch one to suit the occasion. In the mean time the snake's eyes burned with a more pitiless malevolence than before.

Brayton lifted his right foot free of the floor to step backward. That moment he felt a strong aversion to doing so.

"I am accounted brave," he thought; "is bravery, then, no more than pride? Because there are none to witness the shame shall I retreat?"

He was steadying himself with his right hand upon the back of a chair, his foot suspended.

"Nonsense!" he said aloud; "I am not so great a coward as to fear to seem to myself afraid."

He lifted the foot a little higher by slightly bending the knee, and thrust it sharply to the floor—an inch in front of the other! He could not think how that occurred. A trial with the left foot had the same result; it was again in advance of the right. The hand upon the chair back was grasping it; the arm was straight, reaching somewhat backward. One might have said that he was reluctant to lose his hold. The snake's malignant head was still thrust forth from the inner coil as before, the neck level. It had not moved, but its eyes were now electric sparks, radiating an infinity of luminous needles.

The man had an ashy pallor. Again he took a step forward, and another, partly dragging the chair, which when finally released, fell upon the floor with a crash. The man groaned; the snake made neither sound nor motion, but its eyes were two dazzling suns. The reptile itself was wholly concealed by them. They gave off enlarging rings of rich and vivid colors, which at their greatest expansion successively vanished like soap-bubbles; they seemed to approach his very face, and anon were an immeasurable distance away. He heard, somewhere, the continuous throbbing of a great drum, with desultory bursts of far music, inconceivably sweet, like the tones of an æolian harp. He knew it for the sunrise melody of Memnon's statue, and thought he stood in the Nileside reeds hearing with exalted sense that immortal anthem through the silence of the centuries.

The music ceased; rather, it became by insensible degrees the distant roll of a retreating thunderstorm. A landscape, glittering with sun and rain, stretched before him, arched with a vivid rainbow framing in its giant curve a hundred visible cities. In the middle distance a vast serpent, wearing a crown, reared its head out of its voluminous convolutions and looked at him with his dead mother's eyes. Suddenly this enchanting landscape seemed to rise swiftly upward like the drop scene at a theater, and vanished in a blank. Something struck him a hard blow upon the face and breast. He had fallen to the floor; the blood ran from his broken nose and his bruised lips. For a moment he was dazed and stunned, and lay with closed eyes, his face against the floor. In a few moments he had recovered, and then realized that this fall, by withdrawing his eyes, had broken the spell which held him. He felt that now, by keeping his gaze averted, he would be able to retreat. But the thought of the serpent within a few feet of his head, yet unseen—perhaps in the very act of springing upon him and throwing its coils about his throat—was too horrible. He lifted his head, stared again into those baleful eyes, and was again in bondage.

The snake had not moved and appeared somewhat to have

lost its power upon the imagination; the gorgeous illusions of a few moments before were not repeated. Beneath that flat and brainless brow its black, beady eyes simply glittered as at first with an expression unspeakably malignant. It was as if the creature, knowing its triumph assured, had determined to practice no more alluring wiles.

Now ensued a fearful scene. The man, prone upon the floor, within a yard of his enemy, raised the upper part of his body upon his elbows, his head thrown back, his legs extended to their full length. His face was white between its gouts of blood; his eyes were strained open to their uttermost expansion. There was froth upon his lips; it dropped off in flakes. Strong convulsions ran through his body, making almost serpentine undulations. He bent himself at the waist, shifting his legs from side to side. And every movement left him a little nearer to the snake. He thrust his hands forward to brace himself back, yet constantly advanced upon his elbows.

IV

Dr. Druring and his wife sat in the library. The scientist was in rare good humor.

"I have just obtained, by exchange with another collector," he said, "a splendid specimen of the *ophiophagus*."

"And what may that be?" the lady inquired with a somewhat languid interest.

"Why, bless my soul, what profound ignorance! My dear, a man who ascertains after marriage that his wife does not know Greek, is entitled to a divorce. The *ophiophagus* is a snake that eats other snakes."

"I hope it will eat all yours," she said, absently shifting the lamp. "But how does it get the other snakes? By charming them, I suppose."

"That is just like you, dear," said the doctor, with an affectation of petulance. "You know how irritating to me is any allusion to that vulgar superstition about the snake's power of fascination."

The conversation was interrupted by a mighty cry, which rang through the silent house like the voice of a demon shouting in a tomb! Again and yet again it sounded, with terrible distinctness. They sprang to their feet, the man confused, the lady pale and speechless with fright. Almost before the echoes of the last cry had died away the doctor was out of the room, springing up the stairs two steps at a time. In the corridor in front of Brayton's chamber he met some servants who had come from the upper floor. Together they rushed at the door without knocking. It was unfastened and gave way. Brayton lay upon his stomach on the floor, dead. His head and arms were partly concealed under the foot rail of the bed. They pulled the body away, turning it upon the back. The face was daubed with blood and froth, the eyes were wide open, staring —a dreadful sight!

"Died in a fit," said the scientist, bending his knee and placing his hand upon the heart. While in that position he happened to look under the bed. "Good God!" he added; "how did this thing get in here?"

He reached under the bed, pulled out the snake, and flung it, still coiled, to the center of the room, whence with a harsh, shuffling sound, it slid across the polished floor till stopped by the wall, where it lay without motion. It was a stuffed snake; its eyes were two shoe buttons.

A Holy Terror

THERE was an entire lack of interest in the latest arrival at Hurdy-Gurdy. He was not even christened with the picturesquely descriptive nick-name which is so frequently a mining camp's word of welcome to the newcomer. In almost any other camp thereabout this circumstance would of itself have secured him some such appellation as "The White-headed Conundrum," or "No Sarvey"—an expression naïvely supposed to suggest to quick intelligences the Spanish *quien sabe*. He came without provoking a ripple of concern upon the social surface of Hurdy-Gurdy—a place which to the general Californian contempt of men's personal history superadded a local indifference of its own. The time was long past when it was of any importance who came there, or if anybody came. No one was living at Hurdy-Gurdy.

Two years before, the camp had boasted a stirring population of two or three thousand males and not fewer than a dozen females. A majority of the former had done a few weeks' earnest work in demonstrating, to the disgust of the latter, the singularly mendacious character of the person whose ingenious tales of rich gold deposits had lured them thither—work, by the way, in which there was as little mental satisfaction as pecuniary profit; for a bullet from the pistol of a public-spirited citizen had put that imaginative gentleman beyond the reach of aspersion on the third day of the camp's existence. Still, his fiction had a certain foundation in fact, and many had lingered a considerable time in and about Hurdy-Gurdy, though now all had been long gone.

But they had left ample evidence of their sojourn. From the point where Injun Creek falls into the Rio San Juan Smith, up along both banks of the former into the cañon whence it emerges, extended a double row of forlorn shanties that seemed about to fall upon one another's neck to bewail their desolation; while about an equal number appeared to have straggled up the slope on either hand and perched themselves upon commanding eminences, whence they craned forward to

get a good view of the affecting scene. Most of these habitations were emaciated as by famine to the condition of mere
skeletons, about which clung unlovely tatters of what might
have been skin, but was really canvas. The little valley itself, torn
and gashed by pick and shovel, was unhandsome with long,
bending lines of decaying flume resting here and there upon
the summits of sharp ridges, and stilting awkwardly across the
intervals upon unhewn poles. The whole place presented that
raw and forbidding aspect of arrested development which is a
new country's substitute for the solemn grace of ruin wrought
by time. Wherever there remained a patch of the original soil a
rank overgrowth of weeds and brambles had spread upon the
scene, and from its dank, unwholesome shades the visitor curious in such matters might have obtained numberless souvenirs
of the camp's former glory—fellowless boots mantled with
green mould and plethoric of rotting leaves; an occasional old
felt hat; desultory remnants of a flannel shirt; sardine boxes
inhumanly mutilated and a surprising profusion of black bottles
distributed with a truly catholic impartiality, everywhere.

II

The man who had now rediscovered Hurdy-Gurdy was evidently not curious as to its archæology. Nor, as he looked
about him upon the dismal evidences of wasted work and
broken hopes, their dispiriting significance accentuated by the
ironical pomp of a cheap gilding by the rising sun, did he supplement his sigh of weariness by one of sensibility. He simply
removed from the back of his tired burro a miner's outfit a
trifle larger than the animal itself, picketed that creature and
selecting a hatchet from his kit moved off at once across the
dry bed of Injun Creek to the top of a low, gravelly hill beyond.
Stepping across a prostrate fence of brush and boards he
picked up one of the latter, split it into five parts and sharpened
them at one end. He then began a kind of search, occasionally
stooping to examine something with close attention. At last
his patient scrutiny appeared to be rewarded with success, for
he suddenly erected his figure to its full height, made a gesture
of satisfaction, pronounced the word "Scarry" and at once
strode away with long, equal steps, which he counted. Then he

stopped and drove one of his stakes into the earth. He then looked carefully about him, measured off a number of paces over a singularly uneven ground and hammered in another. Pacing off twice the distance at a right angle to his former course he drove down a third, and repeating the process sank home the fourth, and then a fifth. This he split at the top and in the cleft inserted an old letter envelope covered with an intricate system of pencil tracks. In short, he staked off a hill claim in strict accordance with the local mining laws of Hurdy-Gurdy and put up the customary notice.

It is necessary to explain that one of the adjuncts to Hurdy-Gurdy—one to which that metropolis became afterward itself an adjunct—was a cemetery. In the first week of the camp's existence this had been thoughtfully laid out by a committee of citizens. The day after had been signalized by a debate between two members of the committee, with reference to a more eligible site, and on the third day the necropolis was inaugurated by a double funeral. As the camp had waned the cemetery had waxed; and long before the ultimate inhabitant, victorious alike over the insidious malaria and the forthright revolver, had turned the tail of his pack-ass upon Injun Creek the outlying settlement had become a populous if not popular suburb. And now, when the town was fallen into the sere and yellow leaf of an unlovely senility, the graveyard—though somewhat marred by time and circumstance, and not altogether exempt from innovations in grammar and experiments in orthography, to say nothing of the devastating coyote—answered the humble needs of its denizens with reasonable completeness. It comprised a generous two acres of ground, which with commendable thrift but needless care had been selected for its mineral unworth, contained two or three skeleton trees (one of which had a stout lateral branch from which a weather-wasted rope still significantly dangled), half a hundred gravelly mounds, a score of rude headboards displaying the literary peculiarities above mentioned and a struggling colony of prickly pears. Altogether, God's Location, as with characteristic reverence it had been called, could justly boast of an indubitably superior quality of desolation. It was in the most thickly settled part of this interesting demesne that Mr. Jefferson Doman staked off his claim. If in the prosecution of his design he should deem it expedient to remove any of the dead they would have the right to be suitably reinterred.

III

This Mr. Jefferson Doman was from Elizabethtown, New Jersey, where six years before he had left his heart in the keeping of a golden-haired, demure-mannered young woman named Mary Matthews, as collateral security for his return to claim her hand.

"I just *know* you'll never get back alive—you never do succeed in anything," was the remark which illustrated Miss Matthews's notion of what constituted success and, inferentially, her view of the nature of encouragement. She added: "If you don't I'll go to California too. I can put the coins in little bags as you dig them out."

This characteristically feminine theory of auriferous deposits did not commend itself to the masculine intelligence: it was Mr. Doman's belief that gold was found in a liquid state. He deprecated her intent with considerable enthusiasm, suppressed her sobs with a light hand upon her mouth, laughed in her eyes as he kissed away her tears, and with a cheerful "Ta-ta" went to California to labor for her through the long, loveless years, with a strong heart, an alert hope and a steadfast fidelity that never for a moment forgot what it was about. In the mean time, Miss Matthews had granted a monopoly of her humble talent for sacking up coins to Mr. Jo. Seeman, of New York, gambler, by whom it was better appreciated than her commanding genius for unsacking and bestowing them upon his local rivals. Of this latter aptitude, indeed, he manifested his disapproval by an act which secured him the position of clerk of the laundry in the State prison, and for her the *sobriquet* of "Split-faced Moll." At about this time she wrote to Mr. Doman a touching letter of renunciation, inclosing her photograph to prove that she had no longer a right to indulge the dream of becoming Mrs. Doman, and recounting so graphically her fall from a horse that the staid "plug" upon which Mr. Doman had ridden into Red Dog to get the letter made vicarious atonement under the spur all the way back to camp. The letter failed in a signal way to accomplish its object; the fidelity which had before been to Mr. Doman a matter of love and duty was thenceforth a matter of honor also; and the photograph, showing the once pretty face sadly disfigured as by the slash of a knife, was duly instated in his affections and its more comely predecessor treated with contumelious neglect. On being informed of this, Miss Matthews, it is only fair to say, appeared less surprised than from the apparently low estimate of Mr. Doman's generosity which the tone of her former letter attested one would naturally have expected her to be. Soon after, however, her letters grew infrequent, and then ceased altogether.

But Mr. Doman had another correspondent, Mr. Barney Bree, of Hurdy-Gurdy, formerly of Red Dog. This gentleman, although a notable figure among miners, was not a miner. His knowledge of mining consisted mainly in a marvelous command of its slang, to which he made copious contributions, enriching its vocabulary with a wealth of uncommon phrases more remarkable for their aptness than their refinement, and which impressed the unlearned "tenderfoot" with a lively sense of the profundity of their inventor's acquirements. When not entertaining a circle of admiring auditors from San Francisco or the East he could commonly be found pursuing the comparatively obscure industry of sweeping out the various dance houses and purifying the cuspidors.

Barney had apparently but two passions in life—love of Jefferson Doman, who had once been of some service to him, and love of whisky, which certainly had not. He had been among the first in the rush to Hurdy-Gurdy, but had not prospered, and had sunk by degrees to the position of grave digger. This was not a vocation, but Barney in a desultory way turned his trembling hand to it whenever some local misunderstanding at the card table and his own partial recovery from a prolonged debauch occurred coincidently in point of time. One day Mr. Doman received, at Red Dog, a letter with the simple postmark, "Hurdy, Cal.," and being occupied with another matter, carelessly thrust it into a chink of his cabin for future perusal. Some two years later it was accidentally dislodged and he read it. It ran as follows:—

HURDY, June 6.
FRIEND JEFF: I've hit her hard in the boneyard. She's blind and lousy. I'm on the divvy—that's me, and mum's my lay till you toot. Yours,   BARNEY.
P.S.—I've clayed her with Scarry.

With some knowledge of the general mining camp *argot* and of Mr. Bree's private system for the communication of ideas Mr. Doman had no difficulty in understanding by this uncommon epistle that Barney while performing his duty as grave digger had uncovered a quartz ledge with no outcroppings; that it was visibly rich in free gold; that, moved by considerations of friendship, he was willing to accept Mr. Doman as a partner and awaiting that gentleman's declaration of his will in the matter would discreetly keep the discovery a secret. From the postscript it was plainly inferable that in order to conceal the treasure he had buried above it the mortal part of a person named Scarry.

From subsequent events, as related to Mr. Doman at Red Dog, it would appear that before taking this precaution Mr. Bree must have had the thrift to remove a modest competency of the gold; at any rate, it was at about that time that he entered upon that memorable series of potations and treatings which is still one of the cherished traditions of the San Juan Smith country, and is spoken of with respect as far away as Ghost Rock and Lone Hand. At its conclusion some former citizens of Hurdy-Gurdy, for whom he had performed the last kindly office at the cemetery, made room for him among them, and he rested well.

IV

Having finished staking off his claim Mr. Doman walked back to the centre of it and stood again at the spot where his search among the graves had expired in the exclamation, "Scarry." He bent again over the headboard that bore that name and as if to reinforce the senses of sight and hearing ran his forefinger along the rudely carved letters. Re-erecting himself he appended orally to the simple inscription the shockingly forthright epitaph, "She was a holy terror!"

Had Mr. Doman been required to make these words good with proof—as, considering their somewhat censorious character, he doubtless should have been—he would have found himself embarrassed by the absence of reputable witnesses, and hearsay evidence would have been the best he could command. At the time when Scarry had been prevalent in the mining camps thereabout—when, as the editor of the *Hurdy Herald* would have phrased it, she was "in the plenitude of her power"—Mr. Doman's fortunes had been at a low ebb, and he had led the vagrantly laborious life of a prospector. His time had been mostly spent in the mountains, now with one companion, now with another. It was from the admiring recitals of these casual partners, fresh from the various camps, that his judgment of Scarry had been made up; he himself had never had the doubtful advantage of her acquaintance and the precarious distinction of her favor. And when, finally, on the termination of her perverse career at Hurdy-Gurdy he had read in a chance copy of the *Herald* her column-long obituary (written by the local humorist of that lively sheet in the highest style of his art) Doman had paid to her memory and to her historiographer's genius the tribute of a smile and chivalrously forgotten her. Standing now at the grave-side of this mountain Messalina he recalled the leading events of her turbulent career, as he had heard them celebrated at his several campfires, and perhaps with an unconscious attempt at self-justification repeated that she was a holy terror, and sank his pick into her grave up to the handle. At that moment a raven, which had silently settled upon a branch of the blasted tree above his head, solemnly snapped its beak and uttered its mind about the matter with an approving croak.

Pursuing his discovery of free gold with great zeal, which he probably credited to his conscience as a grave digger, Mr. Barney Bree had made an unusually deep sepulcher, and it was near sunset before Mr. Doman, laboring with the leisurely deliberation of one who has "a dead sure thing" and no fear of an adverse claimant's enforcement of a prior right, reached the coffin and uncovered it. When he had done so he was confronted by a difficulty for which he had made no provision; the coffin—a mere flat shell of not very well-preserved redwood boards, apparently—had no handles, and it filled the entire

bottom of the excavation. The best he could do without vio-
lating the decent sanctities of the situation was to make the
excavation sufficiently longer to enable him to stand at the
head of the casket and getting his powerful hands underneath
erect it upon its narrower end; and this he proceeded to do.
The approach of night quickened his efforts. He had no
thought of abandoning his task at this stage to resume it
on the morrow under more advantageous conditions. The feverish stimulation of cupidity and the fascination of terror held
him to his dismal work with an iron authority. He no longer
idled, but wrought with a terrible zeal. His head uncovered,
his outer garments discarded, his shirt opened at the neck and
thrown back from his breast, down which ran sinuous rills of
perspiration, this hardy and impenitent gold-getter and grave-
robber toiled with a giant energy that almost dignified the
character of his horrible purpose; and when the sun fringes had
burned themselves out along the crest line of the western hills,
and the full moon had climbed out of the shadows that lay
along the purple plain, he had erected the coffin upon its foot,
where it stood propped against the end of the open grave.
Then, standing up to his neck in the earth at the opposite extreme of the excavation, as he looked at the coffin upon which
the moonlight now fell with a full illumination he was thrilled
with a sudden terror to observe upon it the startling apparition
of a dark human head—the shadow of his own. For a moment
this simple and natural circumstance unnerved him. The noise
of his labored breathing frightened him, and he tried to still it,
but his bursting lungs would not be denied. Then, laughing
half-audibly and wholly without spirit, he began making movements of his head from side to side, in order to compel the
apparition to repeat them. He found a comforting reassurance
in asserting his command over his own shadow. He was tem-
porizing, making, with unconscious prudence, a dilatory opposition to an impending catastrophe. He felt that invisible
forces of evil were closing in upon him, and he parleyed for
time with the Inevitable.

He now observed in succession several unusual circumstances.
The surface of the coffin upon which his eyes were fastened
was not flat; it presented two distinct ridges, one longitudinal
and the other transverse. Where these intersected at the widest

part there was a corroded metallic plate that reflected the moonlight with a dismal lustre. Along the outer edges of the coffin, at long intervals, were rust-eaten heads of nails. This frail product of the carpenter's art had been put into the grave the wrong side up!

Perhaps it was one of the humors of the camp—a practical manifestation of the facetious spirit that had found literary expression in the topsy-turvy obituary notice from the pen of Hurdy-Gurdy's great humorist. Perhaps it had some occult personal signification impenetrable to understandings uninstructed in local traditions. A more charitable hypothesis is that it was owing to a misadventure on the part of Mr. Barney Bree, who, making the interment unassisted (either by choice for the conservation of his golden secret, or through public apathy), had committed a blunder which he was afterward unable or unconcerned to rectify. However it had come about, poor Scarry had indubitably been put into the earth face downward.

When terror and absurdity make alliance, the effect is frightful. This strong-hearted and daring man, this hardy night worker among the dead, this defiant antagonist of darkness and desolation, succumbed to a ridiculous surprise. He was smitten with a thrilling chill—shivered, and shook his massive shoulders as if to throw off an icy hand. He no longer breathed, and the blood in his veins, unable to abate its impetus, surged hotly beneath his cold skin. Unleavened with oxygen, it mounted to his head and congested his brain. His physical functions had gone over to the enemy; his very heart was arrayed against him. He did not move; he could not have cried out. He needed but a coffin to be dead—as dead as the death that confronted him with only the length of an open grave and the thickness of a rotting plank between.

Then, one by one, his senses returned; the tide of terror that had overwhelmed his faculties began to recede. But with the return of his senses he became singularly unconscious of the object of his fear. He saw the moonlight gilding the coffin, but no longer the coffin that it gilded. Raising his eyes and turning his head, he noted, curiously and with surprise, the black branches of the dead tree, and tried to estimate the length of the weather-worn rope that dangled from its ghostly hand. The monotonous barking of distant coyotes affected him as something he had heard years ago in a dream. An owl flapped awkwardly above him on noiseless wings, and he tried to forecast the direction of its flight when it should encounter the cliff that reared its illuminated front a mile away. His hearing took account of a gopher's stealthy tread in the shadow of the cactus. He was intensely observant; his senses were all alert; but he saw not the coffin. As one can gaze at the sun until it looks black and then vanishes, so his mind, having exhausted its capacities of dread, was no longer conscious of the separate existence of anything dreadful. The Assassin was cloaking the sword.

It was during this lull in the battle that he became sensible of a faint, sickening odor. At first he thought it was that of a rattle-snake, and involuntarily tried to look about his feet. They were nearly invisible in the gloom of the grave. A hoarse, gurgling sound, like the death-rattle in a human throat, seemed to come out of the sky, and a moment later a great, black, angular shadow, like the same sound made visible, dropped curving from the topmost branch of the spectral tree, fluttered for an instant before his face and sailed fiercely away into the mist along the creek.

It was the raven. The incident recalled him to a sense of the situation, and again his eyes sought the upright coffin, now illuminated by the moon for half its length. He saw the gleam of the metallic plate and tried without moving to decipher the inscription. Then he fell to speculating upon what was behind it. His creative imagination presented him a vivid picture. The planks no longer seemed an obstacle to his vision and he saw the livid corpse of the dead woman, standing in grave-clothes, and staring vacantly at him, with lidless, shrunken eyes. The lower jaw was fallen, the upper lip drawn away from the uncovered teeth. He could make out a mottled pattern on the hollow cheeks—the maculations of decay. By some mysterious process his mind reverted for the first time that day to the photograph of Mary Matthews. He contrasted its blonde beauty with the forbidding aspect of this dead face—the most beloved object that he knew with the most hideous that he could conceive.

The Assassin now advanced and displaying the blade laid it

against the victim's throat. That is to say, the man became at first dimly, then definitely, aware of an impressive coincidence —a relation—a parallel between the face on the card and the name on the headboard. The one was disfigured, the other described a disfiguration. The thought took hold of him and shook him. It transformed the face that his imagination had created behind the coffin lid; the contrast became a resemblance; the resemblance grew to identity. Remembering the many descriptions of Scarry's personal appearance that he had heard from the gossips of his camp-fire he tried with imperfect success to recall the exact nature of the disfiguration that had given the woman her ugly name; and what was lacking in his memory fancy supplied, stamping it with the validity of conviction. In the maddening attempt to recall such scraps of the woman's history as he had heard, the muscles of his arms and hands were strained to a painful tension, as by an effort to lift a great weight. His body writhed and twisted with the exertion. The tendons of his neck stood out as tense as whip-cords, and his breath came in short, sharp gasps. The catastrophe could not be much longer delayed, or the agony of anticipation would leave nothing to be done by the *coup de grâce* of verification. The scarred face behind the lid would slay him through the wood.

A movement of the coffin diverted his thought. It came forward to within a foot of his face, growing visibly larger as it approached. The rusted metallic plate, with an inscription illegible in the moonlight, looked him steadily in the eye. Determined not to shrink, he tried to brace his shoulders more firmly against the end of the excavation, and nearly fell backward in the attempt. There was nothing to support him; he had unconsciously moved upon his enemy, clutching the heavy knife that he had drawn from his belt. The coffin had not advanced and he smiled to think it could not retreat. Lifting his knife he struck the heavy hilt against the metal plate with all his power. There was a sharp, ringing percussion, and with a dull clatter the whole decayed coffin lid broke in pieces and came away, falling about his feet. The quick and the dead were face to face—the frenzied, shrieking man—the woman standing tranquil in her silences. She was a holy terror!

V

Some months later a party of men and women belonging to the highest social circles of San Francisco passed through Hurdy-Gurdy on their way to the Yosemite Valley by a new trail. They halted for dinner and during its preparation explored the desolate camp. One of the party had been at Hurdy-Gurdy in the days of its glory. He had, indeed, been one of its prominent citizens; and it used to be said that more money passed over his faro table in any one night than over those of all his competitors in a week; but being now a millionaire engaged in greater enterprises, he did not deem these early successes of sufficient importance to merit the distinction of remark. His invalid wife, a lady famous in San Francisco for the costly nature of her entertainments and her exacting rigor with regard to the social position and "antecedents" of those who attended them, accompanied the expedition. During a stroll among the shanties of the abandoned camp Mr. Porfer directed the attention of his wife and friends to a dead tree on a low hill beyond Injun Creek.

"As I told you," he said, "I passed through this camp in 1852, and was told that no fewer than five men had been hanged here by vigilantes at different times, and all on that tree. If I am not mistaken, a rope is dangling from it yet. Let us go over and see the place."

Mr. Porfer did not add that the rope in question was perhaps the very one from whose fatal embrace his own neck had once had an escape so narrow that an hour's delay in taking himself out of that region would have spanned it.

Proceeding leisurely down the creek to a convenient crossing, the party came upon the cleanly picked skeleton of an animal which Mr. Porfer after due examination pronounced to be that of an ass. The distinguishing ears were gone, but much of the inedible head had been spared by the beasts and birds, and the stout bridle of horsehair was intact, as was the riata, of similar material, connecting it with a picket pin still firmly sunken in the earth. The wooden and metallic elements of a miner's kit lay near by. The customary remarks were made, cynical on the part of the men, sentimental and refined by the lady. A little later they stood by the tree in the cemetery and

Mr. Porfer sufficiently unbent from his dignity to place himself beneath the rotten rope and confidently lay a coil of it about his neck, somewhat, it appeared, to his own satisfaction, but greatly to the horror of his wife, to whose sensibilities the performance gave a smart shock.

An exclamation from one of the party gathered them all about an open grave, at the bottom of which they saw a confused mass of human bones and the broken remnants of a coffin. Coyotes and buzzards had performed the last sad rites for pretty much all else. Two skulls were visible and in order to investigate this somewhat unusual redundancy one of the younger men had the hardihood to spring into the grave and hand them up to another before Mrs. Porfer could indicate her marked disapproval of so shocking an act, which, nevertheless, she did with considerable feeling and in very choice words. Pursuing his search among the dismal débris at the bottom of the grave the young man next handed up a rusted coffin plate, with a rudely cut inscription, which with difficulty Mr. Porfer deciphered and read aloud with an earnest and not altogether unsuccessful attempt at the dramatic effect which he deemed befitting to the occasion and his rhetorical abilities:

> MANUELITA MURPHY.
> Born at the Mission San Pedro—Died in
> Hurdy-Gurdy,
> Aged 47.
> Hell's full of such.

In deference to the piety of the reader and the nerves of Mrs. Porfer's fastidious sisterhood of both sexes let us not touch upon the painful impression produced by this uncommon inscription, further than to say that the elocutionary powers of Mr. Porfer had never before met with so spontaneous and overwhelming recognition.

The next morsel that rewarded the ghoul in the grave was a long tangle of black hair defiled with clay: but this was such an anti-climax that it received little attention. Suddenly, with a short exclamation and a gesture of excitement, the young man unearthed a fragment of grayish rock, and after a hurried inspection handed it up to Mr. Porfer. As the sunlight fell upon it it glittered with a yellow luster—it was thickly studded with gleaming points. Mr. Porfer snatched it, bent his head over it a moment and threw it lightly away with the simple remark:

"Iron pyrites—fool's gold."

The young man in the discovery shaft was a trifle disconcerted, apparently.

Meanwhile, Mrs. Porfer, unable longer to endure the disagreeable business, had walked back to the tree and seated herself at its root. While rearranging a tress of golden hair which had slipped from its confinement she was attracted by what appeared to be and really was the fragment of an old coat. Looking about to assure herself that so unladylike an act was not observed, she thrust her jeweled hand into the exposed breast pocket and drew out a mouldy pocket-book. Its contents were as follows:

One bundle of letters, postmarked "Elizabethtown, New Jersey."

One circle of blonde hair tied with a ribbon.

One photograph of a beautiful girl.

One ditto of same, singularly disfigured.

One name on back of photograph—"Jefferson Doman."

A few moments later a group of anxious gentlemen surrounded Mrs. Porfer as she sat motionless at the foot of the tree, her head dropped forward, her fingers clutching a crushed photograph. Her husband raised her head, exposing a face ghastly white, except the long, deforming cicatrice, familiar to all her friends, which no art could ever hide, and which now traversed the pallor of her countenance like a visible curse.

Mary Matthews Porfer had the bad luck to be dead.

The Suitable Surroundings

THE NIGHT

One midsummer night a farmer's boy living about ten miles from the city of Cincinnati was following a bridle path through a dense and dark forest. He had lost himself while searching for some missing cows, and near midnight was a long way from home, in a part of the country with which he was unfamiliar. But he was a stout-hearted lad, and knowing his general direction from his home, he plunged into the forest without hesitation, guided by the stars. Coming into the bridle path, and observing that it ran in the right direction, he followed it.

The night was clear, but in the woods it was exceedingly dark. It was more by the sense of touch than by that of sight that the lad kept the path. He could not, indeed, very easily go astray; the undergrowth on both sides was so thick as to be almost impenetrable. He had gone into the forest a mile or more when he was surprised to see a feeble gleam of light shining through the foliage skirting the path on his left. The sight of it startled him and set his heart beating audibly.

"The old Breede house is somewhere about here," he said to himself. "This must be the other end of the path which we reach it by from our side. Ugh! what should a light be doing there?"

Nevertheless, he pushed on. A moment later he had emerged from the forest into a small, open space, mostly upgrown to brambles. There were remnants of a rotting fence. A few yards from the trail, in the middle of the "clearing," was the house from which the light came, through an unglazed window. The window had once contained glass, but that and its supporting frame had long ago yielded to missiles flung by hands of venturesome boys to attest alike their courage and their hostility to the supernatural; for the Breede house bore the evil reputation of being haunted. Possibly it was not, but even the hardiest sceptic could not deny that it was deserted—which in rural regions is much the same thing.

Looking at the mysterious dim light shining from the ruined window the boy remembered with apprehension that his own hand had assisted at the destruction. His penitence was of course poignant in proportion to its tardiness and inefficacy. He half expected to be set upon by all the unworldly and bodiless malevolences whom he had outraged by assisting to break alike their windows and their peace. Yet this stubborn lad, shaking in every limb, would not retreat. The blood in his veins was strong and rich with the iron of the frontiersman. He was but two removes from the generation that had subdued the Indian. He started to pass the house.

As he was going by he looked in at the blank window space and saw a strange and terrifying sight,—the figure of a man seated in the centre of the room, at a table upon which lay some loose sheets of paper. The elbows rested on the table, the hands supporting the head, which was uncovered. On each side the fingers were pushed into the hair. The face showed dead-yellow in the light of a single candle a little to one side. The flame illuminated that side of the face, the other was in deep shadow. The man's eyes were fixed upon the blank window space with a stare in which an older and cooler observer might have discerned something of apprehension, but which seemed to the lad altogether soulless. He believed the man to be dead.

The situation was horrible, but not with out its fascination. The boy stopped to note it all. He was weak, faint and trembling; he could feel the blood forsaking his face. Nevertheless, he set his teeth and resolutely advanced to the house. He had no conscious intention—it was the mere courage of terror. He thrust his white face forward into the illuminated opening. At that instant a strange, harsh cry, a shriek, broke upon the silence of the night—the note of a screech-owl. The man sprang to his feet, overturning the table and extinguishing the candle. The boy took to his heels.

THE DAY BEFORE

"Good-morning, Colston. I am in luck, it seems. You have often said that my commendation of your literary work was mere civility, and here you find me absorbed—actually merged—in your latest story in the *Messenger*. Nothing less shocking than your touch upon my shoulder would have roused me to consciousness."

"The proof is stronger than you seem to know," replied the man addressed: "so keen is your eagerness to read my story that you are willing to renounce selfish considerations and forego all the pleasure that you could get from it."

"I don't understand you," said the other, folding the newspaper that he held and putting it into his pocket. "You writers are a queer lot, anyhow. Come, tell me what I have done or omitted in this matter. In what way does the pleasure that I get, or might get, from your work depend on me?"

"In many ways. Let me ask you how you would enjoy your breakfast if you took it in this street car. Suppose the phonograph so perfected as to be able to give you an entire opera,—singing, orchestration, and all; do you think you would get much pleasure out of it if you turned it on at your office during business hours? Do you really care for a serenade by Schubert when you hear it fiddled by an untimely Italian on a morning ferryboat? Are you always cocked and primed for enjoyment? Do you keep every mood on tap, ready to any demand? Let me remind you, sir, that the story which you have done me the honor to begin as a means of becoming oblivious to the discomfort of this car is a ghost story!"

"Well?"

"Well! Has the reader no duties corresponding to his privileges? You have paid five cents for that newspaper. It is yours. You have the right to read it when and where you will. Much of what is in it is neither helped nor harmed by time and place and mood; some of it actually requires to be read at once—while it is fizzing. But my story is not of that character. It is not 'the very latest advices' from Ghostland. You are not expected to keep yourself *au courant* with what is going on in the realm of spooks. The stuff will keep until you have leisure to put yourself into the frame of mind appropriate to the sentiment of the piece—which I respectfully submit that you cannot do in a street car, even if you are the only passenger. The solitude is not of the right sort. An author has rights which the reader is bound to respect."

"For specific example?"

"The right to the reader's undivided attention. To deny him this is immoral. To make him share your attention with the rattle of a street car, the moving panorama of the crowds on the sidewalks, and the buildings beyond—with any of the thousands of distractions which make our customary environment —is to treat him with gross injustice. By God, it is infamous!"

The speaker had risen to his feet and was steadying himself by one of the straps hanging from the roof of the car. The other man looked up at him in sudden astonishment, wondering how so trivial a grievance could seem to justify so strong language. He saw that his friend's face was uncommonly pale and that his eyes glowed like living coals.

"You know what I mean," continued the writer, impetuously crowding his words—"you know what I mean, Marsh. My stuff in this morning's *Messenger* is plainly sub-headed 'A Ghost Story.' That is ample notice to all. Every honorable reader will understand it as prescribing by implication the conditions under which the work is to be read."

The man addressed as Marsh winced a trifle, then asked with a smile: "What conditions? You know that I am only a plain business man who cannot be supposed to understand such things. How, when, where should I read your ghost story?"

"In solitude—at night—by the light of a candle. There are certain emotions which a writer can easily enough excite—such as compassion or merriment. I can move you to tears or laughter under almost any circumstances. But for my ghost story to be effective you must be made to feel fear—at least a strong sense of the supernatural—and that is a difficult matter. I have a right to expect that if you read me at all you will give me a chance; that you will make yourself accessible to the emotion that I try to inspire."

The car had now arrived at its terminus and stopped. The trip just completed was its first for the day and the conversation of the two early passengers had not been interrupted. The streets were yet silent and desolate; the house tops were just touched by the rising sun. As they stepped from the car and walked away together Marsh narrowly eyed his companion, who was reported, like most men of uncommon literary ability, to be addicted to various destructive vices. That is the revenge which dull minds take upon bright ones in resentment of their superiority. Mr. Colston was known as a man of genius. There are honest souls who believe that genius is a mode of excess. It was known that Colston did not drink liquor, but many said that he ate opium. Something in his appearance that morning —a certain wildness of the eyes, an unusual pallor, a thickness and rapidity of speech—were taken by Mr. Marsh to confirm the report. Nevertheless, he had not the self-denial to abandon a subject which he found interesting, however it might excite his friend.

"Do you mean to say," he began, "that if I take the trouble to observe your directions—place myself in the conditions that you demand: solitude, night and a tallow candle—you can with your ghostly work give me an uncomfortable sense of the supernatural, as you call it? Can you accelerate my pulse, make me start at sudden noises, send a nervous chill along my spine and cause my hair to rise?"

Colston turned suddenly and looked him squarely in the eyes as they walked. "You would not dare—you have not the courage," he said. He emphasized the words with a contemptuous gesture. "You are brave enough to read me in a street car, but—in a deserted house—alone—in the forest—at night! Bah! I have a manuscript in my pocket that would kill you."

Marsh was angry. He knew himself courageous, and the words stung him. "If you know such a place," he said, "take me there to-night and leave me your story and a candle. Call for me when I've had time enough to read it and I'll tell you the entire plot and—kick you out of the place."

That is how it occurred that the farmer's boy, looking in at an unglazed window of the Breede house, saw a man sitting in the light of a candle.

THE DAY AFTER

Late in the afternoon of the next day three men and a boy approached the Breede house from that point of the compass toward which the boy had fled the preceding night. The men were in high spirits; they talked very loudly and laughed. They made facetious and good-humored ironical remarks to the boy about his adventure, which evidently they did not believe in. The boy accepted their raillery with seriousness, making no reply. He had a sense of the fitness of things and knew that one who professes to have seen a dead man rise from his seat and blow out a candle is not a credible witness.

Arriving at the house and finding the door unlocked, the party of investigators entered without ceremony. Leading out of the passage into which this door opened was another on the right and one on the left. They entered the room on the left —the one which had the blank front window. Here was the dead body of a man.

It lay partly on one side, with the forearm beneath it, the cheek on the floor. The eyes were wide open; the stare was not an agreeable thing to encounter. The lower jaw had fallen; a little pool of saliva had collected beneath the mouth. An over-thrown table, a partly burned candle, a chair and some paper with writing on it were all else that the room contained. The men looked at the body, touching the face in turn. The boy gravely stood at the head, assuming a look of ownership. It was the proudest moment of his life. One of the men said to him, "You're a good 'un"—a remark which was received by the two others with nods of acquiescence. It was Scepticism apologiz-ing to Truth. Then one of the men took from the floor the sheet of manuscript and stepped to the window, for already the evening shadows were glooming the forest. The song of the whip-poor-will was heard in the distance and a monstrous beetle sped by the window on roaring wings and thundered away out of hearing. The man read:

THE MANUSCRIPT

"Before committing the act which, rightly or wrongly, I have resolved on and appearing before my Maker for judgment, I, James R. Colston, deem it my duty as a journalist to make a statement to the public. My name is, I believe, tolerably well known to the people as a writer of tragic tales, but the somber-est imagination never conceived anything so tragic as my own life and history. Not in incident: my life has been destitute of adventure and action. But my mental career has been lurid with experiences such as kill and damn. I shall not recount them here—some of them are written and ready for publication elsewhere. The object of these lines is to explain to whomsoever may be interested that my death is voluntary—my own act. I shall die at twelve o'clock on the night of the 15th of July—a significant anniversary to me, for it was on that day, and at that hour, that my friend in time and eternity, Charles Breede, performed his vow to me by the same act which his fidelity to our pledge now entails upon me. He took his life in his little house in the Copeton woods. There was the customary verdict of 'temporary insanity.' Had I testified at that inquest—had I told all I knew, they would have called *me* mad!"

Here followed an evidently long passage which the man reading read to himself only. The rest he read aloud.

"I have still a week of life in which to arrange my worldly affairs and prepare for the great change. It is enough, for I have but few affairs and it is now four years since death became an imperative obligation.

"I shall bear this writing on my body; the finder will please hand it to the coroner.

"JAMES R. COLSTON.

"P.S.—Willard Marsh, on this the fatal fifteenth day of July I hand you this manuscript, to be opened and read under the conditions agreed upon, and at the place which I designated. I forego my intention to keep it on my body to explain the manner of my death, which is not important. It will serve to explain the manner of yours. I am to call for you during the night to receive assurance that you have read the manuscript. You know me well enough to expect me. But, my friend, it *will be after twelve o'clock*. May God have mercy on our souls!

"J.R.C."

Before the man who was reading this manuscript had finished, the candle had been picked up and lighted. When the reader had done, he quietly thrust the paper against the flame and despite the protestations of the others held it until it was burnt to ashes. The man who did this, and who afterward placidly endured a severe reprimand from the coroner, was a son-in-law of the late Charles Breede. At the inquest nothing could elicit an intelligent account of what the paper had contained.

FROM "THE TIMES"

"Yesterday the Commissioners of Lunacy committed to the asylum Mr. James R. Colston, a writer of some local reputation, connected with the *Messenger*. It will be remembered that on the evening of the 15th inst. Mr. Colston was given into custody by one of his fellow-lodgers in the Baine House, who had observed him acting very suspiciously, baring his throat and whetting a razor—occasionally trying its edge by actually cutting through the skin of his arm, etc. On being handed over to the police, the unfortunate man made a desperate resistance, and has ever since been so violent that it has been necessary to keep him in a strait-jacket. Most of our esteemed contemporary's other writers are still at large."

The Boarded Window

IN 1830, only a few miles away from what is now the great city of Cincinnati, lay an immense and almost unbroken forest. The whole region was sparsely settled by people of the frontier—restless souls who no sooner had hewn fairly habitable homes out of the wilderness and attained to that degree of prosperity which to-day we should call indigence than impelled by some mysterious impulse of their nature they abandoned all and pushed farther westward, to encounter new perils and privations in the effort to regain the meagre comforts which they had voluntarily renounced. Many of them had already forsaken that region for the remoter settlements, but among those remaining was one who had been of those first arriving. He lived alone in a house of logs surrounded on all sides by the great forest, of whose gloom and silence he seemed a part, for no one had ever known him to smile nor speak a needless word. His simple wants were supplied by the sale or barter of skins of wild animals in the river town, for not a thing did he grow upon the land which, if needful, he might have claimed by right of undisturbed possession. There were evidences of "improvement"—a few acres of ground immediately about the house had once been cleared of its trees, the decayed stumps of which were half concealed by the new growth that had been suffered to repair the ravage wrought by the ax. Apparently the man's zeal for agriculture had burned with a failing flame, expiring in penitential ashes.

The little log house, with its chimney of sticks, its roof of warping clapboards weighted with traversing poles and its "chinking" of clay, had a single door and, directly opposite, a window. The latter, however, was boarded up—nobody could remember a time when it was not. And none knew why it was so closed; certainly not because of the occupant's dislike of light and air, for on those rare occasions when a hunter had passed that lonely spot the recluse had commonly been seen sunning himself on his doorstep if heaven had provided sunshine for his need. I fancy there are few persons living to-day who ever knew the secret of that window, but I am one, as you shall see.

The man's name was said to be Murlock. He was apparently seventy years old, actually about fifty. Something besides years had had a hand in his aging. His hair and long, full beard were white, his gray, lustreless eyes sunken, his face singularly seamed with wrinkles which appeared to belong to two intersecting systems. In figure he was tall and spare, with a stoop of the shoulders—a burden bearer. I never saw him; these particulars I learned from my grandfather, from whom also I got the man's story when I was a lad. He had known him when living near by in that early day.

One day Murlock was found in his cabin, dead. It was not a time and place for coroners and newspapers, and I suppose it was agreed that he had died from natural causes or I should have been told, and should remember. I know only that with what was probably a sense of the fitness of things the body was buried near the cabin, alongside the grave of his wife, who had preceded him by so many years that local tradition had retained hardly a hint of her existence. That closes the final chapter of this true story—excepting, indeed, the circumstance that many years afterward, in company with an equally intrepid spirit, I penetrated to the place and ventured near enough to the ruined cabin to throw a stone against it, and ran away to avoid the ghost which every well-informed boy thereabout knew haunted the spot. But there is an earlier chapter—that supplied by my grandfather.

When Murlock built his cabin and began laying sturdily about with his ax to hew out a farm—the rifle, meanwhile, his means of support—he was young, strong and full of hope. In that eastern country whence he came he had married, as was the fashion, a young woman in all ways worthy of his honest devotion, who shared the dangers and privations of his lot with a willing spirit and light heart. There is no known record of her name; of her charms of mind and person tradition is silent and the doubter is at liberty to entertain his doubt; but God forbid that I should share it! Of their affection and happiness there is abundant assurance in every added day of the man's widowed life; for what but the magnetism of a blessed memory could have chained that venturesome spirit to a lot like that?

One day Murlock returned from gunning in a distant part of the forest to find his wife prostrate with fever, and delirious. There was no physician within miles, no neighbor; nor was she in a condition to be left, to summon help. So he set about the task of nursing her back to health, but at the end of the third day she fell into unconsciousness and so passed away, apparently, with never a gleam of returning reason.

From what we know of a nature like his we may venture to sketch in some of the details of the outline picture drawn by my grandfather. When convinced that she was dead, Murlock had sense enough to remember that the dead must be prepared for burial. In performance of this sacred duty he blundered now and again, did certain things incorrectly, and others which he did correctly were done over and over. His occasional failures to accomplish some simple and ordinary act filled him with astonishment, like that of a drunken man who wonders at the suspension of familiar natural laws. He was surprised, too, that he did not weep—surprised and a little ashamed; surely it is unkind not to weep for the dead. "To-morrow," he said aloud, "I shall have to make the coffin and dig the grave; and then I shall miss her, when she is no longer in sight; but now —she is dead, of course, but it is all right—it *must* be all right, somehow. Things cannot be so bad as they seem."

He stood over the body in the fading light, adjusting the hair and putting the finishing touches to the simple toilet, doing all mechanically, with soulless care. And still through his consciousness ran an undersense of conviction that all was right—that he should have her again as before, and everything explained. He had had no experience in grief; his capacity had not been enlarged by use. His heart could not contain it all, nor his imagination rightly conceive it. He did not know he was so hard struck; *that* knowledge would come later, and never go. Grief is an artist of powers as various as the instruments upon which he plays his dirges for the dead, evoking from some the sharpest, shrillest notes, from others the low, grave chords that throb recurrent like the slow beating of a distant drum. Some natures it startles; some it stupefies. To one it comes like the stroke of an arrow, stinging all the sensibilities to a keener life; to another as the blow of a bludgeon, which in crushing benumbs. We may conceive Murlock to

have been that way affected, for (and here we are upon surer
ground than that of conjecture) no sooner had he finished his
pious work than, sinking into a chair by the side of the table
upon which the body lay, and noting how white the profile
showed in the deepening gloom, he laid his arms upon the
table's edge, and dropped his face into them, tearless yet and
unutterably weary. At that moment came in through the open
window a long, wailing sound like the cry of a lost child in the
far deeps of the darkening wood! But the man did not move.
Again, and nearer than before, sounded that unearthly cry
upon his failing sense. Perhaps it was a wild beast; perhaps it
was a dream. For Murlock was asleep.

Some hours later, as it afterward appeared, this unfaithful
watcher awoke and lifting his head from his arms intently
listened—he knew not why. There in the black darkness by
the side of the dead, recalling all without a shock, he strained
his eyes to see—he knew not what. His senses were all alert, his
breath was suspended, his blood had stilled its tides as if to assist the silence. Who—what had waked him, and where was it?

Suddenly the table shook beneath his arms, and at the same
moment he heard, or fancied that he heard, a light, soft step
—another—sounds as of bare feet upon the floor!

He was terrified beyond the power to cry out or move.
Perforce he waited—waited there in the darkness through
seeming centuries of such dread as one may know, yet live to
tell. He tried vainly to speak the dead woman's name, vainly to
stretch forth his hand across the table to learn if she were there.
His throat was powerless, his arms and hands were like lead.
Then occurred something most frightful. Some heavy body
seemed hurled against the table with an impetus that pushed it
against his breast so sharply as nearly to overthrow him, and at
the same instant he heard and felt the fall of something upon
the floor with so violent a thump that the whole house was
shaken by the impact. A scuffling ensued, and a confusion of
sounds impossible to describe. Murlock had risen to his feet.
Fear had by excess forfeited control of his faculties. He flung
his hands upon the table. Nothing was there!

There is a point at which terror may turn to madness; and
madness incites to action. With no definite intent, from no
motive but the wayward impulse of a madman, Murlock sprang

to the wall, with a little groping seized his loaded rifle, and without aim discharged it. By the flash which lit up the room with a vivid illumination, he saw an enormous panther dragging the dead woman toward the window, its teeth fixed in her throat! Then there were darkness blacker than before, and silence; and when he returned to consciousness the sun was high and the wood vocal with songs of birds.

The body lay near the window, where the beast had left it when frightened away by the flash and report of the rifle. The clothing was deranged, the long hair in disorder, the limbs lay anyhow. From the throat, dreadfully lacerated, had issued a pool of blood not yet entirely coagulated. The ribbon with which he had bound the wrists was broken; the hands were tightly clenched. Between the teeth was a fragment of the animal's ear.

A Lady from Redhorse

I FIND myself more and more interested in him. It is not, I am sure, his—do you know any good noun corresponding to the adjective "handsome"? One does not like to say "beauty" when speaking of a man. He is beautiful enough, Heaven knows; I should not even care to trust you with him—faithfulest of all possible wives that you are—when he looks his best, as he always does. Nor do I think the fascination of his manner has much to do with it. You recollect that the charm of art inheres in that which is undefinable, and to you and me, my dear Irene, I fancy there is rather less of that in the branch of art under consideration than to girls in their first season. I fancy I know how my fine gentleman produces many of his effects and could perhaps give him a pointer on heightening them. Nevertheless, his manner is something truly delightful. I suppose what interests me chiefly is the man's brains. His conversation is the best I have ever heard and altogether unlike any one else's. He seems to know everything, as indeed he ought, for he has been everywhere, read everything, seen all there is to see— sometimes I think rather more than is good for him—and had acquaintance with the *queerest* people. And then his voice— Irene, when I hear it I actually feel as if I ought to have paid at the door, though of course it is my own door.

JULY 3.

I fear my remarks about Dr. Barritz must have been, being thoughtless, very silly, or you would not have written of him with such levity, not to say disrespect. Believe me, dearest, he has more dignity and seriousness (of the kind, I mean, which is not inconsistent with a manner sometimes playful and always charming) than any of the men that you and I ever met. And young Raynor—you knew Raynor at Monterey—tells me that the men all like him and that he is treated with something like deference everywhere. There is a mystery, too—something about his connection with the Blavatsky people in Northern India.

Raynor either would not or could not tell me the particulars. I infer that Dr. Barritz is thought—don't you dare to laugh!—a magician. Could anything be finer than that? An ordinary mystery is not, of course, so good as a scandal, but when it relates to dark and dreadful practices—to the exercise of unearthly powers—could anything be more piquant? It explains, too, the singular influence the man has upon me. It is the undefinable in his art—black art. Seriously, dear, I quite tremble when he looks me full in the eyes with those unfathomable orbs of his, which I have already vainly attempted to describe to you. How dreadful if he has the power to make one fall in love! Do you know if the Blavatsky crowd have that power—outside of Sepoy?

JULY 16.

The strangest thing! Last evening while Auntie was attending one of the hotel hops (I hate them) Dr. Barritz called. It was scandalously late—I actually believe that he had talked with Auntie in the ballroom and learned from her that I was alone. I had been all the evening contriving how to worm out of him the truth about his connection with the Thugs in Sepoy, and all of that black business, but the moment he fixed his eyes on me (for I admitted him, I'm ashamed to say) I was helpless. I trembled, I blushed, I—O Irene, Irene, I love the man beyond expression and you know how it is yourself.

Fancy! I, an ugly duckling from Redhorse—daughter (they say) of old Calamity Jim—certainly his heiress, with no living relation but an absurd old aunt who spoils me a thousand and fifty ways—absolutely destitute of everything but a million dollars and a hope in Paris,—I daring to love a god like him! My dear, if I had you here I could tear your hair out with mortification.

I am convinced that he is aware of my feeling, for he stayed but a few moments, said nothing but what another man might have said half as well, and pretending that he had an engagement went away. I learned to-day (a little bird told me—the bell-bird) that he went straight to bed. How does that strike you as evidence of exemplary habits?

JULY 17.

That little wretch, Raynor, called yesterday and his babble set me almost wild. He never runs down—that is to say, when he exterminates a score of reputations, more or less, he does not pause between one reputation and the next. (By the way, he inquired about you, and his manifestations of interest in you had, I confess, a good deal of *vraisemblance*.) Mr. Raynor observes no game laws; like Death (which he would inflict if slander were fatal) he has all seasons for his own. But I like him, for we knew each other at Redhorse when we were young. He was known in those days as "Giggles," and I—O Irene, can you ever forgive me?—I was called "Gunny." God knows why; perhaps in allusion to the material of my pinafores; perhaps because the name is in alliteration with "Giggles," for Gig and I were inseparable playmates, and the miners may have thought it a delicate civility to recognize some kind of relationship between us.

Later, we took in a third—another of Adversity's brood, who, like Garrick between Tragedy and Comedy, had a chronic inability to adjudicate the rival claims of Frost and Famine. Between him and misery there was seldom anything more than a single suspender and the hope of a meal which would at the same time support life and make it insupportable. He literally picked up a precarious living for himself and an aged mother by "chloriding the dumps," that is to say, the miners permitted him to search the heaps of waste rock for such pieces of "pay ore" as had been overlooked; and these he sacked up and sold at the Syndicate Mill. He became a member of our firm— "Gunny, Giggles, and Dumps" thenceforth—through my favor; for I could not then, nor can I now, be indifferent to his courage and prowess in defending against Giggles the immemorial right of his sex to insult a strange and unprotected female—myself. After old Jim struck it in the Calamity and I began to wear shoes and go to school, and in emulation Giggles took to washing his face and became Jack Raynor, of Wells, Fargo & Co., and old Mrs. Barts was herself chlorided to her fathers, Dumps drifted over to San Juan Smith and turned stage driver, and was killed by road agents, and so forth.

Why do I tell you all this, dear? Because it is heavy on my heart. Because I walk the Valley of Humility. Because I am subduing myself to permanent consciousness of my unworthiness to unloose the latchet of Dr. Barritz's shoe. Because, oh dear, oh dear, there's a cousin of Dumps at this hotel! I haven't spoken to him. I never had much acquaintance with him,—but do you suppose he has recognized me? Do, please give me in your next your candid, sure-enough opinion about it, and say you don't think so. Do you suppose He knows about me already, and that that is why He left me last evening when He saw that I blushed and trembled like a fool under His eyes? You know I can't bribe *all* the newspapers, and I can't go back on anybody who was civil to Gunny at Redhorse—not if I'm pitched out of society into the sea. So the skeleton sometimes rattles behind the door. I never cared much before, as you know, but now—*now* it is not the same. Jack Raynor I am sure of—he will not tell Him. He seems, indeed, to hold Him in such respect as hardly to dare speak to Him at all, and I'm a good deal that way myself. Dear, dear! I wish I had something besides a million dollars! If Jack were three inches taller I'd marry him alive and go back to Redhorse and wear sackcloth again to the end of my miserable days.

JULY 25.

We had a perfectly splendid sunset last evening and I must tell you all about it. I ran away from Auntie and everybody and was walking alone on the beach. I expect you to believe, you infidel! that I had not looked out of my window on the seaward side of the hotel and seen Him walking alone on the beach. If you are not lost to every feeling of womanly delicacy you will accept my statement without question. I soon established myself under my sunshade and had for some time been gazing out dreamily over the sea, when he approached, walking close to the edge of the water—it was ebb tide. I assure you the wet sand actually brightened about his feet! As he approached me he lifted his hat, saying, "Miss Dement, may I sit with you?—or will you walk with me?"

The possibility that neither might be agreeable seems not to have occurred to him. Did you ever know such assurance? Assurance? My dear, it was gall, downright *gall*! Well, I didn't find it wormwood, and replied, with my untutored Redhorse heart in my throat, "I—I shall be pleased to do *anything*."

Could words have been more stupid? There are depths of fatuity in me, friend o' my soul, that are simply bottomless!

He extended his hand, smiling, and I delivered mine into it without a moment's hesitation, and when his fingers closed about it to assist me to my feet the consciousness that it trembled made me blush worse than the red west. I got up, however, and after a while, observing that he had not let go my hand I pulled on it a little, but unsuccessfully. He simply held on, saying nothing, but looking down into my face with some kind of smile—I didn't know—how could I?—whether it was affectionate, derisive, or what, for I did not look at him. How beautiful he was!—with the red fires of the sunset burning in the depths of his eyes. Do you know, dear, if the Thugs and Experts of the Blavatsky region have any special kind of eyes? Ah, you should have seen his superb attitude, the god-like inclination of his head as he stood over me after I had got upon my feet! It was a noble picture, but I soon destroyed it, for I began at once to sink again to the earth. There was only one thing for him to do, and he did it; he supported me with an arm about my waist.

"Miss Dement, are you ill?" he said.

It was not an exclamation; there was neither alarm nor solicitude in it. If he had added: "I suppose that is about what I am expected to say," he would hardly have expressed his sense of the situation more clearly. His manner filled me with shame and indignation, for I was suffering acutely. I wrenched my hand out of his, grasped the arm supporting me and pushing myself free, fell plump into the sand and sat helpless. My hat had fallen off in the struggle and my hair tumbled about my face and shoulders in the most mortifying way.

"Go away from me," I cried, half choking. "O *please* go away, you—you Thug! How dare you think *that* when my leg is asleep?"

I actually said those identical words! And then I broke down and sobbed. Irene, I *blubbered*!

His manner altered in an instant—I could see that much through my fingers and hair. He dropped on one knee beside me, parted the tangle of hair and said in the tenderest way: "My poor girl, God knows I have not intended to pain you.

How should I?—I who love you—I who have loved you for—for years and years!"

He had pulled my wet hands away from my face and was covering them with kisses. My cheeks were like two coals, my whole face was flaming and, I think, steaming. What could I do? I hid it on his shoulder- -there was no other place. And, O my dear friend, how my leg tingled and thrilled, and how I wanted to kick!

We sat so for a long time. He had released one of my hands to pass his arm about me again and I possessed myself of my handkerchief and was drying my eyes and my nose. I would not look up until that was done; he tried in vain to push me a little away and gaze into my face. Presently, when all was right, and it had grown a bit dark, I lifted my head, looked him straight in the eyes and smiled my best—my level best, dear.

"What do you mean," I said, "by 'years and years'?"

"Dearest," he replied, very gravely, very earnestly, "in the absence of the sunken cheeks, the hollow eyes, the lank hair, the slouching gait, the rags, dirt, and youth, can you not—will you not understand? Gunny, I'm Dumps!"

In a moment I was upon my feet and he upon his. I seized him by the lapels of his coat and peered into his handsome face in the deepening darkness. I was breathless with excitement.

"And you are not dead?" I asked, hardly knowing what I said.

"Only dead in love, dear. I recovered from the road agent's bullet, but this, I fear, is fatal."

"But about Jack—Mr. Raynor? Don't you know——"

"I am ashamed to say, darling, that it was through that unworthy person's suggestion that I came here from Vienna."

Irene, they have roped in your affectionate friend,

MARY JANE DEMENT.

P.S.—The worst of it is that there is no mystery; that was the invention of Jack Raynor, to arouse my curiosity. James is not a Thug. He solemnly assures me that in all his wanderings he has never set foot in Sepoy.

The Eyes of the Panther

ONE DOES NOT ALWAYS MARRY WHEN INSANE

A MAN and a woman—nature had done the grouping—sat on a rustic seat, in the late afternoon. The man was middle-aged, slender, swarthy, with the expression of a poet and the complexion of a pirate—a man at whom one would look again. The woman was young, blonde, graceful, with something in her figure and movements suggesting the word "lithe." She was habited in a gray gown with odd brown markings in the texture. She may have been beautiful; one could not readily say, for her eyes denied attention to all else. They were gray-green, long and narrow, with an expression defying analysis. One could only know that they were disquieting. Cleopatra may have had such eyes.

The man and the woman talked.

"Yes," said the woman, "I love you, God knows! But marry you, no. I cannot, will not."

"Irene, you have said that many times, yet always have denied me a reason. I've a right to know, to understand, to feel and prove my fortitude if I have it. Give me a reason."

"For loving you?"

The woman was smiling through her tears and her pallor. That did not stir any sense of humor in the man.

"No; there is no reason for that. A reason for not marrying me. I've a right to know. I must know. I will know!"

He had risen and was standing before her with clenched hands, on his face a frown—it might have been called a scowl. He looked as if he might attempt to learn by strangling her. She smiled no more—merely sat looking up into his face with a fixed, set regard that was utterly without emotion or sentiment. Yet it had something in it that tamed his resentment and made him shiver.

"You are determined to have my reason?" she asked in a tone that was entirely mechanical—a tone that might have been her look made audible.

"If you please—if I'm not asking too much."

Apparently this lord of creation was yielding some part of his dominion over his co-creature.

"Very well, you shall know: I am insane."

The man started, then looked incredulous and was conscious that he ought to be amused. But, again, the sense of humor failed him in his need and despite his disbelief he was profoundly disturbed by that which he did not believe. Between our convictions and our feelings there is no good understanding.

"That is what the physicians would say," the woman continued —"if they knew. I might myself prefer to call it a case of 'possession.' Sit down and hear what I have to say."

The man silently resumed his seat beside her on the rustic bench by the wayside. Over-against them on the eastern side of the valley the hills were already sunset-flushed and the stillness all about was of that peculiar quality that foretells the twilight. Something of its mysterious and significant solemnity had imparted itself to the man's mood. In the spiritual, as in the material world, are signs and presages of night. Rarely meeting her look, and whenever he did so conscious of the indefinable dread with which, despite their feline beauty, her eyes always affected him, Jenner Brading listened in silence to the story told by Irene Marlowe. In deference to the reader's possible prejudice against the artless method of an unpractised historian the author ventures to substitute his own version for hers.

II

A ROOM MAY BE TOO NARROW FOR THREE,
THOUGH ONE IS OUTSIDE

In a little log house containing a single room sparely and rudely furnished, crouching on the floor against one of the walls, was a woman, clasping to her breast a child. Outside, a dense unbroken forest extended for many miles in every direction. This was at night and the room was black dark: no human eye could have discerned the woman and the child. Yet they were observed, narrowly, vigilantly, with never even a momentary slackening of attention; and that is the pivotal fact upon which this narrative turns.

Charles Marlowe was of the class, now extinct in this country, of woodmen pioneers—men who found their most acceptable surroundings in sylvan solitudes that stretched along the eastern slope of the Mississippi Valley, from the Great Lakes to the Gulf of Mexico. For more than a hundred years these men pushed ever westward, generation after generation, with rifle and ax, reclaiming from Nature and her savage children here and there an isolated acreage for the plow, no sooner reclaimed than surrendered to their less venturesome but more thrifty successors. At last they burst through the edge of the forest into the open country and vanished as if they had fallen over a cliff. The woodman pioneer is no more; the pioneer of the plains—he whose easy task it was to subdue for occupancy two-thirds of the country in a single generation—is another and inferior creation. With Charles Marlowe in the wilderness, sharing the dangers, hardships and privations of that strange, unprofitable life, were his wife and child, to whom, in the manner of his class, in which the domestic virtues were a religion, he was passionately attached. The woman was still young enough to be comely, new enough to the awful isolation of her lot to be cheerful. By withholding the large capacity for happiness which the simple satisfactions of the forest life could not have filled, Heaven had dealt honorably with her. In her light household tasks, her child, her husband and her few foolish books, she found abundant provision for her needs.

One morning in midsummer Marlowe took down his rifle from the wooden hooks on the wall and signified his intention of getting game.

"We've meat enough," said the wife; "please don't go out to-day. I dreamed last night, O, such a dreadful thing! I cannot recollect it, but I'm almost sure that it will come to pass if you go out."

It is painful to confess that Marlowe received this solemn statement with less of gravity than was due to the mysterious nature of the calamity foreshadowed. In truth, he laughed.

"Try to remember," he said. "Maybe you dreamed that Baby had lost the power of speech."

The conjecture was obviously suggested by the fact that Baby, clinging to the fringe of his hunting-coat with all her ten pudgy thumbs was at that moment uttering her sense of the situation in a series of exultant goo-goos inspired by sight of her father's raccoon-skin cap.

The woman yielded: lacking the gift of humor she could not hold out against his kindly badinage. So, with a kiss for the mother and a kiss for the child, he left the house and closed the door upon his happiness forever.

At nightfall he had not returned. The woman prepared supper and waited. Then she put Baby to bed and sang softly to her until she slept. By this time the fire on the hearth, at which she had cooked supper, had burned out and the room was lighted by a single candle. This she afterward placed in the open window as a sign and welcome to the hunter if he should approach from that side. She had thoughtfully closed and barred the door against such wild animals as might prefer it to an open window—of the habits of beasts of prey in entering a house uninvited she was not advised, though with true female prevision she may have considered the possibility of their entrance by way of the chimney. As the night wore on she became not less anxious, but more drowsy, and at last rested her arms upon the bed by the child and her head upon the arms. The candle in the window burned down to the socket, sputtered and flared a moment and went out unobserved; for the woman slept and dreamed.

In her dreams she sat beside the cradle of a second child. The first one was dead. The father was dead. The home in the forest was lost and the dwelling in which she lived was unfamiliar. There were heavy oaken doors, always closed, and outside the windows, fastened into the thick stone walls, were iron bars, obviously (so she thought) a provision against Indians. All this she noted with an infinite self-pity, but without surprise—an emotion unknown in dreams. The child in the cradle was invisible under its coverlet which something impelled her to remove. She did so, disclosing the face of a wild animal! In the shock of this dreadful revelation the dreamer awoke, trembling in the darkness of her cabin in the wood.

As a sense of her actual surroundings came slowly back to her she felt for the child that was not a dream, and assured herself by its breathing that all was well with it; nor could she forbear to pass a hand lightly across its face. Then, moved by

some impulse for which she probably could not have accounted, she rose and took the sleeping babe in her arms,
holding it close against her breast. The head of the child's cot
was against the wall to which the woman now turned her back
as she stood. Lifting her eyes she saw two bright objects star-
ring the darkness with a reddish-green glow. She took them to
be two coals on the hearth, but with her returning sense of
direction came the disquieting consciousness that they were
not in that quarter of the room, moreover were too high,
being nearly at the level of the eyes—of her own eyes. For
these were the eyes of a panther.

The beast was at the open window directly opposite and not
five paces away. Nothing but those terrible eyes was visible, but
in the dreadful tumult of her feelings as the situation disclosed
itself to her understanding she somehow knew that the animal
was standing on its hinder feet, supporting itself with its paws
on the window-ledge. That signified a malign interest—not
the mere gratification of an indolent curiosity. The consciousness of the attitude was an added horror, accentuating the
menace of those awful eyes, in whose steadfast fire her strength
and courage were alike consumed. Under their silent questioning she shuddered and turned sick. Her knees failed her, and
by degrees, instinctively striving to avoid a sudden movement
that might bring the beast upon her, she sank to the floor,
crouched against the wall and tried to shield the babe with her
trembling body without withdrawing her gaze from the luminous orbs that were killing her. No thought of her husband
came to her in her agony—no hope nor suggestion of rescue
or escape. Her capacity for thought and feeling had narrowed
to the dimensions of a single emotion—fear of the animal's
spring, of the impact of its body, the buffeting of its great arms,
the feel of its teeth in her throat, the mangling of her babe.
Motionless now and in absolute silence, she awaited her doom,
the moments growing to hours, to years, to ages; and still
those devilish eyes maintained their watch.

Returning to his cabin late at night with a deer on his shoulders Charles Marlowe tried the door. It did not yield. He
knocked; there was no answer. He laid down his deer and went
round to the window. As he turned the angle of the building

he fancied he heard a sound as of stealthy footfalls and a rustling in the undergrowth of the forest, but they were too slight for certainty, even to his practised ear. Approaching the window, and to his surprise finding it open, he threw his leg over the sill and entered. All was darkness and silence. He groped his way to the fire-place, struck a match and lit a candle. Then he looked about. Cowering on the floor against a wall was his wife, clasping his child. As he sprang toward her she rose and broke into laughter, long, loud, and mechanical, devoid of gladness and devoid of sense—the laughter that is not out of keeping with the clanking of a chain. Hardly knowing what he did he extended his arms. She laid the babe in them. It was dead—pressed to death in its mother's embrace.

III
THE THEORY OF THE DEFENSE

That is what occurred during a night in a forest, but not all of it did Irene Marlowe relate to Jenner Brading; not all of it was known to her. When she had concluded the sun was below the horizon and the long summer twilight had begun to deepen in the hollows of the land. For some moments Brading was silent, expecting the narrative to be carried forward to some definite connection with the conversation introducing it; but the narrator was as silent as he, her face averted, her hands clasping and unclasping themselves as they lay in her lap, with a singular suggestion of an activity independent of her will.

"It is a sad, a terrible story," said Brading at last, "but I do not understand. You call Charles Marlowe father; that I know. That he is old before his time, broken by some great sorrow, I have seen, or thought I saw. But, pardon me, you said that you—that you——"

"That I am insane," said the girl, without a movement of head or body.

"But, Irene, you say—please, dear, do not look away from me—you say that the child was dead, not demented."

"Yes, that one—I am the second. I was born three months after that night, my mother being mercifully permitted to lay down her life in giving me mine."

Brading was again silent; he was a trifle dazed and could not at once think of the right thing to say. Her face was still turned away. In his embarrassment he reached impulsively toward the hands that lay closing and unclosing in her lap, but something—he could not have said what—restrained him. He then remembered, vaguely, that he had never altogether cared to take her hand.

"Is it likely," she resumed, "that a person born under such circumstances is like others—is what you call sane?"

Brading did not reply; he was preoccupied with a new thought that was taking shape in his mind—what a scientist would have called an hypothesis; a detective, a theory. It might throw an added light, albeit a lurid one, upon such doubt of her sanity as her own assertion had not dispelled.

The country was still new and, outside the villages, sparsely populated. The professional hunter was still a familiar figure, and among his trophies were heads and pelts of the larger kinds of game. Tales variously credible of nocturnal meetings with savage animals in lonely roads were sometimes current, passed through the customary stages of growth and decay, and were forgotten. A recent addition to these popular apocrypha, originating, apparently, by spontaneous generation in several households, was of a panther which had frightened some of their members by looking in at windows by night. The yarn had caused its little ripple of excitement—had even attained to the distinction of a place in the local newspaper; but Brading had given it no attention. Its likeness to the story to which he had just listened now impressed him as perhaps more than accidental. Was it not possible that the one story had suggested the other—that finding congenial conditions in a morbid mind and a fertile fancy, it had grown to the tragic tale that he had heard?

Brading recalled certain circumstances of the girl's history and disposition, of which, with love's incuriosity, he had hitherto been heedless—such as her solitary life with her father, at whose house no one, apparently, was an acceptable visitor and her strange fear of the night, by which those who knew her best accounted for her never being seen after dark. Surely in such a mind imagination once kindled might burn with a lawless flame, penetrating and enveloping the entire structure. That she was mad, though the conviction gave him the acutest pain, he could no longer doubt; she had only mistaken an effect of her mental disorder for its cause, bringing into imaginary relation with her own personality the vagaries of the local myth-makers. With some vague intention of testing his new "theory," and no very definite notion of how to set about it he said, gravely, but with hesitation:

"Irene, dear, tell me—I beg you will not take offence, but tell me——"

"I have told you," she interrupted, speaking with a passionate earnestness that he had not known her to show—"I have already told you that we cannot marry; is anything else worth saying?"

Before he could stop her she had sprung from her seat and without another word or look was gliding away among the trees toward her father's house. Brading had risen to detain her; he stood watching her in silence until she had vanished in the gloom. Suddenly he started as if he had been shot; his face took on an expression of amazement and alarm: in one of the black shadows into which she had disappeared he had caught a quick, brief glimpse of shining eyes! For an instant he was dazed and irresolute; then he dashed into the wood after her, shouting: "Irene, Irene, look out! The panther! The panther!"

In a moment he had passed through the fringe of forest into open ground and saw the girl's gray skirt vanishing into her father's door. No panther was visible.

IV

AN APPEAL TO THE CONSCIENCE OF GOD

Jenner Brading, attorney-at-law, lived in a cottage at the edge of the town. Directly behind the dwelling was the forest. Being a bachelor, and therefore, by the Draconian moral code of the time and place denied the services of the only species of domestic servant known thereabout, the "hired girl," he boarded at the village hotel, where also was his office. The woodside cottage was merely a lodging maintained—at no great cost, to be sure—as an evidence of prosperity and respectability. It would hardly do for one to whom the local newspaper had pointed with pride as "the foremost jurist of his time" to be "homeless," albeit he may sometimes have suspected that the words "home" and "house" were not strictly synonymous. Indeed, his consciousness of the disparity and his will to harmonize it were matters of logical inference, for it was generally reported that soon after the cottage was built its owner had made a futile venture in the direction of marriage—had, in truth, gone so far as to be rejected by the beautiful but eccentric daughter of Old Man Marlowe, the recluse. This was publicly believed because he had told it himself and she had not—a reversal of the usual order of things which could hardly fail to carry conviction.

Brading's bedroom was at the rear of the house, with a single window facing the forest. One night he was awakened by a noise at that window; he could hardly have said what it was like. With a little thrill of the nerves he sat up in bed and laid hold of the revolver which, with a forethought most commendable in one addicted to the habit of sleeping on the ground floor with an open window, he had put under his pillow. The room was in absolute darkness, but being unterrified he knew where to direct his eyes, and there he held them, awaiting in silence what further might occur. He could now dimly discern the aperture—a square of lighter black. Presently there appeared at its lower edge two gleaming eyes that burned with a malignant lustre inexpressibly terrible! Brading's heart gave a great jump, then seemed to stand still. A chill passed along his spine and through his hair; he felt the blood forsake his cheeks. He could not have cried out—not to save his life; but being a man of courage he would not, to save his life, have done so if he had been able. Some trepidation his coward body might feel, but his spirit was of sterner stuff. Slowly the shining eyes rose with a steady motion that seemed an approach, and slowly rose Brading's right hand, holding the pistol. He fired!

Blinded by the flash and stunned by the report, Brading nevertheless heard, or fancied that he heard, the wild, high scream of the panther, so human in sound, so devilish in suggestion. Leaping from the bed he hastily clothed himself and, pistol in hand, sprang from the door, meeting two or three men who came running up from the road. A brief explanation was followed by a cautious search of the house. The grass was wet with dew; beneath the window it had been trodden and partly leveled for a wide space, from which a devious trail, visible in the light of a lantern, led away into the bushes. One of the men stumbled and fell upon his hands, which as he rose and rubbed them together were slippery. On examination they were seen to be red with blood.

An encounter, unarmed, with a wounded panther was not agreeable to their taste; all but Brading turned back. He, with lantern and pistol, pushed courageously forward into the wood. Passing through a difficult undergrowth he came into a small opening, and there his courage had its reward, for there he found the body of his victim. But it was no panther. What it was is told, even to this day, upon a weather-worn headstone in the village churchyard, and for many years was attested daily at the graveside by the bent figure and sorrow-seamed face of Old Man Marlowe, to whose soul, and to the soul of his strange, unhappy child, peace. Peace and reparation.

CAN SUCH THINGS BE?

CAN SUCH THINGS BE?

The Death of Halpin Frayser

I

For by death is wrought greater change than hath been shown. Whereas in general the spirit that removed cometh back upon occasion, and is sometimes seen of those in flesh (appearing in the form of the body it bore) yet it hath happened that the veritable body without the spirit hath walked. And it is attested of those encountering who have lived to speak thereon that a lich so raised up hath no natural affection, nor remembrance thereof, but only hate. Also, it is known that some spirits which in life were benign become by death evil altogether.—*Hali.*

ONE dark night in midsummer a man waking from a dreamless sleep in a forest lifted his head from the earth, and staring a few moments into the blackness, said: "Catherine Larue." He said nothing more; no reason was known to him why he should have said so much.

The man was Halpin Frayser. He lived in St. Helena, but where he lives now is uncertain, for he is dead. One who practices sleeping in the woods with nothing under him but the dry leaves and the damp earth, and nothing over him but the branches from which the leaves have fallen and the sky from which the earth has fallen, cannot hope for great longevity, and Frayser had already attained the age of thirty-two. There are persons in this world, millions of persons, and far and away the best persons, who regard that as a very advanced age. They are the children. To those who view the voyage of life from the port of departure the bark that has accomplished any considerable distance appears already in close approach to the farther shore. However, it is not certain that Halpin Frayser came to his death by exposure.

He had been all day in the hills west of the Napa Valley, looking for doves and such small game as was in season. Late in the afternoon it had come on to be cloudy, and he had lost his bearings; and although he had only to go always downhill—everywhere the way to safety when one is lost—the absence of trails had so impeded him that he was overtaken by night while still in the forest. Unable in the darkness to penetrate the thickets of manzanita and other undergrowth, utterly bewildered and overcome with fatigue, he had lain down near the root of a large madroño and fallen into a dreamless sleep. It was hours later, in the very middle of the night, that one of God's mysterious messengers, gliding ahead of the incalculable host of his companions sweeping westward with the dawn line, pronounced the awakening word in the ear of the sleeper, who sat upright and spoke, he knew not why, a name, he knew not whose.

Halpin Frayser was not much of a philosopher, nor a scientist. The circumstance that, waking from a deep sleep at night in the midst of a forest, he had spoken aloud a name that he had not in memory and hardly had in mind did not arouse an enlightened curiosity to investigate the phenomenon. He thought it odd, and with a little perfunctory shiver, as if in deference to a seasonal presumption that the night was chill, he lay down again and went to sleep. But his sleep was no longer dreamless.

He thought he was walking along a dusty road that showed white in the gathering darkness of a summer night. Whence and whither it led, and why he traveled it, he did not know, though all seemed simple and natural, as is the way in dreams; for in the Land Beyond the Bed surprises cease from troubling and the judgment is at rest. Soon he came to a parting of the ways; leading from the highway was a road less traveled, having the appearance, indeed, of having been long abandoned, because, he thought, it led to something evil; yet he turned into it without hesitation, impelled by some imperious necessity.

As he pressed forward he became conscious that his way was haunted by invisible existences whom he could not definitely figure to his mind. From among the trees on either side he caught broken and incoherent whispers in a strange tongue which yet he partly understood. They seemed to him fragmentary utterances of a monstrous conspiracy against his body and soul.

It was now long after nightfall, yet the interminable forest through which he journeyed was lit with a wan glimmer having no point of diffusion, for in its mysterious lumination nothing cast a shadow. A shallow pool in the guttered depression of an old wheel rut, as from a recent rain, met his eye with a crimson gleam. He stooped and plunged his hand into it. It stained his fingers; it was blood! Blood, he then observed, was about him everywhere. The weeds growing rankly by the roadside showed it in blots and splashes on their big, broad leaves. Patches of dry dust between the wheelways were pitted and spattered as with a red rain. Defiling the trunks of the trees were broad maculations of crimson, and blood dripped like dew from their foliage.

All this he observed with a terror which seemed not incompatible with the fulfillment of a natural expectation. It seemed to him that it was all in expiation of some crime which, though conscious of his guilt, he could not rightly remember. To the menaces and mysteries of his surroundings the consciousness was an added horror. Vainly he sought by tracing life backward in memory, to reproduce the moment of his sin; scenes and incidents came crowding tumultuously into his mind, one picture effacing another, or commingling with it in confusion and obscurity, but nowhere could he catch a glimpse of what he sought. The failure augmented his terror; he felt as one who has murdered in the dark, not knowing whom nor why. So frightful was the situation—the mysterious light burned with so silent and awful a menace; the noxious plants, the trees that by common consent are invested with a melancholy or baleful character, so openly in his sight conspired against his peace; from overhead and all about came so audible and startling whispers and the sighs of creatures so obviously not of earth—that he could endure it no longer, and with a great effort to break some malign spell that bound his faculties to silence and inaction, he shouted with the full strength of his lungs! His voice broken, it seemed, into an infinite multitude of unfamiliar sounds, went babbling and stammering away into the distant reaches of the forest, died into silence, and all was as before. But he had made a beginning at resistance and was encouraged. He said:

"I will not submit unheard. There may be powers that are not malignant traveling this accursed road. I shall leave them a record and an appeal. I shall relate my wrongs, the persecutions

that I endure—I, a helpless mortal, a penitent, an unoffending
poet!" Halpin Frayser was a poet only as he was a penitent: in
his dream.

Taking from his clothing a small red-leather pocketbook,
one-half of which was leaved for memoranda, he discovered
that he was without a pencil. He broke a twig from a bush,
dipped it into a pool of blood and wrote rapidly. He had hardly
touched the paper with the point of his twig when a low, wild
peal of laughter broke out at a measureless distance away, and
growing ever louder, seemed approaching ever nearer; a soulless, heartless, and unjoyous laugh, like that of the loon, solitary
by the lakeside at midnight; a laugh which culminated in an
unearthly shout close at hand, then died away by slow gradations, as if the accursed being that uttered it had withdrawn
over the verge of the world whence it had come. But the man
felt that this was not so—that it was near by and had not moved.

A strange sensation began slowly to take possession of his
body and his mind. He could not have said which, if any, of
his senses was affected; he felt it rather as a consciousness—a
mysterious mental assurance of some overpowering presence
—some supernatural malevolence different in kind from the
invisible existences that swarmed about him, and superior to
them in power. He knew that it had uttered that hideous
laugh. And now it seemed to be approaching him; from what
direction he did not know—dared not conjecture. All his former fears were forgotten or merged in the gigantic terror that
now held him in thrall. Apart from that, he had but one thought:
to complete his written appeal to the benign powers who, traversing the haunted wood, might some time rescue him if he
should be denied the blessing of annihilation. He wrote with
terrible rapidity, the twig in his fingers rilling blood without
renewal; but in the middle of a sentence his hands denied their
service to his will, his arms fell to his sides, the book to the
earth; and powerless to move or cry out, he found himself staring into the sharply drawn face and blank, dead eyes of his own
mother, standing white and silent in the garments of the
grave!

II

In his youth Halpin Frayser had lived with his parents in Nashville, Tennessee. The Fraysers were well-to-do, having a good position in such society as had survived the wreck wrought by civil war. Their children had the social and educational opportunities of their time and place, and had responded to good associations and instruction with agreeable manners and cultivated minds. Halpin being the youngest and not over robust was perhaps a trifle "spoiled." He had the double disadvantage of a mother's assiduity and a father's neglect. Frayser *père* was what no Southern man of means is not—a politician. His country, or rather his section and State, made demands upon his time and attention so exacting that to those of his family he was compelled to turn an ear partly deafened by the thunder of the political captains and the shouting, his own included.

Young Halpin was of a dreamy, indolent and rather romantic turn, somewhat more addicted to literature than law, the profession to which he was bred. Among those of his relations who professed the modern faith of heredity it was well understood that in him the character of the late Myron Bayne, a maternal great-grandfather, had revisited the glimpses of the moon—by which orb Bayne had in his lifetime been sufficiently affected to be a poet of no small Colonial distinction. If not specially observed, it was observable that while a Frayser who was not the proud possessor of a sumptuous copy of the ancestral "poetical works" (printed at the family expense, and long ago withdrawn from an inhospitable market) was a rare Frayser indeed, there was an illogical indisposition to honor the great deceased in the person of his spiritual successor. Halpin was pretty generally deprecated as an intellectual black sheep who was likely at any moment to disgrace the flock by bleating in meter. The Tennessee Fraysers were a practical folk—not practical in the popular sense of devotion to sordid pursuits, but having a robust contempt for any qualities unfitting a man for the wholesome vocation of politics.

In justice to young Halpin it should be said that while in him were pretty faithfully reproduced most of the mental and moral characteristics ascribed by history and family tradition to the famous Colonial bard, his succession to the gift and faculty divine was purely inferential. Not only had he never been known to court the muse, but in truth he could not have written correctly a line of verse to save himself from the Killer of the Wise. Still, there was no knowing when the dormant faculty might wake and smite the lyre.

In the meantime the young man was rather a loose fish, anyhow. Between him and his mother was the most perfect sympathy, for secretly the lady was herself a devout disciple of the late and great Myron Bayne, though with the tact so generally and justly admired in her sex (despite the hardy calumniators who insist that it is essentially the same thing as cunning) she had always taken care to conceal her weakness from all eyes but those of him who shared it. Their common guilt in respect of that was an added tie between them. If in Halpin's youth his mother had "spoiled" him, he had assuredly done his part toward being spoiled. As he grew to such manhood as is attainable by a Southerner who does not care which way elections go the attachment between him and his beautiful mother—whom from early childhood he had called Katy—became yearly stronger and more tender. In these two romantic natures was manifest in a signal way that neglected phenomenon, the dominance of the sexual element in all the relations of life, strengthening, softening, and beautifying even those of consanguinity. The two were nearly inseparable, and by strangers observing their manner were not infrequently mistaken for lovers.

Entering his mother's boudoir one day Halpin Frayser kissed her upon the forehead, toyed for a moment with a lock of her dark hair which had escaped from its confining pins, and said, with an obvious effort at calmness:

"Would you greatly mind, Katy, if I were called away to California for a few weeks?"

It was hardly needful for Katy to answer with her lips a question to which her telltale cheeks had made instant reply. Evidently she would greatly mind; and the tears, too, sprang into her large brown eyes as corroborative testimony.

"Ah, my son," she said, looking up into his face with infinite tenderness, "I should have known that this was coming. Did I not lie awake a half of the night weeping because, during the other half, Grandfather Bayne had come to me in a dream, and standing by his portrait—young, too, and handsome as that—pointed to yours on the same wall? And when I looked it seemed that I could not see the features; you had been painted with a face cloth, such as we put upon the dead. Your father has laughed at me, but you and I, dear, know that such things are not for nothing. And I saw below the edge of the cloth the marks of hands on your throat—forgive me, but we have not been used to keep such things from each other. Perhaps you have another interpretation. Perhaps it does not mean that you will go to California. Or maybe you will take me with you?"

It must be confessed that this ingenious interpretation of the dream in the light of newly discovered evidence did not wholly commend itself to the son's more logical mind; he had, for the moment at least, a conviction that it foreshadowed a more simple and immediate, if less tragic, disaster than a visit to the Pacific Coast. It was Halpin Frayser's impression that he was to be garroted on his native heath.

"Are there not medicinal springs in California?" Mrs. Frayser resumed before he had time to give her the true reading of the dream—"places where one recovers from rheumatism and neuralgia? Look—my fingers feel so stiff; and I am almost sure they have been giving me great pain while I slept."

She held out her hands for his inspection. What diagnosis of her case the young man may have thought it best to conceal with a smile the historian is unable to state, but for himself he feels bound to say that fingers looking less stiff, and showing fewer evidences of even insensible pain, have seldom been submitted for medical inspection by even the fairest patient desiring a prescription of unfamiliar scenes.

The outcome of it was that of these two odd persons having equally odd notions of duty, the one went to California, as the interest of his client required, and the other remained at home in compliance with a wish that her husband was scarcely conscious of entertaining.

While in San Francisco Halpin Frayser was walking one dark night along the water front of the city, when, with a suddenness that surprised and disconcerted him, he became a sailor. He was in fact "shanghaied" aboard a gallant, gallant ship, and sailed for a far countree. Nor did his misfortunes end with the voyage; for the ship was cast ashore on an island of the South

Pacific, and it was six years afterward when the survivors were taken off by a venturesome trading schooner and brought back to San Francisco.

Though poor in purse, Frayser was no less proud in spirit than he had been in the years that seemed ages and ages ago. He would accept no assistance from strangers, and it was while living with a fellow survivor near the town of St. Helena, awaiting news and remittances from home, that he had gone gunning and dreaming.

III

The apparition confronting the dreamer in the haunted wood —the thing so like, yet so unlike his mother—was horrible! It stirred no love nor longing in his heart; it came unattended with pleasant memories of a golden past—inspired no sentiment of any kind; all the finer emotions were swallowed up in fear. He tried to turn and run from before it, but his legs were as lead; he was unable to lift his feet from the ground. His arms hung helpless at his sides; of his eyes only he retained control, and these he dared not remove from the lusterless orbs of the apparition, which he knew was not a soul without a body, but that most dreadful of all existences infesting that haunted wood—a body without a soul! In its blank stare was neither love, nor pity, nor intelligence—nothing to which to address an appeal for mercy. "An appeal will not lie," he thought, with an absurd reversion to professional slang, making the situation more horrible, as the fire of a cigar might light up a tomb.

For a time, which seemed so long that the world grew gray with age and sin, and the haunted forest, having fulfilled its purpose in this monstrous culmination of its terrors, vanished out of his consciousness with all its sights and sounds, the apparition stood within a pace, regarding him with the mindless malevolence of a wild brute; then thrust its hands forward and sprang upon him with appalling ferocity! The act released his physical energies without unfettering his will; his mind was still spellbound, but his powerful body and agile limbs, endowed with a blind, insensate life of their own, resisted stoutly and well. For an instant he seemed to see this unnatural contest between a dead intelligence and a breathing mechanism only as a spectator—such fancies are in dreams; then he regained his identity almost as if by a leap forward into his body, and the straining automaton had a directing will as alert and fierce as that of its hideous antagonist.

But what mortal can cope with a creature of his dream? The imagination creating the enemy is already vanquished; the combat's result is the combat's cause. Despite his struggles—despite his strength and activity, which seemed wasted in a void, he felt the cold fingers close upon his throat. Borne backward to the earth, he saw above him the dead and drawn face within a hand's breadth of his own, and then all was black. A sound as of the beating of distant drums—a murmur of swarming voices, a sharp, far cry signing all to silence, and Halpin Frayser dreamed that he was dead.

IV

A warm, clear night had been followed by a morning of drenching fog. At about the middle of the afternoon of the preceding day a little whiff of light vapor—a mere thickening of the atmosphere, the ghost of a cloud—had been observed clinging to the western side of Mount St. Helena, away up along the barren altitudes near the summit. It was so thin, so diaphanous, so like a fancy made visible, that one would have said: "Look quickly! in a moment it will be gone."

In a moment it was visibly larger and denser. While with one edge it clung to the mountain, with the other it reached farther and farther out into the air above the lower slopes. At the same time it extended itself to north and south, joining small patches of mist that appeared to come out of the mountainside on exactly the same level, with an intelligent design to be absorbed. And so it grew and grew until the summit was shut out of view from the valley, and over the valley itself was an ever-extending canopy, opaque and gray. At Calistoga, which lies near the head of the valley and the foot of the mountain, there were a starless night and a sunless morning. The fog, sinking into the valley, had reached southward, swallowing up ranch after ranch, until it had blotted out the town of St. Helena, nine miles away. The dust in the road was laid; trees were adrip with moisture; birds sat silent in their coverts; the morning light was wan and ghastly, with neither color nor fire.

Two men left the town of St. Helena at the first glimmer of dawn, and walked along the road northward up the valley toward Calistoga. They carried guns on their shoulders, yet no one having knowledge of such matters could have mistaken them for hunters of bird or beast. They were a deputy sheriff from Napa and a detective from San Francisco—Holker and Jaralson, respectively. Their business was man-hunting.

"How far is it?" inquired Holker, as they strode along, their feet stirring white the dust beneath the damp surface of the road.

"The White Church? Only a half mile farther," the other answered. "By the way," he added, "it is neither white nor a church; it is an abandoned schoolhouse, gray with age and neglect. Religious services were once held in it—when it was white, and there is a graveyard that would delight a poet. Can you guess why I sent for you, and told you to come heeled?"

"Oh, I never have bothered you about things of that kind. I've always found you communicative when the time came. But if I may hazard a guess, you want me to help you arrest one of the corpses in the graveyard."

"You remember Branscom?" said Jaralson, treating his companion's wit with the inattention that it deserved.

"The chap who cut his wife's throat? I ought; I wasted a week's work on him and had my expenses for my trouble. There is a reward of five hundred dollars, but none of us ever got a sight of him. You don't mean to say——"

"Yes, I do. He has been under the noses of you fellows all the time. He comes by night to the old graveyard at the White Church."

"The devil! That's where they buried his wife."

"Well, you fellows might have had sense enough to suspect that he would return to her grave some time."

"The very last place that anyone would have expected him to return to."

"But you had exhausted all the other places. Learning your failure at them, I 'laid for him' there."

"And you found him?"

"Damn it! he found *me*. The rascal got the drop on me—regularly held me up and made me travel. It's God's mercy that he didn't go through me. Oh, he's a good one, and I fancy the half of that reward is enough for me if you're needy."

Holker laughed good humoredly, and explained that his creditors were never more importunate.

"I wanted merely to show you the ground, and arrange a plan with you," the detective explained. "I thought it as well for us to be heeled, even in daylight."

"The man must be insane," said the deputy sheriff. "The reward is for his capture and conviction. If he's mad he won't be convicted."

Mr. Holker was so profoundly affected by that possible failure of justice that he involuntarily stopped in the middle of the road, then resumed his walk with abated zeal.

"Well, he looks it," assented Jaralson. "I'm bound to admit that a more unshaven, unshorn, unkempt, and uneverything wretch I never saw outside the ancient and honorable order of tramps. But I've gone in for him, and can't make up my mind to let go. There's glory in it for us, anyhow. Not another soul knows that he is this side of the Mountains of the Moon."

"All right," Holker said; "we will go and view the ground," and he added, in the words of a once favorite inscription for tombstones: "'where you must shortly lie'—I mean, if old Branscom ever gets tired of you and your impertinent intrusion. By the way, I heard the other day that 'Branscom' was not his real name."

"What is?"

"I can't recall it. I had lost all interest in the wretch, and it did not fix itself in my memory—something like Pardee. The woman whose throat he had the bad taste to cut was a widow when he met her. She had come to California to look up some relatives—there are persons who will do that sometimes. But you know all that."

"Naturally."

"But not knowing the right name, by what happy inspiration did you find the right grave? The man who told me what the name was said it had been cut on the headboard."

"I don't know the right grave." Jaralson was apparently a

trifle reluctant to admit his ignorance of so important a point
of his plan. "I have been watching about the place generally. A
part of our work this morning will be to identify that grave.
Here is the White Church."

For a long distance the road had been bordered by fields on
both sides, but now on the left there was a forest of oaks, ma-
droños, and gigantic spruces whose lower parts only could be
seen, dim and ghostly in the fog. The undergrowth was, in
places, thick, but nowhere impenetrable. For some moments
Holker saw nothing of the building, but as they turned into
the woods it revealed itself in faint gray outline through the
fog, looking huge and far away. A few steps more, and it was
within an arm's length, distinct, dark with moisture, and insignificant in size. It had the usual country-schoolhouse form—
belonged to the packing-box order of architecture; had an
underpinning of stones, a moss-grown roof, and blank window
spaces, whence both glass and sash had long departed. It was
ruined, but not a ruin—a typical Californian substitute for
what are known to guide-bookers abroad as "monuments of
the past." With scarcely a glance at this uninteresting structure
Jaralson moved on into the dripping undergrowth beyond.

"I will show you where he held me up," he said. "This is the
graveyard."

Here and there among the bushes were small inclosures
containing graves, sometimes no more than one. They were
recognized as graves by the discolored stones or rotting boards
at head and foot, leaning at all angles, some prostrate; by the
ruined picket fences surrounding them; or, infrequently, by
the mound itself showing its gravel through the fallen leaves.
In many instances nothing marked the spot where lay the vestiges of some poor mortal—who, leaving "a large circle of
sorrowing friends," had been left by them in turn—except a
depression in the earth, more lasting than that in the spirits of
the mourners. The paths, if any paths had been, were long
obliterated; trees of a considerable size had been permitted to
grow up from the graves and thrust aside with root or branch
the inclosing fences. Over all was that air of abandonment and
decay which seems nowhere so fit and significant as in a village
of the forgotten dead.

As the two men, Jaralson leading, pushed their way through the growth of young trees, that enterprising man suddenly stopped and brought up his shotgun to the height of his breast, uttered a low note of warning, and stood motionless, his eyes fixed upon something ahead. As well as he could, obstructed by brush, his companion, though seeing nothing, imitated the posture and so stood, prepared for what might ensue. A moment later Jaralson moved cautiously forward, the other following.

Under the branches of an enormous spruce lay the dead body of a man. Standing silent above it they noted such particulars as first strike the attention—the face, the attitude, the clothing; whatever most promptly and plainly answers the unspoken question of a sympathetic curiosity.

The body lay upon its back, the legs wide apart. One arm was thrust upward, the other outward; but the latter was bent acutely, and the hand was near the throat. Both hands were tightly clenched. The whole attitude was that of desperate but ineffectual resistance to—what?

Near by lay a shotgun and a game bag through the meshes of which was seen the plumage of shot birds. All about were evidences of a furious struggle; small sprouts of poison-oak were bent and denuded of leaf and bark; dead and rotting leaves had been pushed into heaps and ridges on both sides of the legs by the action of other feet than theirs; alongside the hips were unmistakable impressions of human knees.

The nature of the struggle was made clear by a glance at the dead man's throat and face. While breast and hands were white, those were purple—almost black. The shoulders lay upon a low mound, and the head was turned back at an angle otherwise impossible, the expanded eyes staring blankly backward in a direction opposite to that of the feet. From the froth filling the open mouth the tongue protruded, black and swollen. The throat showed horrible contusions; not mere finger-marks, but bruises and lacerations wrought by two strong hands that must have buried themselves in the yielding flesh, maintaining their terrible grasp until long after death. Breast, throat, face, were wet; the clothing was saturated; drops of water, condensed from the fog, studded the hair and mustache.

All this the two men observed without speaking—almost at a glance. Then Holker said:

"Poor devil! he had a rough deal."

Jaralson was making a vigilant circumspection of the forest, his shotgun held in both hands and at full cock, his finger upon the trigger.

"The work of a maniac," he said, without withdrawing his eyes from the inclosing wood. "It was done by Branscom—Pardee."

Something half hidden by the disturbed leaves on the earth caught Holker's attention. It was a red-leather pocketbook. He picked it up and opened it. It contained leaves of white paper for memoranda, and upon the first leaf was the name "Halpin Frayser." Written in red on several succeeding leaves —scrawled as if in haste and barely legible—were the following lines, which Holker read aloud, while his companion continued scanning the dim gray confines of their narrow world and hearing matter of apprehension in the drip of water from every burdened branch:

> "Enthralled by some mysterious spell, I stood
>   In the lit gloom of an enchanted wood.
>   The cypress there and myrtle twined their boughs,
>   Significant, in baleful brotherhood.
>
> "The brooding willow whispered to the yew;
>   Beneath, the deadly nightshade and the rue,
>   With immortelles self-woven into strange
>   Funereal shapes, and horrid nettles grew.
>
> "No song of bird nor any drone of bees,
>   Nor light leaf lifted by the wholesome breeze:
>   The air was stagnant all, and Silence was
>   A living thing that breathed among the trees.
>
> "Conspiring spirits whispered in the gloom,
>   Half-heard, the stilly secrets of the tomb.
>   With blood the trees were all adrip; the leaves
>   Shone in the witch-light with a ruddy bloom.
>
> "I cried aloud!—the spell, unbroken still,
>   Rested upon my spirit and my will.

> Unsouled, unhearted, hopeless and forlorn,
> I strove with monstrous presages of ill!

"At last the viewless——"

Holker ceased reading; there was no more to read. The manuscript broke off in the middle of a line.

"That sounds like Bayne," said Jaralson, who was something of a scholar in his way. He had abated his vigilance and stood looking down at the body.

"Who's Bayne?" Holker asked rather incuriously.

"Myron Bayne, a chap who flourished in the early years of the nation—more than a century ago. Wrote mighty dismal stuff; I have his collected works. That poem is not among them, but it must have been omitted by mistake."

"It is cold," said Holker; "let us leave here; we must have up the coroner from Napa."

Jaralson said nothing, but made a movement in compliance. Passing the end of the slight elevation of earth upon which the dead man's head and shoulders lay, his foot struck some hard substance under the rotting forest leaves, and he took the trouble to kick it into view. It was a fallen headboard, and painted on it were the hardly decipherable words, "Catharine Larue."

"Larue, Larue!" exclaimed Holker, with sudden animation. "Why, that is the real name of Branscom—not Pardee. And—bless my soul! how it all comes to me—the murdered woman's name had been Frayser!"

"There is some rascally mystery here," said Detective Jaralson. "I hate anything of that kind."

There came to them out of the fog—seemingly from a great distance—the sound of a laugh, a low, deliberate, soulless laugh, which had no more of joy than that of a hyena night-prowling in the desert; a laugh that rose by slow gradation, louder and louder, clearer, more distinct and terrible, until it seemed barely outside the narrow circle of their vision; a laugh so unnatural, so unhuman, so devilish, that it filled those hardy man-hunters with a sense of dread unspeakable! They did not move their weapons nor think of them; the menace of that horrible sound was not of the kind to be met with arms. As it had grown out of silence, so now it died away; from a culminating shout which had seemed almost in their ears, it drew itself away into the distance, until its failing notes, joyless and mechanical to the last, sank to silence at a measureless remove.

The Secret of Macarger's Gulch

NORTHWESTWARDLY from Indian Hill, about nine miles as the crow flies, is Macarger's Gulch. It is not much of a gulch—a mere depression between two wooded ridges of inconsiderable height. From its mouth up to its head—for gulches, like rivers, have an anatomy of their own—the distance does not exceed two miles, and the width at bottom is at only one place more than a dozen yards; for most of the distance on either side of the little brook which drains it in winter, and goes dry in the early spring, there is no level ground at all; the steep slopes of the hills, covered with an almost impenetrable growth of manzanita and chemisal, are parted by nothing but the width of the water course. No one but an occasional enterprising hunter of the vicinity ever goes into Macarger's Gulch, and five miles away it is unknown, even by name. Within that distance in any direction are far more conspicuous topographical features without names, and one might try in vain to ascertain by local inquiry the origin of the name of this one.

About midway between the head and the mouth of Macarger's Gulch, the hill on the right as you ascend is cloven by another gulch, a short dry one, and at the junction of the two is a level space of two or three acres, and there a few years ago stood an old board house containing one small room. How the component parts of the house, few and simple as they were, had been assembled at that almost inaccessible point is a problem in the solution of which there would be greater satisfaction than advantage. Possibly the creek bed is a reformed road. It is certain that the gulch was at one time pretty thoroughly prospected by miners, who must have had some means of getting in with at least pack animals carrying tools and supplies; their profits, apparently, were not such as would have justified any considerable outlay to connect Macarger's Gulch with any center of civilization enjoying the distinction of a sawmill. The house, however, was there, most of it. It lacked a door and a window frame, and the chimney of mud and stones had fallen into an unlovely heap, overgrown with rank weeds. Such humble furniture as there may once have been and much of the lower weatherboarding, had served as fuel in the camp fires of hunters; as had also, probably, the curbing of an old well, which at the time I write of existed in the form of a rather wide but not very deep depression near by.

One afternoon in the summer of 1874, I passed up Macarger's Gulch from the narrow valley into which it opens, by following the dry bed of the brook. I was quail-shooting and had made a bag of about a dozen birds by the time I had reached the house described, of whose existence I was until then unaware. After rather carelessly inspecting the ruin I resumed my sport, and having fairly good success prolonged it until near sunset, when it occurred to me that I was a long way from any human habitation—too far to reach one by nightfall. But in my game bag was food, and the old house would afford shelter, if shelter were needed on a warm and dewless night in the foothills of the Sierra Nevada, where one may sleep in comfort on the pine needles, without covering. I am fond of solitude and love the night, so my resolution to "camp out" was soon taken, and by the time that it was dark I had made my bed of boughs and grasses in a corner of the room and was roasting a quail at a fire that I had kindled on the hearth. The smoke escaped out of the ruined chimney, the light illuminated the room with a kindly glow, and as I ate my simple meal of plain bird and drank the remains of a bottle of red wine which had served me all the afternoon in place of the water, which the region did not supply, I experienced a sense of comfort which better fare and accommodations do not always give.

Nevertheless, there was something lacking. I had a sense of comfort, but not of security. I detected myself staring more frequently at the open doorway and blank window than I could find warrant for doing. Outside these apertures all was black, and I was unable to repress a certain feeling of apprehension as my fancy pictured the outer world and filled it with unfriendly entities, natural and supernatural—chief among which, in their respective classes, were the grizzly bear, which I knew was occasionally still seen in that region, and the ghost, which I had reason to think was not. Unfortunately, our feelings do not always respect the law of probabilities, and to me that evening, the possible and the impossible were equally disquieting.

Everyone who has had experience in the matter must have observed that one confronts the actual and imaginary perils of the night with far less apprehension in the open air than in a house with an open doorway. I felt this now as I lay on my leafy couch in a corner of the room next to the chimney and permitted my fire to die out. So strong became my sense of the presence of something malign and menacing in the place, that I found myself almost unable to withdraw my eyes from the opening, as in the deepening darkness it became more and more indistinct. And when the last little flame flickered and went out I grasped the shotgun which I had laid at my side and actually turned the muzzle in the direction of the now invisible entrance, my thumb on one of the hammers, ready to cock the piece, my breath suspended, my muscles rigid and tense. But later I laid down the weapon with a sense of shame and mortification. What did I fear, and why?—I, to whom the night had been

> a more familiar face
> Than that of man—

I, in whom that element of hereditary superstition from which none of us is altogether free had given to solitude and darkness and silence only a more alluring interest and charm! I was unable to comprehend my folly, and losing in the conjecture the thing conjectured of, I fell asleep. And then I dreamed.

I was in a great city in a foreign land—a city whose people were of my own race, with minor differences of speech and costume; yet precisely what these were I could not say; my sense of them was indistinct. The city was dominated by a great castle upon an overlooking height whose name I knew, but could not speak. I walked through many streets, some broad and straight with high, modern buildings, some narrow, gloomy, and tortuous, between the gables of quaint old houses whose overhanging stories, elaborately ornamented with carvings in wood and stone, almost met above my head.

I sought someone whom I had never seen, yet knew that I should recognize when found. My quest was not aimless and fortuitous; it had a definite method. I turned from one street into another without hesitation and threaded a maze of intricate passages, devoid of the fear of losing my way.

Presently I stopped before a low door in a plain stone house which might have been the dwelling of an artisan of the better sort, and without announcing myself, entered. The room, rather sparely furnished, and lighted by a single window with small diamond-shaped panes, had but two occupants; a man and a woman. They took no notice of my intrusion, a circumstance which, in the manner of dreams, appeared entirely natural. They were not conversing; they sat apart, unoccupied and sullen.

The woman was young and rather stout, with fine large eyes and a certain grave beauty; my memory of her expression is exceedingly vivid, but in dreams one does not observe the details of faces. About her shoulders was a plaid shawl. The man was older, dark, with an evil face made more forbidding by a long scar extending from near the left temple diagonally downward into the black mustache; though in my dreams it seemed rather to haunt the face as a thing apart—I can express it no otherwise—than to belong to it. The moment that I found the man and woman I knew them to be husband and wife.

What followed, I remember indistinctly; all was confused and inconsistent—made so, I think, by gleams of consciousness. It was as if two pictures, the scene of my dream, and my actual surroundings, had been blended, one overlying the other, until the former, gradually fading, disappeared, and I was broad awake in the deserted cabin, entirely and tranquilly conscious of my situation.

My foolish fear was gone, and opening my eyes I saw that my fire, not altogether burned out, had revived by the falling of a stick and was again lighting the room. I had probably slept only a few minutes, but my commonplace dream had somehow so strongly impressed me that I was no longer drowsy; and after a little while I rose, pushed the embers of my fire together, and lighting my pipe proceeded in a rather ludicrously methodical way to meditate upon my vision.

It would have puzzled me then to say in what respect it was worth attention. In the first moment of serious thought that I gave to the matter I recognized the city of my dream as

Edinburgh, where I had never been; so if the dream was a memory it was a memory of pictures and description. The recognition somehow deeply impressed me; it was as if something in my mind insisted rebelliously against will and reason on the importance of all this. And that faculty, whatever it was, asserted also a control of my speech. "Surely," I said aloud, quite involuntarily, "the MacGregors must have come here from Edinburgh."

At the moment, neither the substance of this remark nor the fact of my making it, surprised me in the least; it seemed entirely natural that I should know the name of my dreamfolk and something of their history. But the absurdity of it all soon dawned upon me: I laughed aloud, knocked the ashes from my pipe and again stretched myself upon my bed of boughs and grass, where I lay staring absently into my failing fire, with no further thought of either my dream or my surroundings. Suddenly the single remaining flame crouched for a moment, then, springing upward, lifted itself clear of its embers and expired in air. The darkness was absolute.

At that instant—almost, it seemed, before the gleam of the blaze had faded from my eyes—there was a dull, dead sound, as of some heavy body falling upon the floor, which shook beneath me as I lay. I sprang to a sitting posture and groped at my side for my gun; my notion was that some wild beast had leaped in through the open window. While the flimsy structure was still shaking from the impact I heard the sound of blows, the scuffling of feet upon the floor, and then—it seemed to come from almost within reach of my hand, the sharp shrieking of a woman in mortal agony. So horrible a cry I had never heard nor conceived; it utterly unnerved me; I was conscious for a moment of nothing but my own terror! Fortunately my hand now found the weapon of which it was in search, and the familiar touch somewhat restored me. I leaped to my feet, straining my eyes to pierce the darkness. The violent sounds had ceased, but more terrible than these, I heard, at what seemed long intervals, the faint intermittent gasping of some living, dying thing!

As my eyes grew accustomed to the dim light of the coals in the fireplace, I saw first the shapes of the door and window, looking blacker than the black of the walls. Next, the distinction between wall and floor became discernible, and at last I was sensible to the form and full expanse of the floor from end to end and side to side. Nothing was visible and the silence was unbroken.

With a hand that shook a little, the other still grasping my gun, I restored my fire and made a critical examination of the place. There was nowhere any sign that the cabin had been entered. My own tracks were visible in the dust covering the floor, but there were no others. I relit my pipe, provided fresh fuel by ripping a thin board or two from the inside of the house—I did not care to go into the darkness out of doors—and passed the rest of the night smoking and thinking, and feeding my fire; not for added years of life would I have permitted that little flame to expire again.

Some years afterward I met in Sacramento a man named Morgan, to whom I had a note of introduction from a friend in San Francisco. Dining with him one evening at his home I observed various "trophies" upon the wall, indicating that he was fond of shooting. It turned out that he was, and in relating some of his feats he mentioned having been in the region of my adventure.

"Mr. Morgan," I asked abruptly, "do you know a place up there called Macarger's Gulch?"

"I have good reason to," he replied; "it was I who gave to the newspapers, last year, the accounts of the finding of the skeleton there."

I had not heard of it; the accounts had been published, it appeared, while I was absent in the East.

"By the way," said Morgan, "the name of the gulch is a corruption; it should have been called 'MacGregor's.' My dear," he added, speaking to his wife, "Mr. Elderson has upset his wine."

That was hardly accurate—I had simply dropped it, glass and all.

"There was an old shanty once in the gulch," Morgan resumed when the ruin wrought by my awkwardness had been repaired, "but just previously to my visit it had been blown down, or rather blown away, for its *débris* was scattered all about, the very floor being parted, plank from plank. Between two of the sleepers still in position I and my companion observed the remnant of a plaid shawl, and examining it found that it was wrapped about the shoulders of the body of a woman, of which but little remained besides the bones, partly covered with fragments of clothing, and brown dry skin. But we will spare Mrs. Morgan," he added with a smile. The lady had indeed exhibited signs of disgust rather than sympathy.

"It is necessary to say, however," he went on, "that the skull was fractured in several places, as by blows of some blunt instrument; and that instrument itself—a pick-handle, still stained with blood—lay under the boards near by."

Mr. Morgan turned to his wife. "Pardon me, my dear," he said with affected solemnity, "for mentioning these disagreeable particulars, the natural though regrettable incidents of a conjugal quarrel—resulting, doubtless, from the luckless wife's insubordination."

"I ought to be able to overlook it," the lady replied with composure; "you have so many times asked me to in those very words."

I thought he seemed rather glad to go on with his story.

"From these and other circumstances," he said, "the coroner's jury found that the deceased, Janet MacGregor, came to her death from blows inflicted by some person to the jury unknown; but it was added that the evidence pointed strongly to her husband, Thomas MacGregor, as the guilty person. But Thomas MacGregor has never been found nor heard of. It was learned that the couple came from Edinburgh, but not—my dear, do you not observe that Mr. Elderson's boneplate has water in it?"

I had deposited a chicken bone in my finger bowl.

"In a little cupboard I found a photograph of MacGregor, but it did not lead to his capture."

"Will you let me see it?" I said.

The picture showed a dark man with an evil face made more forbidding by a long scar extending from near the temple diagonally downward into the black mustache.

"By the way, Mr. Elderson," said my affable host, "may I know why you asked about 'Macarger's Gulch'?"

"I lost a mule near there once," I replied, "and the mischance has—has quite—upset me."

"My dear," said Mr. Morgan, with the mechanical intonation of an interpreter translating, "the loss of Mr. Elderson's mule has peppered his coffee."

One Summer Night

THE fact that Henry Armstrong was buried did not seem to him to prove that he was dead: he had always been a hard man to convince. That he really was buried, the testimony of his senses compelled him to admit. His posture—flat upon his back, with his hands crossed upon his stomach and tied with something that he easily broke without profitably altering the situation—the strict confinement of his entire person, the black darkness and profound silence, made a body of evidence impossible to controvert and he accepted it without cavil.

But dead—no; he was only very, very ill. He had, withal, the invalid's apathy and did not greatly concern himself about the uncommon fate that had been allotted to him. No philosopher was he—just a plain, commonplace person gifted, for the time being, with a pathological indifference: the organ that he feared consequences with was torpid. So, with no particular apprehension for his immediate future, he fell asleep and all was peace with Henry Armstrong.

But something was going on overhead. It was a dark summer night, shot through with infrequent shimmers of lightning silently firing a cloud lying low in the west and portending a storm. These brief, stammering illuminations brought out with ghastly distinctness the monuments and headstones of the cemetery and seemed to set them dancing. It was not a night in which any credible witness was likely to be straying about a cemetery, so the three men who were there, digging into the grave of Henry Armstrong, felt reasonably secure.

Two of them were young students from a medical college a few miles away; the third was a gigantic negro known as Jess. For many years Jess had been employed about the cemetery as a man-of-all-work and it was his favorite pleasantry that he knew "every soul in the place." From the nature of what he was now doing it was inferable that the place was not so populous as its register may have shown it to be.

Outside the wall, at the part of the grounds farthest from the public road, were a horse and a light wagon, waiting.

The work of excavation was not difficult: the earth with

which the grave had been loosely filled a few hours before offered little resistance and was soon thrown out. Removal of
the casket from its box was less easy, but it was taken out, for it
was a perquisite of Jess, who carefully unscrewed the cover and
laid it aside, exposing the body in black trousers and white
shirt. At that instant the air sprang to flame, a cracking shock
of thunder shook the stunned world and Henry Armstrong
tranquilly sat up. With inarticulate cries the men fled in terror,
each in a different direction. For nothing on earth could two
of them have been persuaded to return. But Jess was of another
breed.

In the gray of the morning the two students, pallid and haggard from anxiety and with the terror of their adventure still
beating tumultuously in their blood, met at the medical
college.

"You saw it?" cried one.

"God! yes—what are we to do?"

They went around to the rear of the building, where they
saw a horse, attached to a light wagon, hitched to a gatepost
near the door of the dissecting-room. Mechanically they entered the room. On a bench in the obscurity sat the negro Jess.
He rose, grinning, all eyes and teeth.

"I'm waiting for my pay," he said.

Stretched naked on a long table lay the body of Henry
Armstrong, the head defiled with blood and clay from a blow
with a spade.

The Moonlit Road

STATEMENT OF JOEL HETMAN, JR.

I AM the most unfortunate of men. Rich, respected, fairly well educated and of sound health—with many other advantages usually valued by those having them and coveted by those who have them not—I sometimes think that I should be less unhappy if they had been denied me, for then the contrast between my outer and my inner life would not be continually demanding a painful attention. In the stress of privation and the need of effort I might sometimes forget the somber secret ever baffling the conjecture that it compels.

I am the only child of Joel and Julia Hetman. The one was a well-to-do country gentleman, the other a beautiful and accomplished woman to whom he was passionately attached with what I now know to have been a jealous and exacting devotion. The family home was a few miles from Nashville, Tennessee, a large, irregularly built dwelling of no particular order of architecture, a little way off the road, in a park of trees and shrubbery.

At the time of which I write I was nineteen years old, a student at Yale. One day I received a telegram from my father of such urgency that in compliance with its unexplained demand I left at once for home. At the railway station in Nashville a distant relative awaited me to apprise me of the reason for my recall: my mother had been barbarously murdered—why and by whom none could conjecture, but the circumstances were these:

My father had gone to Nashville, intending to return the next afternoon. Something prevented his accomplishing the business in hand, so he returned on the same night, arriving just before the dawn. In his testimony before the coroner he explained that having no latchkey and not caring to disturb the sleeping servants, he had, with no clearly defined intention, gone round to the rear of the house. As he turned an angle of the building, he heard a sound as of a door gently closed, and saw in the darkness, indistinctly, the figure of a man, which

239

instantly disappeared among the trees of the lawn. A hasty
pursuit and brief search of the grounds in the belief that the
trespasser was some one secretly visiting a servant proving
fruitless, he entered at the unlocked door and mounted the
stairs to my mother's chamber. Its door was open, and stepping into black darkness he fell headlong over some heavy object on the floor. I may spare myself the details; it was my poor
mother, dead of strangulation by human hands!

Nothing had been taken from the house, the servants had
heard no sound, and excepting those terrible finger-marks
upon the dead woman's throat—dear God! that I might forget
them!—no trace of the assassin was ever found.

I gave up my studies and remained with my father, who,
naturally, was greatly changed. Always of a sedate, taciturn
disposition, he now fell into so deep a dejection that nothing
could hold his attention, yet anything—a footfall, the sudden
closing of a door—aroused in him a fitful interest; one might
have called it an apprehension. At any small surprise of the
senses he would start visibly and sometimes turn pale, then
relapse into a melancholy apathy deeper than before. I suppose
he was what is called a "nervous wreck." As to me, I was
younger then than now—there is much in that. Youth is Gil-
ead, in which is balm for every wound. Ah, that I might again
dwell in that enchanted land! Unacquainted with grief, I knew
not how to appraise my bereavement; I could not rightly estimate the strength of the stroke.

One night, a few months after the dreadful event, my father
and I walked home from the city. The full moon was about
three hours above the eastern horizon; the entire countryside
had the solemn stillness of a summer night; our footfalls and
the ceaseless song of the katydids were the only sound aloof.
Black shadows of bordering trees lay athwart the road, which,
in the short reaches between, gleamed a ghostly white. As we
approached the gate to our dwelling, whose front was in
shadow, and in which no light shone, my father suddenly
stopped and clutched my arm, saying, hardly above his
breath:

"God! God! what is that?"

"I hear nothing," I replied.

"But see—see!" he said, pointing along the road, directly ahead.

I said: "Nothing is there. Come, father, let us go in—you are ill."

He had released my arm and was standing rigid and motionless in the center of the illuminated roadway, staring like one bereft of sense. His face in the moonlight showed a pallor and fixity inexpressibly distressing. I pulled gently at his sleeve, but he had forgotten my existence. Presently he began to retire backward, step by step, never for an instant removing his eyes from what he saw, or thought he saw. I turned half round to follow, but stood irresolute. I do not recall any feeling of fear, unless a sudden chill was its physical manifestation. It seemed as if an icy wind had touched my face and enfolded my body from head to foot; I could feel the stir of it in my hair.

At that moment my attention was drawn to a light that suddenly streamed from an upper window of the house: one of the servants, awakened by what mysterious premonition of evil who can say, and in obedience to an impulse that she was never able to name, had lit a lamp. When I turned to look for my father he was gone, and in all the years that have passed no whisper of his fate has come across the borderland of conjecture from the realm of the unknown.

II

STATEMENT OF CASPAR GRATTAN

To-day I am said to live; to-morrow, here in this room, will lie a senseless shape of clay that all too long was I. If anyone lift the cloth from the face of that unpleasant thing it will be in gratification of a mere morbid curiosity. Some, doubtless, will go further and inquire, "Who was he?" In this writing I supply the only answer that I am able to make—Caspar Grattan. Surely, that should be enough. The name has served my small need for more than twenty years of a life of unknown length. True, I gave it to myself, but lacking another I had the right. In this world one must have a name; it prevents confusion, even when it does not establish identity. Some, though, are known by numbers, which also seem inadequate distinctions.

One day, for illustration, I was passing along a street of a city, far from here, when I met two men in uniform, one of whom, half pausing and looking curiously into my face, said to his companion, "That man looks like 767." Something in the number seemed familiar and horrible. Moved by an uncontrollable impulse, I sprang into a side street and ran until I fell exhausted in a country lane.

I have never forgotten that number, and always it comes to memory attended by gibbering obscenity, peals of joyless laughter, the clang of iron doors. So I say a name, even if self-bestowed, is better than a number. In the register of the potter's field I shall soon have both. What wealth!

Of him who shall find this paper I must beg a little consideration. It is not the history of my life; the knowledge to write that is denied me. This is only a record of broken and apparently unrelated memories, some of them as distinct and sequent as brilliant beads upon a thread, others remote and strange, having the character of crimson dreams with interspaces blank and black—witch-fires glowing still and red in a great desolation.

Standing upon the shore of eternity, I turn for a last look landward over the course by which I came. There are twenty years of footprints fairly distinct, the impressions of bleeding feet. They lead through poverty and pain, devious and unsure, as of one staggering beneath a burden—

Remote, unfriended, melancholy, slow.

Ah, the poet's prophecy of Me—how admirable, how dreadfully admirable!

Backward beyond the beginning of this *via dolorosa*—this epic of suffering with episodes of sin—I see nothing clearly; it comes out of a cloud. I know that it spans only twenty years, yet I am an old man.

One does not remember one's birth—one has to be told. But with me it was different; life came to me full-handed and dowered me with all my faculties and powers. Of a previous existence I know no more than others, for all have stammering intimations that may be memories and may be dreams. I know only that my first consciousness was of maturity in body and mind—a consciousness accepted without surprise or conjecture. I merely found myself walking in a forest, half-clad, footsore, unutterably weary and hungry. Seeing a farmhouse, I approached and asked for food, which was given me by one who inquired my name. I did not know, yet knew that all had names. Greatly embarrassed, I retreated, and night coming on, lay down in the forest and slept.

The next day I entered a large town which I shall not name. Nor shall I recount further incidents of the life that is now to end—a life of wandering, always and everywhere haunted by an overmastering sense of crime in punishment of wrong and of terror in punishment of crime. Let me see if I can reduce it to narrative.

I seem once to have lived near a great city, a prosperous planter, married to a woman whom I loved and distrusted. We had, it sometimes seems, one child, a youth of brilliant parts and promise. He is at all times a vague figure, never clearly drawn, frequently altogether out of the picture.

One luckless evening it occurred to me to test my wife's fidelity in a vulgar, commonplace way familiar to everyone who has acquaintance with the literature of fact and fiction. I went to the city, telling my wife that I should be absent until the following afternoon. But I returned before daybreak and went to the rear of the house, purposing to enter by a door with which I had secretly so tampered that it would seem to lock, yet not actually fasten. As I approached it, I heard it gently open and close, and saw a man steal away into the darkness. With murder in my heart, I sprang after him, but he had vanished without even the bad luck of identification. Sometimes now I cannot even persuade myself that it was a human being.

Crazed with jealousy and rage, blind and bestial with all the elemental passions of insulted manhood, I entered the house and sprang up the stairs to the door of my wife's chamber. It was closed, but having tampered with its lock also, I easily entered and despite the black darkness soon stood by the side of her bed. My groping hands told me that although disarranged it was unoccupied.

"She is below," I thought, "and terrified by my entrance has evaded me in the darkness of the hall."

With the purpose of seeking her I turned to leave the room, but took a wrong direction—the right one! My foot struck her, cowering in a corner of the room. Instantly my hands were at her throat, stifling a shriek, my knees were upon her struggling body; and there in the darkness, without a word of accusation or reproach, I strangled her till she died!

There ends the dream. I have related it in the past tense, but the present would be the fitter form, for again and again the somber tragedy reenacts itself in my consciousness—over and over I lay the plan, I suffer the confirmation, I redress the wrong. Then all is blank; and afterward the rains beat against the grimy window-panes, or the snows fall upon my scant attire, the wheels rattle in the squalid streets where my life lies in poverty and mean employment. If there is ever sunshine I do not recall it; if there are birds they do not sing.

There is another dream, another vision of the night. I stand among the shadows in a moonlit road. I am aware of another presence, but whose I cannot rightly determine. In the shadow of a great dwelling I catch the gleam of white garments; then the figure of a woman confronts me in the road—my murdered wife! There is death in the face; there are marks upon the throat. The eyes are fixed on mine with an infinite gravity which is not reproach, nor hate, nor menace, nor anything less terrible than recognition. Before this awful apparition I retreat in terror—a terror that is upon me as I write. I can no longer rightly shape the words. See! they—

Now I am calm, but truly there is no more to tell: the incident ends where it began—in darkness and in doubt.

Yes, I am again in control of myself: "the captain of my soul." But that is not respite; it is another stage and phase of expiation. My penance, constant in degree, is mutable in kind: one of its variants is tranquillity. After all, it is only a life-sentence. "To Hell for life"—that is a foolish penalty: the culprit chooses the duration of his punishment. To-day my term expires.

To each and all, the peace that was not mine.

III

STATEMENT OF THE LATE JULIA HETMAN,
THROUGH THE MEDIUM BAYROLLES

I had retired early and fallen almost immediately into a peaceful sleep, from which I awoke with that indefinable sense of peril which is, I think, a common experience in that other, earlier life. Of its unmeaning character, too, I was entirely persuaded, yet that did not banish it. My husband, Joel Hetman, was away from home; the servants slept in another part of the house. But these were familiar conditions; they had never before distressed me. Nevertheless, the strange terror grew so insupportable that conquering my reluctance to move I sat up and lit the lamp at my bedside. Contrary to my expectation this gave me no relief; the light seemed rather an added danger, for I reflected that it would shine out under the door, disclosing my presence to whatever evil thing might lurk outside. You that are still in the flesh, subject to horrors of the imagination, think what a monstrous fear that must be which seeks in darkness security from malevolent existences of the night. That is to spring to close quarters with an unseen enemy —the strategy of despair!

Extinguishing the lamp I pulled the bedclothing about my head and lay trembling and silent, unable to shriek, forgetful to pray. In this pitiable state I must have lain for what you call hours—with us there are no hours, there is no time.

At last it came—a soft, irregular sound of footfalls on the stairs! They were slow, hesitant, uncertain, as of something that did not see its way; to my disordered reason all the more terrifying for that, as the approach of some blind and mindless malevolence to which is no appeal. I even thought that I must have left the hall lamp burning and the groping of this creature proved it a monster of the night. This was foolish and inconsistent with my previous dread of the light, but what would you have? Fear has no brains; it is an idiot. The dismal witness that it bears and the cowardly counsel that it whispers are unrelated. We know this well, we who have passed into the Realm of Terror, who skulk in eternal dusk among the scenes of our former lives, invisible even to ourselves and one another, yet hiding forlorn in lonely places; yearning for speech with our loved ones, yet dumb, and as fearful of them as they of us. Sometimes the disability is removed, the law suspended: by the deathless power of love or hate we break the spell—we are seen by those whom we would warn, console, or punish. What form we seem to them to bear we know not; we know only that we terrify even those whom we most wish to comfort, and from whom we most crave tenderness and sympathy.

Forgive, I pray you, this inconsequent digression by what was once a woman. You who consult us in this imperfect way —you do not understand. You ask foolish questions about things unknown and things forbidden. Much that we know and could impart in our speech is meaningless in yours. We must communicate with you through a stammering intelligence in that small fraction of our language that you yourselves can speak. You think that we are of another world. No, we have knowledge of no world but yours, though for us it holds no sunlight, no warmth, no music, no laughter, no song of birds, nor any companionship. O God! what a thing it is to be a ghost, cowering and shivering in an altered world, a prey to apprehension and despair!

No, I did not die of fright: the Thing turned and went away. I heard it go down the stairs, hurriedly, I thought, as if itself in sudden fear. Then I rose to call for help. Hardly had my shaking hand found the doorknob when—merciful heaven!—I heard it returning. Its footfalls as it remounted the stairs were rapid, heavy and loud; they shook the house. I fled to an angle of the wall and crouched upon the floor. I tried to pray. I tried to call the name of my dear husband. Then I heard the door thrown open. There was an interval of unconsciousness, and when I revived I felt a strangling clutch upon my throat—felt my arms feebly beating against something that bore me backward —felt my tongue thrusting itself from between my teeth! And then I passed into this life.

No, I have no knowledge of what it was. The sum of what we knew at death is the measure of what we know afterward of all that went before. Of this existence we know many things, but no new light falls upon any page of that; in memory is written all of it that we can read. Here are no heights of truth overlooking the confused landscape of that dubitable domain. We still dwell in the Valley of the Shadow, lurk in its desolate places, peering from brambles and thickets at its mad, malign inhabitants. How should we have new knowledge of that fading past?

What I am about to relate happened on a night. We know when it is night, for then you retire to your houses and we can venture from our places of concealment to move unafraid about our old homes, to look in at the windows, even to enter and gaze upon your faces as you sleep. I had lingered long near the dwelling where I had been so cruelly changed to what I am, as we do while any that we love or hate remain. Vainly I had sought some method of manifestation, some way to make my continued existence and my great love and poignant pity understood by my husband and son. Always if they slept they would wake, or if in my desperation I dared approach them when they were awake, would turn toward me the terrible eyes of the living, frightening me by the glances that I sought from the purpose that I held.

On this night I had searched for them without success, fearing to find them; they were nowhere in the house, nor about the moonlit lawn. For, although the sun is lost to us forever, the moon, full-orbed or slender, remains to us. Sometimes it shines by night, sometimes by day, but always it rises and sets, as in that other life.

I left the lawn and moved in the white light and silence along the road, aimless and sorrowing. Suddenly I heard the voice of my poor husband in exclamations of astonishment, with that of my son in reassurance and dissuasion; and there by the shadow of a group of trees they stood—near, so near! Their faces were toward me, the eyes of the elder man fixed upon mine. He saw me—at last, at last, he saw me! In the consciousness of that, my terror fled as a cruel dream. The death-spell was broken: Love had conquered Law! Mad with exultation I shouted—I *must* have shouted, "He sees, he sees: he will understand!" Then, controlling myself, I moved forward, smiling and consciously beautiful, to offer myself to his arms, to comfort him with endearments, and, with my son's hand in mine, to speak words that should restore the broken bonds between the living and the dead.

Alas! alas! his face went white with fear, his eyes were as those of a hunted animal. He backed away from me, as I advanced, and at last turned and fled into the wood—whither, it is not given to me to know.

To my poor boy, left doubly desolate, I have never been able to impart a sense of my presence. Soon he, too, must pass to this Life Invisible and be lost to me forever.

A Diagnosis of Death

"I AM not so superstitious as some of your physicians—men of science, as you are pleased to be called," said Hawver, replying to an accusation that had not been made. "Some of you—only a few, I confess—believe in the immortality of the soul, and in apparitions which you have not the honesty to call ghosts. I go no further than a conviction that the living are sometimes seen where they are not, but have been—where they have lived so long, perhaps so intensely, as to have left their impress on everything about them. I know, indeed, that one's environment may be so affected by one's personality as to yield, long afterward, an image of one's self to the eyes of another. Doubtless the impressing personality has to be the right kind of personality as the perceiving eyes have to be the right kind of eyes—mine, for example."

"Yes, the right kind of eyes, conveying sensations to the wrong kind of brain," said Dr. Frayley, smiling.

"Thank you; one likes to have an expectation gratified; that is about the reply that I supposed you would have the civility to make."

"Pardon me. But you say that you know. That is a good deal to say, don't you think? Perhaps you will not mind the trouble of saying how you learned."

"You will call it an hallucination," Hawver said, "but that does not matter." And he told the story.

"Last summer I went, as you know, to pass the hot weather term in the town of Meridian. The relative at whose house I had intended to stay was ill, so I sought other quarters. After some difficulty I succeeded in renting a vacant dwelling that had been occupied by an eccentric doctor of the name of Mannering, who had gone away years before, no one knew where, not even his agent. He had built the house himself and had lived in it with an old servant for about ten years. His practice, never very extensive, had after a few years been given up entirely. Not only so, but he had withdrawn himself almost altogether from social life and become a recluse. I was told by the village doctor, about the only person with whom he held any relations, that during his retirement he had devoted himself to a single line of study, the result of which he had expounded in a book that did not commend itself to the approval of his professional brethren, who, indeed, considered him not entirely sane. I have not seen the book and cannot now recall the title of it, but I am told that it expounded a rather startling theory. He held that it was possible in the case of many a person in good health to forecast his death with precision, several months in advance of the event. The limit, I think, was eighteen months. There were local tales of his having exerted his powers of prognosis, or perhaps you would say diagnosis; and it was said that in every instance the person whose friends he had warned had died suddenly at the appointed time, and from no assignable cause. All this, however, has nothing to do with what I have to tell; I thought it might amuse a physician.

"The house was furnished, just as he had lived in it. It was a rather gloomy dwelling for one who was neither a recluse nor a student, and I think it gave something of its character to me —perhaps some of its former occupant's character; for always I felt in it a certain melancholy that was not in my natural disposition, nor, I think, due to loneliness. I had no servants that slept in the house, but I have always been, as you know, rather fond of my own society, being much addicted to reading, though little to study. Whatever was the cause, the effect was dejection and a sense of impending evil; this was especially so in Dr. Mannering's study, although that room was the lightest and most airy in the house. The doctor's life-size portrait in oil hung in that room, and seemed completely to dominate it. There was nothing unusual in the picture; the man was evidently rather good looking, about fifty years old, with iron-gray hair, a smooth-shaven face and dark, serious eyes. Something in the picture always drew and held my attention. The man's appearance became familiar to me, and rather 'haunted' me.

"One evening I was passing through this room to my bedroom, with a lamp—there is no gas in Meridian. I stopped as usual before the portrait, which seemed in the lamplight to have a new expression, not easily named, but distinctly uncanny. It interested but did not disturb me. I moved the lamp from one side to the other and observed the effects of the altered light. While so engaged I felt an impulse to turn round.

As I did so I saw a man moving across the room directly toward me! As soon as he came near enough for the lamplight to illuminate the face I saw that it was Dr. Mannering himself; it was as if the portrait were walking!

" 'I beg your pardon,' I said, somewhat coldly, 'but if you knocked I did not hear.'

"He passed me, within an arm's length, lifted his right forefinger, as in warning, and without a word went on out of the room, though I observed his exit no more than I had observed his entrance.

"Of course, I need not tell you that this was what you will call an hallucination and I call an apparition. That room had only two doors, of which one was locked; the other led into a bedroom, from which there was no exit. My feeling on realizing this is not an important part of the incident.

"Doubtless this seems to you a very commonplace 'ghost story'—one constructed on the regular lines laid down by the old masters of the art. If that were so I should not have related it, even if it were true. The man was not dead; I met him to-day in Union street. He passed me in a crowd."

Hawver had finished his story and both men were silent. Dr. Frayley absently drummed on the table with his fingers.

"Did he say anything to-day?" he asked—"anything from which you inferred that he was not dead?"

Hawver stared and did not reply.

"Perhaps," continued Frayley, "he made a sign, a gesture—lifted a finger, as in warning. It's a trick he had—a habit when saying something serious—announcing the result of a diagnosis, for example."

"Yes, he did—just as his apparition had done. But, good God! did you ever know him?"

Hawver was apparently growing nervous.

"I knew him. I have read his book, as will every physician some day. It is one of the most striking and important of the century's contributions to medical science. Yes, I knew him; I attended him in an illness three years ago. He died."

Hawver sprang from his chair, manifestly disturbed. He strode forward and back across the room; then approached his friend, and in a voice not altogether steady, said: "Doctor, have you anything to say to me—as a physician?"

"No, Hawver; you are the healthiest man I ever knew. As a friend I advise you to go to your room. You play the violin like an angel. Play it; play something light and lively. Get this cursed bad business off your mind."

The next day Hawver was found dead in his room, the violin at his neck, the bow upon the strings, his music open before him at Chopin's funeral march.

Moxon's Master

"ARE you serious?—do you really believe that a machine thinks?"

I got no immediate reply; Moxon was apparently intent upon the coals in the grate, touching them deftly here and there with the fire-poker till they signified a sense of his attention by a brighter glow. For several weeks I had been observing in him a growing habit of delay in answering even the most trivial of commonplace questions. His air, however, was that of preoccupation rather than deliberation: one might have said that he had "something on his mind."

Presently he said:

"What is a 'machine'? The word has been variously defined. Here is one definition from a popular dictionary: 'Any instrument or organization by which power is applied and made effective, or a desired effect produced.' Well, then, is not a man a machine? And you will admit that he thinks—or thinks he thinks."

"If you do not wish to answer my question," I said, rather testily, "why not say so?—all that you say is mere evasion. You know well enough that when I say 'machine' I do not mean a man, but something that man has made and controls."

"When it does not control him," he said, rising abruptly and looking out of a window, whence nothing was visible in the blackness of a stormy night. A moment later he turned about and with a smile said: "I beg your pardon; I had no thought of evasion. I considered the dictionary man's unconscious testimony suggestive and worth something in the discussion. I can give your question a direct answer easily enough: I do believe that a machine thinks about the work that it is doing."

That was direct enough, certainly. It was not altogether pleasing, for it tended to confirm a sad suspicion that Moxon's devotion to study and work in his machine-shop had not been good for him. I knew, for one thing, that he suffered from insomnia, and that is no light affliction. Had it affected his mind? His reply to my question seemed to me then evidence that it had; perhaps I should think differently about it now. I was younger then, and among the blessings that are not denied to youth is ignorance. Incited by that great stimulant to controversy, I said:

"And what, pray, does it think with—in the absence of a brain?"

The reply, coming with less than his customary delay, took his favorite form of counter-interrogation:

"With what does a plant think—in the absence of a brain?"

"Ah, plants also belong to the philosopher class! I should be pleased to know some of their conclusions; you may omit the premises."

"Perhaps," he replied, apparently unaffected by my foolish irony, "you may be able to infer their convictions from their acts. I will spare you the familiar examples of the sensitive mimosa, the several insectivorous flowers and those whose stamens bend down and shake their pollen upon the entering bee in order that he may fertilize their distant mates. But observe this. In an open spot in my garden I planted a climbing vine. When it was barely above the surface I set a stake into the soil a yard away. The vine at once made for it, but as it was about to reach it after several days I removed it a few feet. The vine at once altered its course, making an acute angle, and again made for the stake. This manœuvre was repeated several times, but finally, as if discouraged, the vine abandoned the pursuit and ignoring further attempts to divert it traveled to a small tree, further away, which it climbed.

"Roots of the eucalyptus will prolong themselves incredibly in search of moisture. A well-known horticulturist relates that one entered an old drain pipe and followed it until it came to a break, where a section of the pipe had been removed to make way for a stone wall that had been built across its course. The root left the drain and followed the wall until it found an opening where a stone had fallen out. It crept through and following the other side of the wall back to the drain, entered the unexplored part and resumed its journey."

"And all this?"

"Can you miss the significance of it? It shows the consciousness of plants. It proves that they think."

"Even if it did—what then? We were speaking, not of plants, but of machines. They may be composed partly of wood—wood that has no longer vitality—or wholly of metal. Is thought an attribute also of the mineral kingdom?"

"How else do you explain the phenomena, for example, of crystallization?"

"I do not explain them."

"Because you cannot without affirming what you wish to deny, namely, intelligent cooperation among the constituent elements of the crystals. When soldiers form lines, or hollow squares, you call it reason. When wild geese in flight take the form of a letter V you say instinct. When the homogeneous atoms of a mineral, moving freely in solution, arrange themselves into shapes mathematically perfect, or particles of frozen moisture into the symmetrical and beautiful forms of snowflakes, you have nothing to say. You have not even invented a name to conceal your heroic unreason."

Moxon was speaking with unusual animation and earnestness. As he paused I heard in an adjoining room known to me as his "machine-shop," which no one but himself was permitted to enter, a singular thumping sound, as of some one pounding upon a table with an open hand. Moxon heard it at the same moment and, visibly agitated, rose and hurriedly passed into the room whence it came. I thought it odd that any one else should be in there, and my interest in my friend—with doubtless a touch of unwarrantable curiosity—led me to listen intently, though, I am happy to say, not at the keyhole. There were confused sounds, as of a struggle or scuffle; the floor shook. I distinctly heard hard breathing and a hoarse whisper which said "Damn you!" Then all was silent, and presently Moxon reappeared and said, with a rather sorry smile:

"Pardon me for leaving you so abruptly. I have a machine in there that lost its temper and cut up rough."

Fixing my eyes steadily upon his left cheek, which was traversed by four parallel excoriations showing blood, I said:

"How would it do to trim its nails?"

I could have spared myself the jest; he gave it no attention, but seated himself in the chair that he had left and resumed the interrupted monologue as if nothing had occurred:

"Doubtless you do not hold with those (I need not name them to a man of your reading) who have taught that all matter is sentient, that every atom is a living, feeling, conscious being.

I do. There is no such thing as dead, inert matter: it is all alive; all instinct with force, actual and potential; all sensitive to the same forces in its environment and susceptible to the contagion of higher and subtler ones residing in such superior organisms as it may be brought into relation with, as those of man when he is fashioning it into an instrument of his will. It absorbs something of his intelligence and purpose—more of them in proportion to the complexity of the resulting machine and that of its work.

"Do you happen to recall Herbert Spencer's definition of 'Life'? I read it thirty years ago. He may have altered it afterward, for anything I know, but in all that time I have been unable to think of a single word that could profitably be changed or added or removed. It seems to me not only the best definition, but the only possible one.

" 'Life,' he says, 'is a definite combination of heterogeneous changes, both simultaneous and successive, in correspondence with external coexistences and sequences.' "

"That defines the phenomenon," I said, "but gives no hint of its cause."

"That," he replied, "is all that any definition can do. As Mill points out, we know nothing of cause except as an antecedent —nothing of effect except as a consequent. Of certain phenomena, one never occurs without another, which is dissimilar: the first in point of time we call cause, the second, effect. One who had many times seen a rabbit pursued by a dog, and had never seen rabbits and dogs otherwise, would think the rabbit the cause of the dog.

"But I fear," he added, laughing naturally enough, "that my rabbit is leading me a long way from the track of my legitimate quarry: I'm indulging in the pleasure of the chase for its own sake. What I want you to observe is that in Herbert Spencer's definition of 'life' the activity of a machine is included—there is nothing in the definition that is not applicable to it. According to this sharpest of observers and deepest of thinkers, if a man during his period of activity is alive, so is a machine when in operation. As an inventor and constructor of machines I know that to be true."

Moxon was silent for a long time, gazing absently into the fire. It was growing late and I thought it time to be going, but somehow I did not like the notion of leaving him in that isolated house, all alone except for the presence of some person of whose nature my conjectures could go no further than that it was unfriendly, perhaps malign. Leaning toward him and looking earnestly into his eyes while making a motion with my hand through the door of his workshop, I said:

"Moxon, whom have you in there?"

Somewhat to my surprise he laughed lightly and answered without hesitation:

"Nobody; the incident that you have in mind was caused by my folly in leaving a machine in action with nothing to act upon, while I undertook the interminable task of enlightening your understanding. Do you happen to know that Consciousness is the creature of Rhythm?"

"O bother them both!" I replied, rising and laying hold of my overcoat. "I'm going to wish you good night; and I'll add the hope that the machine which you inadvertently left in action will have her gloves on the next time you think it needful to stop her."

Without waiting to observe the effect of my shot I left the house.

Rain was falling, and the darkness was intense. In the sky beyond the crest of a hill toward which I groped my way along precarious plank sidewalks and across miry, unpaved streets I could see the faint glow of the city's lights, but behind me nothing was visible but a single window of Moxon's house. It glowed with what seemed to me a mysterious and fateful meaning. I knew it was an uncurtained aperture in my friend's "machine-shop," and I had little doubt that he had resumed the studies interrupted by his duties as my instructor in mechanical consciousness and the fatherhood of Rhythm. Odd, and in some degree humorous, as his convictions seemed to me at that time, I could not wholly divest myself of the feeling that they had some tragic relation to his life and character— perhaps to his destiny—although I no longer entertained the notion that they were the vagaries of a disordered mind. Whatever might be thought of his views, his exposition of them was too logical for that. Over and over, his last words came back to me: "Consciousness is the creature of Rhythm." Bald and terse as the statement was, I now found it infinitely alluring. At each recurrence it broadened in meaning and deepened in suggestion. Why, here, (I thought) is something upon which to found a philosophy. If consciousness is the product of rhythm all things *are* conscious, for all have motion, and all motion is rhythmic. I wondered if Moxon knew the significance and breadth of his thought—the scope of this momentous generalization; or had he arrived at his philosophic faith by the tortuous and uncertain road of observation?

That faith was then new to me, and all Moxon's expounding had failed to make me a convert; but now it seemed as if a great light shone about me, like that which fell upon Saul of Tarsus; and out there in the storm and darkness and solitude I experienced what Lewes calls "The endless variety and excitement of philosophic thought." I exulted in a new sense of knowledge, a new pride of reason. My feet seemed hardly to touch the earth; it was as if I were uplifted and borne through the air by invisible wings.

Yielding to an impulse to seek further light from him whom I now recognized as my master and guide, I had unconsciously turned about, and almost before I was aware of having done so found myself again at Moxon's door. I was drenched with rain, but felt no discomfort. Unable in my excitement to find the doorbell I instinctively tried the knob. It turned and, entering, I mounted the stairs to the room that I had so recently left. All was dark and silent; Moxon, as I had supposed, was in the adjoining room—the "machine-shop." Groping along the wall until I found the communicating door I knocked loudly several times, but got no response, which I attributed to the uproar outside, for the wind was blowing a gale and dashing the rain against the thin walls in sheets. The drumming upon the shingle roof spanning the unceiled room was loud and incessant.

I had never been invited into the machine-shop—had, indeed, been denied admittance, as had all others, with one exception, a skilled metal worker, of whom no one knew anything except that his name was Haley and his habit silence. But in my spiritual exaltation, discretion and civility were alike forgotten and I opened the door. What I saw took all philosophical speculation out of me in short order.

Moxon sat facing me at the farther side of a small table upon which a single candle made all the light that was in the room.

Opposite him, his back toward me, sat another person. On the table between the two was a chessboard; the men were playing. I knew little of chess, but as only a few pieces were on the board it was obvious that the game was near its close. Moxon was intensely interested—not so much, it seemed to me, in the game as in his antagonist, upon whom he had fixed so intent a look that, standing though I did directly in the line of his vision, I was altogether unobserved. His face was ghastly white, and his eyes glittered like diamonds. Of his antagonist I had only a back view, but that was sufficient; I should not have cared to see his face.

He was apparently not more than five feet in height, with proportions suggesting those of a gorilla—a tremendous breadth of shoulders, thick, short neck and broad, squat head, which had a tangled growth of black hair and was topped with a crimson fez. A tunic of the same color, belted tightly to the waist, reached the seat—apparently a box—upon which he sat; his legs and feet were not seen. His left forearm appeared to rest in his lap; he moved his pieces with his right hand, which seemed disproportionately long.

I had shrunk back and now stood a little to one side of the doorway and in shadow. If Moxon had looked farther than the face of his opponent he could have observed nothing now, except that the door was open. Something forbade me either to enter or to retire, a feeling—I know not how it came—that I was in the presence of an imminent tragedy and might serve my friend by remaining. With a scarcely conscious rebellion against the indelicacy of the act I remained.

The play was rapid. Moxon hardly glanced at the board before making his moves, and to my unskilled eye seemed to move the piece most convenient to his hand, his motions in doing so being quick, nervous and lacking in precision. The response of his antagonist, while equally prompt in the inception, was made with a slow, uniform, mechanical and, I thought, somewhat theatrical movement of the arm, that was a sore trial to my patience. There was something unearthly about it all, and I caught myself shuddering. But I was wet and cold.

Two or three times after moving a piece the stranger slightly inclined his head, and each time I observed that Moxon shifted his king. All at once the thought came to me that the man was dumb. And then that he was a machine—an automaton chess-player! Then I remembered that Moxon had once spoken to me of having invented such a piece of mechanism, though I did not understand that it had actually been constructed. Was all his talk about the consciousness and intelligence of machines merely a prelude to eventual exhibition of this device—only a trick to intensify the effect of its mechanical action upon me in my ignorance of its secret?

A fine end, this, of all my intellectual transports—my "endless variety and excitement of philosophic thought!" I was about to retire in disgust when something occurred to hold my curiosity. I observed a shrug of the thing's great shoulders, as if it were irritated: and so natural was this—so entirely human—that in my new view of the matter it startled me. Nor was that all, for a moment later it struck the table sharply with its clenched hand. At that gesture Moxon seemed even more startled than I: he pushed his chair a little backward, as in alarm.

Presently Moxon, whose play it was, raised his hand high above the board, pounced upon one of his pieces like a sparrow-hawk and with the exclamation "checkmate!" rose quickly to his feet and stepped behind his chair. The automaton sat motionless.

The wind had now gone down, but I heard, at lessening intervals and progressively louder, the rumble and roll of thunder. In the pauses between I now became conscious of a low humming or buzzing which, like the thunder, grew momentarily louder and more distinct. It seemed to come from the body of the automaton, and was unmistakably a whirring of wheels. It gave me the impression of a disordered mechanism which had escaped the repressive and regulating action of some controlling part—an effect such as might be expected if a pawl should be jostled from the teeth of a ratchet-wheel. But before I had time for much conjecture as to its nature my attention was taken by the strange motions of the automaton itself. A slight but continuous convulsion appeared to have possession of it. In body and head it shook like a man with palsy or an ague chill, and the motion augmented every moment until the entire figure was in violent agitation. Suddenly it sprang to its feet and with a movement almost too quick for the eye to follow shot forward across table and chair, with both arms thrust forth to their full length—the posture and lunge of a diver. Moxon tried to throw himself backward out of reach, but he was too late: I saw the horrible thing's hands close upon his throat, his own clutch its wrists. Then the table was over-turned, the candle thrown to the floor and extinguished, and all was black dark. But the noise of the struggle was dreadfully distinct, and most terrible of all were the raucous, squawking sounds made by the strangled man's efforts to breathe. Guided by the infernal hubbub, I sprang to the rescue of my friend, but had hardly taken a stride in the darkness when the whole room blazed with a blinding white light that burned into my brain and heart and memory a vivid picture of the combatants on the floor, Moxon underneath, his throat still in the clutch of those iron hands, his head forced backward, his eyes pro-truding, his mouth wide open and his tongue thrust out; and —horrible contrast!—upon the painted face of his assassin an expression of tranquil and profound thought, as in the solu-tion of a problem in chess! This I observed, then all was black-ness and silence.

Three days later I recovered consciousness in a hospital. As the memory of that tragic night slowly evolved in my ailing brain I recognized in my attendant Moxon's confidential work-man, Haley. Responding to a look he approached, smiling.

"Tell me about it," I managed to say, faintly—"all about it."

"Certainly," he said; "you were carried unconscious from a burning house—Moxon's. Nobody knows how you came to be there. You may have to do a little explaining. The origin of the fire is a bit mysterious, too. My own notion is that the house was struck by lightning."

"And Moxon?"

"Buried yesterday—what was left of him."

Apparently this reticent person could unfold himself on oc-casion. When imparting shocking intelligence to the sick he was affable enough. After some moments of the keenest mental suffering I ventured to ask another question:

"Who rescued me?"

"Well, if that interests you—I did."

"Thank you, Mr. Haley, and may God bless you for it. Did

you rescue, also, that charming product of your skill, the automaton chess-player that murdered its inventor?"

The man was silent a long time, looking away from me. Presently he turned and gravely said:

"Do you know that?"

"I do," I replied; "I saw it done."

That was many years ago. If asked to-day I should answer less confidently.

A Tough Tussle

ONE night in the autumn of 1861 a man sat alone in the heart of a forest in western Virginia. The region was one of the wildest on the continent—the Cheat Mountain country. There was no lack of people close at hand, however; within a mile of where the man sat was the now silent camp of a whole Federal brigade. Somewhere about—it might be still nearer— was a force of the enemy, the numbers unknown. It was this uncertainty as to its numbers and position that accounted for the man's presence in that lonely spot; he was a young officer of a Federal infantry regiment and his business there was to guard his sleeping comrades in the camp against a surprise. He was in command of a detachment of men constituting a picket-guard. These men he had stationed just at nightfall in an irregular line, determined by the nature of the ground, several hundred yards in front of where he now sat. The line ran through the forest, among the rocks and laurel thickets, the men fifteen or twenty paces apart, all in concealment and under injunction of strict silence and unremitting vigilance. In four hours, if nothing occurred, they would be relieved by a fresh detachment from the reserve now resting in care of its captain some distance away to the left and rear. Before stationing his men the young officer of whom we are writing had pointed out to his two sergeants the spot at which he would be found if it should be necessary to consult him, or if his presence at the front line should be required.

It was a quiet enough spot—the fork of an old wood-road, on the two branches of which, prolonging themselves deviously forward in the dim moonlight, the sergeants were themselves stationed, a few paces in rear of the line. If driven sharply back by a sudden onset of the enemy—and pickets are not expected to make a stand after firing—the men would come into the converging roads and naturally following them to their point of intersection could be rallied and "formed." In his small way the author of these dispositions was something of a strategist; if Napoleon had planned as intelligently at Waterloo he would have won that memorable battle and been over-thrown later.

Second-Lieutenant Brainerd Byring was a brave and efficient officer, young and comparatively inexperienced as he was in the business of killing his fellow-men. He had enlisted in the very first days of the war as a private, with no military knowl-edge whatever, had been made first-sergeant of his company on account of his education and engaging manner, and had been lucky enough to lose his captain by a Confederate bullet; in the resulting promotions he had gained a commission. He had been in several engagements, such as they were—at Philippi, Rich Mountain, Carrick's Ford and Greenbrier—and had borne himself with such gallantry as not to attract the at-tention of his superior officers. The exhilaration of battle was agreeable to him, but the sight of the dead, with their clay faces, blank eyes and stiff bodies, which when not unnaturally shrunken were unnaturally swollen, had always intolerably af-fected him. He felt toward them a kind of reasonless antipathy that was something more than the physical and spiritual re-pugnance common to us all. Doubtless this feeling was due to his unusually acute sensibilities—his keen sense of the beauti-ful, which these hideous things outraged. Whatever may have been the cause, he could not look upon a dead body without a loathing which had in it an element of resentment. What others have respected as the dignity of death had to him no existence—was altogether unthinkable. Death was a thing to be hated. It was not picturesque, it had no tender and solemn side—a dismal thing, hideous in all its manifestations and sug-gestions. Lieutenant Byring was a braver man than anybody knew, for nobody knew his horror of that which he was ever ready to incur.

Having posted his men, instructed his sergeants and retired to his station, he seated himself on a log, and with senses all alert began his vigil. For greater ease he loosened his sword-belt and taking his heavy revolver from his holster laid it on the log beside him. He felt very comfortable, though he hardly gave the fact a thought, so intently did he listen for any sound from the front which might have a menacing significance—a shout, a shot, or the footfall of one of his sergeants coming to apprise him of something worth knowing. From the vast, invisible ocean of moonlight overhead fell, here and there, a slender, broken stream that seemed to plash against the intercepting branches and trickle to earth, forming small white pools among the clumps of laurel. But these leaks were few and served only to accentuate the blackness of his environment, which his imagination found it easy to people with all manner of unfamiliar shapes, menacing, uncanny, or merely grotesque.

He to whom the portentous conspiracy of night and solitude and silence in the heart of a great forest is not an unknown experience needs not to be told what another world it all is—how even the most commonplace and familiar objects take on another character. The trees group themselves differently; they draw closer together, as if in fear. The very silence has another quality than the silence of the day. And it is full of half-heard whispers—whispers that startle—ghosts of sounds long dead. There are living sounds, too, such as are never heard under other conditions: notes of strange night-birds, the cries of small animals in sudden encounters with stealthy foes or in their dreams, a rustling in the dead leaves—it may be the leap of a wood-rat, it may be the footfall of a panther. What caused the breaking of that twig?—what the low, alarmed twittering in that bushful of birds? There are sounds without a name, forms without substance, translations in space of objects which have not been seen to move, movements wherein nothing is observed to change its place. Ah, children of the sunlight and the gaslight, how little you know of the world in which you live!

Surrounded at a little distance by armed and watchful friends, Byring felt utterly alone. Yielding himself to the solemn and mysterious spirit of the time and place, he had forgotten the nature of his connection with the visible and audible aspects and phases of the night. The forest was boundless; men and the habitations of men did not exist. The universe was one primeval mystery of darkness, without form and void, himself the sole, dumb questioner of its eternal secret. Absorbed in thoughts born of this mood, he suffered the time to slip away unnoted. Meantime the infrequent patches of white light lying amongst the tree-trunks had undergone changes of size, form and place. In one of them near by, just at the roadside, his eye fell upon an object that he had not previously observed. It was almost before his face as he sat; he could have sworn that it had not before been there. It was partly covered in shadow, but he could see that it was a human figure. Instinctively he adjusted the clasp of his sword-belt and laid hold of his pistol—again he was in a world of war, by occupation an assassin.

The figure did not move. Rising, pistol in hand, he approached. The figure lay upon its back, its upper part in shadow, but standing above it and looking down upon the face, he saw that it was a dead body. He shuddered and turned from it with a feeling of sickness and disgust, resumed his seat upon the log, and forgetting military prudence struck a match and lit a cigar. In the sudden blackness that followed the extinction of the flame he felt a sense of relief; he could no longer see the object of his aversion. Nevertheless, he kept his eyes set in that direction until it appeared again with growing distinctness. It seemed to have moved a trifle nearer.

"Damn the thing!" he muttered. "What does it want?"

It did not appear to be in need of anything but a soul.

Byring turned away his eyes and began humming a tune, but he broke off in the middle of a bar and looked at the dead body. Its presence annoyed him, though he could hardly have had a quieter neighbor. He was conscious, too, of a vague, indefinable feeling that was new to him. It was not fear, but rather a sense of the supernatural—in which he did not at all believe.

"I have inherited it," he said to himself. "I suppose it will require a thousand ages—perhaps ten thousand—for humanity to outgrow this feeling. Where and when did it originate? Away back, probably, in what is called the cradle of the human race—the plains of Central Asia. What we inherit as a superstition our barbarous ancestors must have held as a reasonable conviction. Doubtless they believed themselves justified by facts whose nature we cannot even conjecture in thinking a dead body a malign thing endowed with some strange power of mischief, with perhaps a will and a purpose to exert it. Possibly they had some awful form of religion of which that was one of the chief doctrines, sedulously taught by their priesthood, as ours teach the immortality of the soul. As the Aryans moved slowly on, to and through the Caucasus passes, and spread over Europe, new conditions of life must have resulted in the formulation of new religions. The old belief in the malevolence of the dead body was lost from the creeds and even perished from tradition, but it left its heritage of terror, which is transmitted from generation to generation—is as much a part of us as are our blood and bones."

In following out his thought he had forgotten that which suggested it; but now his eye fell again upon the corpse. The shadow had now altogether uncovered it. He saw the sharp profile, the chin in the air, the whole face, ghastly white in the moonlight. The clothing was gray, the uniform of a Confederate soldier. The coat and waistcoat, unbuttoned, had fallen away on each side, exposing the white shirt. The chest seemed unnaturally prominent, but the abdomen had sunk in, leaving a sharp projection at the line of the lower ribs. The arms were extended, the left knee was thrust upward. The whole posture impressed Byring as having been studied with a view to the horrible.

"Bah!" he exclaimed; "he was an actor—he knows how to be dead."

He drew away his eyes, directing them resolutely along one of the roads leading to the front, and resumed his philosophizing where he had left off.

"It may be that our Central Asian ancestors had not the custom of burial. In that case it is easy to understand their fear of the dead, who really were a menace and an evil. They bred pestilences. Children were taught to avoid the places where they lay, and to run away if by inadvertence they came near a corpse. I think, indeed, I'd better go away from this chap."

He half rose to do so, then remembered that he had told his men in front and the officer in the rear who was to relieve him that he could at any time be found at that spot. It was a matter of pride, too. If he abandoned his post he feared they would think he feared the corpse. He was no coward and he was unwilling to incur anybody's ridicule. So he again seated himself, and to prove his courage looked boldly at the body. The right arm—the one farthest from him—was now in shadow. He could barely see the hand which, he had before observed, lay at the root of a clump of laurel. There had been no change, a fact which gave him a certain comfort, he could not have said why. He did not at once remove his eyes; that which we do not wish to see has a strange fascination, sometimes irresistible. Of the woman who covers her eyes with her hands and looks between the fingers let it be said that the wits have dealt with her not altogether justly.

Byring suddenly became conscious of a pain in his right hand. He withdrew his eyes from his enemy and looked at it. He was grasping the hilt of his drawn sword so tightly that it hurt him. He observed, too, that he was leaning forward in a strained attitude—crouching like a gladiator ready to spring at the throat of an antagonist. His teeth were clenched and he was breathing hard. This matter was soon set right, and as his muscles relaxed and he drew a long breath he felt keenly enough the ludicrousness of the incident. It affected him to laughter. Heavens! what sound was that? what mindless devil was uttering an unholy glee in mockery of human merriment? He sprang to his feet and looked about him, not recognizing his own laugh.

He could no longer conceal from himself the horrible fact of his cowardice; he was thoroughly frightened! He would have run from the spot, but his legs refused their office; they gave way beneath him and he sat again upon the log, violently trembling. His face was wet, his whole body bathed in a chill perspiration. He could not even cry out. Distinctly he heard behind him a stealthy tread, as of some wild animal, and dared not look over his shoulder. Had the soulless living joined forces with the soulless dead?—was it an animal? Ah, if he could but be assured of that! But by no effort of will could he now unfix his gaze from the face of the dead man.

I repeat that Lieutenant Byring was a brave and intelligent man. But what would you have? Shall a man cope, single-handed, with so monstrous an alliance as that of night and solitude and silence and the dead,—while an incalculable host of his own ancestors shriek into the ear of his spirit their coward counsel, sing their doleful death-songs in his heart, and disarm his very blood of all its iron? The odds are too great—courage was not made for so rough use as that.

One sole conviction now had the man in possession: that the body had moved. It lay nearer to the edge of its plot of light—there could be no doubt of it. It had also moved its arms, for, look, they are both in the shadow! A breath of cold air struck Byring full in the face; the boughs of trees above him stirred and moaned. A strongly defined shadow passed across the face of the dead, left it luminous, passed back upon it and left it half obscured. The horrible thing was visibly moving! At that moment a single shot rang out upon the picket-line—a lonelier and louder, though more distant, shot than ever had been heard by mortal ear! It broke the spell of that enchanted man; it slew the silence and the solitude, dispersed the hindering host from Central Asia and released his modern manhood. With a cry like that of some great bird pouncing upon its prey he sprang forward, hot-hearted for action!

Shot after shot now came from the front. There were shoutings and confusion, hoof-beats and desultory cheers. Away to the rear, in the sleeping camp, were a singing of bugles and grumble of drums. Pushing through the thickets on either side the roads came the Federal pickets, in full retreat, firing backward at random as they ran. A straggling group that had followed back one of the roads, as instructed, suddenly sprang away into the bushes as half a hundred horsemen thundered by them, striking wildly with their sabres as they passed. At headlong speed these mounted madmen shot past the spot where Byring had sat, and vanished round an angle of the road, shouting and firing their pistols. A moment later there was a roar of musketry, followed by dropping shots—they had encountered the reserve-guard in line; and back they came in dire confusion, with here and there an empty saddle and many a maddened horse, bullet-stung, snorting and plunging with pain. It was all over—"an affair of out-posts."

The line was reëstablished with fresh men, the roll called, the stragglers were re-formed. The Federal commander with a part of his staff, imperfectly clad, appeared upon the scene, asked a few questions, looked exceedingly wise and retired. After standing at arms for an hour the brigade in camp "swore a prayer or two" and went to bed.

Early the next morning a fatigue-party, commanded by a captain and accompanied by a surgeon, searched the ground for dead and wounded. At the fork of the road, a little to one side, they found two bodies lying close together—that of a

Federal officer and that of a Confederate private. The officer had died of a sword-thrust through the heart, but not, apparently, until he had inflicted upon his enemy no fewer than five dreadful wounds. The dead officer lay on his face in a pool of blood, the weapon still in his breast. They turned him on his back and the surgeon removed it.

"Gad!" said the captain—"It is Byring!"—adding, with a glance at the other, "They had a tough tussle."

The surgeon was examining the sword. It was that of a line officer of Federal infantry—exactly like the one worn by the captain. It was, in fact, Byring's own. The only other weapon discovered was an undischarged revolver in the dead officer's belt.

The surgeon laid down the sword and approached the other body. It was frightfully gashed and stabbed, but there was no blood. He took hold of the left foot and tried to straighten the leg. In the effort the body was displaced. The dead do not wish to be moved—it protested with a faint, sickening odor. Where it had lain were a few maggots, manifesting an imbecile activity.

The surgeon looked at the captain. The captain looked at the surgeon.

One of Twins

A LETTER FOUND AMONG THE PAPERS
OF THE LATE MORTIMER BARR

YOU ask me if in my experience as one of a pair of twins I
ever observed anything unaccountable by the natural laws
with which we have acquaintance. As to that you shall judge;
perhaps we have not all acquaintance with the same natural
laws. You may know some that I do not, and what is to me
unaccountable may be very clear to you.

You knew my brother John—that is, you knew him when
you knew that I was not present; but neither you nor, I believe,
any human being could distinguish between him and me if we
chose to seem alike. Our parents could not; ours is the only
instance of which I have any knowledge of so close resemblance
as that. I speak of my brother John, but I am not at all sure
that his name was not Henry and mine John. We were regularly
christened, but afterward, in the very act of tattooing us with
small distinguishing marks, the operator lost his reckoning;
and although I bear upon my forearm a small "H" and he bore
a "J," it is by no means certain that the letters ought not to
have been transposed. During our boyhood our parents tried
to distinguish us more obviously by our clothing and other
simple devices, but we would so frequently exchange suits and
otherwise circumvent the enemy that they abandoned all such
ineffectual attempts, and during all the years that we lived together at home everybody recognized the difficulty of the situation and made the best of it by calling us both "Jehnry."
I have often wondered at my father's forbearance in not brand-
ing us conspicuously upon our unworthy brows, but as we
were tolerably good boys and used our power of embarrassment and annoyance with commendable moderation, we escaped the iron. My father was, in fact, a singularly good-natured
man, and I think quietly enjoyed nature's practical joke.

Soon after we had come to California, and settled at San
Jose (where the only good fortune that awaited us was our
meeting with so kind a friend as you) the family, as you know,

was broken up by the death of both my parents in the same week. My father died insolvent and the homestead was sacrificed to pay his debts. My sisters returned to relatives in the East, but owing to your kindness John and I, then twenty-two years of age, obtained employment in San Francisco, in different quarters of the town. Circumstances did not permit us to live together, and we saw each other infrequently, sometimes not oftener than once a week. As we had few acquaintances in common, the fact of our extraordinary likeness was little known. I come now to the matter of your inquiry.

One day soon after we had come to this city I was walking down Market street late in the afternoon, when I was accosted by a well-dressed man of middle age, who after greeting me cordially said: "Stevens, I know, of course, that you do not go out much, but I have told my wife about you, and she would be glad to see you at the house. I have a notion, too, that my girls are worth knowing. Suppose you come out to-morrow at six and dine with us, *en famille*; and then if the ladies can't amuse you afterward I'll stand in with a few games of billiards."

This was said with so bright a smile and so engaging a manner that I had not the heart to refuse, and although I had never seen the man in my life I promptly replied: "You are very good, sir, and it will give me great pleasure to accept the invitation. Please present my compliments to Mrs. Margovan and ask her to expect me."

With a shake of the hand and a pleasant parting word the man passed on. That he had mistaken me for my brother was plain enough. That was an error to which I was accustomed and which it was not my habit to rectify unless the matter seemed important. But how had I known that this man's name was Margovan? It certainly is not a name that one would apply to a man at random, with a probability that it would be right. In point of fact, the name was as strange to me as the man.

The next morning I hastened to where my brother was employed and met him coming out of the office with a number of bills that he was to collect. I told him how I had "committed" him and added that if he didn't care to keep the engagement I should be delighted to continue the impersonation.

"That's queer," he said thoughtfully. "Margovan is the only

man in the office here whom I know well and like. When he came in this morning and we had passed the usual greetings some singular impulse prompted me to say: 'Oh, I beg your pardon, Mr. Margovan, but I neglected to ask your address.' I got the address, but what under the sun I was to do with it, I did not know until now. It's good of you to offer to take the consequence of your impudence, but I'll eat that dinner myself, if you please."

He ate a number of dinners at the same place—more than were good for him, I may add without disparaging their quality; for he fell in love with Miss Margovan, proposed marriage to her and was heartlessly accepted.

Several weeks after I had been informed of the engagement, but before it had been convenient for me to make the acquaintance of the young woman and her family, I met one day on Kearney street a handsome but somewhat dissipated-looking man whom something prompted me to follow and watch, which I did without any scruple whatever. He turned up Geary street and followed it until he came to Union square. There he looked at his watch, then entered the square. He loitered about the paths for some time, evidently waiting for someone. Presently he was joined by a fashionably dressed and beautiful young woman and the two walked away up Stockton street, I following. I now felt the necessity of extreme caution, for although the girl was a stranger it seemed to me that she would recognize me at a glance. They made several turns from one street to another and finally, after both had taken a hasty look all about—which I narrowly evaded by stepping into a doorway—they entered a house of which I do not care to state the location. Its location was better than its character.

I protest that my action in playing the spy upon these two strangers was without assignable motive. It was one of which I might or might not be ashamed, according to my estimate of the character of the person finding it out. As an essential part of a narrative educed by your question it is related here without hesitancy or shame.

A week later John took me to the house of his prospective father-in-law, and in Miss Margovan, as you have already surmised, but to my profound astonishment, I recognized the heroine of that discreditable adventure. A gloriously beautiful heroine of a discreditable adventure I must in justice admit that she was; but that fact has only this importance: her beauty was such a surprise to me that it cast a doubt upon her identity with the young woman I had seen before; how could the marvelous fascination of her face have failed to strike me at that time? But no—there was no possibility of error; the difference was due to costume, light and general surroundings.

John and I passed the evening at the house, enduring, with the fortitude of long experience, such delicate enough banter as our likeness naturally suggested. When the young lady and I were left alone for a few minutes I looked her squarely in the face and said with sudden gravity:

"You, too, Miss Margovan, have a double: I saw her last Tuesday afternoon in Union square."

She trained her great gray eyes upon me for a moment, but her glance was a trifle less steady than my own and she withdrew it, fixing it on the tip of her shoe.

"Was she very like me?" she asked, with an indifference which I thought a little overdone.

"So like," said I, "that I greatly admired her, and being unwilling to lose sight of her I confess that I followed her until —Miss Margovan, are you sure that you understand?"

She was now pale, but entirely calm. She again raised her eyes to mine, with a look that did not falter.

"What do you wish me to do?" she asked. "You need not fear to name your terms. I accept them."

It was plain, even in the brief time given me for reflection, that in dealing with this girl ordinary methods would not do, and ordinary exactions were needless.

"Miss Margovan," I said, doubtless with something of the compassion in my voice that I had in my heart, "it is impossible not to think you the victim of some horrible compulsion. Rather than impose new embarrassments upon you I would prefer to aid you to regain your freedom."

She shook her head, sadly and hopelessly, and I continued, with agitation:

"Your beauty unnerves me. I am disarmed by your frankness and your distress. If you are free to act upon conscience you will, I believe, do what you conceive to be best; if you are not —well, Heaven help us all! You have nothing to fear from me but such opposition to this marriage as I can try to justify on—on other grounds."

These were not my exact words, but that was the sense of them, as nearly as my sudden and conflicting emotions permitted me to express it. I rose and left her without another look at her, met the others as they reentered the room and said, as calmly as I could: "I have been bidding Miss Margovan good evening; it is later than I thought."

John decided to go with me. In the street he asked if I had observed anything singular in Julia's manner.

"I thought her ill," I replied; "that is why I left." Nothing more was said.

The next evening I came late to my lodgings. The events of the previous evening had made me nervous and ill; I had tried to cure myself and attain to clear thinking by walking in the open air, but I was oppressed with a horrible presentiment of evil—a presentiment which I could not formulate. It was a chill, foggy night; my clothing and hair were damp and I shook with cold. In my dressing-gown and slippers before a blazing grate of coals I was even more uncomfortable. I no longer shivered but shuddered—there is a difference. The dread of some impending calamity was so strong and dispiriting that I tried to drive it away by inviting a real sorrow—tried to dispel the conception of a terrible future by substituting the memory of a painful past. I recalled the death of my parents and endeavored to fix my mind upon the last sad scenes at their bedsides and their graves. It all seemed vague and unreal, as having occurred ages ago and to another person. Suddenly, striking through my thought and parting it as a tense cord is parted by the stroke of steel—I can think of no other comparison—I heard a sharp cry as of one in mortal agony! The voice was that of my brother and seemed to come from the street outside my window. I sprang to the window and threw it open. A street lamp directly opposite threw a wan and ghastly light upon the wet pavement and the fronts of the houses. A single policeman, with upturned collar, was leaning against a gatepost, quietly smoking a cigar. No one else was in sight. I closed the window and pulled down the shade, seated myself before the fire and tried to fix my mind upon my surroundings. By way of assisting, by performance of some familiar act, I looked at my watch; it marked half-past eleven. Again I heard that awful cry! It seemed in the room—at my side. I was frightened and for some moments had not the power to move. A few minutes later—I have no recollection of the intermediate time—I found myself hurrying along an unfamiliar street as fast as I could walk. I did not know where I was, nor whither I was going, but presently sprang up the steps of a house before which were two or three carriages and in which were moving lights and a subdued confusion of voices. It was the house of Mr. Margovan.

You know, good friend, what had occurred there. In one chamber lay Julia Margovan, hours dead by poison; in another John Stevens, bleeding from a pistol wound in the chest, inflicted by his own hand. As I burst into the room, pushed aside the physicians and laid my hand upon his forehead he unclosed his eyes, stared blankly, closed them slowly and died without a sign.

I knew no more until six weeks afterward, when I had been nursed back to life by your own saintly wife in your own beautiful home. All of that you know, but what you do not know is this—which, however, has no bearing upon the subject of your psychological researches—at least not upon that branch of them in which, with a delicacy and consideration all your own, you have asked for less assistance than I think I have given you:

One moonlight night several years afterward I was passing through Union square. The hour was late and the square deserted. Certain memories of the past naturally came into my mind as I came to the spot where I had once witnessed that fateful assignation, and with that unaccountable perversity which prompts us to dwell upon thoughts of the most painful character I seated myself upon one of the benches to indulge them. A man entered the square and came along the walk toward me. His hands were clasped behind him, his head was bowed; he seemed to observe nothing. As he approached the shadow in which I sat I recognized him as the man whom I had seen meet Julia Margovan years before at that spot. But he was terribly altered—gray, worn and haggard. Dissipation and vice were in evidence in every look; illness was no less apparent. His clothing was in disorder, his hair fell across his forehead in a derangement which was at once uncanny and picturesque. He looked fitter for restraint than liberty—the restraint of a hospital.

With no defined purpose I rose and confronted him. He raised his head and looked me full in the face. I have no words to describe the ghastly change that came over his own; it was a look of unspeakable terror—he thought himself eye to eye with a ghost. But he was a courageous man. "Damn you, John Stevens!" he cried, and lifting his trembling arm he dashed his fist feebly at my face and fell headlong upon the gravel as I walked away.

Somebody found him there, stone-dead. Nothing more is known of him, not even his name. To know of a man that he is dead should be enough.

The Haunted Valley

HOW TREES ARE FELLED IN CHINA

A HALF-MILE north from Jo. Dunfer's, on the road from Hutton's to Mexican Hill, the highway dips into a sunless ravine which opens out on either hand in a half-confidential manner, as if it had a secret to impart at some more convenient season. I never used to ride through it without looking first to the one side and then to the other, to see if the time had arrived for the revelation. If I saw nothing—and I never did see anything—there was no feeling of disappointment, for I knew the disclosure was merely withheld temporarily for some good reason which I had no right to question. That I should one day be taken into full confidence I no more doubted than I doubted the existence of Jo. Dunfer himself, through whose premises the ravine ran.

It was said that Jo. had once undertaken to erect a cabin in some remote part of it, but for some reason had abandoned the enterprise and constructed his present hermaphrodite habitation, half residence and half groggery, at the roadside, upon an extreme corner of his estate; as far away as possible, as if on purpose to show how radically he had changed his mind.

This Jo. Dunfer—or, as he was familiarly known in the neighborhood, Whisky Jo.—was a very important personage in those parts. He was apparently about forty years of age, a long, shock-headed fellow, with a corded face, a gnarled arm and a knotty hand like a bunch of prison-keys. He was a hairy man, with a stoop in his walk, like that of one who is about to spring upon something and rend it.

Next to the peculiarity to which he owed his local appellation, Mr. Dunfer's most obvious characteristic was a deep-seated antipathy to the Chinese. I saw him once in a towering rage because one of his herdsmen had permitted a travel-heated Asian to slake his thirst at the horse-trough in front of the saloon end of Jo.'s establishment. I ventured faintly to remonstrate with Jo. for his unchristian spirit, but he merely explained that there was nothing about Chinamen in the New Testament, and strode away to wreak his displeasure upon his dog, which also, I suppose, the inspired scribes had overlooked.

Some days afterward, finding him sitting alone in his bar-room, I cautiously approached the subject, when, greatly to my relief, the habitual austerity of his expression visibly softened into something that I took for condescension.

"You young Easterners," he said, "are a mile-and-a-half too good for this country, and you don't catch on to our play. People who don't know a Chileño from a Kanaka can afford to hang out liberal ideas about Chinese immigration, but a fellow that has to fight for his bone with a lot of mongrel coolies hasn't any time for foolishness."

This long consumer, who had probably never done an honest day's-work in his life, sprung the lid of a Chinese tobacco-box and with thumb and forefinger forked out a wad like a small haycock. Holding this reinforcement within supporting distance he fired away with renewed confidence.

"They're a flight of devouring locusts, and they're going for everything green in this God blest land, if you want to know."

Here he pushed his reserve into the breach and when his gabble-gear was again disengaged resumed his uplifting discourse.

"I had one of them on this ranch five years ago, and I'll tell you about it, so that you can see the nub of this whole question. I didn't pan out particularly well those days—drank more whisky than was prescribed for me and didn't seem to care for my duty as a patriotic American citizen; so I took that pagan in, as a kind of cook. But when I got religion over at the Hill and they talked of running me for the Legislature it was given to me to see the light. But what was I to do? If I gave him the go somebody else would take him, and mightn't treat him white. *What* was I to do? What would any good Christian do, especially one new to the trade and full to the neck with the brotherhood of Man and the fatherhood of God?"

Jo. paused for a reply, with an expression of unstable satisfaction, as of one who has solved a problem by a distrusted method. Presently he rose and swallowed a glass of whisky from a full bottle on the counter, then resumed his story.

"Besides, he didn't count for much—didn't know anything and gave himself airs. They all do that. I said him nay, but he muled it through on that line while he lasted; but after turning the other cheek seventy and seven times I doctored the dice so that he didn't last forever. And I'm almighty glad I had the sand to do it."

Jo.'s gladness, which somehow did not impress me, was duly and ostentatiously celebrated at the bottle.

"About five years ago I started in to stick up a shack. That was before this one was built, and I put it in another place. I set Ah Wee and a little cuss named Gopher to cutting the timber. Of course I didn't expect Ah Wee to help much, for he had a face like a day in June and big black eyes—I guess maybe they were the damn'dest eyes in this neck o' woods."

While delivering this trenchant thrust at common sense Mr. Dunfer absently regarded a knot-hole in the thin board partition separating the bar from the living-room, as if that were one of the eyes whose size and color had incapacitated his servant for good service.

"Now you Eastern galoots won't believe anything against the yellow devils," he suddenly flamed out with an appearance of earnestness not altogether convincing, "but I tell you that Chink was the perversest scoundrel outside San Francisco. The miserable pig-tail Mongolian went to hewing away at the saplings all round the stems, like a worm o' the dust gnawing a radish. I pointed out his error as patiently as I knew how, and showed him how to cut them on two sides, so as to make them fall right; but no sooner would I turn my back on him, like this"—and he turned it on me, amplifying the illustration by taking some more liquor—"than he was at it again. It was just this way: while I looked at him, *so*"—regarding me rather unsteadily and with evident complexity of vision—"he was all right; but when I looked away, *so*"—taking a long pull at the bottle—"he defied me. Then I'd gaze at him reproachfully, *so*, and butter wouldn't have melted in his mouth."

Doubtless Mr. Dunfer honestly intended the look that he fixed upon me to be merely reproachful, but it was singularly fit to arouse the gravest apprehension in any unarmed person incurring it; and as I had lost all interest in his pointless and interminable narrative, I rose to go. Before I had fairly risen, he had again turned to the counter, and with a barely audible "so," had emptied the bottle at a gulp.

Heavens! what a yell! It was like a Titan in his last, strong agony. Jo. staggered back after emitting it, as a cannon recoils from its own thunder, and then dropped into his chair, as if he had been "knocked in the head" like a beef—his eyes drawn sidewise toward the wall, with a stare of terror. Looking in the same direction, I saw that the knot-hole in the wall had indeed become a human eye—a full, black eye, that glared into my own with an entire lack of expression more awful than the most devilish glitter. I think I must have covered my face with my hands to shut out the horrible illusion, if such it was, and Jo.'s little white man-of-all-work coming into the room broke the spell, and I walked out of the house with a sort of dazed fear that *delirium tremens* might be infectious. My horse was hitched at the watering-trough, and untying him I mounted and gave him his head, too much troubled in mind to note whither he took me.

I did not know what to think of all this, and like every one who does not know what to think I thought a great deal, and to little purpose. The only reflection that seemed at all satisfactory, was, that on the morrow I should be some miles away, with a strong probability of never returning.

A sudden coolness brought me out of my abstraction, and looking up I found myself entering the deep shadows of the ravine. The day was stifling; and this transition from the pitiless, visible heat of the parched fields to the cool gloom, heavy with pungency of cedars and vocal with twittering of the birds that had been driven to its leafy asylum, was exquisitely refreshing. I looked for my mystery, as usual, but not finding the ravine in a communicative mood, dismounted, led my sweating animal into the undergrowth, tied him securely to a tree and sat down upon a rock to meditate.

I began bravely by analyzing my pet superstition about the place. Having resolved it into its constituent elements I arranged them in convenient troops and squadrons, and collecting all the forces of my logic bore down upon them from impregnable premises with the thunder of irresistible conclusions and a great noise of chariots and general intellectual shouting. Then, when my big mental guns had overturned all opposition, and were growling almost inaudibly away on the horizon of pure speculation, the routed enemy straggled in upon their rear, massed silently into a solid phalanx, and captured me, bag and baggage. An indefinable dread came upon me. I rose to shake it off, and began threading the narrow dell by an old, grass-grown cow-path that seemed to flow along the bottom, as a substitute for the brook that Nature had neglected to provide.

The trees among which the path straggled were ordinary, well-behaved plants, a trifle perverted as to trunk and eccentric as to bough, but with nothing unearthly in their general aspect. A few loose bowlders, which had detached themselves from the sides of the depression to set up an independent existence at the bottom, had dammed up the pathway, here and there, but their stony repose had nothing in it of the stillness of death. There was a kind of death-chamber hush in the valley, it is true, and a mysterious whisper above: the wind was just fingering the tops of the trees—that was all.

I had not thought of connecting Jo. Dunfer's drunken narrative with what I now sought, and only when I came into a clear space and stumbled over the level trunks of some small trees did I have the revelation. This was the site of the abandoned "shack." The discovery was verified by noting that some of the rotting stumps were hacked all round, in a most unwoodmanlike way, while others were cut straight across, and the butt ends of the corresponding trunks had the blunt wedge-form given by the axe of a master.

The opening among the trees was not more than thirty paces across. At one side was a little knoll—a natural hillock, bare of shrubbery but covered with wild grass, and on this, standing out of the grass, the headstone of a grave!

I do not remember that I felt anything like surprise at this discovery. I viewed that lonely grave with something of the feeling that Columbus must have had when he saw the hills and headlands of the new world. Before approaching it I leisurely completed my survey of the surroundings. I was even guilty of the affectation of winding my watch at that unusual hour, and with needless care and deliberation. Then I approached my mystery.

The grave—a rather short one—was in somewhat better repair than was consistent with its obvious age and isolation, and my eyes, I dare say, widened a trifle at a clump of unmistakable

garden flowers showing evidence of recent watering. The stone
had clearly enough done duty once as a doorstep. In its front
was carved, or rather dug, an inscription. It read thus:

> AH WEE—CHINAMAN.
> Age unknown. Worked for Jo. Dunfer.
> This monument is erected by him to keep the Chink's
> memory green. Likewise as a warning to Celestials
> not to take on airs. Devil take 'em!
> She Was a Good Egg.

I cannot adequately relate my astonishment at this uncommon inscription! The meagre but sufficient identification of
the deceased; the impudent candor of confession; the brutal
anathema; the ludicrous change of sex and sentiment—all
marked this record as the work of one who must have been at
least as much demented as bereaved. I felt that any further
disclosure would be a paltry anti-climax, and with an unconscious regard for dramatic effect turned squarely about and
walked away. Nor did I return to that part of the county for
four years.

II

WHO DRIVES SANE OXEN SHOULD HIMSELF BE SANE

"Gee-up, there, old Fuddy-Duddy!"

This unique adjuration came from the lips of a queer little
man perched upon a wagonful of firewood, behind a brace of
oxen that were hauling it easily along with a simulation of
mighty effort which had evidently not imposed on their lord
and master. As that gentleman happened at the moment to be
staring me squarely in the face as I stood by the roadside it was
not altogether clear whether he was addressing me or his
beasts; nor could I say if they were named Fuddy and Duddy
and were both subjects of the imperative verb "to gee-up."
Anyhow the command produced no effect on us, and the
queer little man removed his eyes from mine long enough to
spear Fuddy and Duddy alternately with a long pole, remarking, quietly but with feeling: "Dern your skin," as if they enjoyed that integument in common. Observing that my request
for a ride took no attention, and finding myself falling slowly

astern, I placed one foot upon the inner circumference of a hind wheel and was slowly elevated to the level of the hub, whence I boarded the concern, *sans cérémonie*, and scrambling forward seated myself beside the driver—who took no notice of me until he had administered another indiscriminate castigation to his cattle, accompanied with the advice to "buckle down, you derned Incapable!" Then, the master of the outfit (or rather the former master, for I could not suppress a whimsical feeling that the entire establishment was my lawful prize) trained his big, black eyes upon me with an expression strangely, and somewhat unpleasantly, familiar, laid down his rod—which neither blossomed nor turned into a serpent, as I half expected —folded his arms, and gravely demanded, "W'at did you do to W'isky?"

My natural reply would have been that I drank it, but there was something about the query that suggested a hidden significance, and something about the man that did not invite a shallow jest. And so, having no other answer ready, I merely held my tongue, but felt as if I were resting under an imputation of guilt, and that my silence was being construed into a confession.

Just then a cold shadow fell upon my cheek, and caused me to look up. We were descending into my ravine! I can not describe the sensation that came upon me: I had not seen it since it unbosomed itself four years before, and now I felt like one to whom a friend has made some sorrowing confession of crime long past, and who has basely deserted him in consequence. The old memories of Jo. Dunfer, his fragmentary revelation, and the unsatisfying explanatory note by the headstone, came back with singular distinctness. I wondered what had become of Jo., and—I turned sharply round and asked my prisoner. He was intently watching his cattle, and without withdrawing his eyes replied:

"Gee-up, old Terrapin! He lies aside of Ah Wee up the gulch. Like to see it? They always come back to the spot—I've been expectin' you. H-woa!"

At the enunciation of the aspirate, Fuddy-Duddy, the incapable terrapin, came to a dead halt, and before the vowel had died away up the ravine had folded up all his eight legs and lain down in the dusty road, regardless of the effect upon his derned skin. The queer little man slid off his seat to the ground and started up the dell without deigning to look back to see if I was following. But I was.

It was about the same season of the year, and at near the same hour of the day, of my last visit. The jays clamored loudly, and the trees whispered darkly, as before; and I somehow traced in the two sounds a fanciful analogy to the open boastfulness of Mr. Jo. Dunfer's mouth and the mysterious reticence of his manner, and to the mingled hardihood and tenderness of his sole literary production—the epitaph. All things in the valley seemed unchanged, excepting the cow-path, which was almost wholly overgrown with weeds. When we came out into the "clearing," however, there was change enough. Among the stumps and trunks of the fallen saplings, those that had been hacked "China fashion" were no longer distinguishable from those that were cut " 'Melican way." It was as if the Old-World barbarism and the New-World civilization had reconciled their differences by the arbitration of an impartial decay —as is the way of civilizations. The knoll was there, but the Hunnish brambles had overrun and all but obliterated its effete grasses; and the patrician garden-violet had capitulated to his plebeian brother—perhaps had merely reverted to his original type. Another grave—a long, robust mound—had been made beside the first, which seemed to shrink from the comparison; and in the shadow of a new headstone the old one lay prostrate, with its marvelous inscription illegible by accumulation of leaves and soil. In point of literary merit the new was inferior to the old—was even repulsive in its terse and savage jocularity:

JO. DUNFER. DONE FOR.

I turned from it with indifference, and brushing away the leaves from the tablet of the dead pagan restored to light the mocking words which, fresh from their long neglect, seemed to have a certain pathos. My guide, too, appeared to take on an added seriousness as he read it, and I fancied that I could detect beneath his whimsical manner something of manliness, almost of dignity. But while I looked at him his former aspect, so subtly inhuman, so tantalizingly familiar, crept back into his big eyes, repellant and attractive. I resolved to make an end of the mystery if possible.

"My friend," I said, pointing to the smaller grave, "did Jo. Dunfer murder that Chinaman?"

He was leaning against a tree and looking across the open space into the top of another, or into the blue sky beyond. He neither withdrew his eyes, nor altered his posture as he slowly replied:

"No, sir; he justifiably homicided him."

"Then he really did kill him."

"Kill 'im? I should say he did, rather. Doesn't everybody know that? Didn't he stan' up before the coroner's jury and confess it? And didn't they find a verdict of 'Came to 'is death by a wholesome Christian sentiment workin' in the Caucasian breast'? An' didn't the church at the Hill turn W'isky down for it? And didn't the sovereign people elect him Justice of the Peace to get even on the gospelers? I don't know where you were brought up."

"But did Jo. do that because the Chinaman did not, or would not, learn to cut down trees like a white man?"

"Sure!—it stan's so on the record, which makes it true an' legal. My knowin' better doesn't make any difference with legal truth; it wasn't my funeral and I wasn't invited to deliver an oration. But the fact is, W'isky was jealous o' *me*"—and the little wretch actually swelled out like a turkeycock and made a pretense of adjusting an imaginary neck-tie, noting the effect in the palm of his hand, held up before him to represent a mirror.

"Jealous of *you*!" I repeated with ill-mannered astonishment.

"That's what I said. Why not?—don't I look all right?"

He assumed a mocking attitude of studied grace, and twitched the wrinkles out of his threadbare waistcoat. Then, suddenly dropping his voice to a low pitch of singular sweetness, he continued:

"W'isky thought a lot o' that Chink; nobody but me knew how 'e doted on 'im. Couldn't bear 'im out of 'is sight, the derned protoplasm! And w'en 'e came down to this clearin' one day an' found him an' me neglectin' our work—him asleep an' me grapplin a tarantula out of 'is sleeve—W'isky laid hold of my axe and let us have it, good an' hard! I dodged just then, for the spider bit me, but Ah Wee got it bad in the side an' tumbled about like anything. W'isky was just weighin' me out one w'en 'e saw the spider fastened on my finger; then 'e knew he'd made a jack ass of 'imself. He threw away the axe and got down on 'is knees alongside of Ah Wee, who gave a last little kick and opened 'is eyes—he had eyes like mine—an' puttin' up 'is hands drew down W'isky's ugly head and held it there w'ile 'e stayed. That wasn't long, for a tremblin' ran through 'im and 'e gave a bit of a moan an' beat the game."

During the progress of the story the narrator had become transfigured. The comic, or rather, the sardonic element was all out of him, and as he painted that strange scene it was with difficulty that I kept my composure. And this consummate actor had somehow so managed me that the sympathy due to his *dramatis personæ* was given to himself. I stepped forward to grasp his hand, when suddenly a broad grin danced across his face and with a light, mocking laugh he continued:

"W'en W'isky got 'is nut out o' that 'e was a sight to see! All his fine clothes—he dressed mighty blindin' those days—were spoiled everlastin'! 'Is hair was towsled and his face—what I could see of it—was whiter than the ace of lilies. 'E stared once at me, and looked away as if I didn't count; an' then there were shootin' pains chasin' one another from my bitten finger into my head, and it was Gopher to the dark. That's why I wasn't at the inquest."

"But why did you hold your tongue afterward?" I asked.

"It's that kind of tongue," he replied, and not another word would he say about it.

"After that W'isky took to drinkin' harder an' harder, and was rabider an' rabider anti-coolie, but I don't think 'e was ever particularly glad that 'e dispelled Ah Wee. He didn't put on so much dog about it w'en we were alone as w'en he had the ear of a derned Spectacular Extravaganza like you. 'E put up that headstone and gouged the inscription accordin' to his varyin' moods. It took 'im three weeks, workin' between drinks. I gouged his in one day."

"When did Jo. die?" I asked rather absently. The answer took my breath:

"Pretty soon after I looked at him through that knot-hole, w'en you had put something in his w'isky, you derned Borgia!"

Recovering somewhat from my surprise at this astounding charge, I was half-minded to throttle the audacious accuser, but was restrained by a sudden conviction that came to me in the light of a revelation. I fixed a grave look upon him and asked, as calmly as I could: "And when did you go luny?"

"Nine years ago!" he shrieked, throwing out his clenched hands—"nine years ago, w'en that big brute killed the woman who loved him better than she did me!—me who had followed 'er from San Francisco, where 'e won 'er at draw poker!—me who had watched over 'er for years w'en the scoundrel she belonged to was ashamed to acknowledge 'er and treat 'er white! —me who for her sake kept 'is cussed secret till it ate 'im up!—me who w'en you poisoned the beast fulfilled 'is last request to lay 'im alongside 'er and give 'im a stone to the head of 'im! And I've never since seen 'er grave till now, for I didn't want to meet 'im here."

"Meet him? Why, Gopher, my poor fellow, he is dead!"

"That's why I'm afraid of 'im."

I followed the little wretch back to his wagon and wrung his hand at parting. It was now nightfall, and as I stood there at the roadside in the deepening gloom, watching the blank outlines of the receding wagon, a sound was borne to me on the evening wind—a sound as of a series of vigorous thumps— and a voice came out of the night:

"Gee-up, there, you derned old Geranium."

A Jug of Sirup

THIS narrative begins with the death of its hero. Silas Deemer died on the 16th day of July, 1863, and two days later his remains were buried. As he had been personally known to every man, woman and well-grown child in the village, the funeral, as the local newspaper phrased it, "was largely attended." In accordance with a custom of the time and place, the coffin was opened at the graveside and the entire assembly of friends and neighbors filed past, taking a last look at the face of the dead. And then, before the eyes of all, Silas Deemer was put into the ground. Some of the eyes were a trifle dim, but in a general way it may be said that at that interment there was lack of neither observance nor observation; Silas was indubitably dead, and none could have pointed out any ritual delinquency that would have justified him in coming back from the grave. Yet if human testimony is good for anything (and certainly it once put an end to witchcraft in and about Salem) he came back.

I forgot to state that the death and burial of Silas Deemer occurred in the little village of Hillbrook, where he had lived for thirty-one years. He had been what is known in some parts of the Union (which is admittedly a free country) as a "merchant"; that is to say, he kept a retail shop for the sale of such things as are commonly sold in shops of that character. His honesty had never been questioned, so far as is known, and he was held in high esteem by all. The only thing that could be urged against him by the most censorious was a too close attention to business. It was not urged against him, though many another, who manifested it in no greater degree, was less leniently judged. The business to which Silas was devoted was mostly his own—that, possibly, may have made a difference.

At the time of Deemer's death nobody could recollect a single day, Sundays excepted, that he had not passed in his "store," since he had opened it more than a quarter-century before. His health having been perfect during all that time, he had been unable to discern any validity in whatever may or might have been urged to lure him astray from his counter; and it is related that once when he was summoned to the county seat as a witness in an important law case and did not attend, the lawyer who had the hardihood to move that he be "admonished" was solemnly informed that the Court regarded the proposal with "surprise." Judicial surprise being an emotion that attorneys are not commonly ambitious to arouse, the motion was hastily withdrawn and an agreement with the other side effected as to what Mr. Deemer would have said if he had been there—the other side pushing its advantage to the extreme and making the supposititious testimony distinctly damaging to the interests of its proponents. In brief, it was the general feeling in all that region that Silas Deemer was the one immobile verity of Hillbrook, and that his translation in space would precipitate some dismal public ill or strenuous calamity.

Mrs. Deemer and two grown daughters occupied the upper rooms of the building, but Silas had never been known to sleep elsewhere than on a cot behind the counter of the store. And there, quite by accident, he was found one night, dying, and passed away just before the time for taking down the shutters. Though speechless, he appeared conscious, and it was thought by those who knew him best that if the end had unfortunately been delayed beyond the usual hour for opening the store the effect upon him would have been deplorable.

Such had been Silas Deemer—such the fixity and invariety of his life and habit, that the village humorist (who had once attended college) was moved to bestow upon him the sobriquet of "Old Ibidem," and, in the first issue of the local newspaper after the death, to explain without offence that Silas had taken "a day off." It was more than a day, but from the record it appears that well within a month Mr. Deemer made it plain that he had not the leisure to be dead.

One of Hillbrook's most respected citizens was Alvan Creede, a banker. He lived in the finest house in town, kept a carriage and was a most estimable man variously. He knew something of the advantages of travel, too, having been frequently in Boston, and once, it was thought, in New York, though he modestly disclaimed that glittering distinction. The matter is mentioned here merely as a contribution to an understanding of Mr. Creede's worth, for either way it is creditable to him—to his intelligence if he had put himself, even temporarily, into contact with metropolitan culture; to his candor if he had not.

One pleasant summer evening at about the hour of ten Mr. Creede, entering at his garden gate, passed up the gravel walk, which looked very white in the moonlight, mounted the stone steps of his fine house and pausing a moment inserted his latchkey in the door. As he pushed this open he met his wife, who was crossing the passage from the parlor to the library. She greeted him pleasantly and pulling the door further back held it for him to enter. Instead he turned and, looking about his feet in front of the threshold, uttered an exclamation of surprise.

"Why!—what the devil," he said, "has become of that jug?"

"What jug, Alvan?" his wife inquired, not very sympathetically.

"A jug of maple sirup—I brought it along from the store and set it down here to open the door. What the——"

"There, there, Alvan, please don't swear again," said the lady, interrupting. Hillbrook, by the way, is not the only place in Christendom where a vestigial polytheism forbids the taking in vain of the Evil One's name.

The jug of maple sirup which the easy ways of village life had permitted Hillbrook's foremost citizen to carry home from the store was not there.

"Are you quite sure, Alvan?"

"My dear, do you suppose a man does not know when he is carrying a jug? I bought that sirup at Deemer's as I was passing. Deemer himself drew it and lent me the jug, and I——"

The sentence remains to this day unfinished. Mr. Creede staggered into the house, entered the parlor and dropped into an arm-chair, trembling in every limb. He had suddenly remembered that Silas Deemer was three weeks dead.

Mrs. Creede stood by her husband, regarding him with surprise and anxiety.

"For Heaven's sake," she said, "what ails you?"

Mr. Creede's ailment having no obvious relation to the interests of the better land he did not apparently deem it necessary to expound it on that demand; he said nothing—merely stared. There were long moments of silence broken by nothing but the measured ticking of the clock, which seemed somewhat

slower than usual, as if it were civilly granting them an extension of time in which to recover their wits.

"Jane, I have gone mad—that is it." He spoke thickly and
hurriedly. "You should have told me; you must have observed
my symptoms before they became so pronounced that I have
observed them myself. I thought I was passing Deemer's store;
it was open and lit up—that is what I thought; of course it is
never open now. Silas Deemer stood at his desk behind the
counter. My God, Jane, I saw him as distinctly as I see you.
Remembering that you had said you wanted some maple sirup,
I went in and bought some—that is all—I bought two quarts
of maple sirup from Silas Deemer, who is dead and underground, but nevertheless drew that sirup from a cask and handed
it to me in a jug. He talked with me, too, rather gravely, I remember, even more so than was his way, but not a word of
what he said can I now recall. But I saw him—good Lord, I
saw and talked with him—and he is dead! So I thought, but
I'm mad, Jane, I'm as crazy as a beetle; and you have kept it
from me."

This monologue gave the woman time to collect what faculties she had.

"Alvan," she said, "you have given no evidence of insanity,
believe me. This was undoubtedly an illusion—how should it
be anything else? That would be too terrible! But there is no
insanity; you are working too hard at the bank. You should not
have attended the meeting of directors this evening; any one
could see that you were ill; I knew something would occur."

It may have seemed to him that the prophecy had lagged a
bit, awaiting the event, but he said nothing of that, being concerned with his own condition. He was calm now, and could
think coherently.

"Doubtless the phenomenon was subjective," he said, with a
somewhat ludicrous transition to the slang of science. "Granting the possibility of spiritual apparition and even materialization, yet the apparition and materialization of a half-gallon
brown clay jug—a piece of coarse, heavy pottery evolved from
nothing—that is hardly thinkable."

As he finished speaking, a child ran into the room—his little
daughter. She was clad in a bedgown. Hastening to her father
she threw her arms about his neck, saying: "You naughty papa,

you forgot to come in and kiss me. We heard you open the gate and got up and looked out. And, papa dear, Eddy says mayn't he have the little jug when it is empty?"

As the full import of that revelation imparted itself to Alvan Creede's understanding he visibly shuddered. For the child could not have heard a word of the conversation.

The estate of Silas Deemer being in the hands of an administrator who had thought it best to dispose of the "business" the store had been closed ever since the owner's death, the goods having been removed by another "merchant" who had purchased them *en bloc*. The rooms above were vacant as well, for the widow and daughters had gone to another town.

On the evening immediately after Alvan Creede's adventure (which had somehow "got out") a crowd of men, women and children thronged the sidewalk opposite the store. That the place was haunted by the spirit of the late Silas Deemer was now well known to every resident of Hillbrook, though many affected disbelief. Of these the hardiest, and in a general way the youngest, threw stones against the front of the building, the only part accessible, but carefully missed the unshuttered windows. Incredulity had not grown to malice. A few venturesome souls crossed the street and rattled the door in its frame; struck matches and held them near the window; attempted to view the black interior. Some of the spectators invited attention to their wit by shouting and groaning and challenging the ghost to a footrace.

After a considerable time had elapsed without any manifestation, and many of the crowd had gone away, all those remaining began to observe that the interior of the store was suffused with a dim, yellow light. At this all demonstrations ceased; the intrepid souls about the door and windows fell back to the opposite side of the street and were merged in the crowd; the small boys ceased throwing stones. Nobody spoke above his breath; all whispered excitedly and pointed to the now steadily growing light. How long a time had passed since the first faint glow had been observed none could have guessed, but eventually the illumination was bright enough to reveal the whole interior of the store; and there, standing at his desk behind the counter, Silas Deemer was distinctly visible!

The effect upon the crowd was marvelous. It began rapidly

to melt away at both flanks, as the timid left the place. Many ran as fast as their legs would let them; others moved off with greater dignity, turning occasionally to look backward over the shoulder. At last a score or more, mostly men, remained where they were, speechless, staring, excited. The apparition inside gave them no attention; it was apparently occupied with a book of accounts.

Presently three men left the crowd on the sidewalk as if by a common impulse and crossed the street. One of them, a heavy man, was about to set his shoulder against the door when it opened, apparently without human agency, and the courageous investigators passed in. No sooner had they crossed the threshold than they were seen by the awed observers outside to be acting in the most unaccountable way. They thrust out their hands before them, pursued devious courses, came into violent collision with the counter, with boxes and barrels on the floor, and with one another. They turned awkwardly hither and thither and seemed trying to escape, but unable to retrace their steps. Their voices were heard in exclamations and curses. But in no way did the apparition of Silas Deemer manifest an interest in what was going on.

By what impulse the crowd was moved none ever recollected, but the entire mass—men, women, children, dogs—made a simultaneous and tumultuous rush for the entrance. They congested the doorway, pushing for precedence—resolving themselves at length into a line and moving up step by step. By some subtle spiritual or physical alchemy observation had been transmuted into action—the sightseers had become participants in the spectacle—the audience had usurped the stage.

To the only spectator remaining on the other side of the street—Alvan Creede, the banker—the interior of the store with its inpouring crowd continued in full illumination; all the strange things going on there were clearly visible. To those inside all was black darkness. It was as if each person as he was thrust in at the door had been stricken blind, and was maddened by the mischance. They groped with aimless imprecision, tried to force their way out against the current, pushed and elbowed, struck at random, fell and were trampled, rose and trampled in their turn. They seized one another by the garments, the hair, the beard—fought like animals, cursed, shouted, called one another opprobrious and obscene names. When, finally, Alvan Creede had seen the last person of the line pass into that awful tumult the light that had illuminated it was suddenly quenched and all was as black to him as to those within. He turned away and left the place.

In the early morning a curious crowd had gathered about "Deemer's." It was composed partly of those who had run away the night before, but now had the courage of sunshine, partly of honest folk going to their daily toil. The door of the store stood open; the place was vacant, but on the walls, the floor, the furniture, were shreds of clothing and tangles of hair. Hillbrook militant had managed somehow to pull itself out and had gone home to medicine its hurts and swear that it had been all night in bed. On the dusty desk, behind the counter, was the sales-book. The entries in it, in Deemer's handwriting, had ceased on the 16th day of July, the last of his life. There was no record of a later sale to Alvan Creede.

That is the entire story—except that men's passions having subsided and reason having resumed its immemorial sway, it was confessed in Hillbrook that, considering the harmless and honorable character of his first commercial transaction under the new conditions, Silas Deemer, deceased, might properly have been suffered to resume business at the old stand without mobbing. In that judgment the local historian from whose unpublished work these facts are compiled had the thoughtfulness to signify his concurrence.

Staley Fleming's Hallucination

O F two men who were talking one was a physician.

"I sent for you, Doctor," said the other, "but I don't think you can do me any good. May be you can recommend a specialist in psychopathy. I fancy I'm a bit loony."

"You look all right," the physician said.

"You shall judge—I have hallucinations. I wake every night and see in my room, intently watching me, a big black Newfoundland dog with a white forefoot."

"You say you wake; are you sure about that? 'Hallucinations' are sometimes only dreams."

"Oh, I wake, all right. Sometimes I lie still a long time, looking at the dog as earnestly as the dog looks at me—I always leave the light going. When I can't endure it any longer I sit up in bed—and nothing is there!"

"''M, 'm—what is the beast's expression?"

"It seems to me sinister. Of course I know that, except in art, an animal's face in repose has always the same expression. But this is not a real animal. Newfoundland dogs are pretty mild looking, you know; what's the matter with this one?"

"Really, my diagnosis would have no value: I am not going to treat the dog."

The physician laughed at his own pleasantry, but narrowly watched his patient from the corner of his eye. Presently he said: "Fleming, your description of the beast fits the dog of the late Atwell Barton."

Fleming half-rose from his chair, sat again and made a visible attempt at indifference. "I remember Barton," he said; "I believe he was—it was reported that—wasn't there something suspicious in his death?"

Looking squarely now into the eyes of his patient, the physician said: "Three years ago the body of your old enemy, Atwell Barton, was found in the woods near his house and yours. He had been stabbed to death. There have been no arrests; there was no clew. Some of us had 'theories.' I had one. Have you?"

"I? Why, bless your soul, what could I know about it? You remember that I left for Europe almost immediately afterward—a considerable time afterward. In the few weeks since my return you could not expect me to construct a 'theory.' In fact, I have not given the matter a thought. What about his dog?"

"It was first to find the body. It died of starvation on his grave."

We do not know the inexorable law underlying coincidences. Staley Fleming did not, or he would perhaps not have sprung to his feet as the night wind brought in through the open window the long wailing howl of a distant dog. He strode several times across the room in the steadfast gaze of the physician; then, abruptly confronting him, almost shouted: "What has all this to do with my trouble, Dr. Halderman? You forget why you were sent for."

Rising, the physician laid his hand upon his patient's arm and said, gently: "Pardon me. I cannot diagnose your disorder offhand—to-morrow, perhaps. Please go to bed, leaving your door unlocked; I will pass the night here with your books. Can you call me without rising?"

"Yes, there is an electric bell."

"Good. If anything disturbs you push the button without sitting up. Good night."

Comfortably installed in an armchair the man of medicine stared into the glowing coals and thought deeply and long, but apparently to little purpose, for he frequently rose and opening a door leading to the staircase, listened intently; then resumed his seat. Presently, however, he fell asleep, and when he woke it was past midnight. He stirred the failing fire, lifted a book from the table at his side and looked at the title. It was Denneker's "Meditations." He opened it at random and began to read:

"Forasmuch as it is ordained of God that all flesh hath spirit and thereby taketh on spiritual powers, so, also, the spirit hath powers of the flesh, even when it is gone out of the flesh and liveth as a thing apart, as many a violence performed by wraith and lemure sheweth. And there be who say that man is not single in this, but the beasts have the like evil inducement, and——"

The reading was interrupted by a shaking of the house, as by the fall of a heavy object. The reader flung down the book, rushed from the room and mounted the stairs to Fleming's bed-chamber. He tried the door, but contrary to his instructions it was locked. He set his shoulder against it with such force that it gave way. On the floor near the disordered bed, in his night clothes, lay Fleming gasping away his life.

The physician raised the dying man's head from the floor and observed a wound in the throat. "I should have thought of this," he said, believing it suicide.

When the man was dead an examination disclosed the unmistakable marks of an animal's fangs deeply sunken into the jugular vein.

But there was no animal.

A Resumed Identity

THE REVIEW AS A FORM OF WELCOME

ONE summer night a man stood on a low hill overlooking a wide expanse of forest and field. By the full moon hanging low in the west he knew what he might not have known otherwise: that it was near the hour of dawn. A light mist lay along the earth, partly veiling the lower features of the landscape, but above it the taller trees showed in well-defined masses against a clear sky. Two or three farmhouses were visible through the haze, but in none of them, naturally, was a light. Nowhere, indeed, was any sign or suggestion of life except the barking of a distant dog, which, repeated with mechanical iteration, served rather to accentuate than dispel the loneliness of the scene.

The man looked curiously about him on all sides, as one who among familiar surroundings is unable to determine his exact place and part in the scheme of things. It is so, perhaps, that we shall act when, risen from the dead, we await the call to judgment.

A hundred yards away was a straight road, showing white in the moonlight. Endeavoring to orient himself, as a surveyor or navigator might say, the man moved his eyes slowly along its visible length and at a distance of a quarter-mile to the south of his station saw, dim and gray in the haze, a group of horsemen riding to the north. Behind them were men afoot, marching in column, with dimly gleaming rifles aslant above their shoulders. They moved slowly and in silence. Another group of horsemen, another regiment of infantry, another and another—all in unceasing motion toward the man's point of view, past it, and beyond. A battery of artillery followed, the cannoneers riding with folded arms on limber and caisson. And still the interminable procession came out of the obscurity to south and passed into the obscurity to north, with never a sound of voice, nor hoof, nor wheel.

The man could not rightly understand: he thought himself deaf; said so, and heard his own voice, although it had an unfamiliar quality that almost alarmed him; it disappointed his ear's expectancy in the matter of *timbre* and resonance. But he was not deaf, and that for the moment sufficed.

Then he remembered that there are natural phenomena to which some one has given the name "acoustic shadows." If you stand in an acoustic shadow there is one direction from which you will hear nothing. At the battle of Gaines's Mill, one of the fiercest conflicts of the Civil War, with a hundred guns in play, spectators a mile and a half away on the opposite side of the Chickahominy valley heard nothing of what they clearly saw. The bombardment of Port Royal, heard and felt at St. Augustine, a hundred and fifty miles to the south, was inaudible two miles to the north in a still atmosphere. A few days before the surrender at Appomattox a thunderous engagement between the commands of Sheridan and Pickett was unknown to the latter commander, a mile in the rear of his own line.

These instances were not known to the man of whom we write, but less striking ones of the same character had not escaped his observation. He was profoundly disquieted, but for another reason than the uncanny silence of that moonlight march.

"Good Lord!" he said to himself—and again it was as if another had spoken his thought—"if those people are what I take them to be we have lost the battle and they are moving on Nashville!"

Then came a thought of self—an apprehension—a strong sense of personal peril, such as in another we call fear. He stepped quickly into the shadow of a tree. And still the silent battalions moved slowly forward in the haze.

The chill of a sudden breeze upon the back of his neck drew his attention to the quarter whence it came, and turning to the east he saw a faint gray light along the horizon—the first sign of returning day. This increased his apprehension.

"I must get away from here," he thought, "or I shall be discovered and taken."

He moved out of the shadow, walking rapidly toward the graying east. From the safer seclusion of a clump of cedars he looked back. The entire column had passed out of sight: the straight white road lay bare and desolate in the moonlight!

Puzzled before, he was now inexpressibly astonished. So

swift a passing of so slow an army!—he could not comprehend it. Minute after minute passed unnoted; he had lost his sense of time. He sought with a terrible earnestness a solution of the mystery, but sought in vain. When at last he roused himself from his abstraction the sun's rim was visible above the hills, but in the new conditions he found no other light than that of day; his understanding was involved as darkly in doubt as before.

On every side lay cultivated fields showing no sign of war and war's ravages. From the chimneys of the farmhouses thin ascensions of blue smoke signaled preparations for a day's peaceful toil. Having stilled its immemorial allocution to the moon, the watch-dog was assisting a negro who, prefixing a team of mules to the plow, was flatting and sharping content-edly at his task. The hero of this tale stared stupidly at the pastoral picture as if he had never seen such a thing in all his life; then he put his hand to his head, passed it through his hair and, withdrawing it, attentively considered the palm—a singu-lar thing to do. Apparently reassured by the act, he walked confidently toward the road.

II

WHEN YOU HAVE LOST YOUR
LIFE CONSULT A PHYSICIAN

Dr. Stilling Malson, of Murfreesboro, having visited a pa-tient six or seven miles away, on the Nashville road, had re-mained with him all night. At daybreak he set out for home on horseback, as was the custom of doctors of the time and region. He had passed into the neighborhood of Stone's River battle-field when a man approached him from the roadside and sa-luted in the military fashion, with a movement of the right hand to the hat-brim. But the hat was not a military hat, the man was not in uniform and had not a martial bearing. The doctor nodded civilly, half thinking that the stranger's uncom-mon greeting was perhaps in deference to the historic sur-roundings. As the stranger evidently desired speech with him he courteously reined in his horse and waited.

"Sir," said the stranger, "although a civilian, you are perhaps an enemy."

"I am a physician," was the non-committal reply.

"Thank you," said the other. "I am a lieutenant, of the staff of General Hazen." He paused a moment and looked sharply at the person whom he was addressing, then added, "Of the Federal army."

The physician merely nodded.

"Kindly tell me," continued the other, "what has happened here. Where are the armies? Which has won the battle?"

The physician regarded his questioner curiously with half-shut eyes. After a professional scrutiny, prolonged to the limit of politeness, "Pardon me," he said; "one asking information should be willing to impart it. Are you wounded?" he added, smiling.

"Not seriously—it seems."

The man removed the unmilitary hat, put his hand to his head, passed it through his hair and, withdrawing it, attentively considered the palm.

"I was struck by a bullet and have been unconscious. It must have been a light, glancing blow: I find no blood and feel no pain. I will not trouble you for treatment, but will you kindly direct me to my command—to any part of the Federal army— if you know?"

Again the doctor did not immediately reply: he was recalling much that is recorded in the books of his profession—something about lost identity and the effect of familiar scenes in restoring it. At length he looked the man in the face, smiled, and said:

"Lieutenant, you are not wearing the uniform of your rank and service."

At this the man glanced down at his civilian attire, lifted his eyes, and said with hesitation:

"That is true. I—I don't quite understand."

Still regarding him sharply but not unsympathetically the man of science bluntly inquired:

"How old are you?"

"Twenty-three—if that has anything to do with it."

"You don't look it; I should hardly have guessed you to be just that."

The man was growing impatient. "We need not discuss that," he said; "I want to know about the army. Not two hours ago I saw a column of troops moving northward on this road. You must have met them. Be good enough to tell me the color of their clothing, which I was unable to make out, and I'll trouble you no more."

"You are quite sure that you saw them?"

"Sure? My God, sir, I could have counted them!"

"Why, really," said the physician, with an amusing consciousness of his own resemblance to the loquacious barber of the Arabian Nights, "this is very interesting. I met no troops."

The man looked at him coldly, as if he had himself observed the likeness to the barber. "It is plain," he said, "that you do not care to assist me. Sir, you may go to the devil!"

He turned and strode away, very much at random, across the dewy fields, his half-penitent tormentor quietly watching him from his point of vantage in the saddle till he disappeared beyond an array of trees.

III

THE DANGER OF LOOKING INTO A POOL OF WATER

After leaving the road the man slackened his pace, and now went forward, rather deviously, with a distinct feeling of fatigue. He could not account for this, though truly the interminable loquacity of that country doctor offered itself in explanation. Seating himself upon a rock, he laid one hand upon his knee, back upward, and casually looked at it. It was lean and withered. He lifted both hands to his face. It was seamed and furrowed; he could trace the lines with the tips of his fingers. How strange!—a mere bullet-stroke and a brief unconsciousness should not make one a physical wreck.

"I must have been a long time in hospital," he said aloud. "Why, what a fool I am! The battle was in December, and it is now summer!" He laughed. "No wonder that fellow thought me an escaped lunatic. He was wrong: I am only an escaped patient."

At a little distance a small plot of ground enclosed by a stone wall caught his attention. With no very definite intent he rose and went to it. In the center was a square, solid monument of hewn stone. It was brown with age, weather-worn at the angles, spotted with moss and lichen. Between the massive blocks were strips of grass the leverage of whose roots had pushed

them apart. In answer to the challenge of this ambitious structure Time had laid his destroying hand upon it, and it would
soon be "one with Nineveh and Tyre." In an inscription on
one side his eye caught a familiar name. Shaking with excitement, he craned his body across the wall and read:

HAZEN'S BRIGADE

to

The Memory of Its Soldiers

who fell at

Stone River, Dec. 31, 1862.

The man fell back from the wall, faint and sick. Almost
within an arm's length was a little depression in the earth; it
had been filled by a recent rain—a pool of clear water. He crept
to it to revive himself, lifted the upper part of his body on his
trembling arms, thrust forward his head and saw the reflection
of his face, as in a mirror. He uttered a terrible cry. His arms
gave way; he fell, face downward, into the pool and yielded up
the life that had spanned another life.

A Baby Tramp

I F you had seen little Jo standing at the street corner in the rain, you would hardly have admired him. It was apparently an ordinary autumn rainstorm, but the water which fell upon Jo (who was hardly old enough to be either just or unjust, and so perhaps did not come under the law of impartial distribution) appeared to have some property peculiar to itself: one would have said it was dark and adhesive—sticky. But that could hardly be so, even in Blackburg, where things certainly did occur that were a good deal out of the common.

For example, ten or twelve years before, a shower of small frogs had fallen, as is credibly attested by a contemporaneous chronicle, the record concluding with a somewhat obscure statement to the effect that the chronicler considered it good growing-weather for Frenchmen.

Some years later Blackburg had a fall of crimson snow; it is cold in Blackburg when winter is on, and the snows are frequent and deep. There can be no doubt of it—the snow in this instance was of the color of blood and melted into water of the same hue, if water it was, not blood. The phenomenon had attracted wide attention, and science had as many explanations as there were scientists who knew nothing about it. But the men of Blackburg—men who for many years had lived right there where the red snow fell, and might be supposed to know a good deal about the matter—shook their heads and said something would come of it.

And something did, for the next summer was made memorable by the prevalence of a mysterious disease—epidemic, endemic, or the Lord knows what, though the physicians didn't —which carried away a full half of the population. Most of the other half carried themselves away and were slow to return, but finally came back, and were now increasing and multiplying as before, but Blackburg had not since been altogether the same.

Of quite another kind, though equally "out of the common," was the incident of Hetty Parlow's ghost. Hetty Parlow's

304

maiden name had been Brownon, and in Blackburg that meant
more than one would think.

The Brownons had from time immemorial—from the very
earliest of the old colonial days—been the leading family of the
town. It was the richest and it was the best, and Blackburg
would have shed the last drop of its plebeian blood in defense
of the Brownon fair fame. As few of the family's members had
ever been known to live permanently away from Blackburg,
although most of them were educated elsewhere and nearly all
had traveled, there was quite a number of them. The men held
most of the public offices, and the women were foremost in all
good works. Of these latter, Hetty was most beloved by reason
of the sweetness of her disposition, the purity of her character
and her singular personal beauty. She married in Boston a
young scapegrace named Parlow, and like a good Brownon
brought him to Blackburg forthwith and made a man and a
town councilman of him. They had a child which they named
Joseph and dearly loved, as was then the fashion among parents
in all that region. Then they died of the mysterious disorder
already mentioned, and at the age of one whole year Joseph set
up as an orphan.

Unfortunately for Joseph the disease which had cut off his
parents did not stop at that; it went on and extirpated nearly
the whole Brownon contingent and its allies by marriage; and
those who fled did not return. The tradition was broken, the
Brownon estates passed into alien hands and the only Brownons
remaining in that place were underground in Oak Hill Cemetery, where, indeed, was a colony of them powerful enough to
resist the encroachment of surrounding tribes and hold the
best part of the grounds. But about the ghost:

One night, about three years after the death of Hetty Parlow,
a number of the young people of Blackburg were passing Oak
Hill Cemetery in a wagon—if you have been there you will
remember that the road to Greenton runs alongside it on the
south. They had been attending a May Day festival at Greenton; and that serves to fix the date. Altogether there may have
been a dozen, and a jolly party they were, considering the
legacy of gloom left by the town's recent somber experiences.
As they passed the cemetery the man driving suddenly reined

in his team with an exclamation of surprise. It was sufficiently surprising, no doubt, for just ahead, and almost at the roadside, though inside the cemetery, stood the ghost of Hetty Parlow. There could be no doubt of it, for she had been personally known to every youth and maiden in the party. That established the thing's identity; its character as ghost was signified by all the customary signs—the shroud, the long, undone hair, the "far-away look"—everything. This disquieting apparition was stretching out its arms toward the west, as if in supplication for the evening star, which, certainly, was an alluring object, though obviously out of reach. As they all sat silent (so the story goes) every member of that party of merrymakers— they had merry-made on coffee and lemonade only—distinctly heard that ghost call the name "Joey, Joey!" A moment later nothing was there. Of course one does not have to believe all that.

Now, at that moment, as was afterward ascertained, Joey was wandering about in the sagebrush on the opposite side of the continent, near Winnemucca, in the State of Nevada. He had been taken to that town by some good persons distantly related to his dead father, and by them adopted and tenderly cared for. But on that evening the poor child had strayed from home and was lost in the desert.

His after history is involved in obscurity and has gaps which conjecture alone can fill. It is known that he was found by a family of Piute Indians, who kept the little wretch with them for a time and then sold him—actually sold him for money to a woman on one of the east-bound trains, at a station a long way from Winnemucca. The woman professed to have made all manner of inquiries, but all in vain: so, being childless and a widow, she adopted him herself. At this point of his career Jo seemed to be getting a long way from the condition of orphanage; the interposition of a multitude of parents between himself and that woeful state promised him a long immunity from its disadvantages.

Mrs. Darnell, his newest mother, lived in Cleveland, Ohio. But her adopted son did not long remain with her. He was seen one afternoon by a policeman, new to that beat, deliberately toddling away from her house, and being questioned answered that he was "a doin' home." He must have traveled by rail, somehow, for three days later he was in the town of Whiteville, which, as you know, is a long way from Blackburg. His clothing was in pretty fair condition, but he was sinfully dirty. Unable to give any account of himself he was arrested as a vagrant and sentenced to imprisonment in the Infants' Sheltering Home—where he was washed.

Jo ran away from the Infants' Sheltering Home at Whiteville —just took to the woods one day, and the Home knew him no more forever.

We find him next, or rather get back to him, standing forlorn in the cold autumn rain at a suburban street corner in Blackburg; and it seems right to explain now that the raindrops falling upon him there were really not dark and gummy; they only failed to make his face and hands less so. Jo was indeed fearfully and wonderfully besmirched, as by the hand of an artist. And the forlorn little tramp had no shoes; his feet were bare, red, and swollen, and when he walked he limped with both legs. As to clothing—ah, you would hardly have had the skill to name any single garment that he wore, or say by what magic he kept it upon him. That he was cold all over and all through did not admit of a doubt; he knew it himself. Anyone would have been cold there that evening; but, for that reason, no one else was there. How Jo came to be there himself, he could not for the flickering little life of him have told, even if gifted with a vocabulary exceeding a hundred words. From the way he stared about him one could have seen that he had not the faintest notion of where (nor why) he was.

Yet he was not altogether a fool in his day and generation; being cold and hungry, and still able to walk a little by bending his knees very much indeed and putting his feet down toes first, he decided to enter one of the houses which flanked the street at long intervals and looked so bright and warm. But when he attempted to act upon that very sensible decision a burly dog came bowsing out and disputed his right. Inexpressibly frightened and believing, no doubt (with some reason, too) that brutes without meant brutality within, he hobbled away from all the houses, and with gray, wet fields to right of him and gray, wet fields to left of him—with the rain half blinding him and the night coming in mist and darkness, held his way along the road that leads to Greenton. That is to say,

the road leads those to Greenton who succeed in passing the
Oak Hill Cemetery. A considerable number every year do
not.

Jo did not.

They found him there the next morning, very wet, very
cold, but no longer hungry. He had apparently entered the
cemetery gate—hoping, perhaps, that it led to a house where
there was no dog—and gone blundering about in the darkness,
falling over many a grave, no doubt, until he had tired of it all
and given up. The little body lay upon one side, with one
soiled cheek upon one soiled hand, the other hand tucked
away among the rags to make it warm, the other cheek washed
clean and white at last, as for a kiss from one of God's great
angels. It was observed—though nothing was thought of it at
the time, the body being as yet unidentified—that the little
fellow was lying upon the grave of Hetty Parlow. The grave,
however, had not opened to receive him. That is a circumstance which, without actual irreverence, one may wish had
been ordered otherwise.

The Night-Doings at "Deadman's"

A STORY THAT IS UNTRUE

IT was a singularly sharp night, and clear as the heart of a diamond. Clear nights have a trick of being keen. In darkness you may be cold and not know it; when you see, you suffer. This night was bright enough to bite like a serpent. The moon was moving mysteriously along behind the giant pines crowning the South Mountain, striking a cold sparkle from the crusted snow, and bringing out against the black west the ghostly outlines of the Coast Range, beyond which lay the invisible Pacific. The snow had piled itself, in the open spaces along the bottom of the gulch, into long ridges that seemed to heave, and into hills that appeared to toss and scatter spray. The spray was sunlight, twice reflected: dashed once from the moon, once from the snow.

In this snow many of the shanties of the abandoned mining camp were obliterated, (a sailor might have said they had gone down) and at irregular intervals it had overtopped the tall trestles which had once supported a river called a flume; for, of course, "flume" is *flumen*. Among the advantages of which the mountains cannot deprive the gold-hunter is the privilege of speaking Latin. He says of his dead neighbor, "He has gone up the flume." This is not a bad way to say, "His life has returned to the Fountain of Life."

While putting on its armor against the assaults of the wind, this snow had neglected no coign of vantage. Snow pursued by the wind is not wholly unlike a retreating army. In the open field it ranges itself in ranks and battalions; where it can get a foothold it makes a stand; where it can take cover it does so. You may see whole platoons of snow cowering behind a bit of broken wall. The devious old road, hewn out of the mountain side, was full of it. Squadron upon squadron had struggled to escape by this line, when suddenly pursuit had ceased. A more desolate and dreary spot than Deadman's Gulch in a winter midnight it is impossible to imagine. Yet Mr. Hiram Beeson elected to live there, the sole inhabitant.

Away up the side of the North Mountain his little pine-log shanty projected from its single pane of glass a long, thin beam of light, and looked not altogether unlike a black beetle fastened to the hillside with a bright new pin. Within it sat Mr. Beeson himself, before a roaring fire, staring into its hot heart as if he had never before seen such a thing in all his life. He was not a comely man. He was gray; he was ragged and slovenly in his attire; his face was wan and haggard; his eyes were too bright. As to his age, if one had attempted to guess it, one might have said forty-seven, then corrected himself and said seventy-four. He was really twenty-eight. Emaciated he was; as much, perhaps, as he dared be, with a needy undertaker at Bentley's Flat and a new and enterprising coroner at Sonora. Poverty and zeal are an upper and a nether millstone. It is dangerous to make a third in that kind of sandwich.

As Mr. Beeson sat there, with his ragged elbows on his ragged knees, his lean jaws buried in his lean hands, and with no apparent intention of going to bed, he looked as if the slightest movement would tumble him to pieces. Yet during the last hour he had winked no fewer than three times.

There was a sharp rapping at the door. A rap at that time of night and in that weather might have surprised an ordinary mortal who had dwelt two years in the gulch without seeing a human face, and could not fail to know that the country was impassable; but Mr. Beeson did not so much as pull his eyes out of the coals. And even when the door was pushed open he only shrugged a little more closely into himself, as one does who is expecting something that he would rather not see. You may observe this movement in women when, in a mortuary chapel, the coffin is borne up the aisle behind them.

But when a long old man in a blanket overcoat, his head tied up in a handkerchief and nearly his entire face in a muffler, wearing green goggles and with a complexion of glittering whiteness where it could be seen, strode silently into the room, laying a hard, gloved hand on Mr. Beeson's shoulder, the latter so far forgot himself as to look up with an appearance of no small astonishment; whomever he may have been expecting, he had evidently not counted on meeting anyone like this. Nevertheless, the sight of this unexpected guest produced in Mr. Beeson the following sequence: a feeling of astonishment;

a sense of gratification; a sentiment of profound good will. Rising from his seat, he took the knotty hand from his shoulder, and shook it up and down with a fervor quite unaccountable; for in the old man's aspect was nothing to attract, much to repel. However, attraction is too general a property for repulsion to be without it. The most attractive object in the world is the face we instinctively cover with a cloth. When it becomes still more attractive—fascinating—we put seven feet of earth above it.

"Sir," said Mr. Beeson, releasing the old man's hand, which fell passively against his thigh with a quiet clack, "it is an extremely disagreeable night. Pray be seated; I am very glad to see you."

Mr. Beeson spoke with an easy good breeding that one would hardly have expected, considering all things. Indeed, the contrast between his appearance and his manner was sufficiently surprising to be one of the commonest of social phenomena in the mines. The old man advanced a step toward the fire, glowing cavernously in the green goggles. Mr. Beeson resumed:

"You bet your life I am!"

Mr. Beeson's elegance was not too refined; it had made reasonable concessions to local taste. He paused a moment, letting his eyes drop from the muffled head of his guest, down along the row of moldy buttons confining the blanket overcoat, to the greenish cowhide boots powdered with snow, which had begun to melt and run along the floor in little rills. He took an inventory of his guest, and appeared satisfied. Who would not have been? Then he continued:

"The cheer I can offer you is, unfortunately, in keeping with my surroundings; but I shall esteem myself highly favored if it is your pleasure to partake of it, rather than seek better at Bentley's Flat."

With a singular refinement of hospitable humility Mr. Beeson spoke as if a sojourn in his warm cabin on such a night, as compared with walking fourteen miles up to the throat in snow with a cutting crust, would be an intolerable hardship. By way of reply, his guest unbuttoned the blanket overcoat. The host laid fresh fuel on the fire, swept the hearth with the tail of a wolf, and added:

"But *I* think you'd better skedaddle."

The old man took a seat by the fire, spreading his broad soles to the heat without removing his hat. In the mines the hat is seldom removed except when the boots are. Without further remark Mr. Beeson also seated himself in a chair which had been a barrel, and which, retaining much of its original character, seemed to have been designed with a view to preserving his dust if it should please him to crumble. For a moment there was silence; then, from somewhere among the pines, came the snarling yelp of a coyote; and simultaneously the door rattled in its frame. There was no other connection between the two incidents than that the coyote has an aversion to storms, and the wind was rising; yet there seemed somehow a kind of supernatural conspiracy between the two, and Mr. Beeson shuddered with a vague sense of terror. He recovered himself in a moment and again addressed his guest.

"There are strange doings here. I will tell you everything, and then if you decide to go I shall hope to accompany you over the worst of the way; as far as where Baldy Peterson shot Ben Hike—I dare say you know the place."

The old man nodded emphatically, as intimating not merely that he did, but that he did indeed.

"Two years ago," began Mr. Beeson, "I, with two companions, occupied this house; but when the rush to the Flat occurred we left, along with the rest. In ten hours the Gulch was deserted. That evening, however, I discovered I had left behind me a valuable pistol (that is it) and returned for it, passing the night here alone, as I have passed every night since. I must explain that a few days before we left, our Chinese domestic had the misfortune to die while the ground was frozen so hard that it was impossible to dig a grave in the usual way. So, on the day of our hasty departure, we cut through the floor there, and gave him such burial as we could. But before putting him down I had the extremely bad taste to cut off his pigtail and spike it to that beam above his grave, where you may see it at this moment, or, preferably, when warmth has given you leisure for observation.

"I stated, did I not, that the Chinaman came to his death from natural causes? I had, of course, nothing to do with that, and returned through no irresistible attraction, or morbid fascination, but only because I had forgotten a pistol. This is clear to you, is it not, sir?"

The visitor nodded gravely. He appeared to be a man of few words, if any. Mr. Beeson continued:

"According to the Chinese faith, a man is like a kite: he cannot go to heaven without a tail. Well, to shorten this tedious story—which, however, I thought it my duty to relate—on that night, while I was here alone and thinking of anything but him, that Chinaman came back for his pigtail.

"He did not get it."

At this point Mr. Beeson relapsed into blank silence. Perhaps he was fatigued by the unwonted exercise of speaking; perhaps he had conjured up a memory that demanded his undivided attention. The wind was now fairly abroad, and the pines along the mountainside sang with singular distinctness. The narrator continued:

"You say you do not see much in that, and I must confess I do not myself.

"But he keeps coming!"

There was another long silence, during which both stared into the fire without the movement of a limb. Then Mr. Beeson broke out, almost fiercely, fixing his eyes on what he could see of the impassive face of his auditor:

"Give it him? Sir, in this matter I have no intention of troubling anyone for advice. You will pardon me, I am sure"—here he became singularly persuasive—"but I have ventured to nail that pigtail fast, and have assumed the somewhat onerous obligation of guarding it. So it is quite impossible to act on your considerate suggestion.

"Do you play me for a Modoc?"

Nothing could exceed the sudden ferocity with which he thrust this indignant remonstrance into the ear of his guest. It was as if he had struck him on the side of the head with a steel gauntlet. It was a protest, but it was a challenge. To be mistaken for a coward—to be played for a Modoc: these two expressions are one. Sometimes it is a Chinaman. Do you play me for a Chinaman? is a question frequently addressed to the ear of the suddenly dead.

Mr. Beeson's buffet produced no effect, and after a moment's pause, during which the wind thundered in the chimney like the sound of clods upon a coffin, he resumed:

"But, as you say, it is wearing me out. I feel that the life of the last two years has been a mistake—a mistake that corrects itself; you see how. The grave! No; there is no one to dig it. The ground is frozen, too. But you are very welcome. You may say at Bentley's—but that is not important. It was very tough to cut: they braid silk into their pigtails. Kwaagh."

Mr. Beeson was speaking with his eyes shut, and he wandered. His last word was a snore. A moment later he drew a long breath, opened his eyes with an effort, made a single remark, and fell into a deep sleep. What he said was this:

"They are swiping my dust!"

Then the aged stranger, who had not uttered one word since his arrival, arose from his seat and deliberately laid off his outer clothing, looking as angular in his flannels as the late Signorina Festorazzi, an Irish woman, six feet in height, and weighing fifty-six pounds, who used to exhibit herself in her chemise to the people of San Francisco. He then crept into one of the "bunks," having first placed a revolver in easy reach, according to the custom of the country. This revolver he took from a shelf, and it was the one which Mr. Beeson had mentioned as that for which he had returned to the Gulch two years before.

In a few moments Mr. Beeson awoke, and seeing that his guest had retired he did likewise. But before doing so he approached the long, plaited wisp of pagan hair and gave it a powerful tug, to assure himself that it was fast and firm. The two beds—mere shelves covered with blankets not overclean —faced each other from opposite sides of the room, the little square trapdoor that had given access to the Chinaman's grave being midway between. This, by the way, was crossed by a double row of spike-heads. In his resistance to the supernatural, Mr. Beeson had not disdained the use of material precautions.

The fire was now low, the flames burning bluely and petulantly, with occasional flashes, projecting spectral shadows on the walls—shadows that moved mysteriously about, now dividing, now uniting. The shadow of the pendent queue, however, kept moodily apart, near the roof at the further end of the room, looking like a note of admiration. The song of the pines outside had now risen to the dignity of a triumphal hymn. In the pauses the silence was dreadful.

It was during one of these intervals that the trap in the floor began to lift. Slowly and steadily it rose, and slowly and steadily rose the swaddled head of the old man in the bunk to observe it. Then, with a clap that shook the house to its foundation, it was thrown clean back, where it lay with its unsightly spikes pointing threateningly upward. Mr. Beeson awoke, and without rising, pressed his fingers into his eyes. He shuddered; his teeth chattered. His guest was now reclining on one elbow, watching the proceedings with the goggles that glowed like lamps.

Suddenly a howling gust of wind swooped down the chimney, scattering ashes and smoke in all directions, for a moment obscuring everything. When the firelight again illuminated the room there was seen, sitting gingerly on the edge of a stool by the hearthside, a swarthy little man of prepossessing appearance and dressed with faultless taste, nodding to the old man with a friendly and engaging smile. "From San Francisco, evidently," thought Mr. Beeson, who having somewhat recovered from his fright was groping his way to a solution of the evening's events.

But now another actor appeared upon the scene. Out of the square black hole in the middle of the floor protruded the head of the departed Chinaman, his glassy eyes turned upward in their angular slits and fastened on the dangling queue above with a look of yearning unspeakable. Mr. Beeson groaned, and again spread his hands upon his face. A mild odor of opium pervaded the place. The phantom, clad only in a short blue tunic quilted and silken but covered with grave-mold, rose slowly, as if pushed by a weak spiral spring. Its knees were at the level of the floor, when with a quick upward impulse like the silent leaping of a flame it grasped the queue with both hands, drew up its body and took the tip in its horrible yellow teeth. To this it clung in a seeming frenzy, grimacing ghastly, surging and plunging from side to side in its efforts to disengage its property from the beam, but uttering no sound. It was like a corpse artificially convulsed by means of a galvanic battery. The contrast between its superhuman activity and its silence was no less than hideous!

Mr. Beeson cowered in his bed. The swarthy little gentle-man uncrossed his legs, beat an impatient tattoo with the toe of his boot and consulted a heavy gold watch. The old man sat erect and quietly laid hold of the revolver.

Bang!

Like a body cut from the gallows the Chinaman plumped into the black hole below, carrying his tail in his teeth. The trapdoor turned over, shutting down with a snap. The swarthy little gentleman from San Francisco sprang nimbly from his perch, caught something in the air with his hat, as a boy catches a butterfly, and vanished into the chimney as if drawn up by suction.

From away somewhere in the outer darkness floated in through the open door a faint, far cry—a long, sobbing wail, as of a child death-strangled in the desert, or a lost soul borne away by the Adversary. It may have been the coyote.

In the early days of the following spring a party of miners on their way to new diggings passed along the Gulch, and straying through the deserted shanties found in one of them the body of Hiram Beeson, stretched upon a bunk, with a bullet hole through the heart. The ball had evidently been fired from the opposite side of the room, for in one of the oaken beams overhead was a shallow blue dint, where it had struck a knot and been deflected downward to the breast of its victim. Strongly attached to the same beam was what appeared to be an end of a rope of braided horsehair, which had been cut by the bullet in its passage to the knot. Nothing else of interest was noted, excepting a suit of moldy and incongruous cloth-ing, several articles of which were afterward identified by re-spectable witnesses as those in which certain deceased citizens of Deadman's had been buried years before. But it is not easy to understand how that could be, unless, indeed, the garments had been worn as a disguise by Death himself—which is hardly credible.

Beyond the Wall

MANY years ago, on my way from Hongkong to New York, I passed a week in San Francisco. A long time had gone by since I had been in that city, during which my ventures in the Orient had prospered beyond my hope; I was rich and could afford to revisit my own country to renew my friendship with such of the companions of my youth as still lived and remembered me with the old affection. Chief of these, I hoped, was Mohun Dampier, an old schoolmate with whom I had held a desultory correspondence which had long ceased, as is the way of correspondence between men. You may have observed that the indisposition to write a merely social letter is in the ratio of the square of the distance between you and your correspondent. It is a law.

I remembered Dampier as a handsome, strong young fellow of scholarly tastes, with an aversion to work and a marked indifference to many of the things that the world cares for, including wealth, of which, however, he had inherited enough to put him beyond the reach of want. In his family, one of the oldest and most aristocratic in the country, it was, I think, a matter of pride that no member of it had ever been in trade nor politics, nor suffered any kind of distinction. Mohun was a trifle sentimental, and had in him a singular element of superstition, which led him to the study of all manner of occult subjects, although his sane mental health safeguarded him against fantastic and perilous faiths. He made daring incursions into the realm of the unreal without renouncing his residence in the partly surveyed and charted region of what we are pleased to call certitude.

The night of my visit to him was stormy. The Californian winter was on, and the incessant rain plashed in the deserted streets, or, lifted by irregular gusts of wind, was hurled against the houses with incredible fury. With no small difficulty my cabman found the right place, away out toward the ocean beach, in a sparsely populated suburb. The dwelling, a rather ugly one, apparently, stood in the center of its grounds, which as nearly as I could make out in the gloom were destitute of either flowers or grass. Three or four trees, writhing and moaning in the torment of the tempest, appeared to be trying to escape from their dismal environment and take the chance of finding a better one out at sea. The house was a two-story brick structure with a tower, a story higher, at one corner. In a window of that was the only visible light. Something in the appearance of the place made me shudder, a performance that may have been assisted by a rill of rain-water down my back as I scuttled to cover in the doorway.

In answer to my note apprising him of my wish to call, Dampier had written, "Don't ring—open the door and come up." I did so. The staircase was dimly lighted by a single gas-jet at the top of the second flight. I managed to reach the landing without disaster and entered by an open door into the lighted square room of the tower. Dampier came forward in gown and slippers to receive me, giving me the greeting that I wished, and if I had held a thought that it might more fitly have been accorded me at the front door the first look at him dispelled any sense of his inhospitality.

He was not the same. Hardly past middle age, he had gone gray and had acquired a pronounced stoop. His figure was thin and angular, his face deeply lined, his complexion dead-white, without a touch of color. His eyes, unnaturally large, glowed with a fire that was almost uncanny.

He seated me, proffered a cigar, and with grave and obvious sincerity assured me of the pleasure that it gave him to meet me. Some unimportant conversation followed, but all the while I was dominated by a melancholy sense of the great change in him. This he must have perceived, for he suddenly said with a bright enough smile, "You are disappointed in me—*non sum qualis eram*."

I hardly knew what to reply, but managed to say: "Why, really, I don't know: your Latin is about the same."

He brightened again. "No," he said, "being a dead language, it grows in appropriateness. But please have the patience to wait: where I am going there is perhaps a better tongue. Will you care to have a message in it?"

The smile faded as he spoke, and as he concluded he was looking into my eyes with a gravity that distressed me. Yet I would not surrender myself to his mood, nor permit him to see how deeply his prescience of death affected me.

"I fancy that it will be long," I said, "before human speech will cease to serve our need; and then the need, with its possibilities of service, will have passed."

He made no reply, and I too was silent, for the talk had taken a dispiriting turn, yet I knew not how to give it a more agreeable character. Suddenly, in a pause of the storm, when the dead silence was almost startling by contrast with the previous uproar, I heard a gentle tapping, which appeared to come from the wall behind my chair. The sound was such as might have been made by a human hand, not as upon a door by one asking admittance, but rather, I thought, as an agreed signal, an assurance of someone's presence in an adjoining room; most of us, I fancy, have had more experience of such communications than we should care to relate. I glanced at Dampier. If possibly there was something of amusement in the look he did not observe it. He appeared to have forgotten my presence, and was staring at the wall behind me with an expression in his eyes that I am unable to name, although my memory of it is as vivid to-day as was my sense of it then. The situation was embarrassing; I rose to take my leave. At this he seemed to recover himself.

"Please be seated," he said; "it is nothing—no one is there."

But the tapping was repeated, and with the same gentle, slow insistence as before.

"Pardon me," I said, "it is late. May I call to-morrow?"

He smiled—a little mechanically, I thought. "It is very delicate of you," said he, "but quite needless. Really, this is the only room in the tower, and no one is there. At least——" He left the sentence incomplete, rose, and threw up a window, the only opening in the wall from which the sound seemed to come. "See."

Not clearly knowing what else to do I followed him to the window and looked out. A street-lamp some little distance away gave enough light through the murk of the rain that was again falling in torrents to make it entirely plain that "no one was there." In truth there was nothing but the sheer blank wall of the tower.

Dampier closed the window and signing me to my seat resumed his own.

The incident was not in itself particularly mysterious; any one of a dozen explanations was possible (though none has occurred to me), yet it impressed me strangely, the more, perhaps, from my friend's effort to reassure me, which seemed to dignify it with a certain significance and importance. He had proved that no one was there, but in that fact lay all the interest; and he proffered no explanation. His silence was irritating and made me resentful.

"My good friend," I said, somewhat ironically, I fear, "I am not disposed to question your right to harbor as many spooks as you find agreeable to your taste and consistent with your notions of companionship; that is no business of mine. But being just a plain man of affairs, mostly of this world, I find spooks needless to my peace and comfort. I am going to my hotel, where my fellow-guests are still in the flesh."

It was not a very civil speech, but he manifested no feeling about it. "Kindly remain," he said. "I am grateful for your presence here. What you have heard to-night I believe myself to have heard twice before. Now I *know* it was no illusion. That is much to me—more than you know. Have a fresh cigar and a good stock of patience while I tell you the story."

The rain was now falling more steadily, with a low, monotonous susurration, interrupted at long intervals by the sudden slashing of the boughs of the trees as the wind rose and failed. The night was well advanced, but both sympathy and curiosity held me a willing listener to my friend's monologue, which I did not interrupt by a single word from beginning to end.

"Ten years ago," he said, "I occupied a ground-floor apartment in one of a row of houses, all alike, away at the other end of the town, on what we call Rincon Hill. This had been the best quarter of San Francisco, but had fallen into neglect and decay, partly because the primitive character of its domestic architecture no longer suited the maturing tastes of our wealthy citizens, partly because certain public improvements had made a wreck of it. The row of dwellings in one of which I lived stood a little way back from the street, each having a miniature garden, separated from its neighbors by low iron fences and bisected with mathematical precision by a box-bordered gravel walk from gate to door.

"One morning as I was leaving my lodging I observed a young girl entering the adjoining garden on the left. It was a warm day in June, and she was lightly gowned in white. From her shoulders hung a broad straw hat profusely decorated with flowers and wonderfully beribboned in the fashion of the time. My attention was not long held by the exquisite simplicity of her costume, for no one could look at her face and think of anything earthly. Do not fear; I shall not profane it by description; it was beautiful exceedingly. All that I had ever seen or dreamed of loveliness was in that matchless living picture by the hand of the Divine Artist. So deeply did it move me that, without a thought of the impropriety of the act, I unconsciously bared my head, as a devout Catholic or well-bred Protestant uncovers before an image of the Blessed Virgin. The maiden showed no displeasure; she merely turned her glorious dark eyes upon me with a look that made me catch my breath, and without other recognition of my act passed into the house. For a moment I stood motionless, hat in hand, painfully conscious of my rudeness, yet so dominated by the emotion inspired by that vision of incomparable beauty that my penitence was less poignant than it should have been. Then I went my way, leaving my heart behind. In the natural course of things I should probably have remained away until nightfall, but by the middle of the afternoon I was back in the little garden, affecting an interest in the few foolish flowers that I had never before observed. My hope was vain; she did not appear.

"To a night of unrest succeeded a day of expectation and disappointment, but on the day after, as I wandered aimlessly about the neighborhood, I met her. Of course I did not repeat my folly of uncovering, nor venture by even so much as too long a look to manifest an interest in her; yet my heart was beating audibly. I trembled and consciously colored as she turned her big black eyes upon me with a look of obvious recognition entirely devoid of boldness or coquetry.

"I will not weary you with particulars; many times afterward I met the maiden, yet never either addressed her or sought to fix her attention. Nor did I take any action toward making her acquaintance. Perhaps my forbearance, requiring so supreme an effort of self-denial, will not be entirely clear to you. That I was heels over head in love is true, but who can overcome his habit of thought, or reconstruct his character?

"I was what some foolish persons are pleased to call, and others, more foolish, are pleased to be called—an aristocrat; and despite her beauty, her charms and graces, the girl was not of my class. I had learned her name—which it is needless to speak—and something of her family. She was an orphan, a dependent niece of the impossible elderly fat woman in whose lodging-house she lived. My income was small and I lacked the talent for marrying; it is perhaps a gift. An alliance with that family would condemn me to its manner of life, part me from my books and studies, and in a social sense reduce me to the ranks. It is easy to deprecate such considerations as these and I have not retained myself for the defense. Let judgment be entered against me, but in strict justice all my ancestors for generations should be made co-defendants and I be permitted to plead in mitigation of punishment the imperious mandate of heredity. To a mésalliance of that kind every globule of my ancestral blood spoke in opposition. In brief, my tastes, habits, instinct, with whatever of reason my love had left me—all fought against it. Moreover, I was an irreclaimable sentimentalist, and found a subtle charm in an impersonal and spiritual relation which acquaintance might vulgarize and marriage would certainly dispel. No woman, I argued, is what this lovely creature seems. Love is a delicious dream; why should I bring about my own awakening?

"The course dictated by all this sense and sentiment was obvious. Honor, pride, prudence, preservation of my ideals—all commanded me to go away, but for that I was too weak. The utmost that I could do by a mighty effort of will was to cease meeting the girl, and that I did. I even avoided the chance encounters of the garden, leaving my lodging only when I knew that she had gone to her music lessons, and returning after nightfall. Yet all the while I was as one in a trance, indulging the most fascinating fancies and ordering my entire intellectual life in accordance with my dream. Ah, my friend, as one whose actions have a traceable relation to reason, you cannot know the fool's paradise in which I lived.

"One evening the devil put it into my head to be an unspeakable idiot. By apparently careless and purposeless questioning I learned from my gossipy landlady that the young woman's bedroom adjoined my own, a party-wall between. Yielding to a sudden and coarse impulse I gently rapped on the wall. There was no response, naturally, but I was in no mood to accept a rebuke. A madness was upon me and I repeated the folly, the offense, but again ineffectually, and I had the decency to desist.

"An hour later, while absorbed in some of my infernal studies, I heard, or thought I heard, my signal answered. Flinging down my books I sprang to the wall and as steadily as my beating heart would permit gave three slow taps upon it. This time the response was distinct, unmistakable: one, two, three—an exact repetition of my signal. That was all I could elicit, but it was enough—too much.

"The next evening, and for many evenings afterward, that folly went on, I always having 'the last word.' During the whole period I was deliriously happy, but with the perversity of my nature I persevered in my resolution not to see her. Then, as I should have expected, I got no further answers. 'She is disgusted,' I said to myself, 'with what she thinks my timidity in making no more definite advances'; and I resolved to seek her and make her acquaintance and—what? I did not know, nor do I now know, what might have come of it. I know only that I passed days and days trying to meet her, and all in vain; she was invisible as well as inaudible. I haunted the streets where we had met, but she did not come. From my window I watched the garden in front of her house, but she passed neither in nor out. I fell into the deepest dejection, believing that she had gone away, yet took no steps to resolve my doubt by inquiry of my landlady, to whom, indeed, I had taken an unconquerable aversion from her having once spoken of the girl with less of reverence than I thought befitting.

"There came a fateful night. Worn out with emotion, irresolution and despondency, I had retired early and fallen into such sleep as was still possible to me. In the middle of the night something—some malign power bent upon the wrecking of my peace forever—caused me to open my eyes and sit up, wide awake and listening intently for I knew not what. Then I thought I heard a faint tapping on the wall—the mere ghost of the familiar signal. In a few moments it was repeated: one, two, three—no louder than before, but addressing a sense alert and strained to receive it. I was about to reply when the Adversary of Peace again intervened in my affairs with a rascally suggestion of retaliation. She had long and cruelly ignored me; now I would ignore her. Incredible fatuity—may God forgive it! All the rest of the night I lay awake, fortifying my obstinacy with shameless justifications and—listening.

"Late the next morning, as I was leaving the house, I met my landlady, entering.

" 'Good morning, Mr. Dampier,' she said. 'Have you heard the news?'

"I replied in words that I had heard no news; in manner, that I did not care to hear any. The manner escaped her observation.

" 'About the sick young lady next door,' she babbled on. 'What! you did not know? Why, she has been ill for weeks. And now——'

"I almost sprang upon her. 'And now,' I cried, 'now what?'

" 'She is dead.'

"That is not the whole story. In the middle of the night, as I learned later, the patient, awakening from a long stupor after a week of delirium, had asked—it was her last utterance—that her bed be moved to the opposite side of the room. Those in attendance had thought the request a vagary of her delirium, but had complied. And there the poor passing soul had exerted its failing will to restore a broken connection—a golden thread of sentiment between its innocence and a monstrous baseness owning a blind, brutal allegiance to the Law of Self.

"What reparation could I make? Are there masses that can be said for the repose of souls that are abroad such nights as this—spirits 'blown about by the viewless winds'—coming in the storm and darkness with signs and portents, hints of memory and presages of doom?

"This is the third visitation. On the first occasion I was too skeptical to do more than verify by natural methods the character of the incident; on the second, I responded to the signal after it had been several times repeated, but without result. To-night's recurrence completes the 'fatal triad' expounded by Parapelius Necromantius. There is no more to tell."

When Dampier had finished his story I could think of nothing relevant that I cared to say, and to question him would have been a hideous impertinence. I rose and bade him good night in a way to convey to him a sense of my sympathy, which he silently acknowledged by a pressure of the hand. That night, alone with his sorrow and remorse, he passed into the Unknown.

A Psychological Shipwreck

IN the summer of 1874 I was in Liverpool, whither I had gone on business for the mercantile house of Bronson & Jarrett, New York. I am William Jarrett; my partner was Zenas Bronson. The firm failed last year, and unable to endure the fall from affluence to poverty he died.

Having finished my business, and feeling the lassitude and exhaustion incident to its dispatch, I felt that a protracted sea voyage would be both agreeable and beneficial, so instead of embarking for my return on one of the many fine passenger steamers I booked for New York on the sailing vessel *Morrow*, upon which I had shipped a large and valuable invoice of the goods I had bought. The *Morrow* was an English ship with, of course, but little accommodation for passengers, of whom there were only myself, a young woman and her servant, who was a middle-aged negress. I thought it singular that a traveling English girl should be so attended, but she afterward explained to me that the woman had been left with her family by a man and his wife from South Carolina, both of whom had died on the same day at the house of the young lady's father in Devonshire—a circumstance in itself sufficiently uncommon to remain rather distinctly in my memory, even had it not afterward transpired in conversation with the young lady that the name of the man was William Jarrett, the same as my own. I knew that a branch of my family had settled in South Carolina, but of them and their history I was ignorant.

The *Morrow* sailed from the mouth of the Mersey on the 15th of June and for several weeks we had fair breezes and unclouded skies. The skipper, an admirable seaman but nothing more, favored us with very little of his society, except at his table; and the young woman, Miss Janette Harford, and I became very well acquainted. We were, in truth, nearly always together, and being of an introspective turn of mind I often endeavored to analyze and define the novel feeling with which she inspired me—a secret, subtle, but powerful attraction which constantly impelled me to seek her; but the attempt was hopeless. I could only be sure that at least it was not love. Having assured myself of this and being certain that she was quite as whole-hearted, I ventured one evening (I remember it was on the 3d of July) as we sat on deck to ask her, laughingly, if she could assist me to resolve my psychological doubt.

For a moment she was silent, with averted face, and I began to fear I had been extremely rude and indelicate; then she fixed her eyes gravely on my own. In an instant my mind was dominated by as strange a fancy as ever entered human consciousness. It seemed as if she were looking at me, not *with*, but *through*, those eyes—from an immeasurable distance behind them—and that a number of other persons, men, women and children, upon whose faces I caught strangely familiar evanescent expressions, clustered about her, struggling with gentle eagerness to look at me through the same orbs. Ship, ocean, sky—all had vanished. I was conscious of nothing but the figures in this extraordinary and fantastic scene. Then all at once darkness fell upon me, and anon from out of it, as to one who grows accustomed by degrees to a dimmer light, my former surroundings of deck and mast and cordage slowly resolved themselves. Miss Harford had closed her eyes and was leaning back in her chair, apparently asleep, the book she had been reading open in her lap. Impelled by surely I cannot say what motive, I glanced at the top of the page; it was a copy of that rare and curious work, "Denneker's Meditations," and the lady's index finger rested on this passage:

"To sundry it is given to be drawn away, and to be apart from the body for a season; for, as concerning rills which would flow across each other the weaker is borne along by the stronger, so there be certain of kin whose paths intersecting, their souls do bear company, the while their bodies go fore-appointed ways, unknowing."

Miss Harford arose, shuddering; the sun had sunk below the horizon, but it was not cold. There was not a breath of wind; there were no clouds in the sky, yet not a star was visible. A hurried tramping sounded on the deck; the captain, summoned from below, joined the first officer, who stood looking at the barometer. "Good God!" I heard him exclaim.

An hour later the form of Janette Harford, invisible in the darkness and spray, was torn from my grasp by the cruel vortex of the sinking ship, and I fainted in the cordage of the floating mast to which I had lashed myself.

It was by lamplight that I awoke. I lay in a berth amid the familiar surroundings of the stateroom of a steamer. On a couch opposite sat a man, half undressed for bed, reading a book. I recognized the face of my friend Gordon Doyle, whom I had met in Liverpool on the day of my embarkation, when he was himself about to sail on the steamer *City of Prague*, on which he had urged me to accompany him.

After some moments I now spoke his name. He simply said, "Well," and turned a leaf in his book without removing his eyes from the page.

"Doyle," I repeated, "did they save *her*?"

He now deigned to look at me and smiled as if amused. He evidently thought me but half awake.

"Her? Whom do you mean?"

"Janette Harford."

His amusement turned to amazement; he stared at me fixedly, saying nothing.

"You will tell me after a while," I continued; "I suppose you will tell me after a while."

A moment later I asked: "What ship is this?"

Doyle stared again. "The steamer *City of Prague*, bound from Liverpool to New York, three weeks out with a broken shaft. Principal passenger, Mr. Gordon Doyle; ditto lunatic, Mr. William Jarrett. These two distinguished travelers embarked together, but they are about to part, it being the resolute intention of the former to pitch the latter overboard."

I sat bolt upright. "Do you mean to say that I have been for three weeks a passenger on this steamer?"

"Yes, pretty nearly; this is the 3d of July."

"Have I been ill?"

"Right as a trivet all the time, and punctual at your meals."

"My God! Doyle, there is some mystery here; do have the goodness to be serious. Was I not rescued from the wreck of the ship *Morrow*?"

Doyle changed color, and approaching me, laid his fingers

on my wrist. A moment later, "What do you know of Janette Harford?" he asked very calmly.

"First tell me what *you* know of her?"

Mr. Doyle gazed at me for some moments as if thinking what to do, then seating himself again on the couch, said:

"Why should I not? I am engaged to marry Janette Harford, whom I met a year ago in London. Her family, one of the wealthiest in Devonshire, cut up rough about it, and we eloped—are eloping rather, for on the day that you and I walked to the landing stage to go aboard this steamer she and her faithful servant, a negress, passed us, driving to the ship *Morrow*. She would not consent to go in the same vessel with me, and it had been deemed best that she take a sailing vessel in order to avoid observation and lessen the risk of detection. I am now alarmed lest this cursed breaking of our machinery may detain us so long that the *Morrow* will get to New York before us, and the poor girl will not know where to go."

I lay still in my berth—so still I hardly breathed. But the subject was evidently not displeasing to Doyle, and after a short pause he resumed:

"By the way, she is only an adopted daughter of the Harfords. Her mother was killed at their place by being thrown from a horse while hunting, and her father, mad with grief, made away with himself the same day. No one ever claimed the child, and after a reasonable time they adopted her. She has grown up in the belief that she is their daughter."

"Doyle, what book are you reading?"

"Oh, it's called 'Denneker's Meditations.' It's a rum lot, Janette gave it to me; she happened to have two copies. Want to see it?"

He tossed me the volume, which opened as it fell. On one of the exposed pages was a marked passage:

"To sundry it is given to be drawn away, and to be apart from the body for a season; for, as concerning rills which would flow across each other the weaker is borne along by the stronger, so there be certain of kin whose paths intersecting, their souls do bear company, the while their bodies go fore-appointed ways, unknowing."

"She had—she has—a singular taste in reading," I managed to say, mastering my agitation.

"Yes. And now perhaps you will have the kindness to explain how you knew her name and that of the ship she sailed in."

"You talked of her in your sleep," I said.

A week later we were towed into the port of New York. But the *Morrow* was never heard from.

The Middle Toe of the Right Foot

IT is well known that the old Manton house is haunted. In all the rural district near about, and even in the town of Marshall, a mile away, not one person of unbiased mind entertains a doubt of it; incredulity is confined to those opinionated persons who will be called "cranks" as soon as the useful word shall have penetrated the intellectual demesne of the Marshall *Advance*. The evidence that the house is haunted is of two kinds: the testimony of disinterested witnesses who have had ocular proof, and that of the house itself. The former may be disregarded and ruled out on any of the various grounds of objection which may be urged against it by the ingenious; but facts within the observation of all are material and controlling.

In the first place, the Manton house has been unoccupied by mortals for more than ten years, and with its outbuildings is slowly falling into decay—a circumstance which in itself the judicious will hardly venture to ignore. It stands a little way off the loneliest reach of the Marshall and Harriston road, in an opening which was once a farm and is still disfigured with strips of rotting fence and half covered with brambles overrunning a stony and sterile soil long unacquainted with the plow. The house itself is in tolerably good condition, though badly weather-stained and in dire need of attention from the glazier, the smaller male population of the region having attested in the manner of its kind its disapproval of dwelling without dwellers. It is two stories in height, nearly square, its front pierced by a single doorway flanked on each side by a window boarded up to the very top. Corresponding windows above, not protected, serve to admit light and rain to the rooms of the upper floor. Grass and weeds grow pretty rankly all about, and a few shade trees, somewhat the worse for wind, and leaning all in one direction, seem to be making a concerted effort to run away. In short, as the Marshall town humorist explained in the columns of the *Advance*, "the proposition that the Manton house is badly haunted is the only logical conclusion from the premises." The fact that in this dwelling Mr. Manton thought it expedient one night some ten years ago to rise and cut the throats of his wife and two small children, removing at once to another part of the country, has no doubt done its share in directing public attention to the fitness of the place for supernatural phenomena.

To this house, one summer evening, came four men in a wagon. Three of them promptly alighted, and the one who had been driving hitched the team to the only remaining post of what had been a fence. The fourth remained seated in the wagon. "Come," said one of his companions, approaching him, while the others moved away in the direction of the dwelling —"this is the place."

The man addressed did not move. "By God!" he said harshly, "this is a trick, and it looks to me as if you were in it."

"Perhaps I am," the other said, looking him straight in the face and speaking in a tone which had something of contempt in it. "You will remember, however, that the choice of place was with your own assent left to the other side. Of course if you are afraid of spooks——"

"I am afraid of nothing," the man interrupted with another oath, and sprang to the ground. The two then joined the others at the door, which one of them had already opened with some difficulty, caused by rust of lock and hinge. All entered. Inside it was dark, but the man who had unlocked the door produced a candle and matches and made a light. He then unlocked a door on their right as they stood in the passage. This gave them entrance to a large, square room that the candle but dimly lighted. The floor had a thick carpeting of dust, which partly muffled their footfalls. Cobwebs were in the angles of the walls and depended from the ceiling like strips of rotting lace, making undulatory movements in the disturbed air. The room had two windows in adjoining sides, but from neither could anything be seen except the rough inner surfaces of boards a few inches from the glass. There was no fireplace, no furniture; there was nothing: besides the cobwebs and the dust, the four men were the only objects there which were not a part of the structure.

Strange enough they looked in the yellow light of the candle. The one who had so reluctantly alighted was especially spectacular —he might have been called sensational. He was of middle age, heavily built, deep chested and broad shouldered. Looking at his figure, one would have said that he had a giant's strength; at his features, that he would use it like a giant. He was clean shaven, his hair rather closely cropped and gray. His low forehead was seamed with wrinkles above the eyes, and over the nose these became vertical. The heavy black brows followed the same law, saved from meeting only by an upward turn at what would otherwise have been the point of contact. Deeply sunken beneath these, glowed in the obscure light a pair of eyes of uncertain color, but obviously enough too small. There was something forbidding in their expression, which was not bettered by the cruel mouth and wide jaw. The nose was well enough, as noses go; one does not expect much of noses. All that was sinister in the man's face seemed accentuated by an unnatural pallor—he appeared altogether bloodless.

The appearance of the other men was sufficiently commonplace: they were such persons as one meets and forgets that he met. All were younger than the man described, between whom and the eldest of the others, who stood apart, there was apparently no kindly feeling. They avoided looking at each other.

"Gentlemen," said the man holding the candle and keys, "I believe everything is right. Are you ready, Mr. Rosser?"

The man standing apart from the group bowed and smiled.

"And you, Mr. Grossmith?"

The heavy man bowed and scowled.

"You will be pleased to remove your outer clothing."

Their hats, coats, waistcoats and neckwear were soon removed and thrown outside the door, in the passage. The man with the candle now nodded, and the fourth man—he who had urged Grossmith to leave the wagon—produced from the pocket of his overcoat two long, murderous-looking bowie-knives, which he drew now from their leather scabbards.

"They are exactly alike," he said, presenting one to each of the two principals—for by this time the dullest observer would have understood the nature of this meeting. It was to be a duel to the death.

Each combatant took a knife, examined it critically near the candle and tested the strength of blade and handle across his lifted knee. Their persons were then searched in turn, each by the second of the other.

"If it is agreeable to you, Mr. Grossmith," said the man holding the light, "you will place yourself in that corner."

He indicated the angle of the room farthest from the door, whither Grossmith retired, his second parting from him with a grasp of the hand which had nothing of cordiality in it. In the angle nearest the door Mr. Rosser stationed himself, and after a whispered consultation his second left him, joining the other near the door. At that moment the candle was suddenly extinguished, leaving all in profound darkness. This may have been done by a draught from the opened door; whatever the cause, the effect was startling.

"Gentlemen," said a voice which sounded strangely unfamiliar in the altered condition affecting the relations of the senses —"gentlemen, you will not move until you hear the closing of the outer door."

A sound of trampling ensued, then the closing of the inner door; and finally the outer one closed with a concussion which shook the entire building.

A few minutes afterward a belated farmer's boy met a light wagon which was being driven furiously toward the town of Marshall. He declared that behind the two figures on the front seat stood a third, with its hands upon the bowed shoulders of the others, who appeared to struggle vainly to free themselves from its grasp. This figure, unlike the others, was clad in white, and had undoubtedly boarded the wagon as it passed the haunted house. As the lad could boast a considerable former experience with the supernatural thereabouts his word had the weight justly due to the testimony of an expert. The story (in connection with the next day's events) eventually appeared in the *Advance*, with some slight literary embellishments and a concluding intimation that the gentlemen referred to would be allowed the use of the paper's columns for their version of the night's adventure. But the privilege remained without a claimant.

II

The events that led up to this "duel in the dark" were simple enough. One evening three young men of the town of Marshall were sitting in a quiet corner of the porch of the village hotel, smoking and discussing such matters as three educated young men of a Southern village would naturally find interesting. Their names were King, Sancher and Rosser. At a little distance, within easy hearing, but taking no part in the conversation, sat a fourth. He was a stranger to the others. They merely knew that on his arrival by the stage-coach that afternoon he had written in the hotel register the name Robert Grossmith. He had not been observed to speak to anyone except the hotel clerk. He seemed, indeed, singularly fond of his own company—or, as the *personnel* of the *Advance* expressed it, "grossly addicted to evil associations." But then it should be said in justice to the stranger that the *personnel* was himself of a too convivial disposition fairly to judge one differently gifted, and had, moreover, experienced a slight rebuff in an effort at an "interview."

"I hate any kind of deformity in a woman," said King, "whether natural or—acquired. I have a theory that any physical defect has its correlative mental and moral defect."

"I infer, then," said Rosser, gravely, "that a lady lacking the moral advantage of a nose would find the struggle to become Mrs. King an arduous enterprise."

"Of course you may put it that way," was the reply; "but, seriously, I once threw over a most charming girl on learning quite accidentally that she had suffered amputation of a toe. My conduct was brutal if you like, but if I had married that girl I should have been miserable for life and should have made her so."

"Whereas," said Sancher, with a light laugh, "by marrying a gentleman of more liberal views she escaped with a parted throat."

"Ah, you know to whom I refer. Yes, she married Manton, but I don't know about his liberality; I'm not sure but he cut her throat because he discovered that she lacked that excellent thing in woman, the middle toe of the right foot."

"Look at that chap!" said Rosser in a low voice, his eyes fixed upon the stranger.

That chap was obviously listening intently to the conversation.

"Damn his impudence!" muttered King—"what ought we to do?"

"That's an easy one," Rosser replied, rising. "Sir," he continued, addressing the stranger, "I think it would be better if you
would remove your chair to the other end of the veranda. The
presence of gentlemen is evidently an unfamiliar situation to
you."

The man sprang to his feet and strode forward with clenched
hands, his face white with rage. All were now standing. Sancher
stepped between the belligerents.

"You are hasty and unjust," he said to Rosser; "this gentleman has done nothing to deserve such language."

But Rosser would not withdraw a word. By the custom of
the country and the time there could be but one outcome to
the quarrel.

"I demand the satisfaction due to a gentleman," said the
stranger, who had become more calm. "I have not an acquaintance in this region. Perhaps you, sir," bowing to Sancher,
"will be kind enough to represent me in this matter."

Sancher accepted the trust—somewhat reluctantly it must
be confessed, for the man's appearance and manner were not at
all to his liking. King, who during the colloquy had hardly removed his eyes from the stranger's face and had not spoken a
word, consented with a nod to act for Rosser, and the upshot
of it was that, the principals having retired, a meeting was arranged for the next evening. The nature of the arrangements
has been already disclosed. The duel with knives in a dark room
was once a commoner feature of Southwestern life than it is
likely to be again. How thin a veneering of "chivalry" covered
the essential brutality of the code under which such encounters
were possible we shall see.

III

In the blaze of a midsummer noonday the old Manton
house was hardly true to its traditions. It was of the earth,
earthy. The sunshine caressed it warmly and affectionately,
with evident disregard of its bad reputation. The grass green-
ing all the expanse in its front seemed to grow, not rankly, but
with a natural and joyous exuberance, and the weeds blossomed quite like plants. Full of charming lights and shadows
and populous with pleasant-voiced birds, the neglected shade

trees no longer struggled to run away, but bent reverently beneath their burdens of sun and song. Even in the glassless upper windows was an expression of peace and contentment, due to the light within. Over the stony fields the visible heat danced with a lively tremor incompatible with the gravity which is an attribute of the supernatural.

Such was the aspect under which the place presented itself to Sheriff Adams and two other men who had come out from Marshall to look at it. One of these men was Mr. King, the sheriff's deputy; the other, whose name was Brewer, was a brother of the late Mrs. Manton. Under a beneficent law of the State relating to property which has been for a certain period abandoned by an owner whose residence cannot be ascertained, the sheriff was legal custodian of the Manton farm and appurtenances thereunto belonging. His present visit was in mere perfunctory compliance with some order of a court in which Mr. Brewer had an action to get possession of the property as heir to his deceased sister. By a mere coincidence, the visit was made on the day after the night that Deputy King had unlocked the house for another and very different purpose. His presence now was not of his own choosing: he had been ordered to accompany his superior and at the moment could think of nothing more prudent than simulated alacrity in obedience to the command.

Carelessly opening the front door, which to his surprise was not locked, the sheriff was amazed to see, lying on the floor of the passage into which it opened, a confused heap of men's apparel. Examination showed it to consist of two hats, and the same number of coats, waistcoats and scarves, all in a remarkably good state of preservation, albeit somewhat defiled by the dust in which they lay. Mr. Brewer was equally astonished, but Mr. King's emotion is not of record. With a new and lively interest in his own actions the sheriff now unlatched and pushed open a door on the right, and the three entered. The room was apparently vacant—no; as their eyes became accustomed to the dimmer light something was visible in the farthest angle of the wall. It was a human figure—that of a man crouching close in the corner. Something in the attitude made the intruders halt when they had barely passed the threshold. The figure more and more clearly defined itself. The man was upon one knee, his back in the angle of the wall, his shoulders elevated to the level of his ears, his hands before his face, palms outward, the fingers spread and crooked like claws; the white face turned upward on the retracted neck had an expression of unutterable fright, the mouth half open, the eyes incredibly expanded. He was stone dead. Yet, with the exception of a bowie-knife, which had evidently fallen from his own hand, not another object was in the room.

In thick dust that covered the floor were some confused footprints near the door and along the wall through which it opened. Along one of the adjoining walls, too, past the boarded-up windows, was the trail made by the man himself in reaching his corner. Instinctively in approaching the body the three men followed that trail. The sheriff grasped one of the outthrown arms; it was as rigid as iron, and the application of a gentle force rocked the entire body without altering the relation of its parts. Brewer, pale with excitement, gazed intently into the distorted face. "God of mercy!" he suddenly cried, "it is Manton!"

"You are right," said King, with an evident attempt at calmness: "I knew Manton. He then wore a full beard and his hair long, but this is he."

He might have added: "I recognized him when he challenged Rosser. I told Rosser and Sancher who he was before we played him this horrible trick. When Rosser left this dark room at our heels, forgetting his outer clothing in the excitement, and driving away with us in his shirt sleeves—all through the discreditable proceedings we knew whom we were dealing with, murderer and coward that he was!"

But nothing of this did Mr. King say. With his better light he was trying to penetrate the mystery of the man's death. That he had not once moved from the corner where he had been stationed; that his posture was that of neither attack nor defense; that he had dropped his weapon; that he had obviously perished of sheer horror of something that he *saw*—these were circumstances which Mr. King's disturbed intelligence could not rightly comprehend.

Groping in intellectual darkness for a clew to his maze of doubt, his gaze, directed mechanically downward in the way of one who ponders momentous matters, fell upon something which, there, in the light of day and in the presence of living companions, affected him with terror. In the dust of years that lay thick upon the floor—leading from the door by which they had entered, straight across the room to within a yard of Manton's crouching corpse—were three parallel lines of footprints—light but definite impressions of bare feet, the outer ones those of small children, the inner a woman's. From the point at which they ended they did not return; they pointed all one way. Brewer, who had observed them at the same moment, was leaning forward in an attitude of rapt attention, horribly pale.

"Look at that!" he cried, pointing with both hands at the nearest print of the woman's right foot, where she had apparently stopped and stood. "The middle toe is missing—it was Gertrude!"

Gertrude was the late Mrs. Manton, sister to Mr. Brewer.

John Mortonson's Funeral*

JOHN MORTONSON was dead: his lines in "the tragedy 'Man'" had all been spoken and he had left the stage.

The body rested in a fine mahogany coffin fitted with a plate of glass. All arrangements for the funeral had been so well attended to that had the deceased known he would doubtless have approved. The face, as it showed under the glass, was not disagreeable to look upon: it bore a faint smile, and as the death had been painless, had not been distorted beyond the repairing power of the undertaker. At two o'clock of the afternoon the friends were to assemble to pay their last tribute of respect to one who had no further need of friends and respect. The surviving members of the family came severally every few minutes to the casket and wept above the placid features beneath the glass. This did them no good; it did no good to John Mortonson; but in the presence of death reason and philosophy are silent.

As the hour of two approached the friends began to arrive and after offering such consolation to the stricken relatives as the proprieties of the occasion required, solemnly seated themselves about the room with an augmented consciousness of their importance in the scheme funereal. Then the minister came, and in that overshadowing presence the lesser lights went into eclipse. His entrance was followed by that of the widow, whose lamentations filled the room. She approached the casket and after leaning her face against the cold glass for a moment was gently led to a seat near her daughter. Mournfully and low the man of God began his eulogy of the dead, and his doleful voice, mingled with the sobbing which it was its purpose to stimulate and sustain, rose and fell, seemed to come and go, like the sound of a sullen sea. The gloomy day grew darker as he spoke; a curtain of cloud underspread the sky and

*Rough notes of this tale were found among the papers of the late Leigh Bierce. It is printed here with such revision only as the author might himself have made in transcription.

a few drops of rain fell audibly. It seemed as if all nature were weeping for John Mortonson.

When the minister had finished his eulogy with prayer a hymn was sung and the pall-bearers took their places beside the bier. As the last notes of the hymn died away the widow ran to the coffin, cast herself upon it and sobbed hysterically. Gradually, however, she yielded to dissuasion, becoming more composed; and as the minister was in the act of leading her away her eyes sought the face of the dead beneath the glass. She threw up her arms and with a shriek fell backward insensible.

The mourners sprang forward to the coffin, the friends followed, and as the clock on the mantel solemnly struck three all were staring down upon the face of John Mortonson, deceased.

They turned away, sick and faint. One man, trying in his terror to escape the awful sight, stumbled against the coffin so heavily as to knock away one of its frail supports. The coffin fell to the floor, the glass was shattered to bits by the concussion.

From the opening crawled John Mortonson's cat, which lazily leapt to the floor, sat up, tranquilly wiped its crimson muzzle with a forepaw, then walked with dignity from the room.

The Realm of the Unreal

FOR a part of the distance between Auburn and Newcastle the road—first on one side of a creek and then on the other—occupies the whole bottom of the ravine, being partly cut out of the steep hillside, and partly built up with bowlders removed from the creek-bed by the miners. The hills are wooded, the course of the ravine is sinuous. In a dark night careful driving is required in order not to go off into the water. The night that I have in memory was dark, the creek a torrent, swollen by a recent storm. I had driven up from Newcastle and was within about a mile of Auburn in the darkest and narrowest part of the ravine, looking intently ahead of my horse for the roadway. Suddenly I saw a man almost under the animal's nose, and reined in with a jerk that came near setting the creature upon its haunches.

"I beg your pardon," I said; "I did not see you, sir."

"You could hardly be expected to see me," the man replied, civilly, approaching the side of the vehicle; "and the noise of the creek prevented my hearing you."

I at once recognized the voice, although five years had passed since I had heard it. I was not particularly well pleased to hear it now.

"You are Dr. Dorrimore, I think," said I.

"Yes; and you are my good friend Mr. Manrich. I am more than glad to see you—the excess," he added, with a light laugh, "being due to the fact that I am going your way, and naturally expect an invitation to ride with you."

"Which I extend with all my heart."

That was not altogether true.

Dr. Dorrimore thanked me as he seated himself beside me, and I drove cautiously forward, as before. Doubtless it is fancy, but it seems to me now that the remaining distance was made in a chill fog; that I was uncomfortably cold; that the way was longer than ever before, and the town, when we reached it, cheerless, forbidding, and desolate. It must have been early in the evening, yet I do not recollect a light in any of the houses nor a living thing in the streets. Dorrimore explained at some length how he happened to be there, and where he had been during the years that had elapsed since I had seen him. I recall the fact of the narrative, but none of the facts narrated. He had been in foreign countries and had returned—this is all that my memory retains, and this I already knew. As to myself I cannot remember that I spoke a word, though doubtless I did. Of one thing I am distinctly conscious: the man's presence at my side was strangely distasteful and disquieting—so much so that when I at last pulled up under the lights of the Putnam House I experienced a sense of having escaped some spiritual peril of a nature peculiarly forbidding. This sense of relief was somewhat modified by the discovery that Dr. Dorrimore was living at the same hotel.

II

In partial explanation of my feelings regarding Dr. Dorrimore I will relate briefly the circumstances under which I had met him some years before. One evening a half-dozen men of whom I was one were sitting in the library of the Bohemian Club in San Francisco. The conversation had turned to the subject of sleight-of-hand and the feats of the *prestidigitateurs*, one of whom was then exhibiting at a local theatre.

"These fellows are pretenders in a double sense," said one of the party; "they can do nothing which it is worth one's while to be made a dupe by. The humblest wayside juggler in India could mystify them to the verge of lunacy."

"For example, how?" asked another, lighting a cigar.

"For example, by all their common and familiar performances —throwing large objects into the air which never come down; causing plants to sprout, grow visibly and blossom, in bare ground chosen by spectators; putting a man into a wicker basket, piercing him through and through with a sword while he shrieks and bleeds, and then—the basket being opened nothing is there; tossing the free end of a silken ladder into the air, mounting it and disappearing."

"Nonsense!" I said, rather uncivilly, I fear. "You surely do not believe such things?"

"Certainly not: I have seen them too often."

"But I do," said a journalist of considerable local fame as a picturesque reporter. "I have so frequently related them that nothing but observation could shake my conviction. Why, gentlemen, I have my own word for it."

Nobody laughed—all were looking at something behind me. Turning in my seat I saw a man in evening dress who had just entered the room. He was exceedingly dark, almost swarthy, with a thin face, black-bearded to the lips, an abundance of coarse black hair in some disorder, a high nose and eyes that glittered with as soulless an expression as those of a cobra. One of the group rose and introduced him as Dr. Dorrimore, of Calcutta. As each of us was presented in turn he acknowledged the fact with a profound bow in the Oriental manner, but with nothing of Oriental gravity. His smile impressed me as cynical and a trifle contemptuous. His whole demeanor I can describe only as disagreeably engaging.

His presence led the conversation into other channels. He said little—I do not recall anything of what he did say. I thought his voice singularly rich and melodious, but it affected me in the same way as his eyes and smile. In a few minutes I rose to go. He also rose and put on his overcoat.

"Mr. Manrich," he said, "I am going your way."

"The devil you are!" I thought. "How do you know which way I am going?" Then I said, "I shall be pleased to have your company."

We left the building together. No cabs were in sight, the street cars had gone to bed, there was a full moon and the cool night air was delightful; we walked up the California street hill. I took that direction thinking he would naturally wish to take another, toward one of the hotels.

"You do not believe what is told of the Hindu jugglers," he said abruptly.

"How do you know that?" I asked.

Without replying he laid his hand lightly upon my arm and with the other pointed to the stone sidewalk directly in front. There, almost at our feet, lay the dead body of a man, the face upturned and white in the moonlight! A sword whose hilt sparkled with gems stood fixed and upright in the breast; a pool of blood had collected on the stones of the sidewalk.

I was startled and terrified—not only by what I saw, but by the circumstances under which I saw it. Repeatedly during our ascent of the hill my eyes, I thought, had traversed the whole reach of that sidewalk, from street to street. How could they have been insensible to this dreadful object now so conspicuous in the white moonlight?

As my dazed faculties cleared I observed that the body was in evening dress; the overcoat thrown wide open revealed the dresscoat, the white tie, the broad expanse of shirt front pierced by the sword. And—horrible revelation!—the face, except for its pallor, was that of my companion! It was to the minutest detail of dress and feature Dr. Dorrimore himself. Bewildered and horrified, I turned to look for the living man. He was nowhere visible, and with an added terror I retired from the place, down the hill in the direction whence I had come. I had taken but a few strides when a strong grasp upon my shoulder arrested me. I came near crying out with terror: the dead man, the sword still fixed in his breast, stood beside me! Pulling out the sword with his disengaged hand, he flung it from him, the moonlight glinting upon the jewels of its hilt and the unsullied steel of its blade. It fell with a clang upon the sidewalk ahead and—vanished! The man, swarthy as before, relaxed his grasp upon my shoulder and looked at me with the same cynical regard that I had observed on first meeting him. The dead have not that look—it partly restored me, and turning my head backward, I saw the smooth white expanse of sidewalk, unbroken from street to street.

"What is all this nonsense, you devil?" I demanded, fiercely enough, though weak and trembling in every limb.

"It is what some are pleased to call jugglery," he answered, with a light, hard laugh.

He turned down Dupont street and I saw him no more until we met in the Auburn ravine.

III

On the day after my second meeting with Dr. Dorrimore I did not see him: the clerk in the Putnam House explained that a slight illness confined him to his rooms. That afternoon at the railway station I was surprised and made happy by the unexpected arrival of Miss Margaret Corray and her mother, from Oakland.

This is not a love story. I am no storyteller, and love as it is cannot be portrayed in a literature dominated and enthralled by the debasing tyranny which "sentences letters" in the name of the Young Girl. Under the Young Girl's blighting reign— or rather under the rule of those false Ministers of the Censure who have appointed themselves to the custody of her welfare—love

> veils her sacred fires,
> And, unaware, Morality expires,

famished upon the sifted meal and distilled water of a prudish purveyance.

Let it suffice that Miss Corray and I were engaged in marriage. She and her mother went to the hotel at which I lived, and for two weeks I saw her daily. That I was happy needs hardly be said; the only bar to my perfect enjoyment of those golden days was the presence of Dr. Dorrimore, whom I had felt compelled to introduce to the ladies.

By them he was evidently held in favor. What could I say? I knew absolutely nothing to his discredit. His manners were those of a cultivated and considerate gentleman; and to women a man's manner is the man. On one or two occasions when I saw Miss Corray walking with him I was furious, and once had the indiscretion to protest. Asked for reasons, I had none to give and fancied I saw in her expression a shade of contempt for the vagaries of a jealous mind. In time I grew morose and consciously disagreeable, and resolved in my madness to return to San Francisco the next day. Of this, however, I said nothing.

IV

There was at Auburn an old, abandoned cemetery. It was nearly in the heart of the town, yet by night it was as gruesome a place as the most dismal of human moods could crave. The railings about the plats were prostrate, decayed, or altogether gone. Many of the graves were sunken, from others grew sturdy pines, whose roots had committed unspeakable sin. The headstones were fallen and broken across; brambles overran the ground; the fence was mostly gone, and cows and pigs wandered there at will; the place was a dishonor to the living, a calumny on the dead, a blasphemy against God.

The evening of the day on which I had taken my madman's resolution to depart in anger from all that was dear to me found me in that congenial spot. The light of the half moon fell ghostly through the foliage of trees in spots and patches, revealing much that was unsightly, and the black shadows seemed conspiracies withholding to the proper time revelations of darker import. Passing along what had been a gravel path, I saw emerging from shadow the figure of Dr. Dorrimore. I was myself in shadow, and stood still with clenched hands and set teeth, trying to control the impulse to leap upon and strangle him. A moment later a second figure joined him and clung to his arm. It was Margaret Corray!

I cannot rightly relate what occurred. I know that I sprang forward, bent upon murder; I know that I was found in the gray of the morning, bruised and bloody, with finger marks upon my throat. I was taken to the Putnam House, where for days I lay in a delirium. All this I know, for I have been told. And of my own knowledge I know that when consciousness returned with convalescence I sent for the clerk of the hotel.

"Are Mrs. Corray and her daughter still here?" I asked.

"What name did you say?"

"Corray."

"Nobody of that name has been here."

"I beg you will not trifle with me," I said petulantly. "You see that I am all right now; tell me the truth."

"I give you my word," he replied with evident sincerity, "we have had no guests of that name."

His words stupefied me. I lay for a few moments in silence; then I asked: "Where is Dr. Dorrimore?"

"He left on the morning of your fight and has not been heard of since. It was a rough deal he gave you."

V

Such are the facts of this case. Margaret Corray is now my wife. She has never seen Auburn, and during the weeks whose history as it shaped itself in my brain I have endeavored to relate, was living at her home in Oakland, wondering where her lover was and why he did not write. The other day I saw in the Baltimore *Sun* the following paragraph:

"Professor Valentine Dorrimore, the hypnotist, had a large audience last night. The lecturer, who has lived most of his life in India, gave some marvelous exhibitions of his power, hypnotizing anyone who chose to submit himself to the experiment, by merely looking at him. In fact, he twice hypnotized the entire audience (reporters alone exempted), making all entertain the most extraordinary illusions. The most valuable feature of the lecture was the disclosure of the methods of the Hindu jugglers in their famous performances, familiar in the mouths of travelers. The professor declares that these thaumaturgists have acquired such skill in the art which he learned at their feet that they perform their miracles by simply throwing the 'spectators' into a state of hypnosis and telling them what to see and hear. His assertion that a peculiarly susceptible subject may be kept in the realm of the unreal for weeks, months, and even years, dominated by whatever delusions and hallucinations the operator may from time to time suggest, is a trifle disquieting."

John Bartine's Watch

"THE exact time? Good God! my friend, why do you insist? One would think—but what does it matter; it is easily bedtime—isn't that near enough? But, here, if you must set your watch, take mine and see for yourself."

With that he detached his watch—a tremendously heavy, old-fashioned one—from the chain, and handed it to me; then turned away, and walking across the room to a shelf of books, began an examination of their backs. His agitation and evident distress surprised me; they appeared reasonless. Having set my watch by his, I stepped over to where he stood and said, "Thank you."

As he took his timepiece and reattached it to the guard I observed that his hands were unsteady. With a tact upon which I greatly prided myself, I sauntered carelessly to the sideboard and took some brandy and water; then, begging his pardon for my thoughtlessness, asked him to have some and went back to my seat by the fire, leaving him to help himself, as was our custom. He did so and presently joined me at the hearth, as tranquil as ever.

This odd little incident occurred in my apartment, where John Bartine was passing an evening. We had dined together at the club, had come home in a cab and—in short, everything had been done in the most prosaic way; and why John Bartine should break in upon the natural and established order of things to make himself spectacular with a display of emotion, apparently for his own entertainment, I could nowise understand. The more I thought of it, while his brilliant conversational gifts were commending themselves to my inattention, the more curious I grew, and of course had no difficulty in persuading myself that my curiosity was friendly solicitude. That is the disguise that curiosity usually assumes to evade resentment. So I ruined one of the finest sentences of his disregarded monologue by cutting it short without ceremony.

"John Bartine," I said, "you must try to forgive me if I am

wrong, but with the light that I have at present I cannot concede your right to go all to pieces when asked the time o' night. I cannot admit that it is proper to experience a mysterious reluctance to look your own watch in the face and to cherish in my presence, without explanation, painful emotions which are denied to me, and which are none of my business."

To this ridiculous speech Bartine made no immediate reply, but sat looking gravely into the fire. Fearing that I had offended I was about to apologize and beg him to think no more about the matter, when looking me calmly in the eyes he said:

"My dear fellow, the levity of your manner does not at all disguise the hideous impudence of your demand; but happily I had already decided to tell you what you wish to know, and no manifestation of your unworthiness to hear it shall alter my decision. Be good enough to give me your attention and you shall hear all about the matter.

"This watch," he said, "had been in my family for three generations before it fell to me. Its original owner, for whom it was made, was my great-grandfather, Bramwell Olcott Bartine, a wealthy planter of Colonial Virginia, and as stanch a Tory as ever lay awake nights contriving new kinds of maledictions for the head of Mr. Washington, and new methods of aiding and abetting good King George. One day this worthy gentleman had the deep misfortune to perform for his cause a service of capital importance which was not recognized as legitimate by those who suffered its disadvantages. It does not matter what it was, but among its minor consequences was my excellent ancestor's arrest one night in his own house by a party of Mr. Washington's rebels. He was permitted to say farewell to his weeping family, and was then marched away into the darkness which swallowed him up forever. Not the slenderest clew to his fate was ever found. After the war the most diligent inquiry and the offer of large rewards failed to turn up any of his captors or any fact concerning his disappearance. He had disappeared, and that was all."

Something in Bartine's manner that was not in his words—I hardly knew what it was—prompted me to ask:

"What is your view of the matter—of the justice of it?"

"My view of it," he flamed out, bringing his clenched hand

down upon the table as if he had been in a public house dicing with blackguards—"my view of it is that it was a characteristically dastardly assassination by that damned traitor, Washington, and his ragamuffin rebels!"

For some minutes nothing was said: Bartine was recovering his temper, and I waited. Then I said:

"Was that all?"

"No—there was something else. A few weeks after my great-grandfather's arrest his watch was found lying on the porch at the front door of his dwelling. It was wrapped in a sheet of letter paper bearing the name of Rupert Bartine, his only son, my grandfather. I am wearing that watch."

Bartine paused. His usually restless black eyes were staring fixedly into the grate, a point of red light in each, reflected from the glowing coals. He seemed to have forgotten me. A sudden threshing of the branches of a tree outside one of the windows, and almost at the same instant a rattle of rain against the glass, recalled him to a sense of his surroundings. A storm had risen, heralded by a single gust of wind, and in a few moments the steady plash of the water on the pavement was distinctly heard. I hardly know why I relate this incident; it seemed somehow to have a certain significance and relevancy which I am unable now to discern. It at least added an element of seriousness, almost solemnity. Bartine resumed:

"I have a singular feeling toward this watch—a kind of affection for it; I like to have it about me, though partly from its weight, and partly for a reason I shall now explain, I seldom carry it. The reason is this: Every evening when I have it with me I feel an unaccountable desire to open and consult it, even if I can think of no reason for wishing to know the time. But if I yield to it, the moment my eyes rest upon the dial I am filled with a mysterious apprehension—a sense of imminent calamity. And this is the more insupportable the nearer it is to eleven o'clock—by this watch, no matter what the actual hour may be. After the hands have registered eleven the desire to look is gone; I am entirely indifferent. Then I can consult the thing as often as I like, with no more emotion than you feel in looking at your own. Naturally I have trained myself not to look at that watch in the evening before eleven; nothing could induce me.

Your insistence this evening upset me a trifle. I felt very much as I suppose an opium-eater might feel if his yearning for his special and particular kind of hell were re-enforced by opportunity and advice.

"Now that is my story, and I have told it in the interest of your trumpery science; but if on any evening hereafter you observe me wearing this damnable watch, and you have the thoughtfulness to ask me the hour, I shall beg leave to put you to the inconvenience of being knocked down."

His humor did not amuse me. I could see that in relating his delusion he was again somewhat disturbed. His concluding smile was positively ghastly, and his eyes had resumed something more than their old restlessness; they shifted hither and thither about the room with apparent aimlessness and I fancied had taken on a wild expression, such as is sometimes observed in cases of dementia. Perhaps this was my own imagination, but at any rate I was now persuaded that my friend was afflicted with a most singular and interesting monomania. Without, I trust, any abatement of my affectionate solicitude for him as a friend, I began to regard him as a patient, rich in possibilities of profitable study. Why not? Had he not described his delusion in the interest of science? Ah, poor fellow, he was doing more for science than he knew: not only his story but himself was in evidence. I should cure him if I could, of course, but first I should make a little experiment in psychology—nay, the experiment itself might be a step in his restoration.

"That is very frank and friendly of you, Bartine," I said cordially, "and I'm rather proud of your confidence. It is all very odd, certainly. Do you mind showing me the watch?"

He detached it from his waistcoat, chain and all, and passed it to me without a word. The case was of gold, very thick and strong, and singularly engraved. After closely examining the dial and observing that it was nearly twelve o'clock, I opened it at the back and was interested to observe an inner case of ivory, upon which was painted a miniature portrait in that exquisite and delicate manner which was in vogue during the eighteenth century.

"Why, bless my soul!" I exclaimed, feeling a sharp artistic delight—"how under the sun did you get that done? I thought miniature painting on ivory was a lost art."

"That," he replied, gravely smiling, "is not I; it is my excellent great-grandfather, the late Bramwell Olcott Bartine, Esquire, of Virginia. He was younger then than later—about my age, in fact. It is said to resemble me; do you think so?"

"Resemble you? I should say so! Barring the costume, which I supposed you to have assumed out of compliment to the art—or for *vraisemblance*, so to say—and the no mustache, that portrait is you in every feature, line, and expression."

No more was said at that time. Bartine took a book from the table and began reading. I heard outside the incessant plash of the rain in the street. There were occasional hurried footfalls on the sidewalks; and once a slower, heavier tread seemed to cease at my door—a policeman, I thought, seeking shelter in the doorway. The boughs of the trees tapped significantly on the window panes, as if asking for admittance. I remember it all through these years and years of a wiser, graver life.

Seeing myself unobserved, I took the old-fashioned key that dangled from the chain and quickly turned back the hands of the watch a full hour; then, closing the case, I handed Bartine his property and saw him replace it on his person.

"I think you said," I began, with assumed carelessness, "that after eleven the sight of the dial no longer affects you. As it is now nearly twelve"—looking at my own timepiece—"perhaps, if you don't resent my pursuit of proof, you will look at it now."

He smiled good-humoredly, pulled out the watch again, opened it, and instantly sprang to his feet with a cry that Heaven has not had the mercy to permit me to forget! His eyes, their blackness strikingly intensified by the pallor of his face, were fixed upon the watch, which he clutched in both hands. For some time he remained in that attitude without uttering another sound; then, in a voice that I should not have recognized as his, he said:

"Damn you! it is two minutes to eleven!"

I was not unprepared for some such outbreak, and without rising replied, calmly enough:

"I beg your pardon; I must have misread your watch in setting my own by it."

He shut the case with a sharp snap and put the watch in his pocket. He looked at me and made an attempt to smile, but his lower lip quivered and he seemed unable to close his mouth.

His hands, also, were shaking, and he thrust them, clenched, into the pockets of his sack-coat. The courageous spirit was manifestly endeavoring to subdue the coward body. The effort was too great; he began to sway from side to side, as from vertigo, and before I could spring from my chair to support him his knees gave way and he pitched awkwardly forward and fell upon his face. I sprang to assist him to rise; but when John Bartine rises we shall all rise.

The *post-mortem* examination disclosed nothing; every organ was normal and sound. But when the body had been prepared for burial a faint dark circle was seen to have developed around the neck; at least I was so assured by several persons who said they saw it, but of my own knowledge I cannot say if that was true.

Nor can I set limitations to the law of heredity. I do not know that in the spiritual world a sentiment or emotion may not survive the heart that held it, and seek expression in a kindred life, ages removed. Surely, if I were to guess at the fate of Bramwell Olcott Bartine, I should guess that he was hanged at eleven o'clock in the evening, and that he had been allowed several hours in which to prepare for the change.

As to John Bartine, my friend, my patient for five minutes, and—Heaven forgive me!—my victim for eternity, there is no more to say. He is buried, and his watch with him—I saw to that. May God rest his soul in Paradise, and the soul of his Virginian ancestor, if, indeed, they are two souls.

The Damned Thing

ONE DOES NOT ALWAYS EAT WHAT IS ON THE TABLE

B Y the light of a tallow candle which had been placed on one end of a rough table a man was reading something written in a book. It was an old account book, greatly worn; and the writing was not, apparently, very legible, for the man sometimes held the page close to the flame of the candle to get a stronger light on it. The shadow of the book would then throw into obscurity a half of the room, darkening a number of faces and figures; for besides the reader, eight other men were present. Seven of them sat against the rough log walls, silent, motionless, and the room being small, not very far from the table. By extending an arm any one of them could have touched the eighth man, who lay on the table, face upward, partly covered by a sheet, his arms at his sides. He was dead.

The man with the book was not reading aloud, and no one spoke; all seemed to be waiting for something to occur; the dead man only was without expectation. From the blank darkness outside came in, through the aperture that served for a window, all the ever unfamiliar noises of night in the wilderness —the long nameless note of a distant coyote; the stilly pulsing thrill of tireless insects in trees; strange cries of night birds, so different from those of the birds of day; the drone of great blundering beetles, and all that mysterious chorus of small sounds that seem always to have been but half heard when they have suddenly ceased, as if conscious of an indiscretion. But nothing of all this was noted in that company; its members were not overmuch addicted to idle interest in matters of no practical importance; that was obvious in every line of their rugged faces—obvious even in the dim light of the single candle. They were evidently men of the vicinity—farmers and woodsmen.

The person reading was a trifle different; one would have said of him that he was of the world, worldly, albeit there was that in his attire which attested a certain fellowship with the organisms of his environment. His coat would hardly have passed muster in San Francisco; his foot-gear was not of urban origin, and the hat that lay by him on the floor (he was the only one uncovered) was such that if one had considered it as an article of mere personal adornment he would have missed its meaning. In countenance the man was rather prepossessing, with just a hint of sternness; though that he may have assumed or cultivated, as appropriate to one in authority. For he was a coroner. It was by virtue of his office that he had possession of the book in which he was reading; it had been found among the dead man's effects—in his cabin, where the inquest was now taking place.

When the coroner had finished reading he put the book into his breast pocket. At that moment the door was pushed open and a young man entered. He, clearly, was not of mountain birth and breeding: he was clad as those who dwell in cities. His clothing was dusty, however, as from travel. He had, in fact, been riding hard to attend the inquest.

The coroner nodded; no one else greeted him.

"We have waited for you," said the coroner. "It is necessary to have done with this business to-night."

The young man smiled. "I am sorry to have kept you," he said. "I went away, not to evade your summons, but to post to my newspaper an account of what I suppose I am called back to relate."

The coroner smiled.

"The account that you posted to your newspaper," he said, "differs, probably, from that which you will give here under oath."

"That," replied the other, rather hotly and with a visible flush, "is as you please. I used manifold paper and have a copy of what I sent. It was not written as news, for it is incredible, but as fiction. It may go as a part of my testimony under oath."

"But you say it is incredible."

"That is nothing to you, sir, if I also swear that it is true."

The coroner was silent for a time, his eyes upon the floor. The men about the sides of the cabin talked in whispers, but seldom withdrew their gaze from the face of the corpse. Presently the coroner lifted his eyes and said: "We will resume the inquest."

The men removed their hats. The witness was sworn.

"What is your name?" the coroner asked.

"William Harker."

"Age?"

"Twenty-seven."

"You knew the deceased, Hugh Morgan?"

"Yes."

"You were with him when he died?"

"Near him."

"How did that happen—your presence, I mean?"

"I was visiting him at this place to shoot and fish. A part of my purpose, however, was to study him and his odd, solitary way of life. He seemed a good model for a character in fiction. I sometimes write stories."

"I sometimes read them."

"Thank you."

"Stories in general—not yours."

Some of the jurors laughed. Against a sombre background humor shows high lights. Soldiers in the intervals of battle laugh easily, and a jest in the death chamber conquers by surprise.

"Relate the circumstances of this man's death," said the coroner. "You may use any notes or memoranda that you please."

The witness understood. Pulling a manuscript from his breast pocket he held it near the candle and turning the leaves until he found the passage that he wanted began to read.

II

WHAT MAY HAPPEN IN A FIELD OF WILD OATS

" . . . The sun had hardly risen when we left the house. We were looking for quail, each with a shotgun, but we had only one dog. Morgan said that our best ground was beyond a certain ridge that he pointed out, and we crossed it by a trail through the *chaparral*. On the other side was comparatively level ground, thickly covered with wild oats. As we emerged from the *chaparral* Morgan was but a few yards in advance. Suddenly we heard, at a little distance to our right and partly in front, a noise as of some animal thrashing about in the bushes, which we could see were violently agitated.

" 'We've started a deer,' I said. 'I wish we had brought a rifle.'

"Morgan, who had stopped and was intently watching the agitated *chaparral*, said nothing, but had cocked both barrels of his gun and was holding it in readiness to aim. I thought him a trifle excited, which surprised me, for he had a reputation for exceptional coolness, even in moments of sudden and imminent peril.

" 'O, come,' I said. 'You are not going to fill up a deer with quail-shot, are you?'

"Still he did not reply; but catching a sight of his face as he turned it slightly toward me I was struck by the intensity of his look. Then I understood that we had serious business in hand and my first conjecture was that we had 'jumped' a grizzly. I advanced to Morgan's side, cocking my piece as I moved.

"The bushes were now quiet and the sounds had ceased, but Morgan was as attentive to the place as before.

" 'What is it? What the devil is it?' I asked.

" 'That Damned Thing!' he replied, without turning his head. His voice was husky and unnatural. He trembled visibly.

"I was about to speak further, when I observed the wild oats near the place of the disturbance moving in the most inexplicable way. I can hardly describe it. It seemed as if stirred by a streak of wind, which not only bent it, but pressed it down—crushed it so that it did not rise; and this movement was slowly prolonging itself directly toward us.

"Nothing that I had ever seen had affected me so strangely as this unfamiliar and unaccountable phenomenon, yet I am unable to recall any sense of fear. I remember—and tell it here because, singularly enough, I recollected it then—that once in looking carelessly out of an open window I momentarily mistook a small tree close at hand for one of a group of larger trees at a little distance away. It looked the same size as the others, but being more distinctly and sharply defined in mass and detail seemed out of harmony with them. It was a mere falsification of the law of aërial perspective, but it startled, almost terrified me. We so rely upon the orderly operation of familiar natural laws that any seeming suspension of them is noted as a menace to our safety, a warning of unthinkable calamity. So now the apparently causeless movement of the herbage and the slow, undeviating approach of the line of disturbance were distinctly disquieting. My companion appeared actually frightened, and I could hardly credit my senses when I saw him suddenly throw his gun to his shoulder and fire both barrels at the agitated grain! Before the smoke of the discharge had cleared away I heard a loud savage cry—a scream like that of a wild animal—and flinging his gun upon the ground Morgan sprang away and ran swiftly from the spot. At the same instant I was thrown violently to the ground by the impact of something unseen in the smoke—some soft, heavy substance that seemed thrown against me with great force.

"Before I could get upon my feet and recover my gun, which seemed to have been struck from my hands, I heard Morgan crying out as if in mortal agony, and mingling with his cries were such hoarse, savage sounds as one hears from fighting dogs. Inexpressibly terrified, I struggled to my feet and looked in the direction of Morgan's retreat; and may Heaven in mercy spare me from another sight like that! At a distance of less than thirty yards was my friend, down upon one knee, his head thrown back at a frightful angle, hatless, his long hair in disorder and his whole body in violent movement from side to side, backward and forward. His right arm was lifted and seemed to lack the hand—at least, I could see none. The other arm was invisible. At times, as my memory now reports this extraordinary scene, I could discern but a part of his body; it was as if he had been partly blotted out—I cannot otherwise express it—then a shifting of his position would bring it all into view again.

"All this must have occurred within a few seconds, yet in that time Morgan assumed all the postures of a determined wrestler vanquished by superior weight and strength. I saw nothing but him, and him not always distinctly. During the entire incident his shouts and curses were heard, as if through an enveloping uproar of such sounds of rage and fury as I had never heard from the throat of man or brute!

"For a moment only I stood irresolute, then throwing down my gun I ran forward to my friend's assistance. I had a vague belief that he was suffering from a fit, or some form of convulsion. Before I could reach his side he was down and quiet. All sounds had ceased, but with a feeling of such terror as even

these awful events had not inspired I now saw again the mysterious movement of the wild oats, prolonging itself from the
trampled area about the prostrate man toward the edge of a
wood. It was only when it had reached the wood that I was
able to withdraw my eyes and look at my companion. He was
dead."

III
A MAN THOUGH NAKED MAY BE IN RAGS

The coroner rose from his seat and stood beside the dead
man. Lifting an edge of the sheet he pulled it away, exposing
the entire body, altogether naked and showing in the candle-
light a claylike yellow. It had, however, broad maculations of
bluish black, obviously caused by extravasated blood from
contusions. The chest and sides looked as if they had been
beaten with a bludgeon. There were dreadful lacerations; the
skin was torn in strips and shreds.

The coroner moved round to the end of the table and undid
a silk handkerchief which had been passed under the chin and
knotted on the top of the head. When the handkerchief was
drawn away it exposed what had been the throat. Some of the
jurors who had risen to get a better view repented their curiosity and turned away their faces. Witness Harker went to the
open window and leaned out across the sill, faint and sick.
Dropping the handkerchief upon the dead man's neck the
coroner stepped to an angle of the room and from a pile of
clothing produced one garment after another, each of which
he held up a moment for inspection. All were torn, and stiff
with blood. The jurors did not make a closer inspection. They
seemed rather uninterested. They had, in truth, seen all this
before; the only thing that was new to them being Harker's
testimony.

"Gentlemen," the coroner said, "we have no more evidence,
I think. Your duty has been already explained to you; if there is
nothing you wish to ask you may go outside and consider your
verdict."

The foreman rose—a tall, bearded man of sixty, coarsely
clad.

"I should like to ask one question, Mr. Coroner," he said. "What asylum did this yer last witness escape from?"

"Mr. Harker," said the coroner, gravely and tranquilly, "from what asylum did you last escape?"

Harker flushed crimson again, but said nothing, and the seven jurors rose and solemnly filed out of the cabin.

"If you have done insulting me, sir," said Harker, as soon as he and the officer were left alone with the dead man, "I suppose I am at liberty to go?"

"Yes."

Harker started to leave, but paused, with his hand on the door latch. The habit of his profession was strong in him—stronger than his sense of personal dignity. He turned about and said:

"The book that you have there—I recognize it as Morgan's diary. You seemed greatly interested in it; you read in it while I was testifying. May I see it? The public would like——"

"The book will cut no figure in this matter," replied the official, slipping it into his coat pocket; "all the entries in it were made before the writer's death."

As Harker passed out of the house the jury reëntered and stood about the table, on which the now covered corpse showed under the sheet with sharp definition. The foreman seated himself near the candle, produced from his breast pocket a pencil and scrap of paper and wrote rather laboriously the following verdict, which with various degrees of effort all signed:

"We, the jury, do find that the remains come to their death at the hands of a mountain lion, but some of us thinks, all the same, they had fits."

IV

AN EXPLANATION FROM THE TOMB

In the diary of the late Hugh Morgan are certain interesting entries having, possibly, a scientific value as suggestions. At the inquest upon his body the book was not put in evidence; possibly the coroner thought it not worth while to confuse the jury. The date of the first of the entries mentioned cannot be ascertained; the upper part of the leaf is torn away; the part of the entry remaining follows:

". . . would run in a half-circle, keeping his head turned always toward the centre, and again he would stand still, barking furiously. At last he ran away into the brush as fast as he could go. I thought at first that he had gone mad, but on returning to the house found no other alteration in his manner than what was obviously due to fear of punishment.

"Can a dog see with his nose? Do odors impress some cerebral centre with images of the thing that emitted them? . . .

"Sept. 2.—Looking at the stars last night as they rose above the crest of the ridge east of the house, I observed them successively disappear—from left to right. Each was eclipsed but an instant, and only a few at the same time, but along the entire length of the ridge all that were within a degree or two of the crest were blotted out. It was as if something had passed along between me and them; but I could not see it, and the stars were not thick enough to define its outline. Ugh! I don't like this." . . .

Several weeks' entries are missing, three leaves being torn from the book.

"Sept. 27.—It has been about here again—I find evidences of its presence every day. I watched again all last night in the same cover, gun in hand, double-charged with buckshot. In the morning the fresh footprints were there, as before. Yet I would have sworn that I did not sleep—indeed, I hardly sleep at all. It is terrible, insupportable! If these amazing experiences are real I shall go mad; if they are fanciful I am mad already.

"Oct. 3.—I shall not go—it shall not drive me away. No, this is *my* house, *my* land. God hates a coward. . . .

"Oct. 5.—I can stand it no longer; I have invited Harker to pass a few weeks with me—he has a level head. I can judge from his manner if he thinks me mad.

"Oct. 7.—I have the solution of the mystery; it came to me last night—suddenly, as by revelation. How simple—how terribly simple!

"There are sounds that we cannot hear. At either end of the scale are notes that stir no chord of that imperfect instrument, the human ear. They are too high or too grave. I have observed a flock of blackbirds occupying an entire tree-top—the tops of several trees—and all in full song. Suddenly—in a moment—at absolutely the same instant—all spring into the air and fly away. How? They could not all see one another—whole tree-tops intervened. At no point could a leader have been visible to all. There must have been a signal of warning or command, high and shrill above the din, but by me unheard. I have observed, too, the same simultaneous flight when all were silent, among not only blackbirds, but other birds—quail, for example, widely separated by bushes—even on opposite sides of a hill.

"It is known to seamen that a school of whales basking or sporting on the surface of the ocean, miles apart, with the convexity of the earth between, will sometimes dive at the same instant—all gone out of sight in a moment. The signal has been sounded—too grave for the ear of the sailor at the mast-head and his comrades on the deck—who nevertheless feel its vibrations in the ship as the stones of a cathedral are stirred by the bass of the organ.

"As with sounds, so with colors. At each end of the solar spectrum the chemist can detect the presence of what are known as 'actinic' rays. They represent colors—integral colors in the composition of light—which we are unable to discern. The human eye is an imperfect instrument; its range is but a few octaves of the real 'chromatic scale.' I am not mad; there are colors that we cannot see.

"And, God help me! the Damned Thing is of such a color!"

Haïta the Shepherd

IN the heart of Haïta the illusions of youth had not been supplanted by those of age and experience. His thoughts were pure and pleasant, for his life was simple and his soul devoid of ambition. He rose with the sun and went forth to pray at the shrine of Hastur, the god of shepherds, who heard and was pleased. After performance of this pious rite Haïta unbarred the gate of the fold and with a cheerful mind drove his flock afield, eating his morning meal of curds and oat cake as he went, occasionally pausing to add a few berries, cold with dew, or to drink of the waters that came away from the hills to join the stream in the middle of the valley and be borne along with it, he knew not whither.

During the long summer day, as his sheep cropped the good grass which the gods had made to grow for them, or lay with their forelegs doubled under their breasts and chewed the cud, Haïta, reclining in the shadow of a tree, or sitting upon a rock, played so sweet music upon his reed pipe that sometimes from the corner of his eye he got accidental glimpses of the minor sylvan deities, leaning forward out of the copse to hear; but if he looked at them directly they vanished. From this—for he must be thinking if he would not turn into one of his own sheep—he drew the solemn inference that happiness may come if not sought, but if looked for will never be seen; for next to the favor of Hastur, who never disclosed himself, Haïta most valued the friendly interest of his neighbors, the shy immortals of the wood and stream. At nightfall he drove his flock back to the fold, saw that the gate was secure and retired to his cave for refreshment and for dreams.

So passed his life, one day like another, save when the storms uttered the wrath of an offended god. Then Haïta cowered in his cave, his face hidden in his hands, and prayed that he alone might be punished for his sins and the world saved from destruction. Sometimes when there was a great rain, and the stream came out of its banks, compelling him to urge his terrified flock to the uplands, he interceded for the people in the cities which he had been told lay in the plain beyond the two blue hills forming the gateway of his valley.

"It is kind of thee, O Hastur," so he prayed, "to give me mountains so near to my dwelling and my fold that I and my sheep can escape the angry torrents; but the rest of the world thou must thyself deliver in some way that I know not of, or I will no longer worship thee."

And Hastur, knowing that Haïta was a youth who kept his word, spared the cities and turned the waters into the sea.

So he had lived since he could remember. He could not rightly conceive any other mode of existence. The holy hermit who dwelt at the head of the valley, a full hour's journey away, from whom he had heard the tale of the great cities where dwelt people—poor souls!—who had no sheep, gave him no knowledge of that early time, when, so he reasoned, he must have been small and helpless like a lamb.

It was through thinking on these mysteries and marvels, and on that horrible change to silence and decay which he felt sure must some time come to him, as he had seen it come to so many of his flock—as it came to all living things except the birds—that Haïta first became conscious how miserable and hopeless was his lot.

"It is necessary," he said, "that I know whence and how I came; for how can one perform his duties unless able to judge what they are by the way in which he was intrusted with them? And what contentment can I have when I know not how long it is going to last? Perhaps before another sun I may be changed, and then what will become of the sheep? What, indeed, will have become of me?"

Pondering these things Haïta became melancholy and morose. He no longer spoke cheerfully to his flock, nor ran with alacrity to the shrine of Hastur. In every breeze he heard whispers of malign deities whose existence he now first observed. Every cloud was a portent signifying disaster, and the darkness was full of terrors. His reed pipe when applied to his lips gave out no melody, but a dismal wail; the sylvan and riparian intelligences no longer thronged the thicket-side to listen, but fled from the sound, as he knew by the stirred leaves and bent flowers. He relaxed his vigilance and many of his sheep strayed away into the hills and were lost. Those that remained became lean and ill for lack of good pasturage, for he would not seek it for them, but conducted them day after day to the same spot, through mere abstraction, while puzzling about life and death —of immortality he knew not.

One day while indulging in the gloomiest reflections he suddenly sprang from the rock upon which he sat, and with a determined gesture of the right hand exclaimed: "I will no longer be a suppliant for knowledge which the gods withhold. Let them look to it that they do me no wrong. I will do my duty as best I can and if I err upon their own heads be it!"

Suddenly, as he spoke, a great brightness fell about him, causing him to look upward, thinking the sun had burst through a rift in the clouds; but there were no clouds. No more than an arm's length away stood a beautiful maiden. So beautiful she was that the flowers about her feet folded their petals in despair and bent their heads in token of submission; so sweet her look that the humming birds thronged her eyes, thrusting their thirsty bills almost into them, and the wild bees were about her lips. And such was her brightness that the shadows of all objects lay divergent from her feet, turning as she moved.

Haïta was entranced. Rising, he knelt before her in adoration, and she laid her hand upon his head.

"Come," she said in a voice that had the music of all the bells of his flock—"come, thou art not to worship me, who am no goddess, but if thou art truthful and dutiful I will abide with thee."

Haïta seized her hand, and stammering his joy and gratitude arose, and hand in hand they stood and smiled into each other's eyes. He gazed on her with reverence and rapture. He said: "I pray thee, lovely maid, tell me thy name and whence and why thou comest."

At this she laid a warning finger on her lip and began to withdraw. Her beauty underwent a visible alteration that made him shudder, he knew not why, for still she was beautiful. The landscape was darkened by a giant shadow sweeping across the valley with the speed of a vulture. In the obscurity the maiden's figure grew dim and indistinct and her voice seemed to come from a distance, as she said, in a tone of sorrowful reproach:

"Presumptuous and ungrateful youth! must I then so soon leave thee? Would nothing do but thou must at once break the eternal compact?"

Inexpressibly grieved, Haïta fell upon his knees and implored her to remain—rose and sought her in the deepening darkness —ran in circles, calling to her aloud, but all in vain. She was no longer visible, but out of the gloom he heard her voice saying: "Nay, thou shalt not have me by seeking. Go to thy duty, faithless shepherd, or we shall never meet again."

Night had fallen; the wolves were howling in the hills and the terrified sheep crowding about Haïta's feet. In the demands of the hour he forgot his disappointment, drove his sheep to the fold and repairing to the place of worship poured out his heart in gratitude to Hastur for permitting him to save his flock, then retired to his cave and slept.

When Haïta awoke the sun was high and shone in at the cave, illuminating it with a great glory. And there, beside him, sat the maiden. She smiled upon him with a smile that seemed the visible music of his pipe of reeds. He dared not speak, fearing to offend her as before, for he knew not what he could venture to say.

"Because," she said, "thou didst thy duty by the flock, and didst not forget to thank Hastur for staying the wolves of the night, I am come to thee again. Wilt thou have me for a companion?"

"Who would not have thee forever?" replied Haïta. "Oh! never again leave me until—until I—change and become silent and motionless."

Haïta had no word for death.

"I wish, indeed," he continued, "that thou wert of my own sex, that we might wrestle and run races and so never tire of being together."

At these words the maiden arose and passed out of the cave, and Haïta, springing from his couch of fragrant boughs to overtake and detain her, observed to his astonishment that the rain was falling and the stream in the middle of the valley had come out of its banks. The sheep were bleating in terror, for the rising waters had invaded their fold. And there was danger for the unknown cities of the distant plain.

It was many days before Haïta saw the maiden again. One

day he was returning from the head of the valley, where he had
gone with ewe's milk and oat cake and berries for the holy
hermit, who was too old and feeble to provide himself with
food.

"Poor old man!" he said aloud, as he trudged along home-
ward. "I will return to-morrow and bear him on my back to
my own dwelling, where I can care for him. Doubtless it is for
this that Hastur has reared me all these many years, and gives
me health and strength."

As he spoke, the maiden, clad in glittering garments, met
him in the path with a smile that took away his breath.

"I am come again," she said, "to dwell with thee if thou wilt
now have me, for none else will. Thou mayest have learned
wisdom, and art willing to take me as I am, nor care to know."

Haïta threw himself at her feet. "Beautiful being," he cried,
"if thou wilt but deign to accept all the devotion of my heart
and soul—after Hastur be served—it is thine forever. But, alas!
thou art capricious and wayward. Before to-morrow's sun I
may lose thee again. Promise, I beseech thee, that however in
my ignorance I may offend, thou wilt forgive and remain always with me."

Scarcely had he finished speaking when a troop of bears
came out of the hills, racing toward him with crimson mouths
and fiery eyes. The maiden again vanished, and he turned and
fled for his life. Nor did he stop until he was in the cot of the
holy hermit, whence he had set out. Hastily barring the door
against the bears he cast himself upon the ground and wept.

"My son," said the hermit from his couch of straw, freshly
gathered that morning by Haïta's hands, "it is not like thee to
weep for bears—tell me what sorrow hath befallen thee, that
age may minister to the hurts of youth with such balms as it
hath of its wisdom."

Haïta told him all: how thrice he had met the radiant maid,
and thrice she had left him forlorn. He related minutely all
that had passed between them, omitting no word of what had
been said.

When he had ended, the holy hermit was a moment silent,
then said: "My son, I have attended to thy story, and I know the
maiden. I have myself seen her, as have many. Know, then, that
her name, which she would not even permit thee to inquire, is

Happiness. Thou saidst the truth to her, that she is capricious for she imposeth conditions that man can not fulfill, and delinquency is punished by desertion. She cometh only when unsought, and will not be questioned. One manifestation of curiosity, one sign of doubt, one expression of misgiving, and she is away! How long didst thou have her at any time before she fled?"

"Only a single instant," answered Haïta, blushing with shame at the confession. "Each time I drove her away in one moment."

"Unfortunate youth!" said the holy hermit, "but for thine indiscretion thou mightst have had her for two."

An Inhabitant of Carcosa

For there be divers sorts of death—some wherein the body remaineth; and in some it vanisheth quite away with the spirit. This commonly occurreth only in solitude (such is God's will) and, none seeing the end, we say the man is lost, or gone on a long journey—which indeed he hath; but sometimes it hath happened in sight of many, as abundant testimony showeth. In one kind of death the spirit also dieth, and this it hath been known to do while yet the body was in vigor for many years. Sometimes, as is veritably attested, it dieth with the body, but after a season is raised up again in that place where the body did decay.

PONDERING these words of Hali (whom God rest) and questioning their full meaning, as one who, having an intimation, yet doubts if there be not something behind, other than that which he has discerned, I noted not whither I had strayed until a sudden chill wind striking my face revived in me a sense of my surroundings. I observed with astonishment that everything seemed unfamiliar. On every side of me stretched a bleak and desolate expanse of plain, covered with a tall overgrowth of sere grass, which rustled and whistled in the autumn wind with heaven knows what mysterious and disquieting suggestion. Protruded at long intervals above it, stood strangely shaped and somber-colored rocks, which seemed to have an understanding with one another and to exchange looks of uncomfortable significance, as if they had reared their heads to watch the issue of some foreseen event. A few blasted trees here and there appeared as leaders in this malevolent conspiracy of silent expectation.

The day, I thought, must be far advanced, though the sun was invisible; and although sensible that the air was raw and chill my consciousness of that fact was rather mental than physical—I had no feeling of discomfort. Over all the dismal landscape a canopy of low, lead-colored clouds hung like a visible curse. In all this there were a menace and a portent—a hint of evil, an intimation of doom. Bird, beast, or insect there was none. The wind sighed in the bare branches of the dead trees and the gray grass bent to whisper its dread secret to the earth; but no other sound nor motion broke the awful repose of that dismal place.

I observed in the herbage a number of weather-worn stones, evidently shaped with tools. They were broken, covered with moss and half sunken in the earth. Some lay prostrate, some leaned at various angles, none was vertical. They were obviously headstones of graves, though the graves themselves no longer existed as either mounds or depressions; the years had leveled all. Scattered here and there, more massive blocks showed where some pompous tomb or ambitious monument had once flung its feeble defiance at oblivion. So old seemed these relics, these vestiges of vanity and memorials of affection and piety, so battered and worn and stained—so neglected, deserted, forgotten the place, that I could not help thinking myself the discoverer of the burial-ground of a prehistoric race of men whose very name was long extinct.

Filled with these reflections, I was for some time heedless of the sequence of my own experiences, but soon I thought, "How came I hither?" A moment's reflection seemed to make this all clear and explain at the same time, though in a disquieting way, the singular character with which my fancy had invested all that I saw or heard. I was ill. I remembered now that I had been prostrated by a sudden fever, and that my family had told me that in my periods of delirium I had constantly cried out for liberty and air, and had been held in bed to prevent my escape out-of-doors. Now I had eluded the vigilance of my attendants and had wandered hither to—to where? I could not conjecture. Clearly I was at a considerable distance from the city where I dwelt—the ancient and famous city of Carcosa.

No signs of human life were anywhere visible nor audible; no rising smoke, no watchdog's bark, no lowing of cattle, no shouts of children at play—nothing but that dismal burial-place, with its air of mystery and dread, due to my own disordered brain. Was I not becoming again delirious, there beyond human aid? Was it not indeed *all* an illusion of my madness? I called aloud the names of my wives and sons, reached out my hands in search of theirs, even as I walked among the crumbling stones and in the withered grass.

A noise behind me caused me to turn about. A wild animal —a lynx—was approaching. The thought came to me: If I break down here in the desert—if the fever return and I fail, this beast will be at my throat. I sprang toward it, shouting. It trotted tranquilly by within a hand's breadth of me and disappeared behind a rock.

A moment later a man's head appeared to rise out of the ground a short distance away. He was ascending the farther slope of a low hill whose crest was hardly to be distinguished from the general level. His whole figure soon came into view against the background of gray cloud. He was half naked, half clad in skins. His hair was unkempt, his beard long and ragged. In one hand he carried a bow and arrow; the other held a blazing torch with a long trail of black smoke. He walked slowly and with caution, as if he feared falling into some open grave concealed by the tall grass. This strange apparition surprised but did not alarm, and taking such a course as to intercept him I met him almost face to face, accosting him with the familiar salutation, "God keep you."

He gave no heed, nor did he arrest his pace.

"Good stranger," I continued, "I am ill and lost. Direct me, I beseech you, to Carcosa."

The man broke into a barbarous chant in an unknown tongue, passing on and away.

An owl on the branch of a decayed tree hooted dismally and was answered by another in the distance. Looking upward, I saw through a sudden rift in the clouds Aldebaran and the Hyades! In all this there was a hint of night—the lynx, the man with the torch, the owl. Yet I saw—I saw even the stars in absence of the darkness. I saw, but was apparently not seen nor heard. Under what awful spell did I exist?

I seated myself at the root of a great tree, seriously to consider what it were best to do. That I was mad I could no longer doubt, yet recognized a ground of doubt in the conviction. Of fever I had no trace. I had, withal, a sense of exhilaration and vigor altogether unknown to me—a feeling of mental and physical exaltation. My senses seemed all alert; I could feel the air as a ponderous substance; I could hear the silence.

A great root of the giant tree against whose trunk I leaned as I sat held inclosed in its grasp a slab of stone, a part of which protruded into a recess formed by another root. The stone was thus partly protected from the weather, though greatly decomposed. Its edges were worn round, its corners eaten away, its surface deeply furrowed and scaled. Glittering particles of mica were visible in the earth about it—vestiges of its decomposition. This stone had apparently marked the grave out of which the tree had sprung ages ago. The tree's exacting roots had robbed the grave and made the stone a prisoner.

A sudden wind pushed some dry leaves and twigs from the uppermost face of the stone; I saw the low-relief letters of an inscription and bent to read it. God in Heaven! *my* name in full!—the date of *my* birth!—the date of *my* death!

A level shaft of light illuminated the whole side of the tree as I sprang to my feet in terror. The sun was rising in the rosy east. I stood between the tree and his broad red disk—no shadow darkened the trunk!

A chorus of howling wolves saluted the dawn. I saw them sitting on their haunches, singly and in groups, on the summits of irregular mounds and tumuli filling a half of my desert prospect and extending to the horizon. And then I knew that these were ruins of the ancient and famous city of Carcosa.

———

Such are the facts imparted to the medium Bayrolles by the spirit Hoseib Alar Robardin.

The Stranger

A MAN stepped out of the darkness into the little illuminated circle about our failing campfire and seated himself upon a rock.

"You are not the first to explore this region," he said, gravely.

Nobody controverted his statement; he was himself proof of its truth, for he was not of our party and must have been somewhere near when we camped. Moreover, he must have companions not far away; it was not a place where one would be living or traveling alone. For more than a week we had seen, besides ourselves and our animals, only such living things as rattlesnakes and horned toads. In an Arizona desert one does not long coexist with only such creatures as these: one must have pack animals, supplies, arms—"an outfit." And all these imply comrades. It was perhaps a doubt as to what manner of men this unceremonious stranger's comrades might be, together with something in his words interpretable as a challenge, that caused every man of our half-dozen "gentlemen adventurers" to rise to a sitting posture and lay his hand upon a weapon—an act signifying, in that time and place, a policy of expectation. The stranger gave the matter no attention and began again to speak in the same deliberate, uninflected monotone in which he had delivered his first sentence:

"Thirty years ago Ramon Gallegos, William Shaw, George W. Kent and Berry Davis, all of Tucson, crossed the Santa Catalina mountains and traveled due west, as nearly as the configuration of the country permitted. We were prospecting and it was our intention, if we found nothing, to push through to the Gila river at some point near Big Bend, where we understood there was a settlement. We had a good outfit but no guide—just Ramon Gallegos, William Shaw, George W. Kent and Berry Davis."

The man repeated the names slowly and distinctly, as if to fix them in the memories of his audience, every member of which was now attentively observing him, but with a slackened apprehension regarding his possible companions somewhere in the darkness that seemed to enclose us like a black wall; in the manner of this volunteer historian was no suggestion of an unfriendly purpose. His act was rather that of a harmless lunatic than an enemy. We were not so new to the country as not to know that the solitary life of many a plainsman had a tendency to develop eccentricities of conduct and character not always easily distinguishable from mental aberration. A man is like a tree: in a forest of his fellows he will grow as straight as his generic and individual nature permits; alone in the open, he yields to the deforming stresses and tortions that environ him. Some such thoughts were in my mind as I watched the man from the shadow of my hat, pulled low to shut out the firelight. A witless fellow, no doubt, but what could he be doing there in the heart of a desert?

Having undertaken to tell this story, I wish that I could describe the man's appearance; that would be a natural thing to do. Unfortunately, and somewhat strangely, I find myself unable to do so with any degree of confidence, for afterward no two of us agreed as to what he wore and how he looked; and when I try to set down my own impressions they elude me. Anyone can tell some kind of story; narration is one of the elemental powers of the race. But the talent for description is a gift.

Nobody having broken silence the visitor went on to say:

"This country was not then what it is now. There was not a ranch between the Gila and the Gulf. There was a little game here and there in the mountains, and near the infrequent water-holes grass enough to keep our animals from starvation. If we should be so fortunate as to encounter no Indians we might get through. But within a week the purpose of the expedition had altered from discovery of wealth to preservation of life. We had gone too far to go back, for what was ahead could be no worse than what was behind; so we pushed on, riding by night to avoid Indians and the intolerable heat, and concealing ourselves by day as best we could. Sometimes, having exhausted our supply of wild meat and emptied our casks, we were days without food or drink; then a water-hole or a shallow pool in the bottom of an *arroyo* so restored our strength and sanity that we were able to shoot some of the wild animals that sought it also. Sometimes it was a bear, sometimes an antelope, a coyote, a cougar—that was as God pleased; all were food.

"One morning as we skirted a mountain range, seeking a practicable pass, we were attacked by a band of Apaches who had followed our trail up a gulch—it is not far from here. Knowing that they outnumbered us ten to one, they took none of their usual cowardly precautions, but dashed upon us at a gallop, firing and yelling. Fighting was out of the question: we urged our feeble animals up the gulch as far as there was footing for a hoof, then threw ourselves out of our saddles and took to the *chaparral* on one of the slopes, abandoning our entire outfit to the enemy. But we retained our rifles, every man—Ramon Gallegos, William Shaw, George W. Kent and Berry Davis."

"Same old crowd," said the humorist of our party. He was an Eastern man, unfamiliar with the decent observances of social intercourse. A gesture of disapproval from our leader silenced him and the stranger proceeded with his tale:

"The savages dismounted also, and some of them ran up the gulch beyond the point at which we had left it, cutting off further retreat in that direction and forcing us on up the side. Unfortunately the *chaparral* extended only a short distance up the slope, and as we came into the open ground above we took the fire of a dozen rifles; but Apaches shoot badly when in a hurry, and God so willed it that none of us fell. Twenty yards up the slope, beyond the edge of the brush, were vertical cliffs, in which, directly in front of us, was a narrow opening. Into that we ran, finding ourselves in a cavern about as large as an ordinary room in a house. Here for a time we were safe: a single man with a repeating rifle could defend the entrance against all the Apaches in the land. But against hunger and thirst we had no defense. Courage we still had, but hope was a memory.

"Not one of those Indians did we afterward see, but by the smoke and glare of their fires in the gulch we knew that by day and by night they watched with ready rifles in the edge of the bush—knew that if we made a sortie not a man of us would live to take three steps into the open. For three days, watching in turn, we held out before our suffering became insupportable. Then—it was the morning of the fourth day—Ramon Gallegos said:

" 'Senores, I know not well of the good God and what please him. I have live without religion, and I am not acquaint with that of you. Pardon, senores, if I shock you, but for me the time is come to beat the game of the Apache.'

"He knelt upon the rock floor of the cave and pressed his pistol against his temple. 'Madre de Dios,' he said, 'comes now the soul of Ramon Gallegos.'

"And so he left us—William Shaw, George W. Kent and Berry Davis.

"I was the leader: it was for me to speak.

" 'He was a brave man,' I said—'he knew when to die, and how. It is foolish to go mad from thirst and fall by Apache bullets, or be skinned alive—it is in bad taste. Let us join Ramon Gallegos.'

" 'That is right,' said William Shaw.

" 'That is right,' said George W. Kent.

"I straightened the limbs of Ramon Gallegos and put a handkerchief over his face. Then William Shaw said: 'I should like to look like that—a little while.'

"And George W. Kent said that he felt that way, too.

" 'It shall be so,' I said: 'the red devils will wait a week. William Shaw and George W. Kent, draw and kneel.'

"They did so and I stood before them.

" 'Almighty God, our Father,' said I.

" 'Almighty God, our Father,' said William Shaw.

" 'Almighty God, our Father,' said George W. Kent.

" 'Forgive us our sins,' said I.

" 'Forgive us our sins,' said they.

" 'And receive our souls.'

" 'And receive our souls.'

" 'Amen!'

" 'Amen!'

"I laid them beside Ramon Gallegos and covered their faces."

There was a quick commotion on the opposite side of the campfire: one of our party had sprung to his feet, pistol in hand.

"And you!" he shouted—"*you* dared to escape?—you dare to be alive? You cowardly hound, I'll send you to join them if I hang for it!"

But with the leap of a panther the captain was upon him, grasping his wrist. "Hold it in, Sam Yountsey, hold it in!"

We were now all upon our feet—except the stranger, who sat motionless and apparently inattentive. Some one seized Yountsey's other arm.

"Captain," I said, "there is something wrong here. This fellow is either a lunatic or merely a liar—just a plain, every-day liar whom Yountsey has no call to kill. If this man was of that party it had five members, one of whom—probably himself—he has not named."

"Yes," said the captain, releasing the insurgent, who sat down, "there is something—unusual. Years ago four dead bodies of white men, scalped and shamefully mutilated, were found about the mouth of that cave. They are buried there; I have seen the graves—we shall all see them to-morrow."

The stranger rose, standing tall in the light of the expiring fire, which in our breathless attention to his story we had neglected to keep going.

"There were four," he said—"Ramon Gallegos, William Shaw, George W. Kent and Berry Davis."

With this reiterated roll-call of the dead he walked into the darkness and we saw him no more.

At that moment one of our party, who had been on guard, strode in among us, rifle in hand and somewhat excited.

"Captain," he said, "for the last half-hour three men have been standing out there on the *mesa*." He pointed in the direction taken by the stranger. "I could see them distinctly, for the moon is up, but as they had no guns and I had them covered with mine I thought it was their move. They have made none, but, damn it! they have got on to my nerves."

"Go back to your post, and stay till you see them again," said the captain. "The rest of you lie down again, or I'll kick you all into the fire."

The sentinel obediently withdrew, swearing, and did not return. As we were arranging our blankets the fiery Yountsey said: "I beg your pardon, Captain, but who the devil do you take them to be?"

"Ramon Gallegos, William Shaw and George W. Kent."

"But how about Berry Davis? I ought to have shot him."

"Quite needless; you couldn't have made him any deader. Go to sleep."

THE WAYS OF GHOSTS

My peculiar relation to the writer of the following narratives is such that I must ask the reader to overlook the absence of explanation as to how they came into my possession. Withal, my knowledge of him is so meager that I should rather not undertake to say if he were himself persuaded of the truth of what he relates; certainly such inquiries as I have thought it worth while to set about have not in every instance tended to confirmation of the statements made. Yet his style, for the most part devoid alike of artifice and art, almost baldly simple and direct, seems hardly compatible with the disingenuousness of a merely literary intention; one would call it the manner of one more concerned for the fruits of research than for the flowers of expression. In transcribing his notes and fortifying their claim to attention by giving them something of an orderly arrangement, I have conscientiously refrained from embellishing them with such small ornaments of diction as I may have felt myself able to bestow, which would not only have been impertinent, even if pleasing, but would have given me a somewhat closer relation to the work than I should care to have and to avow.—A. B.

Present at a Hanging

A N old man named Daniel Baker, living near Lebanon, Iowa, was suspected by his neighbors of having murdered a peddler who had obtained permission to pass the night at his house. This was in 1853, when peddling was more common in the Western country than it is now, and was attended with considerable danger. The peddler with his pack traversed the country by all manner of lonely roads, and was compelled to rely upon the country people for hospitality. This brought him into relation with queer characters, some of whom were not altogether scrupulous in their methods of making a living, murder being an acceptable means to that end. It occasionally occurred that a peddler with diminished pack and swollen purse would be traced to the lonely dwelling of some rough character and never could be traced beyond. This was so in the case of "old man Baker," as he was always called. (Such names are given in the western "settlements" only to elderly persons who are not esteemed; to the general disrepute of social unworth is affixed the special reproach of age.) A peddler came to his house and none went away—that is all that anybody knew.

Seven years later the Rev. Mr. Cummings, a Baptist minister well known in that part of the country, was driving by Baker's farm one night. It was not very dark: there was a bit of moon somewhere above the light veil of mist that lay along the earth. Mr. Cummings, who was at all times a cheerful person, was whistling a tune, which he would occasionally interrupt to speak a word of friendly encouragement to his horse. As he came to a little bridge across a dry ravine he saw the figure of a man standing upon it, clearly outlined against the gray background of a misty forest. The man had something strapped on his back and carried a heavy stick—obviously an itinerant peddler. His attitude had in it a suggestion of abstraction, like that of a sleepwalker. Mr. Cummings reined in his horse when he arrived in front of him, gave him a pleasant salutation and invited him to a seat in the vehicle—"if you are going my way," he added. The man raised his head, looked him full in the face, but neither answered nor made any further movement. The minister, with good-natured persistence, repeated his invitation. At this the man threw his right hand forward from his side and pointed downward as he stood on the extreme edge of the bridge. Mr. Cummings looked past him, over into the ravine, saw nothing unusual and withdrew his eyes to address the man again. He had disappeared. The horse, which all this time had been uncommonly restless, gave at the same moment a snort of terror and started to run away. Before he had regained control of the animal the minister was at the crest of the hill a hundred yards along. He looked back and saw the figure again, at the same place and in the same attitude as when he had first observed it. Then for the first time he was conscious of a sense of the supernatural and drove home as rapidly as his willing horse would go.

On arriving at home he related his adventure to his family, and early the next morning, accompanied by two neighbors, John White Corwell and Abner Raiser, returned to the spot. They found the body of old man Baker hanging by the neck from one of the beams of the bridge, immediately beneath the spot where the apparition had stood. A thick coating of dust, slightly dampened by the mist, covered the floor of the bridge, but the only footprints were those of Mr. Cummings' horse.

In taking down the body the men disturbed the loose, friable earth of the slope below it, disclosing human bones already nearly uncovered by the action of water and frost. They were identified as those of the lost peddler. At the double inquest the coroner's jury found that Daniel Baker died by his own hand while suffering from temporary insanity, and that Samuel Morritz was murdered by some person or persons to the jury unknown.

A Cold Greeting

T HIS is a story told by the late Benson Foley of San Francisco: "In the summer of 1881 I met a man named James H. Conway, a resident of Franklin, Tennessee. He was visiting San Francisco for his health, deluded man, and brought me a note of introduction from Mr. Lawrence Barting. I had known Barting as a captain in the Federal army during the civil war. At its close he had settled in Franklin, and in time became, I had reason to think, somewhat prominent as a lawyer. Barting had always seemed to me an honorable and truthful man, and the warm friendship which he expressed in his note for Mr. Conway was to me sufficient evidence that the latter was in every way worthy of my confidence and esteem. At dinner one day Conway told me that it had been solemnly agreed between him and Barting that the one who died first should, if possible, communicate with the other from beyond the grave, in some unmistakable way—just how, they had left (wisely, it seemed to me) to be decided by the deceased, according to the opportunities that his altered circumstances might present.

"A few weeks after the conversation in which Mr. Conway spoke of this agreement, I met him one day, walking slowly down Montgomery street, apparently, from his abstracted air, in deep thought. He greeted me coldly with merely a movement of the head and passed on, leaving me standing on the walk, with half-proffered hand, surprised and naturally somewhat piqued. The next day I met him again in the office of the Palace Hotel, and seeing him about to repeat the disagreeable performance of the day before, intercepted him in a doorway, with a friendly salutation, and bluntly requested an explanation of his altered manner. He hesitated a moment; then, looking me frankly in the eyes, said:

" 'I do not think, Mr. Foley, that I have any longer a claim to your friendship, since Mr. Barting appears to have withdrawn his own from me—for what reason, I protest I do not know. If he has not already informed you he probably will do so.'

" 'But,' I replied, 'I have not heard from Mr. Barting.'

" 'Heard from him!' he repeated, with apparent surprise.

'Why, he is here. I met him yesterday ten minutes before meeting you. I gave you exactly the same greeting that he gave me. I met him again not a quarter of an hour ago, and his manner was precisely the same: he merely bowed and passed on. I shall not soon forget your civility to me. Good morning, or—as it may please you—farewell.'

"All this seemed to me singularly considerate and delicate behavior on the part of Mr. Conway.

"As dramatic situations and literary effects are foreign to my purpose I will explain at once that Mr. Barting was dead. He had died in Nashville four days before this conversation. Calling on Mr. Conway, I apprised him of our friend's death, showing him the letters announcing it. He was visibly affected in a way that forbade me to entertain a doubt of his sincerity.

" 'It seems incredible,' he said, after a period of reflection. 'I suppose I must have mistaken another man for Barting, and that man's cold greeting was merely a stranger's civil acknowledgment of my own. I remember, indeed, that he lacked Barting's mustache.'

" 'Doubtless it was another man,' I assented; and the subject was never afterward mentioned between us. But I had in my pocket a photograph of Barting, which had been inclosed in the letter from his widow. It had been taken a week before his death, and was without a mustache."

A Wireless Message

IN the summer of 1896 Mr. William Holt, a wealthy manufacturer of Chicago, was living temporarily in a little town
of central New York, the name of which the writer's memory
has not retained. Mr. Holt had had "trouble with his wife,"
from whom he had parted a year before. Whether the trouble
was anything more serious than "incompatibility of temper,"
he is probably the only living person that knows: he is not addicted to the vice of confidences. Yet he has related the incident herein set down to at least one person without exacting a
pledge of secrecy. He is now living in Europe.

One evening he had left the house of a brother whom he
was visiting, for a stroll in the country. It may be assumed—
whatever the value of the assumption in connection with what
is said to have occurred—that his mind was occupied with reflections on his domestic infelicities and the distressing changes
that they had wrought in his life. Whatever may have been his
thoughts, they so possessed him that he observed neither the
lapse of time nor whither his feet were carrying him; he knew
only that he had passed far beyond the town limits and was
traversing a lonely region by a road that bore no resemblance
to the one by which he had left the village. In brief, he was
"lost."

Realizing his mischance, he smiled; central New York is not
a region of perils, nor does one long remain lost in it. He
turned about and went back the way that he had come. Before
he had gone far he observed that the landscape was growing
more distinct—was brightening. Everything was suffused with
a soft, red glow in which he saw his shadow projected in the
road before him. "The moon is rising," he said to himself. Then
he remembered that it was about the time of the new moon,
and if that tricksy orb was in one of its stages of visibility it had
set long before. He stopped and faced about, seeking the
source of the rapidly broadening light. As he did so, his shadow
turned and lay along the road in front of him as before. The
light still came from behind him. That was surprising; he could

not understand. Again he turned, and again, facing successively to every point of the horizon. Always the shadow was before —always the light behind, "a still and awful red."

Holt was astonished—"dumfounded" is the word that he used in telling it—yet seems to have retained a certain intelligent curiosity. To test the intensity of the light whose nature and cause he could not determine, he took out his watch to see if he could make out the figures on the dial. They were plainly visible, and the hands indicated the hour of eleven o'clock and twenty-five minutes. At that moment the mysterious illumination suddenly flared to an intense, an almost blinding splendor, flushing the entire sky, extinguishing the stars and throwing the monstrous shadow of himself athwart the landscape. In that unearthly illumination he saw near him, but apparently in the air at a considerable elevation, the figure of his wife, clad in her night-clothing and holding to her breast the figure of his child. Her eyes were fixed upon his with an expression which he afterward professed himself unable to name or describe, further than that it was "not of this life."

The flare was momentary, followed by black darkness, in which, however, the apparition still showed white and motionless; then by insensible degrees it faded and vanished, like a bright image on the retina after the closing of the eyes. A peculiarity of the apparition, hardly noted at the time, but afterward recalled, was that it showed only the upper half of the woman's figure: nothing was seen below the waist.

The sudden darkness was comparative, not absolute, for gradually all objects of his environment became again visible.

In the dawn of the morning Holt found himself entering the village at a point opposite to that at which he had left it. He soon arrived at the house of his brother, who hardly knew him. He was wild-eyed, haggard, and gray as a rat. Almost incoherently, he related his night's experience.

"Go to bed, my poor fellow," said his brother, "and—wait. We shall hear more of this."

An hour later came the predestined telegram. Holt's dwelling in one of the suburbs of Chicago had been destroyed by fire. Her escape cut off by the flames, his wife had appeared at an upper window, her child in her arms. There she had stood, motionless, apparently dazed. Just as the firemen had arrived with a ladder, the floor had given way, and she was seen no more.

The moment of this culminating horror was eleven o'clock and twenty-five minutes, standard time.

An Arrest

Having murdered his brother-in-law, Orrin Brower of Kentucky was a fugitive from justice. From the county jail where he had been confined to await his trial he had escaped by knocking down his jailer with an iron bar, robbing him of his keys and, opening the outer door, walking out into the night. The jailer being unarmed, Brower got no weapon with which to defend his recovered liberty. As soon as he was out of the town he had the folly to enter a forest; this was many years ago, when that region was wilder than it is now.

The night was pretty dark, with neither moon nor stars visible, and as Brower had never dwelt thereabout, and knew nothing of the lay of the land, he was, naturally, not long in losing himself. He could not have said if he were getting farther away from the town or going back to it—a most important matter to Orrin Brower. He knew that in either case a posse of citizens with a pack of bloodhounds would soon be on his track and his chance of escape was very slender; but he did not wish to assist in his own pursuit. Even an added hour of freedom was worth having.

Suddenly he emerged from the forest into an old road, and there before him saw, indistinctly, the figure of a man, motionless in the gloom. It was too late to retreat: the fugitive felt that at the first movement back toward the wood he would be, as he afterward explained, "filled with buckshot." So the two stood there like trees, Brower nearly suffocated by the activity of his own heart; the other—the emotions of the other are not recorded.

A moment later—it may have been an hour—the moon sailed into a patch of unclouded sky and the hunted man saw that visible embodiment of Law lift an arm and point significantly toward and beyond him. He understood. Turning his back to his captor, he walked submissively away in the direction indicated, looking to neither the right nor the left; hardly daring to breathe, his head and back actually aching with a prophecy of buckshot.

Brower was as courageous a criminal as ever lived to be

hanged; that was shown by the conditions of awful personal peril in which he had coolly killed his brother-in-law. It is needless to relate them here; they came out at his trial, and the revelation of his calmness in confronting them came near to saving his neck. But what would you have?—when a brave man is beaten, he submits.

So they pursued their journey jailward along the old road through the woods. Only once did Brower venture a turn of the head: just once, when he was in deep shadow and he knew that the other was in moonlight, he looked backward. His captor was Burton Duff, the jailer, as white as death and bearing upon his brow the livid mark of the iron bar. Orrin Brower had no further curiosity.

Eventually they entered the town, which was all alight, but deserted; only the women and children remained, and they were off the streets. Straight toward the jail the criminal held his way. Straight up to the main entrance he walked, laid his hand upon the knob of the heavy iron door, pushed it open without command, entered and found himself in the presence of a half-dozen armed men. Then he turned. Nobody else entered.

On a table in the corridor lay the dead body of Burton Duff.

SOLDIER-FOLK

A Man with Two Lives

HERE is the queer story of David William Duck, related by himself. Duck is an old man living in Aurora, Illinois, where he is universally respected. He is commonly known, however, as "Dead Duck."

"In the autumn of 1866 I was a private soldier of the Eighteenth Infantry. My company was one of those stationed at Fort Phil Kearney, commanded by Colonel Carrington. The country is more or less familiar with the history of that garrison, particularly with the slaughter by the Sioux of a detachment of eighty-one men and officers—not one escaping—through disobedience of orders by its commander, the brave but reckless Captain Fetterman. When that occurred, I was trying to make my way with important dispatches to Fort C. F. Smith, on the Big Horn. As the country swarmed with hostile Indians, I traveled by night and concealed myself as best I could before daybreak. The better to do so, I went afoot, armed with a Henry rifle and carrying three days' rations in my haversack.

"For my second place of concealment I chose what seemed in the darkness a narrow cañon leading through a range of rocky hills. It contained many large bowlders, detached from the slopes of the hills. Behind one of these, in a clump of sage-brush, I made my bed for the day, and soon fell asleep. It seemed as if I had hardly closed my eyes, though in fact it was near midday, when I was awakened by the report of a rifle, the bullet striking the bowlder just above my body. A band of Indians had trailed me and had me nearly surrounded; the shot had been fired with an execrable aim by a fellow who had caught sight of me from the hillside above. The smoke of his rifle betrayed him, and I was no sooner on my feet than he was off his and rolling down the declivity. Then I ran in a stooping posture, dodging among the clumps of sage-brush in a storm of bullets from invisible enemies. The rascals did not rise and pursue, which I thought rather queer, for they must have known by my trail that they had to deal with only one man.

The reason for their inaction was soon made clear. I had not gone a hundred yards before I reached the limit of my run—the head of the gulch which I had mistaken for a cañon. It terminated in a concave breast of rock, nearly vertical and destitute of vegetation. In that cul-de-sac I was caught like a bear in a pen. Pursuit was needless; they had only to wait.

"They waited. For two days and nights, crouching behind a rock topped with a growth of mesquite, and with the cliff at my back, suffering agonies of thirst and absolutely hopeless of deliverance, I fought the fellows at long range, firing occasionally at the smoke of their rifles, as they did at that of mine. Of course, I did not dare to close my eyes at night, and lack of sleep was a keen torture.

"I remember the morning of the third day, which I knew was to be my last. I remember, rather indistinctly, that in my desperation and delirium I sprang out into the open and began firing my repeating rifle without seeing anybody to fire at. And I remember no more of that fight.

"The next thing that I recollect was my pulling myself out of a river just at nightfall. I had not a rag of clothing and knew nothing of my whereabouts, but all that night I traveled, cold and footsore, toward the north. At daybreak I found myself at Fort C. F. Smith, my destination, but without my dispatches. The first man that I met was a sergeant named William Briscoe, whom I knew very well. You can fancy his astonishment at seeing me in that condition, and my own at his asking who the devil I was.

"'Dave Duck,' I answered; 'who should I be?'

"He stared like an owl.

"'You do look it,' he said, and I observed that he drew a little away from me. 'What's up?' he added.

"I told him what had happened to me the day before. He heard me through, still staring; then he said:

"'My dear fellow, if you are Dave Duck I ought to inform you that I buried you two months ago. I was out with a small scouting party and found your body, full of bullet-holes and newly scalped—somewhat mutilated otherwise, too, I am sorry to say—right where you say you made your fight. Come to my tent and I'll show you your clothing and some letters that I took from your person; the commandant has your dispatches.'

"He performed that promise. He showed me the clothing, which I resolutely put on; the letters, which I put into my pocket. He made no objection, then took me to the commandant, who heard my story and coldly ordered Briscoe to take me to the guardhouse. On the way I said:

" 'Bill Briscoe, did you really and truly bury the dead body that you found in these togs?'

" 'Sure,' he answered—'just as I told you. It was Dave Duck, all right; most of us knew him. And now, you damned impostor, you'd better tell me who you are.'

" 'I'd give something to know,' I said.

"A week later, I escaped from the guardhouse and got out of the country as fast as I could. Twice I have been back, seeking for that fateful spot in the hills, but unable to find it."

Three and One Are One

IN the year 1861 Barr Lassiter, a young man of twenty-two, lived with his parents and an elder sister near Carthage, Tennessee. The family were in somewhat humble circumstances, subsisting by cultivation of a small and not very fertile plantation. Owning no slaves, they were not rated among "the best people" of their neighborhood; but they were honest persons of good education, fairly well mannered and as respectable as any family could be if uncredentialed by personal dominion over the sons and daughters of Ham. The elder Lassiter had that severity of manner that so frequently affirms an uncompromising devotion to duty, and conceals a warm and affectionate disposition. He was of the iron of which martyrs are made, but in the heart of the matrix had lurked a nobler metal, fusible at a milder heat, yet never coloring nor softening the hard exterior. By both heredity and environment something of the man's inflexible character had touched the other members of the family; the Lassiter home, though not devoid of domestic affection, was a veritable citadel of duty, and duty —ah, duty is as cruel as death!

When the war came on it found in the family, as in so many others in that State, a divided sentiment; the young man was loyal to the Union, the others savagely hostile. This unhappy division begot an insupportable domestic bitterness, and when the offending son and brother left home with the avowed purpose of joining the Federal army not a hand was laid in his, not a word of farewell was spoken, not a good wish followed him out into the world whither he went to meet with such spirit as he might whatever fate awaited him.

Making his way to Nashville, already occupied by the Army of General Buell, he enlisted in the first organization that he found, a Kentucky regiment of cavalry, and in due time passed through all the stages of military evolution from raw recruit to experienced trooper. A right good trooper he was, too, although in his oral narrative from which this tale is made there was no mention of that; the fact was learned from his surviving comrades. For Barr Lassiter has answered "Here" to the sergeant whose name is Death.

Two years after he had joined it his regiment passed through the region whence he had come. The country thereabout had suffered severely from the ravages of war, having been occupied alternately (and simultaneously) by the belligerent forces, and a sanguinary struggle had occurred in the immediate vicinity of the Lassiter homestead. But of this the young trooper was not aware.

Finding himself in camp near his home, he felt a natural longing to see his parents and sister, hoping that in them, as in him, the unnatural animosities of the period had been softened by time and separation. Obtaining a leave of absence, he set foot in the late summer afternoon, and soon after the rising of the full moon was walking up the gravel path leading to the dwelling in which he had been born.

Soldiers in war age rapidly, and in youth two years are a long time. Barr Lassiter felt himself an old man, and had almost expected to find the place a ruin and a desolation. Nothing, apparently, was changed. At the sight of each dear and familiar object he was profoundly affected. His heart beat audibly, his emotion nearly suffocated him; an ache was in his throat. Unconsciously he quickened his pace until he almost ran, his long shadow making grotesque efforts to keep its place beside him.

The house was unlighted, the door open. As he approached and paused to recover control of himself his father came out and stood bare-headed in the moonlight.

"Father!" cried the young man, springing forward with outstretched hand—"Father!"

The elder man looked him sternly in the face, stood a moment motionless and without a word withdrew into the house. Bitterly disappointed, humiliated, inexpressibly hurt and altogether unnerved, the soldier dropped upon a rustic seat in deep dejection, supporting his head upon his trembling hand. But he would not have it so: he was too good a soldier to accept repulse as defeat. He rose and entered the house, passing directly to the "sitting-room."

It was dimly lighted by an uncurtained east window. On a low stool by the hearthside, the only article of furniture in the place, sat his mother, staring into a fireplace strewn with blackened embers and cold ashes. He spoke to her—tenderly, interrogatively, and with hesitation, but she neither answered, nor moved, nor seemed in any way surprised. True, there had been time for her husband to apprise her of their guilty son's return. He moved nearer and was about to lay his hand upon her arm, when his sister entered from an adjoining room, looked him full in the face, passed him without a sign of recognition and left the room by a door that was partly behind him. He had turned his head to watch her, but when she was gone his eyes again sought his mother. She too had left the place.

Barr Lassiter strode to the door by which he had entered. The moonlight on the lawn was tremulous, as if the sward were a rippling sea. The trees and their black shadows shook as in a breeze. Blended with its borders, the gravel walk seemed unsteady and insecure to step on. This young soldier knew the optical illusions produced by tears. He felt them on his cheek, and saw them sparkle on the breast of his trooper's jacket. He left the house and made his way back to camp.

The next day, with no very definite intention, with no dominant feeling that he could rightly have named, he again sought the spot. Within a half-mile of it he met Bushrod Albro, a former playfellow and schoolmate, who greeted him warmly.

"I am going to visit my home," said the soldier.

The other looked at him rather sharply, but said nothing.

"I know," continued Lassiter, "that my folks have not changed, but——"

"There have been changes," Albro interrupted—"everything changes. I'll go with you if you don't mind. We can talk as we go."

But Albro did not talk.

Instead of a house they found only fire-blackened foundations of stone, enclosing an area of compact ashes pitted by rains.

Lassiter's astonishment was extreme.

"I could not find the right way to tell you," said Albro. "In the fight a year ago your house was burned by a Federal shell."

"And my family—where are they?"

"In Heaven, I hope. All were killed by the shell."

A Baffled Ambuscade

CONNECTING Readyville and Woodbury was a good, hard turnpike nine or ten miles long. Readyville was an outpost of the Federal army at Murfreesboro; Woodbury had the same relation to the Confederate army at Tullahoma. For months after the big battle at Stone River these outposts were in constant quarrel, most of the trouble occurring, naturally, on the turnpike mentioned, between detachments of cavalry. Sometimes the infantry and artillery took a hand in the game by way of showing their good-will.

One night a squadron of Federal horse commanded by Major Seidel, a gallant and skillful officer, moved out from Readyville on an uncommonly hazardous enterprise requiring secrecy, caution and silence.

Passing the infantry pickets, the detachment soon afterward approached two cavalry videttes staring hard into the darkness ahead. There should have been three.

"Where is your other man?" said the major. "I ordered Dunning to be here tonight."

"He rode forward, sir," the man replied. "There was a little firing afterward, but it was a long way to the front."

"It was against orders and against sense for Dunning to do that," said the officer, obviously vexed. "Why did he ride forward?"

"Don't know, sir; he seemed mighty restless. Guess he was skeered."

When this remarkable reasoner and his companion had been absorbed into the expeditionary force, it resumed its advance. Conversation was forbidden; arms and accouterments were denied the right to rattle. The horses' tramping was all that could be heard and the movement was slow in order to have as little as possible of that. It was after midnight and pretty dark, although there was a bit of moon somewhere behind the masses of cloud.

Two or three miles along, the head of the column approached a dense forest of cedars bordering the road on both sides. The major commanded a halt by merely halting, and, evidently himself a bit "skeered," rode on alone to reconnoiter. He was followed, however, by his adjutant and three troopers, who remained a little distance behind and, unseen by him, saw all that occurred.

After riding about a hundred yards toward the forest, the major suddenly and sharply reined in his horse and sat motionless in the saddle. Near the side of the road, in a little open space and hardly ten paces away, stood the figure of a man, dimly visible and as motionless as he. The major's first feeling was that of satisfaction in having left his cavalcade behind; if this were an enemy and should escape he would have little to report. The expedition was as yet undetected.

Some dark object was dimly discernible at the man's feet; the officer could not make it out. With the instinct of the true cavalryman and a particular indisposition to the discharge of firearms, he drew his saber. The man on foot made no movement in answer to the challenge. The situation was tense and a bit dramatic. Suddenly the moon burst through a rift in the clouds and, himself in the shadow of a group of great oaks, the horseman saw the footman clearly, in a patch of white light. It was Trooper Dunning, unarmed and bareheaded. The object at his feet resolved itself into a dead horse, and at a right angle across the animal's neck lay a dead man, face upward in the moonlight.

"Dunning has had the fight of his life," thought the major, and was about to ride forward. Dunning raised his hand, motioning him back with a gesture of warning; then, lowering the arm, he pointed to the place where the road lost itself in the blackness of the cedar forest.

The major understood, and turning his horse rode back to the little group that had followed him and was already moving to the rear in fear of his displeasure, and so returned to the head of his command.

"Dunning is just ahead there," he said to the captain of his leading company. "He has killed his man and will have something to report."

Right patiently they waited, sabers drawn, but Dunning did not come. In an hour the day broke and the whole force moved cautiously forward, its commander not altogether satisfied with his faith in Private Dunning. The expedition had failed, but something remained to be done.

In the little open space off the road they found the fallen horse. At a right angle across the animal's neck face upward, a bullet in the brain, lay the body of Trooper Dunning, stiff as a statue, hours dead.

Examination disclosed abundant evidence that within a half-hour the cedar forest had been occupied by a strong force of Confederate infantry—an ambuscade.

Two Military Executions

IN the spring of the year 1862 General Buell's big army lay in camp, licking itself into shape for the campaign which resulted in the victory at Shiloh. It was a raw, untrained army, although some of its fractions had seen hard enough service, with a good deal of fighting, in the mountains of Western Virginia, and in Kentucky. The war was young and soldiering a new industry, imperfectly understood by the young American of the period, who found some features of it not altogether to his liking. Chief among these was that essential part of discipline, subordination. To one imbued from infancy with the fascinating fallacy that all men are born equal, unquestioning submission to authority is not easily mastered, and the American volunteer soldier in his "green and salad days" is among the worst known. That is how it happened that one of Buell's men, Private Bennett Story Greene, committed the indiscretion of striking his officer. Later in the war he would not have done that; like Sir Andrew Aguecheek, he would have "seen him damned" first. But time for reformation of his military manners was denied him: he was promptly arrested on complaint of the officer, tried by court-martial and sentenced to be shot.

"You might have thrashed me and let it go at that," said the condemned man to the complaining witness; "that is what you used to do at school, when you were plain Will Dudley and I was as good as you. Nobody saw me strike you; discipline would not have suffered much."

"Ben Greene, I guess you are right about that," said the lieutenant. "Will you forgive me? That is what I came to see you about."

There was no reply, and an officer putting his head in at the door of the guard-tent where the conversation had occurred, explained that the time allowed for the interview had expired. The next morning, when in the presence of the whole brigade Private Greene was shot to death by a squad of his comrades, Lieutenant Dudley turned his back upon the sorry performance and muttered a prayer for mercy, in which himself was included.

A few weeks afterward, as Buell's leading division was being ferried over the Tennessee River to assist in succoring Grant's beaten army, night was coming on, black and stormy. Through the wreck of battle the division moved, inch by inch, in the direction of the enemy, who had withdrawn a little to reform his lines. But for the lightning the darkness was absolute. Never for a moment did it cease, and ever when the thunder did not crack and roar were heard the moans of the wounded among whom the men felt their way with their feet, and upon whom they stumbled in the gloom. The dead were there, too—there were dead a-plenty.

In the first faint gray of the morning, when the swarming advance had paused to resume something of definition as a line of battle, and skirmishers had been thrown forward, word was passed along to call the roll. The first sergeant of Lieutenant Dudley's company stepped to the front and began to name the men in alphabetical order. He had no written roll, but a good memory. The men answered to their names as he ran down the alphabet to G.

"Gorham."

"Here!"

"Grayrock."

"Here!"

The sergeant's good memory was affected by habit:

"Greene."

"Here!"

The response was clear, distinct, unmistakable!

A sudden movement, an agitation of the entire company front, as from an electric shock, attested the startling character of the incident. The sergeant paled and paused. The captain strode quickly to his side and said sharply:

"Call that name again."

Apparently the Society for Psychical Research is not first in the field of curiosity concerning the Unknown.

"Bennett Greene."

"Here!"

All faces turned in the direction of the familiar voice; the two men between whom in the order of stature Greene had commonly stood in line turned and squarely confronted each other.

"Once more," commanded the inexorable investigator, and once more came—a trifle tremulously—the name of the dead man:

"Bennett Story Greene."

"Here!"

At that instant a single rifle-shot was heard, away to the front, beyond the skirmish-line, followed, almost attended, by the savage hiss of an approaching bullet which, passing through the line, struck audibly, punctuating as with a full stop the captain's exclamation, "What the devil does it mean?"

Lieutenant Dudley pushed through the ranks from his place in the rear.

"It means this," he said, throwing open his coat and displaying a visibly broadening stain of crimson on his breast. His knees gave way; he fell awkwardly and lay dead.

A little later the regiment was ordered out of line to relieve the congested front, and through some misplay in the game of battle was not again under fire. Nor did Bennett Greene, expert in military executions, ever again signify his presence at one.

SOME HAUNTED HOUSES

The Isle of Pines

FOR many years there lived near the town of Gallipolis, Ohio, an old man named Herman Deluse. Very little was known of his history, for he would neither speak of it himself nor suffer others. It was a common belief among his neighbors that he had been a pirate—if upon any better evidence than his collection of boarding pikes, cutlasses, and ancient flintlock pistols, no one knew. He lived entirely alone in a small house of four rooms, falling rapidly into decay and never repaired further than was required by the weather. It stood on a slight elevation in the midst of a large, stony field overgrown with brambles, and cultivated in patches and only in the most primitive way. It was his only visible property, but could hardly have yielded him a living, simple and few as were his wants. He seemed always to have ready money, and paid cash for all his purchases at the village stores roundabout, seldom buying more than two or three times at the same place until after the lapse of a considerable time. He got no commendation, however, for this equitable distribution of his patronage; people were disposed to regard it as an ineffectual attempt to conceal his possession of so much money. That he had great hoards of ill-gotten gold buried somewhere about his tumbledown dwelling was not reasonably to be doubted by any honest soul conversant with the facts of local tradition and gifted with a sense of the fitness of things.

On the 9th of November, 1867, the old man died; at least his dead body was discovered on the 10th, and physicians testified that death had occurred about twenty-four hours previously—precisely how, they were unable to say; for the *post-mortem* examination showed every organ to be absolutely healthy, with no indication of disorder or violence. According to them, death must have taken place about noonday, yet the body was found in bed. The verdict of the coroner's jury was that he "came to his death by a visitation of God." The body was buried and the public administrator took charge of the estate.

A rigorous search disclosed nothing more than was already known about the dead man, and much patient excavation here and there about the premises by thoughtful and thrifty neighbors went unrewarded. The administrator locked up the house against the time when the property, real and personal, should be sold by law with a view to defraying, partly, the expenses of the sale.

The night of November 20 was boisterous. A furious gale stormed across the country, scourging it with desolating drifts of sleet. Great trees were torn from the earth and hurled across the roads. So wild a night had never been known in all that region, but toward morning the storm had blown itself out of breath and day dawned bright and clear. At about eight o'clock that morning the Rev. Henry Galbraith, a well-known and highly esteemed Lutheran minister, arrived on foot at his house, a mile and a half from the Deluse place. Mr. Galbraith had been for a month in Cincinnati. He had come up the river in a steamboat, and landing at Gallipolis the previous evening had immediately obtained a horse and buggy and set out for home. The violence of the storm had delayed him over night, and in the morning the fallen trees had compelled him to abandon his conveyance and continue his journey afoot.

"But where did you pass the night?" inquired his wife, after he had briefly related his adventure.

"With old Deluse at the 'Isle of Pines,'"* was the laughing reply; "and a glum enough time I had of it. He made no objection to my remaining, but not a word could I get out of him."

Fortunately for the interests of truth there was present at this conversation Mr. Robert Mosely Maren, a lawyer and *littérateur* of Columbus, the same who wrote the delightful "Mellowcraft Papers." Noting, but apparently not sharing, the astonishment caused by Mr. Galbraith's answer this ready-witted person checked by a gesture the exclamations that would naturally have followed, and tranquilly inquired: "How came you to go in there?"

---

*The Isle of Pines was once a famous rendezvous of pirates.

This is Mr. Maren's version of Mr. Galbraith's reply:

"I saw a light moving about the house, and being nearly blinded by the sleet, and half frozen besides, drove in at the gate and put up my horse in the old rail stable, where it is now. I then rapped at the door, and getting no invitation went in without one. The room was dark, but having matches I found a candle and lit it. I tried to enter the adjoining room, but the door was fast, and although I heard the old man's heavy footsteps in there he made no response to my calls. There was no fire on the hearth, so I made one and laying [*sic*] down before it with my overcoat under my head, prepared myself for sleep. Pretty soon the door that I had tried silently opened and the old man came in, carrying a candle. I spoke to him pleasantly, apologizing for my intrusion, but he took no notice of me. He seemed to be searching for something, though his eyes were unmoved in their sockets. I wonder if he ever walks in his sleep. He took a circuit a part of the way round the room, and went out the same way he had come in. Twice more before I slept he came back into the room, acting precisely the same way, and departing as at first. In the intervals I heard him tramping all over the house, his footsteps distinctly audible in the pauses of the storm. When I woke in the morning he had already gone out."

Mr. Maren attempted some further questioning, but was unable longer to restrain the family's tongues; the story of Deluse's death and burial came out, greatly to the good minister's astonishment.

"The explanation of your adventure is very simple," said Mr. Maren. "I don't believe old Deluse walks in his sleep—not in his present one; but you evidently dream in yours."

And to this view of the matter Mr. Galbraith was compelled reluctantly to assent.

Nevertheless, a late hour of the next night found these two gentlemen, accompanied by a son of the minister, in the road in front of the old Deluse house. There was a light inside; it appeared now at one window and now at another. The three men advanced to the door. Just as they reached it there came from the interior a confusion of the most appalling sounds—the clash of weapons, steel against steel, sharp explosions as of firearms, shrieks of women, groans and the curses of men in combat! The investigators stood a moment, irresolute, frightened. Then Mr. Galbraith tried the door. It was fast. But the minister was a man of courage, a man, moreover, of Herculean strength. He retired a pace or two and rushed against the door, striking it with his right shoulder and bursting it from the frame with a loud crash. In a moment the three were inside. Darkness and silence! The only sound was the beating of their hearts.

Mr. Maren had provided himself with matches and a candle. With some difficulty, begotten of his excitement, he made a light, and they proceeded to explore the place, passing from room to room. Everything was in orderly arrangement, as it had been left by the sheriff; nothing had been disturbed. A light coating of dust was everywhere. A back door was partly open, as if by neglect, and their first thought was that the authors of the awful revelry might have escaped. The door was opened, and the light of the candle shone through upon the ground. The expiring effort of the previous night's storm had been a light fall of snow; there were no footprints; the white surface was unbroken. They closed the door and entered the last room of the four that the house contained—that farthest from the road, in an angle of the building. Here the candle in Mr. Maren's hand was suddenly extinguished as by a draught of air. Almost immediately followed the sound of a heavy fall. When the candle had been hastily relighted young Mr. Galbraith was seen prostrate on the floor at a little distance from the others. He was dead. In one hand the body grasped a heavy sack of coins, which later examination showed to be all of old Spanish mintage. Directly over the body as it lay, a board had been torn from its fastenings in the wall, and from the cavity so disclosed it was evident that the bag had been taken.

Another inquest was held: another *post-mortem* examination failed to reveal a probable cause of death. Another verdict of "the visitation of God" left all at liberty to form their own conclusions. Mr. Maren contended that the young man died of excitement.

A Fruitless Assignment

Henry Saylor, who was killed in Covington, in a quarrel with Antonio Finch, was a reporter on the Cincinnati *Commercial*. In the year 1859 a vacant dwelling in Vine street, in Cincinnati, became the center of a local excitement because of the strange sights and sounds said to be observed in it nightly. According to the testimony of many reputable residents of the vicinity these were inconsistent with any other hypothesis than that the house was haunted. Figures with something singularly unfamiliar about them were seen by crowds on the sidewalk to pass in and out. No one could say just where they appeared upon the open lawn on their way to the front door by which they entered, nor at exactly what point they vanished as they came out; or, rather, while each spectator was positive enough about these matters, no two agreed. They were all similarly at variance in their descriptions of the figures themselves. Some of the bolder of the curious throng ventured on several evenings to stand upon the doorsteps to intercept them, or failing in this, get a nearer look at them. These courageous men, it was said, were unable to force the door by their united strength, and always were hurled from the steps by some invisible agency and severely injured; the door immediately afterward opening, apparently of its own volition, to admit or free some ghostly guest. The dwelling was known as the Roscoe house, a family of that name having lived there for some years, and then, one by one, disappeared, the last to leave being an old woman. Stories of foul play and successive murders had always been rife, but never were authenticated.

One day during the prevalence of the excitement Saylor presented himself at the office of the *Commercial* for orders. He received a note from the city editor which read as follows: "Go and pass the night alone in the haunted house in Vine street and if anything occurs worth while make two columns." Saylor obeyed his superior; he could not afford to lose his position on the paper.

Apprising the police of his intention, he effected an entrance through a rear window before dark, walked through the deserted rooms, bare of furniture, dusty and desolate, and seating himself at last in the parlor on an old sofa which he had dragged in from another room watched the deepening of the gloom as night came on. Before it was altogether dark the curious crowd had collected in the street, silent, as a rule, and expectant, with here and there a scoffer uttering his incredulity and courage with scornful remarks or ribald cries. None knew of the anxious watcher inside. He feared to make a light; the uncurtained windows would have betrayed his presence, subjecting him to insult, possibly to injury. Moreover, he was too conscientious to do anything to enfeeble his impressions and unwilling to alter any of the customary conditions under which the manifestations were said to occur.

It was now dark outside, but light from the street faintly illuminated the part of the room that he was in. He had set open every door in the whole interior, above and below, but all the outer ones were locked and bolted. Sudden exclamations from the crowd caused him to spring to the window and look out. He saw the figure of a man moving rapidly across the lawn toward the building—saw it ascend the steps; then a projection of the wall concealed it. There was a noise as of the opening and closing of the hall door; he heard quick, heavy footsteps along the passage—heard them ascend the stairs—heard them on the uncarpeted floor of the chamber immediately overhead.

Saylor promptly drew his pistol, and groping his way up the stairs entered the chamber, dimly lighted from the street. No one was there. He heard footsteps in an adjoining room and entered that. It was dark and silent. He struck his foot against some object on the floor, knelt by it, passed his hand over it. It was a human head—that of a woman. Lifting it by the hair this iron-nerved man returned to the half-lighted room below, carried it near the window and attentively examined it. While so engaged he was half conscious of the rapid opening and closing of the outer door, of footfalls sounding all about him. He raised his eyes from the ghastly object of his attention and saw himself the center of a crowd of men and women dimly seen; the room was thronged with them. He thought the people had broken in.

"Ladies and gentlemen," he said, coolly, "you see me under suspicious circumstances, but——" his voice was drowned in peals of laughter—such laughter as is heard in asylums for the insane. The persons about him pointed at the object in his hand and their merriment increased as he dropped it and it went rolling among their feet. They danced about it with gestures grotesque and attitudes obscene and indescribable. They struck it with their feet, urging it about the room from wall to wall; pushed and overthrew one another in their struggles to kick it; cursed and screamed and sang snatches of ribald songs as the battered head bounded about the room as if in terror and trying to escape. At last it shot out of the door into the hall, followed by all, with tumultuous haste. That moment the door closed with a sharp concussion. Saylor was alone, in dead silence.

Carefully putting away his pistol, which all the time he had held in his hand, he went to a window and looked out. The street was deserted and silent; the lamps were extinguished; the roofs and chimneys of the houses were sharply outlined against the dawn-light in the east. He left the house, the door yielding easily to his hand, and walked to the *Commercial* office. The city editor was still in his office—asleep. Saylor waked him and said: "I have been at the haunted house."

The editor stared blankly as if not wholly awake. "Good God!" he cried, "are you Saylor?"

"Yes—why not?"

The editor made no answer, but continued staring.

"I passed the night there—it seems," said Saylor.

"They say that things were uncommonly quiet out there," the editor said, trifling with a paper-weight upon which he had dropped his eyes, "did anything occur?"

"Nothing whatever."

A Vine on a House

About three miles from the little town of Norton, in Missouri, on the road leading to Maysville, stands an old house that was last occupied by a family named Harding. Since 1886 no one has lived in it, nor is anyone likely to live in it again. Time and the disfavor of persons dwelling thereabout are converting it into a rather picturesque ruin. An observer unacquainted with its history would hardly put it into the category of "haunted houses," yet in all the region round such is its evil reputation. Its windows are without glass, its doorways without doors; there are wide breaches in the shingle roof, and for lack of paint the weatherboarding is a dun gray. But these unfailing signs of the supernatural are partly concealed and greatly softened by the abundant foliage of a large vine overrunning the entire structure. This vine—of a species which no botanist has ever been able to name—has an important part in the story of the house.

The Harding family consisted of Robert Harding, his wife Matilda, Miss Julia Went, who was her sister, and two young children. Robert Harding was a silent, cold-mannered man who made no friends in the neighborhood and apparently cared to make none. He was about forty years old, frugal and industrious, and made a living from the little farm which is now overgrown with brush and brambles. He and his sister-in-law were rather tabooed by their neighbors, who seemed to think that they were seen too frequently together—not entirely their fault, for at these times they evidently did not challenge observation. The moral code of rural Missouri is stern and exacting.

Mrs. Harding was a gentle, sad-eyed woman, lacking a left foot.

At some time in 1884 it became known that she had gone to visit her mother in Iowa. That was what her husband said in reply to inquiries, and his manner of saying it did not encourage further questioning. She never came back, and two years later, without selling his farm or anything that was his, or appointing an agent to look after his interests, or removing his household goods, Harding, with the rest of the family, left the country. Nobody knew whither he went; nobody at that time cared. Naturally, whatever was movable about the place soon disappeared and the deserted house became "haunted" in the manner of its kind.

One summer evening, four or five years later, the Rev. J. Gruber, of Norton, and a Maysville attorney named Hyatt met on horseback in front of the Harding place. Having business matters to discuss, they hitched their animals and going to the house sat on the porch to talk. Some humorous reference to the somber reputation of the place was made and forgotten as soon as uttered, and they talked of their business affairs until it grew almost dark. The evening was oppressively warm, the air stagnant.

Presently both men started from their seats in surprise: a long vine that covered half the front of the house and dangled its branches from the edge of the porch above them was visibly and audibly agitated, shaking violently in every stem and leaf.

"We shall have a storm," Hyatt exclaimed.

Gruber said nothing, but silently directed the other's attention to the foliage of adjacent trees, which showed no movement; even the delicate tips of the boughs silhouetted against the clear sky were motionless. They hastily passed down the steps to what had been a lawn and looked upward at the vine, whose entire length was now visible. It continued in violent agitation, yet they could discern no disturbing cause.

"Let us leave," said the minister.

And leave they did. Forgetting that they had been traveling in opposite directions, they rode away together. They went to Norton, where they related their strange experience to several discreet friends. The next evening, at about the same hour, accompanied by two others whose names are not recalled, they were again on the porch of the Harding house, and again the mysterious phenomenon occurred: the vine was violently agitated while under the closest scrutiny from root to tip, nor did their combined strength applied to the trunk serve to still it. After an hour's observation they retreated, no less wise, it is thought, than when they had come.

No great time was required for these singular facts to rouse the curiosity of the entire neighborhood. By day and by night crowds of persons assembled at the Harding house "seeking a sign." It does not appear that any found it, yet so credible were the witnesses mentioned that none doubted the reality of the "manifestations" to which they testified.

By either a happy inspiration or some destructive design, it was one day proposed—nobody appeared to know from whom the suggestion came—to dig up the vine, and after a good deal of debate this was done. Nothing was found but the root, yet nothing could have been more strange!

For five or six feet from the trunk, which had at the surface of the ground a diameter of several inches, it ran downward, single and straight, into a loose, friable earth; then it divided and subdivided into rootlets, fibers and filaments, most curiously interwoven. When carefully freed from soil they showed a singular formation. In their ramifications and doublings back upon themselves they made a compact network, having in size and shape an amazing resemblance to the human figure. Head, trunk and limbs were there; even the fingers and toes were distinctly defined; and many professed to see in the distribution and arrangement of the fibers in the globular mass representing the head a grotesque suggestion of a face. The figure was horizontal; the smaller roots had begun to unite at the breast.

In point of resemblance to the human form this image was imperfect. At about ten inches from one of the knees, the *cilia* forming that leg had abruptly doubled backward and inward upon their course of growth. The figure lacked the left foot.

There was but one inference—the obvious one; but in the ensuing excitement as many courses of action were proposed as there were incapable counselors. The matter was settled by the sheriff of the county, who as the lawful custodian of the abandoned estate ordered the root replaced and the excavation filled with the earth that had been removed.

Later inquiry brought out only one fact of relevancy and significance: Mrs. Harding had never visited her relatives in Iowa, nor did they know that she was supposed to have done so.

Of Robert Harding and the rest of his family nothing is known. The house retains its evil reputation, but the replanted vine is as orderly and well-behaved a vegetable as a nervous person could wish to sit under of a pleasant night, when the katydids grate out their immemorial revelation and the distant whippoorwill signifies his notion of what ought to be done about it.

At Old Man Eckert's

PHILIP ECKERT lived for many years in an old, weather-stained wooden house about three miles from the little town of Marion, in Vermont. There must be quite a number of persons living who remember him, not unkindly, I trust, and know something of the story that I am about to tell.

"Old Man Eckert," as he was always called, was not of a sociable disposition and lived alone. As he was never known to speak of his own affairs nobody thereabout knew anything of his past, nor of his relatives if he had any. Without being particularly ungracious or repellent in manner or speech, he managed somehow to be immune to impertinent curiosity, yet exempt from the evil repute with which it commonly revenges itself when baffled; so far as I know, Mr. Eckert's renown as a reformed assassin or a retired pirate of the Spanish Main had not reached any ear in Marion. He got his living cultivating a small and not very fertile farm.

One day he disappeared and a prolonged search by his neighbors failed to turn him up or throw any light upon his whereabouts or whyabouts. Nothing indicated preparation to leave: all was as he might have left it to go to the spring for a bucket of water. For a few weeks little else was talked of in that region; then "old man Eckert" became a village tale for the ear of the stranger. I do not know what was done regarding his property—the correct legal thing, doubtless. The house was standing, still vacant and conspicuously unfit, when I last heard of it, some twenty years afterward.

Of course it came to be considered "haunted," and the customary tales were told of moving lights, dolorous sounds and startling apparitions. At one time, about five years after the disappearance, these stories of the supernatural became so rife, or through some attesting circumstances seemed so important, that some of Marion's most serious citizens deemed it well to investigate, and to that end arranged for a night session on the premises. The parties to this undertaking were John Holcomb, an apothecary; Wilson Merle, a lawyer, and Andrus C. Palmer, the teacher of the public school, all men of consequence and repute. They were to meet at Holcomb's house at eight o'clock in the evening of the appointed day and go together to the scene of their vigil, where certain arrangements for their comfort, a provision of fuel and the like, for the season was winter, had been already made.

Palmer did not keep the engagement, and after waiting a half-hour for him the others went to the Eckert house without him. They established themselves in the principal room, before a glowing fire, and without other light than it gave, awaited events. It had been agreed to speak as little as possible: they did not even renew the exchange of views regarding the defection of Palmer, which had occupied their minds on the way.

Probably an hour had passed without incident when they heard (not without emotion, doubtless) the sound of an opening door in the rear of the house, followed by footfalls in the room adjoining that in which they sat. The watchers rose to their feet, but stood firm, prepared for whatever might ensue. A long silence followed—how long neither would afterward undertake to say. Then the door between the two rooms opened and a man entered.

It was Palmer. He was pale, as if from excitement—as pale as the others felt themselves to be. His manner, too, was singularly distrait: he neither responded to their salutations nor so much as looked at them, but walked slowly across the room in the light of the failing fire and opening the front door passed out into the darkness.

It seems to have been the first thought of both men that Palmer was suffering from fright—that something seen, heard or imagined in the back room had deprived him of his senses. Acting on the same friendly impulse both ran after him through the open door. But neither they nor anyone ever again saw or heard of Andrus Palmer!

This much was ascertained the next morning. During the session of Messrs. Holcomb and Merle at the "haunted house" a new snow had fallen to a depth of several inches upon the old. In this snow Palmer's trail from his lodging in the village to the back door of the Eckert house was conspicuous. But there it ended: from the front door nothing led away but the tracks of the two men who swore that he preceded them. Palmer's disappearance was as complete as that of "old man Eckert" himself—whom, indeed, the editor of the local paper somewhat graphically accused of having "reached out and pulled him in."

The Spook House

ON the road leading north from Manchester, in eastern
Kentucky, to Booneville, twenty miles away, stood, in
1862, a wooden plantation house of a somewhat better quality
than most of the dwellings in that region. The house was
destroyed by fire in the year following—probably by some
stragglers from the retreating column of General George W.
Morgan, when he was driven from Cumberland Gap to the
Ohio river by General Kirby Smith. At the time of its destruction, it had for four or five years been vacant. The fields about
it were overgrown with brambles, the fences gone, even the
few negro quarters, and outhouses generally, fallen partly into
ruin by neglect and pillage; for the negroes and poor whites of
the vicinity found in the building and fences an abundant supply of fuel, of which they availed themselves without hesitation, openly and by daylight. By daylight alone; after nightfall
no human being except passing strangers ever went near the
place.

It was known as the "Spook House." That it was tenanted
by evil spirits, visible, audible and active, no one in all that region doubted any more than he doubted what he was told of
Sundays by the traveling preacher. Its owner's opinion of the
matter was unknown; he and his family had disappeared one
night and no trace of them had ever been found. They left
everything—household goods, clothing, provisions, the horses
in the stable, the cows in the field, the negroes in the quarters
—all as it stood; nothing was missing—except a man, a woman,
three girls, a boy and a babe! It was not altogether surprising
that a plantation where seven human beings could be simultaneously effaced and nobody the wiser should be under some
suspicion.

One night in June, 1859, two citizens of Frankfort, Col. J. C.
McArdle, a lawyer, and Judge Myron Veigh, of the State Mili-
tia, were driving from Booneville to Manchester. Their business was so important that they decided to push on, despite
the darkness and the mutterings of an approaching storm,
which eventually broke upon them just as they arrived opposite

415

the "Spook House." The lightning was so incessant that they easily found their way through the gateway and into a shed, where they hitched and unharnessed their team. They then went to the house, through the rain, and knocked at all the doors without getting any response. Attributing this to the continuous uproar of the thunder they pushed at one of the doors, which yielded. They entered without further ceremony and closed the door. That instant they were in darkness and silence. Not a gleam of the lightning's unceasing blaze penetrated the windows or crevices; not a whisper of the awful tumult without reached them there. It was as if they had suddenly been stricken blind and deaf, and McArdle afterward said that for a moment he believed himself to have been killed by a stroke of lightning as he crossed the threshold. The rest of this adventure can as well be related in his own words, from the Frankfort *Advocate* of August 6, 1876:

"When I had somewhat recovered from the dazing effect of the transition from uproar to silence, my first impulse was to reopen the door which I had closed, and from the knob of which I was not conscious of having removed my hand; I felt it distinctly, still in the clasp of my fingers. My notion was to ascertain by stepping again into the storm whether I had been deprived of sight and hearing. I turned the door-knob and pulled open the door. It led into another room!

"This apartment was suffused with a faint greenish light, the source of which I could not determine, making everything distinctly visible, though nothing was sharply defined. Everything, I say, but in truth the only objects within the blank stone walls of that room were human corpses. In number they were perhaps eight or ten—it may well be understood that I did not truly count them. They were of different ages, or rather sizes, from infancy up, and of both sexes. All were prostrate on the floor, excepting one, apparently a young woman, who sat up, her back supported by an angle of the wall. A babe was clasped in the arms of another and older woman. A half-grown lad lay face downward across the legs of a full-bearded man. One or two were nearly naked, and the hand of a young girl held the fragment of a gown which she had torn open at the breast. The bodies were in various stages of decay, all greatly shrunken in face and figure. Some were but little more than skeletons.

"While I stood stupefied with horror by this ghastly spectacle and still holding open the door, by some unaccountable perversity my attention was diverted from the shocking scene and concerned itself with trifles and details. Perhaps my mind, with an instinct of self-preservation, sought relief in matters which would relax its dangerous tension. Among other things, I observed that the door that I was holding open was of heavy iron plates, riveted. Equidistant from one another and from the top and bottom, three strong bolts protruded from the beveled edge. I turned the knob and they were retracted flush with the edge; released it, and they shot out. It was a spring lock. On the inside there was no knob, nor any kind of projection—a smooth surface of iron.

"While noting these things with an interest and attention which it now astonishes me to recall I felt myself thrust aside, and Judge Veigh, whom in the intensity and vicissitudes of my feelings I had altogether forgotten, pushed by me into the room. 'For God's sake,' I cried, 'do not go in there! Let us get out of this dreadful place!'

"He gave no heed to my entreaties, but (as fearless a gentleman as lived in all the South) walked quickly to the center of the room, knelt beside one of the bodies for a closer examination and tenderly raised its blackened and shriveled head in his hands. A strong disagreeable odor came through the doorway, completely overpowering me. My senses reeled; I felt myself falling, and in clutching at the edge of the door for support pushed it shut with a sharp click!

"I remember no more: six weeks later I recovered my reason in a hotel at Manchester, whither I had been taken by strangers the next day. For all these weeks I had suffered from a nervous fever, attended with constant delirium. I had been found lying in the road several miles away from the house; but how I had escaped from it to get there I never knew. On recovery, or as soon as my physicians permitted me to talk, I inquired the fate of Judge Veigh, whom (to quiet me, as I now know) they represented as well and at home.

"No one believed a word of my story, and who can wonder?

And who can imagine my grief when, arriving at my home in Frankfort two months later, I learned that Judge Veigh had never been heard of since that night? I then regretted bitterly the pride which since the first few days after the recovery of my reason had forbidden me to repeat my discredited story and insist upon its truth.

"With all that afterward occurred—the examination of the house; the failure to find any room corresponding to that which I have described; the attempt to have me adjudged insane, and my triumph over my accusers—the readers of the *Advocate* are familiar. After all these years I am still confident that excavations which I have neither the legal right to undertake nor the wealth to make would disclose the secret of the disappearance of my unhappy friend, and possibly of the former occupants and owners of the deserted and now destroyed house. I do not despair of yet bringing about such a search, and it is a source of deep grief to me that it has been delayed by the undeserved hostility and unwise incredulity of the family and friends of the late Judge Veigh."

Colonel McArdle died in Frankfort on the thirteenth day of December, in the year 1879.

The Other Lodgers

"IN order to take that train," said Colonel Levering, sitting in the Waldorf-Astoria hotel, "you will have to remain nearly all night in Atlanta. That is a fine city, but I advise you not to put up at the Breathitt House, one of the principal hotels. It is an old wooden building in urgent need of repairs. There are breaches in the walls that you could throw a cat through. The bedrooms have no locks on the doors, no furniture but a single chair in each, and a bedstead without bedding—just a mattress. Even these meager accommodations you cannot be sure that you will have in monopoly; you must take your chance of being stowed in with a lot of others. Sir, it is a most abominable hotel.

"The night that I passed in it was an uncomfortable night. I got in late and was shown to my room on the ground floor by an apologetic night-clerk with a tallow candle, which he considerately left with me. I was worn out by two days and a night of hard railway travel and had not entirely recovered from a gunshot wound in the head, received in an altercation. Rather than look for better quarters I lay down on the mattress without removing my clothing and fell asleep.

"Along toward morning I awoke. The moon had risen and was shining in at the uncurtained window, illuminating the room with a soft, bluish light which seemed, somehow, a bit spooky, though I dare say it had no uncommon quality; all moonlight is that way if you will observe it. Imagine my surprise and indignation when I saw the floor occupied by at least a dozen other lodgers! I sat up, earnestly damning the management of that unthinkable hotel, and was about to spring from the bed to go and make trouble for the night-clerk—him of the apologetic manner and the tallow candle—when something in the situation affected me with a strange indisposition to move. I suppose I was what a story-writer might call 'frozen with terror.' For those men were obviously all dead!

"They lay on their backs, disposed orderly along three sides of the room, their feet to the walls—against the other wall, farthest from the door, stood my bed and the chair. All the faces were covered, but under their white cloths the features of the two bodies that lay in the square patch of moonlight near the window showed in sharp profile as to nose and chin.

"I thought this a bad dream and tried to cry out, as one does in a nightmare, but could make no sound. At last, with a desperate effort I threw my feet to the floor and passing between the two rows of clouted faces and the two bodies that lay nearest the door, I escaped from the infernal place and ran to the office. The night-clerk was there, behind the desk, sitting in the dim light of another tallow candle—just sitting and staring. He did not rise: my abrupt entrance produced no effect upon him, though I must have looked a veritable corpse myself. It occurred to me then that I had not before really observed the fellow. He was a little chap, with a colorless face and the whitest, blankest eyes I ever saw. He had no more expression than the back of my hand. His clothing was a dirty gray.

" 'Damn you!' I said; 'what do you mean?'

"Just the same, I was shaking like a leaf in the wind and did not recognize my own voice.

"The night-clerk rose, bowed (apologetically) and—well, he was no longer there, and at that moment I felt a hand laid upon my shoulder from behind. Just fancy that if you can! Unspeakably frightened, I turned and saw a portly, kind-faced gentleman, who asked:

" 'What is the matter, my friend?'

"I was not long in telling him, but before I made an end of it he went pale himself. 'See here,' he said, 'are you telling the truth?'

"I had now got myself in hand and terror had given place to indignation. 'If you dare to doubt it,' I said, 'I'll hammer the life out of you!'

" 'No,' he replied, 'don't do that; just sit down till I tell you. This is not a hotel. It used to be; afterward it was a hospital. Now it is unoccupied, awaiting a tenant. The room that you mention was the dead-room—there were always plenty of dead. The fellow that you call the night-clerk used to be that, but later he booked the patients as they were brought in. I don't understand his being here. He has been dead a few weeks.'

" 'And who are you?' I blurted out.

" 'Oh, I look after the premises. I happened to be passing just now, and seeing a light in here came in to investigate. Let us have a look into that room,' he added, lifting the sputtering candle from the desk.

" 'I'll see you at the devil first!' said I, bolting out of the door into the street.

"Sir, that Breathitt House, in Atlanta, is a beastly place! Don't you stop there."

"God forbid! Your account of it certainly does not suggest comfort. By the way, Colonel, when did all that occur?"

"In September, 1864—shortly after the siege."

The Thing at Nolan

To the south of where the road between Leesville and Hardy, in the State of Missouri, crosses the east fork of May Creek stands an abandoned house. Nobody has lived in it since the summer of 1879, and it is fast going to pieces. For some three years before the date mentioned above, it was occupied by the family of Charles May, from one of whose ancestors the creek near which it stands took its name. Mr. May's family consisted of a wife, an adult son and two young girls. The son's name was John—the names of the daughters are unknown to the writer of this sketch.

John May was of a morose and surly disposition, not easily moved to anger, but having an uncommon gift of sullen, implacable hate. His father was quite otherwise; of a sunny, jovial disposition, but with a quick temper like a sudden flame kindled in a wisp of straw, which consumes it in a flash and is no more. He cherished no resentments, and his anger gone, was quick to make overtures for reconciliation. He had a brother living near by who was unlike him in respect of all this, and it was a current witticism in the neighborhood that John had inherited his disposition from his uncle.

One day a misunderstanding arose between father and son, harsh words ensued, and the father struck the son full in the face with his fist. John quietly wiped away the blood that followed the blow, fixed his eyes upon the already penitent offender and said with cold composure, "You will die for that."

The words were overheard by two brothers named Jackson, who were approaching the men at the moment; but seeing them engaged in a quarrel they retired, apparently unobserved. Charles May afterward related the unfortunate occurrence to his wife and explained that he had apologized to the son for the hasty blow, but without avail; the young man not only rejected his overtures, but refused to withdraw his terrible threat. Nevertheless, there was no open rupture of relations: John continued living with the family, and things went on very much as before.

One Sunday morning in June, 1879, about two weeks after

what has been related, May senior left the house immediately after breakfast, taking a spade. He said he was going to make an excavation at a certain spring in a wood about a mile away, so that the cattle could obtain water. John remained in the house for some hours, variously occupied in shaving himself, writing letters and reading a newspaper. His manner was very nearly what it usually was; perhaps he was a trifle more sullen and surly.

At two o'clock he left the house. At five, he returned. For some reason not connected with any interest in his movements, and which is not now recalled, the time of his departure and that of his return were noted by his mother and sisters, as was attested at his trial for murder. It was observed that his clothing was wet in spots, as if (so the prosecution afterward pointed out) he had been removing blood-stains from it. His manner was strange, his look wild. He complained of illness, and going to his room took to his bed.

May senior did not return. Later that evening the nearest neighbors were aroused, and during that night and the following day a search was prosecuted through the wood where the spring was. It resulted in little but the discovery of both men's footprints in the clay about the spring. John May in the meantime had grown rapidly worse with what the local physician called brain fever, and in his delirium raved of murder, but did not say whom he conceived to have been murdered, nor whom he imagined to have done the deed. But his threat was recalled by the brothers Jackson and he was arrested on suspicion and a deputy sheriff put in charge of him at his home. Public opinion ran strongly against him and but for his illness he would probably have been hanged by a mob. As it was, a meeting of the neighbors was held on Tuesday and a committee appointed to watch the case and take such action at any time as circumstances might seem to warrant.

On Wednesday all was changed. From the town of Nolan, eight miles away, came a story which put a quite different light on the matter. Nolan consisted of a school house, a blacksmith's shop, a "store" and a half-dozen dwellings. The store was kept by one Henry Odell, a cousin of the elder May. On the afternoon of the Sunday of May's disappearance Mr. Odell and four of his neighbors, men of credibility, were sitting in the store

smoking and talking. It was a warm day; and both the front
and the back door were open. At about three o'clock Charles
May, who was well known to three of them, entered at the
front door and passed out at the rear. He was without hat or
coat. He did not look at them, nor return their greeting, a
circumstance which did not surprise, for he was evidently seriously hurt. Above the left eyebrow was a wound—a deep gash
from which the blood flowed, covering the whole left side of
the face and neck and saturating his light-gray shirt. Oddly
enough, the thought uppermost in the minds of all was that he
had been fighting and was going to the brook directly at the
back of the store, to wash himself.

Perhaps there was a feeling of delicacy—a backwoods etiquette which restrained them from following him to offer assistance; the court records, from which, mainly, this narrative is
drawn, are silent as to anything but the fact. They waited for
him to return, but he did not return.

Bordering the brook behind the store is a forest extending
for six miles back to the Medicine Lodge Hills. As soon as it
became known in the neighborhood of the missing man's
dwelling that he had been seen in Nolan there was a marked
alteration in public sentiment and feeling. The vigilance committee went out of existence without the formality of a resolution. Search along the wooded bottom lands of May Creek
was stopped and nearly the entire male population of the region took to beating the bush about Nolan and in the Medicine
Lodge Hills. But of the missing man no trace was found.

One of the strangest circumstances of this strange case is the
formal indictment and trial of a man for murder of one whose
body no human being professed to have seen—one not known
to be dead. We are all more or less familiar with the vagaries
and eccentricities of frontier law, but this instance, it is thought,
is unique. However that may be, it is of record that on recovering from his illness John May was indicted for the murder of
his missing father. Counsel for the defense appears not to have
demurred and the case was tried on its merits. The prosecution
was spiritless and perfunctory; the defense easily established—
with regard to the deceased—an *alibi*. If during the time in
which John May must have killed Charles May, if he killed him
at all, Charles May was miles away from where John May must

have been, it is plain that the deceased must have come to his death at the hands of someone else.

John May was acquitted, immediately left the country, and has never been heard of from that day. Shortly afterward his mother and sisters removed to St. Louis. The farm having passed into the possession of a man who owns the land adjoining, and has a dwelling of his own, the May house has ever since been vacant, and has the somber reputation of being haunted.

One day after the May family had left the country, some boys, playing in the woods along May Creek, found concealed under a mass of dead leaves, but partly exposed by the rooting of hogs, a spade, nearly new and bright, except for a spot on one edge, which was rusted and stained with blood. The implement had the initials C. M. cut into the handle.

This discovery renewed, in some degree, the public excitement of a few months before. The earth near the spot where the spade was found was carefully examined, and the result was the finding of the dead body of a man. It had been buried under two or three feet of soil and the spot covered with a layer of dead leaves and twigs. There was but little decomposition, a fact attributed to some preservative property in the mineral-bearing soil.

Above the left eyebrow was a wound—a deep gash from which blood had flowed, covering the whole left side of the face and neck and saturating the light-gray shirt. The skull had been cut through by the blow. The body was that of Charles May.

But what was it that passed through Mr. Odell's store at Nolan?

"MYSTERIOUS DISAPPEARANCES"

The Difficulty of Crossing a Field

ONE morning in July, 1854, a planter named Williamson, living six miles from Selma, Alabama, was sitting with his wife and a child on the veranda of his dwelling. Immediately in front of the house was a lawn, perhaps fifty yards in extent between the house and public road, or, as it was called, the "pike." Beyond this road lay a close-cropped pasture of some ten acres, level and without a tree, rock, or any natural or artificial object on its surface. At the time there was not even a domestic animal in the field. In another field, beyond the pasture, a dozen slaves were at work under an overseer.

Throwing away the stump of a cigar, the planter rose, saying: "I forgot to tell Andrew about those horses." Andrew was the overseer.

Williamson strolled leisurely down the gravel walk, plucking a flower as he went, passed across the road and into the pasture, pausing a moment as he closed the gate leading into it, to greet a passing neighbor, Armour Wren, who lived on an adjoining plantation. Mr. Wren was in an open carriage with his son James, a lad of thirteen. When he had driven some two hundred yards from the point of meeting, Mr. Wren said to his son: "I forgot to tell Mr. Williamson about those horses."

Mr. Wren had sold to Mr. Williamson some horses, which were to have been sent for that day, but for some reason not now remembered it would be inconvenient to deliver them until the morrow. The coachman was directed to drive back, and as the vehicle turned Williamson was seen by all three, walking leisurely across the pasture. At that moment one of the coach horses stumbled and came near falling. It had no more than fairly recovered itself when James Wren cried: "Why, father, what has become of Mr. Williamson?"

It is not the purpose of this narrative to answer that question.

Mr. Wren's strange account of the matter, given under oath in the course of legal proceedings relating to the Williamson estate, here follows:

"My son's exclamation caused me to look toward the spot where I had seen the deceased [*sic*] an instant before, but he was not there, nor was he anywhere visible. I cannot say that at the moment I was greatly startled, or realized the gravity of the occurrence, though I thought it singular. My son, however, was greatly astonished and kept repeating his question in different forms until we arrived at the gate. My black boy Sam was similarly affected, even in a greater degree, but I reckon more by my son's manner than by anything he had himself observed. [This sentence in the testimony was stricken out.] As we got out of the carriage at the gate of the field, and while Sam was hanging [*sic*] the team to the fence, Mrs. Williamson, with her child in her arms and followed by several servants, came running down the walk in great excitement, crying: 'He is gone, he is gone! O God! what an awful thing!' and many other such exclamations, which I do not distinctly recollect. I got from them the impression that they related to something more than the mere disappearance of her husband, even if that had occurred before her eyes. Her manner was wild, but not more so, I think, than was natural under the circumstances. I have no reason to think she had at that time lost her mind. I have never since seen nor heard of Mr. Williamson."

This testimony, as might have been expected, was corroborated in almost every particular by the only other eye-witness (if that is a proper term)—the lad James. Mrs. Williamson had lost her reason and the servants were, of course, not competent to testify. The boy James Wren had declared at first that he *saw* the disappearance, but there is nothing of this in his testimony given in court. None of the field hands working in the field to which Williamson was going had seen him at all, and the most rigorous search of the entire plantation and adjoining country failed to supply a clew. The most monstrous and grotesque fictions, originating with the blacks, were current in that part of the State for many years, and probably are to this day; but what has been here related is all that is certainly known of the matter. The courts decided that Williamson was dead, and his estate was distributed according to law.

An Unfinished Race

JAMES BURNE WORSON was a shoemaker who lived in Leamington, Warwickshire, England. He had a little shop in one of the by-ways leading off the road to Warwick. In his humble sphere he was esteemed an honest man, although like many of his class in English towns he was somewhat addicted to drink. When in liquor he would make foolish wagers. On one of these too frequent occasions he was boasting of his prowess as a pedestrian and athlete, and the outcome was a match against nature. For a stake of one sovereign he undertook to run all the way to Coventry and back, a distance of something more than forty miles. This was on the 3d day of September in 1873. He set out at once, the man with whom he had made the bet—whose name is not remembered—accompanied by Barham Wise, a linen draper, and Hamerson Burns, a photographer, I think, following in a light cart or wagon.

For several miles Worson went on very well, at an easy gait, without apparent fatigue, for he had really great powers of endurance and was not sufficiently intoxicated to enfeeble them. The three men in the wagon kept a short distance in the rear, giving him occasional friendly "chaff" or encouragement, as the spirit moved them. Suddenly—in the very middle of the roadway, not a dozen yards from them, and with their eyes full upon him—the man seemed to stumble, pitched headlong forward, uttered a terrible cry and vanished! He did not fall to the earth—he vanished before touching it. No trace of him was ever discovered.

After remaining at and about the spot for some time, with aimless irresolution, the three men returned to Leamington, told their astonishing story and were afterward taken into custody. But they were of good standing, had always been considered truthful, were sober at the time of the occurrence, and nothing ever transpired to discredit their sworn account of their extraordinary adventure, concerning the truth of which, nevertheless, public opinion was divided, throughout the United Kingdom. If they had something to conceal, their choice of means is certainly one of the most amazing ever made by sane human beings.

Charles Ashmore's Trail

THE family of Christian Ashmore consisted of his wife, his mother, two grown daughters, and a son of sixteen years. They lived in Troy, New York, were well-to-do, respectable persons, and had many friends, some of whom, reading these lines, will doubtless learn for the first time the extraordinary fate of the young man. From Troy the Ashmores moved in 1871 or 1872 to Richmond, Indiana, and a year or two later to the vicinity of Quincy, Illinois, where Mr. Ashmore bought a farm and lived on it. At some little distance from the farmhouse was a spring with a constant flow of clear, cold water, whence the family derived its supply for domestic use at all seasons.

On the evening of the 9th of November in 1878, at about nine o'clock, young Charles Ashmore left the family circle about the hearth, took a tin bucket and started toward the spring. As he did not return, the family became uneasy, and going to the door by which he had left the house, his father called without receiving an answer. He then lighted a lantern and with the eldest daughter, Martha, who insisted on accompanying him, went in search. A light snow had fallen, obliterating the path, but making the young man's trail conspicuous; each footprint was plainly defined. After going a little more than half-way—perhaps seventy-five yards—the father, who was in advance, halted, and elevating his lantern stood peering intently into the darkness ahead.

"What is the matter, father?" the girl asked.

This was the matter: the trail of the young man had abruptly ended, and all beyond was smooth, unbroken snow. The last footprints were as conspicuous as any in the line; the very nail-marks were distinctly visible. Mr. Ashmore looked upward, shading his eyes with his hat held between them and the lantern. The stars were shining; there was not a cloud in the sky; he was denied the explanation which had suggested itself, doubtful as it would have been—a new snowfall with a limit so plainly defined. Taking a wide circuit round the ultimate tracks, so as to leave them undisturbed for further examination, the man proceeded to the spring, the girl following, weak and terrified. Neither had spoken a word of what both had observed. The spring was covered with ice, hours old.

Returning to the house they noted the appearance of the snow on both sides of the trail its entire length. No tracks led away from it.

The morning light showed nothing more. Smooth, spotless, unbroken, the shallow snow lay everywhere.

Four days later the grief-stricken mother herself went to the spring for water. She came back and related that in passing the spot where the footprints had ended she had heard the voice of her son and had been eagerly calling to him, wandering about the place, as she had fancied the voice to be now in one direction, now in another, until she was exhausted with fatigue and emotion. Questioned as to what the voice had said, she was unable to tell, yet averred that the words were perfectly distinct. In a moment the entire family was at the place, but nothing was heard, and the voice was believed to be an hallucination caused by the mother's great anxiety and her disordered nerves. But for months afterward, at irregular intervals of a few days, the voice was heard by the several members of the family, and by others. All declared it unmistakably the voice of Charles Ashmore; all agreed that it seemed to come from a great distance, faintly, yet with entire distinctness of articulation; yet none could determine its direction, nor repeat its words. The intervals of silence grew longer and longer, the voice fainter and farther, and by midsummer it was heard no more.

If anybody knows the fate of Charles Ashmore it is probably his mother. She is dead.

———

SCIENCE TO THE FRONT

In connection with this subject of "mysterious disappearance" —of which every memory is stored with abundant example—it it pertinent to note the belief of Dr. Hern, of Leipsic; not by way of explanation, unless the reader may choose to take it so, but because of its intrinsic interest as a singular speculation. This distinguished scientist has expounded his views in a book entitled "Verschwinden und Seine Theorie," which has attracted some attention, "particularly," says one writer, "among the followers of Hegel, and mathematicians who hold to the actual existence of a so-called non-Euclidean space—that is to say, of space which has more dimensions than length, breadth, and thickness—space in which it would be possible to tie a knot in an endless cord and to turn a rubber ball inside out without 'a solution of its continuity,' or in other words, without breaking or cracking it."

Dr. Hern believes that in the visible world there are void places—*vacua*, and something more—holes, as it were, through which animate and inanimate objects may fall into the invisible world and be seen and heard no more. The theory is something like this: Space is pervaded by luminiferous ether, which is a material thing—as much a substance as air or water, though almost infinitely more attenuated. All force, all forms of energy must be propagated in this; every process must take place in it which takes place at all. But let us suppose that cavities exist in this otherwise universal medium, as caverns exist in the earth, or cells in a Swiss cheese. In such a cavity there would be absolutely nothing. It would be such a vacuum as cannot be artificially produced; for if we pump the air from a receiver there remains the luminiferous ether. Through one of these cavities light could not pass, for there would be nothing to bear it. Sound could not come from it; nothing could be felt in it. It would not have a single one of the conditions necessary to the action of any of our senses. In such a void, in short, nothing whatever could occur. Now, in the words of the writer before quoted—the learned doctor himself nowhere puts it so concisely: "A man inclosed in such a closet could neither see nor be seen; neither hear nor be heard; neither feel nor be felt; neither live nor die, for both life and death are processes which can take place only where there is force, and in empty space no force could exist." Are these the awful conditions (some will ask) under which the friends of the lost are to think of them as existing, and doomed forever to exist?

Baldly and imperfectly as here stated, Dr. Hern's theory, in so far as it professes to be an adequate explanation of "mysterious disappearances," is open to many obvious objections; to fewer as he states it himself in the "spacious volubility" of his book. But even as expounded by its author it does not explain, and in truth is incompatible with some incidents of, the occurrences related in these memoranda: for example, the sound of Charles Ashmore's voice. It is not my duty to indue facts and theories with affinity.

A. B.

THE DEVIL'S DICTIONARY

PREFACE

The Devil's Dictionary was begun in a weekly paper in 1881, and was continued in a desultory way and at long intervals until 1906. In that year a large part of it was published in covers with the title *The Cynic's Word Book*, a name which the author had not the power to reject nor the happiness to approve. To quote the publishers of the present work:

"This more reverent title had previously been forced upon him by the religious scruples of the last newspaper in which a part of the work had appeared, with the natural consequence that when it came out in covers the country already had been flooded by its imitators with a score of 'cynic' books—*The Cynic's This, The Cynic's That*, and *The Cynic'st'Other*. Most of these books were merely stupid, though some of them added the distinction of silliness. Among them, they brought the word 'cynic' into disfavor so deep that any book bearing it was discredited in advance of publication."

Meantime, too, some of the enterprising humorists of the country had helped themselves to such parts of the work as served their needs, and many of its definitions, anecdotes, phrases and so forth, had become more or less current in popular speech. This explanation is made, not with any pride of priority in trifles, but in simple denial of possible charges of plagiarism, which is no trifle. In merely resuming his own the author hopes to be held guiltless by those to whom the work is addressed—enlightened souls who prefer dry wines to sweet, sense to sentiment, wit to humor and clean English to slang.

A conspicuous, and it is hoped not unpleasant, feature of the book is its abundant illustrative quotations from eminent poets, chief of whom is that learned and ingenius cleric, Father Gassalasca Jape, S.J., whose lines bear his initials. To Father Jape's kindly encouragement and assistance the author of the prose text is greatly indebted.

A. B.

A

ABASEMENT, *n.* A decent and customary mental attitude in the presence of wealth or power. Peculiarly appropriate in an employee when addressing an employer.

ABATIS, *n.* Rubbish in front of a fort, to prevent the rubbish outside from molesting the rubbish inside.

ABDICATION, *n.* An act whereby a sovereign attests his sense of the high temperature of the throne.

> Poor Isabella's dead, whose abdication
> Set all tongues wagging in the Spanish nation.
> For that performance 'twere unfair to scold her:
> She wisely left a throne too hot to hold her.
> To History she'll be no royal riddle—
> Merely a plain parched pea that jumped the griddle.
>
> *G. J.*

ABDOMEN, *n.* The temple of the god Stomach, in whose worship, with sacrificial rights, all true men engage. From women this ancient faith commands but a stammering assent. They sometimes minister at the altar in a half-hearted and ineffective way, but true reverence for the one deity that men really adore they know not. If woman had a free hand in the world's marketing the race would become graminivorous.

ABILITY, *n.* The natural equipment to accomplish some small part of the meaner ambitions distinguishing able men from dead ones. In the last analysis ability is commonly found to consist mainly in a high degree of solemnity. Perhaps, however, this impressive quality is rightly appraised; it is no easy task to be solemn.

ABNORMAL, *adj.* Not conforming to standard. In matters of thought and conduct, to be independent is to be abnormal, to be abnormal is to be detested. Wherefore the lexicographer adviseth a striving toward a straiter resemblance to the Average Man than he hath to himself. Whoso attaineth thereto shall have peace, the prospect of death and the hope of Hell.

ABORIGINES, *n.* Persons of little worth found cumbering the soil of a newly discovered country. They soon cease to cumber; they fertilize.

ABRACADABRA.

> By *Abracadabra* we signify
>   An infinite number of things.
> 'Tis the answer to What? and How? and Why?
> And Whence? and Whither?—a word whereby
>   The Truth (with the comfort it brings)
> Is open to all who grope in night,
> Crying for Wisdom's holy light.
>
> Whether the word is a verb or a noun
>   Is knowledge beyond my reach.
> I only know that 'tis handed down
>   From sage to sage,
>   From age to age—
>   An immortal part of speech!
>
> Of an ancient man the tale is told
> That he lived to be ten centuries old,
>   In a cave on a mountain side.
>   (True, he finally died.)
> The fame of his wisdom filled the land,
> For his head was bald, and you'll understand
>   His beard was long and white
>   And his eyes uncommonly bright.
>
> Philosophers gathered from far and near
> To sit at his feet and hear and hear,
>   Though he never was heard
>   To utter a word
>   But *"Abracadabra, abracadab,*
>   *Abracada, abracad,*
>   *Abraca, abrac, abra, ab!"*
>   'Twas all he had,
> 'Twas all they wanted to hear, and each
> Made copious notes of the mystical speech,
>   Which they published next—
>   A trickle of text

In meadow of commentary.
  Mighty big books were these,
  In number, as leaves of trees;
In learning, remarkable—very!

    He's dead,
    As I said,
And the books of the sages have perished,
But his wisdom is sacredly cherished.
In *Abracadabra* it solemnly rings,
Like an ancient bell that forever swings.
    O, I love to hear
    That word make clear
Humanity's General Sense of Things.
               Jamrach Holobom.

ABRIDGE, *v. t.* To shorten.

When in the course of human events it becomes necessary for a people to abridge their king, a decent respect for the opinions of mankind requires that they should declare the causes which impel them to the separation. —*Oliver Cromwell.*

ABRUPT, *adj.* Sudden, without ceremony, like the arrival of a cannon-shot and the departure of the soldier whose interests are most affected by it. Dr. Samuel Johnson beautifully said of another author's ideas that they were "concatenated without abruption."

ABSCOND, *v. i.* To "move in a mysterious way," commonly with the property of another.

    Spring beckons! All things to the call respond;
    The trees are leaving and cashiers abscond.
               Phela Orm.

ABSENT, *adj.* Peculiarly exposed to the tooth of detraction; vilified; hopelessly in the wrong; superseded in the consideration and affection of another.

    To men a man is but a mind. Who cares
    What face he carries or what form he wears?
    But woman's body is the woman. O,
    Stay thou, my sweetheart, and do never go,

But heed the warning words the sage hath said:
A woman absent is a woman dead.

Jogo Tyree.

ABSENTEE, *n.* A person with an income who has had the forethought to remove himself from the sphere of exaction.

ABSOLUTE, *adj.* Independent, irresponsible. An absolute monarchy is one in which the sovereign does as he pleases so long as he pleases the assassins. Not many absolute monarchies are left, most of them having been replaced by limited monarchies, where the sovereign's power for evil (and for good) is greatly curtailed, and by republics, which are governed by chance.

ABSTAINER, *n.* A weak person who yields to the temptation of denying himself a pleasure. A total abstainer is one who abstains from everything but abstention, and especially from inactivity in the affairs of others.

Said a man to a crapulent youth: "I thought
    You a total abstainer, my son."
"So I am, so I am," said the scrapgrace caught—
    "But not, sir, a bigoted one."

G. J.

ABSURDITY, *n.* A statement or belief manifestly inconsistent with one's own opinion.

ACADEME, *n.* An ancient school where morality and philosophy were taught.

ACADEMY, *n.* (from academe). A modern school where football is taught.

ACCIDENT, *n.* An inevitable occurrence due to the action of immutable natural laws.

ACCOMPLICE, *n.* One associated with another in a crime, having guilty knowledge and complicity, as an attorney who defends a criminal, knowing him guilty. This view of the attorney's position in the matter has not hitherto commanded the assent of attorneys, no one having offered them a fee for assenting.

ACCORD, *n*. Harmony.

ACCORDION, *n*. An instrument in harmony with the sentiments of an assassin.

ACCOUNTABILITY, *n*. The mother of caution.

> "My accountability, bear in mind,"
>   Said the Grand Vizier: "Yes, yes,"
> Said the Shah: "I do—'tis the only kind
>   Of ability you possess."
>   *Joram Tate.*

ACCUSE, *v. t.* To affirm another's guilt or unworth; most commonly as a justification of ourselves for having wronged him.

ACEPHALOUS, *adj.* In the surprising condition of the Crusader who absently pulled at his forelock some hours after a Saracen scimitar had, unconsciously to him, passed through his neck, as related by de Joinville.

ACHIEVEMENT, *n*. The death of endeavor and the birth of disgust.

ACKNOWLEDGE, *v. t.* To confess. Acknowledgment of one another's faults is the highest duty imposed by our love of truth.

ACQUAINTANCE, *n*. A person whom we know well enough to borrow from, but not well enough to lend to. A degree of friendship called slight when its object is poor or obscure, and intimate when he is rich or famous.

ACTUALLY, *adv.* Perhaps; possibly.

ADAGE, *n*. Boned wisdom for weak teeth.

ADAMANT, *n.* A mineral frequently found beneath a corset. Soluble in solicitate of gold.

ADDER, *n.* A species of snake. So called from its habit of adding funeral outlays to the other expenses of living.

ADHERENT, *n.* A follower who has not yet obtained all that he expects to get.

ADMINISTRATION, *n.* An ingenious abstraction in politics, designed to receive the kicks and cuffs due to the premier or president. A man of straw, proof against bad-egging and dead-catting.

ADMIRAL, *n.* That part of a war-ship which does the talking while the figure-head does the thinking.

ADMIRATION, *n.* Our polite recognition of another's resemblance to ourselves.

ADMONITION, *n.* Gentle reproof, as with a meat-axe. Friendly warning.

> Consigned, by way of admonition,
> His soul forever to perdition.
> *Judibras.*

ADORE, *v. t.* To venerate expectantly.

ADVICE, *n.* The smallest current coin.

> "The man was in such deep distress,"
> Said Tom, "that I could do no less
> Than give him good advice." Said Jim:
> "If less could have been done for him
> I know you well enough, my son,
> To know that's what you would have done."
> *Jebel Jocordy.*

AFFIANCED, *pp.* Fitted with an ankle-ring for the ball-and-chain.

AFFLICTION, *n.* An acclimatizing process preparing the soul for another and bitter world.

AFRICAN, *n.* A nigger that votes our way.

AGE, *n.* That period of life in which we compound for the vices that we still cherish by reviling those that we have no longer the enterprise to commit.

AGITATOR, *n.* A statesman who shakes the fruit trees of his neighbors—to dislodge the worms.

AIM, *n.* The task we set our wishes to.

> "Cheer up! Have you no aim in life?"
> She tenderly inquired.
> "An aim? Well, no, I haven't, wife;
> The fact is—I have fired."
> *G. J.*

AIR, *n.* A nutritious substance supplied by a bountiful Providence for the fattening of the poor.

ALDERMAN, *n.* An ingenious criminal who covers his secret thieving with a pretence of open marauding.

ALIEN, *n.* An American sovereign in his probationary state.

ALLAH, *n.* The Mahometan Supreme Being, as distinguished from the Christian, Jewish, and so forth.

> Allah's good laws I faithfully have kept,
> And ever for the sins of man have wept;
> And sometimes kneeling in the temple I
> Have reverently crossed my hands and slept.
> *Junker Barlow.*

ALLEGIANCE, *n.*

> This thing Allegiance, as I suppose,
> Is a ring fitted in the subject's nose,
> Whereby that organ is kept rightly pointed
> To smell the sweetness of the Lord's anointed.
> *G. J.*

ALLIANCE, *n.* In international politics, the union of two thieves who have their hands so deeply inserted in each other's pocket that they cannot separately plunder a third.

ALLIGATOR, *n.* The crocodile of America, superior in every detail to the crocodile of the effete monarchies of the Old World. Herodotus says the Indus is, with one exception, the only river that produces crocodiles, but they appear to have gone West and grown up with the other rivers. From the notches on his back the alligator is called a sawrian.

ALONE, *adj.* In bad company.

> In contact, lo! the flint and steel,
> By spark and flame, the thought reveal
> That he the metal, she the stone,
> Had cherished secretly alone.
> *Booley Fito.*

ALTAR, *n.* The place whereon the priest formerly raveled out the small intestine of the sacrificial victim for purposes of divination and cooked its flesh for the gods. The word is now seldom used, except with reference to the sacrifice of their liberty and peace by a male and a female fool.

> They stood before the altar and supplied
> The fire themselves in which their fat was fried.
> In vain the sacrifice!—no god will claim
> An offering burnt with an unholy flame.
> *M. P. Nopput.*

AMBIDEXTROUS, *adj.* Able to pick with equal skill a right-hand pocket or a left.

AMBITION, *n.* An overmastering desire to be vilified by enemies while living and made ridiculous by friends when dead.

AMNESTY, *n.* The state's magnanimity to those offenders whom it would be too expensive to punish.

ANOINT, *v. t.* To grease a king or other great functionary already sufficiently slippery.

As sovereigns are anointed by the priesthood,
So pigs to lead the populace are greased good.
Judibras.

ANTIPATHY, *n*. The sentiment inspired by one's friend's friend.

APHORISM, *n*. Predigested wisdom.

The flabby wine-skin of his brain
Yields to some pathologic strain,
And voids from its unstored abysm
The driblet of an aphorism.
"The Mad Philosopher," 1697.

APOLOGIZE, *v. i.* To lay the foundation for a future offence.

APOSTATE, *n*. A leech who, having penetrated the shell of a turtle only to find that the creature has long been dead, deems it expedient to form a new attachment to a fresh turtle.

APOTHECARY, *n*. The physician's accomplice, undertaker's benefactor and grave worm's provider.

When Jove sent blessings to all men that are,
And Mercury conveyed them in a jar,
That friend of tricksters introduced by stealth
Disease for the apothecary's health,
Whose gratitude impelled him to proclaim:
"My deadliest drug shall bear my patron's name!"
G. J.

APPEAL, *v. t.* In law, to put the dice into the box for another throw.

APPETITE, *n*. An instinct thoughtfully implanted by Providence as a solution to the labor question.

APPLAUSE, *n*. The echo of a platitude.

APRIL FOOL, *n*. The March fool with another month added to his folly.

ARCHBISHOP, *n.* An ecclesiastical dignitary one point holier than a bishop.

> If I were a jolly archbishop,
> On Fridays I'd eat all the fish up—
> Salmon and flounders and smelts;
> On other days everything else.
> *Jodo Rem.*

ARCHITECT, *n.* One who drafts a plan of your house, and plans a draft of your money.

ARDOR, *n.* The quality that distinguishes love without knowledge.

ARENA, *n.* In politics, an imaginary rat-pit in which the statesman wrestles with his record.

ARISTOCRACY, *n.* Government by the best men. (In this sense the word is obsolete; so is that kind of government.) Fellows that wear downy hats and clean shirts—guilty of education and suspected of bank accounts.

ARMOR, *n.* The kind of clothing worn by a man whose tailor is a blacksmith.

ARRAYED, *pp.* Drawn up and given an orderly disposition, as a rioter hanged to a lamppost.

ARREST, *v. t.* Formally to detain one accused of unusualness.

> God made the world in six days and was arrested on the seventh.
> —*The Unauthorized Version.*

ARSENIC, *n.* A kind of cosmetic greatly affected by the ladies, whom it greatly affects in turn.

> "Eat arsenic? Yes, all you get,"
> Consenting, he did speak up;
> " 'Tis better you should eat it, pet,
> Than put it in my teacup."
> *Joel Huck.*

ART, *n.* This word has no definition. Its origin is related as follows by the ingenious Father Gassalasca Jape, S. J.

> One day a wag—what would the wretch be at?—
> Shifted a letter of the cipher RAT,
> And said it was a god's name! Straight arose
> Fantastic priests and postulants (with shows,
> And mysteries, and mummeries, and hymns,
> And disputations dire that lamed their limbs)
> To serve his temple and maintain the fires,
> Expound the law, manipulate the wires.
> Amazed, the populace the rites attend,
> Believe whate'er they cannot comprehend,
> And, inly edified to learn that two
> Half-hairs joined so and so (as Art can do)
> Have sweeter values and a grace more fit
> Than Nature's hairs that never have been split,
> Bring cates and wines for sacrificial feasts,
> And sell their garments to support the priests.

ARTLESSNESS, *n.* A certain engaging quality to which women
attain by long study and severe practice upon the admiring
male, who is pleased to fancy it resembles the candid simplicity of his young.

ASPERSE, *v. t.* Maliciously to ascribe to another vicious actions
which one has not had the temptation and opportunity to
commit.

ASS, *n.* A public singer with a good voice but no ear. In Virginia City, Nevada, he is called the Washoe Canary, in Dakota, the Senator, and everywhere the Donkey. The animal
is widely and variously celebrated in the literature, art and
religion of every age and country; no other so engages and
fires the human imagination as this noble vertebrate. Indeed,
it is doubted by some (Ramasilus, *lib. II., De Clem.*, and
C. Stantatus, *De Temperamente*) if it is not a god; and as
such we know it was worshiped by the Etruscans, and, if we
may believe Macrobious, by the Cupasians also. Of the only
two animals admitted into the Mahometan Paradise along
with the souls of men, the ass that carried Balaam is one, the

dog of the Seven Sleepers the other. This is no small distinction. From what has been written about this beast might be compiled a library of great splendor and magnitude, rivaling that of the Shakespearean cult, and that which clusters about the Bible. It may be said, generally, that all literature is more or less Asinine.

> "Hail, holy Ass!" the quiring angels sing;
> "Priest of Unreason, and of Discords King!
> Great co-Creator, let Thy glory shine:
> God made all else; the Mule, the Mule is thine!"
>
> G. J.

AUCTIONEER, *n.* The man who proclaims with a hammer that he has picked a pocket with his tongue.

AUSTRALIA, *n.* A country lying in the South Sea, whose industrial and commercial development has been unspeakably retarded by an unfortunate dispute among geographers as to whether it is a continent or an island.

AVERNUS, *n.* The lake by which the ancients entered the infernal regions. The fact that access to the infernal regions was obtained by a lake is believed by the learned Marcus Ansello Scrutator to have suggested the Christian rite of baptism by immersion. This, however, has been shown by Lactantius to be an error.

> *Facilis descensus Averni,*
> The poet remarks; and the sense
> Of it is that when down-hill I turn I
> Will get more of punches than pence.
>
> *Jehal Dai Lupe.*

B

BAAL, *n.* An old deity formerly much worshiped under various names. As Baal he was popular with the Phœnicians; as Belus or Bel he had the honor to be served by the priest Berosus, who wrote the famous account of the Deluge; as Babel he had a tower partly erected to his glory on the Plain of Shinar. From Babel comes our English word "babble." Under whatever name worshiped, Baal is the Sun-god. As Beelzebub he is the god of flies, which are begotten of the sun's rays on stagnant water. In Physicia Baal is still worshiped as Bolus, and as Belly he is adored and served with abundant sacrifice by the priests of Guttledom.

BABE or BABY, *n*. A misshapen creature of no particular age, sex, or condition, chiefly remarkable for the violence of the sympathies and antipathies it excites in others, itself without sentiment or emotion. There have been famous babes; for example, little Moses, from whose adventure in the bulrushes the Egyptian hierophants of seven centuries before doubtless derived their idle tale of the child Osiris being preserved on a floating lotus leaf.

> Ere babes were invented
> The girls were contented.
> Now man is tormented
> Until to buy babes he has squandered
> His money. And so I have pondered
> This thing, and thought may be
> 'T were better that Baby
> The First had been eagled or condored.
> *Ro Amil.*

BACCHUS, *n*. A convenient deity invented by the ancients as an excuse for getting drunk.

> Is public worship, then, a sin,
> That for devotions paid to Bacchus
> The lictors dare to run us in,
> And resolutely thump and whack us?
> *Jorace.*

BACK, *n*. That part of your friend which it is your privilege to contemplate in your adversity.

BACKBITE, *v. t.* To speak of a man as you find him when he can't find you.

BAIT, *n.* A preparation that renders the hook more palatable. The best kind is beauty.

BAPTISM, *n.* A sacred rite of such efficacy that he who finds himself in heaven without having undergone it will be unhappy forever. It is performed with water in two ways—by immersion, or plunging, and by aspersion, or sprinkling.

> But whether the plan of immersion
> Is better than simple aspersion
>   Let those immersed
>   And those aspersed
> Decide by the Authorized Version,
> And by matching their agues tertian.
>   *G. J.*

BAROMETER, *n.* An ingenious instrument which indicates what kind of weather we are having.

BARRACK, *n.* A house in which soldiers enjoy a portion of that of which it is their business to deprive others.

BASILISK, *n.* The cockatrice. A sort of serpent hatched from the egg of a cock. The basilisk had a bad eye, and its glance was fatal. Many infidels deny this creature's existence, but Semprello Aurator saw and handled one that had been blinded by lightning as a punishment for having fatally gazed on a lady of rank whom Jupiter loved. Juno afterward restored the reptile's sight and hid it in a cave. Nothing is so well attested by the ancients as the existence of the basilisk, but the cocks have stopped laying.

BASTINADO, *n.* The act of walking on wood without exertion.

BATH, *n.* A kind of mystic ceremony substituted for religious worship, with what spiritual efficacy has not been determined.

> The man who taketh a steam bath
> He loseth all the skin he hath,
> And, for he's boiled a brilliant red,
> Thinketh to cleanliness he's wed,

> Forgetting that his lungs he's soiling
> With dirty vapors of the boiling.
> *Richard Gwow.*

BATTLE, *n.* A method of untying with the teeth of a political knot that would not yield to the tongue.

BEARD, *n.* The hair that is commonly cut off by those who justly execrate the absurd Chinese custom of shaving the head.

BEAUTY, *n.* The power by which a woman charms a lover and terrifies a husband.

BEFRIEND, *v. t.* To make an ingrate.

BEG, *v.* To ask for something with an earnestness proportioned to the belief that it will not be given.

> Who is that, father?

> A mendicant, child,
> Haggard, morose, and unaffable—wild!
> See how he glares through the bars of his cell!
> With Citizen Mendicant all is not well.

> Why did they put him there, father?

> Because
> Obeying his belly he struck at the laws.

> His belly?

> Oh, well, he was starving, my boy—
> A state in which, doubtless, there's little of joy.
> No bite had he eaten for days, and his cry
> Was "Bread!" ever "Bread!"

> What's the matter with pie?

> With little to wear, he had nothing to sell;
> To beg was unlawful—improper as well.

> Why didn't he work?

> He would even have done that,
> But men said: "Get out!" and the State remarked: "Scat!"
> I mention these incidents merely to show

That the vengeance he took was uncommonly low.
Revenge, at the best, is the act of a Siou,
But for trifles—

Pray what did bad Mendicant do?

Stole two loaves of bread to replenish his lack
And tuck out the belly that clung to his back.

Is that *all* father dear?

There is little to tell:
They sent him to jail, and they'll send him to—well,
The company's better than here we can boast,
And there's—

Bread for the needy, dear father?

Um—toast.
Atka Mip.

BEGGAR, *n.* One who has relied on the assistance of his friends.

BEHAVIOR, *n.* Conduct, as determined, not by principle, but by breeding. The word seems to be somewhat loosely used in Dr. Jamrach Holobom's translation of the following lines in the *Dies Iræ*:

Recordare, Jesu pie,
Quod sum causa tuæ viæ.
Ne me perdas illa die.

Pray remember, sacred Savior,
Whose the thoughtless hand that gave your
Death-blow. Pardon such behavior.

BELLADONNA, *n.* In Italian a beautiful lady; in English a deadly poison. A striking example of the essential identity of the two tongues.

BENEDICTINES, *n.* An order of monks otherwise known as black friars.

She thought it a crow, but it turn out to be
A monk of St. Benedict croaking a text.

"Here's one of an order of cooks," said she—
"Black friars in this world, fried black in the next."
"The Devil on Earth" (*London*, 1712).

BENEFACTOR, *n.* One who makes heavy purchases of ingratitude, without, however, materially affecting the price, which is still within the means of all.

BERENICE'S HAIR, *n.* A constellation (*Coma Berenices*) named in honor of one who sacrificed her hair to save her husband.

> Her locks an ancient lady gave
> Her loving husband's life to save;
> And men—they honored so the dame—
> Upon some stars bestowed her name.
>
> But to our modern married fair,
> Who'd give their lords to save their hair,
> No stellar recognition's given.
> There are not stars enough in heaven.
> *G. J.*

BIGAMY, *n.* A mistake in taste for which the wisdom of the future will adjudge a punishment called trigamy.

BIGOT, *n.* One who is obstinately and zealously attached to an opinion that you do not entertain.

BILLINGSGATE, *n.* The invective of an opponent.

BIRTH, *n.* The first and direst of all disasters. As to the nature of it there appears to be no uniformity. Castor and Pollux were born from the egg. Pallas came out of a skull. Galatea was once a block of stone. Peresilis, who wrote in the tenth century, avers that he grew up out of the ground where a priest had spilled holy water. It is known that Arimaxus was derived from a hole in the earth, made by a stroke of lightning. Leucomedon was the son of a cavern in Mount Ætna, and I have myself seen a man come out of a wine cellar.

BLACKGUARD, *n.* A man whose qualities, prepared for display like a box of berries in a market—the fine ones on top—have been opened on the wrong side. An inverted gentleman.

BLANK-VERSE, *n.* Unrhymed iambic pentameters—the most difficult kind of English verse to write acceptably; a kind, therefore, much affected by those who cannot acceptably write any kind.

BODY-SNATCHER, *n.* A robber of grave-worms. One who supplies the young physicians with that with which the old physicians have supplied the undertaker. The hyena.

> "One night," a doctor said, "last fall,
> I and my comrades, four in all,
>   When visiting a graveyard stood
> Within the shadow of a wall.
>
> "While waiting for the moon to sink
> We saw a wild hyena slink
>   About a new-made grave, and then
> Begin to excavate its brink!
>
> "Shocked by the horrid act, we made
> A sally from our ambuscade,
>   And, falling on the unholy beast,
> Dispatched him with a pick and spade."
>   *Bettel K. Jhones.*

BONDSMAN, *n.* A fool who, having property of his own, undertakes to become responsible for that entrusted to another to a third.

Philippe of Orleans wishing to appoint one of his favorites, a dissolute nobleman, to a high office, asked him what security he would be able to give. "I need no bondsmen," he replied, "for I can give you my word of honor." "And pray what may be the value of that?" inquired the amused Regent. "Monsieur, it is worth its weight in gold."

BORE, *n.* A person who talks when you wish him to listen.

BOTANY, *n.* The science of vegetables—those that are not good to eat, as well as those that are. It deals largely with their flowers, which are commonly badly designed, inartistic in color, and ill-smelling.

BOTTLE-NOSED, *adj*. Having a nose created in the image of its maker.

BOUNDARY, *n*. In political geography, an imaginary line between two nations, separating the imaginary rights of one from the imaginary rights of the other.

BOUNTY, *n*. The liberality of one who has much, in permitting one who has nothing to get all that he can.

> A single swallow, it is said, devours ten millions of insects every year. The supplying of these insects I take to be a signal instance of the Creator's bounty in providing for the lives of His creatures. —*Henry Ward Beecher.*

BRAHMA, *n*. He who created the Hindoos, who are preserved by Vishnu and destroyed by Siva—a rather neater division of labor than is found among the deities of some other nations. The Abracadabranese, for example, are created by Sin, maintained by Theft and destroyed by Folly. The priests of Brahma, like those of Abracadabranese, are holy and learned men who are never naughty.

> O Brahma, thou rare old Divinity,
> First Person of the Hindoo Trinity,
> You sit there so calm and securely,
> With feet folded up so demurely—
> You're the First Person Singular, surely.
> *Polydore Smith.*

BRAIN, *n*. An apparatus with which we think what we think. That which distinguishes the man who is content to *be* something from the man who wishes to *do* something. A man of great wealth, or one who has been pitchforked into high station, has commonly such a headful of brain that his neighbors cannot keep their hats on. In our civilization, and under our republican form of government, brain is so highly honored that it is rewarded by exemption from the cares of office.

BRANDY, *n*. A cordial composed of one part thunder-and-lightning, one part remorse, two parts bloody murder, one part death-hell-and-the-grave and four parts clarified Satan. Dose, a headful all the time. Brandy is said by Dr. Johnson to be the drink of heroes. Only a hero will venture to drink it.

BRIDE, *n*. A woman with a fine prospect of happiness behind her.

BRUTE, *n*. See HUSBAND.

C

CAABA, *n*. A large stone presented by the archangel Gabriel to the patriarch Abraham, and preserved at Mecca. The patriarch had perhaps asked the archangel for bread.

CABBAGE, *n*. A familiar kitchen-garden vegetable about as large and wise as a man's head.

The cabbage is so called from Cabagius, a prince who on ascending the throne issued a decree appointing a High Council of Empire consisting of the members of his predecessor's Ministry and the cabbages in the royal garden. When any of his Majesty's measures of state policy miscarried conspicuously it was gravely announced that several members of the High Council had been beheaded, and his murmuring subjects were appeased.

CALAMITY, *n*. A more than commonly plain and unmistakable reminder that the affairs of this life are not of our own ordering. Calamities are of two kinds: misfortune to ourselves, and good fortune to others.

CALLOUS, *adj*. Gifted with great fortitude to bear the evils afflicting another.

When Zeno was told that one of his enemies was no more he was observed to be deeply moved. "What!" said one of his disciples, "you weep at the death of an enemy?" "Ah, 'tis true," replied the great Stoic; "but you should see me smile at the death of a friend."

CALUMNUS, *n.* A graduate of the School for Scandal.

CAMEL, *n.* A quadruped (the *Splaypes humpidorsus*) of great value to the show business. There are two kinds of camels—the camel proper and the camel improper. It is the latter that is always exhibited.

CANNIBAL, *n.* A gastronome of the old school who preserves the simple tastes and adheres to the natural diet of the pre-pork period.

CANNON, *n.* An instrument employed in the rectification of national boundaries.

CANONICALS, *n.* The motley worn by Jesters of the Court of Heaven.

CAPITAL, *n.* The seat of misgovernment. That which provides the fire, the pot, the dinner, the table and the knife and fork for the anarchist; the part of the repast that himself supplies is the disgrace before meat. *Capital Punishment*, a penalty regarding the justice and expediency of which many worthy persons—including all the assassins—entertain grave misgivings.

CARMELITE, *n.* A mendicant friar of the order of Mount Carmel.

> As Death was a-riding out one day,
> Across Mount Carmel he took his way,
>   Where he met a mendicant monk,
>   Some three or four quarters drunk,
> With a holy leer and a pious grin,
> Ragged and fat and as saucy as sin,
>   Who held out his hands and cried:
> "Give, give in Charity's name, I pray.
> Give in the name of the Church. O give,
> Give that her holy sons may live!"
>   And Death replied,
>   Smiling long and wide:
>   "I'll give, holy father, I'll give thee—a ride."

With a rattle and bang
Of his bones, he sprang
From his famous Pale Horse, with his spear;
By the neck and the foot
Seized the fellow, and put
Him astride with his face to the rear.

The Monarch laughed loud with a sound that fell
Like clods on the coffin's sounding shell:
"Ho, ho! A beggar on horseback, they say,
Will ride to the devil!"—and *thump*
Fell the flat of his dart on the rump
Of the charger, which galloped away.

Faster and faster and faster it flew,
Till the rocks and the flocks and the trees that grew
By the road were dim and blended and blue
To the wild, wide eyes
Of the rider—in size
Resembling a couple of blackberry pies.
Death laughed again, as a tomb might laugh
At a burial service spoiled,
And the mourners' intentions foiled
By the body erecting
Its head and objecting
To further proceedings in its behalf.

Many a year and many a day
Have passed since these events away.
The monk has long been a dusty corse,
And Death has never recovered his horse.
For the friar got hold of its tail,
And steered it within the pale
Of the monastery gray,
Where the beast was stabled and fed
With barley and oil and bread
Till fatter it grew than the fattest friar,
And so in due course was appointed Prior.

G. J.

CARNIVOROUS, *adj.* Addicted to the cruelty of devouring the
timorous vegetarian, his heirs and assigns.

CARTESIAN, *adj.* Relating to Descartes, a famous philosopher, author of the celebrated dictum, *Cogito ergo sum*—whereby he was pleased to suppose he demonstrated the reality of human existence. The dictum might be improved, however, thus: *Cogito cogito ergo cogito sum*—"I think that I think, therefore I think that I am;" as close an approach to certainty as any philosopher has yet made.

CAT, *n*. A soft, indestructible automaton provided by nature to be kicked when things go wrong in the domestic circle.

> This is a dog,
> This is a cat.
> This is a frog,
> This is a rat.
> Run, dog, mew, cat,
> Jump, frog, gnaw, rat.
> *Elevenson.*

CAVILER, *n*. A critic of our own work.

CEMETERY, *n*. An isolated suburban spot where mourners match lies, poets write at a target and stone-cutters spell for a wager. The inscriptions following will serve to illustrate the success attained in these Olympian games:

His virtues were so conspicuous that his enemies, unable to overlook them, denied them, and his friends, to whose loose lives they were a rebuke, represented them as vices. They are here commemorated by his family, who shared them.

> In the earth we here prepare a
> Place to lay our little Clara.
> —*Thomas M. and Mary Frazer.*
> P. S.—Gabriel will raise her.

CENTAUR, *n*. One of a race of persons who lived before the division of labor had been carried to such a pitch of differentiation, and who followed the primitive economic maxim, "Every man his own horse." The best of the lot was Chiron, who to the wisdom and virtues of the horse added the fleetness of man. The scripture story of the head of John the Baptist on a charger shows that pagan myths have somewhat sophisticated sacred history.

CERBERUS, *n.* The watch-dog of Hades, whose duty it was to guard the entrance—against whom or what does not clearly appear; everybody, sooner or later, had to go there, and nobody wanted to carry off the entrance. Cerberus is known to have had three heads, and some of the poets have credited him with as many as a hundred. Professor Graybill, whose clerky erudition and profound knowledge of Greek give his opinion great weight, has averaged all the estimates, and makes the number twenty-seven—a judgment that would be entirely conclusive if Professor Graybill had known (*a*) something about dogs, and (*b*) something about arithmetic.

CHILDHOOD, *n.* The period of human life intermediate between the idiocy of infancy and the folly of youth—two removes from the sin of manhood and three from the remorse of age.

CHRISTIAN, *n.* One who believes that the New Testament is a divinely inspired book admirably suited to the spiritual needs of his neighbor. One who follows the teachings of Christ in so far as they are not inconsistent with a life of sin.

> I dreamed I stood upon a hill, and, lo!
> The godly multitudes walked to and fro
> Beneath, in Sabbath garments fitly clad,
> With pious mien, appropriately sad,
> While all the church bells made a solemn din—
> A fire-alarm to those who lived in sin.
> Then saw I gazing thoughtfully below,
> With tranquil face, upon that holy show
> A tall, spare figure in a robe of white,
> Whose eyes diffused a melancholy light.
> "God keep you, stranger," I exclaimed. "You are
> No doubt (your habit shows it) from afar;
> And yet I entertain the hope that you,
> Like these good people, are a Christian too."
> He raised his eyes and with a look so stern
> It made me with a thousand blushes burn
> Replied—his manner with disdain was spiced:
> "What! I a Christian? No, indeed! I'm Christ."
>
> *G. J.*

CIRCUS, *n.* A place where horses, ponies and elephants are permitted to see men, women and children acting the fool.

CLAIRVOYANT, *n.* A person, commonly a woman, who has the power of seeing that which is invisible to her patron—namely, that he is a blockhead.

CLARIONET, *n.* An instrument of torture operated by a person with cotton in his ears. There are two instruments that are worse than a clarionet—two clarionets.

CLERGYMAN, *n.* A man who undertakes the management of our spiritual affairs as a method of bettering his temporal ones.

CLIO, *n.* One of the nine Muses. Clio's function was to preside over history—which she did with great dignity, many of the prominent citizens of Athens occupying seats on the platform, the meetings being addressed by Messrs. Xenophon, Herodotus and other popular speakers.

CLOCK, *n.* A machine of great moral value to man, allaying his concern for the future by reminding him what a lot of time remains to him.

> A busy man complained one day:
> "I get no time!" "What's that you say?"
> Cried out his friend, a lazy quiz;
> "You have, sir, all the time there is.
> There's plenty, too, and don't you doubt it—
> We're never for an hour without it."
> *Purzil Crofe.*

CLOSE-FISTED, *adj.* Unduly desirous of keeping that which many meritorious persons wish to obtain.

> "Close-fisted Scotchman!" Johnson cried
> To thrifty J. Macpherson;
> "See me—I'm ready to divide
> With any worthy person."
>
> Said Jamie: "That is very true—
> The boast requires no backing;

> And all are worthy, sir, to you,
> Who have what you are lacking."
>   *Anita M. Bobe.*

CŒNOBITE, *n*. A man who piously shuts himself up to meditate upon the sin of wickedness; and to keep it fresh in his mind joins a brotherhood of awful examples.

> O Cœnobite, O cœnobite,
>   Monastical gregarian,
> You differ from the anchorite,
>   That solitudinarian:
> With vollied prayers you wound Old Nick;
> With dropping shots he makes him sick.
>   *Quincy Giles.*

COMFORT, *n*. A state of mind produced by contemplation of a neighbor's uneasiness.

COMMENDATION, *n*. The tribute that we pay to achievements that resemble, but do not equal, our own.

COMMERCE, *n*. A kind of transaction in which A plunders from B the goods of C, and for compensation B picks the pocket of D of money belonging to E.

COMMONWEALTH, *n*. An administrative entity operated by an incalculable multitude of political parasites, logically active but fortuitously efficient.

> This commonwealth's capitol's corridors view,
> So thronged with a hungry and indolent crew
> Of clerks, pages, porters and all attachés
> Whom rascals appoint and the populace pays
> That a cat cannot slip through the thicket of shins
> Nor hear its own shriek for the noise of their chins.
> On clerks and on pages, and porters, and all,
> Misfortune attend and disaster befall!
> May life be to them a succession of hurts;
> May fleas by the bushel inhabit their shirts;
> May aches and diseases encamp in their bones,
> Their lungs full of tubercles, bladders of stones;
> May microbes, bacilli, their tissues infest,

And tapeworms securely their bowels digest;
May corn-cobs be snared without hope in their hair,
And frequent impalement their pleasure impair.
Disturbed be their dreams by the awful discourse
Of audible sofas sepulchrally hoarse,
By chairs acrobatic and wavering floors—
The mattress that kicks and the pillow that snores!
Sons of cupidity, cradled in sin!
Your criminal ranks may the death angel thin,
Avenging the friend whom I couldn't work in.

                                                        K. Q.

COMPROMISE, *n.* Such an adjustment of conflicting interests as gives each adversary the satisfaction of thinking he has got what he ought not to have, and is deprived of nothing except what was justly his due.

COMPULSION, *n.* The eloquence of power.

CONDOLE, *v. i.* To show that bereavement is a smaller evil than sympathy.

CONFIDANT, CONFIDANTE, *n.* One entrusted by A with the secrets of B, confided by *him* to C.

CONGRATULATION, *n.* The civility of envy.

CONGRESS, *n.* A body of men who meet to repeal laws.

CONNOISSEUR, *n.* A specialist who knows everything about something and nothing about anything else.
    An old wine-bibber having been smashed in a railway collision, some wine was poured upon his lips to revive him. "Pauillac, 1873," he murmured and died.

CONSERVATIVE, *n.* A statesman who is enamored of existing evils, as distinguished from the Liberal, who wishes to replace them with others.

CONSOLATION, *n.* The knowledge that a better man is more unfortunate than yourself.

CONSUL, *n.* In American politics, a person who having failed to secure an office from the people is given one by the Administration on condition that he leave the country.

CONSULT, *v. i.* To seek another's approval of a course already decided on.

CONTEMPT, *n.* The feeling of a prudent man for an enemy who is too formidable safely to be opposed.

CONTROVERSY, *n.* A battle in which spittle or ink replaces the injurious cannon-ball and the inconsiderate bayonet.

> In controversy with the facile tongue—
> That bloodless warfare of the old and young—
> So seek your adversary to engage
> That on himself he shall exhaust his rage,
> And, like a snake that's fastened to the ground,
> With his own fangs inflict the fatal wound.
> You ask me how this miracle is done?
> Adopt his own opinions, one by one,
> And taunt him to refute them; in his wrath
> He'll sweep them pitilessly from his path.
> Advance then gently all you wish to prove,
> Each proposition prefaced with, "As you've
> So well remarked," or, "As you wisely say,
> And I cannot dispute," or, "By the way,
> This view of it which, better far expressed,
> Runs through your argument." Then leave the rest
> To him, secure that he'll perform his trust
> And prove your views intelligent and just.
> *Conmore Apel Brune.*

CONVENT, *n.* A place of retirement for women who wish for leisure to meditate upon the vice of idleness.

CONVERSATION, *n.* A fair for the display of the minor mental commodities, each exhibitor being too intent upon the arrangement of his own wares to observe those of his neighbor.

CORONATION, *n.* The ceremony of investing a sovereign with

the outward and visible signs of his divine right to be blown skyhigh with a dynamite bomb.

CORPORAL, *n.* A man who occupies the lowest rung of the military ladder.

> Fiercely the battle raged and, sad to tell,
> Our corporal heroically fell!
> Fame from her height looked down upon the brawl
> And said: "He hadn't very far to fall."
> *Giacomo Smith.*

CORPORATION, *n.* An ingenious device for obtaining individual profit without individual responsibility.

CORSAIR, *n.* A politician of the seas.

COURT FOOL, *n.* The plaintiff.

COWARD, *n.* One who in a perilous emergency thinks with his legs.

CRAFT, *n.* A fool's substitute for brains.

CRAYFISH, *n.* A small crustacean very much resembling the lobster, but less indigestible.

> In this small fish I take it that human wisdom is admirably figured and symbolized; for whereas the crayfish doth move only backward, and can have only retrospection, seeing naught but the perils already passed, so the wisdom of man doth not enable him to avoid the follies that beset his course, but only to apprehend their nature afterward. —*Sir James Merivale.*

CREDITOR, *n.* One of a tribe of savages dwelling beyond the Financial Straits and dreaded for their desolating incursions.

CREMONA, *n.* A high-priced violin made in Connecticut.

CRITIC, *n.* A person who boasts himself hard to please because nobody tries to please him.

> There is a land of pure delight,
>   Beyond the Jordan's flood,
> Where saints, apparelled all in white,
>   Fling back the critic's mud.
>
> And as he legs it through the skies,
>   His pelt a sable hue,
> He sorrows sore to recognize
>   The missiles that he threw.
>   *Orrin Goof.*

CROSS, *n.* An ancient religious symbol erroneously supposed to owe its significance to the most solemn event in the history of Christianity, but really antedating it by thousands of years. By many it has been believed to be identical with the *crux ansata* of the ancient phallic worship, but it has been traced even beyond all that we know of that, to the rites of primitive peoples. We have to-day the White Cross as a symbol of chastity, and the Red Cross as a badge of benevolent neutrality in war. Having in mind the former, the reverend Father Gassalasca Jape smites the lyre to the effect following:

> "Be good, be good!" the sisterhood
>   Cry out in holy chorus,
> And, to dissuade from sin, parade
>   Their various charms before us.
>
> But why, O why, has ne'er an eye
>   Seen her of winsome manner
> And youthful grace and pretty face
>   Flaunting the White Cross banner?
>
> Now where's the need of speech and screed
>   To better our behaving?
> A simpler plan for saving man
>   (But, first, is he worth saving?)
>
> Is, dears, when he declines to flee
>   From bad thoughts that beset him,
> Ignores the Law as 't were a straw,
>   And wants to sin—don't let him.

CUI BONO? (Latin) What good would that do *me*?

CUNNING, *n.* The faculty that distinguishes a weak animal or person from a strong one. It brings its possessor much mental satisfaction and great material adversity. An Italian proverb says: "The furrier gets the skins of more foxes than asses."

CUPID, *n.* The so-called god of love. This bastard creation of a barbarous fancy was no doubt inflicted upon mythology for the sins of its deities. Of all unbeautiful and inappropriate conceptions this is the most reasonless and offensive. The notion of symbolizing sexual love by a semisexless babe, and comparing the pains of passion to the wounds of an arrow— of introducing this pudgy homunculus into art grossly to materialize the subtle spirit and suggestion of the work—this is eminently worthy of the age that, giving it birth, laid it on the doorstep of prosperity.

CURIOSITY, *n.* An objectionable quality of the female mind. The desire to know whether or not a woman is cursed with curiosity is one of the most active and insatiable passions of the masculine soul.

CURSE, *v. t.* Energetically to belabor with a verbal slap-stick. This is an operation which in literature, particularly in the drama, is commonly fatal to the victim. Nevertheless, the liability to a cursing is a risk that cuts but a small figure in fixing the rates of life insurance.

CYNIC, *n.* A blackguard whose faulty vision sees things as they are, not as they ought to be. Hence the custom among the Scythians of plucking out a cynic's eyes to improve his vision.

D

DAMN, *v.* A word formerly much used by the Paphlagonians, the meaning of which is lost. By the learned Dr. Dolabelly Gak it is believed to have been a term of satisfaction, implying the highest possible degree of mental tranquillity. Professor Groke, on the contrary, thinks it expressed an emotion of tumultuous delight, because it so frequently occurs in combination with the word *jod* or *god*, meaning "joy." It would be with great diffidence that I should advance an opinion conflicting with that of either of these formidable authorities.

DANCE, *v. i.* To leap about to the sound of tittering music, preferably with arms about your neighbor's wife or daughter. There are many kinds of dances, but all those requiring the participation of the two sexes have two characteristics in common: they are conspicuously innocent, and warmly loved by the vicious.

DANGER, *n.*

> A savage beast which, when it sleeps,
>   Man girds at and despises,
> But takes himself away by leaps
>   And bounds when it arises.
> > *Ambat Delaso.*

DARING, *n.* One of the most conspicuous qualities of a man in security.

DATARY, *n.* A high ecclesiastic official of the Roman Catholic Church, whose important function is to brand the Pope's bulls with the words *Datum Romæ*. He enjoys a princely revenue and the friendship of God.

DAWN, *n.* The time when men of reason go to bed. Certain old men prefer to rise at about that time, taking a cold bath and a long walk with an empty stomach, and otherwise mortifying the flesh. They then point with pride to these practices as the cause of their sturdy health and ripe years; the truth being that they are hearty and old, not because of their habits, but in spite of them. The reason we find only robust persons doing this thing is that it has killed all the others who have tried it.

DAY, *n.* A period of twenty-four hours, mostly misspent. This period is divided into two parts, the day proper and the night, or day improper—the former devoted to sins of business, the latter consecrated to the other sort. These two kinds of social activity overlap.

DEAD, *adj.*

> Done with the work of breathing; done
> With all the world; the mad race run
> Though to the end; the golden goal
> Attained and found to be a hole!
> *Squatol Johnes.*

DEBAUCHEE, *n.* One who has so earnestly pursued pleasure that he has had the misfortune to overtake it.

DEBT, *n.* An ingenious substitute for the chain and whip of the slave-driver.

> As, pent in an aquarium, the troutlet
> Swims round and round his tank to find an outlet,
> Pressing his nose against the glass that holds him,
> Nor ever sees the prison that enfolds him;
> So the poor debtor, seeing naught around him,
> Yet feels the narrow limits that impound him,
> Grieves at his debt and studies to evade it,
> And finds at last he might as well have paid it.
> *Barlow S. Vode.*

DECALOGUE, *n.* A series of commandments, ten in number—just enough to permit an intelligent selection for observance, but not enough to embarrass the choice. Following is the revised edition of the Decalogue, calculated for this meridian.

> Thou shalt no God but me adore:
> 'Twere too expensive to have more.
>
> No images nor idols make
> For Robert Ingersoll to break.
>
> Take not God's name in vain; select
> A time when it will have effect.
>
> Work not on Sabbath days at all,
> But go to see the teams play ball.

> Honor thy parents. That creates
> For life insurance lower rates.

> Kill not, abet not those who kill;
> Thou shalt not pay thy butcher's bill.

> Kiss not thy neighbor's wife, unless
> Thine own thy neighbor doth caress.

> Don't steal; thou'lt never thus compete
> Successfully in business. Cheat.

> Bear not false witness—that is low—
> But "hear 'tis rumored so and so."

> Cover thou naught that thou hast not
> By hook or crook, or somehow, got.
>
> *G. J.*

DECIDE, *v. i.* To succumb to the preponderance of one set of influences over another set.

> A leaf was riven from a tree,
> "I mean to fall to earth," said he.

> The west wind, rising, made him veer.
> "Eastward," said he, "I now shall steer."

> The east wind rose with greater force.
> Said he: "'Twere wise to change my course."

> With equal power they contend.
> He said: "My judgment I suspend."

> Down died the winds; the leaf, elate,
> Cried: "I've decided to fall straight."

> "First thoughts are best?" That's not the moral;
> Just choose your own and we'll not quarrel.

> Howe'er your choice may chance to fall,
> You'll have no hand in it at all.
>
> *G. J.*

DEFAME, *v. t.* To lie about another. To tell the truth about another.

DEFENCELESS, *adj.* Unable to attack.

DEGENERATE, *adj.* Less conspicuously admirable than one's ancestors. The contemporaries of Homer were striking examples of degeneracy; it required ten of them to raise a rock or a riot that one of the heroes of the Trojan war could have raised with ease. Homer never tires of sneering at "men who live in these degenerate days," which is perhaps why they suffered him to beg his bread—a marked instance of returning good for evil, by the way, for if they had forbidden him he would certainly have starved.

DEGRADATION, *n.* One of the stages of moral and social progress from private station to political preferment.

DEINOTHERIUM, *n.* An extinct pachyderm that flourished when the Pterodactyl was in fashion. The latter was a native of Ireland, its name being pronounced Terry Dactyl or Peter O'Dactyl, as the man pronouncing it may chance to have heard it spoken or seen it printed.

DEJEUNER, *n.* The breakfast of an American who has been in Paris. Variously pronounced.

DELEGATION, *n.* In American politics, an article of merchandise that comes in sets.

DELIBERATION, *n.* The act of examining one's bread to determine which side it is buttered on.

DELUGE, *n.* A notable first experiment in baptism which washed away the sins (and sinners) of the world.

DELUSION, *n.* The father of a most respectable family, comprising Enthusiasm, Affection, Self-denial, Faith, Hope, Charity and many other goodly sons and daughters.

> All hail, Delusion! Were it not for thee
> The world turned topsy-turvy we should see;
> For Vice, respectable with cleanly fancies,
> Would fly abandoned Virtue's gross advances.
> *Mumfrey Mappel.*

DENTIST, *n.* A prestidigitator who, putting metal into your mouth, pulls coins out of your pocket.

DEPENDENT, *adj.* Reliant upon another's generosity for the support which you are not in a position to exact from his fears.

DEPUTY, *n.* A male relative of an office-holder, or of his bondsman. The deputy is commonly a beautiful young man, with a red necktie and an intricate system of cobwebs extending from his nose to his desk. When accidentally struck by the janitor's broom, he gives off a cloud of dust.

> "Chief Deputy," the Master cried,
> "To-day the books are to be tried
> By experts and accountants who
> Have been commissioned to go through
> Our office here, to see if we
> Have stolen injudiciously.
> Please have the proper entries made,
> The proper balances displayed,
> Conforming to the whole amount
> Of cash on hand—which they will count.
> I've long admired your punctual way—
> Here at the break and close of day,
> Confronting in your chair the crowd
> Of business men, whose voices loud
> And gestures violent you quell
> By some mysterious, calm spell—
> Some magic lurking in your look
> That brings the noisiest to book
> And spreads a holy and profound
> Tranquillity o'er all around.
> So orderly all's done that they
> Who came to draw remain to pay.
> But now the time demands, at last,
> That you employ your genius vast
> In energies more active. Rise
> And shake the lightnings from your eyes;
> Inspire your underlings, and fling
> Your spirit into everything!"
> The Master's hand here dealt a whack
> Upon the Deputy's bent back,

> When straightway to the floor there fell
> A shrunken globe, a rattling shell,
> A blackened, withered, eyeless head!
> The man had been a twelvemonth dead.
> *Jamrach Holobom.*

DESTINY, *n.* A tyrant's authority for crime and a fool's excuse for failure.

DIAGNOSIS, *n.* A physician's forecast of disease by the patient's pulse and purse.

DIAPHRAGM, *n.* A muscular partition separating disorders of the chest from disorders of the bowels.

DIARY, *n.* A daily record of that part of one's life, which he can relate to himself without blushing.

> Hearst kept a diary wherein were writ
> All that he had of wisdom and of wit.
> So the Recording Angel, when Hearst died,
> Erased all entries of his own and cried:
> "I'll judge you by your diary." Said Hearst:
> "Thank you; 'twill show you I am Saint the First"—
> Straightway producing, jubilant and proud,
> That record from a pocket in his shroud.
> The Angel slowly turned the pages o'er,
> Each stupid line of which he knew before,
> Glooming and gleaming as by turns he hit
> On shallow sentiment and stolen wit;
> Then gravely closed the book and gave it back.
> "My friend, you've wandered from your proper track:
> You'd never be content this side the tomb—
> For big ideas Heaven has little room,
> And Hell's no latitude for making mirth,"
> He said, and kicked the fellow back to earth.
> *"The Mad Philosopher."*

DICTATOR, *n.* The chief of a nation that prefers the pestilence of despotism to the plague of anarchy.

DICTIONARY, *n.* A malevolent literary device for cramping the growth of a language and making it hard and inelastic. This dictionary, however, is a most useful work.

DIE, *n.* The singular of "dice." We seldom hear the word, because there is a prohibitory proverb, "Never say die." At long intervals, however, some one says: "The die is cast," which is not true, for it is cut. The word is found in an immortal couplet by that eminent poet and domestic economist, Senator Depew:

> A cube of cheese no larger than a die
> May bait the trap to catch a nibbling mie.

DIGESTION, *n.* The conversion of victuals into virtues. When the process is imperfect, vices are evolved instead—a circumstance from which that wicked writer, Dr. Jeremiah Blenn, infers that the ladies are the greater sufferers from dyspepsia.

DIPLOMACY, *n.* The patriotic art of lying for one's country.

DISABUSE, *v. t.* To present your neighbor with another and better error than the one which he has deemed it advantageous to embrace.

DISCRIMINATE, *v.i.* To note the particulars in which one person or thing is, if possible, more objectionable than another.

DISCUSSION, *n.* A method of confirming others in their errors.

DISOBEDIENCE, *n.* The silver lining to the cloud of servitude.

DISOBEY, *v. t.* To celebrate with an appropriate ceremony the maturity of a command.

> His right to govern me is clear as day,
> My duty manifest to disobey;
> And if that fit observance e'er I shut
> May I and duty be alike undone.
> *Israfel Brown.*

DISSEMBLE, *v. i.* To put a clean shirt upon the character.

> Let us dissemble. —*Adam.*

DISTANCE, *n.* The only thing that the rich are willing for the poor to call theirs, and keep.

DISTRESS, *n.* A disease incurred by exposure to the prosperity of a friend.

DIVINATION, *n.* The art of nosing out the occult. Divination is of as many kinds as there are fruit-bearing varieties of the flowering dunce and the early fool.

DOG, *n.* A kind of additional or subsidiary Deity designed to catch the overflow and surplus of the world's worship. This Divine Being in some of his smaller and silkier incarnations takes, in the affection of Woman, the place to which there is no human male aspirant. The Dog is a survival—an anachronism. He toils not, neither does he spin, yet Solomon in all his glory never lay upon a door-mat all day long, sunsoaked and fly-fed and fat, while his master worked for the means wherewith to purchase an idle wag of the Solomonic tail, seasoned with a look of tolerant recognition.

DRAGOON, *n.* A soldier who combines dash and steadiness in so equal measure that he makes his advances on foot and his retreats on horseback.

DRAMATIST, *n.* One who adapts plays from the French.

DRUIDS, *n.* Priests and ministers of an ancient Celtic religion which did not disdain to employ the humble allurement of human sacrifice. Very little is now known about the Druids and their faith. Pliny says their religion, originating in Britain, spread eastward as far as Persia. Cæsar says those who desired to study its mysteries went to Britain. Cæsar himself went to Britain, but does not appear to have obtained any high preferment in the Druidical Church, although his talent for human sacrifice was considerable.

Druids performed their religious rites in groves, and knew nothing of church mortgages and the season-ticket system of pew rents. They were, in short, heathens and—as they were once complacently catalogued by a distinguished prelate of the Church of England—Dissenters.

DUCK-BILL, *n.* Your account at your restaurant during the canvas-back season.

DUEL, *n.* A formal ceremony preliminary to the reconciliation of two enemies. Great skill is necessary to its satisfactory observance; if awkwardly performed the most unexpected and deplorable consequences sometimes ensue. A long time ago a man lost his life in a duel.

> That dueling's a gentlemanly vice
> I hold; and wish that it had been my lot
> To live my life out in some favored spot—
> Some country where it is considered nice
> To split a rival like a fish, or slice
> A husband like a spud, or with a shot
> Bring down a debtor doubled in a knot
> And ready to be put upon the ice.
> Some miscreants there are, whom I do long
> To shoot, to stab, or some such way reclaim
> The scurvy rogues to better lives and manners,
> I seem to see them now—a mighty throng.
> It looks as if to challenge *me* they came,
> Jauntily marching with brass bands and banners!
> *Xamba Q. Dar.*

DULLARD, *n.* A member of the reigning dynasty in letters and life. The Dullards came in with Adam, and being both numerous and sturdy have overrun the habitable world. The secret of their power is their insensibility to blows; tickle them with a bludgeon and they laugh with a platitude. The Dullards came originally from Bœotia, whence they were driven by stress of starvation, their dullness having blighted the crops. For some centuries they infested Philistia, and many of them are called Philistines to this day. In the turbulent times of the Crusades they withdrew thence and gradually overspread all Europe, occupying most of the high places in politics, art, literature, science and theology. Since a detachment of Dullards came over with the Pilgrims in the *Mayflower* and made a favorable report of the country, their increase by birth, immigration, and conversion has been rapid and steady. According to the most trustworthy statistics the number of adult Dullards in the United States is but little short of thirty millions, including the statisticians. The intellectual centre of the race is somewhere about Peoria, Illinois, but the New England Dullard is the most shockingly moral.

DUTY, *n.* That which sternly impels us in the direction of profit, along the line of desire.

> Sir Lavender Portwine, in favor at court,
> Was wroth at his master, who'd kissed Lady Port.
> His anger provoked him to take the king's head,
> But duty prevailed, and he took the king's bread,
>   Instead.
>
> *G. J.*

E

EAT, *v. i.* To perform successively (and successfully) the functions of mastication, humectation, and deglutition.

"I was in the drawing-room, enjoying my dinner," said Brillat-Savarin, beginning an anecdote. "What!" interrupted Rochebriant; "eating dinner in a drawing-room?" "I must beg you to observe, monsieur," explained the great gastronome, "that I did not say I was eating my dinner, but enjoying it. I had dined an hour before."

EAVESDROP, *v. i.* Secretly to overhear a catalogue of the crimes and vices of another or yourself.

> A lady with one of her ears applied
> To an open keyhole heard, inside,
> Two female gossips in converse free—
> The subject engaging them was she.
> "I think," said one, "and my husband thinks
> That she's a prying, inquisitive minx!"
> As soon as no more of it she could hear

The lady, indignant, removed her ear.
"I will not stay," she said, with a pout,
"To hear my character lied about!"
Gopete Sherany.

ECCENTRICITY, *n.* A method of distinction so cheap that fools employ it to accentuate their incapacity.

ECONOMY, *n.* Purchasing the barrel of whiskey that you do not need for the price of the cow that you cannot afford.

EDIBLE, *adj.* Good to eat, and wholesome to digest, as a worm to a toad, a toad to a snake, a snake to a pig, a pig to a man, and a man to a worm.

EDITOR, *n.* A person who combines the judicial functions of Minos, Rhadamanthus and Æacus, but is placable with an obolus; a severely virtuous censor, but so charitable withal that he tolerates the virtues of others and the vices of himself; who flings about him the splintering lightning and sturdy thunders of admonition till he resembles a bunch of firecrackers petulantly uttering its mind at the tail of a dog; then straightway murmurs a mild, melodious lay, soft as the cooing of a donkey intoning its prayer to the evening star. Master of mysteries and lord of law, high-pinnacled upon the throne of thought, his face suffused with the dim splendors of the Transfiguration, his legs intertwisted and his tongue a-cheek, the editor spills his will along the paper and cuts it off in lengths to suit. And at intervals from behind the veil of the temple is heard the voice of the foreman demanding three inches of wit and six lines of religious meditation, or bidding him turn off the wisdom and whack up some pathos.

O, the Lord of Law on the Throne of Thought,
    A gilded impostor is he.
Of shreds and patches his robes are wrought,
        His crown is brass,
        Himself is an ass,
    And his power is fiddle-dee-dee.

Prankily, crankily prating of naught,
Silly old quilly old Monarch of Thought.
Public opinion's camp-follower he,
Thundering, blundering, plundering free.
Affected,
Ungracious,
Suspected,
Mendacious,
Respected contemporaree!

J. H. Bumbleshook.

EDUCATION, *n.* That which discloses to the wise and disguises from the foolish their lack of understanding.

EFFECT, *n.* The second of two phenomena which always occur together in the same order. The first, called a Cause, is said to generate the other—which is no more sensible than it would be for one who has never seen a dog except in pursuit of a rabbit to declare the rabbit the cause of a dog.

EGOTIST, *n.* A person of low taste, more interested in himself than in me.

Megaceph, chosen to serve the State
In the halls of legislative debate,
One day with all his credentials came
To the capitol's door and announced his name.
The doorkeeper looked, with a comical twist
Of the face, at the eminent egotist,
And said: "Go away, for we settle here
All manner of questions, knotty and queer,
And we cannot have, when the speaker demands
To be told how every member stands,
A man who to all things under the sky
Assents by eternally voting 'I.'"

EJECTION, *n.* An approved remedy for the disease of garrulity. It is also much used in cases of extreme poverty.

ELECTOR, *n.* One who enjoys the sacred privilege of voting for the man of another man's choice.

ELECTRICITY, *n.* The power that causes all natural phenomena not known to be caused by something else. It is the same thing as lightning, and its famous attempt to strike Dr. Franklin is one of the most picturesque incidents in that great and good man's career. The memory of Dr. Franklin is justly held in great reverence, particularly in France, where a waxen effigy of him was recently on exhibition, bearing the following touching account of his life and services to science:

> "Monsieur Franqulin, inventor of electricity. This illustrious savant, after having made several voyages around the world, died on the Sandwich Islands and was devoured by savages, of whom not a single fragment was ever recovered."

Electricity seems destined to play a most important part in the arts and industries. The question of its economical application to some purposes is still unsettled, but experiment has already proved that it will propel a street car better than a gas jet and give more light than a horse.

ELEGY, *n.* A composition in verse, in which, without employing any of the methods of humor, the writer aims to produce in the reader's mind the dampest kind of dejection. The most famous English example begins somewhat like this:

> The cur foretells the knell of parting day;
> The loafing herd winds slowly o'er the lea;
> The wise man homeward plods; I only stay
> To fiddle-faddle in a minor key.

ELOQUENCE, *n.* The art of orally persuading fools that white is the color that it appears to be. It includes the gift of making any color appear white.

ELYSIUM, *n.* An imaginary delightful country which the ancients foolishly believed to be inhabited by the spirits of the good. This ridiculous and mischievous fable was swept off the face of the earth by the early Christians—may their souls be happy in Heaven!

EMANCIPATION, *n*. A bondman's change from the tyranny of another to the despotism of himself.

> He was a slave: at word he went and came;
>   His iron collar cut him to the bone.
> Then Liberty erased his owner's name,
>   Tightened the rivets and inscribed his own.
>   *G. J.*

EMBALM, *v. t.* To cheat vegetation by locking up the gases upon which it feeds. By embalming their dead and thereby deranging the natural balance between animal and vegetable life, the Egyptians made their once fertile and populous country barren and incapable of supporting more than a meagre crew. The modern metallic burial casket is a step in the same direction, and many a dead man who ought now to be ornamenting his neighbor's lawn as a tree, or enriching his table as a bunch of radishes, is doomed to a long inutility. We shall get him after awhile if we are spared, but in the meantime the violet and rose are languishing for a nibble at his *glutæus maximus.*

EMOTION, *n*. A prostrating disease caused by a determination of the heart to the head. It is sometimes accompanied by a copious discharge of hydrated chloride of sodium from the eyes.

ENCOMIAST, *n*. A special (but not particular) kind of liar.

END, *n*. The position farthest removed on either hand from the Interlocutor.

> The man was perishing apace
>   Who played the tambourine:
> The seal of death was on his face—
>   'Twas pallid, for 'twas clean.
>
> "This is the end," the sick man said
>   In faint and failing tones.
> A moment later he was dead,
>   And Tambourine was Bones.
>   *Tinley Roquot.*

ENOUGH, *pro.* All there is in the world if you like it.

> Enough is as good as a feast—for that matter
> Enougher's as good as a feast for the platter.
> *Arbely C. Strunk.*

ENTERTAINMENT, *n.* Any kind of amusement whose inroads stop short of death by dejection.

ENTHUSIASM, *n.* A distemper of youth, curable by small doses of repentance in connection with outward applications of experience. Byron, who recovered long enough to call it "entuzy-muzy," had a relapse which carried him off—to Missolonghi.

ENVELOPE, *n.* The coffin of a document; the scabbard of a bill; the husk of a remittance; the bed-gown of a love-letter.

ENVY, *n.* Emulation adapted to the meanest capacity.

EPAULET, *n.* An ornamented badge, serving to distinguish a military officer from the enemy—that is to say, from the officer of lower rank to whom his death would give promotion.

EPICURE, *n.* An opponent of Epicurus, an abstemious philosopher who, holding that pleasure should be the chief aim of man, wasted no time in gratification from the senses.

EPIGRAM, *n.* A short, sharp saying in prose or verse, frequently characterized by acidity or acerbity and sometimes by wisdom. Following are some of the more notable epigrams of the learned and ingenious Dr. Jamrach Holobom:

> We know better the needs of ourselves than of others. To serve oneself is economy of administration.

> In each human heart are a tiger, a pig, an ass and a nightingale. Diversity of character is due to their unequal activity.

> There are three sexes; males, females and girls.

> Beauty in women and distinction in men are alike in this: they seem to be the unthinking a kind of credibility.

Women in love are less ashamed than men. They have less to be ashamed of.

While your friend holds you affectionately by both your hands you are safe, for you can watch both his.

EPITAPH, *n.* An inscription on a tomb, showing that virtues acquired by death have a retroactive effect. Following is a touching example:

> Here lie the bones of Parson Platt,
> Wise, pious, humble and all that,
> Who showed us life as all should live it;
> Let that be said—and God forgive it!

ERUDITION, *n.* Dust shaken out of a book into an empty skull.

> So wide his erudition's mighty span,
> He knew Creation's origin and plan
> And only came by accident to grief—
> He thought, poor man, 'twas right to be a thief.
> *Romach Pute.*

ESOTERIC, *adj.* Very particularly abstruse and consummately occult. The ancient philosophies were of two kinds,—*exoteric*, those that the philosophers themselves could partly understand, and *esoteric*, those that nobody could understand. It is the latter that have most profoundly affected modern thought and found greatest acceptance in our time.

ETHNOLOGY, *n.* The science that treats of the various tribes of Man, as robbers, thieves, swindlers, dunces, lunatics, idiots and ethnologists.

EUCHARIST, *n.* A sacred feast of the religious sect of Theophagi.

A dispute once unhappily arose among the members of this sect as to what it was that they ate. In this controversy some five hundred thousand have already been slain, and the question is still unsettled.

EULOGY, *n.* Praise of a person who has either the advantages of wealth and power, or the consideration to be dead.

EVANGELIST, *n.* A bearer of good tidings, particularly (in a religious sense) such as assure us of our own salvation and the damnation of our neighbors.

EVERLASTING, *adj.* Lasting forever. It is with no small diffidence that I venture to offer this brief and elementary definition, for I am not unaware of the existence of a bulky volume by a sometime Bishop of Worcester, entitled, *A Partial Definition of the Word "Everlasting," as Used in the Authorized Version of the Holy Scriptures.* His book was once esteemed of great authority in the Anglican Church, and is still, I understand, studied with pleasure to the mind and profit to the soul.

EXCEPTION, *n.* A thing which takes the liberty to differ from other things of its class, as an honest man, a truthful woman, etc. "The exception proves the rule" is an expression constantly upon the lips of the ignorant, who parrot it from one another with never a thought of its absurdity. In the Latin, "*Exceptio probat regulam*" means that the exception *tests* the rule, puts it to the proof, not *confirms* it. The malefactor who drew the meaning from this excellent dictum and substituted a contrary one of his own exerted an evil power which appears to be immortal.

EXCESS, *n.* In morals, an indulgence that enforces by appropriate penalties the law of moderation.

> Hail, high Excess—especially in wine.
> To thee in worship do I bend the knee
> Who preach abstemiousness unto me—
> My skull thy pulpit, as my paunch thy shrine.
> Precept on precept, aye, and line on line,
> Could ne'er persuade so sweetly to agree
> With reason as thy touch, exact and free,
> Upon my forehead and along my spine.
> At thy command eschewing pleasure's cup,
> With the hot grape I warm no more my wit;
> When on thy stool of penitence I sit
> I'm quite converted, for I can't get up.

> Ungrateful he who afterward would falter
> To make new sacrifices at thine altar!

EXCOMMUNICATION, *n.*

> This "excommunication" is a word
> In speech ecclesiastical oft heard,
> And means the damning, with bell, book and candle,
> Some sinner whose opinions are a scandal—
> A rite permitting Satan to enslave him
> Forever, and forbidding Christ to save him.
> > *Gat Huckle.*

EXECUTIVE, *n.* An officer of the Government, whose duty it is to enforce the wishes of the legislative power until such time as the judicial department shall be pleased to pronounce them invalid and of no effect. Following is an extract from an old book entitled, *The Lunarian Astonished*—Pfeiffer & Co., Boston, 1803:

LUNARIAN: Then when your Congress has passed a law it goes directly to the Supreme Court in order that it may at once be known whether it is constitutional?

TERRESTRIAN: O no; it does not require the approval of the Supreme Court until having perhaps been enforced for many years somebody objects to its operation against himself—I mean his client. The President, if he approves it, begins to execute it at once.

LUNARIAN: Ah, the executive power is a part of the legislative. Do your policemen also have to approve the local ordinances that they enforce?

TERRESTRIAN: Not yet—at least not in their character of constables. Generally speaking, though, all laws require the approval of those whom they are intended to restrain.

LUNARIAN: I see. The death warrant is not valid until signed by the murderer.

TERRESTRIAN: My friend, you put it too strongly; we are not so consistent.

LUNARIAN: But this system of maintaining an expensive judicial machinery to pass upon the validity of laws only after they have long been executed, and then only when brought before the court by some private person—does it not cause great confusion?

TERRESTRIAN: It does.

LUNARIAN: Why then should not your laws, previously to being executed, be validated, not by the signature of your President, but by that of the Chief Justice of the Supreme Court?

TERRESTRIAN: There is no precedent for any such course.

LUNARIAN: Precedent. What is that?

TERRESTRIAN: It has been defined by five hundred lawyers in three volumes each. So how can any one know?

EXHORT, *v. t.* In religious affairs, to put the conscience of another upon the spit and roast it to a nut-brown discomfort.

EXILE, *n.* One who serves his country by residing abroad, yet is not an ambassador.

An English sea-captain being asked if he had read "The Exile of Erin," replied: "No, sir, but I should like to anchor on it." Years afterwards, when he had been hanged as a pirate after a career of unparalleled atrocities, the following memorandum was found in the ship's log that he had kept at the time of his reply:

Aug. 3d, 1842. Made a joke on the ex-Isle of Erin. Coldly received. War with the whole world!

EXISTENCE, *n.*

A transient, horrible, fantastic dream,
Wherein is nothing yet all things do seem:
From which we're wakened by a friendly nudge
Of our bedfellow Death, and cry: "O fudge!"

EXPERIENCE, *n.* The wisdom that enables us to recognize as an undesirable old acquaintance the folly that we have already embraced.

To one who, journeying through night and fog,
Is mired neck-deep in an unwholesome bog,
Experience, like the rising of the dawn,
Reveals the path that he should not have gone.
Joel Frad Bink.

EXPOSTULATION, *n.* One of the many methods by which fools prefer to lose their friends.

EXTINCTION, *n.* The raw material out of which theology created the future state.

F

FAIRY, *n.* A creature, variously fashioned and endowed, that formerly inhabited the meadows and forests. It was nocturnal in its habits, and somewhat addicted to dancing and the theft of children. The fairies are now believed by naturalists to be extinct, though a clergyman of the Church of England saw three near Colchester as lately as 1855, while passing through a park after dining with the lord of the manor. The sight greatly staggered him, and he was so affected that his account of it was incoherent. In the year 1807 a troop of fairies visited a wood near Aix and carried off the daughter of a peasant, who had been seen to enter it with a bundle of clothing. The son of a wealthy *bourgeois* disappeared about the same time, but afterward returned. He had seen the abduction and been in pursuit of the fairies. Justinian Gaux, a writer of the fourteenth century, avers that so great is the fairies' power of transformation that he saw one change itself into two opposing armies and fight a battle with great slaughter, and that the next day, after it had resumed its original shape and gone away, there were seven hundred bodies of the slain which the villagers had to bury. He does not say if any of the wounded recovered. In the time of Henry III, of England, a law was made which prescribed the death penalty for "Kyllynge, wowndynge, or mamynge" a fairy, and it was universally respected.

FAITH, *n.* Belief without evidence in what is told by one who speaks without knowledge, of things without parallel.

FAMOUS, *adj.* Conspicuously miserable.

> Done to a turn on the iron, behold
> Him who to be famous aspired.
> Content? Well, his grill has a plating of gold,
> And his twistings are greatly admired.
> *Hassan Brubuddy.*

FASHION, *n.* A despot whom the wise ridicule and obey.

> A king there was who lost an eye
>   In some excess of passion;
> And straight his courtiers all did try
>   To follow the new fashion.
>
> Each dropped one eyelid when before
>   The throne he ventured, thinking
> 'Twould please the king. That monarch swore
>   He'd slay them all for winking.
>
> What should they do? They were not hot
>   To hazard such disaster;
> They dared not close an eye—dared not
>   See better than their master.
>
> Seeing them lacrymose and glum,
>   A leech consoled the weepers:
> He spread small rags with liquid gum
>   And covered half their peepers.
>
> The court all wore the stuff, the flame
>   Of royal anger dying.
> That's how court-plaster got its name
>   Unless I'm greatly lying.
>
> *Naramy Oof.*

FEAST, *n.* A festival. A religious celebration usually signalized by gluttony and drunkenness, frequently in honor of some holy person distinguished for abstemiousness. In the Roman Catholic Church feasts are "movable" and "immovable," but the celebrants are uniformly immovable until they are full. In their earliest development these entertainments took the form of feasts for the dead; such were held by the Greeks, under the name of *Nemeseia*, by the Aztecs and Peruvians, as in modern times they are popular with the Chinese; though it is believed that the ancient dead, like the modern, were light eaters. Among the many feasts of the Romans was the *Novemdiale*, which was held, according to Livy, whenever stones fell from heaven.

FELON, *n.* A person of greater enterprise than discretion, who in embracing an opportunity has formed an unfortunate attachment.

FEMALE, *n.* One of the opposing, or unfair, sex.

> The Maker, at Creation's birth,
> With living things had stocked the earth.
> From elephants to bats and snails,
> They all were good, for all were males.
> But when the Devil came and saw
> He said: "By Thine eternal law
> Of growth, maturity, decay,
> These all must quickly pass away
> And leave untenanted the earth
> Unless Thou dost establish birth"—
> Then tucked his head beneath his wing
> To laugh—he had no sleeve—the thing
> With deviltry did so accord,
> That he'd suggested to the Lord.
> The Master pondered this advice,
> Then shook and threw the fateful dice
> Wherewith all matters here below
> Are ordered, and observed the throw;
> Then bent His head in awful state,
> Confirming the decree of Fate.
> From every part of earth anew
> The conscious dust consenting flew,
> While rivers from their courses rolled
> To make it plastic for the mould.
> Enough collected (but no more,
> For niggard Nature hoards her store)
> He kneaded it to flexile clay,
> While Nick unseen threw some away.
> And then the various forms He cast,
> Gross organs first and finer last;
> No one at once evolved, but all
> By even touches grew and small
> Degrees advanced, till, shade by shade,
> To match all living things He'd made
> Females, complete in all their parts
> Except (His clay gave out) the hearts.
> "No matter," Satan cried; "with speed

I'll fetch the very hearts they need"—
So flew away and soon brought back
The number needed, in a sack.
That night earth rang with sounds of strife—
Ten million males had each a wife;
That night sweet Peace her pinions spread
O'er Hell—ten million devils dead!
                                        G. J.

FIB, *n.* A lie that has not cut its teeth. An habitual liar's nearest
approach to truth: the perigee of his eccentric orbit.

When David said: "All men are liars," Dave,
    Himself a liar, fibbed like any thief.
    Perhaps he thought to weaken disbelief
By proof that even himself was not a slave
To Truth; though I suspect the aged knave
    Had been of all her servitors the chief
    Had he but known a fig's reluctant leaf
Is more than e'er she wore on land or wave.
No, David served not Naked Truth when he
    Struck that sledge-hammer blow at all his race;
        Nor did he hit the nail upon the head:
For reason shows that it could never be,
    And the facts contradict him to his face.
        Men are not liars all, for some are dead.
                                    Bartle Quinker.

FICKLENESS, *n.* The iterated satiety of an enterprising affection.

FIDDLE, *n.* An instrument to tickle human ears by friction of a
horse's tail on the entrails of a cat.

To Rome said Nero: "If to smoke you turn
I shall not cease to fiddle while you burn."
To Nero Rome replied: "Pray do your worst,
'Tis my excuse that you were fiddling first."
                                    Orm Pludge.

FIDELITY, *n.* A virtue peculiar to those who are about to be
betrayed.

FINANCE, *n.* The art or science of managing revenues and resources for the best advantage of the manager. The pronunciation of this word with the i long and the accent on the first syllable is one of America's most precious discoveries and possessions.

FLAG, *n.* A colored rag borne above troops and hoisted on forts and ships. It appears to serve the same purpose as certain signs that one sees on vacant lots in London—"Rubbish may be shot here."

FLESH, *n.* The Second Person of the secular Trinity.

FLOP, *v.* Suddenly to change one's opinions and go over to another party. The most notable flop on record was that of Saul of Tarsus, who has been severely criticised as a turncoat by some of our partisan journals.

FLY-SPECK, *n.* The prototype of punctuation. It is observed by Garvinus that the systems of punctuation in use by the various literary nations depended originally upon the social habits and general diet of the flies infesting the several countries. These creatures, which have always been distinguished for a neighborly and companionable familiarity with authors, liberally or niggardly embellish the manuscripts in process of growth under the pen, according to their bodily habit, bringing out the sense of the work by a species of interpretation superior to, and independent of, the writer's powers. The "old masters" of literature—that is to say, the early writers whose work is so esteemed by later scribes and critics in the same language—never punctuated at all, but worked right along free-handed, without that abruption of the thought which comes from the use of points. (We observe the same thing in children to-day, whose usage in this particular is a striking and beautiful instance of the law that the infancy of individuals reproduces the methods and stages of development characterizing the infancy of races.) In the work of these primitive scribes all the punctuation is found, by the modern investigator with his optical instruments and chemical tests, to have been inserted by the writers' ingenious and serviceable collaborator, the common house-fly—*Musca male-dicta*. In transcribing these ancient MSS, for the purpose of either making the work their own or preserving what they naturally regard as divine revelations, later writers reverently and accurately copy whatever marks they find upon the papyrus or parchment, to the unspeakable enhancement of the lucidity of the thought and value of the work. Writers contemporary with the copyists naturally avail themselves of the obvious advantages of these marks in their own work, and with such assistance as the flies of their own household may be willing to grant, frequently rival and sometimes surpass the older compositions, in respect at least of punctuation, which is no small glory. Fully to understand the important services that flies perform to literature it is only necessary to lay a page of some popular novelist alongside a saucer of cream-and-molasses in a sunny room and observe "how the wit brightens and the style refines" in accurate proportion to the duration of exposure.

FOLLY, *n.* That "gift and faculty divine" whose creative and controlling energy inspires Man's mind, guides his actions and adorns his life.

> Folly! although Erasmus praised thee once
>   In a thick volume, and all authors known,
>   If not thy glory yet thy power have shown,
> Deign to take homage from thy son who hunts
> Through all thy maze his brothers, fool and dunce,
>   To mend their lives and to sustain his own,
>   However feebly be his arrows thrown,
>
> Howe'er each hide the flying weapons blunts.
> All-Father Folly! be it mine to raise,
>   With lusty lung, here on his western strand
>   With all thine offspring thronged from every land,
> Thyself inspiring me, the song of praise.
> And if too weak, I'll hire, to help me bawl,
> Dick Watson Gilder, gravest of us all.
>   *Aramis Loto Frope.*

FOOL, *n.* A person who pervades the domain of intellectual speculation and diffuses himself through the channels of moral activity. He is omnific, omniform, omnipercipient, omniscience, omnipotent. He it was who invented letters, printing, the railroad, the steamboat, the telegraph, the platitude and the circle of the sciences. He created patriotism and taught the nations war—founded theology, philosophy, law, medicine and Chicago. He established monarchical and republican government. He is from everlasting to everlasting—such as creation's dawn beheld he fooleth now. In the morning of time he sang upon primitive hills, and in the noonday of existence headed the procession of being. His grandmotherly hand was warmly tucked-in the set sun of civilization, and in the twilight he prepares Man's evening meal of milk-and-morality and turns down the covers of the universal grave. And after the rest of us shall have retired for the night of eternal oblivion he will sit up to write a history of human civilization.

FORCE, *n.*

> "Force is but might," the teacher said—
>   "That definition's just."
> The boy said naught but thought instead,
> Remembering his pounded head:
>   "Force is not might but must!"

FOREFINGER, *n.* The finger commonly used in pointing out two malefactors.

FOREORDINATION, *n.* This looks like an easy word to define, but when I consider that pious and learned theologians have spent long lives in explaining it, and written libraries to explain their explanations; when I remember the nations have been divided and bloody battles caused by the difference between foreordination and predestination, and that millions of treasure have been expended in the effort to prove and disprove its compatibility with freedom of the will and the efficacy of prayer, praise, and a religious life,—recalling these awful facts in the history of the word, I stand appalled before the mighty problem of its signification, abase my spiritual eyes, fearing to contemplate its portentous magnitude, reverently uncover and humbly refer it to His Eminence Cardinal Gibbons and His Grace Bishop Potter.

FORGETFULNESS, *n.* A gift of God bestowed upon debtors in compensation for their destitution of conscience.

FORK, *n.* An instrument used chiefly for the purpose of putting dead animals into the mouth. Formerly the knife was employed for this purpose, and by many worthy persons is still thought to have many advantages over the other tool, which, however, they do not altogether reject, but use to assist in charging the knife. The immunity of these persons from swift and awful death is one of the most striking proofs of God's mercy to those that hate Him.

FORMA PAUPERIS (Latin). In the character of a poor person—a method by which a litigant without money for lawyers is considerately permitted to lose his case.

> When Adam long ago in Cupid's awful court
> (For Cupid ruled ere Adam was invented)
> Sued for Eve's favor, says an ancient law report,
> He stood and pleaded unhabilimented.
>
> "You sue *in forma pauperis,* I see," Eve cried;
> "Actions can't here be that way prosecuted."
> So all poor Adam's motions coldly were denied:
> He went away—as he had come—nonsuited.
> G. J.

FRANKALMOIGNE, *n.* The tenure by which a religious corporation holds lands on condition of praying for the soul of the donor. In mediæval times many of the wealthiest fraternities obtained their estates in this simple and cheap manner, and once when Henry VIII of England sent an officer to confiscate certain vast possessions which a fraternity of monks held by frankalmoigne, "What!" said the Prior, "would your master stay our benefactor's soul in Purgatory?" "Ay," said the officer, coldly, "an ye will not pray him thence for naught he must e'en roast." "But look you, my son," persisted the good man, "this act hath rank as robbery of God!" "Nay, nay, good father, my master the king doth but deliver Him from the manifold temptations of too great wealth."

FREEBOOTER, *n.* A conqueror in a small way of business, whose annexations lack the sanctifying merit of magnitude.

FREEDOM, *n.* Exemption from the stress of authority in a beggarly half dozen of restraint's infinite multitude of methods. A political condition that every nation supposes itself to enjoy in virtual monopoly. Liberty. The distinction between freedom and liberty is not accurately known; naturalists have never been able to find a living specimen of either.

> Freedom, as every schoolboy knows,
>   Once shrieked as Kosciusko fell;
> On every wind, indeed, that blows
>   I hear her yell.
>
> She screams whenever monarchs meet,
>   And parliaments as well,
> To bind the chains about her feet
>   And toll her knell.
>
> And when the sovereign people cast
>   The votes they cannot spell,
> Upon the pestilential blast
>   Her clamors swell.
>
> For all to whom the power's given
>   To sway or to compel,
> Among themselves apportion Heaven
>   And give her Hell.
>   *Blary O'Gary.*

FREEMASONS, *n.* An order with secret rites, grotesque ceremonies and fantastic costumes, which, originating in the reign of Charles II, among working artisans of London, has been joined successively by the dead of past centuries in unbroken retrogression until now it embraces all the generations of man on the hither side of Adam and is drumming up distinguished recruits among the pre-Creational inhabitants of Chaos and the Formless Void. The order was founded at different times by Charlemagne, Julius Cæsar, Cyrus, Solomon,

Zoroaster, Confucius, Thothmes, and Buddha. Its emblems and symbols have been found in the Catacombs of Paris and Rome, on the stones of the Parthenon and the Chinese Great Wall, among the temples of Karnak and Palmyra and in the Egyptian Pyramids—always by a Freemason.

FRIENDLESS, *adj.* Having no favors to bestow. Destitute of fortune. Addicted to utterance of truth and common sense.

FRIENDSHIP, *n.* A ship big enough to carry two in fair weather, but only one in foul.

> The sea was calm and the sky was blue;
> Merrily, merrily sailed we two.
>   (High barometer maketh glad.)
> On the tipsy ship, with a dreadful shout,
> The tempest descended and we fell out.
>   (O the walking is nasty bad!)
>   *Armit Huff Bettle.*

FROG, *n.* A reptile with edible legs. The first mention of frogs in profane literature is in Homer's narrative of the war between them and the mice. Skeptical persons have doubted Homer's authorship of the work, but the learned, ingenious and industrious Dr. Schliemann has set the question forever at rest by uncovering the bones of the slain frogs. One of the forms of moral suasion by which Pharaoh was besought to favor the Israelites was a plague of frogs, but Pharaoh, who liked them *fricasées*, remarked, with truly oriental stoicism, that he could stand it as long as the frogs and the Jews could; so the programme was changed. The frog is a diligent songster, having a good voice but no ear. The libretto of his favorite opera, as written by Aristophanes, is brief, simple and effective—"brekekex-koäx"; the music is apparently by that eminent composer, Richard Wagner. Horses have a frog in each hoof—a thoughtful provision of nature, enabling them to shine in a hurdle race.

FRYING-PAN, *n.* One part of the penal apparatus employed in that punitive institution, a woman's kitchen. The frying-pan was invented by Calvin, and by him used in cooking span-long infants that had died without baptism; and observing one day the horrible torment of a tramp who had incautiously pulled a fried babe from the waste-dump and devoured it, it occurred to the great divine to rob death of its terrors by introducing the frying-pan into every household in Geneva. Thence it spread to all corners of the world, and has been of invaluable assistance in the propagation of his sombre faith. The following lines (said to be from the pen of his Grace Bishop Potter) seem to imply that the usefulness of this utensil is not limited to this world; but as the consequences of its employment in this life reach over into the life to come, so also itself may be found on the other side, rewarding its devotees:

> Old Nick was summoned to the skies.
>   Said Peter: "Your intentions
> Are good, but you lack enterprise
>   Concerning new inventions.
>
> "Now, broiling in an ancient plan
>   Of torment, but I hear it
> Reported that the frying-pan
>   Sears best the wicked spirit.
>
> "Go get one—fill it up with fat—
>   Fry sinners brown and good in't."
> "I know a trick worth two o' that,"
>   Said Nick—"I'll cook their food in't."

FUNERAL, *n.* A pageant whereby we attest our respect for the dead by enriching the undertaker, and strengthen our grief by an expenditure that deepens our groans and doubles our tears.

> The savage dies—they sacrifice a horse
> To bear to happy hunting-grounds the corse.
> Our friends expire—we make the money fly
> In hope their souls will chase it to the sky.
>   *Jex Wopley.*

FUTURE, *n.* That period of time in which our affairs prosper, our friends are true and our happiness is assured.

G

GALLOWS, *n.* A stage for the performance of miracle plays, in which the leading actor is translated to heaven. In this country the gallows is chiefly remarkable for the number of persons who escape it.

> Whether on the gallows high
> Or where blood flows the reddest,
> The noblest place for man to die—
> Is where he died the deadest.
> *Old Play.*

GARGOYLE, *n.* A rain-spout projecting from the eaves of mediæval buildings, commonly fashioned into a grotesque caricature of some personal enemy of the architect or owner of the building. This was especially the case in churches and ecclesiastical structures generally, in which the gargoyles presented a perfect rogues' gallery of local heretics and controversialists. Sometimes when a new dean and chapter were installed the old gargoyles were removed and others substituted having a closer relation to the private animosities of the new incumbents.

GARTER, *n.* An elastic band intended to keep a woman from coming out of her stockings and desolating the country.

GENEALOGY, *n.* An account of one's descent from an ancestor who did not particularly care to trace his own.

GENEROUS, *adj.* Originally this word meant noble by birth and was rightly applied to a great multitude of persons. It now means noble by nature and is taking a bit of a rest.

GENTEEL, *adj.* Refined, after the fashion of a gent.

> Observe with care, my son, the distinction I reveal:
> A gentleman is gentle and a gent genteel.
> Heed not the definitions your "Unabridged" presents,
> For dictionary makers are generally gents.
> *G. J.*

GEOGRAPHER, *n.* A chap who can tell you offhand the difference between the outside of the world and the inside.

> Habeam, geographer of wide renown,
> Native of Abu-Keber's ancient town,
> In passing thence along the river Zam
> To the adjacent village of Xelam,
> Bewildered by the multitude of roads,
> Got lost, lived long on migratory toads,
> Then from exposure miserably died,
> And grateful travelers bewailed their guide.
> *Henry Haukhorn.*

GEOLOGY, *n.* The science of the earth's crust—to which, doubtless, will be added that of its interior whenever a man shall come up garrulous out of a well. The geological formations of the globe already noted are catalogued thus: The Primary, or lower one, consists of rocks, bones of mired mules, gas-pipes, miners' tools, antique statues minus the nose, Spanish doubloons and ancestors. The Secondary is largely made up of red worms and moles. The Tertiary comprises railway tracks, patent pavements, grass, snakes, mouldy boots, beer bottles, tomato cans, intoxicated citizens, garbage, anarchists, snap-dogs and fools.

GHOST, *n.* The outward and visible sign of an inward fear.

> He saw a ghost.
> It occupied—that dismal thing!—
> The path that he was following.
> Before he'd time to stop and fly,
> An earthquake trifled with the eye
> That saw a ghost.
> He fell as fall the early good;
> Unmoved that awful vision stood.
> The stars that danced before his ken
> He wildly brushed away, and then
> He saw a post.
> *Jared Macphester.*

Accounting for the uncommon behavior of ghosts, Heine mentions somebody's ingenious theory to the effect that they are as much afraid of us as we of them. Not quite, if I may judge from such tables of comparative speed as I am able to compile from memories of my own experience.

There is one insuperable obstacle to a belief in ghosts. A ghost never comes naked: he appears either in a winding-sheet or "in his habit as he lived." To believe in him, then, is to believe that not only have the dead the power to make themselves visible after there is nothing left of them, but that the same power inheres in textile fabrics. Supposing the products of the loom to have this ability, what object would they have in exercising it? And why does not the apparition of a suit of clothes sometimes walk abroad without a ghost in it? These be riddles of significance. They reach away down and get a convulsive grasp on the very tap-root of this flourishing faith.

GHOUL, *n.* A demon addicted to the reprehensible habit of devouring the dead. The existence of ghouls has been disputed by that class of controversialists who are more concerned to deprive the world of comforting beliefs than to give it anything good in their place. In 1640 Father Secchi saw one in a cemetery near Florence and frightened it away with the sign of the cross. He describes it as gifted with many heads and an uncommon allowance of limbs, and he saw it in more than one place at a time. The good man was coming away from dinner at the time and explains that if he had not been "heavy with eating" he would have seized the demon at all hazards. Atholston relates that a ghoul was caught by some sturdy peasants in a churchyard at Sudbury and ducked in a horsepond. (He appears to think that so distinguished a criminal should have been ducked in a tank of rosewater.) The water turned at once to blood "and so contynues unto ys daye." The pond has since been bled with a ditch. As late as the beginning of the fourteenth century a ghoul was cornered in the crypt of the cathedral at Amiens and the whole population surrounded the place. Twenty armed men with a priest at their head, bearing a crucifix, entered and captured the ghoul, which, thinking to escape by the stratagem, had transformed itself to the semblance of a well known citizen, but was nevertheless hanged, drawn and quartered in the midst of hideous popular orgies. The citizen whose shape the demon had assumed was so affected by the sinister occurrence that he never again showed himself in Amiens and his fate remains a mystery.

GLUTTON, *n*. A person who escapes the evils of moderation by committing dyspepsia.

GNOME, *n*. In North-European mythology, a dwarfish imp inhabiting the interior parts of the earth and having special custody of mineral treasures. Bjorsen, who died in 1765, says gnomes were common enough in the southern parts of Sweden in his boyhood, and he frequently saw them scampering on the hills in the evening twilight. Ludwig Binkerhoof saw three as recently as 1792, in the Black Forest, and Sneddeker avers that in 1803 they drove a party of miners out of a Silesian mine. Basing our computations upon data supplied by these statements, we find that the gnomes were probably extinct as early as 1764.

GNOSTICS, *n*. A sect of philosophers who tried to engineer a fusion between the early Christians and the Platonists. The former would not go into the caucus and the combination failed, greatly to the chagrin of the fusion managers.

GNU, *n*. An animal of South Africa, which in its domesticated state resembles a horse, a buffalo and a stag. In its wild condition it is something like a thunderbolt, an earthquake and a cyclone.

> A hunter from Kew caught a distant view
>   Of a peacefully meditative gnu,
> And he said: "I'll pursue, and my hands imbrue
>   In its blood at a closer interview."
> But that beast did ensue and the hunter it threw
>   O'er the top of a palm that adjacent grew;
> And he said as he flew: "It is well I withdrew
>   Ere, losing my temper, I wickedly slew
>   That really meritorious gnu."
>
> *Jarn Leffer.*

GOOD, *adj.* Sensible, madam, to the worth of this present writer. Alive, sir, to the advantages of letting him alone.

GOOSE, *n.* A bird that supplies quills for writing. These, by some occult process of nature, are penetrated and suffused with various degrees of the bird's intellectual energies and emotional character, so that when inked and drawn mechanically across paper by a person called an "author," there results a very fair and accurate transcript of the fowl's thought and feeling. The difference in geese, as discovered by this ingenious method, is considerable: many are found to have only trivial and insignificant powers, but some are seen to be very great geese indeed.

GORGON, *n.*

> The Gorgon was a maiden bold
> Who turned to stone the Greeks of old
> That looked upon her awful brow.
> We dig them out of ruins now,
> And swear that workmanship so bad
> Proves all the ancient sculptors mad.

GOUT, *n.* A physician's name for the rheumatism of a rich patient.

GRACES, *n.* Three beautiful goddesses, Aglaia, Thalia and Euphrosyne, who attended upon Venus, serving without salary. They were at no expense for board and clothing, for they ate nothing to speak of and dressed according to the weather, wearing whatever breeze happened to be blowing.

GRAMMAR, *n.* A system of pitfalls thoughtfully prepared for the feet of the self-made man, along the path by which he advances to distinction.

GRAPE, *n.*

> Hail noble fruit!—by Homer sung,
>   Anacreon and Khayyam;
> Thy praise is ever on the tongue
>   Of better men than I am.

The lyre my hand has never swept,
  The song I cannot offer:
My humbler service pray accept—
  I'll help to kill the scoffer.

The water-drinkers and the cranks
  Who load their skins with liquor—
I'll gladly bear their belly-tanks
  And tap them with my sticker.

Fill up, fill up, for wisdom cools
  When e'er we let the wine rest.
Here's death to Prohibition's fools,
  And every kind of vine-pest!
                    Jamrach Holobom.

GRAPESHOT, *n.* An argument which the future is preparing in answer to the demands of American Socialism.

GRAVE, *n.* A place in which the dead are laid to await the coming of the medical student.

Beside a lonely grave I stood—
  With brambles 'twas encumbered;
The winds were moaning in the wood,
  Unheard by him who slumbered.

A rustic standing near, I said:
  "He cannot hear it blowing!"
" 'Course not," said he: "the feller's dead—
  He can't hear nowt that's going."

"Too true," I said; "alas, too true—
  No sound his sense can quicken!"
"Well, mister, wot is that to you?—
  The deadster ain't a-kickin'."

I knelt and prayed: "O Father, smile
  On him, and mercy show him!"
That countryman looked on the while,
  And said: "Ye didn't know him."
                    Pobeter Dunk.

GRAVITATION, *n.* The tendency of all bodies to approach one another with a strength proportioned to the quantity of matter they contain—the quantity of matter they contain being ascertained by the strength of their tendency to approach one another. This is a lovely and edifying illustration of how science, having made A the proof of B, makes B the proof of A.

GREAT, *adj.*

> "I'm great," the Lion said—"I reign
> The monarch of the wood and plain!"

> The Elephant replied: "I'm great—
> No quadruped can match my weight!"

> "I'm great—no animal has half
> So long a neck!" said the Giraffe.

> "I'm great," the Kangaroo said—"see
> My femoral muscularity!"

> The 'Possum said: "I'm great—behold,
> My tail is lithe and bald and cold!"

> An Oyster fried was understood
> To say: "I'm great because I'm good!"

> Each reckons greatness to consist
> In that in which he heads the list,

> And Vierick thinks he tops his class
> Because he is the greatest ass.
> *Arion Spurl Doke.*

GUILLOTINE, *n.* A machine which makes a Frenchman shrug his shoulders with good reason.

In his great work on *Divergent Lines of Racial Evolution*, the learned Professor Brayfugle argues from the prevalence of this gesture—the shrug—among Frenchmen, that they are descended from turtles and it is simply a survival of the habit of retracting the head inside the shell. It is with reluctance that I differ with so eminent an authority, but in my judgment (as more elaborately set forth and enforced in my work entitled *Hereditary Emotions*—lib. II, c. XI) the shrug is a poor foundation upon which to build so important a theory, for previously to the Revolution the gesture was unknown. I have not a doubt that it is directly referable to the terror inspired by the guillotine during the period of that instrument's activity.

GUNPOWDER, *n*. An agency employed by civilized nations for the settlement of disputes which might become troublesome if left unadjusted. By most writers the invention of gunpowder is ascribed to the Chinese, but not upon very convincing evidence. Milton says it was invented by the devil to dispel angels with, and this opinion seems to derive some support from the scarcity of angels. Moreover, it has the hearty concurrence of the Hon. James Wilson, Secretary of Agriculture.

Secretary Wilson became interested in gunpowder through an event that occurred on the Government experimental farm in the District of Columbia. One day, several years ago, a rogue imperfectly reverent of the Secretary's profound attainments and personal character presented him with a sack of gunpowder, representing it as the seed of the *Flashawful flabbergastor*, a Patagonian cereal of great commercial value, admirably adapted to this climate. The good Secretary was instructed to spill it along in a furrow and afterward inhume it with soil. This he at once proceeded to do, and had made a continuous line of it all the way across a ten-acre field, when he was made to look backward by a shout from the generous donor, who at once dropped a lighted match into the furrow at the starting-point. Contact with the earth had somewhat dampened the powder, but the startled functionary saw himself pursued by a tall moving pillar of fire and smoke in fierce evolution. He stood for a moment paralyzed and speechless, then he recollected an engagement and, dropping all, absented himself thence with such surprising celerity that to the eyes of spectators along the route selected he appeared like a long, dim streak prolonging itself with inconceivable rapidity through seven villages, and audibly refusing to be comforted. "Great Scott! what is that?" cried a surveyor's chainman, shading his eyes and gazing at the fading line of agriculturist which bisected his visible horizon.

"That," said the surveyor, carelessly glancing at the phenomenon and again centering his attention upon his instrument, "is the Meridian of Washington."

H

HABEAS CORPUS, *n.* A writ by which a man may be taken out
of jail when confined for the wrong crime.

HABIT, *n.* A shackle for the free.

HADES, *n.* The lower world; the residence of departed spirits;
the place where the dead live.

Among the ancients the idea of Hades was not synonymous with our Hell, many of the most respectable men of
antiquity residing there in a very comfortable kind of way.
Indeed, the Elysian Fields themselves were a part of Hades,
though they have since been removed to Paris. When the
Jacobean version of the New Testament was in process of
evolution the pious and learned men engaged in the work
insisted by a majority vote on translating the Greek word
"Ἀδης" as "Hell"; but a conscientious minority member
secretly possessed himself of the record and struck out the
objectionable word wherever he could find it. At the next
meeting, the Bishop of Salisbury, looking over the work,
suddenly sprang to his feet and said with considerable excitement: "Gentlemen, somebody has been razing 'Hell'
here!" Years afterward the good prelate's death was made
sweet by the reflection that he had been the means (under
Providence) of making an important, serviceable and immortal addition to the phraseology of the English tongue.

HAG, *n.* An elderly lady whom you do not happen to like;
sometimes called, also, a hen, or cat. Old witches, sorcer-
esses, etc., were called hags from the belief that their heads
were surrounded by a kind of baleful lumination or nimbus—hag being the popular name of that peculiar electrical
light sometimes observed in the hair. At one time hag was
not a word of reproach: Drayton speaks of a "beautiful hag,

all smiles," much as Shakespeare said, "sweet wench." It would not now be proper to call your sweetheart a hag—that compliment is reserved for the use of her grandchildren.

HALF, *n.* One of two equal parts into which a thing may be divided, or considered as divided. In the fourteenth century a heated discussion arose among theologists and philosophers as to whether Omniscience could part an object into three halves; and the pious Father Aldrovinus publicly prayed in the cathedral at Rouen that God would demonstrate the affirmative of the proposition in some signal and unmistakable way, and particularly (if it should please Him) upon the body of that hardy blasphemer, Manutius Procinus, who maintained the negative. Procinus, however, was spared to die of the bite of a viper.

HALO, *n.* Properly, a luminous ring encircling an astronomical body, but not infrequently confounded with "aureola," or "nimbus," a somewhat similar phenomenon worn as a headdress by divinities and saints. The halo is a purely optical illusion, produced by moisture in the air, in the manner of a rainbow; but the aureola is conferred as a sign of superior sanctity, in the same way as a bishop's mitre, or the Pope's tiara. In the painting of the Nativity, by Szedgkin, a pious artist of Pesth, not only do the Virgin and the Child wear the nimbus, but an ass nibbling hay from the sacred manger is similarly decorated and, to his lasting honor be it said, appears to bear his unaccustomed dignity with a truly saintly grace.

HAND, *n.* A singular instrument worn at the end of the human arm and commonly thrust into somebody's pocket.

HANDKERCHIEF, *n.* A small square of silk or linen, used in various ignoble offices about the face and especially serviceable at funerals to conceal the lack of tears. The handkerchief is of recent invention; our ancestors knew nothing of it and intrusted its duties to the sleeve. Shakespeare's introducing it into the play of "Othello" is an anachronism: Desdemona dried her nose with her skirt, as Dr. Mary Walker and other reformers have done with their coattails in our own day—an evidence that revolutions sometimes go backward.

HANGMAN, *n*. An officer of the law charged with duties of the highest dignity and utmost gravity, and held in hereditary disesteem by a populace having a criminal ancestry. In some of the American States his functions are now performed by an electrician, as in New Jersey, where executions by electricity have recently been ordered—the first instance known to this lexicographer of anybody questioning the expediency of hanging Jerseymen.

HAPPINESS, *n*. An agreeable sensation arising from contemplating the misery of another.

HARANGUE, *n*. A speech by an opponent, who is known as an harangue-outang.

HARBOR, *n*. A place where ships taking shelter from storms are exposed to the fury of the customs.

HARMONISTS, *n*. A sect of Protestants, now extinct, who came from Europe in the beginning of the last century and were distinguished for the bitterness of their internal controversies and dissensions.

HASH, *x*. There is no definition for this word—nobody knows what hash is.

HATCHET, *n*. A young axe, known among Indians as a Thomashawk.

> "O bury the hatchet, irascible Red,
> For peace is a blessing," the White Man said.
>   The Savage concurred, and that weapon interred,
> With imposing rites, in the White Man's head.
>   *John Lukkus.*

HATRED, *n.* A sentiment appropriate to the occasion of another's superiority.

HEAD-MONEY, *n.* A capitation tax, or poll-tax.

> In ancient times there lived a king
> Whose tax-collectors could not wring
> From all his subjects gold enough
> To make the royal way less rough.
> For pleasure's highway, like the dames
> Whose premises adjoin it, claims
> Perpetual repairing. So
> The tax-collectors in a row
> Appeared before the throne to pray
> Their master to devise some way
> To swell the revenue. "So great,"
> Said they, "are the demands of state
> A tithe of all that we collect
> Will scarcely meet them. Pray reflect:
> How, if one-tenth we must resign,
> Can we exist on t'other nine?"
> The monarch asked them in reply:
> "Has it occurred to you to try
> The advantage of economy?"
> "It has," the spokesman said: "we sold
> All of our gray garrotes of gold;
> With plated-ware we now compress
> The necks of those whom we assess.
> Plain iron forceps we employ
> To mitigate the miser's joy
> Who hoards, with greed that never tires,
> That which your Majesty requires."
> Deep lines of thought were seen to plow
> Their way across the royal brow.
> "Your state is desperate, no question;
> Pray favor me with a suggestion."
> "O King of Men," the spokesman said,
> "If you'll impose upon each head
> A tax, the augmented revenue
> We'll cheerfully divide with you."
> As flashes of the sun illume
> The parted storm-cloud's sullen gloom,

The king smiled grimly. "I decree
That it be so—and, not to be
In generosity outdone,
Declare you, each and every one,
Exempted from the operation
Of this new law of capitation.
But lest the people censure me
Because they're bound and you are free,
'Twere well some clever scheme were laid
By you this poll-tax to evade.
I'll leave you now while you confer
With my most trusted minister."
The monarch from the throne-room walked
And straightway in among them stalked
A silent man, with brow concealed,
Bare-armed—his gleaming axe revealed!

                                        G. J.

HEARSE, *n.* Death's baby-carriage.

HEART, *n.* An automatic, muscular blood-pump. Figuratively, this useful organ is said to be the seat of emotions and sentiments—a very pretty fancy which, however, is nothing but a survival of a once universal belief. It is now known that the sentiments and emotions reside in the stomach, being evolved from food by chemical action of the gastric fluid. The exact process by which a beefsteak becomes a feeling—tender or not, according to the age of the animal from which it was cut; the successive stages of elaboration through which a caviar sandwich is transmuted to a quaint fancy and reappears as a pungent epigram; the marvelous functional methods of converting a hard-boiled egg into religious contrition, or a cream-puff into a sigh of sensibility—these things have been patiently ascertained by M. Pasteur, and by him expounded with convincing lucidity. (See, also, my monograph, *The Essential Identity of the Spiritual Affections and Certain Intestinal Gases Freed in Digestion*—4to, 687 pp.) In a scientific work entitled, I believe, *Delectatio Demonorum* (John Camden Hotton, London, 1873) this view of the sentiments receives a striking illustration; and for further light consult Professor Dam's famous treatise on *Love as a Product of Alimentary Maceration.*

HEAT, *n.*

> Heat, says Professor Tyndall, is a mode
>   Of motion, but I know now how he's proving
> His point; but this I know—hot words bestowed
>   With skill will set the human fist a-moving,
> And where it stops the stars burn free and wild.
> *Crede expertum*—I have seen them, child.
>   *Gorton Swope.*

HEATHEN, *n.* A benighted creature who has the folly to worship something that he can see and feel. According to Professor Howison, of the California State University, Hebrews are heathens.

> "The Hebrews are heathens!" says Howison. He's
>   A Christian philosopher. I'm
> A scurril agnostical chap, if you please,
>   Addicted too much to the crime
>   Of religious discussion in my rhyme.
>
> Though Hebrew and Howison cannot agree
>   On a *modus vivendi*—not they!—
> Yet Heaven has had the designing of me,
>   And I haven't been reared in a way
>   To joy in the thick of the fray.
>
> For this of my creed is the soul and the gist,
>   And the truth of it I aver:
> Who differs from me in his faith is an 'ist,
>   And 'ite, an 'ic, or an 'er—
>   And I'm down upon him or her!
>
> Let Howison urge with perfunctory chin
>   Toleration—that's all very well,
> But a roast is "nuts" to his nostril thin,
>   And he's running—I know by the smell—
>   A secret and personal Hell!
>   *Bissell Gip.*

HEAVEN, *n.* A place where the wicked cease from troubling

you with talk of their personal affairs, and the good listen with attention while you expound your own.

HEBREW, *n.* A male Jew, as distinguished from the Shebrew, an altogether superior creation.

HELPMATE, *n.* A wife, or bitter half.

> "Now, why is yer wife called a helpmate, Pat?"
>   Says the priest. "Since the time o' yer wooin'
> She's niver assisted in what ye were at—
>   For it's naught ye are ever doin'."
>
> "That's true of yer Riverence," Patrick replies,
>   And no sign of contrition envinces;
> "But, bedad, it's a fact which the word implies,
>   For she helps to mate the expinses!"
>   *Marley Wottel.*

HEMP, *n.* A plant from whose fibrous bark is made an article of neckwear which is frequently put on after public speaking in the open air and prevents the wearer from taking cold.

HERMIT, *n.* A person whose vices and follies are not sociable.

HERS, *pron.* His.

HIBERNATE, *v. i.* To pass the winter season in domestic seclusion. There have been many singular popular notions about the hibernation of various animals. Many believe that the bear hibernates during the whole winter and subsists by mechanically sucking its paws. It is admitted that it comes out of its retirement in the spring so lean that it has to try twice before it can cast a shadow. Three or four centuries ago, in England, no fact was better attested than that swallows passed the winter months in the mud at the bottom of the brooks, clinging together in globular masses. They have apparently been compelled to give up the custom on account of the foulness of the brooks. Sotus Escobius discovered in Central Asia a whole nation of people who hibernate. By some investigators, the fasting of Lent is supposed to have been originally a modified form of hibernation, to which the Church gave a religious significance; but this view was strenuously opposed by that eminent authority, Bishop Kip, who did not wish any honors denied to the memory of the Founder of his family.

HIPPOGRIFF, *n*. An animal (now extinct) which was half horse and half griffin. The griffin was itself a compound creature, half lion and half eagle. The hippogriff was actually, therefore, only one-quarter eagle, which is two dollars and fifty cents in gold. The study of zoology is full of surprises.

HISTORIAN, *n*. A broad-gauge gossip.

HISTORY, *n*. An account mostly false, of events mostly unimportant, which are brought about by rulers mostly knaves, and soldiers mostly fools.

> Of Roman history, great Niebuhr's shown
> 'Tis nine-tenths lying. Faith, I wish 'twere known,
> Ere we accept great Niebuhr as a guide,
> Wherein he blundered and how much he lied.
> *Salder Bupp.*

HOG, *n*. A bird remarkable for the catholicity of its appetite and serving to illustrate that of ours. Among the Mahometans and Jews, the hog is not in favor as an article of diet, but is respected for the delicacy of its habits, the beauty of its plumage and the melody of its voice. It is chiefly as a songster that the fowl is esteemed; a cage of him in full chorus has been known to draw tears from two persons at once. The scientific name of this dicky-bird is *Porcus Rockefelleri*. Mr. Rockefeller did not discover the hog, but it is considered his by right of resemblance.

HOMICIDE, *n*. The slaying of one human being by another. There are four kinds of homicide: felonious, excusable, justifiable, and praiseworthy, but it makes no great difference to the person slain whether he fell by one kind or another—the classification is for advantage of the lawyers.

HOMILETICS, *n.* The science of adapting sermons to the spiritual needs, capacities and conditions of the congregation.

> So skilled the parson was in homiletics
> That all his moral purges and emetics
> To medicine the spirit were compounded
> With a most just discrimination founded
> Upon a rigorous examination
> Of tongue and pulse and heart and respiration.
> Then, having diagnosed each one's condition,
> His scriptural specifics this physician
> Administered—his pills so efficacious
> And pukes of disposition so vivacious
> That souls afflicted with ten kinds of Adam
> Were convalescent ere they knew they had 'em.
> But Slander's tongue—itself all coated—uttered
> Her bilious mind and scandalously muttered
> That in the case of patients having money
> The pills were sugar and the pukes were honey.
> *Biography of Bishop Potter.*

HOMŒOPATHIST, *n.* The humorist of the medical profession.

HOMŒOPATHY, *n.* A school of medicine midway between Allopathy and Christian Science. To the last both the others are distinctly inferior, for Christian Science will cure imaginary diseases, and they can not.

HONORABLE, *adj.* Afflicted with an impediment in one's reach. In legislative bodies it is customary to mention all members as honorable; as, "the honorable gentleman is a scurvy cur."

HOPE, *n.* Desire and expectation rolled into one.

> Delicious Hope! when naught to man is left—
> Of fortune destitute, of friends bereft;
> When even his dog deserts him, and his goat
> With tranquil disaffection chews his coat
> While yet it hangs upon his back; then thou,
> The star far-flaming on thine angel brow,
> Descendest, radiant, from the skies to hint
> The promise of a clerkship in the Mint.
> *Fogarty Weffing.*

HOSPITALITY, *n.* The virtue which induces us to feed and lodge certain persons who are not in need of food and lodging.

HOSTILITY, *n.* A peculiarly sharp and specially applied sense of the earth's overpopulation. Hostility is classed as active and passive; as (respectively) the feeling of a woman for her female friends, and that which she entertains for all the rest of her sex.

HOURI, *n.* A comely female inhabiting the Mohammedan Paradise to make things cheery for the good Mussulman, whose belief in her existence marks a noble discontent with his earthly spouse, whom he denies a soul. By that good lady the Houris are said to be held in deficient esteem.

HOUSE, *n.* A hollow edifice erected for the habitation of man, rat, mouse, beetle, cockroach, fly, mosquito, flea, bacillus and microbe. *House of Correction*, a place of reward for political and personal service, and for the detention of offenders and appropriations. *House of God*, a building with a steeple and a mortgage on it. *House-dog*, a pestilent beast kept on domestic premises to insult persons passing by and appal the hardy visitor. *House-maid*, a youngerly person of the opposing sex employed to be variously disagreeable and ingeniously unclean in the station in which it has pleased God to place her.

HOUSELESS, *adj.* Having paid all taxes on household goods.

HOVEL, *n.* The fruit of a flower called the Palace.

> Twaddle had a hovel,
>   Twiddle had a palace;
>   Twaddle said: "I'll grovel
>   Or he'll think I bear him malice"—
> A sentiment as novel
>   As a castor on a chalice.
>
>   Down upon the middle
>   Of his legs fell Twaddle
>   And astonished Mr. Twiddle,
>   Who began to lift his noddle.

> Feed upon the fiddle-
> Faddle flummery, unswaddle
> A new-born self-sufficiency and think himself a model.
> > *G. J.*

HUMANITY, *n.* The human race, collectively, exclusive of the anthropoid poets.

HUMORIST, *n.* A plague that would have softened down the hoar austerity of Pharaoh's heart and persuaded him to dismiss Israel with his best wishes, cat-quick.

> Lo! the poor humorist, whose tortured mind
> See jokes in crowds, though still to gloom inclined—
> Whose simple appetite, untaught to stray,
> His brains, renewed by night, consumes by day.
> He thinks, admitted to an equal sty,
> A graceful hog would bear his company.
> > *Alexander Poke.*

HURRICANE, *n.* An atmospheric demonstration once very common but now generally abandoned for the tornado and cyclone. The hurricane is still in popular use in the West Indies and is preferred by certain old-fashioned sea-captains. It is also used in the construction of the upper decks of steamboats, but generally speaking, the hurricane's usefulness has outlasted it.

HURRY, *n.* The dispatch of bunglers.

HUSBAND, *n.* One who, having dined, is charged with the care of the plate.

HYBRID, *n.* A pooled issue.

HYDRA, *n.* A kind of animal that the ancients catalogued under many heads.

HYENA, *n.* A beast held in reverence by some oriental nations from its habit of frequenting at night the burial-places of the dead. But the medical student does that.

HYPOCHONDRIASIS, *n.* Depression of one's own spirits.

> Some heaps of trash upon a vacant lot
> Where long the village rubbish had been shot
> Displayed a sign among the stuff and stumps—
> "Hypochondriasis." It meant The Dumps.
> *Bogul S. Purvy.*

HYPOCRITE, *n.* One who, professing virtues that he does not respect, secures the advantage of seeming to be what he depises.

I

I is the first letter of the alphabet, the first word of the language, the first thought of the mind, the first object of affection. In grammar it is a pronoun of the first person and singular number. Its plural is said to be *We*, but how there can be more than one myself is doubtless clearer to the grammarians than it is to the author of this incomparable dictionary. Conception of two myselves is difficult, but fine. The frank yet graceful use of "I" distinguishes a good writer from a bad; the latter carries it with the manner of a thief trying to cloak his loot.

ICHOR, *n.* A fluid that serves the gods and goddesses in place of blood.

> Fair Venus, speared by Diomed,
> Restrained the raging chief and said:
> "Behold, rash mortal, whom you've bled—
> Your soul's stained white with ichorshed!"
> *Mary Doke.*

ICONOCLAST, *n.* A breaker of idols, the worshipers whereof are imperfectly gratified by the performance, and most strenuously protest that he unbuildeth but doth not reëdify, that he pulleth down but pileth not up. For the poor things would have other idols in place of those he thwacketh upon the mazzard and dispelleth. But the iconoclast saith: "Ye shall have none at all, for ye need them not; and if the rebuilder fooleth round hereabout, behold I will depress the head of him and sit thereon till he squawk it."

IDIOT, *n.* A member of a large and powerful tribe whose influence in human affairs has always been dominant and controlling. The Idiot's activity is not confined to any special field of thought or action, but "pervades and regulates the whole." He has the last word in everything; his decision is unappealable. He sets the fashions of opinion and taste, dictates the limitations of speech and circumscribes conduct with a dead-line.

IDLENESS, *n.* A model farm where the devil experiments with seeds of new sins and promotes the growth of staple vices.

IGNORAMUS, *n.* A person unacquainted with certain kinds of knowledge familiar to yourself, and having certain other kinds that you know nothing about.

> Dumble was an ignoramus,
> Mumble was for learning famous.
> Mumble said one day to Dumble:
> "Ignorance should be more humble.
> Not a spark have you of knowledge
> That was got in any college."
> Dumble said to Mumble: "Truly
> You're self-satisfied unduly.
> Of things in college I'm denied
> A knowledge—you of all beside."
> *Borelli.*

ILLUMINATI, *n.* A sect of Spanish heretics of the latter part of the sixteenth century; so called because they were light weights—*cunctationes illuminati.*

ILLUSTRIOUS, *adj.* Suitably placed for the shafts of malice, envy and detraction.

IMAGINATION, *n.* A warehouse of facts, with poet and liar in joint ownership.

IMBECILITY, *n.* A kind of divine inspiration, or sacred fire affecting censorious critics of this dictionary.

IMMIGRANT, *n.* An unenlightened person who thinks one country better than another.

IMMODEST, *adj.* Having a strong sense of one's own merit, coupled with a feeble conception of worth in others.

> There was once a man in Ispahan
>   Ever and ever so long ago,
> And he had a head, the phrenologists said,
>   That fitted him for a show.
>
> For his modesty's bump was so large a lump
>   (Nature, they said, had taken a freak)
> That its summit stood far above the wood
>   Of his hair, like a mountain peak.
>
> So modest a man in all Ispahan,
>   Over and over again they swore—
> So humble and meek, you would vainly seek;
>   None ever was found before.
>
> Meantime the hump of that awful bump
>   Into the heavens contrived to get
> To so great a height that they called the wight
>   The man with a minaret.
>
> There wasn't a man in all Ispahan
>   Prouder, or louder in praise of his chump:
> With a tireless tongue and a brazen lung
>   He bragged of that beautiful bump
>
> Till the Shah in a rage sent a trusty page
>   Bearing a sack and a bow-string too,
> And that gentle child explained as he smiled:
>   "A little present for you."
>
> The saddest man in all Ispahan,
>   Sniffed at the gift, yet accepted the same.
> "If I'd lived," said he, "my humility
>   Had given me deathless fame!"
>   *Sukker Uffro.*

IMMORAL, *adj.* Inexpedient. Whatever in the long run and with regard to the greater number of instances men find to be generally inexpedient comes to be considered wrong, wicked, immoral. If man's notions of right and wrong have any other basis than this of expediency; if they originated, or could have originated, in any other way; if actions have in themselves a moral character apart from, and nowise dependent on, their consequences—then all philosophy is a lie and reason a disorder of the mind.

IMMORTALITY, *n.*

> A toy which people cry for,
> And on their knees apply for,
> Dispute, contend and lie for,
>   And if allowed
>   Would be right proud
> Eternally to die for.
>   *G. J.*

IMPALE, *v. t.* In popular usage to pierce with any weapon which remains fixed in the wound. This, however, is inaccurate; to impale is, properly, to put to death by thrusting an upright sharp stake into the body, the victim being left in a sitting posture. This was a common mode of punishment among many of the nations of antiquity, and is still in high favor in China and other parts of Asia. Down to the beginning of the fifteenth century it was widely employed in "churching" heretics and schismatics. Wolecraft calls it the "stoole of re-pentynge," and among the common people it was jocularly known as "riding the one legged horse." Ludwig Salzmann informs us that in Thibet impalement is considered the most appropriate punishment for crimes against religion; and although in China it is sometimes awarded for secular offences, it is most frequently adjudged in cases of sacrilege. To the person in actual experience of impalement it must be a matter of minor importance by what kind of civil or religious dissent he was made acquainted with its discomforts; but doubtless he would feel a certain satisfaction if able to contemplate himself in the character of a weather-cock on the spire of the True Church.

IMPARTIAL, *adj.* Unable to perceive any promise of personal advantage from espousing either side of a controversy or adopting either of two conflicting opinions.

IMPENITENCE, *n.* A state of mind intermediate in point of time between sin and punishment.

IMPIETY, *n.* Your irreverence toward my deity.

IMPOSITION, *n.* The act of blessing or consecrating by the laying on of hands—a ceremony common to many ecclesiastical systems, but performed with the frankest sincerity by the sect known as Thieves.

> "Lo! by the laying on of hands,"
>   Say parson, priest and dervise,
> "We consecrate your cash and lands
>   To ecclesiastic service.
> No doubt you'll swear till all is blue
> At such an imposition. Do."
>   *Pollo Doncas.*

IMPOSTOR, *n.* A rival aspirant to public honors.

IMPROBABILITY, *n.*

> His tale he told with a solemn face
> And a tender, melancholy grace.
>   Improbable 'twas, no doubt,
>   When you came to think it out,
>   But the fascinated crowd
>   Their deep surprise avowed
> And all with a single voice averred
> 'Twas the most amazing thing they'd heard—
> All save one who spake never a word,
>   But sat as mum
>   As if deaf and dumb,
> Serene, indifferent and unstirred.
>   Then all the others turned to him
>   And scrutinized him limb from limb—
>   Scanned him alive;
>   But he seemed to thrive

And tranquiler grow each minute,
    As if there were nothing in it.
"What! what!" cried one, "are you not amazed
At what our friend has told?" He raised
Soberly then his eyes and gazed
        In a natural way
        And proceeded to say,
As he crossed his feet on the mantel-shelf:
"O no—not at all; I'm a liar myself."

IMPROVIDENCE, *n.* Provision for the needs of to-day from the revenues of to-morrow.

IMPUNITY, *n.* Wealth.

INADMISSIBLE, *adj.* Not competent to be considered. Said of certain kinds of testimony which juries are supposed to be unfit to be entrusted with, and which judges, therefore, rule out, even of proceedings before themselves alone. Hearsay evidence is inadmissible because the person quoted was unsworn and is not before the court for examination; yet most momentous actions, military, political, commercial and of every other kind, are daily undertaken on hearsay evidence. There is no religion in the world that has any other basis than hearsay evidence. Revelation is hearsay evidence; that the Scriptures are the word of God we have only the testimony of men long dead whose identity is not clearly established and who are not known to have been sworn in any sense. Under the rules of evidence as they now exist in this country, no single assertion in the Bible has in its support any evidence admissible in a court of law. It cannot be proved that the battle of Blenheim ever was fought, that there was such a person as Julius Caesar, such an empire as Assyria.

But as records of courts of justice are admissible, it can easily be proved that powerful and malevolent magicians once existed and were a scourge to mankind. The evidence (including confession) upon which certain women were convicted of witchcraft and executed was without a flaw; it is still unimpeachable. The judges' decisions based on it were sound in logic and in law. Nothing in any existing court was ever more thoroughly proved than the charges of witchcraft and sorcery for which so many suffered death. If there were no witches, human testimony and human reason are alike destitute of value.

IN'ARDS, *n.* The stomach, heart, soul and other bowels. Many eminent investigators do not class the soul as an in'ard, but that acute observer and renowned authority, Dr. Gunsaulus, is persuaded that the mysterious organ known as the spleen is nothing less than our immortal part. To the contrary, Professor Garrett P. Servis holds that man's soul is that prolongation of his spinal marrow which forms the pith of his no tail; and for demonstration of his faith points confidently to the fact that tailed animals have no souls. Concerning these two theories, it is best to suspend judgment by believing both.

INAUSPICIOUSLY, *adv.* In an unpromising manner, the auspices being unfavorable. Among the Romans it was customary before undertaking any important action or enterprise to obtain from the augurs, or state prophets, some hint of its probable outcome; and one of their favorite and most trustworthy modes of divination consisted in observing the flight of birds—the omens thence derived being called *auspices.* Newspaper reporters and certain miscreant lexicographers have decided that the word—always in the plural—shall mean "patronage" or "management"; as, "The festivities were under the auspices of the Ancient and Honorable Order of Body-Snatchers"; or, "The hilarities were auspicated by the Knights of Hunger."

> A Roman slave appeared one day
> Before the Augur. "Tell me, pray,
> If—" here the Augur, smiling, made
> A checking gesture and displayed
> His open palm, which plainly itched,
> For visibly its surface twitched.
> A *denarius* (the Latin nickel)
> Successfully allayed the tickle,
> And then the slave proceeded: "Please
> Inform me whether Fate decrees

Success or failure in what I
To-night (if it be dark) shall try.
Its nature? Never mind—I think
'Tis writ on this"—and with a wink
Which darkened half the earth, he drew
Another denarius to view,
Its shining face attentive scanned,
Then slipped it into the good man's hand,
Who with great gravity said: "Wait
While I retire to question Fate."
That holy person then withdrew
His sacred clay and, passing through
The temple's rearward gate, cried "Shoo!"
Waving his robe of office. Straight
Each sacred peacock and its mate
(Maintained for Juno's favor) fled
With clamor from the trees o'erhead,
Where they were perching for the night.
The temple's roof received their flight,
For thither they would always go,
When danger threatened them below.
Back to the slave the Augur went:
"My son, forecasting the event
By flight of birds, I must confess
The auspices deny success."
That slave retired, a sadder man,
Abandoning his secret plan—
Which was (as well the crafty seer
Had from the first divined) to clear
The wall and fraudulently seize
On Juno's poultry in the trees.

G. J.

INCOME, *n.* The natural and rational gauge and measure of
respectability, the commonly accepted standards being artificial, arbitrary and fallacious; for, as "Sir Sycophas Chryso-
later" in the play has justly remarked, "the true use and
function of property (in whatsoever it consisteth—coins, or
land, or houses, or merchant-stuff, or anything which may be
named as holden of right to one's own subservience) as also
of honors, titles, preferments and place, and all favor and acquaintance of persons of quality or ableness, are but to get

money. Hence it followeth that all things are truly to be rated as of worth in measure of their serviceableness to that end; and their possessors should take rank in agreement thereto, neither the lord of an unproducing manor, howsoever broad and ancient, nor he who bears an unremunerate dignity, nor yet the pauper favorite of a king, being esteemed of level excellency with him whose riches are of daily accretion; and hardly should they whose wealth is barren claim and rightly take more honor than the poor and unworthy."

INCOMPATIBILITY, *n.* In matrimony a similarity of tastes, particularly the taste for domination. Incompatibility may, however, consist of a meek-eyed matron living just around the corner. It has even been known to wear a moustache.

INCOMPOSSIBLE, *adj.* Unable to exist if something else exists. Two things are incompossible when the world of being has scope enough for one of them, but not enough for both—as Walt Whitman's poetry and God's mercy to man. Incompossibility, it will be seen, is only incompatibility let loose. Instead of such low language as "Go heel yourself—I mean to kill you on sight," the words, "Sir, we are incompossible," would convey an equally significant intimation and in stately courtesy are altogether superior.

INCUBUS, *n.* One of a race of highly improper demons who, though probably not wholly extinct, may be said to have seen their best nights. For a complete account of *incubi* and *succubi*, including *incubæ*, and *succubæ*, see the *Liber Demonorum* of Protassus (Paris, 1328), which contains much curious information that would be out of place in a dictionary intended as a text-book for the public schools.

Victor Hugo relates that in the Channel Islands Satan himself—tempted more than elsewhere by the beauty of the women, doubtless—sometimes plays at *incubus*, greatly to the inconvenience and alarm of the good dames who wish to be loyal to their marriage vows, generally speaking. A certain lady applied to the parish priest to learn how they might, in the dark, distinguish the hardy intruder from their husbands.

The holy man said they must feel his brow for horns; but Hugo is ungallant enough to hint a doubt of the efficacy of the test.

INCUMBENT, *n.* A person of the liveliest interest to the out-cumbents.

INDECISION, *n.* The chief element of success; "for whereas," saith Sir Thomas Brewbold, "there is but one way to do nothing and divers way to do something, whereof, to a surety, only one is the right way, it followeth that he who from indecision standeth still hath not so many chances of going astray as he who pusheth forwards"—a most clear and satisfactory exposition of the matter.

"Your prompt decision to attack," said General Grant on a certain occasion to General Gordon Granger, "was admirable; you had but five minutes to make up your mind in."

"Yes, sir," answered the victorious subordinate, "it is a great thing to know exactly what to do in an emergency. When in doubt whether to attack or retreat I never hesitate a moment—I toss us a copper."

"Do you mean to say that's what you did this time?"

"Yes, General; but for Heaven's sake don't reprimand me: I disobeyed the coin."

INDIFFERENT, *adj.* Imperfectly sensible to distinctions among things.

> "You tiresome man!" cried Indolentio's wife,
> "You've grown indifferent to all in life."
> "Indifferent?" he drawled with a slow smile;
> "I would be, dear, but it is not worth while."
> *Apuleius M. Gokul.*

INDIGESTION, *n.* A disease which the patient and his friends frequently mistake for deep religious conviction and concern for the salvation of mankind. As the simple Red Man of the western wild put it, with, it must be confessed, a certain force: "Plenty well, no pray; big bellyache, heap God."

INDISCRETION, *n.* The guilt of woman.

INEXPEDIENT, *adj.* Not calculated to advance one's interests.

INFANCY, *n.* The period of our lives when, according to Wordsworth, "Heaven lies about us." The world begins lying about us pretty soon afterward.

INFERIÆ, *n.* (Latin.) Among the Greeks and Romans, sacrifices for propitation of the *Dii Manes*, or souls of the dead heroes; for the pious ancients could not invent enough gods to satisfy their spiritual needs, and had to have a number of makeshift deities, or, as a sailor might say, jury-gods, which they made out of the most unpromising materials. It was while sacrificing a bullock to the spirit of Agamemnon that Laiaides, a priest of Aulis, was favored with an audience of that illustrious warrior's shade, who prophetically recounted to him the birth of Christ and the triumph of Christianity, giving him also a rapid but tolerably complete review of events down to the reign of Saint Louis. The narrative ended abruptly at that point, owing to the inconsiderate crowing of a cock, which compelled the ghosted King of Men to scamper back to Hades. There is a fine mediæval flavor to this story, and as it has not been traced back further than Père Brateille, a pious but obscure writer at the court of Saint Louis, we shall probably not err on the side of presumption in considering it apocryphal, though Monsignor Capel's judgment of the matter might be different; and to that I bow—wow.

INFIDEL, *n.* In New York, one who does not believe in the Christian religion; in Constantinople, one who does. (See GIAOUR.) A kind of scoundrel imperfectly reverent of, and niggardly contributory to, divines, ecclesiastics, popes, parsons, canons, monks, mollahs, voodoos, presbyters, hierophants, prelates, obeah-men, abbés, nuns, missionaries, exhorters, deacons, friars, hadjis, high-priests, muezzins, brahmins, medicine-men, confessors, eminences, elders, primates, prebendaries, pilgrims, prophets, imaums, beneficiaries, clerks, vicars-choral, archbishops, bishops, abbots, priors, preachers, padres, abbotesses, caloyers, palmers, curates, patriarchs, bonezs, santons, beadsmen, canonesses, residentiaries, diocesans, deans, subdeans, rural deans, abdals, charm-sellers, archdeacons, hierarchs, class-leaders, incumbents, capitulars, sheiks, talapoins, postulants, scribes, gooroos, precentors, beadles, fakeers, sextons, reverences, revivalists, cenobites, perpetual curates, chaplains, mudjoes, readers, novices, vicars, pastors, rabbis, ulemas, lamas, sacristans, vergers, dervises, lectors, church wardens, cardinals, prioresses, suffragans, acolytes, rectors, curés, sophis, mutifs and pumpums.

INFLUENCE, *n.* In politics, a visionary *quo* given in exchange for a substantial *quid*.

INFRALAPSARIAN, *n.* One who ventures to believe that Adam need not have sinned unless he had a mind to—in opposition to the Supralapsarians, who hold that that luckless person's fall was decreed from the beginning. Infralapsarians are sometimes called Sublapsarians without material effect upon the importance and lucidity of their views about Adam.

> Two theologues once, as they wended their way
> To chapel, engaged in colloquial fray—
> An earnest logomachy, bitter as gall,
> Concerning poor Adam and what made him fall.
> "'Twas Predestination," cried one—"for the Lord
> Decreed he should fall of his own accord."
> "Not so—'twas Free will," the other maintained,
> "Which led him to choose what the Lord had ordained."
> So fierce and so fiery grew the debate
> That nothing but bloodshed their dudgeon could sate;
> So off flew their cassocks and caps to the ground
> And, moved by the spirit, their hands went round.
> Ere either had proved his theology right
> By winning, or even beginning, the fight,
> A gray old professor of Latin came by,
> A staff in his hand and a scowl in his eye,
> And learning the cause of their quarrel (for still
> As they clumsily sparred they disputed with skill
> Of foreordinational freedom of will)

Cried: "Sirrahs! this reasonless warfare compose:
Atwixt ye's no difference worthy of blows.
The sects ye belong to—I'm ready to swear
Ye wrongly interpret the names that they bear.
You—Infralapsarian son of a clown!—
Should only contend that Adam slipped down;
While *you*—you Supralapsarian pup!—
Should nothing aver but that Adam slipped up."
It's all the same whether up or down
You slip on a peel of banana brown.
Even Adam analyzed not his blunder,
But thought he had slipped on a peal of thunder!

G. J.

INGRATE, *n.* One who receives a benefit from another, or is otherwise an object of charity.

"All men are ingrates," sneered the cynic. "Nay,"
    The good philanthropist replied;
"I did great service to a man one day
Who never since has cursed me to repay,
    Nor vilified."

"Ho!" cried the cynic, "lead me to him straight—
    With veneration I am overcome,
And fain would have his blessing." "Sad your fate—
He cannot bless you, for I grieve to state
    The man is dumb."

Ariel Selp.

INJURY, *n.* An offense next in degree of enormity to a slight.

INJUSTICE, *n.* A burden which of all those that we load upon others and carry ourselves is lightest in the hands and heaviest upon the back.

INK, *n.* A villainous compound of tannogallate of iron, gum-arabic and water, chiefly used to facilitate the infection of idiocy and promote intellectual crime. The properties of ink are peculiar and contradictory: it may be used to make reputations and unmake them; to blacken them and to make them white; but it is most generally and acceptably employed as a mortar to bind together the stones of an edifice of fame, and as a whitewash to conceal afterward the rascal quality of the material. There are men called journalists who have established ink baths which some persons pay money to get into, others to get out of. Not infrequently it occurs that a person who has paid to get in pays twice as much to get out.

INNATE, *adj.* Natural, inherent—as innate ideas, that is to say, ideas that we are born with, having had them previously imparted to us. The doctrine of innate ideas is one of the most admirable faiths of philosophy, being itself an innate idea and therefore inaccessible to disproof, though Locke foolishly supposed himself to have given it "a black eye." Among innate ideas may be mentioned the belief in one's ability to conduct a newspaper, in the greatness of one's country, in the superiority of one's civilization, in the importance of one's personal affairs and in the interesting nature of one's diseases.

INSCRIPTION, *n.* Something written on another thing. Inscriptions are of many kinds, but mostly memorial, intended to commemorate the fame of some illustrious person and hand down to distant ages the record of his services and virtues. To this class of inscriptions belongs the name of John Smith, penciled on the Washington monument. Following are examples of memorial inscriptions on tombstones: (See EPITAPH.)

> "In the sky my soul is found,
> And my body in the ground.
> By and by my body'll rise
> To my spirit in the skies,
> Soaring up to Heaven's gate.
> 1878."

"Sacred to the memory of Jeremiah Tree. Cut down May 9th, 1862, aged 27 yrs. 4 mos. and 12 ds. Indigenous."

> "Affliction sore long time she boar,
> Phisicians was in vain,

Till Deth released the dear deceased
And left her a remain.
Gone to join Ananias in the regions of bliss."

"The clay that rests beneath this stone
As Silas Wood was widely known.
Now, lying here, I ask what good
It was to me to be S. Wood.
O Man, let not ambition trouble you,
Is the advice of Silas W."

"Richard Haymon, of Heaven. Fell to Earth Jan. 20, 1807, and had the dust brushed off him Oct. 3, 1874."

INSECTIVORA, *n.*

"See," cries the chorus of admiring preachers,
"How Providence provides for all His creatures!"
"His care," the gnat said, "even the insects follows:
For us He has provided wrens and swallows."
Sempen Railey.

INSURANCE, *n.* An ingenious modern game of chance in which the player is permitted to enjoy the comfortable conviction that he is beating the man who keeps the table.

INSURANCE AGENT: My dear sir, that is a fine house—pray let me insure it.

HOUSE OWNER: With pleasure. Please make the annual premium so low that by the time when, according to the tables of your actuary, it will probably be destroyed by fire I will have paid you considerably less than the face of the policy.

INSURANCE AGENT: O dear, no—we could not afford to do that. We must fix the premium so that you will have paid more.

HOUSE OWNER: How, then, can *I* afford *that*?

INSURANCE AGENT: Why, your house may burn down at any time. There was Smith's house, for example, which—

HOUSE OWNER: Spare me—there were Brown's house, on the contrary, and Jones's house, and Robinson's house, which—

INSURANCE AGENT: Spare *me!*

HOUSE OWNER: Let us understand each other. You want me to pay you money on the supposition that something will occur previously to the time set by yourself for its occurrence. In other words, you expect me to bet that my house will not last so long as you say that it will probably last.

INSURANCE AGENT: But if your house burns without insurance it will be a total loss.

HOUSE OWNER: Beg your pardon—by your own actuary's tables I shall probably have saved, when it burns, all the premiums I would otherwise have paid to you—amounting to more than the face of the policy they would have bought. But suppose it to burn, uninsured, before the time upon which your figures are based. If I could not afford that, how could you if it were insured?

INSURANCE AGENT: O, we should make ourselves whole from our luckier ventures with other clients. Virtually, they pay your loss.

HOUSE OWNER: And virtually, then, don't I help to pay their losses? Are not their houses as likely as mine to burn before they have paid you as much as you must pay them? The case stands this way: you expect to take more money from your clients than you pay to them, do you not?

INSURANCE AGENT: Certainly; if we did not—

HOUSE OWNER: I would not trust you with my money. Very well, then. If it is *certain*, with reference to the whole body of your clients, that they lose money on you it is *probable*, with reference to any one of them, that *he* will. It is these individual probabilities that make the aggregate certainty.

INSURANCE AGENT: I will not deny it—but look at the figures in this pamph—

HOUSE OWNER: Heaven forbid!

INSURANCE AGENT: You spoke of saving the premiums which you would otherwise pay to me. Will you not be more likely to squander them? We offer you an incentive to thrift.

HOUSE OWNER: The willingness of A to take care of B's money is not peculiar to insurance, but as a charitable institution you command esteem. Deign to accept its expression from a Deserving Object.

INSURRECTION, *n.* An unsuccessful revolution. Disaffection's failure to substitute misrule for bad government.

INTENTION, *n.* The mind's sense of the prevalence of one set of influences over another set; an effect whose cause is the imminence, immediate or remote, of the performance of an involuntary act.

INTERPRETER, *n.* One who enables two persons of different languages to understand each other by repeating to each what it would have been to the interpreter's advantage for the other to have said.

INTERREGNUM, *n.* The period during which a monarchical country is governed by a warm spot on the cushion of the throne. The experiment of letting the spot grow cold has commonly been attended by most unhappy results from the zeal of many worthy persons to make it warm again.

INTIMACY, *n.* A relation into which fools are providentially drawn for their mutual destruction.

> Two Seidlitz powders, one in blue
> And one in white, together drew,
> And having each a pleasant sense
> Of t'other powder's excellence,
> Forsook their jackets for the snug
> Enjoyment of a common mug.
> So close their intimacy grew
> One paper would have held the two.
> To confidences straight they fell,
> Less anxious each to hear than tell;
> Then each remorsefully confessed
> To all the virtues he possessed,
> Acknowledging he had them in
> So high degree it was a sin.
> The more they said, the more they felt
> Their spirits with emotion melt,
> Till tears of sentiment expressed
> Their feelings. Then they effervesced!
> So Nature executes her feats
> Of wrath on friends and sympathetes
> The good old rule who won't apply,
> That you are you and I am I.

INTRODUCTION, *n.* A social ceremony invented by the devil for the gratification of his servants and the plaguing of his enemies. The introduction attains its most malevolent development in this country, being, indeed, closely related to our political system. Every American being the equal of every other American, it follows that everybody has the right to know everybody else, which implies the right to introduce without request or permission. The Declaration of Independence should have read thus:

"We hold these truths to be self-evident: that all men are created equal; that they are endowed by their Creator with certain inalienable rights; that among these are life, and the right to make that of another miserable by thrusting upon him an incalculable quantity of acquaintances; liberty, particularly the liberty to introduce persons to one another without first ascertaining if they are not already acquainted as enemies; and the pursuit of another's happiness with a running pack of strangers."

INVENTOR, *n.* A person who makes an ingenious arrangement of wheels, levers and springs, and believes it civilization.

IRRELIGION, *n.* The principal one of the great faiths of the world.

ITCH, *n.* The patriotism of a Scotchman.

J

J is a consonant in English, but some nations use it as a vowel—than which nothing could be more absurd. Its original form, which has been but slightly modified, was that of the tail of a subdued dog, and it was not a letter but a character, standing for a Latin verb, *jacere*, "to throw," because when a stone is thrown at a dog the dog's tail assumes that shape. This is the origin of the letter, as expounded by the renowned Dr. Jocolpus Bumer, of the University of Belgrade, who established his conclusions on the subject in a work of three quarto volumes and committed suicide on being reminded that the j in the Roman alphabet had originally no curl.

JEALOUS, *adj.* Unduly concerned about the preservation of that which can be lost only if not worth keeping.

JESTER, *n.* An officer formerly attached to a king's household, whose business it was to amuse the court by ludicrous actions and utterances, the absurdity being attested by his motley costume. The king himself being attired with dignity, it took the world some centuries to discover that his own conduct and decrees were sufficiently ridiculous for the amusement not only of his court but of all mankind. The jester was commonly called a fool, but the poets and romancers have ever delighted to represent him as a singularly wise and witty person. In the circus of to-day the melancholy ghost of the court fool effects the dejection of humbler audiences with the same jests wherewith in life he gloomed the marble hall, panged the patrician sense of humor and tapped the tank of royal tears.

> The widow-queen of Portugal
>   Had an audacious jester
> Who entered the confessional
>   Disguised, and there confessed her.
>
> "Father," she said, "thine ear bend down—
>   My sins are more than scarlet:
> I love my fool—blaspheming clown,
>   And common, base-born varlet."
>
> "Daughter," the mimic priest replied,
>   "That sin, indeed, is awful:
> The church's pardon is denied
>   To love that is unlawful.
>
> "But since thy stubborn heart will be
>   For him forever pleading,
> Thou'dst better make him, by decree,
>   A man of birth and breeding."
>
> She made the fool a duke, in hope
>   With Heaven's taboo to palter;
> Then told a priest, who told the Pope,
>   Who damned her from the altar!
>   *Barel Dort.*

JEWS-HARP, *n.* An unmusical instrument, played by holding it fast with the teeth and trying to brush it away with the finger.

JOSS-STICKS, *n.* Small sticks burned by the Chinese in their pagan tomfoolery, in imitation of certain sacred rites of our holy religion.

JUSTICE, *n.* A commodity which in a more or less adulterated condition the State sells to the citizen as a reward for his allegiance, taxes and personal service.

K

K is a consonant that we get from the Greeks, but it can be traced away back beyond them to the Cerathians, a small commercial nation inhabiting the peninsula of Smero. In their tongue it was called *Klatch*, which means "destroyed." The form of the letter was originally precisely that of our H, but the erudite Dr. Snedeker explains that it was altered to its present shape to commemorate the destruction of the great temple of Jarute by an earthquake, *circa* 730 B.C. This building was famous for the two lofty columns of its portico, one of which was broken in half by the catastrophe, the other remaining intact. As the earlier form of the letter is supposed to have been suggested by these pillars, so, it is thought by the great antiquary, its later was adopted as a simple and natural—not to say touching—means of keeping the calamity ever in the national memory. It is not known if the name of the letter was altered as an additional mnemonic, or if the name was always *Klatch* and the destruction one of nature's puns. As each theory seems probable enough, I see no objection to believing both—and Dr. Snedeker arrayed himself on that side of the question.

KEEP, *v. t.*

> He willed away his whole estate,
>   And then in death he fell asleep,
> Murmuring: "Well, at any rate,
>   My name unblemished I shall keep."
> But when upon the tomb 'twas wrought
> Whose was it?—for the dead keep naught.
>   *Durang Gophel Arn.*

KILL, *v. t.* To create a vacancy without nominating a successor.

KILT, *n*. A costume sometimes worn by Scotchmen in America and Americans in Scotland.

KINDNESS, *n*. A brief preface to ten volumes of exaction.

KING, *n*. A male person commonly known in America as a "crowned head," although he never wears a crown and has usually no head to speak of.

> A king, in times long, long gone by,
>   Said to his lazy jester:
> "If I were you and you were I
> My moments merrily would fly—
>   No care nor grief to pester."
>
> "The reason, Sire, that you would thrive,"
>   The fool said—"if you'll hear it—
> Is that of all the fools alive
> Who own you for their sovereign, I've
>   The most forgiving spirit."
>   *Oogum Bem.*

KING'S EVIL, *n*. A malady that was formerly cured by the touch of the sovereign, but has now to be treated by the physicians. Thus "the most pious Edward" of England used to lay his royal hand upon his ailing subjects and make them whole—

> a crowd of wretched souls
> That stay his cure: their malady convinces
> The great essay of art; but at his touch,
> Such sanctity hath Heaven given his hand,
> They presently amend,

as the "Doctor" in *Macbeth* hath it. This useful property of the royal hand could, it appears, be transmitted along with other crown properties; for according to "Malcolm,"

> 'tis spoken,
> To the succeeding royalty he leaves
> The healing benediction.

But the gift somewhere dropped out of the line of succession: the later sovereigns of England have not been tactual healers, and the disease once honored with the name "king's evil" now bears the humbler one of "scrofula," from *scrofa*, a sow. The date and author of the following epigram are known only to the author of this dictionary, but it is old enough to show that the jest about Scotland's national disorder is not a thing of yesterday.

> Y^e Kynge his evill in me laye,
> Wh. he of Scottlande charmed awaye.
> He layde his hand on mine and sayd:
> "Be gone!" Y^e ill no longer stayd.
> But O ye wofull plyght in wh.
> I'm now y-pight: I have ye itche!

The superstition that maladies can be cured by royal taction is dead, but like many a departed conviction it has left a monument of custom to keep its memory green. The practice of forming in line and shaking the President's hand had no other origin, and when that great dignitary bestows his healing salutation on

> strangely visited people,
> All swoln and ulcerous, pitiful to the eye,
> The mere despair of surgery,

he and his patients are handing along an extinguished torch which once was kindled at the altar-fire of a faith long held by all classes of men. It is a beautiful and edifying "survival" —one which brings the sainted past close home to our "business and bosoms."

KISS, *n.* A word invented by the poets as a rhyme for "bliss." It is supposed to signify, in a general way, some kind of rite or ceremony appertaining to a good understanding; but the manner of its performance is unknown to this lexicographer.

KLEPTOMANIAC, *n.* A rich thief.

KNIGHT, *n.*

> Once a warrior gentle of birth,
> Then a person of civic worth,
> Now a fellow to move our mirth.

Warrior, person, and fellow—no more:
We must knight our dogs to get any lower.
Brave Knights Kennelers then shall be,
Noble Knights of the Golden Flea,
Knights of the Order of St. Steboy,
Knights of St. Gorge and Sir Knights Jawy.
God speed the day when this knighting fad
Shall go to the dogs and the dogs go mad.

KORAN, *n.* A book which the Mohammedans foolishly believe to have been written by divine inspiration, but which Christians know to be a wicked imposture, contradictory to the Holy Scriptures.

L

LABOR, *n.* One of the processes by which A acquires property for B.

LAND, *n.* A part of the earth's surface, considered as property. The theory that land is property subject to private ownership and control is the foundation of modern society, and is eminently worthy of the superstructure. Carried to its logical conclusion, it means that some have the right to prevent others from living; for the right to own implies the right exclusively to occupy; and in fact laws of trespass are enacted wherever property in land is recognized. It follows that if the whole area of *terra firma* is owned by A, B and C, there will be no place for D, E, F and G to be born, or, born as trespassers, to exist.

A life on the ocean wave,
   A home on the rolling deep,
For the spark that nature gave
   I have there the right to keep.

They give me the cat-o'-nine
   Whenever I go ashore.
Then ho! for the flashing brine—
   I'm a natural commodore!
         Dodle.

LANGUAGE, *n*. The music with which we charm the serpents guarding another's treasure.

LAOCOON, *n*. A famous piece of antique scripture representing a priest of that name and his two sons in the folds of two enormous serpents. The skill and diligence with which the old man and lads support the serpents and keep them up to their work have been justly regarded as one of the noblest artistic illustrations of the mastery of human intelligence over brute inertia.

LAP, *n*. One of the most important organs of the female system —an admirable provision of nature for the repose of infancy, but chiefly useful in rural festivities to support plates of cold chicken and heads of adult males. The male of our species has a rudimentary lap, imperfectly developed and in no way contributing to the animal's substantial welfare.

LAST, *n*. A shoemaker's implement, named by a frowning Providence as opportunity to the maker of puns.

> Ah, punster, would my lot were cast,
>   Where the cobbler is unknown,
> So that I might forget his last
>   And hear your own.
> *Gargo Repsky.*

LAUGHTER, *n*. An interior convulsion, producing a distortion of the features and accompanied by inarticulate noises. It is infectious and, though intermittent, incurable. Liability to attacks of laughter is one of the characteristics distinguishing man from the animals—these being not only inaccessible to the provocation of his example, but impregnable to the microbes having original jurisdiction in bestowal of the disease. Whether laughter could be imparted to animals by inoculation from the human patient is a question that has not been answered by experimentation. Dr. Meir Witchell holds that the infectious character of laughter is due to instantaneous fermentation of *sputa* diffused in a spray. From this peculiarity he names the disorder *Convulsio spargens*.

LAUREATE, *adj.* Crowned with leaves of the laurel. In England the Poet Laureate is an officer of the sovereign's court, acting as dancing skeleton at every royal feast and singing-mute at every royal funeral. Of all incumbents of that high office, Robert Southey had the most notable knack at drugging the Samson of public joy and cutting his hair to the quick; and he had an artistic color-sense which enabled him so to blacken a public grief as to give it the aspect of a national crime.

LAUREL, *n.* The *laurus*, a vegetable dedicated to Apollo, and formerly defoliated to wreathe the brows of victors and such poets as had influence at court. (*Vide supra.*)

LAW, *n.*

> Once Law was sitting on the bench,
>   And Mercy knelt a-weeping.
> "Clear out!" he cried, "disordered wench!
>   Nor come before me creeping.
> Upon your knees if you appear,
> 'Tis plain you have no standing here."
>
> Then Justice came. His Honor cried:
>   "*Your* status?—devil seize you!"
> "*Amica curiae*," she replied—
>   "Friend of the court, so please you."
> "Begone!" he shouted—"there's the door—
> I never saw your face before!"
>
> G. J.

LAWFUL, *adj.* Compatible with the will of a judge having jurisdiction.

LAWYER, *n.* One skilled in circumvention of the law.

LAZINESS, *n.* Unwarranted repose of manner in a person of low degree.

LEAD, *n.* A heavy blue-gray metal much used in giving stability to light lovers—particularly to those who love not wisely but other men's wives. Lead is also of great service as a

counterpoise to an argument of such weight that it turns the
scale of debate the wrong way. An interesting fact in the
chemistry of international controversy is that at the point of
contact of two patriotisms lead is precipitated in great quantities.

> Hail, holy Lead!—of human feuds the great
>   And universal arbiter; endowed
>   With penetration to pierce any cloud
> Fogging the field of controversial hate,
> And with a swift, inevitable, straight,
>   Searching precision find the unavowed
>   But vital point. Thy judgment, when allowed
> By the chirurgeon, settles the debate.
> O useful metal!—were it not for thee
>   We'd grapple one another's ears alway:
> But when we hear thee buzzing like a bee
>   We, like old Muhlenberg, "care not to stay."
> And when the quick have run away like pellets
> Jack Satan smelts the dead to make new bullets.

LEARNING, *n*. The kind of ignorance distinguishing the studious.

LECTURER, *n*. One with his hand in your pocket, his tongue in
your ear and his faith in your patience.

LEGACY, *n*. A gift from one who is legging it out of this vale of
tears.

LEONINE, *adj*. Unlike a menagerie lion. Leonine verses are
those in which a word in the middle of a line rhymes with a
word at the end, as in this famous passage from Bella Peeler
Silcox:

> The electric light invades the dunnest deep of Hades.
> Cries Pluto, 'twixt his snores: "O tempora! O mores!"

It should be explained that Mrs. Silcox does not undertake to teach the pronunciation of the Greek and Latin
tongues. Leonine verses are so called in honor of a poet
named Leo, whom prosodists appear to find a pleasure in

believing to have been the first to discover that a rhyming couplet could be run into a single line.

LETTUCE, *n*. An herb of the genus *Lactuca*, "Wherewith," says that pious gastronome, Hengist Pelly, "God has been pleased to reward the good and punish the wicked. For by his inner light the righteous man has discerned a manner of compounding for it a dressing to the appetency whereof a multitude of gustible condiments conspire, being reconciled and ameliorated with profusion of oil, the entire comestible making glad the heart of the godly and causing his face to shine. But the person of spiritual unworth is successfully tempted of the Adversary to eat of lettuce with destitution of oil, mustard, egg, salt and garlic, and with a rascal bath of vinegar polluted with sugar. Wherefore the person of spiritual unworth suffers an intestinal pang of strange complexity and raises the song."

LEVIATHAN, *n*. An enormous aquatic animal mentioned by Job. Some suppose it to have been the whale, but that distinguished ichthyologer, Dr. Jordan, of Stanford University, maintains with considerable heat that it was a species of gigantic Tadpole (*Thaddeus Polandensis*) or Polliwig—*Maria pseudo-hirsuta*. For an exhaustive description and history of the Tadpole consult the famous monograph of Jane Porter, *Thaddeus of Warsaw*.

LEXICOGRAPHER, *n*. A pestilent fellow who, under the pretense of recording some particular stage in the development of a language, does what he can to arrest its growth, stiffen its flexibility and mechanize its methods. For your lexicographer, having written his dictionary, comes to be considered "as one having authority," whereas his function is only to make a record, not to give a law. The natural servility of the human understanding having invested him with judicial power, surrenders its right of reason and submits itself to a chronicle as if it were a statute. Let the dictionary (for example) mark a good word as "obsolete" or "obsolescent" and few men thereafter venture to use it, whatever their need of it and however desirable its restoration to favor—whereby the process of improverishment is accelerated and speech decays. On the contrary, the bold and discerning writer who, recognizing the truth that language must grow by innovation if it grow at all, makes new words and uses the old in an unfamiliar sense, has no following and is tartly reminded that "it isn't in the dictionary"—although down to the time of the first lexicographer (Heaven forgive him!) no author ever had used a word that *was* in the dictionary. In the golden prime and high noon of English speech; when from the lips of the great Elizabethans fell words that made their own meaning and carried it in their very sound; when a Shakespeare and a Bacon were possible, and the language now rapidly perishing at one end and slowly renewed at the other was in vigorous growth and hardy preservation—sweeter than honey and stronger than a lion—the lexicographer was a person unknown, the dictionary a creation which his Creator had not created him to create.

> God said: "Let Spirit perish into Form,"
> And lexicographers arose, a swarm!
> Thought fled and left her clothing, which they took,
> And catalogued each garment in a book.
> Now, from her leafy covert when she cries:
> "Give me my clothes and I'll return," they rise
> And scan the list, and say without compassion:
> "Excuse us—they are mostly out of fashion."
> *Sigismund Smith.*

LIAR, *n.* A lawyer with a roving commission.

LIBERTY, *n.* One of Imagination's most precious possessions.

> The rising People, hot and out of breath,
> Roared round the palace: "Liberty or death!"
> "If death will do," the King said, "let me reign;
> You'll have, I'm sure, no reason to complain."
> *Martha Braymance.*

LICKSPITTLE, *n.* A useful functionary, not infrequently found editing a newspaper. In his character of editor he is closely allied to the blackmailer by the tie of occasional identity; for in truth the lickspittle is only the blackmailer under another aspect, though the latter is frequently found as an independent species. Lickspittling is more detestable than blackmailing, precisely as the business of a confidence man is more detestable than that of a highway robber; and the parallel maintains itself throughout, for whereas few robbers will cheat, every sneak will plunder if he dare.

LIFE, *n*. A spiritual pickle preserving the body from decay. We live in daily apprehension of its loss; yet when lost it is not missed. The question, "Is life worth living?" has been much discussed; particularly by those who think it is not, many of whom have written at great length in support of their view and by careful observance of the laws of health enjoyed for long terms of years the honors of successful controversy.

> "Life's not worth living, and that's the truth,"
> Carelessly caroled the golden youth.
> In manhood still he maintained that view
> And held it more strongly the older he grew.
> When kicked by a jackass at eighty-three,
> "Go fetch me a surgeon at once!" cried he.
> *Han Soper.*

LIGHTHOUSE, *n*. A tall building on the seashore in which the government maintains a lamp and the friend of a politician.

LIMB, *n*. The branch of a tree or the leg of an American woman.

> 'Twas a pair of boots that the lady bought,
>   And the salesman laced them tight
>   To a very remarkable height—
> Higher, indeed, than I think he ought—
>   Higher than *can* be right.
> For the Bible declares—but never mind:
>   It is hardly fit
> To censure freely and fault to find
> With others for sins that I'm not inclined
>   Myself to commit.
> Each has his weakness, and though my own
>   Is freedom from every sin,
>   It still were unfair to pitch in,

Discharging the first censorious stone.
Besides, the truth compels me to say,
The boots in question were *made* that way.
As he drew the lace she made a grimace,
  And blushingly said to him:
"This boot, I'm sure, is too high to endure,
It hurts my—hurts my—limb."
The salesman smiled in a manner mild,
Like an artless, undesigning child;
Then, checking himself, to his face he gave
A look as sorrowful as the grave,
  Though he didn't care two figs
For her pains and throes,
As he stroked her toes,
Remarking with speech and manner just
Befitting his calling: "Madam, I trust
  That it doesn't hurt your twigs."
                              B. Percival Dike.

LINEN, *n.* "A kind of cloth the making of which, when made of hemp, entails a great waste of hemp."—*Calcraft the Hangman.*

LITIGANT, *n.* A person about to give up his skin for the hope of retaining his bones.

LITIGATION, *n.* A machine which you go into as a pig and come out of as a sausage.

LIVER, *n.* A large red organ thoughtfully provided by nature to be bilious with. The sentiments and emotions which every literary anatomist now knows to haunt the heart were anciently believed to infest the liver; and even Gascoygne, speaking of the emotional side of human nature, calls it "our hepaticall parte." It was at one time considered the seat of life; hence its name—liver, the thing we live with. The liver is heaven's best gift to the goose; without it that bird would be unable to supply us with the Strasbourg *pâté.*

LL.D. Letters indicating the degree *Legumptionorum Doctor,* one learned in laws, gifted with legal gumption. Some suspicion is cast upon this derivation by the fact that the title was formerly *££.d.*, and conferred only upon gentlemen distinguished for their wealth. At the date of this writing Columbia University is considering the expediency of making another degree for clergymen, in place of the old D.D.—*Damnator Diaboli*. The new honor will be known as *Sanctorum Custus*, and written *$$c*. The name of the Rev. John Satan has been suggested as a suitable recipient by a lover of consistency, who points out that Professor Harry Thurston Peck has long enjoyed the advantage of a degree.

LOCK-AND-KEY, *n.* The distinguishing device of civilization and enlightenment.

LODGER, *n.* A less popular name for the Second Person of that delectable newspaper Trinity, the Roomer, the Bedder and the Mealer.

LOGANIMITY, *n.* The disposition to endure injury with meek forbearance while maturing a plan of revenge.

LOGIC, *n.* The art of thinking and reasoning in strict accordance with the limitations and incapacities of the human misunderstanding. The basic of logic is the syllogism, consisting of a major and a minor premise and a conclusion —thus:

Major Premise: Sixty men can do a piece of work sixty times as quickly as one man.

Minor Premise: One man can dig a posthole in sixty seconds; therefore—

Conclusion: Sixty men can dig a posthole in one second.

This may be called the syllogism arithmetical, in which, by combining logic and mathematics, we obtain a double certainty and are twice blessed.

LOGOMACHY, *n.* A war in which the weapons are words and the wounds punctures in the swim-bladder of self-esteem—a kind of contest in which, the vanquished being unconscious of defeat, the victor is denied the reward of success.

> 'Tis said by divers of the scholar-men
> That poor Salmasius died of Milton's pen.
> Alas! we cannot know if this is true,
> For reading Milton's wit we perish too.

LONGEVITY, *n.* Uncommon extension of the fear of death.

LOOKING-GLASS, *n.* A vitreous plane upon which to display a fleeting show for man's disillusion given.

The King of Manchuria had a magic looking-glass, whereon whoso looked saw, not his own image, but only that of the king. A certain courtier who had long enjoyed the king's favor and was thereby enriched beyond any other subject of the realm, said to the king: "Give me, I pray, thy wonderful mirror, so that when absent out of thine august presence I may yet do homage before thy visible shadow, prostrating myself night and morning in the glory of thy benign countenance, as which nothing has so divine splendor, O Noonday Sun of the Universe!"

Pleased with the speech, the king commanded that the mirror be conveyed to the courtier's palace; but after, having gone thither without apprisal, he found it in an apartment where was naught but idle lumber. And the mirror was dimmed with dust and overlaced with cobwebs. This so angered him that he fisted it hard, shattering the glass, and was sorely hurt. Enraged all the more by this mischance, he commanded that the ungrateful courtier be thrown into prison, and that the glass be repaired and taken back to his own palace; and this was done. But when the king looked again on the mirror he saw not his image as before, but only the figure of a crowned ass, having a bloody bandage on one of its hinder hooves—as the artificers and all who had looked upon it had before discerned but feared to report. Taught wisdom and charity, the king restored his courtier to liberty, had the mirror set into the back of the throne and reigned many years with justice and humility; and one day when he fell asleep in death while on the throne, the whole court saw in the mirror the luminous figure of an angel, which remains to this day.

LOQUACITY, *n*. A disorder which renders the sufferer unable to curb his tongue when you wish to talk.

LORD, *n*. In American society, an English tourist above the state of a costermonger, as, lord 'Aberdasher, Lord Hartisan and so forth. The traveling Briton of lesser degree is addressed as "Sir," as, Sir 'Arry Donkiboi, of 'Amstead 'Eath. The word "Lord" is sometimes used, also, as a title of the Supreme Being; but this is thought to be rather flattery than true reverence.

> Miss Sallie Ann Splurge, of her own accord,
> Wedded a wandering English lord—
> Wedded and took him to dwell with her "paw,"
> A parent who throve by the practice of Draw.
> Lord Cadde I don't hesitate to declare
> Unworthy the father-in-legal care
> Of that elderly sport, notwithstanding the truth
> That Cadde had renounced all the follies of youth;
> For, sad to relate, he'd arrived at the stage
> Of existence that's marked by the vices of age.
> Among them, cupidity caused him to urge
> Repeated demands on the pocket of Splurge,
> Till, wrecked in his fortune, that gentleman saw
> Inadequate aid in the practice of Draw,
> And took, as a means of augmenting his pelf,
> To the business of being a lord himself.
> His neat-fitting garments he wilfully shed
> And sacked himself strangely in checks instead;
> Denuded his chin, but retained at each ear
> A whisker that looked like a blasted career.
> He painted his neck an incarnadine hue
> Each morning and varnished it all that he knew.
> The moony monocular set in his eye
> Appeared to be scanning the Sweet Bye-and-Bye.
> His head was enroofed with a billycock hat,
> And his low-necked shoes were aduncous and flat.
> In speech he eschewed his American ways,
> Denying his nose to the use of his A's
> And dulling their edge till the delicate sense
> Of a babe at their temper could take no offence.
> His H's—'twas most inexpressibly sweet,

> The patter they made as they fell at his feet!
> Re-outfitted thus, Mr. Splurge without fear
> Began as Lord Splurge his recouping career.
> Alas, the Divinity shaping his end
> Entertained other views and decided to send
> His lordship in horror, despair and dismay
> From the land of the nobleman's natural prey.
> For, smit with his Old World ways, Lady Cadde
> Fell—suffering Cæsar!—in love with her dad!
>   G. J.

LORE, *n.* Learning—particularly that sort which is not derived from a regular course of instruction but comes of the reading of occult books, or by nature. This latter is commonly designated as folk-lore and embraces popularly myths and superstitions. In Baring-Gould's *Curious Myths of the Middle Ages* the reader will find many of these traced backward, through various peoples on converging lines, toward a common origin in remote antiquity. Among these are the fables of "Teddy the Giant Killer," "The Sleeping John Sharp Williams," "Little Red Riding Hood and the Sugar Trust," "Beauty and the Brisbane," "The Seven Aldermen of Ephesus," "Rip Van Fairbanks," and so forth. The fable with Goethe so affectingly relates under the title of "The Erl-King" was known two thousand years ago in Greece as "The Demos and the Infant Industry." One of the most general and ancient of these myths is that Arabian tale of "Ali Baba and the Forty Rockefellers."

LOSS, *n.* Privation of that which we had, or had not. Thus, in the latter sense, it is said of a defeated candidate that he "lost his election"; and of that eminent man, the poet Gilder, that he has "lost his mind." It is in the former and more legitimate sense, that the word is used in the famous epitaph:

> Here Huntington's ashes long have lain
> Whose loss is our own eternal gain,
> For while he exercised all his powers
> Whatever he gained, the loss was ours.

LOVE, *n.* A temporary insanity curable by marriage or by removal of the patient from the influences under which he incurred the disorder. This disease, like *caries* and many other ailments, is prevalent only among civilized races living under artificial conditions; barbarous nations breathing pure air and eating simple food enjoy immunity from its ravages. It is sometimes fatal, but more frequently to the physician than to the patient.

LOW-BRED, *adj.* "Raised" instead of brought up.

LUMINARY, *n.* One who throws light upon a subject; as an editor by not writing about it.

LUNARIAN, *n.* An inhabitant of the moon, as distinguished from Lunatic, one whom the moon inhabits. The Lunarians have been described by Lucian, Locke and other observers, but without much agreement. For example, Bragellos avers their anatomical identity with Man, but Professor Newcomb says they are more like the hill tribes of Vermont.

LYRE, *n.* An ancient instrument of torture. The word is now used in a figurative sense to denote the poetic faculty, as in the following fiery lines of our great poet, Ella Wheeler Wilcox:

> I sit astride Parnassus with my lyre,
> And pick with care the disobedient wire.
> That stupid shepherd lolling on his crook
> With deaf attention scarcely deigns to look.
> I bide my time, and it shall come at length,
> When, with a Titan's energy and strength,
> I'll grab a fistful of the strings, and O,
> The world shall suffer when I let them go!
> *Farquharson Harris.*

M

MACE, *n.* A staff of office signifying authority. Its form, that of a heavy club, indicates its original purpose and use in dissuading from dissent.

MACHINATION, *n.* The method employed by one's opponents

in baffling one's open and honorable efforts to do the right thing.

> So plain the advantages of machination
> It constitutes a moral obligation,
> And honest wolves who think upon't with loathing
> Feel bound to don the sheep's deceptive clothing.
> So prospers still the diplomatic art,
> And Satan bows, with hand upon his heart.
>
> *R.S.K.*

MACROBIAN, *n.* One forgotten of the gods and living to a great age. History is abundantly supplied with examples, from Methuselah to Old Parr, but some notable instances of longevity are less well known. A Calabrian peasant named Coloni, born in 1753, lived so long that he had what he considered a glimpse of the dawn of universal peace. Scanavius relates that he knew an archbishop who was so old that he could remember a time when he did not deserve hanging. In 1566 a linen draper of Bristol, England, declared that he had lived five hundred years, and that in all that time he had never told a lie. There are instances of longevity (*macrobiosis*) in our own country. Senator Chauncey Depew is old enough to know better. The editor of *The American*, a newspaper in New York City, has a memory that goes back to the time when he was a rascal, but not to the fact. The President of the United States was born so long ago that many of the friends of his youth have risen to high political and military preferment without the assistance of personal merit. The verses following were written by a macrobian:

> When I was young the world was fair
>   And amiable and sunny.
> A brightness was in all the air,
>   In all the waters, honey.
>   The jokes were fine and funny,
> The statesmen honest in their views,
>   And in their lives, as well,
> And when you heard a bit of news
>   'Twas true enough to tell.
> Men were not ranting, shouting, reeking,
> Nor women "generally speaking."

The Summer then was long indeed:
    It lasted one whole season!
The sparkling Winter gave no heed
    When ordered by Unreason
    To bring the early peas on.
Now, where the dickens is the sense
    In calling that a year
Which does no more than just commence
    Before the end is near?
When I was young the year extended
From month to month until it ended.

I know not why the world has changed
    To something dark and dreary,
And everything is now arranged
    To make a fellow weary.
    The Weather Man—I fear he
Has much to do with it, for, sure,
    The air is not the same:
It chokes you when it is impure,
    When pure it makes you lame.
With windows closed you are asthmatic;
Open, neuralgic or sciatic.

Well, I suppose this new régime
    Of dun degeneration
Seems eviler than it would seem
    To a better observation,
    And has for compensation
Some blessings in a deep disguise
    Which mortal sight has failed
To pierce, although to angels' eyes
    They're visible unveiled.
If Age is such a boon, good land!
He's costumed by a master hand!
                Venable Strigg.

MAD, *adj.* Affected with a high degree of intellectual independence; not conforming to standards of thought, speech and action derived by the conformants from study of themselves; at odds with the majority; in short, unusual. It is noteworthy that persons are pronounced mad by officials destitute of evidence that themselves are sane. For illustration, this present (and illustrious) lexicographer is no firmer in the faith of his own sanity than is any inmate of any madhouse in the land; yet for aught he knows to the contrary, instead of the lofty occupation that seems to him to be engaging his powers he may really be beating his hands against the window bars of an asylum and declaring himself Noah Webster, to the innocent delight of many thoughtless spectators.

MAGDALENE, *n.* An inhabitant of Magdala. Popularly, a woman found out. This definition of the word has the authority of ignorance, Mary of Magdala being another person than the penitent woman mentioned by St. Luke. It has also the official sanction of the governments of Great Britain and the United States. In England the word is pronounced Maudlin, whence maudlin, adjective, unpleasantly sentimental. With their Maudlin for Magdalene, and their Bedlam for Bethlehem, the English may justly boast themselves the greatest of revisers.

MAGIC, *n.* An art of converting superstition into coin. There are other arts serving the same high purpose, but the discreet lexicographer does not name them.

MAGNET, *n.* Something acted upon by magnetism.

MAGNETISM, *n.* Something acting upon a magnet.
  The two definitions immediately foregoing are condensed from the works of one thousand eminent scientists, who have illuminated the subject with a great white light, to the inexpressible advancement of human knowledge.

MAGNIFICENT, *adj.* Having a grandeur or splendor superior to that to which the spectator is accustomed, as the ears of an ass, to a rabbit, or the glory of a glowworm, to a maggot.

MAGNITUDE, *n.* Size. Magnitude being purely relative, nothing is large and nothing small. If everything in the universe were increased in bulk one thousand diameters nothing would be any larger than it was before, but if one thing remain unchanged all the others would be larger than they had been. To an understanding familiar with the relativity of magnitude and distance the spaces and masses of the astronomer would be no more impressive than those of the microscopist. For anything we know to the contrary, the visible universe may be a small part of an atom, with its component ions, floating in the life-fluid (luminiferous ether) of some animal. Possibly the wee creatures peopling the corpuscles of our own blood are overcome with the proper emotion when contemplating the unthinkable distance from one of these to another.

MAGPIE, *n.* A bird whose thievish disposition suggested to someone that it might be taught to talk.

MAIDEN, *n.* A young person of the unfair sex addicted to clewless conduct and views that madden to crime. The genus has a wide geographical distribution, being found wherever sought and deplored wherever found. The maiden is not altogether unpleasing to the eye, nor (without her piano and her views) insupportable to the ear, though in respect to comeliness distinctly inferior to the rainbow, and, with regard to the part of her that is audible, beaten out of the field by the canary—which, also, is more portable.

> A lovelorn maiden she sat and sang—
> This quaint, sweet song sang she:
> "It's O for a youth with a football bang
> And a muscle fair to see!
> The Captain he
> Of a team to be!
> On the gridiron he shall shine,
> A monarch by right divine,
> And never to roast on it—me!"
> *Opoline Jones.*

MAJESTY, *n.* The state and title of a king. Regarded with a just contempt by the Most Eminent Grand Masters, Grand Chancellors, Great Incohonees and Imperial Potentates of the ancient and honorable orders of republican America.

MALE, *n.* A member of the unconsidered, or negligible sex. The male of the human race is commonly known (to the female) as Mere Man. The genus has two varieties: good providers and bad providers.

MALEFACTOR, *n.* The chief factor in the progress of the human race.

MALTHUSIAN, *adj.* Pertaining to Malthus and his doctrines. Malthus believed in artificially limiting population, but found that it could not be done by talking. One of the most practical exponents of the Malthusian idea was Herod of Judea, though all the famous soldiers have been of the same way of thinking.

MAMMALIA, *n. pl.* A family of vertebrate animals whose females in a state of nature suckle their young, but when civilized and enlightened put them out to nurse, or use the bottle.

MAMMON, *n.* The god of the world's leading religion. The chief temple is in the holy city of New York.

> He swore that all other religions were gammon,
> And wore out his knees in the worship of Mammon.
> *Jared Oopf.*

MAN, *n.* An animal so lost in rapturous contemplation of what he thinks he is as to overlook what he indubitably ought to be. His chief occupation is extermination of other animals and his own species, which, however, multiplies with such insistent rapidity as to infest the whole habitable earth and Canada.

> When the world was young and Man was new,
>   And everything was pleasant,
> Distinctions Nature never drew
>   'Mongst kings and priest and peasant.
>   We're not that way at present,
> Save here in this Republic, where
>   We have that old régime,
> For all are kings, however bare
>   Their backs, howe'er extreme
> Their hunger. And, indeed, each has a voice
> To accept the tyrant of his party's choice.

> A citizen who would not vote,
>   And, therefore, was detested,
> Was one day with a tarry coat
>   (With feathers backed and breasted)
>   By patriots invested.
> "It is your duty," cried the crowd,
>   "Your ballot true to cast
> For the man o' your choice." He humbly bowed,
>   And explained his wicked past:
> "That's what I very gladly would have done,
> Dear patriots, but he has never run."
> *Apperton Duke.*

MANES, *n.* The immortal parts of dead Greeks and Romans. They were in a state of dull discomfort until the bodies from which they had exhaled were buried and burned; and they seem not to have been particularly happy afterward.

MANICHEISM, *n.* The ancient Persian doctrine of an incessant warfare between Good and Evil. When Good gave up the fight the Persians joined the victorious Opposition.

MANNA, *n.* A food miraculously given to the Israelites in the wilderness. When it was no longer supplied to them they settled down and tilled the soil, fertilizing it, as a rule, with the bodies of the original occupants.

MARRIAGE, *n.* The state or condition of a community consisting of a master, a mistress and two slaves, making in all, two.

MARTYR, *n.* One who moves along the line of least reluctance to a desired death.

MATERIAL, *adj.* Having an actual existence, as distinguished from an imaginary one. Important.

> Material things I know, or feel, or see;
> All else is immaterial to me.
> *Jamarach Holobom.*

MAUSOLEUM, *n.* The final and funniest folly of the rich.

MAYONNAISE, *n.* One of the sauces which serve the French in place of a state religion.

ME, *pro.* The objectionable case of I. The personal pronoun in English has three cases, the dominative, the objectionable and the oppressive. Each is all three.

MEANDER, *n.* To proceed sinuously and aimlessly. The word is the ancient name of a river about one hundred and fifty miles south of Troy, which turned and twisted in the effort to get out of hearing when the Greeks and Trojans boasted of their prowess.

MEDAL, *n.* A small metal disk given as a reward for virtues, attainments or services more or less authentic.

It is related of Bismark, who had been awarded a medal for gallantly rescuing a drowning person, that, being asked the meaning of the medal, he replied: "I save lives sometimes." And sometimes he didn't.

MEDICINE, *n.* A stone flung down the Bowery to kill a dog in Broadway.

MEEKNESS, *n.* Uncommon patience in planning a revenge that is worth while.

> M is for Moses,
>   Who slew the Egyptian.
> As sweet as a rose is
> The meekness of Moses.
> No monument shows his
>   Post-mortem inscription,
> But M is for Moses,
>   Who slew the Egyptian.
> *The Biographical Alphabet.*

MEERSCHAUM, *n.* (Literally, seafoam, and by many erroneously supposed to be made of it.) A fine white clay, which for convenience in coloring it brown is made into tobacco pipes and smoked by the workmen engaged in that industry. The purpose of coloring it has not been disclosed by the manufacturers.

> There was a youth (you've heard before,
>   This woful tale, may be),
> Who bought a meerschaum pipe and swore
>   That color it would he!
>
> He shut himself from the world away,
>   Nor any soul he saw.
> He smoked by night, he smoked by day,
>   As hard as he could draw.
>
> His dog died moaning in the wrath
>   Of winds that blew aloof;
> The weeds were in the gravel path,
>   The owl was on the roof.
>
> "He's gone afar, he'll come no more,"
>   The neighbors sadly say.
> And so they batter in the door
>   To take his goods away.
>
> Dead, pipe in mouth, the youngster lay,
>   Nut-brown in face and limb.
> "That pipe's a lovely white," they say,
>   "But it has colored him!"
>
> The moral there's small need to sing—
>   'Tis plain as day to you:
> Don't play your game on any thing
>   That is a gamester too.
>   *Martin Bulstrode.*

MENDACIOUS, *adj.* Addicted to rhetoric.

MERCHANT, *n.* One engaged in a commercial pursuit. A commercial pursuit is one in which the thing pursued is a dollar.

MERCY, *n.* An attribute beloved of detected offenders.

MESMERISM, *n.* Hypnotism before it wore good clothes, kept a carriage and asked Incredulity to dinner.

METROPOLIS, *n.* A stronghold of provincialism.

MILLENNIUM, *n.* The period of a thousand years when the lid is to be screwed down, with all reformers on the under side.

MIND, *n.* A mysterious form of matter secreted by the brain. Its chief activity consists in the endeavor to ascertain its own nature, the futility of the attempt being due to the fact that it has nothing but itself to know itself with. From the Latin *mens,* a fact unknown to that honest shoe-seller, who, observing that his learned competitor over the way had displayed the motto "*Mens conscia recti,*" emblazoned his own shop front with the words "Men's, women's and children's conscia recti."

MINE, *adj.* Belonging to me if I can hold or seize it.

MINISTER, *n.* An agent of a higher power with a lower responsibility. In diplomacy an officer sent into a foreign country as the visible embodiment of his sovereign's hostility. His principal qualification is a degree of plausible inveracity next below that of an ambassador.

MINOR, *adj.* Less objectionable.

MINSTREL, *adj.* Formerly a poet, singer or musician; now a nigger with a color less than skin deep and a humor more than flesh and blood can bear.

MIRACLE, *n.* An act or event out of the order of nature and unaccountable, as beating a normal hand of four kings and an ace with four aces and a king.

MISCREANT, *n.* A person of the highest degree of unworth. Etymologically, the word means unbeliever, and its present signification may be regarded as theology's noblest contribution to the development of our language.

MISDEMEANOR, *n.* An infraction of the law having less dignity than a felony and constituting no claim to admittance into the best criminal society.

> By misdemeanors he essayed to climb
> Into the aristocracy of crime.
> O, woe was him!—with manner chill and grand
> "Captains of industry" refused his hand,
> "Kings of finance" denied him recognition
> And "railway magnates" jeered his low condition.
> He robbed a bank to make himself respected.
> They still rebuffed him, for he was detected.
> > *S. V. Hanipur.*

MISERICORDE, *n.* A dagger which in mediæval warfare was used by the foot soldier to remind an unhorsed knight that he was mortal.

MISFORTUNE, *n.* The kind of fortune that never misses.

MISS, *n.* The title with which we brand unmarried women to indicate that they are in the market. Miss, Missis (Mrs.) and Mister (Mr.) are the three most distinctly disagreeable words in the language, in sound and sense. Two are corruptions of Mistress, the other of Master. In the general abolition of social titles in this our country they miraculously escaped to plague us. If we must have them let us be consistent and give one to the unmarried man. I venture to suggest Mush, abbreviated to Mh.

MOLECULE, *n.* The ultimate, indivisible unit of matter. It is distinguished from the corpuscle, also the ultimate, indivisible unit of matter, by a closer resemblance to the atom, also the ultimate, indivisible unit of matter. Three great scientific theories of the structure of the universe are the molecular, the corpuscular and the atomic. A fourth affirms, with Haeckel, the condensation of precipitation of matter from ether— whose existence is proved by the condensation or precipitation. The present trend of scientific thought is toward the theory of ions. The ion differs from the molecule, the corpuscle and the atom in that it is an ion. A fifth theory is held by idiots, but it is doubtful if they know any more about the matter than the others.

MONAD, *n.* The ultimate, indivisible unit of matter. (See *Molecule.*) According to Leibnitz, as nearly as he seems willing to be understood, the monad has body without bulk, and mind without manifestation—Leibnitz knows him by the innate power of considering. He has founded upon him a theory of the universe, which the creature bears without resentment, for the monad is a gentlman. Small as he is, the monad contains all the powers and possibilities needful to his evolution into a German philosopher of the first class—altogether a very capable little fellow. He is not to be confounded with the microbe, or bacillus; by its inability to discern him, a good microscope shows him to be of an entirely distinct species.

MONARCH, *n.* A person engaged in reigning. Formerly the monarch ruled, as the derivation of the word attests, and as many subjects have had occasion to learn. In Russia and the Orient the monarch has still a considerable influence in public affairs and in the disposition of the human head, but in western Europe political administration is mostly entrusted to his ministers, he being somewhat preoccupied with reflections relating to the status of his own head.

MONARCHICAL GOVERNMENT, *n.* Government.

MONDAY, *n.* In Christian countries, the day after the baseball game.

MONEY, *n.* A blessing that is of no advantage to us excepting when we part with it. An evidence of culture and a passport to polite society. Supportable property.

MONKEY, *n.* An arboreal animal which makes itself at home in genealogical trees.

MONOSYLLABIC, *adj.* Composed of words of one syllable, for literary babes who never tire of testifying their delight in the vapid compound by appropriate googoogling. The words are commonly Saxon—that is to say, words of a barbarous people destitute of ideas and incapable of any but the most elementary sentiments and emotions.

> The man who writes in Saxon
> Is the man to use an ax on.
> *Judibras.*

MONSIGNOR, *n.* A high ecclesiastical title, of which the Founder of our religion overlooked the advantages.

MONUMENT, *n.* A structure intended to commemorate something which either needs no commemoration or cannot be commemorated.

> The bones of Agammemnon are a show,
> And ruined is his royal monument,

but Agammemnon's fame suffers no diminution in consequence. The monument custom has its *reductiones ad absurdum* in monuments "to the unknown dead"—that is to say, monuments to perpetuate the memory of those who have left no memory.

MORAL, *adj.* Conforming to a local and mutable standard of right. Having the quality of general expediency.

> It is sayd there be a raunge of mountaynes in the Easte, on one syde of the which certayn conducts are immorall, yet on the other syde they are holden in good esteeme; wherebye the mountayneer is much conveenyenced, for it is given to him to goe downe eyther way and act as it shall suite his moode, withouten offence.
> —*Gooke's Meditations.*

MORE, *adj.* The comparative degree of too much.

MOUSE, *n.* An animal which strews its path with fainting women. As in Rome Christians were thrown to the lions, so centuries earlier in Otumwee, the most ancient and famous city of the world, female heretics were thrown to the mice. Jakak-Zotp, the historian, the only Otumwump whose writings have descended to us, says that these martyrs met their death with little dignity and much exertion. He even attempts to exculpate the mice (such is the malice of bigotry) by declaring that the unfortunate women perished, some from exhaustion, some of broken necks from falling over their own feet, and some from lack of restoratives. The mice, he avers, enjoyed the pleasures of the chase with composure. But if "Roman history is nine-tenths lying," we can hardly expect a smaller proportion of that rhetorical figure in the annals of a people capable of so incredible cruelty to a lovely woman; for a hard heart has a false tongue.

MOUSQUETAIRE, *n.* A long glove covering a part of the arm. Worn in New Jersey. But "mousquetaire" is a might poor way to spell muskeeter.

MOUTH, *n.* In man, the gateway to the soul; in woman, the outlet of the heart.

MUGWUMP, *n.* In politics one afflicted with self-respect and addicted to the vice of independence. A term of contempt.

MULATTO, *n.* A child of two races, ashamed of both.

MULTITUDE, *n.* A crowd; the source of political wisdom and virtue. In a republic, the object of the statesman's adoration. "In a multitude of counsellors there is wisdom," saith the proverb. If many men of equal individual wisdom are wiser than any one of them, it must be that they acquire the excess of wisdom by the mere act of getting together. Whence comes it? Obviously from nowhere—as well say that a range of mountains is higher than the single mountains composing it. A multitude is as wise as its wisest member if it obey him; if not, it is no wiser than its most foolish.

MUMMY, *n.* An ancient Egyptian, formerly in universal use among modern civilized nations as medicine, and now engaged in supplying art with an excellent pigment. He is handy, too, in museums in gratifying the vulgar curiosity that serves to distinguish man from the lower animals.

> By means of the Mummy, mankind, it is said,
> Attests to the gods its respect for the dead.
> We plunder his tomb, be he sinner or saint,
> Distil him for physic and grind him for paint,
> Exhibit for money his poor, shrunken frame,
> And with levity flock to the scene of the shame.
> O, tell me, ye gods, for the use of my rhyme:
> For respecting the dead what's the limit of time?
> *Scopas Brune.*

MUSTANG, *n.* An indocile horse of the western plains. In English society, the American wife of an English nobleman.

MYRMIDON, *n.* A follower of Achilles—particularly when he didn't lead.

MYTHOLOGY, *n.* The body of a primitive people's beliefs concerning its origin, early history, heroes, deities and so forth, as distinguished from the true accounts which it invents later.

N

NECTAR, *n.* A drink served at banquets of the Olympian deities. The secret of its preparation is lost, but the modern Kentuckians believe that they come pretty near to a knowledge of its chief ingredient.

> Juno drank a cup of nectar,
> But the draught did not affect her.
> Juno drank a cup of rye—
> Then she bade herself good-bye.
> *J. G.*

NEGRO, *n.* The *pièce de résistance* in the American political problem. Representing him by the letter *n*, the Republicans begin to build their equation thus: "Let *n*=the white man." This, however, appears to give an unsatisfactory solution.

NEIGHBOR, *n.* One whom we are commanded to love as ourselves, and who does all he knows how to make us disobedient.

NEPOTISM, *n.* Appointing your grandmother to office for the good of the party.

NEWTONIAN, *adj.* Pertaining to a philosophy of the universe invented by Newton, who discovered that an apple will fall to the ground, but was unable to say why. His successors and disciples have advanced so far as to be able to say when.

NIHILIST, *n.* A Russian who denies the existence of anything but Tolstoi. The leader of the school is Tolstoi.

NIRVANA, *n.* In the Buddhist religion, a state of pleasurable annihilation awarded to the wise, particularly to those wise enough to understand it.

NOBLEMAN, *n.* Nature's provision for wealthy American maids ambitious to incur social distinction and suffer high life.

NOISE, *n.* A stench in the ear. Undomesticated music. The chief product and authenticating sign of civilization.

NOMINATE, *v.* To designate for the heaviest political assessment. To put forward a suitable person to incur the mud-gobbing and deadcatting of the opposition.

NOMINEE, *n.* A modest gentleman shrinking from the distinction of private life and diligently seeking the honorable obscurity of public office.

NON-COMBATANT, *n.* A dead Quaker.

NONSENSE, *n.* The objections that are urged against this excellent dictionary.

NOSE, *n.* The extreme outpost of the face. From the circumstance that great conquerors have great noses, Getius, whose writings antedate the age of humor, calls the nose the organ of quell. It has been observed that one's nose is never so happy as when thrust into the affairs of another, from which some physiologists have drawn the inference that the nose is devoid of the sense of smell.

> There's a man with a Nose,
>   And wherever he goes
> The people run from him and shout:
>   "No cotton have we
>   For our ears if so be
> He blow that interminous snout!"

> So the lawyers applied
>   For injunction. "Denied,"
> Said the Judge: "the defendant prefixion,
>   Whate'er it portend,
>   Appears to transcend
> The bounds of this court's jurisdiction."
>   *Arpad Singiny.*

NOTORIETY, *n.* The fame of one's competitor for public honors. The kind of renown most accessible and acceptable to mediocrity. A Jacob's-ladder leading to the vaudeville stage, with angels ascending and descending.

NOUMENON, *n.* That which exists, as distinguished from that which merely seems to exist, the latter being a phenomenon. The noumenon is a bit difficult to locate; it can be apprehended only by a process of reasoning—which is a phenomenon. Nevertheless, the discovery and exposition of noumena offer a rich field for what Lewes calls "the endless variety and excitement of philosophic thought." Hurrah (therefore) for the noumenon!

NOVEL, *n.* A short story padded. A species of composition bearing the same relation to literature that the panorama bears to art. As it is too long to be read at a sitting the impressions made by its successive parts are successively effaced, as in the panorama. Unity, totality of effect, is impossible; for besides the few pages last read all that is carried in mind is the mere plot of what has gone before. To the romance the novel is what photography is to painting. Its distinguishing principle, probability, corresponds to the literal actuality of the photograph and puts it distinctly into the category of reporting; whereas the free wing of the romancer enables him to mount to such altitudes of imagination as he may be fitted to attain; and the first three essentials of the literary art are imagination, imagination and imagination. The art of writing novels, such as it was, is long dead everywhere except in Russia, where it is new. Peace to its ashes—some of which have a large sale.

NOVEMBER, *n.* The eleventh twelfth of a weariness.

O

OATH, *n.* In law, a solemn appeal to the Deity, made binding upon the conscience by a penalty for perjury.

OBLIVION, *n.* The state or condition in which the wicked cease from struggling and the dreary are at rest. Fame's eternal dumping ground. Cold storage for high hopes. A place where ambitious authors meet their works without pride and their betters without envy. A dormitory without an alarm clock.

OBSERVATORY, *n.* A place where astronomers conjecture away the guesses of their predecessors.

OBSESSED, *pp.* Vexed by an evil spirit, like the Gadarene swine and other critics. Obsession was once more common than it is now. Arasthus tells of a peasant who was occupied by a different devil for every day in the week, and on Sundays by two. They were frequently seen, always walking in his shadow, when he had one, but were finally driven away by the village notary, a holy man; but they took the peasant with them, for he vanished utterly. A devil thrown out of a woman by the Archbishop of Rheims ran through the streets, pursued by a hundred persons, until the open country was reached, where by a leap higher than a church spire he escaped into a bird. A chaplain in Cromwell's army exorcised a soldier's obsessing devil by throwing the soldier into the water, when the devil came to the surface. The soldier, unfortunately, did not.

OBSOLETE, *adj.* No longer used by the timid. Said chiefly of words. A word which some lexicographer has marked obsolete is ever thereafter an object of dread and loathing to the fool writer, but if it is a good word and has no exact modern equivalent equally good, it is good enough for the good writer. Indeed, a writer's attitude toward "obsolete" words is as true a measure of his literary ability as anything except the character of his work. A dictionary of obsolete and obsolescent words would not only be singularly rich in strong and sweet parts of speech; it would add large possessions to the vocabulary of every competent writer who might not happen to be a competent reader.

OBSTINATE, *adj.* Inaccessible to the truth as it is manifest in the splendor and stress of our advocacy.

The popular type and exponent of obstinacy is the mule, a most intelligent animal.

OCCASIONAL, *adj.* Afflicting us with greater or less frequency. That, however, is not the sense in which the word is used in the phrase "occasional verses," which are verses written for an "occasion," such as an anniversary, a celebration or other event. True, they afflict us a little worse than other sorts of verse, but their name has no reference to irregular recurrence.

OCCIDENT, *n.* The part of the world lying west (or east) of the Orient. It is largely inhabited by Christians, a powerful subtribe of the Hypocrites, whose principal industries are murder and cheating, which they are pleased to call "war" and "commerce." These, also, are the principal industries of the Orient.

OCEAN, *n.* A body of water occupying about two-thirds of a world made for man—who has no gills.

OFFENSIVE, *adj.* Generating disagreeable emotions or sensations, as the advance of an army against its enemy.

"Were the enemy's tactics offensive?" the king asked. "I

should say so!" replied the unsuccessful general. "The black-guard wouldn't come out of his works!"

OLD, *adj.* In that stage of usefulness which is not inconsistent with general inefficiency, as an *old man*. Discredited by lapse of time and offensive to the popular taste, as an *old* book.

> "Old books? The devil take them!" Goby said.
> "Fresh every day must be my books and bread."
> Nature herself approves the Goby rule
> And gives us every moment a fresh fool.
> *Harley Shum.*

OLEAGINOUS, *adj.* Oily, smooth, sleek.

Disraeli once described the manner of Bishop Wilberforce as "unctuous, oleaginous, saponaceous." And the good prelate was ever afterward known as Soapy Sam. For every man there is something in the vocabulary that would stick to him like a second skin. His enemies have only to find it.

OLYMPIAN, *adj.* Relating to a mountain in Thessaly, once inhabited by gods, now a repository of yellowing newspapers, beer bottles and mutilated sardine cans, attesting the presence of the tourist and his appetite.

> His name the smirking tourist scrawls
> Upon Minerva's temple walls,
> Where thundered once Olympian Zeus,
> And marks his appetite's abuse.
> *Averil Joop.*

OMEN, *n.* A sign that something will happen if nothing happens.

ONCE, *adv.* Enough.

OPERA, *n.* A play representing life in another world, whose inhabitants have no speech but song, no motions but gestures and no postures but attitudes. All acting is simulation, and the word *simulation* is from *simia*, an ape; but in opera the actor takes for his model *Simia audibilis* (or *Pithecanthropos stentor*)—the ape that howls.

> The actor apes a man—at least in shape;
> The opera performer apes an ape.

OPIATE, *n.* An unlocked door in the prison of Identity. It leads into the jail yard.

OPPORTUNITY, *n.* A favorable occasion for grasping a disappointment.

OPPOSE, *v.* To assist with obstructions and objections.

> How lonely he who thinks to vex
> With badinage the Solemn Sex!
> Of levity, Mere Man, beware;
> None but the Grave deserve the Unfair.
>   *Percy P. Orminder.*

OPPOSITION, *n.* In politics the party that prevents the Government from running amuck by hamstringing it.

The King of Ghargaroo, who had been abroad to study the science of government, appointed one hundred of his fattest subjects as members of a parliament to make laws for the collection of revenue. Forty of these he named the Party of Opposition and had his Prime Minister carefully instruct them in their duty of opposing every royal measure. Nevertheless, the first one that was submitted passed unanimously. Greatly displeased, the King vetoed it, informing the Opposition that if they did that again they would pay for their obstinacy with their heads. The entire forty promptly disemboweled themselves.

"What shall we do now?" the King asked. "Liberal institutions cannot be maintained without a party of Opposition."

"Splendor of the universe," replied the Prime Minister, "it is true these dogs of darkness have no longer their credentials, but all is not lost. Leave the matter to this worm of the dust."

So the Minister had the bodies of his Majesty's Opposition embalmed and stuffed with straw, put back into the seats of power and nailed there. Forty votes were recorded against every bill and the nation prospered. But one day a bill imposing a tax on warts was defeated—the members of the Government party had not been nailed to their seats! This so enraged the King that the Prime Minister was put to death, the parliament was dissolved with a battery of artillery, and government of the people, by the people, for the people perished from Ghargaroo.

OPTIMISM, *n.* The doctrine, or belief, that everything is beautiful, including what is ugly, everything good, especially the bad, and everything right that is wrong. It is held with greatest tenacity by those most accustomed to the mischance of falling into adversity, and is most acceptably expounded with the grin that apes a smile. Being a blind faith, it is inaccessible to the light of disproof—an intellectual disorder, yielding to no treatment but death. It is hereditary, but fortunately not contagious.

OPTIMIST, *n.* A proponent of the doctrine that black is white.
    A pessimist applied to God for relief.
    "Ah, you wish me to restore your hope and cheerfulness," said God.
    "No," replied the petitioner, "I wish you to create something that would justify them."
    "The world is all created," said God, "but you have overlooked something—the mortality of the optimist."

ORATORY, *n.* A conspiracy between speech and action to cheat the understanding. A tyranny tempered by stenography.

ORPHAN, *n.* A living person whom death has deprived of the power of filial ingratitude—a privation appealing with a particular eloquence to all that is sympathetic in human nature. When young the orphan is commonly sent to an asylum, where by careful cultivation of its rudimentary sense of locality it is taught to know its place. It is then instructed in the arts of dependence and servitude and eventually turned loose to prey upon the world as a bootblack or scullery maid.

ORTHODOX, *n.* An ox wearing the popular religious joke.

ORTHOGRAPHY, *n.* The science of spelling by the eye instead of the ear. Advocated with more heat than light by the outmates of every asylum for the insane. They have had to concede a few things since the time of Chaucer, but are none the less hot in defence of those to be conceded hereafter.

> A spelling reformer indicted
> For fudge was before the court cicted.
>   The judge said: "Enough—
>   His candle we'll snough,
> And his sepulchre shall not be whicted."

OSTRICH, *n.* A large bird to which (for its sins, doubtless) nature has denied that hinder toe in which so many pious naturalists have seen a conspicuous evidence of design. The absence of a good working pair of wings is no defect, for, as has been ingeniously pointed out, the ostrich does not fly.

OTHERWISE, *adv.* No better.

OUTCOME, *n.* A particular type of disappointment. By the kind of intelligence that sees in an exception a proof of the rule the wisdom of an act is judged by the outcome, the result. This is immortal nonsense; the wisdom of an act is to be judged by the light that the doer had when he performed it.

OUTDO, *v. t.* To make an enemy.

OUT-OF-DOORS, *n.* That part of one's environment upon which no government has been able to collect taxes. Chiefly useful to inspire poets.

> I climbed to the top of a mountain one day
>   To see the sun setting in glory,
> And I thought, as I looked at his vanishing ray,
>   Of a perfectly splendid story.
>
> 'Twas about an old man and the ass he bestrode
>   Till the strength of the beast was o'ertested;
> Then the man would carry him miles on the road
>   Till Neddy was pretty well rested.

The moon rising solemnly over the crest
Of the hills to the east of my station
Displayed her broad disk to the darkening west
Like a visible new creation.

And I thought of a joke (and I laughed till I cried)
Of an idle young woman who tarried
About a church-door for a look at the bride,
Although 'twas herself that was married.

To poets all Nature is pregnant with grand
Ideas—with thought and emotion.
I pity the dunces who don't understand
The speech of earth, heaven and ocean.
Stromboli Smith.

OVATION, *n.* In ancient Rome, a definite, formal pageant in honor of one who had been disserviceable to the enemies of the nation. A lesser "triumph." In modern English the word is improperly used to signify any loose and spontaneous expression of popular homage to the hero of the hour and place.

"I had an ovation!" the actor man said,
But I thought it uncommonly queer,
That people and critics by him had been led
By the ear.

The Latin lexicon makes his absurd
Assertion as plain as a peg;
In "ovum" we find the true root of the word.
It means egg.
Dudley Spink.

OVEREAT, *v.* To dine.

Hail, Gastronome, Apostle of Excess,
Well skilled to overeat without distress!
Thy great invention, the unfatal feast,
Shows Man's superiority to Beast.
John Boop.

OVERWORK, *n.* A dangerous disorder affecting high public functionaries who want to go fishing.

Owe, *v.* To have (and to hold) a debt. The word formerly signified not indebtedness, but possession; it meant "own," and in the minds of debtors there is still a good deal of confusion between assets and liabilities.

Oyster, *n.* A slimy, gobby shellfish which civilization gives men the hardihood to eat without removing its entrails! The shells are sometimes given to the poor.

P

Pain, *n.* An uncomfortable frame of mind that may have a physical basis in something that is being done to the body, or may be purely mental, caused by the good fortune of another.

Painting, *n.* The art of protecting flat surfaces from the weather and exposing them to the critic.

Formerly, painting and sculpture were combined in the same work: the ancients painted their statues. The only present alliance between the two arts is that the modern painter chisels his patrons.

Palace, *n.* A fine and costly residence, particularly that of a great official. The residence of a high dignitary of the Christian Church is called a palace; that of the Founder of his religion was known as a field, or wayside. There is progress.

Palm, *n.* A species of tree having several varieties, of which the familiar "itching palm" (*Palma hominis*) is most widely distributed and sedulously cultivated. This noble vegetable exudes a kind of invisible gum, which may be detected by applying to the bark a piece of gold or silver. The metal will adhere with remarkable tenacity. The fruit of the itching palm is so bitter and unsatisfying that a considerable percentage of it is sometimes given away in what are known as "benefactions."

Palmistry, *n.* The 947th method (according to Mimbleshaw's

classification) of obtaining money by false pretences. It consists in "reading character" in the wrinkles made by closing the hand. The pretence is not altogether false; character can really be read very accurately in this way, for the wrinkles in every hand submitted plainly spell the word "dupe." The imposture consists in not reading it aloud.

PANDEMONIUM, *n.* Literally, the Place of All the Demons. Most of them have escaped into politics and finance, and the place is now used as a lecture hall by the Audible Reformer. When disturbed by his voice the ancient echoes clamor appropriate responses most gratifying to his pride of distinction.

PANTALOONS, *n.* A nether habiliment of the adult civilized male. The garment is tubular and unprovided with hinges at the points of flexion. Supposed to have been invented by a humorist. Called "trousers" by the enlightened and "pants" by the unworthy.

PANTHEISM, *n.* The doctrine that everything is God, in contradistinction to the doctrine that God is everything.

PANTOMIME, *n.* A play in which the story is told without violence to the language. The least disagreeable form of dramatic action.

PARDON, *v.* To remit a penalty and restore to a life of crime. To add to the lure of crime the temptation of ingratitude.

PASSPORT, *n.* A document treacherously inflicted upon a citizen going abroad, exposing him as an alien and pointing him out for special reprobation and outrage.

PAST, *n.* That part of Eternity with some small fraction of which we have a slight and regrettable acquaintance. A moving line called the Present parts it from an imaginary period known as the Future. These two grand divisions of Eternity, of which the one is continually effacing the other, are entirely unlike. The one is dark with sorrow and disappointment, the other bright with prosperity and joy. The Past is the region of sobs, the Future is the realm of song. In the one crouches Memory, clad in sackcloth and ashes, mumbling penitential prayer; in the sunshine of the other Hope flies with a free wing, beckoning to temples of success and bowers of ease. Yet the Past is the Future of yesterday, the Future is the Past of to-morrow. They are one—the knowledge and the dream.

PASTIME, *n.* A device for promoting dejection. Gentle exercise for intellectual debility.

PATIENCE, *n.* A minor form of despair, disguised as a virtue.

PATRIOT, *n.* One to whom the interests of a part seem superior to those of the whole. The dupe of statesmen and the tool of conquerors.

PATRIOTISM, *n.* Combustible rubbish ready to the torch of any one ambitious to illuminate his name.

In Dr. Johnson's famous dictionary patriotism is defined as the last resort of a scoundrel. With all due respect to an enlightened but inferior lexicographer I beg to submit that it is the first.

PEACE, *n.* In international affairs, a period of cheating between two periods of fighting.

> O, what's the loud uproar assailing
>   Mine ears without cease?
> 'Tis the voice of the hopeful, all-hailing
>   The horrors of peace.
>
> Ah, Peace Universal; they woo it—
>   Would marry it, too.
> If only they knew how to do it
>   'Twere easy to do.
>
> They're working by night and by day
>   On their problem, like moles.
> Have mercy, O Heaven, I pray,
>   On their meddlesome souls!
>   *Ro Amil.*

PEDESTRIAN, *n.* The variable (an audible) part of the roadway for an automobile.

PEDIGREE, *n.* The known part of the route from an arboreal ancestor with a swim bladder to an urban descendant with a cigarette.

PENITENT, *adj.* Undergoing or awaiting punishment.

PERFECTION, *n.* An imaginary state or quality distinguished from the actual by an element known as excellence; an attribute of the critic.

 The editor of an English magazine having received a letter pointing out the erroneous nature of his views and style, and signed "Perfection," promptly wrote at the foot of the letter: "I don't agree with you," and mailed it to Matthew Arnold.

PERIPATETIC, *adj.* Walking about. Relating to the philosophy of Aristotle, who, while expounding it, moved from place to place in order to avoid his pupil's objections. A needless precaution—they knew no more of the matter than he.

PERORATION, *n.* The explosion of an oratorical rocket. It dazzles, but to an observer having the wrong kind of nose its most conspicuous peculiarity is the smell of the several kinds of powder used in preparing it.

PERSEVERANCE, *n.* A lowly virtue whereby mediocrity achieves an inglorious success.

> "Persevere, persevere!" cry the homilists all,
> Themselves, day and night, persevering to bawl.
> "Remember the fable of tortoise and hare—
> The one at the goal while the other is—where?"
> Why, back there in Dreamland, renewing his lease
> Of life, all his muscles preserving the peace,
> The goal and the rival forgotten alike,
> And the long fatigue of the needless hike.
> His spirit a-squat in the grass and the dew
> Of the dogless Land beyond the Stew,

He sleeps, like a saint in a holy place,
A winner of all that is good in a race.

Sukker Uffro.

PESSIMISM, *n.* A philosophy forced upon the convictions of the observer by the disheartening prevalence of the optimist with his scarecrow hope and his unsightly smile.

PHILANTHROPIST, *n.* A rich (and usually bald) old gentleman who has trained himself to grin while his conscience is picking his pocket.

PHILISTINE, *n.* One whose mind is the creature of its environment, following the fashion in thought, feeling and sentiment. He is sometimes learned, frequently prosperous, commonly clean and always solemn.

PHILOSOPHY, *n.* A route of many roads leading from nowhere to nothing.

PHŒNIX, *n.* The classical prototype of the modern "small hot bird."

PHONOGRAPH, *n.* An irritating toy that restores life to dead noises.

PHOTOGRAPH, *n.* A picture painted by the sun without instruction in art. It is a little better than the work of an Apache, but not quite so good as that of a Cheyenne.

PHRENOLOGY, *n.* The science of picking the pocket through the scalp. It consists in locating and exploiting the organ that one is a dupe with.

PHYSICIAN, *n.* One upon whom we set our hopes when ill and our dogs when well.

PHYSIOGNOMY, *n.* The art of determining the character of another by the resemblances and differences between his face and our own, which is the standard of excellence.

> "There is no art," says Shakespeare, foolish man,
>   "To read the mind's construction in the face."
> The physiognomists his portrait scan,
>   And say: "How little wisdom here we trace!
> He knew his face disclosed his mind and heart,
> So, in his own defence, denied our art."
> *Lavatar Shunk.*

PIANO, *n.* A parlor utensil for subduing the impenitent visitor. It is operated by depressing the keys of the machine and the spirits of the audience.

PICKANINNY, *n.* The young of the *Procyanthropos*, or *Americanus dominans.* It is small, black and charged with political fatalities.

PICTURE, *n.* A representation in two dimensions of something wearisome in three.

> "Behold great Daubert's picture here on view—
> Taken from Life." If that description's true,
> Grant, heavenly Powers, that I be taken, too.
> *Jali Hane.*

PIE, *n.* An advance agent of the reaper whose name is Indigestion.

> Cold pie was highly esteemed by the remains.—*The Rev. Dr. Mucker, in a Funeral Sermon Over a British Nobleman.*

> Cold pie is a detestable
> American comestible.
> That's why I'm done—or undone—
> So far from that dear London.
> —*From the Headstone of a British Nobleman,*
>   *in Kalamazoo.*

PIETY, *n.* Reverence for the Supreme Being, based upon His supposed resemblance to man.

> The pig is taught by sermons and epistles
> To think the God of Swine has snout and bristles.
> *Judibras.*

PIG, *n.* An animal (*Porcus omnivorus*) closely allied to the human race by the splendor and vivacity of its appetite, which, however, is inferior in scope, for it sticks at pig.

PIGMY, *n.* One of a tribe of very small men found by ancient travelers in many parts of the world, but by modern in Central Africa only. The Pigmies are so called to distinguish them from the bulkier Caucasians—who are Hogmies.

PILGRIM, *n.* A traveler that is taken seriously. A Pilgrim Father was one who, leaving Europe in 1620 because not permitted to sing psalms through his nose, followed it to Massachusetts, where he could personate God according to the dictates of his conscience.

PILLORY, *n.* A mechanical device for inflicting personal distinction —prototype of the modern newspaper conducted by persons of austere virtues and blameless lives.

PIRACY, *n.* Commerce without its folly-swaddles, just as God made it.

PITIFUL, *adj.* The state of an enemy or opponent after an imaginary encounter with oneself.

PITY, *n.* A failing sense of exemption, inspired by contrast.

PLAGIARISM, *n.* A literary coincidence compounded of a discreditable priority and an honorable subsequence.

PLAGIARIZE, *v.* To take the thought or style of another writer whom one has never, never read.

PLAGUE, *n.* In ancient times a general punishment of the innocent for admonition of their ruler, as in the familiar instance of Pharaoh the Immune. The plague as we of to-day have the happiness to know it is merely Nature's fortuitous manifestation of her purposeless objectionableness.

PLAN, *v. t.* To bother about the best method of accomplishing an accidental result.

PLATITUDE, *n.* The fundamental element and special glory of popular literature. A thought that snores in words that smoke. The wisdom of a million fools in the diction of a dullard. A fossil sentiment in artificial rock. A moral without the fable. All that is mortal of a departed truth. A demi-tasse of milk-and-mortality. The Pope's-nose of a featherless peacock. A jelly-fish withering on the shore of the sea of thought. The cackle surviving the egg. A desiccated epigram.

PLATONIC, *adj.* Pertaining to the philosophy of Socrates. Platonic Love is a fool's name for the affection between a disability and a frost.

PLAUDITS, *n.* Coins with which the populace pays those who tickle and devour it.

PLEASE, *v.* To lay the foundation for a superstructure of imposition.

PLEASURE, *n.* The least hateful form of dejection.

PLEBEIAN, *n.* An ancient Roman who in the blood of his country stained nothing but his hands. Distinguished from the Patrician, who was a saturated solution.

PLEBISCITE, *n.* A popular vote to ascertain the will of the sovereign.

PLENIPOTENTIARY, *adj.* Having full power. A Minister Plenipotentiary is a diplomatist possessing absolute authority on condition that he never exert it.

PLEONASM, *n.* An army of words escorting a corporal of thought.

PLOW, *n.* An implement that cries aloud for hands accustomed to the pen.

PLUNDER, *v.* To take the property of another without observing the decent and customary reticences of theft. To effect a change of ownership with the candid concomitance of a brass band. To wrest the wealth of A from B and leave C lamenting a vanished opportunity.

POCKET, *n.* The cradle of motive and the grave of conscience. In woman this organ is lacking; so she acts without motive, and her conscience, denied burial, remains ever alive, confessing the sins of others.

POETRY, *n.* A form of expression peculiar to the Land beyond the Magazines.

POKER, *n.* A game said to be played with cards for some purpose to this lexicographer unknown.

POLICE, *n.* An armed force for protection and participation.

POLITENESS, *n.* The most acceptable hypocrisy.

POLITICIAN, *n.* An eel in the fundamental mud upon which the superstructure of organized society is reared. When he wriggles he mistakes the agitation of his tail for the trembling of the edifice. As compared with the statesman, he suffers the disadvantage of being alive.

POLITICS, *n.* A strife of interests masquerading as a contest of principles. The conduct of public affairs for private advantage.

POLYGAMY, *n.* A house of atonement, or expiatory chapel, fitted with several stools of repentance, as distinguished from monogamy, which has but one.

POPULIST, *n.* A fossil patriot of the early agricultural period, found in the old red soapstone underlying Kansas; characterized by an uncommon spread of ear, which some naturalists contend gave him the power of flight, though Professors Morse and Whitney, pursuing independent lines of thought, have ingeniously pointed out that had he possessed it he would have gone elsewhere. In the picturesque speech of his period, some fragments of which have come down to us, he was known as "The Matter with Kansas."

PORTABLE, *adj.* Exposed to a mutable ownership through vicissitudes of possession.

> His light estate, if neither he did make it
> Nor yet its former guardian forsake it,
> Is portable impropery, I take it.
> *Worgum Slupsky.*

PORTUGUESE, *n. pl.* A species of geese indigenous to Portugal. They are mostly without feathers and imperfectly edible, even when stuffed with garlic.

POSITIVE, *adj.* Mistaken at the top of one's voice.

POSITIVISM, *n.* A philosophy that denies our knowledge of the Real and affirms our ignorance of the Apparent. Its longest exponent is Comte, its broadest Mill and its thickest Spencer.

POSTERITY, *n.* An appellate court which reverses the judgment of a popular author's contemporaries, the appellant being his obscure competitor.

POTABLE, *n.* Suitable for drinking. Water is said to be potable; indeed, some declare it our natural beverage, although even they find it palatable only when suffering from the recurrent disorder known as thirst, for which it is a medicine. Upon nothing has so great and diligent ingenuity been brought to bear in all ages and in all countries, except the most uncivilized, as upon the invention of substitutes for water. To hold that this general aversion to that liquid has no basis in the preservative instinct of the race is to be unscientific—and without science we are as the snakes and toads.

POVERTY, *n.* A file provided for the teeth of the rats of reform.

The number of plans for its abolition equals that of the re-formers who suffer from it, plus that of the philosophers who know nothing about it. Its victims are distinguished by possession of all the virtues and by their faith in leaders seeking to conduct them into a prosperity where they believe these to be unknown.

PRAY, *v.* To ask that the laws of the universe be annulled in behalf of a single petitioner confessedly unworthy.

PRE-ADAMITE, *n.* One of an experimental and apparently unsatisfactory race that antedated Creation and lived under conditions not easily conceived. Melsius believed them to have inhabited "the Void" and to have been something intermediate between fishes and birds. Little is known of them beyond the fact that they supplied Cain with a wife and theologians with a controversy.

PRECEDENT, *n.* In Law, a previous decision, rule or practice which, in the absence of a definite statute, has whatever force and authority a Judge may choose to give it, thereby greatly simplifying his task of doing as he pleases. As there are precedents for everything, he has only to ignore those that make against his interest and accentuate those in the line of his desire. Invention of the precedent elevates the trial-at-law from the low estate of a fortuitous ordeal to the noble attitude of a dirigible arbitrament.

PRECIPITATE, *adj.* Anteprandial.

> Precipitate in all, this sinner
> Took action first, and then his dinner.
> *Judibras.*

PREDESTINATION, *n.* The doctrine that all things occur according to programme. This doctrine should not be confused with that of foreordination, which means that all things are programmed, but does not affirm their occurrence, that being only an implication from other doctrines by which this is entailed. The difference is great enough to have deluged Christendom with ink, to say nothing of the gore. With the distinction of the two doctrines kept well in mind, and a reverent belief in both, one may hope to escape perdition if spared.

PREDICAMENT, *n*. The wage of consistency.

PREDILECTION, *n*. The preparatory stage of disillusion.

PRE-EXISTENCE, *n*. An unnoted factor in creation.

PREFERENCE, *n*. A sentiment, or frame of mind, induced by the erroneous belief that one thing is better than another.

An ancient philosopher, expounding his conviction that life is no better than death, was asked by a disciple why, then, he did not die. "Because," he replied, "death is no better than life."

It is longer.

PREHISTORIC, *adj.* Belonging to an early period and a museum. Antedating the art and practice of perpetuating falsehood.

> He lived in a period prehistoric,
> When all was absurd and phantasmagoric.
> Born later, when Clio, celestial recorder,
> Set down great events in succession and order,
> He surely had seen nothing droll or fortuitous
> In anything here but the lies that she threw at us.
> *Orpheus Bowen.*

PREJUDICE, *n*. A vagrant opinion without visible means of support.

PRELATE, *n*. A church officer having a superior degree of holiness and a fat preferment. One of Heaven's aristocracy. A gentleman of God.

PREROGATIVE, *n*. A sovereign's right to do wrong.

PRESBYTERIAN, *n*. One who holds the conviction that the government authorities of the Church should be called presbyters.

PRESCRIPTION, *n*. A physician's guess at what will best prolong the situation with least harm to the patient.

PRESENT, *n*. That part of eternity dividing the domain of disappointment from the realm of hope.

PRESENTABLE, *adj*. Hideously appareled after the manner of the time and place.

In Boorioboola-Gha a man is presentable on occasions of ceremony if he have his abdomen painted a bright blue and wear a cow's tail; in New York he may, if it please him, omit the paint, but after sunset he must wear two tails made of the wool of a sheep and dyed black.

PRESIDE, *v*. To guide the action of a deliberative body to a desirable result. In Journalese, to perform upon a musical instrument; as, "He presided at the piccolo."

> The Headliner, holding the copy in hand,
>   Read with a solemn face:
> "The music was very uncommonly grand—
>   The best that was every provided,
>   For our townsman Brown presided
>   At the organ with skill and grace."
> The Headliner discontinued to read,
>   And, spreading the paper down
> On the desk, he dashed in at the top of the screed:
>   "Great playing by President Brown."
>   *Orpheus Bowen.*

PRESIDENCY, *n*. The greased pig in the field game of American politics.

PRESIDENT, *n*. The leading figure in a small group of men of whom—and of whom only—it is positively known that immense numbers of their countrymen did not want any of them for President.

> If that's an honor surely 'tis a greater
> To have been a simple and undamned spectator.
> Behold in me a man of mark and note
> Whom no elector e'er denied a vote!—
> An undiscredited, unhooted gent
> Who might, for all we know, be President
> By acclamation. Cheer, ye varlets, cheer—
> I'm passing with a wide and open ear!
> *Jonathan Fomry.*

PREVARICATOR, *n.* A liar in the caterpillar state.

PRICE, *n.* Value, plus a reasonable sum for the wear and tear of conscience in demanding it.

PRIMATE, *n.* The head of a church, especially a State church supported by involuntary contributions. The Primate of England is the Archbishop of Canterbury, an amiable old gentleman, who occupies Lambeth Palace when living and Westminster Abbey when dead. He is commonly dead.

PRISON, *n.* A place of punishments and rewards. The poet assures us that—

> "Stone walls do not a prison make,"

but a combination of the stone wall, the political parasite and the moral instructor is no garden of sweets.

PRIVATE, *n.* A military gentleman with a field-marshal's baton in his knapsack and an impediment in his hope.

PROBOSCIS, *n.* The rudimentary organ of an elephant which serves him in place of the knife-and-fork that Evolution has as yet denied him. For purposes of humor it is popularly called a trunk.

Asked how he knew that an elephant was going on a journey, the illustrious Jo. Miller cast a reproachful look upon his tormentor, and answered, absently: "When it is ajar," and threw himself from a high promontory into the sea. Thus perished in his pride the most famous humorist of antiquity, leaving to mankind a heritage of woe! No successor worthy of the title has appeared, though Mr. Edward Bok, of *The Ladies' Home Journal,* is much respected for the purity and sweetness of his personal character.

PROJECTILE, *n.* The final arbiter in international disputes. Formerly these disputes were settled by physical contact of the disputants, with such simple arguments as the rudimentary logic of the times could supply—the sword, the spear, and so forth. With the growth of prudence in military affairs the projectile came more and more into favor, and is now held in high esteem by the most courageous. Its capital defect is that it requires personal attendance at the point of propulsion.

PROOF, *n.* Evidence having a shade more of plausibility than of unlikelihood. The testimony of two credible witnesses as opposed to that of only one.

PROOF-READER, *n.* A malefactor who atones for making your writing nonsense by permitting the compositor to make it unintelligible.

PROPERTY, *n.* Any material thing, having no particular value, that may be held by A against the cupidity of B. Whatever gratifies the passion for possession in one and disappoints it in all others. The object of man's brief rapacity and long indifference.

PROPHECY, *n.* The art and practice of selling one's credibility for future delivery.

PROSPECT, *n.* An outlook, usually forbidding. An expectation, usually forbidden.

> Blow, blow, ye spicy breezes—
>   O'er Ceylon blow your breath,
> Where every prospect pleases,
>   Save only that of death.
>   *Bishop Sheber.*

PROVIDENTIAL, *adj.* Unexpectedly and conspicuously beneficial to the person so describing it.

PRUDE, *n.* A bawd hiding behind the back of her demeanor.

PUBLISH, *n.* In literary affairs, to become the fundamental element in a cone of critics.

PUSH, *n.* One of the two things mainly conducive to success,
especially in politics. The other is Pull.

PYRRHONISM, *n.* An ancient philosophy, named for its inventor. It consisted of an absolute disbelief in everything but
Pyrrhonism. Its modern professors have added that.

Q

QUEEN, *n.* A woman by whom the realm is ruled when there is
a king, and through whom it is ruled when there is not.

QUILL, *n.* An implement of torture yielded by a goose and
commonly wielded by an ass. This use of the quill is now
obsolete, but its modern equivalent, the steel pen, is wielded
by the same everlasting Presence.

QUIVER, *n.* A portable sheath in which the ancient statesman
and the aboriginal lawyer carried their lighter arguments.

> He extracted from his quiver,
>   Did this controversial Roman,
> An argument well fitted
> To the question as submitted,
> Then addressed it to the liver,
>   Of the unpersuaded foeman.
>   *Oglum P. Boomp.*

QUIXOTIC, *adj.* Absurdly chivalric, like Don Quixote. An in-
sight into the beauty and excellence of this incomparable
adjective is unhappily denied to him who has the misfortune
to know that the gentleman's name is pronounced
Ke-ho-tay.

When ignorance from out our lives can banish
Philology, 'tis folly to know Spanish.
Juan Smith.

QUORUM, *n.* A sufficient number of members of a deliberative body to have their own way and their own way of having it. In the United States Senate a quorum consists of the chairman of the Committee on Finance and a messenger from the White House; in the House of Representatives, of the Speaker and the devil.

QUOTATION, *n.* The act of repeating erroneously the words of another. The words erroneously repeated.

Intent on making his quotation truer,
He sought the page infallible of Brewer,
Then made a solemn vow that he would be
Condemned eternally. Ah, me, ah, me!
Stumpo Gaker.

QUOTIENT, *n.* A number showing how many times a sum of money belonging to one person is contained in the pocket of another—usually about as many times as it can be got there.

R

RABBLE, *n.* In a republic, those who exercise a supreme authority tempered by fraudulent elections. The rabble is like the sacred Simurgh, of Arabian fable—omnipotent on condition that it do nothing. (The word is Aristocratese, and has no exact equivalent in our tongue, but means, as nearly as may be, "soaring swine.")

RACK, *n.* An argumentative implement formerly much used in persuading devotees of a false faith to embrace the living truth. As a call to the unconverted the rack never had any particular efficacy, and is now held in light popular esteem.

RADICALISM, *n.* The conservatism of to-morrow injected into the affairs of to-day.

RADIUM, *n.* A mineral that gives off heat and stimulates the organ that a scientist is a fool with.

RAILROAD, *n.* The chief of many mechanical devices enabling us to get away from where we are to where we are no better off. For this purpose the railroad is held in highest favor by the optimist, for it permits him to make the transit with great expedition.

RAMSHACKLE, *adj.* Pertaining to a certain order of architecture, otherwise known as the Normal American. Most of the public buildings of the United States are of the Ramshackle order, though some of our earlier architects preferred the Ironic. Recent additions to the White House in Washington are Theo-Doric, the ecclesiastic order of the Dorians. They are exceedingly fine and cost one hundred dollars a brick.

RANK, *n.* Relative elevation in the scale of human worth.

> He held at court a rank so high
> That other noblemen asked why.
> "Because," 'twas answered, "others lack
> His skill to scratch the royal back."
> *Aramis Jukes.*

RANSOM, *n.* The purchase of that which neither belongs to the seller, nor can belong to the buyer. The most unprofitable of investments.

RAPACITY, *n.* Providence without industry. The thrift of power.

RAREBIT, *n.* A Welsh rabbit, in the speech of the humorless, who point out that it is not a rabbit. To whom it may be solemnly explained that the comestible known as toad-in-a-hole is really not a toad, and that *riz-de-veau à la financière* is not the smile of a calf prepared after the recipe of a she banker.

RASCAL, *n.* A fool considered under another aspect.

RASCALITY, *n.* Stupidity militant. The activity of a clouded intellect.

RASH, *adj*. Insensible to the value of our advice.

> "Now lay your bet with mine, nor let
>   These gamblers take your cash."
> "Nay, this child makes no bet." "Great snakes!
>   How can you be so rash?"
>   *Bootle P. Gish.*

RATIONAL, *adj*. Devoid of all delusions save those of observation, experience and reflection.

RATTLESNAKE, *n*. Our prostrate brother, *Homo ventrambulans.*

RAZOR, *n*. An instrument used by the Caucasian to enhance his beauty, by the Mongolian to make a guy of himself, and by the Afro-American to affirm his worth.

REACH, *n*. The radius of action of the human hand. The area within which it is possible (and customary) to gratify directly the propensity to provide.

> This is a truth, as old as the hills,
>   That life and experience teach:
> The poor man suffers that keenest of ills,
>   An impediment in his reach.
>   *G. J.*

READING, *n*. The general body of what one reads. In our country it consists, as a rule, of Indiana novels, short stories in "dialect" and humor in slang.

> We know by one's reading
> His learning and breeding;
> By what draws his laughter
> We know his Hereafter.
> Read nothing, laugh never—
> The Sphinx was less clever!
>   *Jupiter Muke.*

REALISM, *n*. The art of depicting nature as it is seen by toads. The charm suffusing a landscape painted by a mole, or a story written by a measuring-worm.

REALITY, *n.* The dream of a mad philosopher. That which would remain in the cupel if one should assay a phantom. The nucleus of a vacuum.

REALLY, *adv.* Apparently.

REAR, *n.* In American military matters, that exposed part of the army that is nearest to Congress.

REASON, *v. i.* To weight probabilities in the scales of desire.

REASON, *n.* Propensitate of prejudice.

REASONABLE, *adj.* Accessible to the infection of our own opinions. Hospitable to persuasion, dissuasion and evasion.

REBEL, *n.* A proponent of a new misrule who has failed to establish it.

RECOLLECT, *v.* To recall with additions something not previously known.

RECONCILIATION, *n.* A suspension of hostilities. An armed truce for the purpose of digging up the dead.

RECONSIDER, *v.* To seek a justification for a decision already made.

RECOUNT, *n.* In American politics, another throw of the dice, accorded to the player against whom they are loaded.

RECREATION, *n.* A particular kind of dejection to relieve a general fatigue.

RECRUIT, *n.* A person distinguishable from a civilian by his uniform and from a soldier by his gait.

> Fresh from the farm or factory or street,
> His marching, in pursuit or in retreat,
>   Were an impressive martial spectacle
> Except for two impediments—his feet.
>   *Thompson Johnson.*

RECTOR, *n.* In the Church of England, the Third Person of the parochial Trinity, the Curate and the Vicar being the other two.

REDEMPTION, *n.* Deliverance of sinners from the penalty of their sin, through their murder of the deity against whom they sinned. The doctrine of Redemption is the fundamental mystery of our holy religion, and whoso believeth in it shall not perish, but have everlasting life in which to try to understand it.

> We must awake Man's spirit from its sin,
>   And take some special measure for redeeming it;
> Though hard indeed the task to get it in
>   Among the angels any way but teaming it,
>   Or purify it otherwise than steaming it.
> I'm awkward at Redemption—a beginner:
> My method is to crucify the sinner.
>   *Golgo Brone.*

REDRESS, *n.* Reparation without satisfaction.

Among the Anglo-Saxons a subject conceiving himself wronged by the king was permitted, on proving his injury, to beat a brazen image of the royal offender with a switch that was afterward applied to his own naked back. The latter rite was performed by the public hangman, and it assured moderation in the plaintiff's choice of a switch.

RED-SKIN, *n.* A North American Indian, whose skin is not red—at least not on the outside.

REDUNDANT, *adj.* Superfluous; needless; *de trop*.

> The Sultan said: "There's evidence abundant
> To prove this unbelieving dog redundant."
> To whom the Grand Vizier, with mien impressive,
> Replied: "His head, at least, appears excessive."
>   *Habeeb Suleiman.*

Mr. Debs is a redundant citizen. —*Theodore Roosevelt.*

REFERENDUM, *n.* A law for submission of proposed legislation to a popular vote to learn the nonsensus of public opinion.

REFLECTION, *n.* An action of the mind whereby we obtain a clearer view of our relation to the things of yesterday and are able to avoid the perils that we shall not again encounter.

REFORM, *v.* A thing that mostly satisfies reformers opposed to reformation.

REFUGE, *n.* Anything assuring protection to one in peril. Moses and Joshua provided six cities of refuge—Bezer, Golan, Ramoth, Kadesh, Schekem and Hebron—to which one who had taken life inadvertently could flee when hunted by relatives of the deceased. This admirable expedient supplied him with wholesome exercise and enabled them to enjoy the pleasures of the chase; whereby the soul of the dead man was appropriately honored by observances akin to the funeral games of early Greece.

REFUSAL, *n.* Denial of something desired; as an elderly maiden's hand in marriage, to a rich and handsome suitor; a valuable franchise to a rich corporation, by an alderman; absolution to an impenitent king, by a priest, and so forth. Refusals are graded in a descending scale of finality thus: the refusal absolute, the refusal conditional, the refusal tentative and the refusal feminine. The last is called by some casuists the refusal assentive.

REGALIA, *n.* Distinguishing insignia, jewels and costume of such ancient and honorable orders as Knights of Adam; Visionaries of Detectable Bosh; the Ancient Order of Modern Troglodytes; the League of Holy Humbug; the Golden Phalanx of Phalangers; the Genteel Society of Expurgated Hoodlums; the Mystic Alliance of Gorgeous Regalians; Knights and Ladies of the Yellow Dog; the Oriental Order of Sons of the West; the Blatherhood of Insufferable Stuff; Warriors of the Long Bow; Guardians of the Great Horn Spoon; the Band of Brutes; the Impenitent Order of Wife-Beaters; the Sublime Legion of Flamboyant Conspicuants; Worshipers at the Electroplated Shrine; Shining Inaccessibles; Fee-Faw-Fummers of the Inimitable Grip; Jannissaries of the Broad-Blown Peacock; Plumed Increscencies of the

Magic Temple; the Grand Cabal of Able-Bodied Sedentarians; Associated Deities of the Butter Trade; the Garden of Galoots; the Affectionate Fraternity of Men Similarly Warted; the Flashing Astonishers; Ladies of Horror; Coöperative Association for Breaking into the Spotlight; Dukes of Eden; Disciples Militant of the Hidden Faith; Knights-Champions of the Domestic Dog; the Holy Gregarians; the Resolute Optimists; the Ancient Sodality of Inhospitable Hogs; Associated Sovereigns of Mendacity; Dukes-Guardian of the Mystic Cess-Pool; the Society for Prevention of Prevalence; Kings of Drink; Polite Federation of Gents-Consequential; the Mysterious Order of the Undecipherable Scroll; Uniformed Rank of Lousy Cats; Monarchs of Worth and Hunger; Sons of the South Star; Prelates of the Tub-and-Sword.

RELIGION, *n.* A daughter of Hope and Fear, explaining to Ignorance the nature of the Unknowable.

"What is your religion my son?" inquired the Archbishop of Rheims.

"Pardon, monseigneur," replied Rochebriant; "I am ashamed of it."

"Then why do you not become an atheist?"

"Impossible! I should be ashamed of atheism."

"In that case, monsieur, you should join the Protestants."

RELIQUARY, *n.* A receptacle for such sacred objects as pieces of the true cross, short-ribs of the saints, the ears of Balaam's ass, the lung of the cock that called Peter to repentance and so forth. Reliquaries are commonly of metal, and provided with a lock to prevent the contents from coming out and performing miracles at unseasonable times. A feather from the wing of the Angel of the Annunciation once escaped during a sermon in Saint Peter's and so tickled the noses of the congregation that they woke and sneezed with great vehemence three times each. It is related in the "Gesta Sanctorum" that a sacristan in the Canterbury cathedral surprised the head of Saint Dennis in the library. Reprimanded by its stern custodian, it explained that it was seeking a body of doctrine. This unseemly levity so enraged the diocesan that the offender was publicly anathematized, thrown into the

Stour and replaced by another head of Saint Dennis, brought from Rome.

RENOWN, *n.* A degree of distinction between notoriety and fame—a little more supportable than the one and a little more intolerable than the other. Sometimes it is conferred by an unfriendly and inconsiderate hand.

> I touched the harp in every key,
>   But found no heeding ear;
> And then Ithuriel touched me
>   With a revealing spear.
>
> Not all my genius, great as 'tis,
>   Could urge me out of night.
> I felt the faint appulse of his,
>   And leapt into the light!
>   *W. J. Candleton.*

REPARATION, *n.* Satisfaction that is made for a wrong and deducted from the satisfaction felt in committing it.

REPARTEE, *n.* Prudent insult in retort. Practiced by gentlemen with a constitutional aversion to violence, but a strong disposition to offend. In a war of words, the tactics of the North American Indian.

REPENTANCE, *n.* The faithful attendant and follower of Punishment. It is usually manifest in a degree of reformation that is not inconsistent with continuity of sin.

> Desirous to avoid the pains of Hell,
> You will repent and join the Church, Parnell?
> How needless!—Nick will keep you off the coals
> And add you to the woes of other souls.
>   *Jomater Abemy.*

REPLICA, *n.* A reproduction of a work of art, by the artist that made the original. It is so called to distinguish it from a "copy," which is made by another artist. When the two are made with equal skill the replica is the more valuable, for it is supposed to be more beautiful than it looks.

REPORTER, *n.* A writer who guesses his way to the truth and dispels it with a tempest of words.

> "More dear than all my bosom knows, O thou
> Whose 'lips are sealed' and will not disavow!"
> So sang the blithe reporter-man as grew
> Beneath his hand the leg-long "interview."
> *Barson Maith.*

REPOSE, *v. i.* To cease from troubling.

REPRESENTATIVE, *n.* In national politics, a member of the Lower House in this world, and without discernible hope of promotion in the next.

REPROBATION, *n.* In theology, the state of a luckless mortal prenatally damned. The doctrine of reprobation was taught by Calvin, whose joy in it was somewhat marred by the sad sincerity of his conviction that although some are foredoomed to perdition, others are predestined to salvation.

REPUBLIC, *n.* A nation in which, the thing governing and the thing governed being the same, there is only a permitted authority to enforce an optional obedience. In a republic the foundation of public order is the ever lessening habit of submission inherited from ancestors who, being truly governed, submitted because they had to. There are as many kinds of republics as there are gradations between the despotism whence they came and the anarchy whither they lead.

REQUIEM, *n.* A mass for the dead which the minor poets assure us the winds sing o'er the graves of their favorites. Sometimes, by way of providing a varied entertainment, they sing a dirge.

RESIDENT, *adj.* Unable to leave.

RESIGN, *v. t.* To renounce an honor for an advantage. To renounce an advantage for a greater advantage.

> 'Twas rumored Leonard Wood had signed
> A true renunciation

> Of title, rank and every kind
>   Of military station—
>   Each honorable station.
>
> By his example fired—inclined
>   To noble emulation,
> The country humbly was resigned
>   To Leonard's resignation—
>   His Christian resignation.
>   *Politian Greame.*

RESOLUTE, *adj.* Obstinate in a course that we approve.

RESPECTABILITY, *n.* The offspring of a *liaison* between a bald head and a bank account.

RESPIRATOR, *n.* An apparatus fitted over the nose and mouth of an inhabitant of London, whereby to filter the visible universe in its passage to the lungs.

RESPITE, *n.* A suspension of hostilities against a sentenced assassin, to enable the Executive to determine whether the murder may not have been done by the prosecuting attorney. Any break in the continuity of a disagreeable expectation.

> Altgeld upon his incandescent bed
> Lay, an attendant demon at his head.
>
> "O cruel cook, pray grant me some relief—
> Some respite from the roast, however brief.
>
> "Remember how on earth I pardoned all
> Your friends in Illinois when held in thrall."
>
> "Unhappy soul! for that alone you squirm
> O'er fire unquenched, a never-dying worm.
>
> "Yet, for I pity your uneasy state,
> Your doom I'll mollify and pains abate.
>
> "Naught, for a season, shall your comfort mar,
> Not even the memory of who you are."
>
> Throughout eternal space dread silence fell;
> Heaven trembled as Compassion entered Hell.

"As long, sweet demon, let my respite be
As, governing down here, I'd respite thee."

"As long, poor soul, as any of the pack
You thrust from jail consumed in getting back."

A genial chill affected Altgeld's hide
While they were turning him on t'other side.
Joel Spate Woop.

RESPLENDENT, *adj.* Like a simple American citizen beduking himself in his lodge, or affirming his consequence in the Scheme of Things as an elemental unit of a parade.

The Knights of Dominion were so resplendent in their velvet-and-gold that their masters would hardly have known them. —*"Chronicles of the Classes."*

RESPOND, *v. i.* To make answer, or disclose otherwise a consciousness of having inspired an interest in what Herbert Spencer calls "external coexistences," as Satan "squat like a toad" at the ear of Eve, responded to the touch of the angel's spear. To respond in damages is to contribute to the maintenance of the plaintiff's attorney and, incidentally, to the gratification of the plaintiff.

RESPONSIBILITY, *n.* A detachable burden easily shifted to the shoulders of God, Fate, Fortune, Luck or one's neighbor. In the days of astrology it was customary to unload it upon a star.

Alas, things ain't what we should see
If Eve had let that apple be;
And many a feller which had ought
To set with monarchses of thought,
Or play some rosy little game
With battle-chaps on fields of fame,
Is downed by his unlucky star,
And hollers: "Peanuts!—here you are!"
"The Sturdy Beggar."

RESTITUTION, *n.* The founding or endowing of universities and public libraries by gift or bequest.

RESTITUTOR, *n.* Benefactor; philanthropist.

RETALIATION, *n.* The natural rock upon which is reared the Temple of Law.

RETRIBUTION, *n.* A rain of fire-and-brimstone that falls alike upon the just and such of the unjust as have not procured shelter by evicting them.

In the lines following, addressed to an Emperor in exile by Father Gassalasca Jape, the reverend poet appears to hint his sense of the imprudence of turning about to face Retribution when it is taking exercise:

> What, what! Dom Pedro, you desire to go
>   Back to Brazil to end your days in quiet?
> Why, what assurance have you 'twould be so?
>   'Tis not so long since you were in a riot,
>   And your dear subjects showed a will to fly at
> Your throat and shake you like a rat. You know
> That empires are ungrateful; are you certain
> Republics are less handy to get hurt in?

REVEILLE, *n.* A signal to sleeping soldiers to dream of battlefields no more, but get up and have their blue noses counted. In the American army it is ingeniously called "rev-e-lee," and to that pronunciation our countrymen have pledged their lives, their misfortunes and their sacred dishonor.

REVELATION, *n.* A famous book in which St. John the Divine concealed all that he knew. The revealing is done by the commentators, who know nothing.

REVERENCE, *n.* The spiritual attitude of a man to a god and a dog to a man.

REVIEW, *v. t.*

> To set your wisdom (holding not a doubt of it,
>   Although in truth there's neither bone nor skin to it)
> At work upon a book, and so read out of it
>   The qualities that you have first read into it.

REVOLUTION, *n*. In politics, an abrupt change in the form of misgovernment. Specifically, in American history, the substitution of the rule of an Administration for that of a Ministry, whereby the welfare and happiness of the people were advanced a full half-inch. Revolutions are usually accompanied by a considerable effusion of blood, but are accounted worth it—this appraisement being made by beneficiaries whose blood had not the mischance to be shed. The French revolution is of incalculable value to the Socialist of to-day; when he pulls the string actuating its bones its gestures are inexpressibly terrifying to gory tyrants suspected of fomenting law and order.

RHADOMANCER, *n*. One who uses a divining-rod in prospecting for precious metals in the pocket of a fool.

RIBALDRY, *n*. Censorious language by another concerning oneself.

RIBROASTER, *n*. Censorious language by oneself concerning another. The word is of classical refinement, and is even said to have been used in a fable by Georgius Coadjutor, one of the most fastidious writers of the fifteenth century—commonly, indeed, regarded as the founder of the Fastidiotic School.

RICE-WATER, *n*. A mystic beverage secretly used by our most popular novelists and poets to regulate the imagination and narcotize the conscience. It is said to be rich in both obtundite and lethargine, and is brewed in a midnight fog by a fat witch of the Dismal Swamp.

RICH, *adj*. Holding in trust and subject to an accounting the property of the indolent, the incompetent, the unthrifty, the envious and the luckless. That is the view that prevails in the underworld, where the Brotherhood of Man finds its most logical development and candid advocacy. To denizens of the midworld the word means good and wise.

RICHES, *n.*

> A gift from Heaven signifying, "This is my beloved son, in whom I am well pleased." —*John D. Rockefeller.*
> The reward of toil and virtue. —*J. P. Morgan.*
> The savings of many in the hands of one. —*Eugene Debs.*

To these excellent definitions the inspired lexicographer feels that he can add nothing of value.

RIDICULE, *n.* Words designed to show that the person of whom they are uttered is devoid of the dignity of character distinguishing him who utters them. It may be graphic, mimetic or merely rident. Shaftesbury is quoted as having pronounced it the test of truth—a ridiculous assertion, for many a solemn fallacy has undergone centuries of ridicule with no abatement of its popular acceptance. What, for example, has been more valorously derided than the doctrine of Infant Respectability?

RIGHT, *n.* Legitimate authority to be, to do or to have; as the right to be a king, the right to do one's neighbor, the right to have measles, and the like. The first of these rights was once universally believed to be derived directly from the will of God; and this is still sometimes affirmed *in partibus infidelium* outside the enlightened realms of Democracy; as the well known lines of Sir Abednego Bink, following:

> By what right, then, do royal rulers rule?
>   Whose is the sanction of their state and pow'r?
> He surely were as stubborn as a mule
>   Who, God unwilling, could maintain an hour
> His uninvited session on the throne, or air
> His pride securely in the Presidential chair.
>
> Whatever is is so by Right Divine;
>   Whate'er occurs, God wills it so. Good land!
> It were a wondrous thing if His design
>   A fool could baffle or a rogue withstand!
> If so, then God, I say (intending no offence)
> Is guilty of contributory negligence.

RIGHTEOUSNESS, *n.* A sturdy virtue that was once found

among the Pantidoodles inhabiting the lower part of the peninsula of Oque. Some feeble attempts were made by returned missionaries to introduce it into several European countries, but it appears to have been imperfectly expounded. An example of this faulty exposition is found in the only extant sermon of the pious Bishop Rowley, a characteristic passage from which is here given:

"Now righteousness consisteth not merely in a holy state of mind, nor yet in performance of religious rites and obedience to the letter of the law. It is not enough that one be pious and just: one must see to it that others also are in the same state; and to this end compulsion is a proper means. Forasmuch as my injustice may work ill to another, so by his injustice may evil be wrought upon still another, the which it is as manifestly my duty to estop as to forestall mine own tort. Wherefore if I would be righteous I am bound to restrain my neighbor, by force if needful, in all those injurious enterprises from which, through a better disposition and by the help of Heaven, I do myself refrain."

RIME, *n.* Agreeing sounds in the terminals of verse, mostly bad. The verses themselves, as distinguished from prose, mostly dull. Usually (and wickedly) spelled "rhyme."

RIMER, *n.* A poet regarded with indifference or disesteem.

> The rimer quenches his unheeded fires,
> The sound surceases and the sense expires.
> Then the domestic dog, to east and west,
> Expounds the passions burning in his breast.
> The rising moon o'er that enchanted land
> Pauses to hear and yearns to understand.
> *Mowbray Myles.*

RIOT, *n.* A popular entertainment given to the military by innocent bystanders.

R. I. P. A careless abbreviation of *requiescat in pace*, attesting an indolent goodwill to the dead. According to the learned Dr. Drigge, however, the letters originally meant nothing more than *reductus in pulvis.*

RITE, *n.* A religious or semi-religious ceremony fixed by law, precept or custom, with the essential oil of sincerity carefully squeezed out of it.

RITUALISM, *n.* A Dutch Garden of God where He may walk in rectilinear freedom, keeping off the grass.

ROAD, *n.* A strip of land along which one may pass from where it is too tiresome to be to where it is futile to go.

> All roads, howsoe'er they diverge, lead to Rome,
> Whence, thank the good Lord, at least one leads back home.
> > *Borey the Bald.*

ROBBER, *n.* A candid man of affairs.

It is related of Voltaire that one night he and some traveling companions lodged at a wayside inn. The surroundings were suggestive, and after supper they agreed to tell robber stories in turn. When Voltaire's turn came he said: "Once there was a Farmer-General of the Revenues." Saying nothing more, he was encouraged to continue. "That," he said, "is the story."

ROMANCE, *n.* Fiction that owes no allegiance to the God of Things as They Are. In the novel the writer's thought is tethered to probability, as a domestic horse to the hitching-post, but in romance it ranges at will over the entire region of the imagination—free, lawless, immune to bit and rein. Your novelist is a poor creature, as Carlyle might say—a mere reporter. He may invent his characters and plot, but he must not imagine anything taking place that might not occur, albeit his entire narrative is candidly a lie. Why he imposes this hard condition on himself, and "drags at each remove a lengthening chain" of his own forging he can explain in ten thick volumes without illuminating by so much as a candle's ray the black profound of his own ignorance of the matter. There are great novels, for great writers have "laid waste their powers" to write them, but it remains true that far and away the most fascinating fiction that we have is "The Thousand and One Nights."

ROPE, *n*. An obsolescent appliance for reminding assassins that they too are mortal. It is put about the neck and remains in place one's whole life long. It has been largely superseded by a more complex electrical device worn upon another part of the person; and this is rapidly giving place to an apparatus known as the preachment.

ROSTRUM, *n*. In Latin, the beak of a bird or the prow of a ship. In America, a place from which a candidate for office energetically expounds the wisdom, virtue and power of the rabble.

ROUNDHEAD, *n*. A member of the Parliamentarian party in the English civil war—so called from his habit of wearing his hair short, whereas his enemy, the Cavalier, wore his long. There were other points of difference between them, but the fashion in hair was the fundamental cause of quarrel. The Cavaliers were royalists because the king, an indolent fellow, found it more convenient to let his hair grow than to wash his neck. This the Roundheads, who were mostly barbers and soap-boilers, deemed an injury to trade, and the royal neck was therefore the object of their particular indignation. Descendants of the belligerents now wear their hair all alike, but the fires of animosity enkindled in that ancient strife smoulder to this day beneath the snows of British civility.

RUBBISH, *n*. Worthless matter, such as the religions, philosophies, literatures, arts and sciences of the tribes infesting the regions lying due south from Boreaplas.

RUIN, *v*. To destroy. Specifically, to destroy a maid's belief in the virtue of maids.

RUM, *n*. Generically, fiery liquors that produce madness in total abstainers.

RUMOR, *n*. A favorite weapon of the assassins of character.

> Sharp, irresistible by mail or shield,
> By guard unparried as by flight unstayed,

O serviceable Rumor, let me wield
   Against my enemy no other blade.
His be the terror of a foe unseen,
   His the inutile hand upon the hilt,
And mine the deadly tongue, long, slender, keen,
   Hinting a rumor of some ancient guilt.
So shall I slay the wretch without a blow,
Spare me to celebrate his overthrow,
And nurse my valor for another foe.
                Joel Buxter.

RUSSIAN, *n.* A person with a Caucasian body and a Mongolian soul. A Tartar Emetic.

S

SABBATH, *n.* A weekly festival having its origin in the fact that God made the world in six days and was arrested on the seventh. Among the Jews observance of the day was enforced by a Commandment of which this is the Christian version: "Remember the seventh day to make thy neighbor keep it wholly." To the Creator it seemed fit and expedient that the Sabbath should be the last day of the week, but the Early Fathers of the Church held other views. So great is the sanctity of the day that even where the Lord holds a doubtful and precarious jurisdiction over those who go down to (and down into) the sea it is reverently recognized, as is manifest in the following deep-water version of the Fourth Commandment:

Six days shalt thou labor and do all thou art able,
And on the seventh holystone the deck and scrape the cable.

Decks are no longer holystoned, but the cable still supplies the captain with opportunity to attest a pious respect for the divine ordinance.

SACERDOTALIST, *n.* One who holds the belief that a clergyman is a priest. Denial of this momentous doctrine is the hardiest challenge that is now flung into the teeth of the Episcopalian church by the Neo-Dictionarians.

SACRAMENT, *n.* A solemn religious ceremony to which several degrees of authority and significance are attached. Rome has seven sacraments, but the Protestant churches, being less prosperous, feel that they can afford only two, and these of inferior sanctity. Some of the smaller sects have no sacraments at all—for which mean economy they will indubitably be damned.

SACRED, *adj.* Dedicated to some religious purpose; having a divine character; inspiring solemn thoughts or emotions; as, the Dalai Lama of Thibet; the Moogum of M'bwango; the temple of Apes in Ceylon; the Cow in India; the Crocodile, the Cat and the Onion of ancient Egypt; the Mufti of Moosh; the hair of the dog that bit Noah, etc.

> All things are either sacred or profane.
> The former to ecclesiasts bring gain;
> The latter to the devil appertain.
> *Dumbo Omohundro.*

SAFETY-LUTCH, *n.* A mechanical device acting automatically to prevent the fall of an elevator, or cage, in case of an accident to the hoisting apparatus.

> Once I seen a human ruin
> In a elevator-well,
> And his members was bestrewin'
> All the place where he had fell.
>
> And I says, apostrophisin'
> That uncommon woful wreck:
> "Your position's so surprisin'
> That I tremble for your neck!"
>
> Then that ruin, smilin' sadly
> And impressive, up and spoke:
> "Well, I wouldn't tremble badly,
> For it's been a fortnight broke."
>
> Then, for further comprehension
> Of his attitude, he begs
> I will focus my attention
> On his various arms and legs—

How they all are contumacious;
    Where they each, respective, lie;
How one trotter proves ungracious,
    T'other one an *alibi*.

These particulars is mentioned
    For to show his dismal state,
Which I wasn't first intentioned
    To specifical relate.

None is worser to be dreaded
    That I ever have heard tell
Than the gent's who there was spreaded
    In that elevator-well.

Now this tale is allegoric—
    It is figurative all,
For the well is metaphoric
    And the feller didn't fall.

I opine it isn't moral
    For a writer-man to cheat,
And despise to wear a laurel
    As was gotten by deceit.

For 'tis Politics intended
    By the elevator, mind,
It will boost a person splendid
    If his talent is the kind.

Col. Bryan had the talent
    (For the busted man is him)
And it shot him up right gallant
    Till his head begun to swim.

Then the rope it broke above him
    And he painful come to earth
Where there's nobody to love him
    For his detrimented worth.

Though he's livin' none would know him,
    Or at leastwise not as such.
Moral of this woful poem:
    Frequent oil your safety-clutch.
                            Porfer Poog.

SAINT, *n.* A dead sinner revised and edited.

The Duchess of Orleans relates that the irreverent old calumniator, Marshal Villeroi, who in his youth had known St. Francis de Sales, said, on hearing him called saint: "I am delighted to hear that Monsieur de Sales is a saint. He was fond of saying indelicate things, and used to cheat at cards. In other respects he was a perfect gentleman, though a fool."

SALACITY, *n.* A certain literary quality frequently observed in popular novels, especially in those written by women and young girls, who give it another name and think that in introducing it they are occupying a neglected field of letters and reaping an overlooked harvest. If they have the misfortune to live long enough they are tormented with a desire to burn their sheaves.

SALAMANDER, *n.* Originally a reptile inhabiting fire; later, an anthropomorphous immortal, but still a pyrophile. Salamanders are now believed to be extinct, the last one of which we have an account having been seen in Carcassonne by the Abbe Belloc, who exorcised it with a bucket of holy water.

SANDLOTTER, *n.* A vertebrate mammal holding the political views of Denis Kearney, a notorious demagogue of San Francisco, whose audiences gathered in the open spaces (sandlots) of the town. True to the traditions of his species, this leader of the proletariat was finally bought off by his law-and-order enemies, living prosperously silent and dying impenitently rich. But before his treason he imposed upon California a constitution that was a confection of sin in a diction of solecisms. The similarity between the words "sandlotter" and "sansculotte" is problematically significant, but indubitably suggestive.

SARCOPHAGUS, *n.* Among the Greeks a coffin which being made of a certain kind of carnivorous stone, had the peculiar property of devouring the body placed in it. The sarcophagus known to modern obsequiographers is commonly a product of the carpenter's art.

SATAN, *n.* One of the Creator's lamentable mistakes, repented in sashcloth and axes. Being instated as an archangel, Satan made himself multifariously objectionable and was finally expelled from Heaven. Halfway in his descent he paused, bent his head in thought a moment and at last went back. "There is one favor that I should like to ask," said he.

"Name it."

"Man, I understand, is about to be created. He will need laws."

"What, wretch! you his appointed adversary, charged from the dawn of eternity with hatred of his soul—you ask for the right to make his laws?"

"Pardon; what I have to ask is that he be permitted to make them himself."

It was so ordered.

SATIETY, *n.* The feeling that one has for the plate after he has eaten its contents, madam.

SATIRE, *n.* An obsolete kind of literary composition in which the vices and follies of the author's enemies were expounded with imperfect tenderness. In this country satire never had more than a sickly and uncertain existence, for the soul of it is wit, wherein we are dolefully deficient, the humor that we mistake for it, like all humor, being tolerant and sympathetic. Moreover, although Americans are "endowed by their Creator" with abundant vice and folly, it is not generally known that these are reprehensible qualities, wherefore the satirist is popularly regarded as a sour-spirited knave, and his every victim's outcry for codefendants evokes a national assent.

> Hail Satire! be thy praises ever sung
> In the dead language of a mummy's tongue,
> For thou thyself art dead, and damned as well—
> Thy spirit (usefully employed) in Hell.
> Had it been such as consecrates the Bible
> Thou hadst not perished by the law of libel.
> *Barney Stims.*

SATYR, *n.* One of the few characters of the Grecian mythology accorded recognition in the Hebrew. (Leviticus, xvii, 7.) The satyr was at first a member of the dissolute community acknowledging a loose allegiance to Dionysius, but underwent many transformations and improvements. Not infrequently he is confounded with the faun, a later and decenter creation of the Romans, who was less like a man and more like a goat.

Sauce, *n.* The one infallible sign of civilization and enlightenment. A people with no sauces has one thousand vices; a people with one sauce has only nine hundred and ninety-nine. For every sauce invented and accepted a vice is renounced and forgiven.

Saw, *n.* A trite popular saying, or proverb. (Figurative and colloquial.) So called because it makes its way into a wooden head. Following are examples of old saws fitted with new teeth.

A penny saved is a penny to squander.

A man is known by the company that he organizes.

A bad workman quarrels with the man who calls him that.

A bird in the hand is worth what it will bring.

Better late than before anybody has invited you.

Example is better than following it.

Half a loaf is better than a whole one if there is much else.

Think twice before you speak to a friend in need.

What is worth doing is worth the trouble of asking somebody to do it.

Least said is soonest disavowed.

He laughs best who laughs least.

Speak of the Devil and he will hear about it.

Of two evils choose to be the least.

Strike while your employer has a big contract.

Where there's a will there's a won't.

SCARABÆUS, *n.* The sacred beetle of the ancient Egyptians, allied to our familiar "tumble-bug." It was supposed to symbolize immortality, the fact that God knew why giving it its peculiar sanctity. Its habit of incubating its eggs in a ball of ordure may also have commended it to the favor of the priesthood, and may some day assure it an equal reverence among ourselves. True, the American beetle is an inferior beetle, but the American priest is an inferior priest.

SCARABEE, *n.* The same as scarabæus.

> He fell by his own hand
>> Beneath the great oak tree.
> He'd traveled in a foreign land.
> He tried to make her understand
> The dance that's called the Saraband,
>> But he called it Scarabee.
> He had called it so through an afternoon,
> And she, the light of his harem if so might be,
>   Had smiled and said naught. O the body was fair to see,
> All frosted there in the shine o' the moon—
>> Dead for a Scarabee
> And a recollection that came too late.
>> O Fate!
>> They buried him where he lay,
>> He sleeps awaiting the Day,
>> In state,
> And two Possible Puns, moon-eyed and wan,
> Gloom over the grave and then move on.
>> Dead for a Scarabee!
>>> *Fernando Tapple.*

SCARIFICATION, *n.* A form of penance practised by the mediæval pious. The rite was performed, sometimes with a knife, sometimes with a hot iron, but always, says Arsenius Asceticus, acceptably if the penitent spared himself no pain nor harmless disfigurement. Scarification, with other crude penances, has now been superseded by benefaction. The founding of a library or endowment of a university is said to yield to the penitent a sharper and more lasting pain than is conferred by the knife or iron, and is therefore a surer means of grace. There are, however, two grave objections to it as a penitential method: the good that it does and the taint of justice.

SCEPTER, *n.* A king's staff of office, the sign and symbol of his authority. It was originally a mace with which the sovereign admonished his jester and vetoed ministerial measures by breaking the bones of their proponents.

SCIMETAR, *n.* A curved sword of exceeding keenness, in the conduct of which certain Orientals attain a surprising proficiency, as the incident here related will serve to show. The account is translated from the Japanese of Shusi Itama, a famous writer of the thirteenth century.

When the great Gichi-Kuktai was Mikado he condemned to decapitation Jijiji Ri, a high officer of the Court. Soon after the hour appointed for performance of the rite what was his Majesty's surprise to see calmly approaching the throne the man who should have been at that time ten minutes dead!

"Seventeen hundred impossible dragons!" shouted the enraged monarch. "Did I not sentence you to stand in the market-place and have your head struck off by the public executioner at three o'clock? And is it not now 3:10?"

"Son of a thousand illustrious deities," answered the condemned minister, "all that you say is so true that the truth is a lie in comparison. But your heavenly Majesty's sunny and vitalizing wishes have been pestilently disregarded. With joy I ran and placed my unworthy body in the market-place. The executioner appeared with his bare scimetar, ostentatiously whirled it in air, and then, tapping me lightly upon the neck, strode away, pelted by the populace, with whom I was ever a favorite. I am come to pray for justice upon his own dishonorable and treasonous head."

"To what regiment of executioners does the black-boweled caitiff belong?" asked the Mikado.

"To the gallant Ninety-eight Hundred and Thirty-seventh—I know the man. His name is Sakko-Samshi."

"Let him be brought before me," said the Mikado to an attendant, and a half-hour later the culprit stood in the Presence.

"Thou bastard son of a three-legged hunchback without thumbs!" roared the sovereign—"why didst thou but lightly tap the neck that it should have been thy pleasure to sever?"

"Lord of Cranes of Cherry Blooms," replied the executioner, unmoved, "command him to blow his nose with his fingers."

Being commanded, Jijiji Ri laid hold of his nose and trumpeted like an elephant, all expecting to see the severed head flung violently from him. Nothing occurred: the performance prospered peacefully to the close, without incident.

All eyes were now turned on the executioner, who had grown as white as the snows on the summit of Fujiama. His legs trembled and his breath came in gasps of terror.

"Several kinds of spike-tailed brass lions!" he cried; "I am a ruined and disgraced swordsman! I struck the villain feebly because in flourishing the scimetar I had accidentally passed it through my own neck! Father of the Moon, I resign my office."

So saying, he grasped his top-knot, lifted off his head, and advancing to the throne laid it humbly at the Mikado's feet.

SCRAP-BOOK, *n.* A book that is commonly edited by a fool. Many persons of some small distinction compile scrap-books containing whatever they happen to read about themselves or employ others to collect. One of these egotists was addressed in the lines following, by Agamemnon Melancthon Peters:

> Dear Frank, that scrap-book where you boast
>   You keep a record true
> Of every kind of peppered roast
>   That's made of you;
>
> Wherein you paste the printed gibes
>   That revel round your name,
> Thinking the laughter of the scribes
>   Attests your fame;
>
> Where all the pictures you arrange
>   That comic pencils trace—
> Your funny figure and your strange
>   Semitic face—
>
> Pray lend it me. Wit I have not,
>   Nor art, but there I'll list
> The daily drubbings you'd have got
>   Had God a fist.

SCRIBBLER, *n.* A professional writer whose views are antagonistic to one's own.

SCRIPTURES, *n.* The sacred books of our holy religion, as distinguished from the false and profane writings on which all other faiths are based.

SEAL, *n.* A mark impressed upon certain kinds of documents to attest their authenticity and authority. Sometimes it is stamped upon wax, and attached to the paper, sometimes into the paper itself. Sealing, in this sense, is a survival of an ancient custom of inscribing important papers with cabalistic words or signs to give them a magical efficacy independent of the authority that they represent. In the British museum are preserved many ancient papers, mostly of a sacerdotal character, validated by necromantic pentagrams and other devices, frequently initial letters of words to conjure with; and in many instances these are attached in the same way that seals are appended now. As nearly every reasonless and apparently meaningless custom, rite or observance of modern times had origin in some remote utility, it is pleasing to note an example of ancient nonsense evolving in the process of ages into something really useful. Our word "sincere" is derived from *sine cero*, without wax, but the learned are not in agreement as to whether this refers to the absence of the cabalistic signs, or to that of the wax with which letters were formerly closed from public scrutiny. Either view of the matter will serve one in immediate need of an hypothesis. The initials L. S., commonly appended to signatures of legal documents, mean *locum sigillis*, the place of the seal, although the seal is no longer used—an admirable example of conservatism distinguishing Man from the beasts that perish. The words *locum sigillis* are humbly suggested as a suitable motto for the Pribyloff Islands whenever they shall take their place as a sovereign State of the American Union.

SEINE, *n.* A kind of net for effecting an involuntary change of environment. For fish it is made strong and coarse, but women are more easily taken with a singularly delicate fabric weighted with small, cut stones.

> The devil casting a seine of lace,
>   (With precious stones 'twas weighted)
> Drew it into the landing place
> And its contents calculated.
>
> All souls of women were in that sack—
>   A draft miraculous, precious!
> But ere he could throw it across his back
> They'd all escaped through the meshes.
>   *Baruch de Loppis.*

SELF-ESTEEM, *n.* An erroneous appraisement.

SELF-EVIDENT, *adj.* Evident to one's self and to nobody else.

SELFISH, *adj.* Devoid of consideration for the selfishness of others.

SENATE, *n.* A body of elderly gentlemen charged with high duties and misdemeanors.

SERIAL, *n.* A literary work, usually a story that is not true, creeping through several issues of a newspaper or magazine. Frequently appended to each instalment is a "synposis of preceding chapters" for those who have not read them, but a direr need is a synposis of succeeding chapters for those who do not intend to read *them.* A synposis of the entire work would be still better.

    The late James F. Bowman was writing a serial tale for a weekly paper in collaboration with a genius whose name has not come down to us. They wrote, not jointly but alternately, Bowman supplying the instalment for one week, his friend for the next, and so on, world without end, they hoped. Unfortunately they quarreled, and one Monday morning when Bowman read the paper to prepare himself for his task, he found his work cut out for him in a way to surprise and pain him. His collaborator had embarked every character of the narrative on a ship and sunk them all in the deepest part of the Atlantic.

SEVERALTY, *n.* Separateness, as, lands in severalty, *i.e.,* lands held individually, not in joint ownership. Certain tribes of Indians are believed now to be sufficiently civilized to have in severalty the lands that they have hitherto held as tribal organizations, and could not sell to the Whites for waxen beads and potato whiskey.

> Lo! the poor Indian whose unsuited mind
> Saw death before, hell and the grave behind;
> Whom thrifty settler ne'er besought to stay—
> His small belongings their appointed prey;
> Whom Dispossession, with alluring wile,
> Persuaded elsewhere every little while!
> His fire unquenched and his undying worm
> By "land in severalty" (charming term!)
> Are cooled and killed, respectively, at last,
> And he to his new holding anchored fast!

SHERIFF, *n.* In America the chief executive office of a country, whose most characteristic duties, in some of the Western and Southern States, are the catching and hanging of rogues.

> John Elmer Pettibone Cajee
> (I write of him with little glee)
> Was just as bad as he could be.
>
> 'Twas frequently remarked: "I swon!
> The sun has never looked upon
> So bad a man as Neighbor John."
>
> A sinner through and through, he had
> This added fault: it made him mad
> To know another man was bad.
>
> In such a case he thought it right
> To rise at any hour of night
> And quench that wicked person's light.
>
> Despite the town's entreaties, he
> Would hale him to the nearest tree
> And leave him swinging wide and free.
>
> Or sometimes, if the humor came,
> A luckless wight's reluctant frame
> Was given to the cheerful flame.

While it was turning nice and brown,
All unconcerned John met the frown
Of that austere and righteous town.

"How sad," his neighbors said, "that he
So scornful of the law should be—
An anar c, h, i, s, t."

(That is the way that they preferred
To utter the abhorrent word,
So strong the aversion that it stirred.)

"Resolved," they said, continuing,
"That Badman John must cease this thing
Of having his unlawful fling.

"Now, by these sacred relics"—here
Each man had out a souvenir
Got at a lynching yesteryear—

"By these we swear he shall forsake
His ways, nor cause our hearts to ache
By sins of rope and torch and stake.

"We'll tie his red right hand until
He'll have small freedom to fulfil
The mandates of his lawless will."

So, in convention then and there,
They named him Sheriff. The affair
Was opened, it is said, with prayer.
                    J. Milton Sloluck.

SIREN, *n.* One of several musical prodigies famous for a vain attempt to dissuade Odysseus from a life on the ocean wave. Figuratively, any lady of splendid promise, dissembled purpose and disappointing performance.

SLANG, *n.* The grunt of the human hog (*Pignoramus intolerabilis*) with an audible memory. The speech of one who utters with his tongue what he thinks with his ear, and feels the pride of a creator in accomplishing the feat of a parrot. A means (under Providence) of setting up as a wit without a capital of sense.

SMITHAREEN, *n.* A fragment, a decomponent part, a remain.

The word is used variously, but in the following verses on a noted female reformer who opposed bicycle-riding by women because it "led them to the devil" it is seen at its best:

> The wheels go round without a sound—
>   The maidens hold high revel;
> In sinful mood, insanely gay,
> True spinsters spin adown the way
>   From duty to the devil!
> They laugh, they sing, and—ting-a-ling!
>   Their bells go all the morning;
> Their lanterns bright bestar the night
>   Pedestrians a-warning.
> With lifted hands Miss Charlotte stands,
>   Good-Lording and O-mying,
> Her rheumatism forgotten quite,
>   Her fat with anger frying.
> She blocks the path that leads to wrath,
>   Jack Satan's power defying.
> The wheels go round without a sound
>   The lights burn red and blue and green.
> What's this that's found upon the ground?
> Poor Charlotte Smith's a smithareen!
>
> > *John William Yope.*

SOPHISTRY, *n.* The controversial method of an opponent, distinguished from one's own by superior insincerity and fooling. This method is that of the later Sophists, a Grecian sect of philosophers who began by teaching wisdom, prudence, science, art and, in brief, whatever men ought to know, but lost themselves in a maze of quibbles and a fog of words.

> His bad opponent's "facts" he sweeps away,
> And drags his sophistry to light of day;
> Then swears they're pushed to madness who resort
> To falsehood of so desperate a sort.
> Not so; like sods upon a dead man's breast,
> He lies most lightly who the least is pressed.
>
> > *Polydore Smith.*

SORCERY, *n.* The ancient prototype and forerunner of political influence. It was, however, deemed less respectable and sometimes was punished by torture and death. Augustine Nicholas

relates that a poor peasant who had been accused of sorcery
was put to the torture to compel a confession. After enduring a few gentle agonies the suffering simpleton admitted
his guilt, but naively asked his tormentors if it were not possible to be a sorcerer without knowing it.

SOUL, *n.* A spiritual entity concerning which there hath been
brave disputation. Plato held that those souls which in a previous state of existence (antedating Athens) had obtained
the clearest glimpses of eternal truth entered into the bodies
of persons who became philosophers. Plato was himself a
philosopher. The souls that had least contemplated divine
truth animated the bodies of usurpers and despots. Dionysius I, who had threatened to decapitate the broad-browed
philosopher, was a usurper and a despot. Plato, doubtless,
was not the first to construct a system of philosophy that
could be quoted against his enemies; certainly he was not
the last.

   "Concerning the nature of the soul," saith the renowned
author of *Diversiones Sanctorum,* "there hath been hardly
more argument than that of its place in the body. Mine own
belief is that the soul hath her seat in the abdomen—in
which faith we may discern and interpret a truth hitherto
unintelligible, namely that the glutton is of all men most devout. He is said in the Scripture to 'make a god of his belly'
—why, then, should he not be pious, having ever his Deity
with him to freshen his faith? Who so well as he can know
the might and majesty that he shrines? Truly and soberly,
the soul and the stomach are one Divine Entity; and such
was the belief of Promasius, who nevertheless erred in denying it immortality. He had observed that its visible and material substance failed and decayed with the rest of the body
after death, but of its immaterial essence he knew nothing.
This is what we call the Appetite, and it survives the wreck
and reek of mortality, to be rewarded or punished in another
world, according to what it hath demanded in the flesh. The
Appetite whose coarse clamoring was for the unwholesome
viands of the general market and the public refectory shall
be cast into eternal famine, whilst that which firmly though
civilly insisted on ortolans, caviare, terrapin, anchovies, *pâtés*

de foie gras and all such Christian comestibles shall flesh its spiritual tooth in the souls of them forever and ever, and wreak its divine thirst upon the immortal parts of the rarest and richest wines ever quaffed here below. Such is my religious faith, though I grieve to confess that neither His Holiness the Pope nor His Grace the Archbishop of Canterbury (whom I equally and profoundly revere) will assent to its dissemination."

SPOOKER, *n.* A writer whose imagination concerns itself with supernatural phenomena, especially the doings of spooks. One of the most illustrious spookers of our time is Mr. William D. Howells, who introduces a well-credentialed reader to as respectable and mannerly a company of spooks as one could wish to meet. To the terror that invests the chairman of a district school board, the Howells ghost adds something of the mystery enveloping a farmer from another township.

STORY, *n.* A narrative, commonly untrue. The truth of the stories here following has, however, not been successfully impeached.

One evening Mr. Rudolph Block, of New York, found himself seated at dinner alongside Mr. Percival Pollard, the distinguished critic.

"Mr. Pollard," said he, "my book, *The Biography of a Dead Cow*, is published anonymously, but you can hardly be ignorant of its authorship. Yet in reviewing it you speak of it as the work of the Idiot of the Century. Do you think that fair criticism?"

"I am very sorry, sir," replied the critic, amiably, "but it did not occur to me that you really might not wish the public to know who wrote it."

Mr. W. C. Morrow, who used to live in San Jose, California, was addicted to writing ghost stories which made the reader feel as if a stream of lizards, fresh from the ice, were streaking it up his back and hiding in his hair. San Jose was at that time believed to be haunted by the visible spirit of a noted bandit named Vasquez, who had been hanged there. The town was not very well lighted, and it is putting it mildly to say that San Jose was reluctant to be out o' nights. One particularly dark night two gentlemen were abroad in the loneliest spot within the city limits, talking loudly to keep up their courage, when they came upon Mr. J. J. Owen, a well-known journalist.

"Why, Owen," said one, "what brings you here on such a night as this? You told me that this is one of Vasquez' favorite haunts! And you are a believer. Aren't you afraid to be out?"

"My dear fellow," the journalist replied with a drear autumnal cadence in his speech, like the moan of a leaf-laden wind, "I am afraid to be in. I have one of Will Morrow's stories in my pocket and I don't dare to go where there is light enough to read it."

Rear-Admiral Schley and Representative Charles F. Joy were standing near the Peace Monument, in Washington, discussing the question, Is success a failure? Mr. Joy suddenly broke off in the middle of an eloquent sentence, exclaiming: "Hello! I've heard that band before. Santlemann's, I think."

"I don't hear any band," said Schley.

"Come to think, I don't either," said Joy; "but I see General Miles coming down the avenue, and that pageant always affects me in the same way as a brass band. One has to scrutinize one's impressions pretty closely, or one will mistake their origin."

While the Admiral was digesting this hasty meal of philosophy General Miles passed in review, a spectacle of impressive dignity. When the tail of the seeming procession had passed and the two observers had recovered from the transient blindness caused by its effulgence——

"He seems to be enjoying himself," said the Admiral.

"There is nothing," assented Joy, thoughtfully, "that he enjoys one-half so well."

The illustrious statesman, Champ Clark, once lived about a mile from the village of Jebigue, in Missouri. One day he rode into town on a favorite mule, and, hitching the beast on the sunny side of a street, in front of a saloon, he went inside in his character of teetotaler, to apprise the barkeeper that wine is a mocker. It was a dreadfully hot day. Pretty soon a neighbor came in and seeing Clark, said:

"Champ, it is not right to leave that mule out there in the sun. He'll roast, sure!—he was smoking as I passed him."

"O, he's all right," said Clark, lightly; "he's an inveterate smoker."

The neighbor took a lemonade, but shook his head and repeated that it was not right.

He was a conspirator. There had been a fire the night before: a stable just around the corner had burned and a number of horses had put on their immortality, among them a young colt, which was roasted to a rich nut-brown. Some of the boys had turned Mr. Clark's mule loose and substituted the mortal part of the colt. Presently another man entered the saloon.

"For mercy's sake!" he said, taking it with sugar, "do remove that mule, barkeeper: it smells."

"Yes," interposed Clark, "that animal has the best nose in Missouri. But if he doesn't mind, you shouldn't."

In the course of human events Mr. Clark went out, and there, apparently, lay the incinerated and shrunken remains of his charger. The boys did not have any fun out of Mr. Clarke, who looked at the body and, with the non-committal expression to which he owes so much of his political preferment, went away. But walking home late that night he saw his mule standing silent and solemn by the wayside in the misty moonlight. Mentioning the name of Helen Blazes with uncommon emphasis, Mr. Clark took the back track as hard as ever he could hook it, and passed the night in town.

General H. H. Wotherspoon, president of the Army War College, has a pet rib-nosed baboon, an animal of uncommon intelligence but imperfectly beautiful. Returning to his apartment one evening, the General was surprised and pained to find Adam (for so the creature is named, the general being a Darwinian) sitting up for him and wearing his master's best uniform coat, epaulettes and all.

"You confounded remote ancestor!" thundered the great strategist, "what do you mean by being out of bed after taps?—and with my coat on!"

Adam rose and with a reproachful look got down on all fours in the manner of his kind and, scuffling across the room to a table, returned with a visiting-card: General Barry had called and, judging by an empty champagne bottle and several cigar-stumps, had been hospitably entertained while waiting. The general apologized to his faithful progenitor and retired. The next day he met General Barry, who said:

"Spoon, old man, when leaving you last evening I forgot to ask you about those excellent cigars. Where did you get them?"

General Wotherspoon did not deign to reply, but walked away.

"Pardon me, please," said Barry, moving after him; "I was joking of course. Why, I knew it was not you before I had been in the room fifteen minutes."

SUCCESS, *n.* The one unpardonable sin against one's fellows. In literature, and particularly in poetry, the elements of success are exceedingly simple, and are admirably set forth in the following lines by the reverend Father Gassalasca Jape, entitled, for some mysterious reason, "John A. Joyce."

> The bard who would prosper must carry a book,
>   Do his thinking in prose and wear
> A crimson cravat, a far-away look
>   And a head of hexameter hair.
> Be thin in your thought and your body'll be fat;
> If you wear your hair long you needn't your hat.

SUFFRAGE, *n.* Expression of opinion by means of a ballot. The right of suffrage (which is held to be both a privilege and a duty) means, as commonly interpreted, the right to vote for the man of another man's choice, and is highly prized. Refusal to do so has the bad name of "incivism." The incivilian, however, cannot be properly arraigned for his crime, for there is no legitimate accuser. If the accuser is himself guilty he has no standing in the court of opinion; if not, he profits by the crime, for A's abstention from voting gives greater weight to the vote of B. By female suffrage is meant the right of a woman to vote as some man tells her to. It is based on female responsibility, which is somewhat limited. The woman most eager to jump out of her petticoat to assert her rights is first to jump back into it when threatened with a switching for misusing them.

SYCOPHANT, *n.* One who approaches Greatness on his belly so that he may not be commanded to turn and be kicked. He is sometimes an editor.

> As the lean leech, its victim found, is pleased
> To fix itself upon a part diseased
> Till, its black hide distended with bad blood,
> It drops to die of surfeit in the mud,
> So the base sycophant with joy descries
> His neighbor's weak spot and his mouth applies,
> Gorges and prospers like the leech, although,
> Unlike that reptile, he will not let go.
> Gelasma, if it paid you to devote
> Your talent to the service of a goat,
> Showing by forceful logic that its beard
> Is more than Aaron's fit to be revered;
> If to the task of honoring its smell
> Profit had prompted you, and love as well,
> The world would benefit at last by you
> And wealthy malefactors weep anew—
> Your favor for a moment's space denied
> And to the nobler object turned aside.
> Is't not enough that thrifty millionaires
> Who loot in freight and spoliate in fares,
> Or, cursed with consciences that bid them fly
> To safer villainies of darker dye,
> Forswearing robbery and fain, instead,
> To steal (they call it "cornering") our bread
> May see you groveling their boots to lick
> And begging for the favor of a kick?
> Still must you follow to the bitter end
> Your sycophantic disposition's trend,
> And in your eagerness to please the rich
> Hunt hungry sinners to their final ditch?
> In Morgan's praise you smite the sounding wire,

And sing hosannas to great Havemeyer!
What's Satan done that him you should eschew?
He too is reeking rich—deducting *you*.

SYLLOGISM, *n*. A logical formula consisting of a major and a minor assumption and an inconsequent. (See LOGIC.)

SYLPH, *n*. An immaterial but visible being that inhabited the air when the air was an element and before it was fatally polluted with factory smoke, sewer gas and similar products of civilization. Sylphs were allied to gnomes, nymphs and salamanders, which dwelt, respectively, in earth, water and fire, all now insalubrious. Sylphs, like fowls of the air, were male and female, to no purpose, apparently, for if they had progeny they must have nested in inaccessible places, none of the chicks having ever been seen.

SYMBOL, *n*. Something that is supposed to typify or stand for something else. Many symbols are mere "survivals"—things which having no longer any utility continue to exist because we have inherited the tendency to make them; as funereal urns carved on memorial monuments. They were once real urns holding the ashes of the dead. We cannot stop making them, but we can give them a name that conceals our helplessness.

SYMBOLIC, *adj*. Pertaining to symbols and the use and interpretation of symbols.

They say 'tis conscience feels compunction;
I hold that that's the stomach's function,
For of the sinner I have noted
That when he's sinned he's somewhat bloated,
Or ill some other ghastly fashion
Within that bowel of compassion.
True, I believe the only sinner
Is he that eats a shabby dinner.
You know how Adam with good reason,
For eating apples out of season,
Was "cursed." But that is all symbolic:
The truth is, Adam had the colic.

                                              G. J.

T

T, the twentieth letter of the English alphabet, was by the Greeks absurdly called *tau*. In the alphabet whence ours comes it had the form of the rude corkscrew of the period, and when it stood alone (which was more than the Phœnicians could always do) signified *Tallegal*, translated by the learned Dr. Brownrigg, "tanglefoot."

TABLE D'HÔTE, *n.* A caterer's thrifty concession to the universal passion for irresponsibility.

> Old Paunchinello, freshly wed,
>   Took Madam P. to table,
> And there deliriously fed
>   As fast as he was able.
>
> "I dote upon good grub," he cried,
>   Intent upon its throatage.
> "Ah, yes," said the neglected bride,
>   "You're in your *table d'hôtage*."
>   *Associated Poets.*

TAIL, *n.* The part of an animal's spine that has transcended its natural limitations to set up an independent existence in a world of its own. Excepting in its fœtal state, Man is without a tail, a privation of which he attests an hereditary and uneasy consciousness by the coat-skirt of the male and the train of the female, and by a marked tendency to ornament that part of his attire where the tail should be, and indubitably once was. This tendency is most observable in the female of the species, in whom the ancestral sense is strong and persistent. The tailed men described by Lord Monboddo are now generally regarded as a product of an imagination unusually susceptible to influences generated in the golden age of our pithecan past.

TAKE, *v. t.* To acquire, frequently by force but preferably by stealth.

TALK, *v. t.* To commit an indiscretion without temptation, from an impulse without purpose.

TARIFF, *n.* A scale of taxes on imports, designed to protect the domestic producer against the greed of his consumer.

> The Enemy of Human Souls
> Sat grieving at the cost of coals;
> For Hell had been annexed of late,
> And was a sovereign Southern State.
>
> "It were no more than right," said he,
> "That I should get my fuel free.
> The duty, neither just nor wise,
> Compels me to economize—
> Whereby my broilers, every one,
> Are execrably underdone.
> What would they have?—although I yearn
> To do them nicely to a turn,
> I can't afford an honest heat.
> This tariff makes even devils cheat!
> I'm ruined, and my humble trade
> All rascals may at will invade:
> Beneath my nose the public press
> Outdoes me in sulphureousness;
> The bar ingeniously applies
> To my undoing my own lies;
> My medicines the doctors use
> (Albeit vainly) to refuse
> To me my fair and rightful prey
> And keep their own in shape to pay;
> The preachers by example teach
> What, scorning to perform, I preach;
> And statesmen, aping me, all make
> More promises than they can break.
> Against such competition I
> Lift up a disregarded cry.
> Since all ignore my just complaint,
> By Hokey-Pokey! I'll turn saint!"
> Now, the Republicans, who all
> Are saints, began at once to bawl
> Against *his* competition; so
> There was a devil of a go!
> They locked horns with him, tête-à-tête
> In acrimonious debate,
> Till Democrats, forlorn and lone,
> Had hopes of coming by their own.

That evil to avert, in haste
The two belligerents embraced;
But since 'twere wicked to relax
A tittle of the Sacred Tax,
'Twas finally agreed to grant
The bold Insurgent-protestant
A bounty on each soul that fell
Into his ineffectual Hell.

Edam Smith.

TECHNICALITY, *n.* In an English court a man named Home was tried for slander in having accused a neighbor of murder. His exact words were: "Sir Thomas Holt hath taken a cleaver and stricken his cook upon the head, so that one side of the head fell upon one shoulder and the other side upon the other shoulder." The defendant was acquitted by instruction of the court, the learned judges holding that the words did not charge murder, for they did not affirm the death of the cook, that being only an inference.

TEDIUM, *n.* Ennui, the state or condition of one that is bored. Many fanciful derivations of the word have been affirmed, but so high an authority as Father Jape says that it comes from a very obvious source—the first words of the ancient Latin hymn *Te Deum Laudamus.* In this apparently natural derivation there is something that saddens.

TEETOTALER, *n.* One who abstains from strong drink, sometimes totally, sometimes tolerably totally.

TELEPHONE, *n.* An invention of the devil which abrogates some of the advantages of making a disagreeable person keep his distance.

TELESCOPE, *n.* A device having a relation to the eye similar to that of the telephone to the ear, enabling distant objects to plague us with a multitude of needless details. Luckily it is unprovided with a bell summoning us to the sacrifice.

TENACITY, *n.* A certain quality of the human hand in its relation

to the coin of the realm. It attains its highest development
in the hand of authority and is considered a serviceable
equipment for a career in politics. The following illustrative
lines were written of a Californian gentleman in high political preferment, who has passed to his accounting:

> Of such tenacity his grip
> That nothing from his hand can slip.
> Well-buttered eels you may o'erwhelm
> In tubs of liquid slippery-elm
> In vain—from his detaining pinch
> They cannot struggle half an inch!
> 'Tis lucky that he so is planned
> That breath he draws not with his hand,
> For if he did, so great his greed
> He'd draw his last with eager speed.
> Nay, that were well, you say. Not so
> He'd draw but never let it go!

THEOSOPHY, *n.* An ancient faith having all the certitude of religion and all the mystery of science. The modern Theosophist
holds, with the Buddhists, that we live an incalculable number of times on this earth, in as many several bodies, because
one life is not long enough for our complete spiritual development; that is, a single lifetime does not suffice for us to
become as wise and good as we choose to wish to become.
To be absolutely wise and good—that is perfection; and the
Theosophist is so keen-sighted as to have observed that everything desirous of improvement eventually attains perfection.
Less competent observers are disposed to except cats, which
seem neither wiser nor better than they were last year. The
greatest and fattest of recent Theosophists was the late
Madame Blavatsky, who had no cat.

TIGHTS, *n.* An habiliment of the stage designed to reinforce
the general acclamation of the press agent with a particular
publicity. Public attention was once somewhat diverted from
this garment to Miss Lillian Russell's refusal to wear it, and
many were the conjectures as to her motive, the guess of
Miss Pauline Hall showing a high order of ingenuity and sustained reflection. It was Miss Hall's belief that nature had

not endowed Miss Russell with beautiful legs. This theory was impossible of acceptance by the male understanding, but the conception of a faulty female leg was of so prodigious originality as to rank among the most brilliant feats of philosophical speculation! It is strange that in all the controversy regarding Miss Russell's aversion to tights no one seems to have thought to ascribe it to what was known among the ancients as "modesty." The nature of that sentiment is now imperfectly understood, and possibly incapable of exposition with the vocabulary that remains to us. The study of lost arts has, however, been recently revived and some of the arts themselves recovered. This is an epoch of *renaissances*, and there is ground for hope that the primitive "blush" may be dragged from its hiding-place amongst the tombs of antiquity and hissed on to the stage.

TOMB, *n.* The House of Indifference. Tombs are now by common consent invested with a certain sanctity, but when they have been long tenanted it is considered no sin to break them open and rifle them, the famous Egyptologist, Dr. Huggyns, explaining that a tomb may be innocently "glened" as soon as its occupant is done "smellynge," the soul being then all exhaled. This reasonable view is now generally accepted by archæologists, whereby the noble science of Curiosity has been greatly dignified.

TOPE, *v.* To tipple, booze, swill, soak, guzzle, lush, bib, or swig. In the individual, toping is regarded with disesteem, but toping nations are in the forefront of civilization and power. When pitted against the hard-drinking Christians the abstemious Mahometans go down like grass before the scythe. In India one hundred thousand beef-eating and brandy-and-soda guzzling Britons hold in subjection two hundred and fifty million vegetarian abstainers of the same Aryan race. With what an easy grace the whisky-loving American pushed the temperate Spaniard out of his possessions! From the time when the Berserkers ravaged all the coasts of western Europe and lay drunk in every conquered port it has been the same way: everywhere the nations that drink too much are observed to fight rather well and not too righteously. Wherefore the estimable old ladies who abolished the canteen from the American army may justly boast of having materially augmented the nation's military power.

TORTOISE, *n.* A creature thoughtfully created to supply occasion for the following lines by the illustrious Ambat Delaso:

TO MY PET TORTOISE

My friend, you are not graceful—not at all;
Your gait's between a stagger and a sprawl.

Nor are you beautiful: your head's a snake's
To look at, and I do not doubt it aches.

As to your feet, they'd make an angel weep.
'Tis true you take them in whene'er you sleep.

No, you're not pretty, but you have, I own,
A certain firmness—mostly you're backbone.

Firmness and strength (you have a giant's thews)
Are virtues that the great know how to use—

I wish that they did not; yet, on the whole,
You lack—excuse my mentioning it—Soul.

So, to be candid, unreserved and true,
I'd rather you were I than I were you.

Perhaps, however, in a time to be,
When Man's extinct, a better world may see

Your progeny in power and control,
Due to the genesis and growth of Soul.

So I salute you as a reptile grand
Predestined to regenerate the land.

Father of Possibilities, O deign
To accept the homage of a dying reign!

In the far region of the unforeknown
I dream a tortoise upon every throne.

I see an Emperor his head withdraw
Into his carapace for fear of Law;

A King who carries something else than fat,
Howe'er acceptably he carries that;

A President not strenuously bent
On punishment of audible dissent—

Who never shot (it were a vain attack)
An armed or unarmed tortoise in the back;

Subjects and citizens that feel no need
To make the March of Mind a wild stampede;

All progress slow, contemplative, sedate,
And "Take your time" the word, in Church and State.

O Tortoise, 'tis a happy, happy dream,
My glorious testudinous régime!

I wish in Eden you'd brought this about
By slouching in and chasing Adam out.

TREE, *n.* A tall vegetable intended by nature to serve as a penal apparatus, though through a miscarriage of justice most trees bear only a negligible fruit, or none at all. When naturally fruited, the tree is a beneficent agency of civilization and an important factor in public morals. In the stern West and the sensitive South its fruit (white and black respectively) though not eaten, is agreeable to the public taste and, though not exported, profitable to the general welfare. That the legitimate relation of the tree to justice was no discovery of Judge Lynch (who, indeed, conceded it no primacy over the lamp-post and the bridge-girder) is made plain by the following passage from Morryster, who antedated him by two centuries:

While in yᵗ londe I was carried to see yᵉ Ghogo tree, whereof I had hearde moch talk; but sayynge yᵗ I saw naught remarkabyll in it, yᵉ hed manne of yᵉ villayge where it grewe made answer as followeth:

"Yᵉ tree is not nowe in fruite, but in his seasonne you shall see dependynge fr. his braunches all soch as have affroynted yᵉ King his Majesty."

And I was furder tolde yᵗ yᵉ worde "Ghogo" sygnifyeth in yʳ tong yᵉ same as "rapscal" in our owne. —*Trauvells in yᵉ Easte:*

TRIAL, *n.* A formal inquiry designed to prove and put upon record the blameless characters of judges, advocates and jurors. In order to effect this purpose it is necessary to supply a contrast in the person of one who is called the defendant, the prisoner, or the accused. If the contrast is made sufficiently clear this person is made to undergo such an affliction as will give the virtuous gentlemen a comfortable sense of their immunity, added to that of their worth. In our day the accused is usually a human being, or a socialist, but in mediæval times, animals, fishes, reptiles and insects were brought to trial. A beast that had taken human life, or practiced sorcery, was duly arrested, tried and, if condemned, put to death by the public executioner. Insects ravaging grain fields, orchards or vineyards were cited to appeal by counsel before a civil tribunal, and after testimony, argument and condemnation, if they continued *in contumaciam* the matter was taken to a high ecclesiastical court, where they were solemnly excommunicated and anathematized. In a street of Toledo, some pigs that had wickedly run between the viceroy's legs, upsetting him, were arrested on a warrant, tried and punished. In Naples an ass was condemned to be burned at the stake, but the sentence appears not to have been executed. D'Addosio relates from the court records many trials of pigs, bulls, horses, cocks, dogs, goats, etc., greatly, it is believed, to the betterment of their conduct and morals. In 1451 a suit was brought against the leeches infesting some ponds about Berne, and the Bishop of Lausanne, instructed by the faculty of Heidelberg University, directed that some of "the aquatic worms" be brought before the local magistracy. This was done and the leeches, both present and absent, were ordered to leave the places that they had infested within three days on pain of incurring "the malediction of God." In the voluminous records of this *cause célèbre* nothing is found to show whether the offenders braved the punishment, or departed forthwith out of that inhospitable jurisdiction.

TRICHINOSIS, *n.* The pig's reply to proponents of porcophagy.

Moses Mendlessohn having fallen ill sent for a Christian physician, who at once diagnosed the philosopher's disorder as trichinosis, but tactfully gave it another name. "You need an immediate change of diet," he said; "you must eat six ounces of pork every other day."

"Pork?" shrieked the patient—"pork? Nothing shall induce me to touch it!"

"Do you mean that?" the doctor gravely asked.

"I swear it!"

"Good!—then I will undertake to cure you."

TRINITY, *n*. In the multiplex theism of certain Christian churches, three entirely distinct deities consistent with only one. Subordinate deities of the polytheistic faith, such as devils and angels, are not dowered with the power of combination, and must urge individually their claims to adoration and propitiation. The Trinity is one of the most sublime mysteries of our holy religion. In rejecting it because it is incomprehensible, Unitarians betray their inadequate sense of theological fundamentals. In religion we believe only what we do not understand, except in the instance of an intelligible doctrine that contradicts an incomprehensible one. In that case we believe the former as a part of the latter.

TROGLODYTE, *n*. Specifically, a cave-dweller of the paleolithic period, after the Tree and before the Flat. A famous community of troglodytes dwelt with David in the Cave of Adullam. The colony consisted of "every one that was in distress, and every one that was in debt, and every one that was discontented"—in brief, all the Socialists of Judah.

TRUCE, *n*. Friendship.

TRUST, *n*. In American politics, a large corporation composed in greater part of thrifty working men, widows of small means, orphans in the care of guardians and the courts, with many similar malefactors and public enemies.

TRUTH, *n*. An ingenious compound of desirability and appearance. Discovery of truth is the sole purpose of philosophy, which is the most ancient occupation of the human mind and has a fair prospect of existing with increasing activity to the end of time.

TRUTHFUL, *adj.* Dumb and illiterate.

TURKEY, *n.* A large bird whose flesh when eaten on certain religious anniversaries has the peculiar property of attesting piety and gratitude. Incidentally, it is pretty good eating.

TWICE, *adv.* Once too often.

TYPE, *n.* Pestilent bits of metal suspected of destroying civilization and enlightenment, despite their obvious agency in this incomparable dictionary.

TZETZE (or TSETSE) FLY, *n.* An African insect (*Glossina morsitans*) whose bite is commonly regarded as nature's most efficacious remedy for insomnia, though some patients prefer that of the American novelist (*Mendax interminabilis.*)

U

UBIQUITY, *n.* The gift or power of being in all places at one time, but not in all places at all times, which is omnipresence, an attribute of God and the luminiferous ether only. This important distinction between ubiquity and omnipresence was not clear to the mediæval Church and there was much bloodshed about it. Certain Lutherans, who affirmed the presence everywhere of Christ's body were known as Ubiquitarians. For this error they were doubtless damned, for Christ's body is present only in the eucharist, though that sacrament may be performed in more than one place simultaneously. In recent times ubiquity has not always been understood—not even by Sir Boyle Roche, for example, who held that a man cannot be in two places at once unless he is a bird.

UGLINESS, *n.* A gift of the gods to certain women, entailing virtue without humility.

ULTIMATUM, *n.* In diplomacy, a last demand before resorting to concessions.

Having received an ultimatum from Austria, the Turkish Ministry met to consider it.

"O servant of the Prophet," said the Sheik of the Imperial Chibouk to the Mamoosh of the Invincible Army, "how many unconquerable soldiers have we in arms?"

"Upholder of the Faith," that dignitary replied after examining his memoranda, "they are in numbers as the leaves of the forest!"

"And how many impenetrable battleships strike terror to the hearts of all Christian swine?" he asked the Imaum of the Ever Victorious Navy.

"Uncle of the Full Moon," was the reply, "deign to know that they are as the waves of the ocean, the sands of the desert and the stars of Heaven!"

For eight hours the broad brow of the Sheik of the Imperial Chibouk was corrugated with evidences of deep thought: he was calculating the chances of war. Then, "Sons of angels," he said, "the die is cast! I shall suggest to the Ulema of the Imperial Ear that he advise inaction. In the name of Allah, the council is adjourned."

UN-AMERICAN, *adj.* Wicked, intolerable, heathenish.

UNCTION, *n.* An oiling, or greasing. The rite of extreme unction consists in touching with oil consecrated by a bishop several parts of the body of one engaged in dying. Marbury relates that after the rite had been administered to a certain wicked English nobleman it was discovered that the oil had not been properly consecrated and no other could be obtained. When informed of this the sick man said in anger: "Then I'll be damned if I die!"

"My son," said the priest, "this is what we fear."

UNDERSTANDING, *n.* A cerebral secretion that enables one having it to know a house from a horse by the roof on the house. Its nature and laws have been exhaustively expounded by Locke, who rode a house, and Kant, who lived in a horse.

His understanding was so keen
That all things which he'd felt, heard, seen,
He could interpret without fail
If he was in or out of jail.
He wrote at Inspiration's call
Deep disquisitions on them all,
Then, pent at last in an asylum,
Performed the service to compile 'em.
So great a writer, all men swore,
They never had not read before.
Jorrock Wormley.

UNITARIAN, *n.* One who denies the divinity of a Trinitarian.

UNIVERSALIST, *n.* One who foregoes the advantage of a Hell for persons of another faith.

URBANITY, *n.* The kind of civility that urban observers ascribe to dwellers in all cities but New York. Its commonest expression is heard in the words, "I beg your pardon," and it is not inconsistent with disregard of the rights of others.

The owner of a powder mill
Was musing on a distant hill—
    Something his mind foreboded—
When from the cloudless sky there fell
A deviled human kidney! Well,
    The man's mill had exploded.
His hat he lifted from his head;
"I beg your pardon, sir," he said;
    "I didn't know 'twas loaded."
Swatkin.

USAGE, *n.* The First Person of the literary Trinity, the Second and Third being Custom and Conventionality. Imbued with a decent reverence for this Holy Triad an industrious writer may hope to produce books that will live as long as the fashion.

UXORIOUSNESS, *n.* A perverted affection that has strayed to one's own wife.

V

VALOR, *n.* A soldierly compound of vanity, duty and the gambler's hope.

"Why have you halted?" roared the commander of a division at Chickamauga, who had ordered a charge; "move forward, sir, at once."

"General," said the commander of the delinquent brigade, "I am persuaded that any further display of valor by my troops will bring them into collision with the enemy."

VANITY, *n.* The tribute of a fool to the worth of the nearest ass.

> They say that hens do cackle loudest when
>   There's nothing vital in the eggs they've laid;
>   And there are hens, professing to have made
> A study of mankind, who say that men
> Whose business 'tis to drive the tongue or pen
>   Make the most clamorous fanfaronade
>   O'er their most worthless work; and I'm afraid
> They're not entirely different from the hen.
> Lo! the drum-major in his coat of gold,
>   His blazing breeches and high-towering cap—
> Imperiously pompous, grandly bold,
>   Grim, resolute, an awe-inspiring chap!
> Who'd think this gorgeous creature's only virtue
> Is that in battle he will never hurt you?
> *Hannibal Hunsiker.*

VIRTUES, *n. pl.* Certain abstentions.

VITUPERATION, *n.* Satire, as understood by dunces and all such as suffer from an impediment in their wit.

VOTE, *n.* The instrument and symbol of a freeman's power to make a fool of himself and a wreck of his country.

W

W (double U) has, of all the letters in our alphabet, the only cumbrous name, the names of the others being monosyllabic. This advantage of the Roman alphabet over the Grecian is the more valued after audibly spelling out some simple Greek word, like εκιχοριαμβικός. Still, it is now thought by the learned that other agencies than the difference of the two alphabets may have been concerned in the decline of "the glory that was Greece" and the rise of "the grandeur that was Rome." There can be no doubt, however, that by simplifying the name of W (calling it "wow," for example) our civilization could be, if not promoted, at least better endured.

WALL STREET, *n.* A symbol of sin for every devil to rebuke. That Wall Street is a den of thieves is a belief that serves every unsuccessful thief in place of a hope in Heaven. Even the great and good Andrew Carnegie has made his profession of faith in the matter.

> Carnegie the dauntless has uttered his call
> To battle: "The brokers are parasites all!"
> Carnegie, Carnegie, you'll never prevail;
> Keep the wind of your slogan to belly your sail,
> Go back to your isle of perpetual brume,
> Silence your pibroch, doff tartan and plume:
> Ben Lomond is calling his son from the fray—
> Fly, fly from the region of Wall Street away!
> While still you're possessed of a single baubee
> (I wish it were pledged to endowment of me)
> 'Twere wise to retreat from the wars of finance
> Lest its value decline ere your credit advance.
> For a man 'twixt a king of finance and the sea,
> Carnegie, Carnegie, your tongue is too free!
> *Anonymus Bink.*

WAR, *n.* A by-product of the arts of peace. The most menacing political condition is a period of international amity. The student of history who has not been taught to expect the unexpected may justly boast himself inaccessible to the light. "In time of peace prepare for war" has a deeper meaning than is commonly discerned; it means, not merely that all things earthly have an end—that change is the one immutable and eternal law—but that the soil of peace is thickly sown with seeds of war and singularly suited to their germination and growth. It was when Kubla Khan had decreed his "stately pleasure dome"—when, that is to say, there were peace and fat feasting in Xanadu—that he

> heard from far
> Ancestral voices prophesying war.

One of the greatest of poets, Coleridge was one of the wisest of men, and it was not for nothing that he read us this parable. Let us have a little less of "hands across the sea," and a little more of that elemental distrust that is the security of nations. War loves to come like a thief in the night; professions of eternal amity provide the night.

WASHINGTONIAN, *n.* A Potomac tribesman who exchanged the privilege of governing himself for the advantage of good government. In justice to him it should be said that he did not want to.

> They took away his vote and gave instead
> The right, when he had earned, to *eat* his bread.
> In vain—he clamors for his "boss," poor soul,
> To come again and part him from his roll.
> *Offenbach Stutz.*

WEAKNESSES, *n. pl.* Certain primal powers of Tyrant Woman wherewith she holds dominion over the male of her species, binding him to the service of her will and paralyzing his rebellious energies.

WEATHER, *n.* The climate of an hour. A permanent topic of conversation among persons whom it does not interest, but who have inherited the tendency to chatter about it from naked arboreal ancestors whom it keenly concerned. The setting up of official weather bureaus and their maintenance in mendacity prove that even governments are accessible to suasion by the rude forefathers of the jungle.

Once I dipt into the future far as human eye could see,
And I saw the Chief Forecaster, dead as any one can be—
Dead and damned and shut in Hades as a liar from his birth,
With a record of unreason seldom paralleled on earth.

While I looked he reared him solemnly, that incandescent youth,
From the coals that he'd preferred to the advantages of truth.
He cast his eyes about him and above him; then he wrote
On a slab of thin asbestos what I venture here to quote—
For I read it in the rose-light of the everlasting glow:
"Cloudy; variable winds, with local showers; cooler; snow."

Halcyon Jones.

WEDDING, *n.* A ceremony at which two persons undertake to become one, one undertakes to become nothing, and nothing undertakes to become supportable.

WEREWOLF, *n.* A wolf that was once, or is sometimes, a man. All werewolves are of evil disposition, having assumed a bestial form to gratify a beastial appetite, but some, transformed by sorcery, are as humane as is consistent with an acquired taste for human flesh.

Some Bavarian peasants having caught a wolf one evening, tied it to a post by the tail and went to bed. The next morning nothing was there! Greatly perplexed, they consulted the local priest, who told them that their captive was undoubtedly a werewolf and had resumed its human form during the night. "The next time that you take a wolf," the good man said, "see that you chain it by the leg, and in the morning you will find a Lutheran."

WHANGDEPOOTENAWAH, *n.* In the Ojibwa tongue, disaster; an unexpected affliction that strikes hard.

> Should you ask me whence this laughter,
> Whence this audible big-smiling,
> With its labial extension,
> With its maxillar distortion
> And its diaphragmic rhythmus
> Like the billowing of ocean,
> Like the shaking of a carpet,
> I should answer, I should tell you:
> From the great deeps of the spirit,
> From the unplummeted abysmus
> Of the soul this laughter welleth
> As the fountain, the gug-guggle,

Like the river from the cañon,
To entoken and give warning
That my present mood is sunny.
Should you ask me further question—
Why the great deeps of the spirit,
Why the unplummeted abysmus
Of the soul extrudes this laughter,
This all audible big-smiling,
I should answer, I should tell you
With a white heart, tumpitumpy,
With a true tongue, honest Injun:
William Bryan, he has Caught It,
Caught the Whangdepootenawah!

Is't the sandhill crane, the shankank,
Standing in the marsh, the kneedeep,
Standing silent in the kneedeep
With his wing-tips crossed behind him
And his neck close-reefed before him,
With his bill, his william, buried
In the down upon his bosom,
With his head retracted inly,
While his shoulders overlook it?
Does the sandhill crane, the shankank,
Shiver grayly in the north wind,
Wishing he had died when little,
As the sparrow, the chipchip, does?
No 'tis not the Shankank standing,
Standing in the gray and dismal
Marsh, the gray and dismal kneedeep.
No, 'tis peerless William Bryan
Realizing that he's Caught It,
Caught the Whangdepootenawah!

WHEAT, *n.* A cereal from which a tolerably good whisky can with some difficulty be made, and which is used also for bread. The French are said to eat more bread *per capita* of population than any other people, which is natural, for only they know how to make the stuff palatable.

WHITE, *adj.* and *n.* Black.

WIDOW, *n.* A pathetic figure that the Christian world has

agreed to take humorously, although Christ's tenderness towards widows was one of the most marked features of his character.

WINE, *n.* Fermented grape-juice known to the Women's Christian Union as "liquor," sometimes as "rum." Wine, madam, is God's next best gift to man.

WIT, *n.* The salt with which the American humorist spoils his intellectual cookery by leaving it out.

WITCH, *n.* (1) Any ugly and repulsive old woman, in a wicked league with the devil. (2) A beautiful and attractive young woman, in wickedness a league beyond the devil.

WITTICISM, *n.* A sharp and clever remark, usually quoted, and seldom noted; what the Philistine is pleased to call a "joke."

WOMAN, *n.* An animal usually living in the vicinity of Man, and having a rudimentary susceptibility to domestication. It is credited by many of the elder zoölogists with a certain vestigial docility acquired in a former state of seclusion, but naturalists of the postsusananthony period, having no knowledge of the seclusion, deny the virtue and declare that such as creation's dawn beheld, it roareth now. The species is the most widely distributed of all beasts of prey, infesting all habitable parts of the globe, from Greenland's spicy mountains to India's moral strand. The popular name (wolfman) is incorrect, for the creature is of the cat kind. The woman is lithe and graceful in its movement, especially the American variety (*Felis pugnans*), is omnivorous and can be taught not to talk. —*Balthasar Pober.*

WORMS'-MEAT, *n.* The finished product of which we are the raw material. The contents of the Taj Mahal, the Tombeau Napoleon and the Granitarium. Worms'-meat is usually outlasted by the structure that houses it, but "this too must pass away." Probably the silliest work in which a human being can engage is construction of a tomb for himself. The solemn purpose cannot dignify, but only accentuates by contrast the foreknown futility.

> Ambitious fool! so mad to be a show!
> How profitless the labor you bestow
>   Upon a dwelling whose magnificence
> The tenant neither can admire nor know.
>
> Build deep, build high, build massive as you can,
> The wanton grass-roots will defeat the plan
>   By shouldering asunder all the stones
> In what to you would be a moment's span.
>
> Time to the dead so all unreckoned flies
> That when your marble all is dust, arise,
>   If wakened, stretch your limbs and yawn—
> You'll think you scarcely can have closed your eyes.
>
> What though of all man's works your tomb alone
> Should stand till Time himself be overthrown?
>   Would it advantage you to dwell therein
> Forever as a stain upon a stone?
>
> *Joel Huck.*

WORSHIP, *n.* Homo Creator's testimony to the sound construction and fine finish of Deus Creatus. A popular form of abjection, having an element of pride.

WRATH, *n.* Anger of a superior quality and degree, appropriate to exalted characters and momentous occasions; as, "the wrath of God," "the day of wrath," etc. Amongst the ancients the wrath of kings was deemed sacred, for it could usually command the agency of some god for its fit manifestation, as could also that of a priest. The Greeks before Troy were so harried by Apollo that they jumped out of the frying-pan of the wrath of Chryses into the fire of the wrath of Achilles, though Agamemnon, the sole offender, was neither fried nor roasted. A similar noted immunity was that of David when he incurred the wrath of Yahveh by numbering his people, seventy thousand of whom paid the penalty with their lives. God is now Love, and a director of the census performs his work without apprehension of disaster.

X

X in our alphabet being a needless letter has an added invincibility to the attacks of the spelling reformers, and like them, will doubtless last as long as the language. X is the sacred symbol of ten dollars, and in such words as Xmas, Xn, etc., stands for Christ, not, as is popularly supposed, because it represents a cross, but because the corresponding letter in the Greek alphabet is the initial of his name—Χριστός. If it represented a cross it would stand for St. Andrew, who "testified" upon one of that shape. In the algebra of psychology x stands for Woman's mind. Words beginning with X are Grecian and will not be defined in this standard English dictionary.

Y

YANKEE, *n.* In Europe, an American. In the Northern States of our Union, a New Englander. In the Southern States the word is unknown. (See DAMYANK.)

YEAR, *n.* A period of three hundred and sixty-five disappointments.

YESTERDAY, *n.* The infancy of youth, the youth of manhood, the entire past of age.

> But yesterday I should have thought me blest
>   To stand high-pinnacled upon the peak
>   Of middle life and look adown the bleak
> And unfamiliar foreslope to the West,
> Where solemn shadows all the land invest
>   And stilly voices, half-remembered, speak
>   Unfinished prophecy, and witch-fires freak
> The haunted twilight of the Dark of Rest.
> Yea, yesterday my soul was all aflame
>   To stay the shadow on the dial's face
> At manhood's noonmark! Now, in God His name
>   I chide aloud the little interspace
> Disparting me from Certitude, and fain
> Would know the dream and vision ne'er again.
>   *Baruch Arnegriff.*

It is said that in his last illness the poet Arnegriff was attended at different times by seven doctors.

YOKE, *n.* An implement, madam, to whose Latin name, *jugum,* we owe one of the most illuminating words in our language —a word that defines the matrimonial situation with precision, point and poignancy. A thousand apologies for withholding it.

YOUTH, *n.* The Period of Possibility, when Archimedes finds a fulcrum, Cassandra has a following and seven cities compete for the honor of endowing a living Homer.

Youth is the true Saturnian Reign, the Golden Age on earth again, when figs are grown on thistles, and pigs betailed with whistles and, wearing silken bristles, live ever in clover, and cows fly over, delivering milk at every door, and Justice never is heard to snore, and every assassin is made a ghost and, howling, is cast into Baltimost!

Polydore Smith.

Z

ZANY, *n.* A popular character in old Italian plays, who imitated with ludicrous incompetence the *buffone,* or clown, and was therefore the ape of an ape; for the clown himself imitated the serious characters of the play. The zany was progenitor to the specialist in humor, as we to-day have the unhappiness to know him. In the zany we see an example of creation; in the humorist, of transmission. Another excellent specimen of the modern zany is the curate, who apes the rector, who apes the bishop, who apes the archbishop, who apes the devil.

ZANZIBARI, *n.* An inhabitant of the Sultanate of Zanzibar, off the eastern coast of Africa. The Zanzibaris, a warlike people, are best known in this country through a threatening diplomatic incident that occurred a few years ago. The American consul at the capital occupied a dwelling that faced the sea, with a sandy beach between. Greatly to the scandal of this official's family, and against repeated remonstrances of the official himself, the people of the city persisted in using the beach for bathing. One day a woman came down to the edge of the water and was stooping to remove her attire (a pair of sandals) when the consul, incensed beyond restraint, fired a charge of bird-shot into the most conspicuous part of her person. Unfortunately for the existing *entente cordiale* between two great nations, she was the Sultana.

ZEAL, *n.* A certain nervous disorder afflicting the young and inexperienced. A passion that goeth before a sprawl.

> When Zeal sought Gratitude for his reward
> He went away exclaiming: "O my Lord!"
> "What do you want?" the Lord asked, bending down.
> "An ointment for my cracked and bleeding crown."
> *Jum Coople.*

ZENITH, *n.* A point in the heavens directly overhead to a man standing or a growing cabbage. A man in bed or a cabbage in the pot is not considered as having a zenith, though from this view of the matter there was once a considerable dissent among the learned, some holding that the posture of the body was immaterial. These were called Horizontalists, their opponents, Verticalists. The Horizontalist heresy was finally extinguished by Xanobus, the philosopher-king of Abara, a zealous Verticalist. Entering an assembly of philosophers who were debating the matter, he cast a severed human head at the feet of his opponents and asked them to determine its zenith, explaining that its body was hanging by the heels outside. Observing that it was the head of their leader, the Horizontalists hastened to profess themselves converted to whatever opinion the Crown might be pleased to hold, and Horizontalism took its place among *fides defuncti.*

ZEUS, *n.* The chief of Grecian gods, adored by the Romans as Jupiter and by the modern Americans as God, Gold, Mob and Dog. Some explorers who have touched upon the shores of America, and one who professes to have penetrated a considerable distance into the interior, have thought that these four names stand for as many distinct deities, but in his monumental work on Surviving Faiths, Frumpp insists that the natives are monotheists, each having no other god than himself, whom he worships under many sacred names.

ZIGZAG, *v. t.* To move forward uncertainly, from side to side, as one carrying the white man's burden. (From *zed*, *z*, and *jag*, an Icelandic word of unknown meaning.)

> He zedjagged so uncomen wyde
> Thet non coude pas on eyder syde;
> So, to com saufly thruh, I been
> Constreynet for to doodge betwene.
> *Munwele.*

ZOOLOGY, *n.* The science and history of the animal kingdom, including its king, the House Fly (*Musca maledicta.*) The father of Zoölogy was Aristotle, as is universally conceded, but the name of its mother has not come down to us. Two of the science's most illustrious expounders were Buffon and Oliver Goldsmith, from both of whom we learn (*L'Histoire générale des animaux* and *A History of Animated Nature*) that the domestic cow sheds its horns every two years.

BITS OF AUTOBIOGRAPHY

On a Mountain

THEY say that the lumberman has looked upon the Cheat Mountain country and seen that it is good, and I hear that some wealthy gentlemen have been there and made a game preserve. There must be lumber and, I suppose, sport, but some things one could wish were ordered otherwise. Looking back upon it through the haze of near half a century, I see that region as a veritable realm of enchantment; the Alleghanies as the Delectable Mountains. I note again their dim, blue billows, ridge after ridge interminable, beyond purple valleys full of sleep, "in which it seemèd always afternoon." Miles and miles away, where the lift of earth meets the stoop of sky, I discern an imperfection in the tint, a faint graying of the blue above the main range—the smoke of an enemy's camp.

It was in the autumn of that "most immemorial year," the 1861st of our Lord, and of our Heroic Age the first, that a small brigade of raw troops—troops were all raw in those days—had been pushed in across the Ohio border and after various vicissitudes of fortune and mismanagement found itself, greatly to its own surprise, at Cheat Mountain Pass, holding a road that ran from Nowhere to the southeast. Some of us had served through the summer in the "three-months' regiments," which responded to the President's first call for troops. We were regarded by the others with profound respect as "old soldiers." (Our ages, if equalized, would, I fancy, have given about twenty years to each man.) We gave ourselves, this aristocracy of service, no end of military airs; some of us even going to the extreme of keeping our jackets buttoned and our hair combed. We had been in action, too; had shot off a Confederate leg at Philippi, "the first battle of the war," and had lost as many as a dozen men at Laurel Hill and Carrick's Ford, whither the enemy had fled in trying, Heaven knows why, to get away from us. We now "brought to the task" of subduing the Rebellion a patriotism which never for a moment doubted that a rebel was a fiend accursed of God and the angels—one for whose extirpation by force and arms each youth of us considered himself specially "raised up."

It was a strange country. Nine in ten of us had never seen a mountain, nor a hill as high as a church spire, until we had crossed the Ohio River. In power upon the emotions nothing, I think, is comparable to a first sight of mountains. To a member of a plains-tribe, born and reared on the flats of Ohio or Indiana, a mountain region was a perpetual miracle. Space seemed to have taken on a new dimension; areas to have not only length and breadth, but thickness.

Modern literature is full of evidence that our great grandfathers looked upon mountains with aversion and horror. The poets of even the seventeenth century never tire of damning them in good, set terms. If they had had the unhappiness to read the opening lines of "The Pleasures of Hope," they would assuredly have thought Master Campbell had gone funny and should be shut up lest he do himself an injury.

The flatlanders who invaded the Cheat Mountain country had been suckled in another creed, and to them western Virginia —there was, as yet, no West Virginia—was an enchanted land. How we reveled in its savage beauties! With what pure delight we inhaled its fragrances of spruce and pine! How we stared with something like awe at its clumps of laurel!—real laurel, as we understood the matter, whose foliage had been once accounted excellent for the heads of illustrious Romans and such —mayhap to reduce the swelling. We carved its roots into finger-rings and pipes. We gathered spruce-gum and sent it to our sweethearts in letters. We ascended every hill within our picket-lines and called it a "peak."

And, by the way, during those halcyon days (the halcyon was there, too, chattering above every creek, as he is all over the world) we fought another battle. It has not got into history, but it had a real objective existence, although by a felicitous afterthought called by us who were defeated a "reconnaissance in force." Its short and simple annals are that we marched a long way and lay down before a fortified camp of the enemy at the farther edge of a valley. Our commander had the forethought to see that we lay well out of range of the small-arms of the period. A disadvantage of this arrangement was that the enemy was out of reach of us as well, for our rifles were no better than his. Unfortunately—one might almost say unfairly—he had a few pieces of artillery very well protected, and with those he mauled us to the eminent satisfaction of his mind and heart. So we parted from him in anger and returned to our own place, leaving our dead—not many.

Among them was a chap belonging to my company, named Abbott; it is not odd that I recollect it, for there was something unusual in the manner of Abbott's taking off. He was lying flat upon his stomach and was killed by being struck in the side by a nearly spent cannon-shot that came rolling in among us. The shot remained in him until removed. It was a solid round-shot, evidently cast in some private foundry, whose proprietor, setting the laws of thrift above those of ballistics, had put his "imprint" upon it: it bore, in slightly sunken letters, the name "Abbott." That is what I was told—I was not present.

It was after this, when the nights had acquired a trick of biting and the morning sun appeared to shiver with cold, that we moved up to the summit of Cheat Mountain to guard the pass through which nobody wanted to go. Here we slew the forest and built us giant habitations (astride the road from Nowhere to the southeast) commodious to lodge an army and fitly loopholed for discomfiture of the adversary. The long logs that it was our pride to cut and carry! The accuracy with which we laid them one upon another, hewn to the line and bullet-proof! The Cyclopean doors that we hung, with sliding bolts fit to be "the mast of some great admiral"! And when we had "made the pile complete" some marplot of the Regular Army came that way and chatted a few moments with our commander, and we made an earthwork away off on one side of the road (leaving the other side to take care of itself) and camped outside it in tents! But the Regular Army fellow had not the heart to suggest the demolition of our Towers of Babel, and the foundations remain to this day to attest the genius of the American volunteer soldiery.

We were the original game-preservers of the Cheat Mountain region, for although we hunted in season and out of season over as wide an area as we dared to cover we took less game, probably, than would have been taken by a certain single hunter of disloyal views whom we scared away. There were bear galore and deer in quantity, and many a winter day, in snow up to his knees, did the writer of this pass in tracking bruin to his den, where, I am bound to say, I commonly left him. I agreed with my lamented friend, the late Robert Weeks, poet:

> Pursuit may be, it seems to me,
> Perfect without possession.

There can be no doubt that the wealthy sportsmen who have made a preserve of the Cheat Mountain region will find plenty of game if it has not died since 1861. We left it there.

Yet hunting and idling were not the whole of life's programme up there on that wild ridge with its shaggy pelt of spruce and firs, and in the riparian lowlands that it parted. We had a bit of war now and again. There was an occasional "affair of outposts"; sometimes a hazardous scout into the enemy's country, ordered, I fear, more to keep up the appearance of doing something than with a hope of accomplishing a military result. But one day it was bruited about that a movement in force was to be made on the enemy's position miles away, at the summit of the main ridge of the Alleghanies—the camp whose faint blue smoke we had watched for weary days. The movement was made, as was the fashion in those 'prentice days of warfare, in two columns, which were to pounce upon the foeman from opposite sides at the same moment. Led over unknown roads by untrusty guides, encountering obstacles not foreseen—miles apart and without communication, the two columns invariably failed to execute the movement with requisite secrecy and precision. The enemy, in enjoyment of that inestimable military advantage known in civilian speech as being "surrounded," always beat the attacking columns one at a time or, turning red-handed from the wreck of the first, frightened the other away.

All one bright wintry day we marched down from our eyrie; all one bright wintry night we climbed the great wooded ridge opposite. How romantic it all was; the sunset valleys full of visible sleep; the glades suffused and interpenetrated with moonlight; the long valley of the Greenbrier stretching away to we knew not what silent cities; the river itself unseen under its "astral body" of mist! Then there was the "spice of danger."

Once we heard shots in front; then there was a long wait. As we trudged on we passed something—some things—lying by the wayside. During another wait we examined them, curiously lifting the blankets from their yellow-clay faces. How repulsive they looked with their blood-smears, their blank, staring eyes, their teeth uncovered by contraction of the lips! The frost had begun already to whiten their deranged clothing. We were as patriotic as ever, but we did not wish to be that way. For an hour afterward the injunction of silence in the ranks was needless.

*

Repassing the spot the next day, a beaten, dispirited and exhausted force, feeble from fatigue and savage from defeat, some of us had life enough left, such as it was, to observe that these bodies had altered their position. They appeared also to have thrown off some of their clothing, which lay near by, in disorder. Their expression, too, had an added blankness—they had no faces.

As soon as the head of our straggling column had reached the spot a desultory firing had begun. One might have thought the living paid honors to the dead. No; the firing was a military execution; the condemned, a herd of galloping swine. They had eaten our fallen, but—touching magnanimity!—we did not eat theirs.

The shooting of several kinds was very good in the Cheat Mountain country, even in 1861.

What I Saw of Shiloh

I

THIS is a simple story of a battle; such a tale as may be told by a soldier who is no writer to a reader who is no soldier.

The morning of Sunday, the sixth day of April, 1862, was bright and warm. Reveille had been sounded rather late, for the troops, wearied with long marching, were to have a day of rest. The men were idling about the embers of their bivouac fires; some preparing breakfast, others looking carelessly to the condition of their arms and accoutrements, against the inevitable inspection; still others were chatting with indolent dogmatism on that never-failing theme, the end and object of the campaign. Sentinels paced up and down the confused front with a lounging freedom of mien and stride that would not have been tolerated at another time. A few of them limped unsoldierly in deference to blistered feet. At a little distance in rear of the stacked arms were a few tents out of which frowsy-headed officers occasionally peered, languidly calling to their servants to fetch a basin of water, dust a coat or polish a scabbard. Trim young mounted orderlies, bearing dispatches obviously unimportant, urged their lazy nags by devious ways amongst the men, enduring with unconcern their good-humored raillery, the penalty of superior station. Little negroes of not very clearly defined status and function lolled on their stomachs, kicking their long, bare heels in the sunshine, or slumbered peacefully, unaware of the practical waggery prepared by white hands for their undoing.

Presently the flag hanging limp and lifeless at headquarters was seen to lift itself spiritedly from the staff. At the same instant was heard a dull, distant sound like the heavy breathing of some great animal below the horizon. The flag had lifted its head to listen. There was a momentary lull in the hum of the human swarm; then, as the flag drooped the hush passed away. But there were some hundreds more men on their feet than before; some thousands of hearts beating with a quicker pulse.

Again the flag made a warning sign, and again the breeze bore to our ears the long, deep sighing of iron lungs. The division, as if it had received the sharp word of command, sprang to its feet, and stood in groups at "attention." Even the little blacks got up. I have since seen similar effects produced by earthquakes; I am not sure but the ground was trembling then. The mess-cooks, wise in their generation, lifted the steaming camp-kettles off the fire and stood by to cast out. The mounted orderlies had somehow disappeared. Officers came ducking from beneath their tents and gathered in groups. Headquarters had become a swarming hive.

The sound of the great guns now came in regular throb-bings—the strong, full pulse of the fever of battle. The flag flapped excitedly, shaking out its blazonry of stars and stripes with a sort of fierce delight. Toward the knot of officers in its shadow dashed from somewhere—he seemed to have burst out of the ground in a cloud of dust—a mounted aide-de-camp, and on the instant rose the sharp, clear notes of a bugle, caught up and repeated, and passed on by other bugles, until the level reaches of brown fields, the line of woods trending away to far hills, and the unseen valleys beyond were "telling of the sound," the farther, fainter strains half drowned in ring-ing cheers as the men ran to range themselves behind the stacks of arms. For this call was not the wearisome "general" before which the tents go down; it was the exhilarating "assembly," which goes to the heart as wine and stirs the blood like the kisses of a beautiful woman. Who that has heard it calling to him above the grumble of great guns can forget the wild intoxica-tion of its music?

II

The Confederate forces in Kentucky and Tennessee had suf-fered a series of reverses, culminating in the loss of Nashville. The blow was severe: immense quantities of war material had fallen to the victor, together with all the important strategic points. General Johnston withdrew Beauregard's army to Corinth, in northern Mississippi, where he hoped so to recruit and equip it as to enable it to assume the offensive and retake the lost territory.

The town of Corinth was a wretched place—the capital of a swamp. It is a two days' march west of the Tennessee River, which here and for a hundred and fifty miles farther, to where it falls into the Ohio at Paducah, runs nearly north. It is navigable to this point—that is to say, to Pittsburg Landing, where Corinth got to it by a road worn through a thickly wooded country seamed with ravines and bayous, rising nobody knows where and running into the river under sylvan arches heavily draped with Spanish moss. In some places they were obstructed by fallen trees. The Corinth road was at certain seasons a branch of the Tennessee River. Its mouth was Pittsburg Landing. Here in 1862 were some fields and a house or two; now there are a national cemetery and other improvements.

It was at Pittsburg Landing that Grant established his army, with a river in his rear and two toy steamboats as a means of communication with the east side, whither General Buell with thirty thousand men was moving from Nashville to join him. The question has been asked, Why did General Grant occupy the enemy's side of the river in the face of a superior force before the arrival of Buell? Buell had a long way to come; perhaps Grant was weary of waiting. Certainly Johnston was, for in the gray of the morning of April 6th, when Buell's leading division was *en bivouac* near the little town of Savannah, eight or ten miles below, the Confederate forces, having moved out of Corinth two days before, fell upon Grant's advance brigades and destroyed them. Grant was at Savannah, but hastened to the Landing in time to find his camps in the hands of the enemy and the remnants of his beaten army cooped up with an impassable river at their backs for moral support. I have related how the news of this affair came to us at Savannah. It came on the wind—a messenger that does not bear copious details.

III

On the side of the Tennessee River, over against Pittsburg Landing, are some low bare hills, partly inclosed by a forest. In the dusk of the evening of April 6 this open space, as seen from the other side of the stream—whence, indeed, it was anxiously watched by thousands of eyes, to many of which it grew dark long before the sun went down—would have appeared to have been ruled in long, dark lines, with new lines being constantly drawn across. These lines were the regiments of Buell's leading division, which having moved up from Savannah through a country presenting nothing but interminable swamps and pathless "bottom lands," with rank overgrowths of jungle, was arriving at the scene of action breathless, footsore and faint with hunger. It had been a terrible race; some regiments had lost a third of their number from fatigue, the men dropping from the ranks as if shot, and left to recover or die at their leisure. Nor was the scene to which they had been invited likely to inspire the moral confidence that medicines physical fatigue. True, the air was full of thunder and the earth was trembling beneath their feet; and if there is truth in the theory of the conversion of force, these men were storing up energy from every shock that burst its waves upon their bodies. Perhaps this theory may better than another explain the tremendous endurance of men in battle. But the eyes reported only matter for despair.

Before us ran the turbulent river, vexed with plunging shells and obscured in spots by blue sheets of low-lying smoke. The two little steamers were doing their duty well. They came over to us empty and went back crowded, sitting very low in the water, apparently on the point of capsizing. The farther edge of the water could not be seen; the boats came out of the obscurity, took on their passengers and vanished in the darkness. But on the heights above, the battle was burning brightly enough; a thousand lights kindled and expired in every second of time. There were broad flushings in the sky, against which the branches of the trees showed black. Sudden flames burst out here and there, singly and in dozens. Fleeting streaks of fire crossed over to us by way of welcome. These expired in blinding flashes and fierce little rolls of smoke, attended with the peculiar metallic ring of bursting shells, and followed by the musical humming of the fragments as they struck into the ground on every side, making us wince, but doing little harm. The air was full of noises. To the right and the left the musketry rattled smartly and petulantly; directly in front it sighed and growled. To the experienced ear this meant that the death-line was an arc of which the river was the chord. There were deep, shaking explosions and smart shocks; the whisper of stray bullets and the hurtle of conical shells; the rush of round shot. There were faint, desultory cheers, such as announce a momentary or partial triumph. Occasionally, against the glare behind the trees, could be seen moving black figures, singularly distinct but apparently no longer than a thumb. They seemed to me ludicrously like the figures of demons in old allegorical prints of hell. To destroy these and all their belongings the enemy needed but another hour of daylight; the steamers in that case would have been doing him fine service by bringing more fish to his net. Those of us who had the good fortune to arrive late could then have eaten our teeth in impotent rage. Nay, to make his victory sure it did not need that the sun should pause in the heavens; one of the many random shots falling into the river would have done the business had chance directed it into the engine-room of a steamer. You can perhaps fancy the anxiety with which we watched them leaping down.

But we had two other allies besides the night. Just where the enemy had pushed his right flank to the river was the mouth of a wide bayou, and here two gunboats had taken station. They too were of the toy sort, plated perhaps with railway metals, perhaps with boiler-iron. They staggered under a heavy gun or two each. The bayou made an opening in the high bank of the river. The bank was a parapet, behind which the gunboats crouched, firing up the bayou as through an embrasure. The enemy was at this disadvantage: he could not get at the gunboats, and he could advance only by exposing his flank to their ponderous missiles, one of which would have broken a half-mile of his bones and made nothing of it. Very annoying this must have been—these twenty gunners beating back an army because a sluggish creek had been pleased to fall into a river at one point rather than another. Such is the part that accident may play in the game of war.

As a spectacle this was rather fine. We could just discern the black bodies of these boats, looking very much like turtles. But when they let off their big guns there was a conflagration. The river shuddered in its banks, and hurried on, bloody, wounded, terrified! Objects a mile away sprang toward our eyes as a snake strikes at the face of its victim. The report stung us to the brain, but we blessed it audibly. Then we could hear the great shell tearing away through the air until the sound died out in the distance; then, a surprisingly long time afterward, a dull, distant explosion and a sudden silence of small-arms told their own tale.

IV

There was, I remember, no elephant on the boat that passed us across that evening, nor, I think, any hippopotamus. These would have been out of place. We had, however, a woman. Whether the baby was somewhere on board I did not learn. She was a fine creature, this woman; somebody's wife. Her mission, as she understood it, was to inspire the failing heart with courage; and when she selected mine I felt less flattered by her preference than astonished by her penetration. How did she learn? She stood on the upper deck with the red blaze of battle bathing her beautiful face, the twinkle of a thousand rifles mirrored in her eyes; and displaying a small ivory-handled pistol, she told me in a sentence punctuated by the thunder of great guns that if it came to the worst she would do her duty like a man! I am proud to remember that I took off my hat to this little fool.

V

Along the sheltered strip of beach between the river bank and the water was a confused mass of humanity—several thousands of men. They were mostly unarmed; many were wounded; some dead. All the camp-following tribes were there; all the cowards; a few officers. Not one of them knew where his regiment was, nor if he had a regiment. Many had not. These men were defeated, beaten, cowed. They were deaf to duty and dead to shame. A more demented crew never drifted to the rear of broken battalions. They would have stood in their tracks and been shot down to a man by a provost-marshal's guard, but they could not have been urged up that bank. An army's bravest men are its cowards. The death which they would not meet at the hands of the enemy they will meet at the hands of their officers, with never a flinching.

Whenever a steamboat would land, this abominable mob had to be kept off her with bayonets; when she pulled away, they sprang on her and were pushed by scores into the water, where they were suffered to drown one another in their own way. The men disembarking insulted them, shoved them, struck them. In return they expressed their unholy delight in the certainty of our destruction by the enemy.

By the time my regiment had reached the plateau night had put an end to the struggle. A sputter of rifles would break out now and then, followed perhaps by a spiritless hurrah. Occasionally a shell from a far-away battery would come pitching down somewhere near, with a whir crescendo, or flit above our heads with a whisper like that made by the wings of a night bird, to smother itself in the river. But there was no more fighting. The gunboats, however, blazed away at set intervals all night long, just to make the enemy uncomfortable and break him of his rest.

For us there was no rest. Foot by foot we moved through the dusky fields, we knew not whither. There were men all about us, but no camp-fires; to have made a blaze would have been madness. The men were of strange regiments; they mentioned the names of unknown generals. They gathered in groups by the wayside, asking eagerly our numbers. They recounted the depressing incidents of the day. A thoughtful officer shut their mouths with a sharp word as he passed; a wise one coming after encouraged them to repeat their doleful tale all along the line.

Hidden in hollows and behind clumps of rank brambles were large tents, dimly lighted with candles, but looking comfortable. The kind of comfort they supplied was indicated by pairs of men entering and reappearing, bearing litters; by low moans from within and by long rows of dead with covered faces outside. These tents were constantly receiving the wounded, yet were never full; they were continually ejecting the dead, yet were never empty. It was as if the helpless had been carried in and murdered, that they might not hamper those whose business it was to fall to-morrow.

The night was now black-dark; as is usual after a battle, it had begun to rain. Still we moved; we were being put into position by somebody. Inch by inch we crept along, treading on one another's heels by way of keeping together. Commands were passed along the line in whispers; more commonly none were given. When the men had pressed so closely together that they could advance no farther they stood stock-still, sheltering the locks of their rifles with their ponchos. In this position many fell asleep. When those in front suddenly stepped away those in the rear, roused by the tramping, hastened after with such zeal that the line was soon choked again. Evidently the head of the division was being piloted at a snail's pace by some one who did not feel sure of his ground. Very often we struck our feet against the dead; more frequently against those who still had spirit enough to resent it with a moan. These were lifted carefully to one side and abandoned. Some had sense enough to ask in their weak way for water. Absurd! Their clothes were soaken, their hair dank; their white faces, dimly discernible, were clammy and cold. Besides, none of us had any water. There was plenty coming, though, for before midnight a thunderstorm broke upon us with great violence. The rain, which had for hours been a dull drizzle, fell with a copiousness that stifled us; we moved in running water up to our ankles. Happily, we were in a forest of great trees heavily "decorated" with Spanish moss, or with an enemy standing to his guns the disclosures of the lightning might have been inconvenient. As it was, the incessant blaze enabled us to consult our watches and encouraged us by displaying our numbers; our black, sinuous line, creeping like a giant serpent beneath the trees, was apparently interminable. I am almost ashamed to say how sweet I found the companionship of those coarse men.

So the long night wore away, and as the glimmer of morning crept in through the forest we found ourselves in a more open country. But where? Not a sign of battle was here. The trees were neither splintered nor scarred, the underbrush was unmown, the ground had no footprints but our own. It was as if we had broken into glades sacred to eternal silence. I should not have been surprised to see sleek leopards come fawning about our feet, and milk-white deer confront us with human eyes.

A few inaudible commands from an invisible leader had placed us in order of battle. But where was the enemy? Where, too, were the riddled regiments that we had come to save? Had our other divisions arrived during the night and passed the river to assist us? or were we to oppose our paltry five thousand breasts to an army flushed with victory? What protected our right? Who lay upon our left? Was there really anything in our front?

There came, borne to us on the raw morning air, the long, weird note of a bugle. It was directly before us. It rose with a low, clear, deliberate warble, and seemed to float in the gray sky like the note of a lark. The bugle calls of the Federal and the Confederate armies were the same: it was the "assembly"! As it died away I observed that the atmosphere had suffered a change; despite the equilibrium established by the storm, it was electric. Wings were growing on blistered feet. Bruised muscles and jolted bones, shoulders pounded by the cruel knapsack, eyelids leaden from lack of sleep—all were pervaded by the subtle fluid, all were unconscious of their clay. The men thrust forward their heads, expanded their eyes and clenched their teeth. They breathed hard, as if throttled by tugging at the leash. If you had laid your hand in the beard or hair of one of these men it would have crackled and shot sparks.

VI

I suppose the country lying between Corinth and Pittsburg Landing could boast a few inhabitants other than alligators. What manner of people they were it is impossible to say, inasmuch as the fighting dispersed, or possibly exterminated them; perhaps in merely classing them as non-saurian I shall describe them with sufficient particularity and at the same time avert from myself the natural suspicion attaching to a writer who points out to persons who do not know him the peculiarities of persons whom he does not know. One thing, however, I hope I may without offense affirm of these swamp-dwellers— they were pious. To what deity their veneration was given— whether, like the Egyptians, they worshiped the crocodile, or, like other Americans, adored themselves, I do not presume to guess. But whoever, or whatever, may have been the divinity whose ends they shaped, unto Him, or It, they had builded a temple. This humble edifice, centrally situated in the heart of a solitude, and conveniently accessible to the supersylvan crow, had been christened Shiloh Chapel, whence the name of the battle. The fact of a Christian church—assuming it to have been

a Christian church—giving name to a wholesale cutting of
Christian throats by Christian hands need not be dwelt on
here; the frequency of its recurrence in the history of our species has somewhat abated the moral interest that would otherwise attach to it.

VII

Owing to the darkness, the storm and the absence of a road,
it had been impossible to move the artillery from the open
ground about the Landing. The privation was much greater in
a moral than in a material sense. The infantry soldier feels a
confidence in this cumbrous arm quite unwarranted by its actual achievements in thinning out the opposition. There is
something that inspires confidence in the way a gun dashes up
to the front, shoving fifty or a hundred men to one side as if it
said, "Permit *me*!" Then it squares its shoulders, calmly dislo-
cates a joint in its back, sends away its twenty-four legs and
settles down with a quiet rattle which says as plainly as possible,
"I've come to stay." There is a superb scorn in its grimly defiant attitude, with its nose in the air; it appears not so much to
threaten the enemy as deride him.

Our batteries were probably toiling after us somewhere; we
could only hope the enemy might delay his attack until they
should arrive. "He may delay his defense if he like," said a
sententious young officer to whom I had imparted this natural
wish. He had read the signs aright; the words were hardly
spoken when a group of staff officers about the brigade commander shot away in divergent lines as if scattered by a whirlwind, and galloping each to the commander of a regiment
gave the word. There was a momentary confusion of tongues,
a thin line of skirmishers detached itself from the compact
front and pushed forward, followed by its diminutive reserves
of half a company each—one of which platoons it was my fortune to command. When the straggling line of skirmishers had
swept four or five hundred yards ahead, "See," said one of my
comrades, "she moves!" She did indeed, and in fine style, her
front as straight as a string, her reserve regiments in columns
doubled on the center, following in true subordination; no

braying of brass to apprise the enemy, no fifing and drumming
to amuse him; no ostentation of gaudy flags; no nonsense. This
was a matter of business.

In a few moments we had passed out of the singular oasis
that had so marvelously escaped the desolation of battle, and
now the evidences of the previous day's struggle were present
in profusion. The ground was tolerably level here, the forest
less dense, mostly clear of undergrowth, and occasionally opening out into small natural meadows. Here and there were small
pools—mere discs of rainwater with a tinge of blood. Riven
and torn with cannon-shot, the trunks of the trees protruded
bunches of splinters like hands, the fingers above the wound
interlacing with those below. Large branches had been lopped,
and hung their green heads to the ground, or swung critically
in their netting of vines, as in a hammock. Many had been cut
clean off and their masses of foliage seriously impeded the
progress of the troops. The bark of these trees, from the root
upward to a height of ten or twenty feet, was so thickly pierced
with bullets and grape that one could not have laid a hand on
it without covering several punctures. None had escaped. How
the human body survives a storm like this must be explained
by the fact that it is exposed to it but a few moments at a time,
whereas these grand old trees had had no one to take their
places, from the rising to the going down of the sun. Angular
bits of iron, concavo-convex, sticking in the sides of muddy
depressions, showed where shells had exploded in their furrows. Knapsacks, canteens, haversacks distended with soaken
and swollen biscuits, gaping to disgorge, blankets beaten into
the soil by the rain, rifles with bent barrels or splintered stocks,
waist-belts, hats and the omnipresent sardine-box—all the
wretched debris of the battle still littered the spongy earth as
far as one could see, in every direction. Dead horses were everywhere; a few disabled caissons, or limbers, reclining on one
elbow, as it were; ammunition wagons standing disconsolate
behind four or six sprawling mules. Men? There were men
enough; all dead, apparently, except one, who lay near where I
had halted my platoon to await the slower movement of the
line—a Federal sergeant, variously hurt, who had been a fine
giant in his time. He lay face upward, taking in his breath in
convulsive, rattling snorts, and blowing it out in sputters of

froth which crawled creamily down his cheeks, piling itself alongside his neck and ears. A bullet had clipped a groove in his skull, above the temple; from this the brain protruded in bosses, dropping off in flakes and strings. I had not previously known one could get on, even in this unsatisfactory fashion, with so little brain. One of my men, whom I knew for a womanish fellow, asked if he should put his bayonet through him. Inexpressibly shocked by the cold-blooded proposal, I told him I thought not; it was unusual, and too many were looking.

VIII

It was plain that the enemy had retreated to Corinth. The arrival of our fresh troops and their successful passage of the river had disheartened him. Three or four of his gray cavalry videttes moving amongst the trees on the crest of a hill in our front, and galloping out of sight at the crack of our skirmishers' rifles, confirmed us in the belief; an army face to face with its enemy does not employ cavalry to watch its front. True, they might be a general and his staff. Crowning this rise we found a level field, a quarter of a mile in width; beyond it a gentle acclivity, covered with an undergrowth of young oaks, impervious to sight. We pushed on into the open, but the division halted at the edge. Having orders to conform to its movements, we halted too; but that did not suit; we received an intimation to proceed. I had performed this sort of service before, and in the exercise of my discretion deployed my platoon, pushing it forward at a run, with trailed arms, to strengthen the skirmish line, which I overtook some thirty or forty yards from the wood. Then—I can't describe it—the forest seemed all at once to flame up and disappear with a crash like that of a great wave upon the beach—a crash that expired in hot hissings, and the sickening "spat" of lead against flesh. A dozen of my brave fellows tumbled over like ten-pins. Some struggled to their feet, only to go down again, and yet again. Those who stood fired into the smoking brush and doggedly retired. We had expected to find, at most, a line of skirmishers similar to our own; it was with a view to overcoming them by a sudden *coup* at the moment of collision that I had thrown forward my little reserve. What we had found was a line of battle, coolly holding its fire till it could count our teeth. There was no more to be done but get back across the open ground, every superficial yard of which was throwing up its little jet of mud provoked by an impinging bullet. We got back, most of us, and I shall never forget the ludicrous incident of a young officer who had taken part in the affair walking up to his colonel, who had been a calm and apparently impartial spectator, and gravely reporting: "The enemy is in force just beyond this field, sir."

IX

In subordination to the design of this narrative, as defined by its title, the incidents related necessarily group themselves about my own personality as a center; and, as this center, during the few terrible hours of the engagement, maintained a variably constant relation to the open field already mentioned, it is important that the reader should bear in mind the topographical and tactical features of the local situation. The hither side of the field was occupied by the front of my brigade—a length of two regiments in line, with proper intervals for field batteries. During the entire fight the enemy held the slight wooded acclivity beyond. The debatable ground to the right and left of the open was broken and thickly wooded for miles, in some places quite inaccessible to artillery and at very few points offering opportunities for its successful employment. As a consequence of this the two sides of the field were soon studded thickly with confronting guns, which flamed away at one another with amazing zeal and rather startling effect. Of course, an infantry attack delivered from either side was not to be thought of when the covered flanks offered inducements so unquestionably superior; and I believe the riddled bodies of my poor skirmishers were the only ones left on this "neutral ground" that day. But there was a very pretty line of dead continually growing in our rear, and doubtless the enemy had at his back a similar encouragement.

The configuration of the ground offered us no protection. By lying flat on our faces between the guns we were screened from view by a straggling row of brambles, which marked the course of an obsolete fence; but the enemy's grape was sharper than his eyes, and it was poor consolation to know that his gunners could not see what they were doing, so long as they did it. The shock of our own pieces nearly deafened us, but in the brief intervals we could hear the battle roaring and stammering in the dark reaches of the forest to the right and left, where our other divisions were dashing themselves again and again into the smoking jungle. What would we not have given to join them in their brave, hopeless task! But to lie inglorious beneath showers of shrapnel darting divergent from the unassailable sky—meekly to be blown out of life by level gusts of grape—to clench our teeth and shrink helpless before big shot pushing noisily through the consenting air—this was horrible! "Lie down, there!" a captain would shout, and then get up himself to see that his order was obeyed. "Captain, take cover, sir!" the lieutenant-colonel would shriek, pacing up and down in the most exposed position that he could find.

O those cursed guns!—not the enemy's, but our own. Had it not been for them, we might have died like men. They must be supported, forsooth, the feeble, boasting bullies! It was impossible to conceive that these pieces were doing the enemy as excellent a mischief as his were doing us; they seemed to raise their "cloud by day" solely to direct aright the streaming procession of Confederate missiles. They no longer inspired confidence, but begot apprehension; and it was with grim satisfaction that I saw the carriage of one and another smashed into matchwood by a whooping shot and bundled out of the line.

X

The dense forests wholly or partly in which were fought so many battles of the Civil War, lay upon the earth in each autumn a thick deposit of dead leaves and stems, the decay of which forms a soil of surprising depth and richness. In dry weather the upper stratum is as inflammable as tinder. A fire once kindled in it will spread with a slow, persistent advance as far as local conditions permit, leaving a bed of light ashes beneath which the less combustible accretions of previous years will smolder until extinguished by rains. In many of the engagements of the war the fallen leaves took fire and roasted the fallen men. At Shiloh, during the first day's fighting, wide tracts of woodland were burned over in this way and scores of wounded who might have recovered perished in slow torture. I remember a deep ravine a little to the left and rear of the field I have described, in which, by some mad freak of heroic incompetence, a part of an Illinois regiment had been surrounded, and refusing to surrender was destroyed, as it very well deserved. My regiment having at last been relieved at the guns and moved over to the heights above this ravine for no obvious purpose, I obtained leave to go down into the valley of death and gratify a reprehensible curiosity.

Forbidding enough it was in every way. The fire had swept every superficial foot of it, and at every step I sank into ashes to the ankle. It had contained a thick undergrowth of young saplings, every one of which had been severed by a bullet, the foliage of the prostrate tops being afterward burnt and the stumps charred. Death had put his sickle into this thicket and fire had gleaned the field. Along a line which was not that of extreme depression, but was at every point significantly equidistant from the heights on either hand, lay the bodies, half buried in ashes; some in the unlovely looseness of attitude denoting sudden death by the bullet, but by far the greater number in postures of agony that told of the tormenting flame. Their clothing was half burnt away—their hair and beard entirely; the rain had come too late to save their nails. Some were swollen to double girth; others shriveled to manikins. According to degree of exposure, their faces were bloated and black or yellow and shrunken. The contraction of muscles which had given them claws for hands had cursed each countenance with a hideous grin. Faugh! I cannot catalogue the charms of these gallant gentlemen who had got what they enlisted for.

XI

It was now three o'clock in the afternoon, and raining. For fifteen hours we had been wet to the skin. Chilled, sleepy, hungry and disappointed—profoundly disgusted with the inglorious part to which they had been condemned—the men of my regiment did everything doggedly. The spirit had gone quite out of them. Blue sheets of powder smoke, drifting amongst the trees, settling against the hillsides and beaten into nothingness by the falling rain, filled the air with their peculiar pungent odor, but it no longer stimulated. For miles on either hand could be heard the hoarse murmur of the battle, breaking out near by with frightful distinctness, or sinking to a murmur in the distance; and the one sound aroused no more attention than the other.

We had been placed again in rear of those guns, but even they and their iron antagonists seemed to have tired of their feud, pounding away at one another with amiable infrequency. The right of the regiment extended a little beyond the field. On the prolongation of the line in that direction were some regiments of another division, with one in reserve. A third of a mile back lay the remnant of somebody's brigade looking to its wounds. The line of forest bounding this end of the field stretched as straight as a wall from the right of my regiment to Heaven knows what regiment of the enemy. There suddenly appeared, marching down along this wall, not more than two hundred yards in our front, a dozen files of gray-clad men with rifles on the right shoulder. At an interval of fifty yards they were followed by perhaps half as many more; and in fair supporting distance of these stalked with confident mien a single man! There seemed to me something indescribably ludicrous in the advance of this handful of men upon an army, albeit with their left flank protected by a forest. It does not so impress me now. They were the exposed flanks of three lines of infantry, each half a mile in length. In a moment our gunners had grappled with the nearest pieces, swung them half round, and were pouring streams of canister into the invaded wood. The infantry rose in masses, springing into line. Our threatened regiments stood like a wall, their loaded rifles at "ready," their bayonets hanging quietly in the scabbards. The right wing of my own regiment was thrown slightly backward to threaten the flank of the assault. The battered brigade away to the rear pulled itself together.

Then the storm burst. A great gray cloud seemed to spring out of the forest into the faces of the waiting battalions. It was received with a crash that made the very trees turn up their leaves. For one instant the assailants paused above their dead, then struggled forward, their bayonets glittering in the eyes that shone behind the smoke. One moment, and those unmoved men in blue would be impaled. What were they about? Why did they not fix bayonets? Were they stunned by their own volley? Their inaction was maddening! Another tremendous crash!—the rear rank had fired! Humanity, thank Heaven! is not made for this, and the shattered gray mass drew back a score of paces, opening a feeble fire. Lead had scored its old-time victory over steel; the heroic had broken its great heart against the commonplace. There are those who say that it is sometimes otherwise.

All this had taken but a minute of time, and now the second Confederate line swept down and poured in its fire. The line of blue staggered and gave way; in those two terrific volleys it seemed to have quite poured out its spirit. To this deadly work our reserve regiment now came up with a run. It was surprising to see it spitting fire with never a sound, for such was the infernal din that the ear could take in no more. This fearful scene was enacted within fifty paces of our toes, but we were rooted to the ground as if we had grown there. But now our commanding officer rode from behind us to the front, waved his hand with the courteous gesture that says *après vous*, and with a barely audible cheer we sprang into the fight. Again the smoking front of gray receded, and again, as the enemy's third line emerged from its leafy covert, it pushed forward across the piles of dead and wounded to threaten with protruded steel. Never was seen so striking a proof of the paramount importance of numbers. Within an area of three hundred yards by fifty there struggled for front places no fewer than six regiments; and the accession of each, after the first collision, had it not been immediately counterpoised, would have turned the scale.

As matters stood, we were now very evenly matched, and how long we might have held out God only knows. But all at once something appeared to have gone wrong with the enemy's left; our men had somewhere pierced his line. A moment later his whole front gave way, and springing forward with fixed bayonets we pushed him in utter confusion back to his original line. Here, among the tents from which Grant's people had been expelled the day before, our broken and disordered regiments inextricably intermingled, and drunken with the wine of triumph, dashed confidently against a pair of trim battalions, provoking a tempest of hissing lead that made us stagger under its very weight. The sharp onset of another against our flank sent us whirling back with fire at our heels and fresh foes in merciless pursuit—who in their turn were broken upon the front of the invalided brigade previously mentioned, which had moved up from the rear to assist in this lively work.

As we rallied to reform behind our beloved guns and noted the ridiculous brevity of our line—as we sank from sheer fatigue, and tried to moderate the terrific thumping of our hearts —as we caught our breath to ask who had seen such-and-such a comrade, and laughed hysterically at the reply—there swept past us and over us into the open field a long regiment with fixed bayonets and rifles on the right shoulder. Another followed, and another; two—three—four! Heavens! where do all these men come from, and why did they not come before? How grandly and confidently they go sweeping on like long blue waves of ocean chasing one another to the cruel rocks! Involuntarily we draw in our weary feet beneath us as we sit, ready to spring up and interpose our breasts when these gallant lines shall come back to us across the terrible field, and sift brokenly through among the trees with spouting fires at their backs. We still our breathing to catch the full grandeur of the volleys that are to tear them to shreds. Minute after minute passes and the sound does not come. Then for the first time we note that the silence of the whole region is not comparative, but absolute. Have we become stone deaf? See; here comes a stretcher-bearer, and there a surgeon! Good heavens! a chaplain!

The battle was indeed at an end.

XII

And this was, O so long ago! How they come back to me —dimly and brokenly, but with what a magic spell—those years of youth when I was soldiering! Again I hear the far warble of blown bugles. Again I see the tall, blue smoke of camp-fires ascending from the dim valleys of Wonderland. There steals upon my sense the ghost of an odor from pines that canopy the ambuscade. I feel upon my cheek the morning mist that shrouds the hostile camp unaware of its doom, and my blood stirs at the ringing rifle-shot of the solitary sentinel.

Unfamiliar landscapes, glittering with sunshine or sullen with rain, come to me demanding recognition, pass, vanish and give place to others. Here in the night stretches a wide and blasted field studded with half-extinct fires burning redly with I know not what presage of evil. Again I shudder as I note its desolation and its awful silence. Where was it? To what monstrous inharmony of death was it the visible prelude?

O days when all the world was beautiful and strange; when unfamiliar constellations burned in the Southern midnights, and the mocking-bird poured out his heart in the moon-gilded magnolia; when there was something new under a new sun; will your fine, far memories ever cease to lay contrasting pictures athwart the harsher features of this later world, accentuating the ugliness of the longer and tamer life? Is it not strange that the phantoms of a blood-stained period have so airy a grace and look with so tender eyes?—that I recall with difficulty the danger and death and horrors of the time, and without effort all that was gracious and picturesque? Ah, Youth, there is no such wizard as thou! Give me but one touch of thine artist hand upon the dull canvas of the Present; gild for but one moment the drear and somber scenes of to-day, and I will willingly surrender an other life than the one that I should have thrown away at Shiloh.

A Little of Chickamauga

THE history of that awful struggle is well known—I have not the intention to record it here, but only to relate some part of what I saw of it; my purpose not instruction, but entertainment.

I was an officer of the staff of a Federal brigade. Chickamauga was not my first battle by many, for although hardly more than a boy in years, I had served at the front from the beginning of the trouble, and had seen enough of war to give me a fair understanding of it. We knew well enough that there was to be a fight: the fact that we did not want one would have told us that, for Bragg always retired when we wanted to fight and fought when we most desired peace. We had manœuvred him out of Chattanooga, but had not manœuvred our entire army into it, and he fell back so sullenly that those of us who followed, keeping him actually in sight, were a good deal more concerned about effecting a junction with the rest of our army than to push the pursuit. By the time that Rosecrans had got his three scattered corps together we were a long way from Chattanooga, with our line of communication with it so exposed that Bragg turned to seize it. Chickamauga was a fight for possession of a road.

Back along this road raced Crittenden's corps, with those of Thomas and McCook, which had not before traversed it. The whole army was moving by its left.

There was sharp fighting all along and all day, for the forest was so dense that the hostile lines came almost into contact before fighting was possible. One instance was particularly horrible. After some hours of close engagement my brigade, with foul pieces and exhausted cartridge boxes, was relieved and withdrawn to the road to protect several batteries of artillery— probably two dozen pieces—which commanded an open field in the rear of our line. Before our weary and virtually disarmed men had actually reached the guns the line in front gave way, fell back behind the guns and went on, the Lord knows whither. A moment later the field was gray with Confederates in pursuit. Then the guns opened fire with grape and canister and for perhaps five minutes—it seemed an hour—nothing could be heard but the infernal din of their discharge and nothing seen through the smoke but a great ascension of dust from the smitten soil. When all was over, and the dust cloud had lifted, the spectacle was too dreadful to describe. The Confederates were still there—all of them, it seemed—some almost under the muzzles of the guns. But not a man of all these brave fellows was on his feet, and so thickly were all covered with dust that they looked as if they had been reclothed in yellow.

"We bury our dead," said a gunner, grimly, though doubtless all were afterward dug out, for some were partly alive.

To a "day of danger" succeeded a "night of waking." The enemy, everywhere held back from the road, continued to stretch his line northward in the hope to overlap us and put himself between us and Chattanooga. We neither saw nor heard his movement, but any man with half a head would have known that he was making it, and we met it by a parallel movement to our left. By morning we had edged along a good way and thrown up rude intrenchments at a little distance from the road, on the threatened side. The day was not very far advanced when we were attacked furiously all along the line, beginning at the left. When repulsed, the enemy came again and again— his persistence was dispiriting. He seemed to be using against us the law of probabilities: of so many efforts one would eventually succeed.

One did, and it was my luck to see it win. I had been sent by my chief, General Hazen, to order up some artillery ammunition and rode away to the right and rear in search of it. Finding an ordnance train I obtained from the officer in charge a few wagons loaded with what I wanted, but he seemed in doubt as to our occupancy of the region across which I proposed to guide them. Although assured that I had just traversed it, and that it lay immediately behind Wood's division, he insisted on riding to the top of the ridge behind which his train lay and overlooking the ground. We did so, when to my astonishment I saw the entire country in front swarming with Confederates; the very earth seemed to be moving toward us! They came on in thousands, and so rapidly that we had barely time to turn tail and gallop down the hill and away, leaving them in possession of the train, many of the wagons being upset by frantic efforts to put them about. By what miracle that officer had sensed the situation I did not learn, for we parted company then and there and I never again saw him.

By a misunderstanding Wood's division had been withdrawn from our line of battle just as the enemy was making an assault. Through the gap of half a mile the Confederates charged without opposition, cutting our army clean in two. The right divisions were broken up and with General Rosecrans in their midst fled how they could across the country, eventually bringing up in Chattanooga, whence Rosecrans telegraphed to Washington the destruction of the rest of his army. The rest of his army was standing its ground.

A good deal of nonsense used to be talked about the heroism of General Garfield, who, caught in the rout of the right, nevertheless went back and joined the undefeated left under General Thomas. There was no great heroism in it; that is what every man should have done, including the commander of the army. We could hear Thomas's guns going—those of us who had ears for them—and all that was needful was to make a sufficiently wide detour and then move toward the sound. I did so myself, and have never felt that it ought to make me President. Moreover, on my way I met General Negley, and my duties as topographical engineer having given me some knowledge of the lay of the land offered to pilot him back to glory or the grave. I am sorry to say my good offices were rejected a little uncivilly, which I charitably attributed to the general's obvious absence of mind. His mind, I think, was in Nashville, behind a breastwork.

Unable to find my brigade, I reported to General Thomas, who directed me to remain with him. He had assumed command of all the forces still intact and was pretty closely beset. The battle was fierce and continuous, the enemy extending his lines farther and farther around our right, toward our line of retreat. We could not meet the extension otherwise than by "refusing" our right flank and letting him inclose us; which but for gallant Gordon Granger he would inevitably have done.

This was the way of it. Looking across the fields in our rear (rather longingly) I had the happy distinction of a discoverer. What I saw was the shimmer of sunlight on metal: lines of troops were coming in behind us! The distance was too great, the atmosphere too hazy to distinguish the color of their uniform, even with a glass. Reporting my momentous "find" I was directed by the general to go and see who they were. Galloping toward them until near enough to see that they were of our kidney I hastened back with the glad tidings and was sent again, to guide them to the general's position.

It was General Granger with two strong brigades of the reserve, moving soldier-like toward the sound of heavy firing. Meeting him and his staff I directed him to Thomas, and unable to think of anything better to do decided to go visiting. I knew I had a brother in that gang—an officer of an Ohio battery. I soon found him near the head of a column, and as we moved forward we had a comfortable chat amongst such of the enemy's bullets as had inconsiderately been fired too high. The incident was a trifle marred by one of them unhorsing another officer of the battery, whom we propped against a tree and left. A few moments later Granger's force was put in on the right and the fighting was terrific!

By accident I now found Hazen's brigade—or what remained of it—which had made a half-mile march to add itself to the unrouted at the memorable Snodgrass Hill. Hazen's first remark to me was an inquiry about that artillery ammunition that he had sent me for.

It was needed badly enough, as were other kinds: for the last hour or two of that interminable day Granger's were the only men that had enough ammunition to make a five minutes' fight. Had the Confederates made one more general attack we should have had to meet them with the bayonet alone. I don't know why they did not; probably they were short of ammunition. I know, though, that while the sun was taking its own time to set we lived through the agony of at least one death each, waiting for them to come on.

At last it grew too dark to fight. Then away to our left and rear some of Bragg's people set up "the rebel yell." It was taken up successively and passed round to our front, along our right and in behind us again, until it seemed almost to have got to the point whence it started. It was the ugliest sound that any mortal ever heard—even a mortal exhausted and unnerved by two days of hard fighting, without sleep, without rest, without food and without hope. There was, however, a space somewhere at the back of us across which that horrible yell did not prolong itself; and through that we finally retired in profound silence and dejection, unmolested.

To those of us who have survived the attacks of both Bragg and Time, and who keep in memory the dear dead comrades whom we left upon that fateful field, the place means much. May it mean something less to the younger men whose tents are now pitched where, with bended heads and clasped hands, God's great angels stood invisible among the heroes in blue and the heroes in gray, sleeping their last sleep in the woods of Chickamauga.

1898.

The Crime at Pickett's Mill

THERE is a class of events which by their very nature, and despite any intrinsic interest that they may possess, are foredoomed to oblivion. They are merged in the general story of those greater events of which they were a part, as the thunder of a billow breaking on a distant beach is unnoted in the continuous roar. To how many having knowledge of the battles of our Civil War does the name Pickett's Mill suggest acts of heroism and devotion performed in scenes of awful carnage to accomplish the impossible? Buried in the official reports of the victors there are indeed imperfect accounts of the engagement: the vanquished have not thought it expedient to relate it. It is ignored by General Sherman in his memoirs, yet Sherman ordered it. General Howard wrote an account of the campaign of which it was an incident, and dismissed it in a single sentence; yet General Howard planned it, and it was fought as an isolated and independent action under his eye. Whether it was so trifling an affair as to justify this inattention let the reader judge.

The fight occurred on the 27th of May, 1864, while the armies of Generals Sherman and Johnston confronted each other near Dallas, Georgia, during the memorable "Atlanta campaign." For three weeks we had been pushing the Confederates southward, partly by manœuvring, partly by fighting, out of Dalton, out of Resaca, through Adairsville, Kingston and Cassville. Each army offered battle everywhere, but would accept it only on its own terms. At Dallas Johnston made another stand and Sherman, facing the hostile line, began his customary manœuvring for an advantage. General Wood's division of Howard's corps occupied a position opposite the Confederate right. Johnston finding himself on the 26th overlapped by Schofield, still farther to Wood's left, retired his right (Polk) across a creek, whither we followed him into the woods with a deal of desultory bickering, and at nightfall had established the new lines at nearly a right angle with the old—Schofield reaching well around and threatening the Confederate rear.

The civilian reader must not suppose when he reads accounts

of military operations in which relative positions of the forces are defined, as in the foregoing passages, that these were matters of general knowledge to those engaged. Such statements are commonly made, even by those high in command, in the light of later disclosures, such as the enemy's official reports. It is seldom, indeed, that a subordinate officer knows anything about the disposition of the enemy's forces—except that it is unaimable—or precisely whom he is fighting. As to the rank and file, they can know nothing more of the matter than the arms they carry. They hardly know what troops are upon their own right or left the length of a regiment away. If it is a cloudy day they are ignorant even of the points of the compass. It may be said, generally, that a soldier's knowledge of what is going on about him is coterminous with his official relation to it and his personal connection with it; what is going on in front of him he does not know at all until he learns it afterward.

At nine o'clock on the morning of the 27th Wood's division was withdrawn and replaced by Stanley's. Supported by Johnson's division, it moved at ten o'clock to the left, in the rear of Schofield, a distance of four miles through a forest, and at two o'clock in the afternoon had reached a position where General Howard believed himself free to move in behind the enemy's forces and attack them in the rear, or at least, striking them in the flank, crush his way along their line in the direction of its length, throw them into confusion and prepare an easy victory for a supporting attack in front. In selecting General Howard for this bold adventure General Sherman was doubtless not unmindful of Chancellorsville, where Stonewall Jackson had executed a similar manœuvre for Howard's instruction. Experience is a normal school: it teaches how to teach.

There are some differences to be noted. At Chancellorsville it was Jackson who attacked; at Pickett's Mill, Howard. At Chancellorsville it was Howard who was assailed; at Pickett's Mill, Hood. The significance of the first distinction is doubled by that of the second.

The attack, it was understood, was to be made in column of brigades, Hazen's brigade of Wood's division leading. That such was at least Hazen's understanding I learned from his own lips during the movement, as I was an officer of his staff. But after a march of less than a mile an hour and a further delay of

three hours at the end of it to acquaint the enemy of our intention to surprise him, our single shrunken brigade of fifteen
hundred men was sent forward without support to double up
the army of General Johnston. "We will put in Hazen and see
what success he has." In these words of General Wood to
General Howard we were first apprised of the true nature of
the distinction about to be conferred upon us.

General W. B. Hazen, a born fighter, an educated soldier,
after the war Chief Signal Officer of the Army and now long
dead, was the best hated man that I ever knew, and his very
memory is a terror to every unworthy soul in the service. His
was a stormy life: he was in trouble all round. Grant, Sherman,
Sheridan and a countless multitude of the less eminent luckless
had the misfortune, at one time and another, to incur his disfavor, and he tried to punish them all. He was always—after the
war—the central figure of a court-martial or a Congressional inquiry, was accused of everything, from stealing to cowardice,
was banished to obscure posts, "jumped on" by the press,
traduced in public and in private, and always emerged trium-
phant. While Signal Officer, he went up against the Secretary
of War and put him to the controversial sword. He convicted
Sheridan of falsehood, Sherman of barbarism, Grant of inefficiency. He was aggressive, arrogant, tyrannical, honorable, truthful, courageous—a skillful soldier, a faithful friend and one
of the most exasperating of men. Duty was his religion, and
like the Moslem he proselyted with the sword. His missionary
efforts were directed chiefly against the spiritual darkness of his
superiors in rank, though he would turn aside from pursuit of
his erring commander to set a chicken-thieving orderly astride
a wooden horse, with a heavy stone attached to each foot.
"Hazen," said a brother brigadier, "is a synonym of insubordination." For my commander and my friend, my master in the
art of war, now unable to answer for himself, let this fact answer: when he heard Wood say they would put him in and see
what success he would have in defeating an army—when he
saw Howard assent—he uttered never a word, rode to the head
of his feeble brigade and patiently awaited the command to
go. Only by a look which I knew how to read did he betray his
sense of the criminal blunder.

The enemy had now had seven hours in which to learn of the movement and prepare to meet it. General Johnston says:

"The Federal troops extended their intrenched line [we did not intrench] so rapidly to their left that it was found necessary to transfer Cleburne's division to Hardee's corps to our right, where it was formed on the prolongation of Polk's line."

General Hood, commanding the enemy's right corps, says:

"On the morning of the 27th the enemy were known to be rapidly extending their left, attempting to turn my right as they extended. Cleburne was deployed to meet them, and at half-past five P.M. a very stubborn attack was made on this division, extending to the right, where Major-General Wheeler with his cavalry division was engaging them. The assault was continued with great determination upon both Cleburne and Wheeler."

That, then, was the situation: a weak brigade of fifteen hundred men, with masses of idle troops behind in the character of audience, waiting for the word to march a quarter-mile up hill through almost impassable tangles of underwood, along and across precipitous ravines, and attack breastworks constructed at leisure and manned with two divisions of troops as good as themselves. True, we did not know all this, but if any man on that ground besides Wood and Howard expected a "walkover" his must have been a singularly hopeful disposition. As topographical engineer it had been my duty to make a hasty examination of the ground in front. In doing so I had pushed far enough forward through the forest to hear distinctly the murmur of the enemy awaiting us, and this had been duly reported; but from our lines nothing could be heard but the wind among the trees and the songs of birds. Some one said it was a pity to frighten them, but there would necessarily be more or less noise. We laughed at that: men awaiting death on the battle-field laugh easily, though not infectiously.

The brigade was formed in four battalions, two in front and two in rear. This gave us a front of about two hundred yards. The right front battalion was commanded by Colonel R. L. Kimberly of the 41st Ohio, the left by Colonel O. H. Payne of the 124th Ohio, the rear battalions by Colonel J. C. Foy, 23d Kentucky, and Colonel W. W. Berry, 5th Kentucky—all brave and skillful officers, tested by experience on many fields. The whole command (known as the Second Brigade, Third Division, Fourth Corps) consisted of no fewer than nine regiments, reduced by long service to an average of less than two hundred men each. With full ranks and only the necessary details for special duty we should have had some eight thousand rifles in line.

We moved forward. In less than one minute the trim battalions had become simply a swarm of men struggling through the undergrowth of the forest, pushing and crowding. The front was irregularly serrated, the strongest and bravest in advance, the others following in fan-like formations, variable and inconstant, ever defining themselves anew. For the first two hundred yards our course lay along the left bank of a small creek in a deep ravine, our left battalions sweeping along its steep slope. Then we came to the fork of the ravine. A part of us crossed below, the rest above, passing over both branches, the regiments inextricably intermingled, rendering all military formation impossible. The color-bearers kept well to the front with their flags, closely furled, aslant backward over their shoulders. Displayed, they would have been torn to rags by the boughs of the trees. Horses were all sent to the rear; the general and staff and all the field officers toiled along on foot as best they could. "We shall halt and form when we get out of this," said an aide-de-camp.

Suddenly there were a ringing rattle of musketry, the familiar hissing of bullets, and before us the interspaces of the forest were all blue with smoke. Hoarse, fierce yells broke out of a thousand throats. The forward fringe of brave and hardy assailants was arrested in its mutable extensions; the edge of our swarm grew dense and clearly defined as the foremost halted, and the rest pressed forward to align themselves beside them, all firing. The uproar was deafening; the air was sibilant with streams and sheets of missiles. In the steady, unvarying roar of small-arms the frequent shock of the cannon was rather felt than heard, but the gusts of grape which they blew into that populous wood were audible enough, screaming among the trees and cracking against their stems and branches. We had, of course, no artillery to reply.

Our brave color-bearers were now all in the forefront of

battle in the open, for the enemy had cleared a space in front of his breastworks. They held the colors erect, shook out their glories, waved them forward and back to keep them spread, for there was no wind. From where I stood, at the right of the line—we had "halted and formed," indeed—I could see six of our flags at one time. Occasionally one would go down, only to be instantly lifted by other hands.

I must here quote again from General Johnston's account of this engagement, for nothing could more truly indicate the resolute nature of the attack than the Confederate belief that it was made by the whole Fourth Corps, instead of one weak brigade:

"The Fourth Corps came on in deep order and assailed the Texans with great vigor, receiving their close and accurate fire with the fortitude always exhibited by General Sherman's troops in the actions of this campaign. . . . The Federal troops approached within a few yards of the Confederates, but at last were forced to give way by their storm of well-directed bullets, and fell back to the shelter of a hollow near and behind them. They left hundreds of corpses within twenty paces of the Confederate line. When the United States troops paused in their advance within fifteen paces of the Texan front rank one of their color-bearers planted his colors eight or ten feet in front of his regiment, and was instantly shot dead. A soldier sprang forward to his place and fell also as he grasped the color-staff. A second and third followed successively, and each received death as speedily as his predecessors. A fourth, however, seized and bore back the object of soldierly devotion."

Such incidents have occurred in battle from time to time since men began to venerate the symbols of their cause, but they are not commonly related by the enemy. If General Johnston had known that his veteran divisions were throwing their successive lines against fewer than fifteen hundred men his glowing tribute to his enemy's valor could hardly have been more generously expressed. I can attest the truth of his soldierly praise: I saw the occurrence that he relates and regret that I am unable to recall even the name of the regiment whose colors were so gallantly saved.

Early in my military experience I used to ask myself how it was that brave troops could retreat while still their courage was high. As long as a man is not disabled he can go forward; can it be anything but fear that makes him stop and finally retire? Are there signs by which he can infallibly know the struggle to be hopeless? In this engagement, as in others, my doubts were answered as to the fact; the explanation is still obscure. In many instances which have come under my observation, when hostile lines of infantry engage at close range and the assailants afterward retire, there was a "dead-line" beyond which no man advanced but to fall. Not a soul of them ever reached the enemy's front to be bayoneted or captured. It was a matter of the difference of three or four paces—too small a distance to affect the accuracy of aim. In these affairs no aim is taken at individual antagonists; the soldier delivers his fire at the thickest mass in his front. The fire is, of course, as deadly at twenty paces as at fifteen; at fifteen as at ten. Nevertheless, there is the "dead-line," with its well-defined edge of corpses—those of the bravest. Where both lines are fighting without cover—as in a charge met by a counter-charge—each has its "dead-line," and between the two is a clear space—neutral ground, devoid of dead, for the living cannot reach it to fall there.

I observed this phenomenon at Pickett's Mill. Standing at the right of the line I had an unobstructed view of the narrow, open space across which the two lines fought. It was dim with smoke, but not greatly obscured: the smoke rose and spread in sheets among the branches of the trees. Most of our men fought kneeling as they fired, many of them behind trees, stones and whatever cover they could get, but there were considerable groups that stood. Occasionally one of these groups, which had endured the storm of missiles for moments without perceptible reduction, would push forward, moved by a common despair, and wholly detach itself from the line. In a second every man of the group would be down. There had been no visible movement of the enemy, no audible change in the awful, even roar of the firing—yet all were down. Frequently the dim figure of an individual soldier would be seen to spring away from his comrades, advancing alone toward that fateful interspace, with leveled bayonet. He got no farther than the farthest of his predecessors. Of the "hundreds of corpses within twenty paces of the Confederate line," I venture to say that a third were within fifteen paces, and not one within ten.

It is the perception—perhaps unconscious—of this inexplicable phenomenon that causes the still unharmed, still vigorous and still courageous soldier to retire without having come into actual contact with his foe. He sees, or feels, that he *cannot*. His bayonet is a useless weapon for slaughter; its purpose is a moral one. Its mandate exhausted, he sheathes it and trusts to the bullet. That failing, he retreats. He has done all that he could do with such appliances as he has.

No command to fall back was given, none could have been heard. Man by man, the survivors withdrew at will, sifting through the trees into the cover of the ravines, among the wounded who could drag themselves back; among the skulkers whom nothing could have dragged forward. The left of our short line had fought at the corner of a cornfield, the fence along the right side of which was parallel to the direction of our retreat. As the disorganized groups fell back along this fence on the wooded side, they were attacked by a flanking force of the enemy moving through the field in a direction nearly parallel with what had been our front. This force, I infer from General Johnston's account, consisted of the brigade of General Lowry, or two Arkansas regiments under Colonel Baucum. I had been sent by General Hazen to that point and arrived in time to witness this formidable movement. But already our retreating men, in obedience to their officers, their courage and their instinct of self-preservation, had formed along the fence and opened fire. The apparently slight advantage of the imperfect cover and the open range worked its customary miracle: the assault, a singularly spiritless one, considering the advantages it promised and that it was made by an organized and victorious force against a broken and retreating one, was checked. The assailants actually retired, and if they afterward renewed the movement they encountered none but our dead and wounded.

The battle, as a battle, was at an end, but there was still some slaughtering that it was possible to incur before nightfall; and as the wreck of our brigade drifted back through the forest we met the brigade (Gibson's) which, had the attack been made in column, as it should have been, would have been but five minutes behind our heels, with another five minutes behind its own. As it was, just forty-five minutes had elapsed, during which the enemy had destroyed us and was now ready to perform the same kindly office for our successors. Neither Gibson nor the brigade which was sent to his "relief" as tardily as he to ours accomplished, or could have hoped to accomplish, anything whatever. I did not note their movements, having other duties, but Hazen in his "Narrative of Military Service" says:

"I witnessed the attack of the two brigades following my own, and none of these (troops) advanced nearer than one hundred yards of the enemy's works. They went in at a run, and as organizations were broken in less than a minute."

Nevertheless their losses were considerable, including several hundred prisoners taken from a sheltered place whence they did not care to rise and run. The entire loss was about fourteen hundred men, of whom nearly one-half fell killed and wounded in Hazen's brigade in less than thirty minutes of actual fighting.

General Johnston says:

"The Federal dead lying near our line were counted by many persons, officers and soldiers. According to these counts there were seven hundred of them."

This is obviously erroneous, though I have not the means at hand to ascertain the true number. I remember that we were all astonished at the uncommonly large proportion of dead to wounded—a consequence of the uncommonly close range at which most of the fighting was done.

The action took its name from a water-power mill near by. This was on a branch of a stream having, I am sorry to say, the prosaic name of Pumpkin Vine Creek. I have my own reasons for suggesting that the name of that water-course be altered to Sunday-School Run.

Four Days in Dixie

URING a part of the month of October, 1864, the Federal and Confederate armies of Sherman and Hood respectively, having performed a surprising and resultless series of marches and countermarches since the fall of Atlanta, confronted each other along the separating line of the Coosa River in the vicinity of Gaylesville, Alabama. Here for several days they remained at rest—at least most of the infantry and artillery did; what the cavalry was doing nobody but itself ever knew or greatly cared. It was an interregnum of expectancy between two régimes of activity.

I was on the staff of Colonel McConnell, who commanded an infantry brigade in the absence of its regular commander. McConnell was a good man, but he did not keep a very tight rein upon the half dozen restless and reckless young fellows who (for his sins) constituted his "military family." In most matters we followed the trend of our desires, which commonly ran in the direction of adventure—it did not greatly matter what kind. In pursuance of this policy of escapades, one bright Sunday morning Lieutenant Cobb, an aide-de-camp, and I mounted and set out to "seek our fortunes," as the story books have it. Striking into a road of which we knew nothing except that it led toward the river, we followed it for a mile or such a matter, when we found our advance interrupted by a considerable creek, which we must ford or go back. We consulted a moment and then rode at it as hard as we could, possibly in the belief that a high momentum would act as it does in the instance of a skater passing over thin ice. Cobb was fortunate enough to get across comparatively dry, but his hapless companion was utterly submerged. The disaster was all the greater from my having on a resplendent new uniform, of which I had been pardonably vain. Ah, what a gorgeous new uniform it never was again!

A half-hour devoted to wringing my clothing and dry-charging my revolver, and we were away. A brisk canter of a half-hour under the arches of the trees brought us to the river, where it was our ill luck to find a boat and three soldiers of our brigade. These men had been for several hours concealed in the brush patiently watching the opposite bank in the amiable hope of getting a shot at some unwary Confederate, but had seen none. For a great distance up and down the stream on the other side, and for at least a mile back from it, extended corn-fields. Beyond the cornfields, on slightly higher ground, was a thin forest, with breaks here and there in its continuity, denoting plantations, probably. No houses were in sight, and no camps. We knew that it was the enemy's ground, but whether his forces were disposed along the slightly higher country bordering the bottom lands, or at strategic points miles back, as ours were, we knew no more than the least curious private in our army. In any case the river line would naturally be picketed or patrolled. But the charm of the unknown was upon us: the mysterious exerted its old-time fascination, beckoning to us from that silent shore so peaceful and dreamy in the beauty of the quiet Sunday morning. The temptation was strong and we fell. The soldiers were as eager for the hazard as we, and readily volunteered for the madmen's enterprise. Concealing our horses in a cane-brake, we unmoored the boat and rowed across unmolested.

Arrived at a kind of "landing" on the other side, our first care was so to secure the boat under the bank as to favor a hasty re-embarking in case we should be so unfortunate as to incur the natural consequence of our act; then, following an old road through the ranks of standing corn, we moved in force upon the Confederate position, five strong, with an armament of three Springfield rifles and two Colt's revolvers. We had not the further advantage of music and banners. One thing favored the expedition, giving it an apparent assurance of success: it was well officered—an officer to each man and a half.

After marching about a mile we came into a neck of woods and crossed an intersecting road which showed no wheel-tracks, but was rich in hoof-prints. We observed them and kept right on about our business, whatever that may have been. A few hundred yards farther brought us to a plantation bordering our road upon the right. The fields, as was the Southern fashion at that period of the war, were uncultivated and over-grown with brambles. A large white house stood at some little distance from the road; we saw women and children and a few negroes there. On our left ran the thin forest, pervious to cavalry. Directly ahead an ascent in the road formed a crest beyond which we could see nothing.

On this crest suddenly appeared two horsemen in gray, sharply outlined against the sky—men and animals looking gigantic. At the same instant a jingling and tramping were audible behind us, and turning in that direction I saw a score of mounted men moving forward at a trot. In the meantime the giants on the crest had multiplied surprisingly. Our invasion of the Gulf States had apparently failed.

There was lively work in the next few seconds. The shots were thick and fast—and uncommonly loud; none, I think, from our side. Cobb was on the extreme left of our advance, I on the right—about two paces apart. He instantly dived into the wood. The three men and I climbed across the fence somehow and struck out across the field—actuated, doubtless, by an intelligent forethought: men on horseback could not immediately follow. Passing near the house, now swarming like a hive of bees, we made for a swamp two or three hundred yards away, where I concealed myself in a jungle, the others continuing—as a defeated commander would put it—to fall back. In my cover, where I lay panting like a hare, I could hear a deal of shouting and hard riding and an occasional shot. I heard some one calling dogs, and the thought of bloodhounds added its fine suggestiveness to the other fancies appropriate to the occasion.

Finding myself unpursued after the lapse of what seemed an hour, but was probably a few minutes, I cautiously sought a place where, still concealed, I could obtain a view of the field of glory. The only enemy in sight was a group of horsemen on a hill a quarter of a mile away. Toward this group a woman was running, followed by the eyes of everybody about the house. I thought she had discovered my hiding-place and was going to "give me away." Taking to my hands and knees I crept as rapidly as possible among the clumps of brambles directly back toward the point in the road where we had met the enemy and failed to make him ours. There I dragged myself into a patch of briars within ten feet of the road, where I lay undiscovered during the remainder of the day, listening to a variety of disparaging remarks upon Yankee valor and to dispiriting declarations of intention conditional on my capture, as members of the

Opposition passed and repassed and paused in the road to discuss the morning's events. In this way I learned that the three privates had been headed off and caught within ten minutes. Their destination would naturally be Andersonville; what further became of them God knows. Their captors passed the day making a careful canvass of the swamp for me.

When night had fallen I cautiously left my place of concealment, dodged across the road into the woods and made for the river through the mile of corn. Such corn! It towered above me like a forest, shutting out all the starlight except what came from directly overhead. Many of the ears were a yard out of reach. One who has never seen an Alabama river-bottom cornfield has not exhausted nature's surprises; nor will he know what solitude is until he explores one in a moonless night.

I came at last to the river bank with its fringe of trees and willows and canes. My intention was to swim across, but the current was swift, the water forbiddingly dark and cold. A mist obscured the other bank. I could not, indeed, see the water more than a few yards out. It was a hazardous and horrible undertaking, and I gave it up, following cautiously along the bank in search of the spot where we had moored the boat. True, it was hardly likely that the landing was now unguarded, or, if so, that the boat was still there. Cobb had undoubtedly made for it, having an even more urgent need than I; but hope springs eternal in the human breast, and there was a chance that he had been killed before reaching it. I came at last into the road that we had taken and consumed half the night in cautiously approaching the landing, pistol in hand and heart in mouth. The boat was gone! I continued my journey along the stream—in search of another.

My clothing was still damp from my morning bath, my teeth rattled with cold, but I kept on along the stream until I reached the limit of the cornfields and entered a dense wood. Through this I groped my way, inch by inch, when, suddenly emerging from a thicket into a space slightly more open, I came upon a smoldering camp-fire surrounded by prostrate figures of men, upon one of whom I had almost trodden. A sentinel, who ought to have been shot, sat by the embers, his carbine across his lap, his chin upon his breast. Just beyond was a group of unsaddled horses. The men were asleep; the sentinel was asleep;

the horses were asleep. There was something indescribably uncanny about it all. For a moment I believed them all lifeless, and O'Hara's familiar line, "The bivouac of the dead," quoted itself in my consciousness. The emotion that I felt was that inspired by a sense of the supernatural; of the actual and imminent peril of my position I had no thought. When at last it occurred to me I felt it as a welcome relief, and stepping silently back into the shadow retraced my course without having awakened a soul. The vividness with which I can now recall that scene is to me one of the marvels of memory.

Getting my bearings again with some difficulty, I now made a wide detour to the left, in the hope of passing around this outpost and striking the river beyond. In this mad attempt I ran upon a more vigilant sentinel, posted in the heart of a thicket, who fired at me without challenge. To a soldier an unexpected shot ringing out at dead of night is fraught with an awful significance. In my circumstances—cut off from my comrades, groping about an unknown country, surrounded by invisible perils which such a signal would call into eager activity —the flash and shock of that firearm were unspeakably dreadful! In any case I should and ought to have fled, and did so; but how much or little of conscious prudence there was in the prompting I do not care to discover by analysis of memory. I went back into the corn, found the river, followed it back a long way and mounted into the fork of a low tree. There I perched until the dawn, a most uncomfortable bird.

In the gray light of the morning I discovered that I was opposite an island of considerable length, separated from the mainland by a narrow and shallow channel, which I promptly waded. The island was low and flat, covered with an almost impenetrable cane-brake interlaced with vines. Working my way through these to the other side, I obtained another look at God's country—Shermany, so to speak. There were no visible inhabitants. The forest and the water met. This did not deter me. For the chill of the water I had no further care, and laying off my boots and outer clothing I prepared to swim. A strange thing now occurred—more accurately, a familiar thing occurred at a strange moment. A black cloud seemed to pass before my eyes—the water, the trees, the sky, all vanished in a profound darkness. I heard the roaring of a great cataract, felt the earth sinking from beneath my feet. Then I heard and felt no more.

At the battle of Kennesaw Mountain in the previous June I had been badly wounded in the head, and for three months was incapacitated for service. In truth, I had done no actual duty since, being then, as for many years afterward, subject to fits of fainting, sometimes without assignable immediate cause, but mostly when suffering from exposure, excitement or excessive fatigue. This combination of them all had broken me down —most opportunely, it would seem.

When I regained my consciousness the sun was high. I was still giddy and half blind. To have taken to the water would have been madness; I must have a raft. Exploring my island, I found a pen of slender logs: an old structure without roof or rafters, built for what purpose I do not know. Several of these logs I managed with patient toil to detach and convey to the water, where I floated them, lashing them together with vines. Just before sunset my raft was complete and freighted with my outer clothing, boots and pistol. Having shipped the last article, I returned into the brake, seeking something from which to improvise a paddle. While peering about I heard a sharp metallic click—the cocking of a rifle! I was a prisoner.

The history of this great disaster to the Union arms is brief and simple. A Confederate "home guard," hearing something going on upon the island, rode across, concealed his horse and still-hunted me. And, reader, when you are "held up" in the same way may it be by as fine a fellow. He not only spared my life, but even overlooked a feeble and ungrateful after-attempt upon his own (the particulars of which I shall not relate), merely exacting my word of honor that I would not again try to escape while in his custody. Escape! I could not have escaped a new-born babe.

At my captor's house that evening there was a reception, attended by the élite of the whole vicinity. A Yankee officer in full fig—minus only the boots, which could not be got on to his swollen feet—was something worth seeing, and those who came to scoff remained to stare. What most interested them, I think, was my eating—an entertainment that was prolonged to a late hour. They were a trifle disappointed by the absence of horns, hoof and tail, but bore their chagrin with good-natured fortitude. Among my visitors was a charming young woman from the plantation where we had met the foe the day before —the same lady whom I had suspected of an intention to reveal my hiding-place. She had had no such design; she had run over to the group of horsemen to learn if her father had been hurt—by whom, I should like to know. No restraint was put upon me; my captor even left me with the women and children and went off for instructions as to what disposition he should make of me. Altogether the reception was "a pronounced success," though it is to be regretted that the guest of the evening had the incivility to fall dead asleep in the midst of the festivities, and was put to bed by sympathetic and, he has reason to believe, fair hands.

The next morning I was started off to the rear in custody of two mounted men, heavily armed. They had another prisoner, picked up in some raid beyond the river. He was a most offensive brute—a foreigner of some mongrel sort, with just sufficient command of our tongue to show that he could not control his own. We traveled all day, meeting occasional small bodies of cavalrymen, by whom, with one exception—a Texan officer—I was civilly treated. My guards said, however, that if we should chance to meet Jeff Gatewood he would probably take me from them and hang me to the nearest tree; and once or twice, hearing horsemen approach, they directed me to stand aside, concealed in the brush, one of them remaining near by to keep an eye on me, the other going forward with my fellow-prisoner, for whose neck they seemed to have less tenderness, and whom I heartily wished well hanged.

Jeff Gatewood was a "guerrilla" chief of local notoriety, who was a greater terror to his friends than to his other foes. My guards related almost incredible tales of his cruelties and infamies. By their account it was into his camp that I had blundered on Sunday night.

We put up for the night at a farmhouse, having gone not more than fifteen miles, owing to the condition of my feet. Here we got a bite of supper and were permitted to lie before the fire. My fellow-prisoner took off his boots and was soon sound asleep. I took off nothing and, despite exhaustion, remained equally sound awake. One of the guards also removed his footgear and outer clothing, placed his weapons under his neck and slept the sleep of innocence; the other sat in the chimney corner on watch. The house was a double log cabin, with an open space between the two parts, roofed over—a common type of habitation in that region. The room we were in had its entrance in this open space, the fireplace opposite, at the end. Beside the door was a bed, occupied by the old man of the house and his wife. It was partly curtained off from the room.

In an hour or two the chap on watch began to yawn, then to nod. Pretty soon he stretched himself on the floor, facing us, pistol in hand. For a while he supported himself on his elbow, then laid his head on his arm, blinking like an owl. I performed an occasional snore, watching him narrowly between my eye-lashes from the shadow of my arm. The inevitable occurred—he slept audibly.

A half-hour later I rose quietly to my feet, particularly care-ful not to disturb the blackguard at my side, and moved as si-lently as possible to the door. Despite my care the latch clicked. The old lady sat bolt upright in bed and stared at me. She was too late. I sprang through the door and struck out for the nearest point of woods, in a direction previously selected, vault-ing fences like an accomplished gymnast and followed by a multitude of dogs. It is said that the State of Alabama has more dogs than school-children, and that they cost more for their keep. The estimate of cost is probably too high.

Looking backward as I ran, I saw and heard the place in a turmoil and uproar; and to my joy the old man, evidently oblivious to the facts of the situation, was lifting up his voice and calling his dogs. They were good dogs: they went back; otherwise the malicious old rascal would have had my skeleton. Again the traditional bloodhound did not materialize. Other pursuit there was no reason to fear; my foreign gentleman would occupy the attention of one of the soldiers, and in the darkness of the forest I could easily elude the other, or, if need be, get him at a disadvantage. In point of fact there was no pursuit.

I now took my course by the north star (which I can never sufficiently bless), avoiding all roads and open places about houses, laboriously boring my way through forests, driving myself like a wedge into brush and bramble, swimming every stream I came to (some of them more than once, probably), and pulling myself out of the water by boughs and briars—whatever could be grasped. Let any one try to go a little way across even the most familiar country on a moonless night, and he will have an experience to remember. By dawn I had probably not made three miles. My clothing and skin were alike in rags.

During the day I was compelled to make wide detours to avoid even the fields, unless they were of corn; but in other respects the going was distinctly better. A light breakfast of raw sweet potatoes and persimmons cheered the inner man; a good part of the outer was decorating the several thorns, boughs and sharp rocks along my sylvan wake.

Late in the afternoon I found the river, at what point it was impossible to say. After a half-hour's rest, concluding with a fervent prayer that I might go to the bottom, I swam across. Creeping up the bank and holding my course still northward through a dense undergrowth, I suddenly reeled into a dusty highway and saw a more heavenly vision than ever the eyes of a dying saint were blessed withal—two patriots in blue carrying a stolen pig slung upon a pole!

Late that evening Colonel McConnell and his staff were chatting by a camp-fire in front of his headquarters. They were in a pleasant humor: some one had just finished a funny story about a man cut in two by a cannon-shot. Suddenly something staggered in among them from the outer darkness and fell into the fire. Somebody dragged it out by what seemed to be a leg. They turned the animal on its back and examined it—they were no cowards.

"What is it, Cobb?" said the chief, who had not taken the trouble to rise.

"I don't know, Colonel, but thank God it is dead!"

It was not.

What Occurred at Franklin

FOR several days, in snow and rain, General Schofield's little army had crouched in its hastily constructed defenses at Columbia, Tennessee. It had retreated in hot haste from Pulaski, thirty miles to the south, arriving just in time to foil Hood, who, marching from Florence, Alabama, by another road, with a force of more than double our strength, had hoped to intercept us. Had he succeeded, he would indubitably have bagged the whole bunch of us. As it was, he simply took position in front of us and gave us plenty of employment, but did not attack; he knew a trick worth two of that.

Duck River was directly in our rear; I suppose both our flanks rested on it. The town was between them. One night—that of November 27, 1864—we pulled up stakes and crossed to the north bank to continue our retreat to Nashville, where Thomas and safety lay—such safety as is known in war. It was high time too, for before noon of the next day Forrest's cavalry forded the river a few miles above us and began pushing back our own horse toward Spring Hill, ten miles in our rear, on our only road. Why our infantry was not immediately put in motion toward the threatened point, so vital to our safety, General Schofield could have told better than I. Howbeit, we lay there inactive all day.

The next morning—a bright and beautiful one—the brigade of Colonel P. Sidney Post was thrown out, up the river four or five miles, to see what it could see. What it saw was Hood's head-of-column coming over on a pontoon bridge, and a right pretty spectacle it would have been to one whom it did not concern. It concerned us rather keenly.

As a member of Colonel Post's staff, I was naturally favored with a good view of the performance. We formed in line of battle at a distance of perhaps a half-mile from the bridge-head, but that unending column of gray and steel gave us no more attention than if we had been a crowd of farmer-folk. Why should it? It had only to face to the left to be itself a line of battle. Meantime it had more urgent business on hand than brushing away a small brigade whose only offense was curiosity; it was making for Spring Hill with all its legs and wheels. Hour after hour we watched that unceasing flow of infantry and artillery toward the rear of our army. It was an unnerving spectacle, yet we never for a moment doubted that, acting on the intelligence supplied by our succession of couriers, our entire force was moving rapidly to the point of contact. The battle of Spring Hill was obviously decreed. Obviously, too, our brigade of observation would be among the last to have a hand in it. The thought annoyed us, made us restless and resentful. Our mounted men rode forward and back behind the line, nervous and distressed; the men in the ranks sought relief in frequent changes of posture, in shifting their weight from one leg to the other, in needless inspection of their weapons and in that unfailing resource of the discontented soldier, audible damning of those in the saddles of authority. But never for more than a moment at a time did any one remove his eyes from that fascinating and portentous pageant.

Toward evening we were recalled, to learn that of our five divisions of infantry, with their batteries, numbering twenty-three thousand men, only one—Stanley's, four thousand weak—had been sent to Spring Hill to meet that formidable movement of Hood's three veteran corps! Why Stanley was not immediately effaced is still a matter of controversy. Hood, who was early on the ground, declared that he gave the needful orders and tried vainly to enforce them; Cheatham, in command of his leading corps, that he did not. Doubtless the dispute is still being carried on between these chieftains from their beds of asphodel and moly in Elysium. So much is certain: Stanley drove away Forrest and successfully held the junction of the roads against Cleburne's division, the only infantry that attacked him.

That night the entire Confederate army lay within a half mile of our road, while we all sneaked by, infantry, artillery, and trains. The enemy's camp-fires shone redly—miles of them—seemingly only a stone's throw from our hurrying column. His men were plainly visible about them, cooking their suppers—a sight so incredible that many of our own, thinking them friends, strayed over to them and did not return. At intervals of a few hundred yards we passed dim figures on horseback by the roadside, enjoining silence. Needless precaution; we could not have spoken if we had tried, for our hearts were in our throats. But fools are

God's peculiar care, and one of his protective methods is the stupidity of other fools. By daybreak our last man and last wagon had passed the fateful spot unchallenged, and our first were entering Franklin, ten miles away. Despite spirited cavalry attacks on trains and rear-guard, all were in Franklin by noon and such of the men as could be kept awake were throwing up a slight line of defense, inclosing the town.

Franklin lies—or at that time did lie; I know not what exploration might now disclose—on the south bank of a small river, the Harpeth by name. For two miles southward was a nearly flat, open plain, extending to a range of low hills through which passed the turnpike by which we had come. From some bluffs on the precipitous north bank of the river was a commanding overlook of all this open ground, which, although more than a mile away, seemed almost at one's feet. On this elevated ground the wagon-train had been parked and General Schofield had stationed himself—the former for security, the latter for outlook. Both were guarded by General Wood's infantry division, of which my brigade was a part. "We are in beautiful luck," said a member of the division staff. With some prevision of what was to come and a lively recollection of the nervous strain of helpless observation, I did not think it luck. In the activity of battle one does not feel one's hair going gray with vicissitudes of emotion.

For some reason to the writer unknown General Schofield had brought along with him General D. S. Stanley, who commanded two of his divisions—ours and another, which was not "in luck." In the ensuing battle, when this excellent officer could stand the strain no longer, he bolted across the bridge like a shot and found relief in the hell below, where he was promptly tumbled out of the saddle by a bullet.

Our line, with its reserve brigades, was about a mile and a half long, both flanks on the river, above and below the town—a mere bridge-head. It did not look a very formidable obstacle to the march of an army of more than forty thousand men. In a more tranquil temper than his failure at Spring Hill had put him into Hood would probably have passed around our left and turned us out with ease—which would justly have entitled him to the Humane Society's great gold medal. Apparently that was not his day for saving life.

About the middle of the afternoon our field-glasses picked up the Confederate head-of-column emerging from the range of hills previously mentioned, where it is cut by the Columbia road. But—ominous circumstance!—it did not come on. It turned to its left, at a right angle, moving along the base of the hills, parallel to our line. Other heads-of-column came through other gaps and over the crests farther along, impudently deploying on the level ground with a spectacular display of flags and glitter of arms. I do not remember that they were molested, even by the guns of General Wagner, who had been foolishly posted with two small brigades across the turnpike, a half-mile in our front, where he was needless for apprisal and powerless for resistance. My recollection is that our fellows down there in their shallow trenches noted these portentous dispositions without the least manifestation of incivility. As a matter of fact, many of them were permitted by their compassionate officers to sleep. And truly it was good weather for that: sleep was in the very atmosphere. The sun burned crimson in a gray-blue sky through a delicate Indian-summer haze, as beautiful as a day-dream in paradise. If one had been given to moralizing one might have found material a-plenty for homilies in the contrast between that peaceful autumn afternoon and the bloody business that it had in hand. If any good chaplain failed to "improve the occasion" let us hope that he lived to lament in sack-cloth-of-gold and ashes-of-roses his intellectual unthrift.

The putting of that army into battle shape—its change from columns into lines—could not have occupied more than an hour or two, yet it seemed an eternity. Its leisurely evolutions were irritating, but at last it moved forward with atoning rapidity and the fight was on. First, the storm struck Wagner's isolated brigades, which, vanishing in fire and smoke, instantly reappeared as a confused mass of fugitives inextricably intermingled with their pursuers. They had not stayed the advance a moment, and as might have been foreseen were now a peril to the main line, which could protect itself only by the slaughter of its friends. To the right and left, however, our guns got into play, and simultaneously a furious infantry fire broke out along the entire front, the paralyzed center excepted. But nothing could stay those gallant rebels from a hand-to-hand encounter with bayonet and butt, and it was accorded to them with hearty good-will.

Meantime Wagner's conquerors were pouring across the breastwork like water over a dam. The guns that had spared the fugitives had now no time to fire; their infantry supports gave way and for a space of more than two hundred yards in the very center of our line the assailants, mad with exultation, had everything their own way. From the right and the left their gray masses converged into the gap, pushed through, and then, spreading, turned our men out of the works so hardly held against the attack in their front. From our viewpoint on the bluff we could mark the constant widening of the gap, the steady encroachment of that blazing and smoking mass against its disordered opposition.

"It is all up with us," said Captain Dawson, of Wood's staff; "I am going to have a quiet smoke."

I do not doubt that he supposed himself to have borne the heat and burden of the strife. In the midst of his preparations for a smoke he paused and looked again—a new tumult of musketry had broken loose. Colonel Emerson Opdycke had rushed his reserve brigade into the *mêlée* and was bitterly disputing the Confederate advantage. Other fresh regiments joined in the countercharge, commanderless groups of retreating men returned to their work, and there ensued a hand-to-hand contest of incredible fury. Two long, irregular, mutable, and tumultuous blurs of color were consuming each other's edge along the line of contact. Such devil's work does not last long, and we had the great joy to see it ending, not as it began, but "more nearly to the heart's desire." Slowly the mobile blur moved away from the town, and presently the gray half of it dissolved into its elemental units, all in slow recession. The retaken guns in the embrasures pushed up towering clouds of white smoke; to east and to west along the reoccupied parapet ran a line of misty red till the spitfire crest was without a break from flank to flank. Probably there was some Yankee cheering, as doubtless there had been the "rebel yell," but my memory recalls neither. There are many battles in a war, and many incidents in a battle: one does not recollect everything. Possibly I have not a retentive ear.

While this lively work had been doing in the center, there had been no lack of diligence elsewhere, and now all were as busy as bees. I have read of many "successive attacks"—"charge after charge"—but I think the only assaults after the first were those of the second Confederate lines and possibly some of the reserves; certainly there were no visible abatement and renewal of effort anywhere except where the men who had been pushed out of the works backward tried to reenter. And all the time there was fighting.

After resetting their line the victors could not clear their front, for the baffled assailants would not desist. All over the open country in their rear, clear back to the base of the hills, drifted the wreck of battle, the wounded that were able to walk; and through the receding throng pushed forward, here and there, horsemen with orders and footmen whom we knew to be bearing ammunition. There were no wagons, no caissons: the enemy was not using, and could not use, his artillery. Along the line of fire we could see, dimly in the smoke, mounted officers, singly and in small groups, attempting to force their horses across the slight parapet, but all went down. Of this devoted band was the gallant General Adams, whose body was found upon the slope, and whose animal's forefeet were actually inside the crest. General Cleburne lay a few paces farther out, and five or six other general officers sprawled elsewhere. It was a great day for Confederates in the line of promotion.

For many minutes at a time broad spaces of battle were veiled in smoke. Of what might be occurring there conjecture gave a terrifying report. In a visible peril observation is a kind of defense; against the unseen we lift a trembling hand. Always from these regions of obscurity we expected the worst, but always the lifted cloud revealed an unaltered situation.

The assailants began to give way. There was no general retreat; at many points the fight continued, with lessening ferocity and lengthening range, well into the night. It became an affair of twinkling musketry and broad flares of artillery; then it sank to silence in the dark.

Under orders to continue his retreat, Schofield could now do so unmolested: Hood had suffered so terrible a loss in life and *morale* that he was in no condition for effective pursuit. As

at Spring Hill, daybreak found us on the road with all our impedimenta except some of our wounded, and that night we
encamped under the protecting guns of Thomas, at Nashville.
Our gallant enemy audaciously followed, and fortified himself
within rifle-reach, where he remained for two weeks without
firing a gun and was then destroyed.

'Way Down in Alabam'

A T the break-up of the great Rebellion I found myself at Selma, Alabama, still in the service of the United States, and although my duties were now purely civil my treatment was not uniformly so, and I am not surprised that it was not. I was a minor official in the Treasury Department, engaged in performance of duties exceedingly disagreeable not only to the people of the vicinity, but to myself as well. They consisted in the collection and custody of "captured and abandoned property." The Treasury had covered pretty nearly the entire area of "the States lately in rebellion" with a hierarchy of officials, consisting, as nearly as memory serves, of one supervising agent and a multitude of special agents. Each special agent held dominion over a collection district and was allowed an "agency aide" to assist him in his purposeful activity, besides such clerks, laborers and so forth as he could persuade himself to need. My humble position was that of agency aide. When the special agent was present for duty I was his chief executive officer; in his absence I represented him (with greater or less fidelity to the original and to my conscience) and was invested with his powers. In the Selma agency the property that we were expected to seize and defend as best we might was mostly plantations (whose owners had disappeared; some were dead, others in hiding) and cotton. The country was full of cotton which had been sold to the Confederate Government, but not removed from the plantations to take its chance of export through the blockade. It had been decided that it now belonged to the United States. It was worth about five hundred dollars a bale—say one dollar a pound. The world agreed that that was a pretty good price for cotton.

Naturally the original owners, having received nothing for their product but Confederate money which the result of the war had made worthless, manifested an unamiable reluctance to give it up, for if they could market it for themselves it would more than recoup them for all their losses in the war. They had therefore exercised a considerable ingenuity in effacing all record of its transfer to the Confederate Government, obliterating the marks on the bales, and hiding these away in swamps and other inconspicuous places, fortifying their claims to private ownership with appalling affidavits and "covering their tracks" in an infinite variety of ways generally.

In effecting their purpose they encountered many difficulties. Cotton in bales is not very portable property; it requires for movement and concealment a good deal of coöperation by persons having no interest in keeping the secret and easily accessible to the blandishments of those interested in tracing it. The negroes, by whom the work was necessarily done, were zealous to pay for emancipation by fidelity to the new *régime*, and many poor devils among them forfeited their lives by services performed with more loyalty than discretion. Railways—even those having a more than nominal equipment of rails and rolling stock—were unavailable for secret conveyance of the cotton. Navigating the Alabama and Tombigbee rivers were a few small steamboats, the half-dozen pilots familiar with these streams exacting one hundred dollars a day for their services; but our agents, backed by military authority, were at all the principal shipping points and no boat could leave without their consent. The port of Mobile was in our hands and the lower waters were patrolled by gunboats. Cotton might, indeed, be dumped down a "slide" by night at some private landing and fall upon the deck of a steamer idling innocently below. It might even arrive at Mobile, but secretly to transfer it to a deep-water vessel and get it out of the country—that was a dream.

On the movement of private cotton we put no restrictions; and such were the freight rates that it was possible to purchase a steamboat at Mobile, go up the river in ballast, bring down a cargo of cotton and make a handsome profit, after deducting the cost of the boat and all expenses of the venture, including the wage of the pilot. With no great knowledge of "business" I venture to think that in Alabama in the latter part of the year of grace 1865 commercial conditions were hardly normal.

Nor were social conditions what I trust they have now become. There was no law in the country except of the unsatisfactory sort known as "martial," and that was effective only within areas covered by the guns of isolated forts and the physical activities of their small garrisons. True, there were the immemorial laws of self-preservation and retaliation, both of which were liberally interpreted. The latter was faithfully administered, mostly against straggling Federal soldiers and too zealous government officials. When my chief had been ordered to Selma he had arrived just in time to act as sole mourner at the funeral of his predecessor—who had had the bad luck to interpret his instructions in a sense that was disagreeable to a gentleman whose interests were affected by the interpretation. Early one pleasant morning shortly afterward two United States marshals were observed by the roadside in a suburb of the town. They looked comfortable enough there in the sunshine, but each

> had that across his throat
> Which you had hardly cared to see.

When dispatched on business of a delicate nature men in the service of the agency had a significant trick of disappearing—they were of "the unreturning brave." Really the mortality among the unacclimated in the Selma district at that time was excessive. When my chief and I parted at dinner time (our palates were not in harmony) we commonly shook hands and tried to say something memorable that was worthy to serve as "last words." We had been in the army together and had many a time gone into battle without having taken that precaution in the interest of history.

Of course the better class of the people were not accountable for this state of affairs, and I do not remember that I greatly blamed the others. The country was full of the "elements of combustion." The people were impoverished and smarting with a sense of defeat. Organized resistance was no longer possible, but many men trained to the use of arms did not consider themselves included in the surrender and conscientiously believed it both right and expedient to prolong the struggle by private enterprise. Many, no doubt, made the easy and natural transition from soldiering to assassination by insensible degrees, unconscious of the moral difference, such as it is. Selma was little better than a ruin; in the concluding period of the war General Wilson's cavalry had raided it and nearly destroyed it, and the work begun by the battery had been completed by the torch. The conflagration was generally attributed to the negroes, who certainly augmented it, for a number of those suspected of the crime were flung into the flames by the maddened

populace. None the less were the Yankee invaders held respon
sible.

Every Northern man represented some form or phase of an
authority which these luckless people horribly hated, and to
which they submitted only because, and in so far as, they had
to. Fancy such a community, utterly without the restraints of
law and with no means of ascertaining public opinion—for
newspapers were not—denied even the moral advantage of the
pulpit! Considering what human nature has the misfortune to
be, it is wonderful that there was so little of violence and crime.

As the carcass invites the vulture, this prostrate land drew
adventurers from all points of the compass. Many, I am sorry
to say, were in the service of the United States Government.
Truth to tell, the special agents of the Treasury were themselves, as a body, not altogether spotless. I could name some
of them, and some of their assistants, who made large fortunes
by their opportunities. The special agents were allowed one-
fourth of the value of the confiscated cotton for expenses of
collection—none too much, considering the arduous and perilous character of the service; but the plan opened up such
possibilities of fraud as have seldom been accorded by any system of conducting the public business, and never without disastrous results to official morality. Against bribery no provision
could have provided an adequate safeguard; the magnitude of
the interests involved was too great, the administration of the
trust too loose and irresponsible. The system as it was, hastily
devised in the storm and stress of a closing war, broke down in
the end, and it is doubtful if the Government might not more
profitably have let the "captured and abandoned property"
alone.

As an instance of the temptations to which we were exposed,
and of our tactical dispositions in resistance, I venture to relate
a single experience of my own. During an absence of my chief
I got upon the trail of a lot of cotton—seven hundred bales, as
nearly as I now recollect—which had been hidden with so exceptional ingenuity that I was unable to trace it. One day there
came to my office two well-dressed and mannerly fellows who
suffered me to infer that they knew all about this cotton and
controlled it. When our conference on the subject ended it was
past dinner time and they civilly invited me to dine with them,

which, in hope of eliciting information over the wine, I did. I knew well enough that they indulged a similar selfish hope, so I had no scruples about using their hospitality to their disadvantage if I could. The subject, however, was not mentioned at table, and we were all singularly abstemious in the matter of champagne—so much so that as we rose from a rather long session at the board we disclosed our sense of the ludicrousness of the situation by laughing outright. Nevertheless, neither party would accept defeat, and for the next few weeks the war of hospitality was fast and furious. We dined together nearly every day, sometimes at my expense, sometimes at theirs. We drove, rode, walked, played at billiards and made many a night of it; but youth and temperance (in drink) pulled me through without serious inroads on my health. We had early come to an understanding and a deadlock. Failing to get the slenderest clew to the location of the cotton I offered them one-fourth if they would surrender it or disclose its hiding-place; they offered me one-fourth if I would sign a permit for its shipment as private property.

All things have an end, and this amusing contest finally closed. Over the remains of a farewell dinner, unusually luxurious, as befitted the occasion, we parted with expressions of mutual esteem—not, I hope, altogether insincere, and the ultimate fate of the cotton is to me unknown. Up to the date of my departure from the agency not a bale of it had either come into possession of the Government or found an outlet. I am sometimes disloyal enough to indulge myself in the hope that they baffled my successors as skilfully as they did me. One cannot help feeling a certain tenderness for men who know and value a good dinner.

Another corrupt proposal that I had the good fortune to be afraid to entertain came, as it were, from within. There was a dare-devil fellow whom, as I know him to be dead, I feel justified in naming Jack Harris. He was engaged in all manner of speculative ventures on his own account, but the special agent had so frequently employed him in "enterprises of great pith and moment" that he was in a certain sense and to a certain extent one of us. He seemed to me at the time unique, but shortly afterward I had learned to classify him as a type of the Californian adventurer with whose peculiarities of manner, speech and disposition most of us are to-day familiar enough. He never spoke of his past, having doubtless good reasons for reticence, but any one learned in Western slang—a knowledge then denied me—would have catalogued him with infallible accuracy. He was a rather large, strong fellow, swarthy, black-bearded, black-eyed, black-hearted and entertaining, no end; ignorant with an ignorance whose frankness redeemed it from offensiveness, vulgar with a vulgarity that expressed itself in such metaphors and similes as would have made its peace with the most implacable refinement. He drank hard, gambled high, swore like a parrot, scoffed at everything, was openly and proudly a rascal, did not know the meaning of fear, borrowed money abundantly, and squandered it with royal disregard. Desiring one day to go to Mobile, but reluctant to leave Montgomery and its pleasures—unwilling to quit certainty for hope—he persuaded the captain of a loaded steamboat to wait four days for him at an expense of $400 a day; and lest time should hang too heavy on the obliging skipper's hands, Jack permitted him to share the orgies gratis. But that is not my story.

One day Jack came to me with a rather more sinful proposal than he had heretofore done me the honor to submit. He knew of about a thousand bales of cotton, some of it private property, some of it confiscable, stored at various points on the banks of the Alabama. He had a steamboat in readiness, "with a gallant, gallant crew," and he proposed to drop quietly down to the various landings by night, seize the cotton, load it on his boat and make off down the river. What he wanted from me, and was willing to pay for, was only my official signature to some blank shipping permits; or if I would accompany the expedition and share its fortunes no papers would be necessary. In declining this truly generous offer I felt that I owed it to Jack to give him a reason that he was capable of understanding, so I explained to him the arrangements at Mobile, which would prevent him from transferring his cargo to a ship and getting the necessary papers permitting her to sail. He was astonished and, I think, pained by my simplicity. Did I think him a fool? He did not purpose—not he—to tranship at all: the perfected plan was to dispense with all hampering formality by slipping through Mobile Bay in the black of the night and navigating his laden river craft across the Gulf to Havana! The rascal was in dead earnest, and that natural timidity of disposition which compelled me to withhold my coöperation greatly lowered me in his esteem, I fear.

It was in Cuba, by the way, that Jack came to grief some years later. He was one of the crew of the filibustering vessel *Virginius*, and was captured and shot along with the others. Something in his demeanor as he knelt in the line to receive the fatal fusillade prompted a priest to inquire his religion. "I am an atheist, by God!" said Jack, and with this quiet profession of faith that gentle spirit winged its way to other tropics.

Having expounded with some particularity the precarious tenure by which I held my office and my life in those "thrilling regions" where my duties lay, I ought to explain by what unhappy chance I am still able to afflict the reader. There lived in Selma a certain once wealthy and still influential citizen, whose two sons, of about my own age, had served as officers in the Confederate Army. I will designate them simply as Charles and Frank. They were types of a class now, I fear, almost extinct. Born and bred in luxury and knowing nothing of the seamy side of life—except, indeed, what they had learned in the war—well educated, brave, generous, sensitive to points of honor, and of engaging manners, these brothers were by all respected, by many loved and by some feared. For they had quick fingers upon the pistol-trigger withal, and would rather fight a duel than eat—nay, drink. Nor were they over-particular about the combat taking the form of a duel—almost any form was good enough. I made their acquaintance by chance and cultivated it for the pleasure it gave me. It was long afterward that I gave a thought to its advantages; but from the time that I became generally known as their friend my safety was assured through all that region; an army with banners could not have given me the same immunity from danger, obstruction or even insult in the performance of my disagreeable duties. What glorious fellows they were, to be sure—these my late antagonists of the dark days when, God forgive us, we were trying to cut one another's throat. To this day I feel a sense of regret when I think of my instrumentality, however small, in depriving the world of many such men in the criminal insanity that we call battle.

Life in Selma became worth living even as the chance of living it augmented. With my new friends and a friend of theirs, whose name—the more shame to me—I cannot now recall, but should not write here if I could, I passed most of my leisure hours. At the houses of themselves and their friends I did most of my dining; and, heaven be praised! there was no necessity for moderation in wine. In their society I committed my sins, and together beneath that noble orb unknown to colder skies, the Southern moon, we atoned for them by acts of devotion performed with song and lute beneath the shrine window of many a local divinity.

One night we had an adventure. We were out late—so late that it was night only astronomically. The streets were "deserted and drear," and, of course, unlighted—the late Confederacy had no gas and no oil. Nevertheless, we saw that we were followed. A man keeping at a fixed distance behind turned as we turned, paused as we paused, and pursued as we moved on. We stopped, went back and remonstrated; asked his intentions in, I dare say, no gentle words. He gave us no reply, but as we left him he followed. Again we stopped, and I felt my pistol plucked out of my pocket. Frank had unceremoniously possessed himself of it and was advancing on the enemy. I do not remember if I had any wish to interpose a protest—anyhow there was no time. Frank fired and the man fell. In a moment all the chamber-windows in the street were thrown open with a head visible (and audible) in each. We told Frank to go home, which to our surprise he did; the rest of us, assisted by somebody's private policeman—who afterward apprised us that we were in arrest—carried the man to a hotel. It was found that his leg was broken above the knee, and the next day it was amputated. We paid his surgeon and his hotel bill, and when he had sufficiently recovered sent him to an address which he gave us in Mobile; but not a word could anybody get out of him as to who he had the misfortune to be, or why he had persisted, against the light, in following a quartet of stray revelers.

On the morning of the shooting, when everything possible had been done for the comfort of the victim, we three accomplices were released on our own recognizance by an old gentleman of severe aspect, who had resumed his function of justice of the peace where he had laid it down during the war. I did not then know that he had no more legal authority than I had myself, and I was somewhat disturbed in mind as I reflected on the possibilities of the situation. The opportunity to get rid of an offensive Federal official must of course be very tempting, and after all the shooting was a trifle hasty and not altogether justifiable.

On the day appointed for our preliminary examination, all of us except Frank were released and put on the witness-stand. We gave a true and congruent history of the affair. The hold-over justice listened to it all very patiently and then, with commendable brevity and directness of action, fined Frank five dollars and costs for disorderly conduct. There was no appeal.

There were queer characters in Alabama in those days, as you shall see. Once upon a time the special agent and I started down the Tombigbee River with a steamboat load of government cotton—some six hundred bales. At one of the military stations we took on a guard of a dozen or fifteen soldiers under command of a non-commissioned officer. One evening, just before dusk, as we were rounding a bend where the current set strongly against the left bank of the stream and the channel lay close to that shore, we were suddenly saluted with a volley of bullets and buckshot from that direction. The din of the firing, the rattle and crash of the missiles splintering the woodwork and the jingle of broken glass made a very rude arousing from the tranquil indolence of a warm afternoon on the sluggish Tombigbee. The left bank, which at this point was a trifle higher than the hurricane deck of a steamer, was now swarming with men who, almost near enough to jump aboard, looked unreasonably large and active as they sprang about from cover to cover, pouring in their fire. At the first volley the pilot had deserted his wheel, as well he might, and the boat, drifting in to the bank under the boughs of a tree, was helpless. Her jackstaff and yawl were carried away, her guards broken in, and her deck-load of cotton was tumbling into the stream a dozen bales at once. The captain was nowhere to be seen, the engineer had evidently abandoned his post and the special agent had gone to hunt up the soldiers. I happened to be on the hurricane deck, armed with a revolver, which I fired as rapidly as I could, listening all the time for the fire of the soldiers—and listening in vain. It transpired later that they had not a cartridge among them; and of all helpless mortals a soldier without a cartridge is the most imbecile. But all this time the continuous rattle of the enemy's guns and the petulant pop of my own pocket firearm were punctuated, as it were, by pretty regularly recurring loud explosions, as of a small cannon. They came from somewhere forward—I supposed from the opposition, as I knew we had no artillery on board.

The failure of our military guard made the situation somewhat grave. For two of us, at least, capture meant hanging out of hand. I had never been hanged in all my life and was not enamored of the prospect. Fortunately for us the bandits had selected their point of attack without military foresight. Immediately below them a bayou, impassable to them, let into the river. The moment we had drifted below it we were safe from boarding and capture. The captain was found in hiding and an empty pistol at his ear persuaded him to resume command of his vessel; the engineer and pilot were encouraged to go back to their posts and after some remarkably long minutes, during which we were under an increasingly long-range fire, we got under way. A few cotton bales piled about the pilot-house made us tolerably safe from that sort of thing in the future and then we took account of our damages. Nobody had been killed and only a few were wounded. This gratifying result was attributable to the fact that, being unarmed, nearly everybody had dived below at the first fire and taken cover among the cotton bales. While issuing a multitude of needless commands from the front of the hurricane-deck I looked below, and there, stretched out at full length on his stomach, lay a long, ungainly person, clad in faded butternut, bare-headed, his long, lank hair falling down each side of his neck, his coat-tails similarly parted, and his enormous feet spreading their soles to the blue sky. He had an old-fashioned horse-pistol, some two feet long, which he was in the act of sighting across his left palm for a parting shot at the now distant assailants. A more ludicrous figure I never saw; I laughed outright; but when his weapon went off it was matter for gratitude to be above it instead of before it. It was the "cannon" whose note I had marked all through the unequal fray.

The fellow was a returned Confederate whom we had taken on at one of the upper landings as our only passenger; we were dead-heading him to Mobile. He was undoubtedly in hearty sympathy with the enemy, and I at first suspected him of collusion, but circumstances not necessary to detail here rendered this impossible. Moreover, I had distinctly seen one of the "guer-rillas" fall and remain down after my own weapon was empty, and no man else on board except the passenger had fired a shot or had a shot to fire. When everything had been made snug again, and we were gliding along under the stars, without ap-prehension; when I had counted fifty-odd bullet holes through the pilot-house (which had not received the attention that by its prominence and importance it was justly entitled to) and everybody was variously boasting his prowess, I approached my butternut comrade-in-arms and thanked him for his kindly aid. "But," said I, "how the devil does it happen that *you* fight *that* crowd?"

"Wal, Cap," he drawled, as he rubbed the powder grime from his antique artillery, "I allowed it was mouty clever in you-all to take me on, seein' I hadn't ary cent, so I thought I'd jist kinder work my passage."

Working for an Empress

IN the spring of 1874 I was living in the pretty English town of Leamington, a place that will be remembered by most Americans who have visited the grave of Shakespeare at Stratford-on-Avon, or by personal inspection of the ruins of Kenilworth Castle have verified their knowledge of English history derived from Scott's incomparable romance. I was at that time connected with several London newspapers, among them the *Figaro*, a small weekly publication, semi-humorous, semi-theatrical, with a remarkable aptitude for managing the political affairs of France in the interest of the Imperialists. This last peculiarity it owed to the personal sympathies of its editor and proprietor, Mr. James Mortimer, a gentleman who for some twenty years before the overthrow of the Empire had lived in Paris. Mr. Mortimer had been a personal friend of the Emperor and Empress, and on the flight of the latter to England had rendered her important service; and after the release of the Emperor from captivity among the Germans Mr. Mortimer was a frequent visitor to the imperial exiles at Chiselhurst.

One day at Leamington my London mail brought a letter from Mr. Mortimer, informing me that he intended to publish a new satirical journal, which he wished me to write. I was to do all the writing, he the editing; and it would not be necessary for me to come up to London; I could send manuscript by mail. The new journal was not to appear at stated periods, but "occasionally." Would I submit to him a list of suitable titles for it, from which he could make a selection?

With some surprise at what seemed to me the singularly whimsical and unbusiness-like features of the enterprise I wrote him earnestly advising him either to abandon it or materially to modify his plan. I represented to him that such a journal, so conducted, could not in my judgment succeed; but he was obdurate and after a good deal of correspondence I consented to do all the writing if he was willing to do all the losing money. I submitted a number of names which I thought suitable for the paper, but all were rejected, and he finally wrote that he had decided to call the new journal *The Lantern*. This decision elicited from me another energetic protest. The title was not original, but obviously borrowed from M. Rochefort's famous journal, *La Lanterne*. True, that publication was dead, and its audacious editor deported to New Caledonia with his Communistic following; but the name could hardly be agreeable to Mr. Mortimer's Imperialist friends, particularly the Empress—the Emperor was then dead. To my surprise Mr. Mortimer not only adhered to his resolution but suggested the propriety of my taking M. Rochefort's late lamented journal as a model for our own. This I flatly declined to do and carried my point; I was delighted to promise, however, that the new paper should resemble the old in one particular: it should be irritatingly disrespectful of existing institutions and exalted personages.

On the 18th of May, 1874, there was published at the corner of St. Bride Street and Shoe Lane, E.C., London, the first number of "*The Lantern*—Appearing Occasionally. Illuminated by Faustin. Price, sixpence." It was a twelve-page paper with four pages of superb illustrations in six colors. I winced when I contemplated its artistic and mechanical excellence, for I knew at what a price that quality had been obtained. A gold mine would be required to maintain that journal, and that journal could by no means ever be itself a gold mine. A copy lies before me as I write and noting it critically I cannot help thinking that the illuminated title-page of this pioneer in the field of chromatic journalism is the finest thing of the kind that ever came from a press.

Of the literary contents I am less qualified for judgment, inasmuch as I wrote every line in the paper. It may perhaps be said without immodesty that the new "candidate for popular favor" was not distinguished by servile flattery of the British character and meek subservience to the British Government, as might perhaps be inferred from the following extract from an article on General Sir Garnet Wolseley, who had just received the thanks of his Sovereign and a munificent reward from Parliament for his successful plundering expedition through Ashantee:

"We feel a comfortable sense of satisfaction in the thought that *The Lantern* will never fail to shed the light of its loyal approval upon any unworthy act by which our country shall secure an adequate and permanent advantage. When the great heart of England is stirred by quick cupidity to profitable crime, far be it from us to lift our palms in deprecation. In the wrangle for existence nations, equally with individuals, work by diverse means to a common end—the spoiling of the weak; and when by whatever of outrage we have pushed a feeble competitor to the wall, in Heaven's name let us pin him fast and relieve his pockets of the material good to which, in bestowing it upon him, the bountiful Lord has invited our thieving hand. But these Ashantee women were not worth garroting. Their fallals, precious to them, are worthless to us; the entire loot fetched only £11,000—of which sum the man who brought home the trinkets took a little more than four halves. We submit that with practiced agents in every corner of the world and a watchful government at home this great commercial nation might dispose of its honor to better advantage."

With the candor of repentance it may now be confessed that, however unscrupulous it may be abroad, a government which tolerates this kind of criticism cannot rightly be charged with tyranny at home.

By way (as I supposed) of gratitude to M. Rochefort for the use of the title of his defunct journal it had been suggested by Mr. Mortimer that he be given a little wholesome admonition here and there in the paper and I had cheerfully complied. M. Rochefort had escaped from New Caledonia some months before. A disagreeable cartoon was devised for his discomfort and he received a number of such delicate attentions as that following, which in the issue of July 15th greeted him on his arrival in England along with his distinguished compatriot, M. Pascal Grousset:

"M. Rochefort is a gentleman who has lost his standing. There have been greater falls than his. Kings before now have become servitors, honest men bandits, thieves communists. Insignificant in his fortunes as in his abilities, M. Rochefort, who was never very high, is not now very low—he has avoided the falsehood of extremes: never quite a count, he is now but half a convict. Having missed the eminence that would have given him calumniation, he is also denied the obscurity that would bring misconstruction. He is not even a *misérable*; he is a person. It is curious to note how persistently this man has perverted his gifts. With talents that might have corrupted pan-egyric, he preferred to refine detraction; fitted to disgrace the *salon*, he has elected to adorn the cell; the qualities that would have endeared him to a blackguard he has wasted upon Pascal Grousset.

"As we write, it is reported that this person is in England. It is further affirmed that it is his intention to proceed to Belgium or Switzerland to fight certain journalists who have not had the courtesy to suppress the truth about him, though he never told it of them. We presume, however, this rumor is false; M. Rochefort must retain enough of the knowledge he acquired when he was esteemed a gentleman to be aware that a meeting between him and a journalist is now impossible. This is the more to be regretted, because M. Paul de Cassagnac would have much pleasure in taking M. Rochefort's life and we in la-menting his fall.

"M. Rochefort, we believe, is already suffering from an un-healed wound. It is his mouth."

There was a good deal of such "scurril jesting" in the paper, especially in a department called "Prattle." There were verses on all manner of subjects—mostly the nobility and their works and ways, from the viewpoint of disapproval—and epigrams, generally ill-humorous, like the following, headed "*Novum Organum*":

> "In Bacon see the culminating prime
> Of British intellect and British crime.
> He died, and Nature, settling his affairs,
> Parted his powers among us, his heirs:
> To each a pinch of common-sense, for seed,
> And, to develop it, a pinch of greed.
> Each frugal heir, to make the gift suffice,
> Buries the talent to manure the vice."

When the first issue of *The Lantern* appeared I wrote to Mr. Mortimer, again urging him to modify his plans and alter the character of the journal. He replied that it suited him as it was and he would let me know when to prepare "copy" for the second number. That eventually appeared on July 15th. I never was instructed to prepare any more copy, and there has been, I believe, no further issue of that interesting sheet as yet.

Taking a retrospective view of this singular venture in journalism, one day, the explanation of the whole matter came to my understanding in the light of a revelation, and was confirmed later by Mr. Mortimer.

In the days when Napoleon III was at the zenith of his glory and power there was a thorn in his side. It was the pen of M. Henri Rochefort, le Comte de Luçay, journalist and communard. Despite fines, "suppressions," and imprisonments, this gifted writer and unscrupulous blackguard had, as every one knows, made incessant war upon the Empire and all its *personnel*. The bitter and unfair attacks of his paper, *La Lanterne*, made life at the Tuilleries exceedingly uncomfortable. His rancor against the Empress was something horrible, and went to the length of denying the legitimacy of the Prince Imperial. His existence was a menace and a terror to the illustrious lady, even when she was in exile at Chiselhurst and he in confinement on the distant island of New Caledonia. When the news of his escape from that penal colony arrived at Chiselhurst the widowed Empress was in despair; and when, on his way to England, he announced his intention of reviving *La Lanterne* in London (of course he dared not cross the borders of France) she was utterly prostrated by the fear of his pitiless animosity. But what could she do? Not prevent the revival of his dreadful newspaper, certainly, but—well, she could send for Mr. Mortimer. That ingenious gentleman was not long at a loss for an expedient that would accomplish what was possible. He shut Rochefort out of London by forestalling him. At the very time when Mortimer was asking me to suggest a suitable name for the new satirical journal he had already registered at Stationers' Hall—that is to say, copyrighted—the title of *The Lantern*, a precaution which M. Rochefort's French friends had neglected to take, although they had expended thousands of pounds in a plant for their venture. Mr. Mortimer cruelly permitted them to go on with their costly preparations, and the first intimation they had that the field was occupied came from the newsdealers selling *The Lantern*. After some futile attempts at relief and redress, M. Rochefort took himself off and set up his paper in Belgium.

The expenses of *The Lantern*—including a generous *douceur* to myself—were all defrayed by the Empress. She was the sole owner of it and, I was gratified to learn, took so lively an interest in her venture that a special French edition was printed for her private reading. I was told that she especially enjoyed the articles on M. le Comte de Luçay, though I dare say some of the delicate subtleties of their literary style were lost in translation.

Being in London later in the year, I received through Mortimer an invitation to visit the poor lady, *en famille*, at Chiselhurst; but as the iron rules of imperial etiquette, even in exile, required that the hospitable request be made in the form of a "command," my republican independence took alarm and I had the incivility to disobey; and I still think it a sufficient distinction to be probably the only American journalist who was ever employed by an Empress in so congenial a pursuit as the pursuit of another journalist.

Across the Plains

THAT noted pioneer, General John Bidwell, of California, once made a longish step up the western slope of our American Parnassus by an account of his journey "across the plains" seven years before the lamented Mr. Marshall had found the least and worst of all possible reasons for making the "trek." General Bidwell had not the distinction to be a great writer, but in order to command admiration and respect in that province of the Republic of Letters which lies in the Sacramento Valley above the mouth of the Yuba the gift of writing greatly is a needless endowment. Nevertheless I read his narrative with an interest which on analysis turns out to be a by-product of personal experience: among my youthful indiscretions was a journey over much of the same ground, which I took in much the same way—as did many thousands before and after.

It was a far cry from 1841 to 1866, yet the country between the Missouri River and the Sierra Nevada had not greatly improved: civilization had halted at the river, awaiting transportation. A railroad had set out from Omaha westward, and another at Sacramento was solemnly considering the impossible suggestion of going eastward to meet it. There were lunatics in those days, as there are in these. I left the one road a few miles out of the Nebraskan village and met the other at Dutch Flat, in California.

Waste no compassion on the loneliness of my journey: a thriving colony of Mormons had planted itself in the valley of Salt Lake and there were "forts" at a few points along the way, where ambitious young army officers passed the best years of their lives guarding live stock and teaching the mysteries of Hardee's tactics to that alien patriot, the American regular. There was a dusty wagon road, bordered with bones—not always those of animals—with an occasional mound, sometimes dignified with a warped and rotting head-board bearing an illegible inscription. (One inscription not entirely illegible is said to have concluded with this touching tribute to the worth of the departed: "He was a good egg." Another was: "He done his damnedest.") In other particulars the "Great American Desert" of our fathers was very like what it was when General Bidwell's party traversed it with that hereditary instinct, that delicacy of spiritual nose which served the Western man of that day in place of a map and guide-book. Westward the course of empire had taken its way, but excepting these poor vestiges it had for some fifteen hundred miles left no trace of its march. The Indian of the plains had as yet seen little to unsettle his assurance of everlasting dominion. Of the slender lines of metal creeping slowly toward him from East and West he knew little; and had he known more, how could he have foreseen their momentous effect upon his "ancient solitary reign"?

I remember very well, as so many must, some of the marked features of the route that General Bidwell mentions. One of the most imposing of these is Court House Rock, near the North Platte. Surely no object of such dignity ever had a more belittling name—given it in good faith no doubt by some untraveled wight whose county court-house was the most "reverend pile" of which he had any conception. It should have been called the Titan's Castle. What a gracious memory I have of the pomp and splendor of its aspect, with the crimson glories of the setting sun fringing its outlines, illuminating its western walls like the glow of Mammon's fires for the witches' revel in the Hartz, and flung like banners from its crest!

I suppose Court House Rock is familiar enough and commonplace enough to the dwellers in that land (riparian tribes once infesting the low lands of Ohio and Indiana and the flats of Iowa), but to me, tipsy with youth, full-fed on Mayne Reid's romances, and now first entering the enchanted region that he so charmingly lied about, it was a revelation and a dream. I wish that anything in the heavens, on the earth, or in the waters under the earth would give me now such an emotion as I experienced in the shadow of that "great rock in a weary land."

I was not a pilgrim, but an engineer *attaché* to an expedition through Dakota and Montana, to inspect some new military posts. The expedition consisted, where the Indians preserved the peace, of the late General W. B. Hazen, myself, a cook and a teamster; elsewhere we had an escort of cavalry. My duty, as I was given to understand it, was to amuse the general and other large game, make myself as comfortable as possible without too much discomfort to others, and when in an unknown country survey and map our route for the benefit of those who might come after. The posts which the general was to inspect had recently been established along a military road, one end of which was at the North Platte and the other—there was no other end; up about Fort C. F. Smith at the foot of the Big-Horn Mountains the road became a buffalo trail and was lost in the weeds. But it was a useful road, for by leaving it before going too far one could reach a place near the headwaters of the Yellowstone, where the National Park is now.

By a master stroke of military humor we were ordered to return (to Washington) via Salt Lake City, San Francisco and Panama. I obeyed until I got as far as San Francisco, where, finding myself appointed to a second lieutenancy in the Regular Army, ingratitude, more strong than traitors' arms, quite vanquished me: I resigned, parted from Hazen more in sorrow than in anger and remained in California.

I have thought since that this may have been a youthful error: the Government probably meant no harm, and if I had served long enough I might have become a captain. In time, if I lived, I should naturally have become the senior captain of the Army; and then if there were another war and any of the field officers did me the favor to paunch a bullet I should become the junior major, certain of another step upward as soon as a number of my superiors equal to the whole number of majors should be killed, resign or die of old age—enchanting prospect! But I am getting a long way off the trail.

It was near Fort C. F. Smith that we found our first buffaloes, and abundant they were. We had to guard our camp at night with fire and sword to keep them from biting us as they grazed. Actually one of them half-scalped a teamster as he lay dreaming of home with his long fair hair commingled with the toothsome grass. His utterances as the well-meaning beast lifted him from the ground and tried to shake the earth from his roots were neither wise nor sweet, but they made a profound impression on the herd, which, arching its multitude of tails, absented itself to pastures new like an army with banners.

At Fort C. F. Smith we parted with our *impedimenta*, and with an escort of about two dozen cavalrymen and a few pack animals struck out on horseback through an unexplored country northwest for old Fort Benton, on the upper Missouri. The journey was not without its perils. Our only guide was my compass; we knew nothing of the natural obstacles that we must encounter; the Indians were on the warpath, and our course led us through the very heart of their country. Luckily for us they were gathering their clans into one great army for a descent upon the posts that we had left behind; a little later some three thousand of them moved upon Fort Phil Kearney, lured a force of ninety men and officers outside and slaughtered them to the last man. This was one of the posts that we had inspected, and the officers killed had hospitably entertained us.

In that lively and interesting book, "Indian Fights and Fighters," Dr. Cyrus Townsend Brady says of this "outpost of civilization":

"The most careful watchfulness was necessary at all hours of the day and night. The wood trains to fetch logs to the sawmills were heavily guarded. There was fighting all the time. Casualties among the men were by no means rare. At first it was difficult to keep men within the limits of the camp; but stragglers who failed to return, and some who had been cut off, scalped and left for dead, but who had crawled back to die, convinced every one of the wisdom of the commanding officer's repeated orders and cautions. To chronicle the constant succession of petty skirmishes would be wearisome; yet they often resulted in torture and loss of life on the part of the soldiers, although the Indians in most instances suffered the more severely."

In a footnote the author relates this characteristic instance of the Government's inability to understand: "Just when the alarms were most frequent a messenger came to the headquarters, announcing that a train *en route* from Fort Laramie, with special messengers from that post, was corraled by Indians, and demanded immediate help. An entire company of infantry in wagons, with a mountain howitzer and several rounds of grapeshot, was hastened to their relief. It proved to be a train with mail from the Laramie Commission, announcing the confirmation of a 'satisfactory treaty of peace with all the Indians of the Northwest,' and assuring the district commander of the fact. The messenger was brought in in safety, and *peace* lasted until his message was delivered. So much was gained—that the messenger did not lose his scalp."

Through this interesting environment our expeditionary

force of four men had moved to the relief of the beleaguered post, but finding it impossible to "raise the siege" had—with a score of troopers—pushed on to Fort C. F. Smith, and thence into the Unknown.

The first part of this new journey was well enough; there were game and water. Where we swam the Yellowstone we had an abundance of both, for the entire river valley, two or three miles wide, was dotted with elk. There were hundreds. As we advanced they became scarce; buffalo became scarce; bear, deer, rabbits, sage-hens, even prairie dogs gave out, and we were near starving. Water gave out too, and starvation was a welcome state: our hunger was so much less disagreeable than our thirst that it was a real treat.

However, we got to Benton, Heaven knows how and why, but we were a sorry-looking lot, though our scalps were intact. If in all that region there is a mountain that I have not climbed, a river that I have not swum, an alkali pool that I have not thrust my muzzle into, or an Indian that I have not shuddered to think about, I am ready to go back in a Pullman sleeper and do my duty.

From Fort Benton we came down through Helena and Virginia City, Montana—then new mining camps—to Salt Lake, thence westward to California. Our last bivouac was on the old camp of the Donner party, where, in the flickering lights and dancing shadows made by our camp-fire, I first heard the story of that awful winter, and in the fragrance of the meat upon the coals fancied I could detect something significantly uncanny. The meat which the Donner party had cooked at that spot was not quite like ours. Pardon: I mean it was not like that which we cooked.

The Mirage

S INCE the overland railways have long been carrying many thousands of persons across the elevated plateaus of the continent the mirage in many of its customary aspects has become pretty well known to great numbers of persons all over the Union, and the tales of early observers who came "der blains agross" are received with a less frigid inhospitality than they formerly were by incredulous pioneers who had come "der Horn aroundt," as the illustrious Hans Breitmann phrases it; but in its rarer and more marvelous manifestations, the mirage is still a rock upon which many a reputation for veracity is wrecked remediless. With an ambition intrepidly to brave this disaster, and possibly share it with the hundreds of devoted souls whose disregard of the injunction never to tell an incredible truth has branded them as hardy and impenitent liars, I purpose to note here a few of the more remarkable illusions by which my own sense of sight has been befooled by the freaks of the enchanter.

It is apart from my purpose to explain the mirage scientifically, and not altogether in my power. Every schoolboy can do so, I suppose, to the satisfaction of his teacher if the teacher has not himself seen the phenomenon, or has seen it only in the broken, feeble and evanescent phases familiar to the overland passenger; but for my part I am unable to understand how the simple causes affirmed in the text-books sufficiently account for the infinite variety and complexity of some of the effects said to be produced by them. But of this the reader shall judge for himself.

One summer morning in the upper North Platte country I rose from my blankets, performed the pious acts of sun-worship by yawning toward the east, kicked together the parted embers of my camp-fire, and bethought me of water for my ablutions. We had gone into bivouac late in the night on the open plain, and without any clear notion of where we were. There were a half-dozen of us, our chief on a tour of inspection of the new military posts in Wyoming. I accompanied the expedition as surveyor. Having an aspiration for water I naturally looked about to see what might be the prospect of obtaining it, and to my surprise and delight saw a long line of willows, apparently some three hundred yards away. Willows implied water, and snatching up a camp-kettle I started forward without taking the trouble to put on my coat and hat. For the first mile or two I preserved a certain cheerful hopefulness; but when the sun had risen farther toward the meridian and began to affect my bare head most uncomfortably, and the picketed horses at the camp were hull down on the horizon in the rear, and the willows in front increased their pace out of all proportion to mine, I began to grow discouraged and sat down on a stone to wish myself back. Perceiving that the willows also had halted for breath I determined to make a dash at them, leaving the camp-kettle behind to make its way back to camp as best it could. I was now traveling "flying light," and had no doubt of my ability to overtake the enemy, which had, however, disappeared over the crest of a low sandhill. Ascending this I was treated to a surprise. Right ahead of me lay a barren waste of sand extending to the right and left as far as I could see. Its width in the direction that I was going I judged to be about twenty miles. On its farther border the cactus plain began again, sloping gradually upward to the horizon, along which was a fringe of cedar trees—the willows of my vision! In that country a cedar will not grow within thirty miles of water if it knows it.

On my return journey I coldly ignored the appeals of the camp-kettle, and when I met the rescuing party which had been for some hours trailing me made no allusion to the real purpose of my excursion. When the chief asked if I purposed to enter a plea of temporary insanity I replied that I would reserve my defense for the present; and in fact I never did disclose it until now.

I had afterward the satisfaction of seeing the chief, an experienced plainsman, consume a full hour, rifle in hand, working round to the leeward of a dead coyote in the sure and certain hope of bagging a sleeping buffalo. Mirage or no mirage, you must not too implicitly trust your eyes in the fantastic atmosphere of the high plains.

I remember that one forenoon I looked forward to the base of the Big Horn Mountains and selected a most engaging nook for the night's camp. My good opinion of it was confirmed when we reached it three days later. The deception in this instance was due to nothing but the marvelous lucidity of the atmosphere and the absence of objects of known dimensions, and these sources of error are sometimes sufficient of themselves to produce the most incredible illusions. When they are in alliance with the mirage the combination's pranks are bewildering.

One of the most grotesque and least comfortable of my experiences with the magicians of the air occurred near the forks of the Platte. There had been a tremendous thunder-storm, lasting all night. In the morning my party set forward over the soaken prairie under a cloudless sky intensely blue. I was riding in advance, absorbed in thought, when I was suddenly roused to a sense of material things by exclamations of astonishment and apprehension from the men behind. Looking forward, I beheld a truly terrifying spectacle. Immediately in front, at a distance, apparently, of not more than a quarter-mile, was a long line of the most formidable looking monsters that the imagination ever conceived. They were taller than trees. In them the elements of nature seemed so fantastically and discordantly confused and blended, compounded, too, with architectural and mechanical details, that they partook of the triple character of animals, houses and machines. Legs they had, that an army of elephants could have marched among; bodies that ships might have sailed beneath; heads about which eagles might have delighted to soar, and ears—they were singularly well gifted with ears. But wheels also they were endowed with, and vast sides of blank wall; the wheels as large as the ring of a circus, the walls white and high as cliffs of chalk along an English coast. Among them, on them, beneath, in and a part of them, were figures and fragments of figures of gigantic men. All were inextricably interblended and superposed—a man's head and shoulders blazoned on the side of an animal; a wheel with legs for spokes rolling along the creature's back; a vast section of wall, having no contact with the earth, but (with a tail hanging from its rear, like a note of admiration) moving along the line, obscuring here an anatomical horror and disclosing there a mechanical nightmare. In short, this appalling procession, which was crossing our road with astonishing rapidity, seemed made up of unassigned and unassorted units, out of which some imaginative god might be about to create a world of giants, ready supplied with some of the appliances of a high civilization. Yet the whole apparition had so shadowy and spectral a look that the terror it inspired was itself vague and indefinite, like the terror of a dream. It affected our horses as well as ourselves; they extended their necks and threw forward their ears. For some moments we sat in our saddles surveying the hideous and extravagant spectacle without a word, and our tongues were loosened only when it began rapidly to diminish and recede, and at last was resolved into a train of mules and wagons, barely visible on the horizon. They were miles away and outlined against the blue sky.

I then remembered what my astonishment had not permitted me closely to note—that this pageant had appeared to move along parallel to the foot of a slope extending upward and backward to an immense height, intersected with rivers and presenting all the features of a prairie landscape. The mirage had in effect contracted the entire space between us and the train to a pistol-shot in breadth, and had made a background for its horrible picture by lifting into view Heaven knows how great an extent of country below our horizon. Does refraction account for all this? To this day I cannot without vexation remember the childish astonishment that prevented me from observing the really interesting features of the spectacle and kept my eyes fixed with a foolish distension on a lot of distorted mules, teamsters and wagons.

One of the commonest and best known tricks of the mirage is that of overlaying a dry landscape with ponds and lakes, and by a truly interesting and appropriate coincidence one or more travelers perishing of thirst seem always to be present, properly to appreciate the humor of the deception; but when a gentleman whose narrative suggested this article averred that he had seen these illusory lakes navigated by phantom boats filled with visionary persons he was, I daresay, thought to be drawing the long bow, even by many miragists in good standing. For aught I know he may have been. I can only attest the entirely credible character of the statement.

Away up at the headwaters of the Missouri, near the British possessions, I found myself one afternoon rather unexpectedly on the shore of an ocean. At less than a gunshot from where I stood was as plainly defined a seabeach as one could wish to see. The eye could follow it in either direction, with all its bays, inlets and promontories, to the horizon. The sea was studded with islands, and these with tall trees of many kinds, both islands and trees being reflected in the water with absolute fidelity. On many of the islands were houses, showing white beneath the trees, and on one which lay farthest out seaward was a considerable city, with towers, domes and clusters of steeples. There were ships in the offing whose sails glistened in the sunlight and, closer in, several boats of novel but graceful design, crowded with human figures, moved smoothly among the lesser islands, impelled by some power invisible from my point of view, each boat attended by its inverted reflection "crowding up beneath the keel." It must be admitted that the voyagers were habited after a somewhat uncommon fashion—almost unearthly, I may say—and were so grouped that at my distance I could not clearly distinguish their individual limbs and attitudes. Their features were, of course, entirely invisible. None the less, they were plainly human beings—what other creatures would be boating? Of the other features of the scene—the coast, islands, trees, houses, city and ships hull-down in the offing—I distinctly affirm an absolute identity of visible aspect with those to which we are accustomed in the realm of reality; imagination had simply nothing to do with the matter. True, I had not recently had the advantage of seeing any such objects, except trees, and these had been mighty poor specimens, but, like Macduff, I "could not but remember such things were," nor had I forgotten how they looked.

Of course I was not for an instant deceived by all this: I knew that under it all lay a particularly forbidding and inhospitable expanse of sagebrush and cactus, peopled with nothing more nearly akin to me than prairie dogs, ground owls and jackass rabbits—that with these exceptions the desert was as desolate as the environment of Ozymandias' "vast and trunkless legs of stone." But as a show it was surely the most enchanting that human eyes had ever looked on, and after more years than I care to count it remains one of memory's most precious possessions. The one thing which always somewhat impairs the illusion in such instances—the absence of the horizon water-line—did not greatly abate the *vraisemblance* in this, for the large island in the distance nearly closed the view seaward, and the ships occupied most of the remaining space. I had but to fancy a slight haze on the farther water, and all was right and regular. For more than a half-hour this charming picture remained intact; then ugly patches of plain began to show through, the islands with their palms and temples slowly dissolved, the boats foundered with every soul on board, the sea drifted over the headlands in a most unwaterlike way, and inside the hour since,

> like stout Cortez, when with eagle eyes
> He stared at the Pacific, and all his men
> Looked at each other with a wild surmise,
> Silent upon a peak in Darien,

I had discovered this unknown sea all this insubstantial pageant had faded like the baseless fabric of the vision that it was and left not a rack behind.

In some of its minor manifestations the mirage is sometimes seen on the western coast of our continent, in the bay of San Francisco, for example, causing no small surprise to the untraveled and unread observer, and no small pain to the spirits of purer fire who are fated to be caught within earshot and hear him pronounce it a "mirridge." I have seen Goat Island without visible means of support and Red Rock suspended in midair like the coffin of the Prophet. Looking up toward Mare Island one most ungracious morning when a barbarous norther had purged the air of every stain and the human soul of every virtue, I saw San Pablo Bay margined with cliffs whose altitude must have exceeded considerably that from whose dizzy verge old eyeless Gloster, falling in a heap at his own feet, supposed himself to have sailed like a stone.

One more instance and "I've done, i' faith." Gliding along down the Hudson River one hot summer afternoon in a steamboat, I went out on the afterguard for a breath of fresh air, but there was none to be had. The surface of the river was like oil and the steamer's hull slipped through it with surprisingly little disturbance. Her tremor was for once hardly perceptible; the beating of her paddles was subdued to an almost inaudible rhythm. The air seemed what we call "hollow" and had apparently hardly enough tenuity to convey sounds. Everywhere on the surface of the glassy stream were visible undulations of heat, and the light steam of evaporation lay along the sluggish water and hung like a veil between the eye and the bank. Seated in an armchair and overcome by the heat and the droning of some prosy passengers near by, I fell asleep. When I awoke the guards were crowded with passengers in a high state of excitement, pointing and craning shoreward. Looking in the same direction I saw, through the haze, the sharp outlines of a city in gray silhouette. Roofs, spires, pinnacles, chimneys, angles of wall—all were there, cleanly cut out against the air.

"What is it?" I cried, springing to my feet.

"That, sir," replied a passenger stolidly, "is Poughkeepsie."

It was.

A Sole Survivor

A MONG the arts and sciences, the art of Sole Surviving is one of the most interesting, as (to the artist) it is by far the most important. It is not altogether an art, perhaps, for success in it is largely due to accident. One may study how solely to survive, yet, having an imperfect natural aptitude, may fail of proficiency and be early cut off. To the contrary, one little skilled in its methods, and not even well grounded in its fundamental principles, may, by taking the trouble to have been born with a suitable constitution, attain to a considerable eminence in the art. Without undue immodesty, I think I may fairly claim some distinction in it myself, although I have not regularly acquired it as one acquires knowledge and skill in writing, painting and playing the flute. O yes, I am a notable Sole Survivor, and some of my work in that way attracts great attention, mostly my own.

You would naturally expect, then, to find in me one who has experienced all manner of disaster at sea and the several kinds of calamity incident to a life on dry land. It would seem a just inference from my Sole Survivorship that I am familiar with railroad wrecks, inundations (though these are hardly dry-land phenomena), pestilences, earthquakes, conflagrations and other forms of what the reporters delight to call "a holocaust." This is not entirely true; I have never been shipwrecked, never assisted as "unfortunate sufferer" at a fire or railway collision, and know of the ravages of epidemics only by hearsay. The most destructive *temblor* of which I have had a personal experience decreased the population of San Francisco by fewer, probably, than ten thousand persons, of whom not more than a dozen were killed; the others moved out of town. It is true that I once followed the perilous trade of a soldier, but my eminence in Sole Surviving is of a later growth and not specially the product of the sword.

Opening the portfolio of memory, I draw out picture after picture—"figure-pieces"—groups of forms and faces whereof mine only now remains, somewhat the worse for wear.

Here are three young men lolling at ease on a grassy bank.

One, a handsome, dark-eyed chap, with a forehead like that of a Grecian god, raises his body on his elbow, looks straight away to the horizon, where some black trees hold captive certain vestiges of sunset as if they had torn away the plumage of a flight of flamingoes, and says: "Fellows, I mean to be rich. I shall see every country worth seeing. I shall taste every pleasure worth having. When old, I shall become a hermit."

Said another slender youth, fair-haired: "I shall become President and execute a *coup d'etat* making myself an absolute monarch. I shall then issue a decree requiring that all hermits be put to death."

The third said nothing. Was he restrained by some prescient sense of the perishable nature of the material upon which he was expected to inscribe the record of his hopes? However it may have been, he flicked his shoe with a hazel switch and kept his own counsel. For twenty years he has been the Sole Survivor of the group.

The scene changes. Six men are on horseback on a hill—a general and his staff. Below, in the gray fog of a winter morning, an army, which has left its intrenchments, is moving upon those of the enemy—creeping silently into position. In an hour the whole wide valley for miles to left and right will be all aroar with musketry stricken to seeming silence now and again by thunder claps of big guns. In the meantime the risen sun has burned a way through the fog, splendoring a part of the beleaguered city.

"Look at that, General," says an aide; "it is like enchantment."

"Go and enchant Colonel Post," said the general, without taking his field-glass from his eyes, "and tell him to pitch in as soon as he hears Smith's guns."

All laughed. But to-day I laugh alone. I am the Sole Survivor.

It would be easy to fill many pages with instances of Sole Survival, from my own experience. I could mention extinct groups composed wholly (myself excepted) of the opposing sex, all of whom, with the same exception, have long ceased their opposition, their warfare accomplished, their pretty noses blue and chill under the daisies. They were good girls, too, mostly,

Heaven rest them! There were Maud and Lizzie and Nanette (ah, Nanette, indeed; she is the deadest of the whole bright band) and Emeline and—but really this is not discreet; one should not survive and tell.

The flame of a camp-fire stands up tall and straight toward the black sky. We feed it constantly with sage brush. A circling wall of darkness closes us in; but turn your back to the fire and walk a little away and you shall see the serrated summit-line of snow-capped mountains, ghastly cold in the moonlight. They are in all directions; everywhere they efface the great gold stars near the horizon, leaving the little green ones of the mid-heaven trembling viciously, as bleak as steel. At irregular intervals we hear the distant howling of a wolf—now on this side and again on that. We check our talk to listen; we cast quick glances toward our weapons, our saddles, our picketed horses: the wolves may be of the variety known as Sioux, and there are but four of us.

"What would you do, Jim," said Hazen, "if we were surrounded by Indians?"

Jim Beckwourth was our guide—a life-long frontiersman, an old man "beated and chopped with tanned antiquity." He had at one time been a chief of the Crows.

"I'd spit on that fire," said Jim Beckwourth.

The old man has gone, I hope, where there is no fire to be quenched. And Hazen, and the chap with whom I shared my blanket that winter night on the plains—both gone. One might suppose that I would feel something of the natural exultation of a Sole Survivor; but as Byron found that

> our thoughts take wildest flight
> Even at the moment when they should array
> Themselves in pensive order,

so I find that they sometimes array themselves in pensive order, even at the moment when they ought to be most hilarious.

Of reminiscences there is no end. I have a vast store of them laid up, wherewith to wile away the tedious years of my anecdotage—whenever it shall please Heaven to make me old. Some years that I passed in London as a working journalist are particularly rich in them. Ah! "we were a gallant company" in those days.

I am told that the English are heavy thinkers and dull talkers. My recollection is different; speaking from that, I should say they are no end clever with their tongues. Certainly I have not elsewhere heard such brilliant talk as among the artists and writers of London. Of course they were a picked lot; some of them had attained to some eminence in the world of intellect; others have achieved it since. But they were not all English by many. London draws the best brains of Ireland and Scotland, and there is always a small American contingent, mostly correspondents of the big New York journals.

The typical London journalist is a gentleman. He is usually a graduate of one or the other of the great universities. He is well paid and holds his position, whatever it may be, by a less precarious tenure than his American congener. He rather moves than "dabbles" in literature, and not uncommonly takes a hand at some of the many forms of art. On the whole, he is a good fellow, too, with a skeptical mind, a cynical tongue, and a warm heart. I found these men agreeable, hospitable, intelligent, amusing. We worked too hard, dined too well, frequented too many clubs, and went to bed too late in the forenoon. We were overmuch addicted to shedding the blood of the grape. In short, we diligently, conscientiously, and with a perverse satisfaction burned the candle of life at both ends and in the middle.

This was many a year ago. To-day a list of these men's names with a cross against that of each one whom I know to be dead would look like a Roman Catholic cemetery. I could dine all the survivors at the table on which I write, and I should like to do so. But the dead ones, I must say, were the best diners.

But about Sole Surviving. There was a London publisher named John Camden Hotten. Among American writers he had a pretty dark reputation as a "pirate." They accused him of republishing their books without their assent, which, in absence of international copyright, he had a legal, and it seems to me (a "sufferer") a moral right to do. Through sympathy with their foreign confrères British writers also held him in high disesteem.

I knew Hotten very well, and one day I stood by what purported to be his body, which afterward I assisted to bury in the cemetery at Highgate. I am sure that it was his body, for I was uncommonly careful in the matter of identification, for a very good reason, which you shall know.

Aside from his "piracy," Hotten had a wide renown as "a hard man to deal with." For several months before his death he had owed me one hundred pounds sterling, and he could not possibly have been more reluctant to part with anything but a larger sum. Even to this day in reviewing the intelligent methods—ranging from delicate finesse to frank effrontery—by which that good man kept me out of mine own I am prostrated with admiration and consumed with envy. Finally by a lucky chance I got him at a disadvantage and seeing my power he sent his manager—a fellow named Chatto, who as a member of the firm of Chatto & Windus afterward succeeded to his business and methods—to negotiate. I was the most implacable creditor in the United Kingdom, and after two mortal hours of me in my most acidulated mood Chatto pulled out a check for the full amount, ready signed by Hotten in anticipation of defeat. Before handing it to me Chatto said: "This check is dated next Saturday. Of course you will not present it until then."

To this I cheerfully consented.

"And now," said Chatto, rising to go, "as everything is satisfactory I hope you will go out to Hotten's house and have a friendly talk. It is his wish."

On Saturday morning I went. In pursuance, doubtless, of his design when he antedated that check he had died of a pork pie promptly on the stroke of twelve o'clock the night before —which invalidated the check! I have met American publishers who thought they knew something about the business of drinking champagne out of writers' skulls. If this narrative— which, upon my soul, is every word true—teaches them humility by showing that genuine commercial sagacity is not bounded by geographical lines it will have served its purpose.

Having assured myself that Mr. Hotten was really no more, I drove furiously bankward, hoping that the sad tidings had not preceded me—and they had not.

Alas! on the route was a certain tap-room greatly frequented by authors, artists, newspaper men and "gentlemen of wit and pleasure about town."

Sitting about the customary table were a half-dozen or more choice spirits—George Augustus Sala, Henry Sampson, Tom Hood the younger, Captain Mayne Reid, and others less known to fame. I am sorry to say my somber news affected these sinners in a way that was shocking. Their levity was a thing to shudder at. As Sir Boyle Roche might have said, it grated harshly upon an ear that had a dubious check in its pocket. Having uttered their hilarious minds by word of mouth all they knew how, these hardy and impenitent offenders set about writing "appropriate epitaphs." Thank Heaven, all but one of these have escaped my memory, one that I wrote myself. At the close of the rites, several hours later, I resumed my movement against the bank. Too late—the old, old story of the hare and the tortoise was told again. The "heavy news" had overtaken and passed me as I loitered by the wayside.

All attended the funeral—Sala, Sampson, Hood, Reid, and the undistinguished others, including this present Sole Survivor of the group. As each cast his handful of earth upon the coffin I am very sure that, like Lord Brougham on a somewhat similar occasion, we all felt more than we cared to express. On the death of a political antagonist whom he had not treated with much consideration his lordship was asked, rather rudely, "Have you no regrets now that he is gone?"

After a moment of thoughtful silence he replied, with gravity, "Yes; I favor his return."

One night in the summer of 1880 I was driving in a light wagon through the wildest part of the Black Hills in South Dakota. I had left Deadwood and was well on my way to Rockerville with thirty thousand dollars on my person, belonging to a mining company of which I was the general manager. Naturally, I had taken the precaution to telegraph my secretary at Rockerville to meet me at Rapid City, then a small town, on another route; the telegram was intended to mislead the "gentlemen of the road" whom I knew to be watching my movements, and who might possibly have a confederate in the telegraph office. Beside me on the seat of the wagon sat Boone May.

Permit me to explain the situation. Several months before, it had been the custom to send a "treasure-coach" twice a week from Deadwood to Sidney, Nebraska. Also, it had been the custom to have this coach captured and plundered by "road agents." So intolerable had this practice become—even iron-clad coaches loopholed for rifles proving a vain device—that the mine owners had adopted the more practicable plan of importing from California a half-dozen of the most famous "shotgun messengers" of Wells, Fargo & Co.—fearless and trusty fellows with an instinct for killing, a readiness of resource that was an intuition, and a sense of direction that put a shot where it would do the most good more accurately than the most careful aim. Their feats of marksmanship were so incredible that seeing was scarcely believing.

In a few weeks these chaps had put the road agents out of business and out of life, for they attacked them wherever found. One sunny Sunday morning two of them strolling down a street of Deadwood recognized five or six of the rascals, ran back to their hotel for their rifles, and returning killed them all!

Boone May was one of these avengers. When I employed him, as a messenger, he was under indictment for murder. He had trailed a "road agent" across, the Bad Lands for hundreds of miles, brought him back to within a few miles of Deadwood and picketed him out for the night. The desperate man, tied as he was, had attempted to escape, and May found it expedient to shoot and bury him. The grave by the roadside is perhaps still pointed out to the curious. May gave himself up, was formally charged with murder, released on his own recognizance, and I had to give him leave of absence to go to court and be acquitted. Some of the New York directors of my company having been good enough to signify their disapproval of my action in employing "such a man," I could do no less than make some recognition of their dissent, and thenceforth he was borne upon the pay-rolls as "Boone May, Murderer." Now let me get back to my story.

I knew the road fairly well, for I had previously traveled it by night, on horseback, my pockets bulging with currency and my free hand holding a cocked revolver the entire distance of fifty miles. To make the journey by wagon with a companion was luxury. Still, the drizzle of rain was uncomfortable. May sat hunched up beside me, a rubber poncho over his shoulders and a Winchester rifle in its leathern case between his knees. I thought him a trifle off his guard, but said nothing. The road, barely visible, was rocky, the wagon rattled, and alongside ran a roaring stream. Suddenly we heard through it all the clinking of a horse's shoes directly behind, and simultaneously the short, sharp words of authority: "Throw up your hands!"

With an involuntary jerk at the reins I brought my team to its haunches and reached for my revolver. Quite needless: with the quickest movement that I had ever seen in anything but a cat—almost before the words were out of the horseman's mouth—May had thrown himself backward across the back of the seat, face upward, and the muzzle of his rifle was within a yard of the fellow's breast! What further occurred among the three of us there in the gloom of the forest has, I fancy, never been accurately related.

Boone May is long dead of yellow fever in Brazil, and I am the Sole Survivor.

There was a famous *prima donna* with whom it was my good fortune to cross the Atlantic to New York. In truth I was charged by a friend of both with the agreeable duty of caring for her safety and comfort. Madame was gracious, clever, altogether charming, and before the voyage was two days old a half-dozen of the men aboard, whom she had permitted me to present, were heels over head in love with her, as I was myself.

Our competition for her favor did not make us enemies; on the contrary we were drawn together into something like an offensive and defensive alliance by a common sorrow—the successful rivalry of a singularly handsome Italian who sat next her at table. So assiduous was he in his attentions that my office as the lady's guide, philosopher and friend was nearly a sinecure, and as to the others, they had hardly one chance a day to prove their devotion: that enterprising son of Italy dominated the entire situation. By some diabolical prevision he anticipated Madame's every need and wish—placed her reclining-chair in the most sheltered spots on deck, smothered her in layer upon layer of wraps, and conducted himself, generally, in the most inconsiderate way. Worse still, Madame accepted his good offices with a shameless grace "which said as plain as whisper in the ear" that there was a perfect understanding between them. What made it harder to bear was the fellow's faulty civility to the rest of us; he seemed hardly aware of our existence.

Our indignation was not loud, but deep. Every day in the smoking-room we contrived the most ingenious and monstrous plans for his undoing in this world and the next; the least cruel being a project to lure him to the upper deck on a dark night and send him unshriven to his account by way of the lee rail; but as none of us knew enough Italian to tell him the needful falsehood that scheme of justice came to nothing, as did all the others. At the wharf in New York we parted from Madame more in sorrow than in anger, and from her conquering cavalier with polite manifestations of the contempt we did not feel.

That evening I called on her at her hotel, facing Union Square. Soon after my arrival there was an audible commotion out in front: the populace, headed by a brass band and incited, doubtless, by pure love of art, had arrived to do honor to the great singer. There was music—a serenade—followed by shoutings of the lady's name. She seemed a trifle nervous, but I led her to the balcony, where she made a very pretty little speech, piquant with her most charming accent. When the tumult and shouting had died we re-entered her apartment to resume our conversation. Would it please monsieur to have a glass of wine? It would. She left the room for a moment; then came the wine and glasses on a tray, borne by that impossible Italian! He had a napkin across his arm—he was a servant.

Barring some of the band and the populace, I am doubtless the Sole Survivor, for Madame has for a number of years had a permanent engagement Above, and my faith in Divine Justice does not permit me to think that the servile wretch who cast down the mighty from their seat among the Sons of Hope was suffered to live out the other half of his days.

A dinner of seven in an old London tavern—a good dinner, the memory whereof is not yet effaced from the tablets of the palate. A soup, a plate of white-bait be-lemoned and red-peppered with exactness, a huge joint of roast beef, from which we sliced at will, flanked by various bottles of old dry Sherry and crusty Port—such Port! (And we are expected to be patriots in a country where it cannot be procured! And the Portuguese are expected to love the country which, having it, sends it away!) That was the dinner—O, there was Stilton cheese; it were shameful not to mention the Stilton. Good, wholesome, and toothsome it was, rich and nutty. The Stilton that we get here, clouted in tin-foil, is monstrous poor stuff, hardly better than our American sort. After dinner there were walnuts and coffee and cigars. I cannot say much for the cigars; they are not over-good in England: too long at sea, I suppose.

On the whole, it was a memorable dinner. Even its nonessential features were satisfactory. The waiter was fascinatingly solemn, the floor snowily sanded, the company sufficiently distinguished in literature and art for me to keep track of them through the newspapers. They are dead—as dead as Queen Anne, every mother's son of them! I am in my favorite rôle of Sole Survivor. It has become habitual to me; I rather like it.

Of the company were two eminent gastronomes—call them Messrs. Guttle and Swig—who so acridly hated each other that nothing but a good dinner could bring them under the same roof. (They had had a quarrel, I think, about the merit of a certain Amontillado—which, by the way, one insisted, despite Edgar Allan Poe, who certainly knew too much of whiskey to know much of wine, *is* a Sherry.) After the cloth had been removed and the coffee, walnuts and cigars brought in, the company stood, and to an air extemporaneously composed by Guttle, sang the following shocking and reprehensible song, which had been written during the proceedings by this present Sole Survivor. It will serve as fitly to conclude this feast of unreason as it did that:

THE SONG

Jack Satan's the greatest of gods,
   And Hell is the best of abodes.
'Tis reached through the Valley of Clods
   By seventy beautiful roads.
Hurrah for the Seventy Roads!
   Hurrah for the clods that resound
   With a hollow, thundering sound!
Hurrah for the Best of Abodes!

We'll serve him as long as we've breath—
    Jack Satan, the greatest of gods.
To all of his enemies, death!—
    A home in the Valley of Clods.
Hurrah for the thunder of clods
    That smother the souls of his foes!
    Hurrah for the spirit that goes
To dwell with the Greatest of Gods!

SELECTED STORIES

Mrs. Dennison's Head

W HILE I was employed in the Bank of Loan and Discount (said Mr. Applegarth, smiling the smile with which he always prefaced a nice old story), there was another clerk there, named Dennison—a quiet, reticent fellow, the very soul of truth, and a great favourite with us all. He always wore crape on his hat, and once when asked for whom he was in mourning he replied his wife, and seemed much affected. We all expressed our sympathy as delicately as possible, and no more was said upon the subject. Some weeks after this he seemed to have arrived at that stage of tempered grief at which it becomes a relief to give sorrow words—to speak of the departed one to sympathizing friends; for one day he voluntarily began talking of his bereavement, and of the terrible calamity by which his wife had been deprived of her head!

This sharpened our curiosity to the keenest edge; but of course we controlled it, hoping he would volunteer some further information with regard to so singular a misfortune; but when day after day went by and he did not allude to the matter, we got worked up into a fever of excitement about it. One evening after Dennison had gone, we held a kind of political meeting about it, at which all possible and impossible methods of decapitation were suggested as the ones to which Mrs. D. probably owed her extraordinary demise. I am sorry to add that we so far forgot the grave character of the event as to lay small wagers that it was done this way or that way; that it was accidental or premeditated; that she had had a hand in it herself or that it was wrought by circumstances beyond her control. All was mere conjecture, however; but from that time Dennison, as the custodian of a secret upon which we had staked our cash, was an object of more than usual interest. It wasn't entirely that, either; aside from our paltry wagers, we felt a consuming curiosity to know the truth for its own sake. Each set himself to work to elicit the dread secret in some way; and the misdirected ingenuity we developed was wonderful. All sorts of pious devices were resorted to to entice poor Dennison into clearing up the mystery. By a thousand indirect methods we sought to entrap him into divulging all. History, fiction, poesy —all were laid under contribution, and from Goliah down, through Charles I., to Sam Spigger, a local celebrity who got his head entangled in mill machinery, every one who had ever mourned the loss of a head received his due share of attention during office hours. The regularity with which we introduced, and the pertinacity with which we stuck to, this one topic came near getting us all discharged; for one day the cashier came out of his private office and intimated that if we valued our situations the subject of hanging would afford us the means of retaining them. He added that he always selected his subordinates with an eye to their conversational abilities, but variety of subject was as desirable, at times, as exhaustive treatment.

During all this discussion Dennison, albeit he had evinced from the first a singular interest in the theme, and shirked not his fair share of the conversation, never once seemed to understand that it had any reference to himself. His frank truthful nature was quite unable to detect the personal significance of the subject. It was plain that nothing short of a definite inquiry would elicit the information we were dying to obtain; and at a "caucus," one evening, we drew lots to determine who should openly propound it. The choice fell upon me.

Next morning we were at the bank somewhat earlier than usual, waiting impatiently for Dennison and the time to open the doors: they always arrived together. When Dennison stepped into the room, bowing in his engaging manner to each clerk as he passed to his own desk, I confronted him, shaking him warmly by the hand. At that moment all the others fell to writing and figuring with unusual avidity, as if thinking of anything under the sun except Dennison's wife's head.

"Oh, Dennison," I began, as carelessly as I could manage it; "speaking of decapitation reminds me of something I would like to ask you. I have intended asking it several times, but it has always slipped my memory. Of course you will pardon me if it is not a fair question."

As if by magic, the scratching of pens died away, leaving a dead silence which quite disconcerted me; but I blundered on:

"I heard the other day—that is, you said—or it was in the newspapers—or somewhere—something about your poor wife, you understand—about her losing her head. Would you mind telling me how such a distressing accident—if it was an accident—occurred?"

When I had finished, Dennison walked straight past me as if he didn't see me, went round the counter to his stool, and perched himself gravely on the top of it, facing the other clerks. Then he began speaking, calmly, and without apparent emotion:

"Gentlemen, I have long desired to speak of this thing, but you gave me no encouragement, and I naturally supposed you were indifferent. I now thank you all for the friendly interest you take in my affairs. I will satisfy your curiosity upon this point at once, if you will promise never hereafter to allude to the matter, and to ask not a single question now."

We all promised upon our sacred honour, and collected about him with the utmost eagerness. He bent his head a moment, then raised it, quietly saying:

"My poor wife's head was bitten off!"

"By what?" we all exclaimed eagerly, with suspended breath.

He gave us a look full of reproach, turned to his desk, and went at his work.

We went at ours.

The Man Overboard

THE good ship *Nupple-duck* was drifting rapidly upon a
sunken coral reef, which seemed to extend a reasonless
number of leagues to the right and left without a break, and I
was reading Macaulay's "Naseby Fight" to the man at the wheel.
Everything was, in fact, going on as nicely as heart could wish,
when Captain Abersouth, standing on the companion-stair,
poked his head above deck and asked where we were. Pausing
in my reading, I informed him that we had got as far as the
disastrous repulse of Prince Rupert's cavalry, adding that if he
would have the goodness to hold his jaw we should be making
it awkward for the wounded in about three minutes, and he
might bear a hand at the pockets of the slain. Just then the ship
struck heavily, and went down!

Calling another ship, I stepped aboard, and gave directions
to be taken to No. 900 Tottenham Court Road, where I had
an aunt; then, walking aft to the man at the wheel, asked him
if he would like to hear me read "Naseby Fight." He thought
he would: he would like to hear that, and then I might pass on
to something else—Kinglake's "Crimean War," the proceedings at the trial of Warren Hastings, or some such trifle, just to
wile away the time till eight bells.

All this time heavy clouds had been gathering along the horizon directly in front of the ship, and a deputation of passengers now came to the man at the wheel to demand that she be
put about, or she would run into them, which the spokesman
explained would be unusual. I thought at the time that it certainly was not the regular thing to do, but, as I was myself only
a passenger, did not deem it expedient to take a part in the
heated discussion that ensued; and, after all, it did not seem
likely that the weather in those clouds would be much worse
than that in Tottenham Court Road, where I had an aunt.

It was finally decided to refer the matter to arbitration, and
after many names had been submitted and rejected by both
sides, it was agreed that the captain of the ship should act as

arbitrator if his consent could be obtained, and I was delegated to conduct the negotiations to that end. With considerable difficulty, I persuaded him to accept the responsibility.

He was a feeble-minded sort of fellow named Troutbeck, who was always in a funk lest he should make enemies; never reflecting that most men would a little rather be his enemies than not. He had once been the ship's cook, but had cooked so poisonously ill that he had been forcibly transferred from galley to quarter-deck by the dyspeptic survivors of his culinary career.

The little captain went aft with me to listen to arguments of the dissatisfied passengers and the obstinate steersman, as to whether we should take our chances in the clouds, or tail off and run for the opposite horizon; but on approaching the wheel, we found both helmsman and passengers in a condition of profound astonishment, rolling their eyes about towards every point of the compass, and shaking their heads in hopeless perplexity. It was rather remarkable, certainly: the bank of cloud which had worried the landsmen was now directly astern, and the ship was cutting along lively in her own wake, toward the point from which she had come, and straight away from Tottenham Court Road! Everybody declared it was a miracle; the chaplain was piped up for prayers, and the man at the wheel was as truly penitent as if he had been detected robbing an empty poor-box.

The explanation was simple enough, and dawned upon me the moment I saw how matters stood. During the dispute between the helmsman and the deputation, the former had renounced his wheel to gesticulate, and I, thinking no harm, had amused myself, during a rather tedious debate, by revolving the thing this way and that, and had unconsciously put the ship about. By a coincidence not unusual in low latitudes, the wind had effected a corresponding transposition at the same time, and was now bowling us as merrily back toward the place where I had embarked, as it had previously wafted us in the direction of Tottenham Court Road, where I had an aunt. I must here so far anticipate, as to explain that some years later these various incidents—particularly the reading of "Naseby Fight" —led to the adoption, in our mercantile marine, of a rule which I believe is still extant, to the effect that one must not speak to the man at the wheel unless the man at the wheel speaks first.

II

It is only by inadvertence that I have omitted the information that the vessel in which I was now a pervading influence was the *Bonnyclabber* (Troutbeck, master), of Malvern Heights.

The *Bonnyclabber's* reactionary course had now brought her to the spot at which I had taken passage. Passengers and crew, fatigued by their somewhat awkward attempts to manifest their gratitude for our miraculous deliverance from the cloud-bank, were snoring peacefully in unconsidered attitudes about the deck, when the lookout man, perched on the supreme extremity of the mainmast, consuming a cold sausage, began an apparently preconcerted series of extraordinary and unimaginable noises. He coughed, sneezed, and barked simultaneously— bleated in one breath, and cackled in the next—sputteringly shrieked, and chatteringly squealed, with a bass of suffocated roars. There were desolutory vocal explosions, tapering off in long wails, half smothered in unintelligible small-talk. He whistled, wheezed, and trumpeted; began to sharp, thought better of it and flatted; neighed like a horse, and then thundered like a drum! Through it all he continued making incomprehensible signals with one hand while clutching his throat with the other. Presently he gave it up, and silently descended to the deck.

By this time we were all attention; and no sooner had he set foot amongst us, than he was assailed with a tempest of questions which, had they been visible, would have resembled a flight of pigeons. He made no reply—not even by a look, but passed through our enclosing mass with a grim, defiant step, a face deathly white, and a set of the jaw as of one repressing an ambitious dinner, or ignoring a venomous toothache. For the poor man was choking!

Passing down the companion-way, the patient sought the surgeon's cabin, with the ship's company at his heels. The surgeon was fast asleep, the lark-like performance at the masthead having been inaudible in that lower region. While some of us were holding a whisky-bottle to the medical nose, in order to apprise the medical intelligence of the demand upon it, the patient seated himself in statuesque silence. By this time his pallor, which was but the mark of a determined mind, had given place to a fervent crimson, which visibly deepened into a pronounced purple, and was ultimately superseded by a clouded blue, shot through with opalescent gleams, and smitten with variable streaks of black. The face was swollen and shapeless, the neck puffy. The eyes protruded like pegs of a hat-stand.

Pretty soon the doctor was got awake, and after making a careful examination of his patient, remarking that it was a lovely case of *stopupagus æsophagi*, took a tool and set to work, producing with no difficulty a cold sausage of the size, figure, and general bearing of a somewhat self-important banana. The operation had been performed amid breathless silence, but the moment it was concluded the patient, whose neck and head had visibly collapsed, sprang to his feet and shouted:

"Man overboard!"

That is what he had been trying to say.

There was a confused rush to the upper deck, and everybody flung something over the ship's side—a life-belt, a chicken-coop, a coil of rope, a spar, an old sail, a pocket handkerchief, an iron crowbar—any movable article which it was thought might be useful to a drowning man who had followed the vessel during the hour that had elapsed since the initial alarm at the mast-head. In a few moments the ship was pretty nearly dismantled of everything that could be easily renounced, and some excitable passenger having cut away the boats there was nothing more that we could do, though the chaplain explained that if the ill-fated gentleman in the wet did not turn up after a while it was his intention to stand at the stern and read the burial service of the Church of England.

Presently it occurred to some ingenious person to inquire who had gone overboard, and all hands being mustered and the roll called, to our great chagrin every man answered to his name, passengers and all! Captain Troutbeck, however, held that in a matter of so great importance a simple roll-call was insufficient, and with an assertion of authority that was encouraging insisted that every person on board be separately sworn.

The result was the same; nobody was missing and the captain, begging pardon for having doubted our veracity, retired to his cabin to avoid further responsibility, but expressed a hope that for the purpose of having everything properly recorded in the log-book we would apprise him of any further action that we might think it advisable to take. I smiled as I remembered that in the interest of the unknown gentleman whose peril we had overestimated I had flung the log-book over the ship's side.

Soon afterward I felt suddenly inspired with one of those great ideas that come to most men only once or twice in a lifetime, and to the ordinary story teller never. Hastily reconvening the ship's company I mounted the capstan and thus addressed them:

"Shipmates, there has been a mistake. In the fervor of an ill-considered compassion we have made pretty free with certain movable property of an eminent firm of shipowners of Malvern Heights. For this we shall undoubtedly be called to account if we are ever so fortunate as to drop anchor in Tottenham Court Road, where I have an aunt. It would add strength to our defence if we could show to the satisfaction of a jury of our peers that in heeding the sacred promptings of humanity we had acted with some small degree of common sense. If, for example, we could make it appear that there really was a man overboard, who might have been comforted and sustained by the material consolation that we so lavishly dispensed in the form of buoyant articles belonging to others, the British heart would find in that fact a mitigating circumstance pleading eloquently in our favor. Gentlemen and ship's officers, I venture to propose that we do now throw a man overboard."

The effect was electrical: the motion was carried by acclamation and there was a unanimous rush for the now wretched mariner whose false alarm at the masthead was the cause of our embarrassment, but on second thoughts it was decided to substitute Captain Troutbeck, as less generally useful and more undeviatingly in error. The sailor had made one mistake of considerable magnitude, but the captain's entire existence was a mistake altogether. He was fetched up from his cabin and chucked over.

At 900 Tottenham Road Court lived an aunt of mine—a good old lady who had brought me up by hand and taught me many wholesome lessons in morality, which in my later life have proved of extreme value. Foremost among these I may mention her solemn and oft-repeated injunction never to tell a lie without a definite and specific reason for doing so. Many years' experience in the violation of this principle enables me to speak with authority as to its general soundness. I have, therefore, much pleasure in making a slight correction in the preceding chapter of this tolerably true history. It was there affirmed that I threw the *Bonnyclabber's* log-book into the sea. The statement is entirely false, and I can discover no reason for having made it that will for a moment weigh against those I now have for the preservation of that log-book.

The progress of the story has developed new necessities, and I now find it convenient to quote from that book passages which it could not have contained if cast into the sea at the time stated; for if thrown upon the resources of my imagination I might find the temptation to exaggerate too strong to be resisted.

It is needless to worry the reader with those entries in the book referring to events already related. Our record will begin on the day of the captain's consignment to the deep, after which era I made the entries myself.

"June 22nd.—Not much doing in the way of gales, but heavy swells left over from some previous blow. Latitude and longitude not notably different from last observation. Ship laboring a trifle, owing to lack of top-hamper, everything of that kind having been cut away in consequence of Captain Troutbeck having accidently fallen overboard while fishing from the bowsprit. Also threw over cargo and everything that we could spare. Miss our sails rather, but if they save our dear captain, we shall be content. Weather flagrant.

"23d.—Nothing from Captain Troutbeck. Dead calm—also dead whale. The passengers having become preposterous in various ways, Mr. Martin, the chief officer, had three of the ringleaders tied up and rope's-ended. He thought it advisable also to flog an equal number of the crew, by way of being impartial. Weather ludicrous.

"24th.—Captain still prefers to stop away, and does not telegraph. The 'captain of the foretop'—there isn't any foretop now—was put in irons to-day by Mr. Martin for eating cold sausage while on look-out. Mr. Martin has flogged the steward, who had neglected to holy-stone the binnacle and paint the dead-lights. The steward is a good fellow all the same. Weather iniquitous.

"25th.—Can't think whatever has become of Captain Trout-beck. He must be getting hungry by this time; for although he has his fishing-tackle with him, he has no bait. Mr. Martin inspected the entries in this book to-day. He is a most excellent and humane officer. Weather inexcusable.

"26th.—All hope of hearing from the Captain has been abandoned. We have sacrificed everything to save him; but now, if we could procure the loan of a mast and some sails, we should proceed on our voyage. Mr. Martin has knocked the coxswain overboard for sneezing. He is an experienced seaman, a capable officer, and a Christian gentleman—damn his eyes! Weather tormenting.

"27th.—Another inspection of this book by Mr. Martin. Farewell, vain world! Break it gently to my aunt in Tottenham Court Road."

In the concluding sentences of this record, as it now lies before me, the handwriting is not very legible: they were penned under circumstances singularly unfavorable. Mr. Martin stood behind me with his eyes fixed on the page; and in order to secure a better view, had twisted the machinery of the engine he called his hand into the hair of my head, depressing that globe to such an extent that my nose was flattened against the surface of the table, and I had no small difficulty in discerning the lines through my eyebrows. I was not accustomed to writing in that position: it had not been taught in the only school that I ever attended. I therefore felt justified in bringing the record to a somewhat abrupt close, and immediately went on deck with Mr. Martin, he preceding me up the companion-stairs on foot, I following, not on horseback, but on my own, the connection between us being maintained without important alteration.

Arriving on deck, I thought it advisable, in the interest of peace and quietness, to pursue him in the same manner to the side of the ship, where I parted from him forever with many expressions of regret, which might have been heard at a considerable distance.

Of the subsequent fate of the *Bonnyclabber*, I can only say that the log-book from which I have quoted was found some years later in the stomach of a whale, along with some shreds of clothing, a few buttons and several decayed life-belts. It contained only one new entry, in a straggling handwriting, as if it had been penned in the dark:

"july2th foundered svivors rescude by wale wether stuffy no nues from capting trowtbeck Sammle martin cheef Ofcer."

Let us now take a retrospective glance at the situation. The ship *Nupple-duck*, (Abersouth, master) had, it will be remembered, gone down with all on board except me. I had escaped on the ship *Bonnyclabber* (Troutbeck) which I had quitted owing to a misunderstanding with the chief officer, and was now unattached. That is how matters stood when, rising on an unusually high wave, and casting my eye in the direction of Tottenham Court Road—that is, backward along the course pursued by the *Bonnyclabber* and toward the spot at which the *Nupple-duck* had been swallowed up—I saw a quantity of what appeared to be wreckage. It turned out to be some of the stuff that we had thrown overboard under a misapprehension. The several articles had been compiled and, so to speak, carefully edited. They were, in fact, lashed together, forming a raft. On a stool in the center of it—not, apparently navigating it, but rather with the subdued and dignified bearing of a passenger, sat Captain Abersouth, of the *Nupple-duck*, reading a novel.

Our meeting was not cordial. He remembered me as a man of literary taste superior to his own and harbored resentment, and although he made no opposition to my taking passage with him I could see that his acquiescence was due rather to his muscular inferiority than to the circumstance that I was damp and taking cold. Merely acknowledging his presence with a nod as I climbed aboard, I seated myself and inquired if he would care to hear the concluding stanzas of "Naseby Fight."

"No," he replied, looking up from his novel, "no, Claude Reginald Gump, writer of sea stories, I've done with you. When you sank the *Nupple-duck* some days ago you probably thought that you had made an end of me. That was clever of you, but I came to the surface and followed the other ship—the one on which you escaped. It was I that the sailor saw from the masthead. I saw him see me. It was for me that all that stuff was hove overboard. Good—I made it into this raft. It was, I think, the next day that I passed the floating body of a man whom I recognized as my old friend Billy Troutbeck—he used to be a cook on a man-o'-war. It gives me pleasure to be the means of saving your life, but I eschew you. The moment that we reach port our paths part. You remember that in the very first sentence of this story you began to drive my ship, the *Nupple-duck*, on to a reef of coral."

I was compelled to confess that this was true, and he continued his inhospitable reproaches:

"Before you had written half a column you sent her to the bottom, with me and the crew. But *you*—you escaped."

"That is true," I replied; "I cannot deny that the facts are correctly stated."

"And in a story before that, you took me and my mates of the ship *Camel* into the heart of the South Polar Sea and left us frozen dead in the ice, like flies in amber. But you did not leave yourself there—you escaped."

"Really, Captain," I said, "your memory is singularly accurate, considering the many hardships that you have had to undergo; many a man would have gone mad."

"And a long time before that," Captain Abersouth resumed, after a pause, more, apparently, to con his memory than to enjoy my good opinion of it, "you lost me at sea—look here; I didn't read anything but George Eliot at that time, but I'm *told* that you lost me at sea in the *Mudlark*. Have I been misinformed?"

I could not say he had been misinformed.

"You yourself escaped on that occasion, I think."

It was true. Being usually the hero of my own stories, I commonly do manage to live through one, in order to figure to advantage in the next. It is from artistic necessity: no reader would take much interest in a hero who was dead before the beginning of the tale. I endeavored to explain this to Captain Abersouth. He shook his head.

"No," said he, "it's cowardly, that's the way I look at it."

Suddenly an effulgent idea began to dawn upon me, and I let it have its way until my mind was perfectly luminous. Then I rose from my seat, and frowning down into the upturned face of my accuser, spoke in severe and rasping accents thus:

"Captain Abersouth, in the various perils you and I have encountered together in the classical literature of the period, if I have always escaped and you have always perished; if I lost you at sea in the *Mudlark*, froze you into the ice at the South Pole in the *Camel* and drowned you in the *Nupple-duck*, pray be good enough to tell me whom I have the honor to address."

It was a blow to the poor man: no one was ever so disconcerted. Flinging aside his novel, he put up his hands and began to scratch his head and think. It was beautiful to see him think, but it seemed to distress him and pointing significantly over the side of the raft I suggested as delicately as possible that it was time to act. He rose to his feet and fixing upon me a look of reproach which I shall remember as long as I can, cast himself into the deep. As to me—I escaped.

Jupiter Doke, Brigadier-General

From the Secretary of War to the Hon. Jupiter Doke, Hardpan Crossroads, Posey County, Illinois.

WASHINGTON, November 3, 1861.

HAVING faith in your patriotism and ability, the President has been pleased to appoint you a brigadier-general of volunteers. Do you accept?

From the Hon. Jupiter Doke to the Secretary of War.

HARDPAN, ILLINOIS, November 9, 1861.

It is the proudest moment of my life. The office is one which should be neither sought nor declined. In times that try men's souls the patriot knows no North, no South, no East, no West. His motto should be: "My country, my whole country and nothing but my country." I accept the great trust confided in me by a free and intelligent people, and with a firm reliance on the principles of constitutional liberty, and invoking the guidance of an all-wise Providence, Ruler of Nations, shall labor so to discharge it as to leave no blot upon my political escutcheon. Say to his Excellency, the successor of the immortal Washington in the Seat of Power, that the patronage of my office will be bestowed with an eye single to securing the greatest good to the greatest number, the stability of republican institutions and the triumph of the party in all elections; and to this I pledge my life, my fortune and my sacred honor. I shall at once prepare an appropriate response to the speech of the chairman of the committee deputed to inform me of my appointment, and I trust the sentiments therein expressed will strike a sympathetic chord in the public heart, as well as command the Executive approval.

From the Secretary of War to Major-General Blount Wardorg, Commanding the Military Department of Eastern Kentucky.

WASHINGTON, November 14, 1861.

I have assigned to your department Brigadier-General Jupiter

Doke, who will soon proceed to Distilleryville, on the Little Buttermilk River, and take command of the Illinois Brigade at that point, reporting to you by letter for orders. Is the route from Covington by way of Bluegrass, Opossum Corners and Horsecave still infested with bushwhackers, as reported in your last dispatch? I have a plan for cleaning them out.

From Major-General Blount Wardorg to the Secretary of War.

LOUISVILLE, KENTUCKY, November 20, 1861.

The name and services of Brigadier-General Doke are unfamiliar to me, but I shall be pleased to have the advantage of his skill. The route from Covington to Distilleryville *via* Opossum Corners and Horsecave I have been compelled to abandon to the enemy, whose guerilla warfare made it possible to keep it open without detaching too many troops from the front. The brigade at Distilleryville is supplied by steamboats up the Little Buttermilk.

From the Secretary of War to Brigadier-General Jupiter Doke, Hardpan, Illinois.

WASHINGTON, November 26, 1861.

I deeply regret that your commission had been forwarded by mail before the receipt of your letter of acceptance; so we must dispense with the formality of official notification to you by a committee. The President is highly gratified by the noble and patriotic sentiments of your letter, and directs that you proceed at once to your command at Distilleryville, Kentucky, and there report by letter to Major-General Wardorg at Louisville, for orders. It is important that the strictest secrecy be observed regarding your movements until you have passed Covington, as it is desired to hold the enemy in front of Distilleryville until you are within three days of him. Then if your approach is known it will operate as a demonstration against his right and cause him to strengthen it with his left now at Memphis, Tennessee, which it is desirable to capture first. Go by way of Bluegrass, Opossum Corners and Horsecave. All officers are expected to be in full uniform when *en route* to the front.

From Brigadier-General Jupiter Doke to the Secretary of War.

COVINGTON, KENTUCKY, December 7, 1861.

I arrived yesterday at this point, and have given my proxy to Joel Briller, Esq., my wife's cousin, and a staunch Republican, who will worthily represent Posey County in field and forum. He points with pride to a stainless record in the halls of legislation, which have often echoed to his soul-stirring eloquence on questions which lie at the very foundation of popular government. He has been called the Patrick Henry of Hardpan, where he has done yeoman's service in the cause of civil and religious liberty. Mr. Briller left for Distilleryville last evening, and the standard bearer of the Democratic host confronting that stronghold of freedom will find him a lion in his path. I have been asked to remain here and deliver some addresses to the people in a local contest involving issues of paramount importance. That duty being performed, I shall in person enter the arena of armed debate and move in the direction of the heaviest firing, burning my ships behind me. I forward by this mail to his Excellency the President a request for the appointment of my son, Jabez Leonidas Doke, as postmaster at Hardpan. I would take it, sir, as a great favor if you would give the application a strong oral indorsement, as the appointment is in the line of reform. Be kind enough to inform me what are the emoluments of the office I hold in the military arm, and if they are by salary or fees. Are there any perquisites? My mileage account will be transmitted monthly.

From Brigadier-General Jupiter Doke to Major General Blount Wardorg.

DISTILLERYVILLE, KENTUCKY,
January 12, 1862.

I arrived on the tented field yesterday by steamboat, the recent storms having inundated the landscape, covering, I understand, the greater part of a congressional district. I am pained to find that Joel Briller, Esq., a prominent citizen of Posey County, Illinois, and a far-seeing statesman who held my proxy, and who a month ago should have been thundering at the gates of Disunion, has not been heard from, and has doubtless been sacrificed upon the altar of his country. In him the American people lose a bulwark of freedom. I would respectfully move that you designate a committee to draw up resolutions of respect to his memory, and that the office holders and men under your command wear the usual badge of mourning for thirty days. I shall at once place myself at the head of affairs here, and am now ready to entertain any suggestions which you may make, looking to the better enforcement of the laws in this commonwealth. The militant Democrats on the other side of the river appear to be contemplating extreme measures. They have two large cannons facing this way, and yesterday morning, I am told, some of them came down to the water's edge and remained in session for some time, making infamous allegations.

From the Diary of Brigadier-General Jupiter Doke, at Distilleryville, Kentucky.

January 12, 1862.—On my arrival yesterday at the Henry Clay Hotel (named in honor of the late far-seeing statesman) I was waited on by a delegation consisting of the three colonels intrusted with the command of the regiments of my brigade. It was an occasion that will be memorable in the political annals of America. Forwarded copies of the speeches to the Posey *Maverick*, to be spread upon the record of the ages. The gentlemen composing the delegation unanimously reaffirmed their devotion to the principles of national unity and the Republican party. Was gratified to recognize in them men of political prominence and untarnished escutcheons. At the subsequent banquet, sentiments of lofty patriotism were expressed. Wrote to Mr. Wardorg at Louisville for instructions.

January 13, 1862.—Leased a prominent residence (the former incumbent being absent in arms against his country) for the term of one year, and wrote at once for Mrs. Brigadier-General Doke and the vital issues—excepting Jabez Leonidas. In the camp of treason opposite here there are supposed to be three thousand misguided men laying the ax at the root of the tree of liberty. They have a clear majority, many of our men having returned without leave to their constituents. We could probably not poll more than two thousand votes. Have advised my heads of regiments to make a canvass of those remaining, all bolters to be read out of the phalanx.

January 14, 1862.—Wrote to the President, asking for the contract to supply this command with firearms and regalia through my brother-in-law, prominently identified with the manufacturing interests of the country. Club of cannon soldiers arrived at Jayhawk, three miles back from here, on their way to join us in battle array. Marched my whole brigade to Jayhawk to escort them into town, but their chairman, mistaking us for the opposing party, opened fire on the head of the procession and by the extraordinary noise of the cannon balls (I had no conception of it!) so frightened my horse that I was unseated without a contest. The meeting adjourned in disorder and returning to camp I found that a deputation of the enemy had crossed the river in our absence and made a division of the loaves and fishes. Wrote to the President, applying for the Gubernatorial Chair of the Territory of Idaho.

From Editorial Article in the Posey, Illinois, "Maverick," January 20, 1862.

Brigadier-General Doke's thrilling account, in another column, of the Battle of Distilleryville will make the heart of every loyal Illinoisian leap with exultation. The brilliant exploit marks an era in military history, and as General Doke says, "lays broad and deep the foundations of American prowess in arms." As none of the troops engaged, except the gallant author-chieftain (a host in himself) hails from Posey County, he justly considered that a list of the fallen would only occupy our valuable space to the exclusion of more important matter, but his account of the strategic ruse by which he apparently abandoned his camp and so inveigled a perfidious enemy into it for the purpose of murdering the sick, the unfortunate *countertempus* at Jayhawk, the subsequent dash upon a trapped enemy flushed with a supposed success, driving their terrified legions across an impassable river which precluded pursuit—all these "moving accidents by flood and field" are related with a pen of fire and have all the terrible interest of romance.

Verily, truth is stranger than fiction and the pen is mightier than the sword. When by the graphic power of the art preservative of all arts we are brought face to face with such glorious events as these, the *Maverick's* enterprise in securing for its thousands of readers the services of so distinguished a contributor as the Great Captain who made the history as well as wrote it seems a matter of almost secondary importance. For President in 1864 (subject to the decision of the Republican National Convention) Brigadier-General Jupiter Doke, of Illinois!

From Major-General Blount Wardorg to Brigadier-General Jupiter Doke.

LOUISVILLE, January 22, 1862.
Your letter apprising me of your arrival at Distilleryville was delayed in transmission, having only just been received (open) through the courtesy of the Confederate department commander under a flag of truce. He begs me to assure you that he would consider it an act of cruelty to trouble you, and I think it would be. Maintain, however, a threatening attitude, but at the least pressure retire. Your position is simply an outpost which it is not intended to hold.

From Major-General Blount Wardorg to the Secretary of War.

LOUISVILLE, January 23, 1862.
I have certain information that the enemy has concentrated twenty thousand troops of all arms on the Little Buttermilk. According to your assignment, General Doke is in command of the small brigade of raw troops opposing them. It is no part of my plan to contest the enemy's advance at that point, but I cannot hold myself responsible for any reverses to the brigade mentioned, under its present commander. I think him a fool.

From the Secretary of War to Major-General Blount Wardorg.

WASHINGTON, February 1, 1862.
The President has great faith in General Doke. If your estimate of him is correct, however, he would seem to be singularly well placed where he now is, as your plans appear to contemplate

a considerable sacrifice for whatever advantages you expect to gain.

From Brigadier-General Jupiter Doke to Major-General Blount Wardorg.

DISTILLERYVILLE, February 1, 1862.

To-morrow I shall remove my headquarters to Jayhawk in order to point the way whenever my brigade retires from Distilleryville, as foreshadowed by your letter of the 22d ult. I have appointed a Committee on Retreat, the minutes of whose first meeting I transmit to you. You will perceive that the committee having been duly organized by the election of a chairman and secretary, a resolution (prepared by myself) was adopted, to the effect that in case treason again raises her hideous head on this side of the river every man of the brigade is to mount a mule, the procession to move promptly in the direction of Louisville and the loyal North. In preparation for such an emergency I have for some time been collecting mules from the resident Democracy, and have on hand 2300 in a field at Jayhawk. Eternal vigilance is the price of liberty!

From Major-General Gibeon J. Buxter, C. S. A., to the Confederate Secretary of War.

BUNG STATION, KENTUCKY,
February 4, 1862.

On the night of the 2d inst., our entire force, consisting of 25,000 men and thirty-two field pieces, under command of Major-General Simmons B. Flood, crossed by a ford to the north side of Little Buttermilk River at a point three miles above Distilleryville and moved obliquely down and away from the stream, to strike the Covington turnpike at Jayhawk; the object being, as you know, to capture Covington, destroy Cincinnati and occupy the Ohio Valley. For some months there had been in our front only a small brigade of undisciplined troops, apparently without a commander, who were useful to us, for by not disturbing them we could create an impression of our weakness. But the movement on Jayhawk having isolated them, I was about to detach an Alabama regiment to bring them in, my division being the leading one, when an earth-shaking rumble was felt and heard, and suddenly the head-of-column was struck by one of the terrible tornadoes for which this region is famous, and utterly annihilated. The tornado, I believe, passed along the entire length of the road back to the ford, dispersing or destroying our entire army; but of this I cannot be sure, for I was lifted from the earth insensible and blown back to the south side of the river. Continuous firing all night on the north side and the reports of such of our men as have recrossed at the ford convince me that the Yankee brigade has exterminated the disabled survivors. Our loss has been uncommonly heavy. Of my own division of 15,000 infantry, the casualties—killed, wounded, captured, and missing—are 14,994. Of General Dolliver Billow's division, 11,200 strong, I can find but two officers and a nigger cook. Of the artillery, 800 men, none has reported on this side of the river. General Flood is dead. I have assumed command of the expeditionary force, but owing to the heavy losses have deemed it advisable to contract my line of supplies as rapidly as possible. I shall push southward to-morrow morning early. The purposes of the campaign have been as yet but partly accomplished.

From Major-General Dolliver Billows, C. S. A., to the Confederate Secretary of War.

BUHAC, KENTUCKY, February 5, 1862.

. . . But during the 2d they had, unknown to us, been re-inforced by fifty thousand cavalry, and being apprised of our movement by a spy, this vast body was drawn up in the darkness at Jayhawk, and as the head of our column reached that point at about 11 P.M., fell upon it with astonishing fury, destroying the division of General Buxter in an instant. General Baumschank's brigade of artillery, which was in the rear, may have escaped—I did not wait to see, but withdrew my division to the river at a point several miles above the ford, and at day-light ferried it across on two fence rails lashed together with a suspender. Its losses, from an effective strength of 11,200, are 11,199. General Buxter is dead. I am changing my base to Mobile, Alabama.

From Brigadier-General Schneddeker Baumschank, C. S. A., to the Confederate Secretary of War.

IODINE, KENTUCKY, February 6, 1862.
. . . Yoost den somdings occur, I know nod vot it vos—somdings mackneefcent, but it vas nod vor—und I finds meinselluf, afder leedle viles, in dis blace, midout a hors und mit no men und goons. Sheneral Peelows is deadt. You will blease be so goot as to resign me—I vights no more in a dam gontry vere I gets vipped und knows nod how it vos done.

Resolutions of Congress, February 15, 1862.

Resolved, That the thanks of Congress are due, and hereby tendered, to Brigadier-General Jupiter Doke and the gallant men under his command for their unparalleled feat of attacking —themselves only 2000 strong—an army of 25,000 men and utterly overthrowing it, killing 5327, making prisoners of 19,003, of whom more than half were wounded, taking 32 guns, 20,000 stand of small arms and, in short, the enemy's entire equipment.

Resolved, That for this unexampled victory the President be requested to designate a day of thanksgiving and public cele-bration of religious rites in the various churches.

Resolved, That he be requested, in further commemoration of the great event, and in reward of the gallant spirits whose deeds have added such imperishable lustre to the American arms, to appoint, with the advice and consent of the Senate, the following officer:

One major-general.

Statement of Mr. Hannibal Alcazar Peyton, of Jayhawk, Ken-tucky.

Dat wus a almighty dark night, sho', and dese yere ole eyes aint wuf shuks, but I's got a year like a sque'l, an' w'en I cotch de mummer o' v'ices I knowed dat gang b'long on de far side o' de ribber. So I jes' runs in de house an' wakes Marse Doke an' tells him: "Skin outer dis fo' yo' life!" An' de Lo'd bress my soul! ef dat man didn' go right fru de winder in his shir' tail an' break for to cross de mule patch! An' dem twenty-free hunerd mules dey jes' t'nk it is de debble hese'f wid de brandin' iron, an' dey bu'st outen dat patch like a yarthquake, an' pile inter de upper ford road, an' flash down it five deep, an' it full o' Confed'rates from en' to en'! . . .

A Bottomless Grave

M Y name is John Brenwalter. My father, a drunkard, had a patent for an invention for making coffee-berries out of clay; but he was an honest man and would not himself engage in the manufacture. He was, therefore, only moderately wealthy, his royalties from his really valuable invention bringing him hardly enough to pay his expenses of litigation with rogues guilty of infringement. So I lacked many advantages enjoyed by the children of unscrupulous and dishonorable parents, and had it not been for a noble and devoted mother, who neglected all my brothers and sisters and personally supervised my education, should have grown up in ignorance and been compelled to teach school. To be the favorite child of a good woman is better than gold.

When I was nineteen years of age my father had the misfortune to die. He had always had perfect health, and his death, which occurred at the dinner table without a moment's warning, surprised no one more than himself. He had that very morning been notified that a patent had been granted him for a device to burst open safes by hydraulic pressure, without noise. The Commissioner of Patents had pronounced it the most ingenious, effective and generally meritorious invention that had ever been submitted to him, and my father had naturally looked forward to an old age of prosperity and honor. His sudden death was, therefore, a deep disappointment to him; but my mother, whose piety and resignation to the will of Heaven were conspicuous virtues of her character, was apparently less affected. At the close of the meal, when my poor father's body had been removed from the floor, she called us all into an adjoining room and addressed us as follows:

"My children, the uncommon occurrence that you have just witnessed is one of the most disagreeable incidents in a good man's life, and one in which I take little pleasure, I assure you. I beg you to believe that I had no hand in bringing it about. Of course," she added, after a pause, during which her eyes were cast down in deep thought, "of course it is better that he is dead."

She uttered this with so evident a sense of its obviousness as a self-evident truth that none of us had the courage to brave her surprise by asking an explanation. My mother's air of surprise when any of us went wrong in any way was very terrible to us. One day, when in a fit of peevish temper, I had taken the liberty to cut off the baby's ear, her simple words, "John, you surprise me!" appeared to me so sharp a reproof that after a sleepless night I went to her in tears, and throwing myself at her feet, exclaimed: "Mother, forgive me for surprising you." So now we all—including the one-eared baby—felt that it would keep matters smoother to accept without question the statement that it was better, somehow, for our dear father to be dead. My mother continued:

"I must tell you, my children, that in a case of sudden and mysterious death the law requires the Coroner to come and cut the body into pieces and submit them to a number of men who, having inspected them, pronounce the person dead. For this the Coroner gets a large sum of money. I wish to avoid that painful formality in this instance; it is one which never had the approval of—of the remains. John"—here my mother turned her angel face to me—"you are an educated lad, and very discreet. You have now an opportunity to show your gratitude for all the sacrifices that your education has entailed upon the rest of us. John, go and remove the Coroner."

Inexpressibly delighted by this proof of my mother's confidence, and by the chance to distinguish myself by an act that squared with my natural disposition, I knelt before her, carried her hand to my lips and bathed it with tears of sensibility. Before five o'clock that afternoon I had removed the Coroner.

I was immediately arrested and thrown into jail, where I passed a most uncomfortable night, being unable to sleep because of the profanity of my fellow-prisoners, two clergymen, whose theological training had given them a fertility of impious ideas and a command of blasphemous language altogether unparalleled. But along toward morning the jailer, who, sleeping in an adjoining room, had been equally disturbed, entered the cell and with a fearful oath warned the reverend gentlemen that if he heard any more swearing their sacred calling would not prevent him from turning them into the street. After that they moderated their objectionable conversation, substituting an accordion, and I slept the peaceful and refreshing sleep of youth and innocence.

The next morning I was taken before the Superior Judge, sitting as a committing magistrate, and put upon my preliminary examination. I pleaded not guilty, adding that the man whom I had murdered was a notorious Democrat. (My good mother was a Republican, and from early childhood I had been carefully instructed by her in the principles of honest government and the necessity of suppressing factional opposition.) The Judge, elected by a Republican ballot-box with a sliding bottom, was visibly impressed by the cogency of my plea and offered me a cigarette.

"May it please your Honor," began the District Attorney, "I do not deem it necessary to submit any evidence in this case. Under the law of the land you sit here as a committing magistrate. It is therefore your duty to commit. Testimony and argument alike would imply a doubt that your Honor means to perform your sworn duty. That is my case."

My counsel, a brother of the deceased Coroner, rose and said: "May it please the Court, my learned friend on the other side has so well and eloquently stated the law governing in this case that it only remains for me to inquire to what extent it has been already complied with. It is true, your Honor is a committing magistrate, and as such it is your duty to commit—what? That is a matter which the law has wisely and justly left to your own discretion, and wisely you have discharged already every obligation that the law imposes. Since I have known your Honor you have done nothing but commit. You have committed embracery, theft, arson, perjury, adultery, murder—every crime in the calendar and every excess known to the sensual and depraved, including my learned friend, the District Attorney. You have done your whole duty as a committing magistrate, and as there is no evidence against this worthy young man, my client, I move that he be discharged."

An impressive silence ensued. The Judge arose, put on the black cap and in a voice trembling with emotion sentenced me to life and liberty. Then turning to my counsel he said, coldly but significantly:

"I will see you later."

The next morning the lawyer who had so conscientiously

defended me against a charge of murdering his own brother —with whom he had a quarrel about some land—had disappeared and his fate is to this day unknown.

In the meantime my poor father's body had been secretly buried at midnight in the back yard of his late residence, with his late boots on and the contents of his late stomach unanalyzed. "He was opposed to display," said my dear mother, as she finished tamping down the earth above him and assisted the children to litter the place with straw; "his instincts were all domestic and he loved a quiet life."

My mother's application for letters of administraition stated that she had good reason to believe that the deceased was dead, for he had not come home to his meals for several days; but the Judge of the Crowbait Court—as she ever afterward contemptuously called it—decided that the proof of death was insufficient, and put the estate into the hands of the Public Administrator, who was his son-in-law. It was found that the liabilities were exactly balanced by the assets; there was left only the patent for the device for bursting open safes without noise, by hydraulic pressure and this had passed into the ownership of the Probate Judge and the Public Administraitor—as my dear mother preferred to spell it. Thus, within a few brief months a worthy and respectable family was reduced from prosperity to crime; necessity compelled us to go to work.

In the selection of occupations we were governed by a variety of considerations, such as personal fitness, inclination, and so forth. My mother opened a select private school for instruction in the art of changing the spots upon leopard-skin rugs; my eldest brother, George Henry, who had a turn for music, became a bugler in a neighboring asylum for deaf mutes; my sister, Mary Maria, took orders for Professor Pumpernickel's Essence of Latchkeys for flavoring mineral springs, and I set up as an adjuster and gilder of crossbeams for gibbets. The other children, too young for labor, continued to steal small articles exposed in front of shops, as they had been taught.

In our intervals of leisure we decoyed travelers into our house and buried the bodies in a cellar.

In one part of this cellar we kept wines, liquors and provisions. From the rapidity of their disappearance we acquired the superstitious belief that the spirits of the persons buried there came at dead of night and held a festival. It was at least certain that frequently of a morning we would discover fragments of pickled meats, canned goods and such débris, littering the place, although it had been securely locked and barred against human intrusion. It was proposed to remove the provisions and store them elsewhere, but our dear mother, always generous and hospitable, said it was better to endure the loss than risk exposure: if the ghosts were denied this trifling gratification they might set on foot an investigation, which would overthrow our scheme of the division of labor, by diverting the energies of the whole family into the single industry pursued by me—we might all decorate the cross-beams of gibbets. We accepted her decision with filial submission, due to our reverence for her worldly wisdom and the purity of her character.

One night while we were all in the cellar—none dared to enter it alone—engaged in bestowing upon the Mayor of an adjoining town the solemn offices of Christian burial, my mother and the younger children, holding a candle each, while George Henry and I labored with a spade and pick, my sister Mary Maria uttered a shriek and covered her eyes with her hands. We were all dreadfully startled and the Mayor's obsequies were instantly suspended, while with pale faces and in trembling tones we begged her to say what had alarmed her. The younger children were so agitated that they held their candles unsteadily, and the waving shadows of our figures danced with uncouth and grotesque movements on the walls and flung themselves into the most uncanny attitudes. The face of the dead man, now gleaming ghastly in the light, and now extinguished by some floating shadow, appeared at each emergence to have taken on a new and more forbidding expression, a maligner menace. Frightened even more than ourselves by the girl's scream, rats raced in multitudes about the place, squeaking shrilly, or starred the black opacity of some distant corner with steadfast eyes, mere points of green light, matching the faint phosphorescence of decay that filled the half-dug grave and seemed the visible manifestation of that faint odor of mortality which tainted the unwholesome air. The children now sobbed and clung about the limbs of their elders, dropping their candles, and we were near being left in total darkness, except for that sinister light, which slowly welled upward from the disturbed earth and overflowed the edges of the grave like a fountain.

Meanwhile my sister, crouching in the earth that had been thrown out of the excavation, had removed her hands from her face and was staring with expanded eyes into an obscure space between two wine casks.

"There it is!—there it is!" she shrieked, pointing; "God in heaven! can't you see it?"

And there indeed it was!—a human figure, dimly discernible in the gloom—a figure that wavered from side to side as if about to fall, clutching at the wine-casks for support, had stepped unsteadily forward and for one moment stood revealed in the light of our remaining candles; then it surged heavily and fell prone upon the earth. In that moment we had all recognized the figure, the face and bearing of our father—dead these ten months and buried by our own hands!—our father indubitably risen and ghastly drunk!

On the incidents of our precipitate flight from that horrible place—on the extinction of all human sentiment in that tumultuous, mad scramble up the damp and mouldy stairs—slipping, falling, pulling one another down and clambering over one another's back—the lights extinguished, babes trampled beneath the feet of their strong brothers and hurled backward to death by a mother's arm!—on all this I do not dare to dwell. My mother, my eldest brother and sister and I escaped; the others remained below, to perish of their wounds, or of their terror—some, perhaps, by flame. For within an hour we four, hastily gathering together what money and jewels we had and what clothing we could carry, fired the dwelling and fled by its light into the hills. We did not even pause to collect the insurance, and my dear mother said on her death-bed, years afterward in a distant land, that this was the only sin of omission that lay upon her conscience. Her confessor, a holy man, assured her that under the circumstances Heaven would pardon the neglect.

About ten years after our removal from the scenes of my childhood I, then a prosperous forger, returned in disguise to the spot with a view to obtaining, if possible, some treasure belonging to us, which had been buried in the cellar. I may say that I was unsuccessful: the discovery of many human bones in the ruins had set the authorities digging for more. They had found the treasure and had kept it for their honesty. The house had not been rebuilt; the whole suburb was, in fact, a desolation. So many unearthly sights and sounds had been reported thereabout that nobody would live there. As there was none to question nor molest, I resolved to gratify my filial piety by gazing once more upon the face of my beloved father, if indeed our eyes had deceived us and he was still in his grave. I remembered, too, that he had always worn an enormous diamond ring, and never having seen it nor heard of it since his death, I had reason to think he might have been buried in it. Procuring a spade, I soon located the grave in what had been the backyard and began digging. When I had got down about four feet the whole bottom fell out of the grave and I was precipitated into a large drain, falling through a long hole in its crumbling arch. There was no body, nor any vestige of one.

Unable to get out of the excavation, I crept through the drain, and having with some difficulty removed a mass of charred rubbish and blackened masonry that choked it, emerged into what had been that fateful cellar.

All was clear. My father, whatever had caused him to be "taken bad" at his meal (and I think my sainted mother could have thrown some light upon that matter) had indubitably been buried alive. The grave having been accidentally dug above the forgotten drain, and down almost to the crown of its arch, and no coffin having been used, his struggles on reviving had broken the rotten masonry and he had fallen through, escaping finally into the cellar. Feeling that he was not welcome in his own house, yet having no other, he had lived in subterranean seclusion, a witness to our thrift and a pensioner on our providence. It was he who had eaten our food; it was he who had drunk our wine—he was no better than a thief! In a moment of intoxication, and feeling, no doubt, that need of companionship which is the one sympathetic link between a drunken man and his race, he had left his place of concealment at a strangely inopportune time, entailing the most deplorable consequences upon those nearest and dearest to him—a blunder that had almost the dignity of crime.

For the Ahkoond

IN the year 4591 I accepted from his gracious Majesty the
Ahkoond of Citrusia a commission to explore the unknown
region lying to the eastward of the Ultimate Hills, the range
which that learned archæologist, Simeon Tucker, affirms to be
identical with the "Rocky Mountains" of the ancients. For this
proof of his Majesty's favor I was indebted, doubtless, to a
certain distinction that I had been fortunate enough to acquire
by explorations in the heart of Darkest Europe. His Majesty
kindly offered to raise and equip a large expeditionary force to
accompany me, and I was given the widest discretion in the
matter of outfit; I could draw upon the royal treasury for any
sum that I might require, and upon the royal university for
all the scientific apparatus and assistance necessary to my purpose. Declining these encumbrances, I took my electric rifle
and a portable waterproof case containing a few simple instruments and writing materials and set out. Among the instruments was, of course, an aerial isochronophone which I set by
the one in the Ahkoond's private dining-room at the palace.
His Majesty invariably dined alone at 18 o'clock, and sat at table six hours: it was my intention to send him all my reports at
the hour of 23, just as dessert would be served, and he would
be in a proper frame of mind to appreciate my discoveries and
my services to the crown.

At 9 o'clock on the 13th of Meijh I left Sanf Rachisco and
after a tedious journey of nearly fifty minutes arrived at Bolosson, the eastern terminus of the magnetic tube, on the summit
of the Ultimate Hills. According to Tucker this was anciently a
station on the Central Peaceful Railway, and was called "German," in honor of an illustrious dancing master. Prof. Nupper,
however, says it was the ancient Nevraska, the capital of Ki-
kago, and geographers generally have accepted that view.

Finding nothing at Bolosson to interest me except a fine
view of the volcano Carlema, then in active eruption, I shouldered my electric rifle and with my case of instruments strapped
upon my back plunged at once into the wilderness, down the

eastern slope. As I descended the character of the vegetation altered. The pines of the higher altitudes gave place to oaks, these to ash, beech and maple. To these succeeded the tamarack and such trees as affect a moist and marshy habitat; and finally, when for four months I had been steadily descending, I found myself in a primeval flora consisting mainly of giant ferns, some of them as much as twenty *surindas* in diameter. They grew upon the margins of vast stagnant lakes which I was compelled to navigate by means of rude rafts made from their trunks lashed together with vines.

In the fauna of the region that I had traversed I had noted changes corresponding to those in the flora. On the upper slope there was nothing but the mountain sheep, but I passed successively through the habitats of the bear, the deer and the horse. This last mentioned creature, which our naturalists have believed long extinct, and which Dorbley declares our ancestors domesticated, I found in vast numbers on high table lands covered with grass upon which it feeds. The animal answers the current description of the horse very nearly, but all that I saw were destitute of the horns, and none had the characteristic forked tail. This member, on the contrary, is a tassel of straight wiry hair, reaching nearly to the ground—a surprising sight. Lower still I came upon the mastodon, the lion, the tiger, hippopotamus and alligator, all differing very little from those infesting Central Europe, as described in my "Travels in the Forgotten Continent."

In the lake region where I now found myself, the waters abounded with ichthyosauri, and along the margins the iguanodon dragged his obscene bulk in indolent immunity. Great flocks of pterodactyls, their bodies as large as those of oxen and their necks enormously long, clamored and fought in the air, the broad membranes of their wings making a singular musical humming, unlike anything that I had ever heard. Between them and the ichthyosauri there was incessant battle, and I was constantly reminded of the ancient poet's splendid and original comparison of man to

> dragons of the prime
> That tare each other in their slime.

When brought down with my electric rifle and properly roasted, the pterodactyl proved very good eating, particularly the pads of the toes.

In urging my raft along the shore line of one of the stagnant lagoons one day I was surprised to find a broad rock jutting out from the shore, its upper surface some ten *coprets* above the water. Disembarking, I ascended it, and on examination recognized it as the remnant of an immense mountain which at one time must have been 5,000 *coprets* in height and doubtless the dominating peak of a long range. From the striations all over it I discovered that it had been worn away to its present trivial size by glacial action. Opening my case of instruments, I took out my petrochronologue and applied it to the worn and scratched surface of the rock. The indicator at once pointed to K 59 xpc 1/2! At this astonishing result I was nearly overcome by excitement: the last erosions of the ice-masses upon this vestige of a stupendous mountain range which they had worn away, had been made as recently as the year 1945! Hastily applying my nymograph, I found that the name of this particular mountain at the time when it began to be enveloped in the mass of ice moving down upon it from the north, was "Pike's Peak." Other observations with other instruments showed that at that time the country circumjacent to it had been inhabited by a partly civilized race of people known as Galoots, the name of their capital city being Denver.

That evening at the hour of 23 I set up my aerial isochronophone* and reported to his gracious Majesty the Ahkoond as follows:

"*Sire*: I have the honor to report that I have made a startling discovery. The primeval region into which I have penetrated, as I informed you yesterday—the ichthyosaurus belt—was peopled by tribes considerably advanced in some of the arts almost within historic times: in 1920. They were exterminated by a glacial period not exceeding one hundred and twenty-five years in duration. Your Majesty can conceive the magnitude

---

*This satire was published in the San Francisco *Examiner* many years before the invention of wireless telegraphy; so I retain my own name for the instrument.—A. B.

and violence of the natural forces which overwhelmed their country with moving sheets of ice not less that 5,000 *coprets* in thickness, grinding down every eminence, destroying (of course) all animal and vegetable life and leaving the region a fathomless bog of detritus. Out of this vast sea of mud Nature has had to evolve another creation, beginning *de novo*, with her lowest forms. It has long been known, your Majesty, that the region east of the Ultimate Hills, between them and the Wintry Sea, was once the seat of an ancient civilization, some scraps and shreds of whose history, arts and literature have been wafted to us across the gulf of time; but it was reserved for your gracious Majesty, through me, your humble and unworthy instrument, to ascertain the astonishing fact that these were a pre-glacial people—that between them and us stands, as it were, a wall of impenetrable ice. That all local records of this unfortunate race have perished your Majesty needs not to be told: we can supplement our present imperfect knowledge of them by instrumental observation only."

To this message I received the following extraordinary reply:

"All right—another bottle of—ice goes: push on—this cheese is too—spare no effort to—hand me those nuts—learn all you can—damn you!"

His most gracious Majesty was being served with dessert, and served badly.

I now resolved to go directly north toward the source of the ice-flow and investigate its cause, but examining my barometer found that I was more than 8,000 *coprets* below the sea-level; the moving ice had not only ground down the face of the country, planing off the eminences and filling the depressions, but its enormous weight had caused the earth's crust to sag, and with the lessening of the weight from evaporation it had not recovered.

I had no desire to continue in this depression, as I should in going north, for I should find nothing but lakes, marshes and ferneries, infested with the same primitive and monstrous forms of life. So I continued my course eastward and soon had the satisfaction to find myself meeting the sluggish current of such streams as I encountered in my way. By vigorous use of the new double-distance telepode, which enables the wearer to step eighty *surindas* instead of forty, as with the instrument in popular use, I was soon again at a considerable elevation above the sea-level and nearly 200 *prastams* from "Pike's Peak." A little farther along the water courses began to flow to the eastward. The flora and fauna had again altered in character, and now began to grow sparse; the soil was thin and arid, and in a week I found myself in a region absolutely destitute of organic life and without a vestige of soil. All was barren rock. The surface for hundreds of *prastams*, as I continued my advance, was nearly level, with a slight dip to the eastward. The rock was singularly striated, the scratches arranged concentrically and in helicoidal curves. This circumstance puzzled me and I resolved to take some more instrumental observations, bitterly regretting my improvidence in not availing myself of the Ahkoond's permission to bring with me such apparatus and assistants as would have given me knowledge vastly more copious and accurate than I could acquire with my simple pocket appliances.

I need not here go into the details of my observations with such instruments as I had, nor into the calculations of which these observations were the basic data. Suffice it that after two months' labor I reported the results to his Majesty in Sanf Rachisco in the words following:

"*Sire*: It is my high privilege to apprise you of my arrival on the western slope of a mighty depression running through the center of the continent north and south, formerly known as the Mississippi Valley. It was once the seat of a thriving and prosperous population known as the Pukes, but is now a vast expanse of bare rock, from which every particle of soil and everything movable, including people, animals and vegetation, have been lifted by terrific cyclones and scattered afar, falling in other lands and at sea in the form of what was called meteoric dust! I find that these terrible phenomena began to occur about the year 1860, and lasted, with increasing frequency and power, through a century, culminating about the middle of that glacial period which saw the extinction of the Galoots and their neighboring tribes. There was, of course, a close connection between the two malefic phenomena, both, doubtless, being due to the same cause, which I have been unable to trace. A cyclone, I venture to remind your gracious Majesty, is a mighty whirlwind, accompanied by the most startling meteorological phenomena, such as electrical disturbances, floods of falling water, darkness and so forth. It moves with great speed, sucking up everything and reducing it to powder. In many days' journey I have not found a square *copret* of the country that did not suffer a visitation. If any human being escaped he must speedily have perished from starvation. For some twenty centuries the Pukes have been an extinct race, and their country a desolation in which no living thing can dwell, unless, like me, it is supplied with Dr. Blobob's Condensed Life-pills."

The Ahkoond replied that he was pleased to feel the most poignant grief for the fate of the unfortunate Pukes, and if I should by chance find the ancient king of the country I was to do my best to revive him with the patent resuscitator and present him the assurances of his Majesty's distinguished consideration; but as the politoscope showed that the nation had been a republic I gave myself no trouble in the matter.

My next report was made six months later and was in substance this:

"*Sire*: I address your Majesty from a point 430 *coprets* vertically above the site of the famous ancient city of Buffalo, once the capital of a powerful nation called the Smugwumps. I can approach no nearer because of the hardness of the snow, which is very firmly packed. For hundreds of *prastams* in every direction, and for thousands to the north and west, the land is covered with this substance, which, as your Majesty is doubtless aware, is extremely cold to the touch, but by application of sufficient heat can be turned into water. It falls from the heavens, and is believed by the learned among your Majesty's subjects to have a sidereal origin.

"The Smugwumps were a hardy and intelligent race, but they entertained the vain delusion that they could subdue Nature. Their year was divided into two seasons—summer and winter, the former warm, the latter cold. About the beginning of the nineteenth century according to my archæthermograph, the summers began to grow shorter and hotter, the winters longer and colder. At every point in their country, and every day in the year, when they had not the hottest weather ever known in that place, they had the coldest. When they were not dying by hundreds from sunstroke they were dying by thousands from frost. But these heroic and devoted people struggled on, believing that they were becoming acclimated faster than the climate was becoming insupportable. Those called away on business were even afflicted with nostalgia, and with a fatal infatuation returned to grill or freeze, according to the season of their arrival. Finally there was no summer at all, though the last flash of heat slew several millions and set most of their cities afire, and winter reigned eternal.

"The Smugwumps were now keenly sensible of the perils environing them, and, abandoning their homes, endeavored to reach their kindred, the Californians, on the western side of the continent in what is now your Majesty's ever-blessed realm. But it was too late: the snow growing deeper and deeper day by day, besieged them in their towns and dwellings, and they were unable to escape. The last one of them perished about the year 1943, and may God have mercy on his fool soul!"

To this dispatch the Ahkoond replied that it was the royal opinion that the Smugwumps were served very well right.

Some weeks later I reported thus:

"*Sire*: The country which your Majesty's munificence is enabling your devoted servant to explore extends southward and southwestward from Smugwumpia many hundreds of *prastams*, its eastern and southern borders being the Wintry Sea and the Fiery Gulf, respectively. The population in ancient times was composed of Whites and Blacks in about equal numbers and of about equal moral worth—at least that is the record on the dial of my ethnograph when set for the twentieth century and given a southern exposure. The Whites were called Crackers and the Blacks known as Coons.

"I find here none of the barrenness and desolation characterizing the land of the ancient Pukes, and the climate is not so rigorous and thrilling as that of the country of the late

Smugwumps. It is, indeed, rather agreeable in point of temperature, and the soil being fertile exceedingly, the whole land is covered with a dense and rank vegetation. I have yet to find a square *smig* of it that is open ground, or one that is not the lair of some savage beast, the haunt of some venomous reptile, or the roost of some offensive bird. Crackers and Coons alike are long extinct, and these are their successors.

"Nothing could be more forbidding and unwholesome than these interminable jungles, with their horrible wealth of organic life in its most objectionable forms. By repeated observations with the necrohistoriograph I find that the inhabitants of this country, who had always been more or less dead, were wholly extirpated contemporaneously with the disastrous events which swept away the Galoots, the Pukes and the Smugwumps. The agency of their effacement was an endemic disorder known as yellow fever. The ravages of this frightful disease were of frequent recurrence, every point of the country being a center of infection; but in some seasons it was worse than in others. Once in every half century at first, and afterward every year* it broke out somewhere and swept over wide areas with such fatal effect that there were not enough of the living to plunder the dead; but at the first frost it would subside. During the ensuing two or three months of immunity the stupid survivors returned to the infected homes from which they had fled and were ready for the next outbreak. Emigration would have saved them all, but although the Californians (over whose happy and prosperous descendants your Majesty has the goodness to reign) invited them again and again to their beautiful land, where sickness and death were hardly known, they would not go, and by the year 1946 the last one of them, may it please your gracious Majesty, was dead and damned."

Having spoken this into the transmitter of the aerial isochronophone at the usual hour of 23 o'clock I applied the receiver to my ear, confidently expecting the customary commendation.

---

*At one time it was foolishly believed that the disease had been eradicated by slapping the mosquitoes which were thought to produce it; but a few years later it broke out with greater violence than ever before, although the mosquitoes had left the country.

Imagine my astonishment and dismay when my master's well-remembered voice was heard in utterance of the most awful imprecations on me and my work, followed by appalling threats against my life!

The Ahkoond had changed his dinner-time to five hours later and I had been speaking into the ears of an empty stomach!

My Favorite Murder

Having murdered my mother under circumstances of singular atrocity, I was arrested and put upon my trial, which lasted seven years. In charging the jury, the judge of the Court of Acquittal remarked that it was one of the most ghastly crimes that he had ever been called upon to explain away.

At this, my attorney rose and said:

"May it please your Honor, crimes are ghastly or agreeable only by comparison. If you were familiar with the details of my client's previous murder of his uncle you would discern in his later offense (if offense it may be called) something in the nature of tender forbearance and filial consideration for the feelings of the victim. The appalling ferocity of the former assassination was indeed inconsistent with any hypothesis but that of guilt; and had it not been for the fact that the honorable judge before whom he was tried was the president of a life insurance company that took risks on hanging, and in which my client held a policy, it is hard to see how he could decently have been acquitted. If your Honor would like to hear about it for instruction and guidance of your Honor's mind, this unfortunate man, my client, will consent to give himself the pain of relating it under oath."

The district attorney said: "Your Honor, I object. Such a statement would be in the nature of evidence, and the testimony in this case is closed. The prisoner's statement should have been introduced three years ago, in the spring of 1881."

"In a statutory sense," said the judge, "you are right, and in the Court of Objections and Technicalities you would get a ruling in your favor. But not in a Court of Acquittal. The objection is overruled."

"I except," said the district attorney.

"You cannot do that," the judge said. "I must remind you that in order to take an exception you must first get this case transferred for a time to the Court of Exceptions on a formal motion duly supported by affidavits. A motion to that effect by your predecessor in office was denied by me during the first year of this trial. Mr. Clerk, swear the prisoner."

The customary oath having been administered, I made the following statement, which impressed the judge with so strong a sense of the comparative triviality of the offense for which I was on trial that he made no further search for mitigating circumstances, but simply instructed the jury to acquit, and I left the court, without a stain upon my reputation:

"I was born in 1856 in Kalamakee, Mich., of honest and reputable parents, one of whom Heaven has mercifully spared to comfort me in my later years. In 1867 the family came to California and settled near Nigger Head, where my father opened a road agency and prospered beyond the dreams of avarice. He was a reticent, saturnine man then, though his increasing years have now somewhat relaxed the austerity of his disposition, and I believe that nothing but his memory of the sad event for which I am now on trial prevents him from manifesting a genuine hilarity.

"Four years after we had set up the road agency an itinerant preacher came along, and having no other way to pay for the night's lodging that we gave him, favored us with an exhortation of such power that, praise God, we were all converted to religion. My father at once sent for his brother, the Hon. William Ridley of Stockton, and on his arrival turned over the agency to him, charging him nothing for the franchise nor plant—the latter consisting of a Winchester rifle, a sawed-off shotgun, and an assortment of masks made out of flour sacks. The family then moved to Ghost Rock and opened a dance house. It was called 'The Saints' Rest Hurdy-Gurdy,' and the proceedings each night began with prayer. It was there that my now sainted mother, by her grace in the dance, acquired the *sobriquet* of 'The Bucking Walrus.'

"In the fall of '75 I had occasion to visit Coyote, on the road to Mahala, and took the stage at Ghost Rock. There were four other passengers. About three miles beyond Nigger Head, persons whom I identified as my Uncle William and his two sons held up the stage. Finding nothing in the express box, they went through the passengers. I acted a most honorable part in the affair, placing myself in line with the others, holding up my hands and permitting myself to be deprived of forty dollars and a gold watch. From my behavior no one could have suspected that I knew the gentlemen who gave the entertainment.

A few days later, when I went to Nigger Head and asked for
the return of my money and watch my uncle and cousins swore
they knew nothing of the matter, and they affected a belief that
my father and I had done the job ourselves in dishonest violation of commercial good faith. Uncle William even threatened
to retaliate by starting an opposition dance house at Ghost
Rock. As 'The Saints' Rest' had become rather unpopular, I
saw that this would assuredly ruin it and prove a paying enterprise, so I told my uncle that I was willing to overlook the past
if he would take me into the scheme and keep the partnership
a secret from my father. This fair offer he rejected, and I then
perceived that it would be better and more satisfactory if he
were dead.

"My plans to that end were soon perfected, and communicating them to my dear parents I had the gratification of receiving their approval. My father said he was proud of me, and
my mother promised that although her religion forbade her to
assist in taking human life I should have the advantage of her
prayers for my success. As a preliminary measure looking to
my security in case of detection I made an application for
membership in that powerful order, the Knights of Murder,
and in due course was received as a member of the Ghost Rock
commandery. On the day that my probation ended I was for
the first time permitted to inspect the records of the order and
learn who belonged to it—all the rites of initiation having been
conducted in masks. Fancy my delight when, in looking over
the roll of membership, I found the third name to be that of my
uncle, who indeed was junior vice-chancellor of the order! Here
was an opportunity exceeding my wildest dreams—to murder
I could add insubordination and treachery. It was what my
good mother would have called 'a special Providence.'

"At about this time something occurred which caused my cup
of joy, already full, to overflow on all sides, a circular cataract of
bliss. Three men, strangers in that locality, were arrested for the
stage robbery in which I had lost my money and watch. They
were brought to trial and, despite my efforts to clear them and
fasten the guilt upon three of the most respectable and worthy
citizens of Ghost Rock, convicted on the clearest proof. The
murder would now be as wanton and reasonless as I could wish.

"One morning I shouldered my Winchester rifle, and going

over to my uncle's house, near Nigger Head, asked my Aunt Mary, his wife, if he were at home, adding that I had come to kill him. My aunt replied with her peculiar smile that so many gentlemen called on that errand and were afterward carried away without having performed it that I must excuse her for doubting my good faith in the matter. She said it did not look as if I would kill anybody, so, as a proof of good faith I leveled my rifle and wounded a Chinaman who happened to be passing the house. She said she knew whole families that could do a thing of that kind, but Bill Ridley was a horse of another color. She said, however, that I would find him over on the other side of the creek in the sheep lot; and she added that she hoped the best man would win.

"My Aunt Mary was one of the most fair-minded women that I have ever met.

I found my uncle down on his knees engaged in skinning a sheep. Seeing that he had neither gun nor pistol handy I had not the heart to shoot him, so I approached him, greeted him pleasantly and struck him a powerful blow on the head with the butt of my rifle. I have a very good delivery and Uncle William lay down on his side, then rolled over on his back, spread out his fingers and shivered. Before he could recover the use of his limbs I seized the knife that he had been using and cut his hamstrings. You know, doubtless, that when you sever the *tendo Achillis* the patient has no further use of his leg; it is just the same as if he had no leg. Well, I parted them both, and when he revived he was at my service. As soon as he comprehended the situation, he said:

" 'Samuel, you have got the drop on me and can afford to be generous. I have only one thing to ask of you, and that is that you carry me to the house and finish me in the bosom of my family.'

"I told him I thought that a pretty reasonable request and I would do so if he would let me put him into a wheat sack; he would be easier to carry that way and if we were seen by the neighbors *en route* it would cause less remark. He agreed to that, and going to the barn I got a sack. This, however, did not fit him; it was too short and much wider than he; so I bent his legs, forced his knees up against his breast and got him into it that way, tying the sack above his head. He was a heavy man and I had all that I could do to get him on my back, but I staggered along for some distance until I came to a swing that some of the children had suspended to the branch of an oak. Here I laid him down and sat upon him to rest, and the sight of the rope gave me a happy inspiration. In twenty minutes my uncle, still in the sack, swung free to the sport of the wind.

"I had taken down the rope, tied one end tightly about the mouth of the bag, thrown the other across the limb and hauled him up about five feet from the ground. Fastening the other end of the rope also about the mouth of the sack, I had the satisfaction to see my uncle converted into a large, fine pendulum. I must add that he was not himself entirely aware of the nature of the change that he had undergone in his relation to the exterior world, though in justice to a good man's memory I ought to say that I do not think he would in any case have wasted much of my time in vain remonstrance.

"Uncle William had a ram that was famous in all that region as a fighter. It was in a state of chronic constitutional indignation. Some deep disappointment in early life had soured its disposition and it had declared war upon the whole world. To say that it would butt anything accessible is but faintly to express the nature and scope of its military activity: the universe was its antagonist; its methods that of a projectile. It fought like the angels and devils, in mid-air, cleaving the atmosphere like a bird, describing a parabolic curve and descending upon its victim at just the exact angle of incidence to make the most of its velocity and weight. Its momentum, calculated in foot-tons, was something incredible. It had been seen to destroy a four year old bull by a single impact upon that animal's gnarly forehead. No stone wall had ever been known to resist its downward swoop; there were no trees tough enough to stay it; it would splinter them into matchwood and defile their leafy honors in the dust. This irascible and implacable brute—this incarnate thunderbolt—this monster of the upper deep, I had seen reposing in the shade of an adjacent tree, dreaming dreams of conquest and glory. It was with a view to summoning it forth to the field of honor that I suspended its master in the manner described.

"Having completed my preparations, I imparted to the avuncular pendulum a gentle oscillation, and retiring to cover behind a contiguous rock, lifted up my voice in a long rasping cry whose diminishing final note was drowned in a noise like that of a swearing cat, which emanated from the sack. Instantly that formidable sheep was upon its feet and had taken in the military situation at a glance. In a few moments it had approached, stamping, to within fifty yards of the swinging foeman, who, now retreating and anon advancing, seemed to invite the fray. Suddenly I saw the beast's head drop earthward as if depressed by the weight of its enormous horns; then a dim, white, wavy streak of sheep prolonged itself from that spot in a generally horizontal direction to within about four yards of a point immediately beneath the enemy. There it struck sharply upward, and before it had faded from my gaze at the place whence it had set out I heard a horrible thump and a piercing scream, and my poor uncle shot forward, with a slack rope higher than the limb to which he was attached. Here the rope tautened with a jerk, arresting his flight, and back he swung in a breathless curve to the other end of his arc. The ram had fallen, a heap of indistinguishable legs, wool and horns, but pulling itself together and dodging as its antagonist swept downward it retired at random, alternately shaking its head and stamping its fore-feet. When it had backed about the same distance as that from which it had delivered the assault it paused again, bowed its head as if in prayer for victory and again shot forward, dimly visibly as before—a prolonging white streak with monstrous undulations, ending with a sharp ascension. Its course this time was at a right angle to its former one, and its impatience so great that it struck the enemy before he had nearly reached the lowest point of his arc. In consequence he went flying around and around in a horizontal circle whose radius was about equal to half the length of the rope, which I forgot to say was nearly twenty feet long. His shrieks, *crescendo* in approach and *diminuendo* in recession, made the rapidity of his revolution more obvious to the ear than to the eye. He had evidently not yet been struck in a vital spot. His posture in the sack and the distance from the ground at which he hung compelled the ram to operate upon his lower extremities and the end of his back. Like a plant that has struck its root into some poisonous mineral, my poor uncle was dying slowly upward.

"After delivering its second blow the ram had not again

retired. The fever of battle burned hot in its heart; its brain was intoxicated with the wine of strife. Like a pugilist who in his rage forgets his skill and fights ineffectively at half-arm's length, the angry beast endeavoured to reach its fleeting foe by awkward vertical leaps as he passed overhead, sometimes, indeed, succeeding in striking him feebly, but more frequently overthrown by its own misguided eagerness. But as the impetus was exhausted and the man's circles narrowed in scope and diminished in speed, bringing him nearer to the ground, these tactics produced better results, eliciting a superior quality of screams, which I greatly enjoyed.

"Suddenly, as if the bugles had sung truce, the ram suspended hostilities and walked away, thoughtfully wrinkling and smoothing its great aquiline nose, and occasionally cropping a bunch of grass and slowly munching it. It seemed to have tired of war's alarms and resolved to beat the sword into a plowshare and cultivate the arts of peace. Steadily it held its course away from the field of fame until it had gained a distance of nearly a quarter of a mile. There it stopped and stood with its rear to the foe, chewing its cud and apparently half asleep. I observed, however, an occasional slight turn of its head, as if its apathy were more affected than real.

"Meanwhile Uncle William's shrieks had abated with his motion, and nothing was heard from him but long, low moans, and at long intervals my name, uttered in pleading tones exceedingly grateful to my ear. Evidently the man had not the faintest notion of what was being done to him, and was inexpressibly terrified. When Death comes cloaked in mystery he is terrible indeed. Little by little my uncle's oscillations diminished, and finally he hung motionless. I went to him and was about to give him the *coup de grâce*, when I heard and felt a succession of smart shocks which shook the ground like a series of light earthquakes, and turning in the direction of the ram, saw a long cloud of dust approaching me with inconceivable rapidity and alarming effect! At a distance of some thirty yards away it stopped short, and from the near end of it rose into the air what I at first thought a great white bird. Its ascent was so smooth and easy and regular that I could not realize its extraordinary celerity, and was lost in admiration of its grace. To this day the impression remains that it was a slow, deliberate movement, the ram—for it was that animal—being upborne by some power other than its own impetus, and supported through the successive stages of its flight with infinite tenderness and care. My eyes followed its progress through the air with unspeakable pleasure, all the greater by contrast with my former terror of its approach by land. Onward and upward the noble animal sailed, its head bent down almost between its knees, its fore-feet thrown back, its hinder legs trailing to rear like the legs of a soaring heron.

"At a height of forty or fifty feet, as fond recollection presents it to view, it attained its zenith and appeared to remain an instant stationary; then, tilting suddenly forward without altering the relative position of its parts, it shot downward on a steeper and steeper course with augmenting velocity, passed immediately above me with a noise like the rush of a cannon shot and struck my poor uncle almost squarely on the top of the head! So frightful was the impact that not only the man's neck was broken, but the rope too; and the body of the deceased, forced against the earth, was crushed to pulp beneath the awful front of that meteoric sheep! The concussion stopped all the clocks between Lone Hand and Dutch Dan's, and Professor Davidson, a disinguished authority in matters seismic, who happened to be in the vicinity, promptly explained that the vibrations were from the north to southwest.

"Altogether, I cannot help thinking that in point of artistic atrocity my murder of Uncle William has seldom been excelled."

Oil of Dog

M Y name is Boffer Bings. I was born of honest parents in one of the humbler walks of life, my father being a manufacturer of dog-oil and my mother having a small studio in the shadow of the village church, where she disposed of unwelcome babes. In my boyhood I was trained to habits of industry; I not only assisted my father in procuring dogs for his vats, but was frequently employed by my mother to carry away the debris of her work in the studio. In performance of this duty I sometimes had need of all my natural intelligence for all the law officers of the vicinity were opposed to my mother's business. They were not elected on an opposition ticket, and the matter had never been made a political issue; it just happened so. My father's business of making dog-oil was, naturally, less unpopular, though the owners of missing dogs sometimes regarded him with suspicion, which was reflected, to some extent, upon me. My father had, as silent partners, all the physicians of the town, who seldom wrote a prescription which did not contain what they were pleased to designate as *Ol. can.* It is really the most valuable medicine ever discovered. But most persons are unwilling to make personal sacrifices for the afflicted, and it was evident that many of the fattest dogs in town had been forbidden to play with me—a fact which pained my young sensibilities, and at one time came near driving me to become a pirate.

Looking back upon those days, I cannot but regret, at times, that by indirectly bringing my beloved parents to their death I was the author of misfortunes profoundly affecting my future.

One evening while passing my father's oil factory with the body of a foundling from my mother's studio I saw a constable who seemed to be closely watching my movements. Young as I was, I had learned that a constable's acts, of whatever apparent character, are prompted by the most reprehensible motives, and I avoided him by dodging into the oilery by a side door which happened to stand ajar. I locked it at once and was alone with my dead. My father had retired for the night. The only light in the place came from the furnace, which glowed a deep,

798

rich crimson under one of the vats, casting ruddy reflections
on the walls. Within the cauldron the oil still rolled in indolent
ebullition, occasionally pushing to the surface a piece of dog.
Seating myself to wait for the constable to go away, I held the
naked body of the foundling in my lap and tenderly stroked its
short, silken hair. Ah, how beautiful it was! Even at that early
age I was passionately fond of children, and as I looked upon
this cherub I could almost find it in my heart to wish that the
small, red wound upon its breast—the work of my dear mother
—had not been mortal.

It had been my custom to throw the babes into the river
which nature had thoughtfully provided for the purpose, but
that night I did not dare to leave the oilery for fear of the constable. "After all," I said to myself, "it cannot greatly matter if
I put it into this cauldron. My father will never know the bones
from those of a puppy, and the few deaths which may result
from administering another kind of oil for the incomparable *ol.
can.* are not important in a population which increases so rapidly." In short, I took the first step in crime and brought myself
untold sorrow by casting the babe into the cauldron.

The next day, somewhat to my surprise, my father, rubbing
his hands with satisfaction, informed me and my mother that
he had obtained the finest quality of oil that was ever seen; that
the physicians to whom he had shown samples had so pronounced it. He added that he had no knowledge as to how the
result was obtained; the dogs had been treated in all respects as
usual, and were of an ordinary breed. I deemed it my duty to
explain—which I did, though palsied would have been my
tongue if I could have foreseen the consequences. Bewailing
their previous ignorance of the advantages of combining their
industries, my parents at once took measures to repair the
error. My mother removed her studio to a wing of the factory
building and my duties in connection with the business ceased;
I was no longer required to dispose of the bodies of the small
superfluous, and there was no need of alluring dogs to their
doom, for my father discarded them altogether, though they
still had an honorable place in the name of the oil. So suddenly
thrown into idleness, I might naturally have been expected to
become vicious and dissolute, but I did not. The holy influence of my dear mother was ever about me to protect me from

the temptations which beset youth, and my father was a deacon in a church. Alas, that through my fault these estimable persons should have come to so bad an end!

Finding a double profit in her business, my mother now devoted herself to it with a new assiduity. She removed not only superfluous and unwelcome babes to order, but went out into the highways and byways, gathering in children of a larger growth, and even such adults as she could entice to the oilery. My father, too, enamored of the superior quality of oil produced, purveyed for his vats with diligence and zeal. The conversion of their neighbors into dog-oil became, in short, the one passion of their lives—an absorbing and overwhelming greed took possession of their souls and served them in place of a hope in Heaven—by which, also, they were inspired.

So enterprising had they now become that a public meeting was held and resolutions passed severely censuring them. It was intimated by the chairman that any further raids upon the population would be met in a spirit of hostility. My poor parents left the meeting broken-hearted, desperate and, I believe, not altogether sane. Anyhow, I deemed it prudent not to enter the oilery with them that night, but slept outside in a stable.

At about midnight some mysterious impulse caused me to rise and peer through a window into the furnace-room, where I knew my father now slept. The fires were burning as brightly as if the following day's harvest had been expected to be abundant. One of the large cauldrons was slowly "walloping" with a mysterious appearance of self-restraint, as if it bided its time to put forth its full energy. My father was not in bed; he had risen in his night clothes and was preparing a noose in a strong cord. From the looks which he cast at the door of my mother's bedroom I knew too well the purpose that he had in mind. Speechless and motionless with terror, I could do nothing in prevention or warning. Suddenly the door of my mother's apartment was opened, noiselessly, and the two confronted each other, both apparently surprised. The lady, also, was in her night clothes, and she held in her right hand the tool of her trade, a long, narrow-bladed dagger.

She, too, had been unable to deny herself the last profit which the unfriendly action of the citizens and my absence had left her. For one instant they looked into each other's blazing eyes and then sprang together with indescribable fury. Round and round the room they struggled, the man cursing, the woman shrieking, both fighting like demons—she to strike him with the dagger, he to strangle her with his great bare hands. I know not how long I had the unhappiness to observe this disagreeable instance of domestic infelicity, but at last, after a more than usually vigorous struggle, the combatants suddenly moved apart.

My father's breast and my mother's weapon showed evidences of contact. For another instant they glared at each other in the most unamiable way; then my poor, wounded father, feeling the hand of death upon him, leaped forward, unmindful of resistance, grasped my dear mother in his arms, dragged her to the side of the boiling cauldron, collected all his failing energies, and sprang in with her! In a moment, both had disappeared and were adding their oil to that of the committee of citizens who had called the day before with an invitation to the public meeting.

Convinced that these unhappy events closed to me every avenue to an honorable career in that town, I removed to the famous city of Otumwee, where these memoirs are written with a heart full of remorse for a heedless act entailing so dismal a commercial disaster.

Ashes of the Beacon

AN HISTORICAL MONOGRAPH WRITTEN IN 4930

OF the many causes that conspired to bring about the lamentable failure of "self-government" in ancient America the most general and comprehensive was, of course, the impracticable nature of the system itself. In the light of modern culture, and instructed by history, we readily discern the folly of those crude ideas upon which the ancient Americans based what they knew as "republican institutions," and maintained, as long as maintenance was possible, with something of a religious fervor, even when the results were visibly disastrous.

To us of to-day it is clear that the word "self-government" involves a contradiction, for government means control by something other than the thing to be controlled. When the thing governed is the same as the thing governing there is no government, though for a time there may be, as in the case under consideration there was, a considerable degree of forbearance, giving a misleading appearance of public order. This, however, soon must, as in fact it soon did, pass away with the delusion that gave it birth. The habit of obedience to written law, inculcated by generations of respect for actual government able to enforce its authority, will persist for a long time, with an ever lessening power upon the imagination of the people; but there comes a time when the tradition is forgotten and the delusion exhausted. When men perceive that nothing is restraining them but their consent to be restrained, then at last there is nothing to obstruct the free play of that selfishness which is the dominant characteristic and fundamental motive of human nature and human action respectively. Politics, which may have had something of the character of a contest of principles, becomes a struggle of interests, and its methods are frankly serviceable to personal and class advantage. Patriotism and respect for law pass like a tale that is told. Anarchy, no longer disguised as "government by consent," reveals his hidden hand, and in the words of our greatest living poet,

lets the curtain fall,
And universal darkness buries all!

The ancient Americans were a composite people; their blood was a blend of all the strains known in their time. Their government, while they had one, being merely a loose and mutable expression of the desires and caprices of the majority—that is to say, of the ignorant, restless and reckless—gave the freest rein and play to all the primal instincts and elemental passions of the race. In so far and for so long as it had any restraining force, it was only the restraint of the present over the power of the past—that of a new habit over an old and insistent tendency ever seeking expression in large liberties and indulgences impatient of control. In the history of that unhappy people, therefore, we see unveiled the workings of the human will in its most lawless state, without fear of authority or care of consequence. Nothing could be more instructive.

Of the American form of government, although itself the greatest of evils afflicting the victims of those that it entailed, but little needs to be said here; it has perished from the earth, a system discredited by an unbroken record of failure in all parts of the world, from the earliest historic times to its final extinction. Of living students of political history not one professes to see in it anything but a mischievous creation of theorists and visionaries—persons whom our gracious sovereign has deigned to brand for the world's contempt as "dupes of hope purveying to sons of greed." The political philosopher of to-day is spared the trouble of pointing out the fallacies of republican government, as the mathematician is spared that of demonstrating the absurdity of the convergence of parallel lines; yet the ancient Americans not only clung to their error with a blind, unquestioning faith, even when groaning under its most insupportable burdens, but seem to have believed it of divine origin. It was thought by them to have been established by the god Washington, whose worship, with that of such *dii minores* as Gufferson, Jaxon and Lincon (identical probably with the Hebru Abrem) runs like a shining thread through all the warp and woof of the stuff that garmented their moral nakedness. Some stones, very curiously inscribed in many tongues,

were found by the explorer Droyhors in the wilderness bordering the river Bhitt (supposed by him to be the ancient Potomac) as lately as the reign of Barukam IV. These stones
appear to be fragments of a monument or temple erected to
the glory of Washington in his divine character of Founder and
Preserver of republican institutions. If this tutelary deity of the
ancient Americans really invented representative government
they were not the first by many to whom he imparted the malign secret of its inauguration and denied that of its maintenance.

Although many of the causes which finally, in combination,
brought about the downfall of the great American republic
were in operation from the beginning—being, as has been said,
inherent in the system—it was not until the year 1995 (as the
ancients for some reason not now known reckoned time) that
the collapse of the vast, formless fabric was complete. In that
year the defeat and massacre of the last army of law and order
in the lava beds of California extinguished the final fires of
enlightened patriotism and quenched in blood the monarchical
revival. Thenceforth armed opposition to anarchy was confined
to desultory and insignificant warfare waged by small gangs of
mercenaries in the service of wealthy individuals and equally
feeble bands of proscripts fighting for their lives. In that year,
too, "the Three Presidents" were driven from their capitals,
Cincinnati, New Orleans and Duluth, their armies dissolving
by desertion and themselves meeting death at the hands of the
populace.

The turbulent period between 1920 and 1995, with its incalculable waste of blood and treasure, its dreadful conflicts of
armies and more dreadful massacres by passionate mobs, its ka-
leidoscopic changes of government and incessant effacement
and redrawing of boundaries of states, its interminable tale of
political assassinations and proscriptions—all the horrors incident
to intestinal wars of a naturally lawless race—had so exhausted
and dispirited the surviving protagonists of legitimate government that they could make no further head against the inevitable,
and were glad indeed and most fortunate to accept life on any
terms that they could obtain.

But the purpose of this sketch is not bald narration of historic fact, but examination of antecedent germinal conditions;

not to recount calamitous events familiar to students of that faulty civilization, but to trace, as well as the meager record will permit, the genesis and development of the causes that brought them about. Historians in our time have left little undone in the matter of narration of political and military phenomena. In Golpek's "Decline and Fall of the American Republics," in Soseby's "History of Political Fallacies," in Holobom's "Monarchical Renasence," and notably in Gunkux's immortal work, "The Rise, Progress, Failure and Extinction of The Connected States of America" the fruits of research have been garnered, a considerable harvest. The events are set forth with such conscientiousness and particularity as to have exhausted the possibilities of narration. It remains only to expound causes and point the awful moral.

To a delinquent observation it may seem needless to point out the inherent defects of a system of government which the logic of events has swept like political rubbish from the face of the earth, but we must not forget that ages before the inception of the American republics and that of France and Ireland this form of government had been discredited by emphatic failures among the most enlightened and powerful nations of antiquity: the Greeks, the Romans, and long before them (as we now know) the Egyptians and the Chinese. To the lesson of these failures the founders of the eighteenth and nineteenth century republics were blind and deaf. Have we then reason to believe that our posterity will be wiser because instructed by a greater number of examples? And is the number of examples which they will have in memory really greater? Already the instances of China, Egypt, Greece and Rome are almost lost in the mists of antiquity; they are known, except by infrequent report, to the archæologist only, and but dimly and uncertainly to him. The brief and imperfect record of yesterdays which we call History is like that traveling vine of India which, taking new root as it advances, decays at one end while it grows at the other, and so is constantly perishing and finally lost in all the spaces which it has over-passed.

From the few and precious writings that have descended to us from the early period of the American republic we get a clear if fragmentary view of the disorders and lawlessness affecting that strange and unhappy nation. Leaving the historically famous "labor troubles" for more extended consideration, we may summarize here a few of the results of hardly more than a century and a quarter of "self-government" as it existed on this continent just previously to the awful end. At the beginning of the "twentieth century" a careful study by trustworthy contemporary statisticians of the public records and those apparently private ones known as "newspapers" showed that in a population of about 80,000,000 the annual number of homicides was not less than 10,000; and this continued year after year to increase, not only absolutely, but proportionately, until, in the words of Dumbleshaw, who is thought to have written his famous "Memoirs of a Survivor" in the year 1908 of their era, "it would seem that the practice of suicide is a needless custom, for if a man but have patience his neighbor is sure to put him out of his misery." Of the 10,000 assassins less than three per cent. were punished, further than by incidental imprisonment if unable to give bail while awaiting trial. If the chief end of government is the citizen's security of life and his protection from aggression, what kind of government do these appalling figures disclose? Yet so infatuated with their imaginary "liberty" were these singular people that the contemplation of all this crime abated nothing of the volume and persistence of their patriotic ululations, and affected not their faith in the perfection of their system. They were like a man standing on a rock already submerged by the rising tide, and calling to his neighbors on adjacent cliffs to observe his superior security.

When three men engage in an undertaking in which they have an equal interest, and in the direction of which they have equal power, it necessarily results that any action approved by two of them, with or without the assent of the third, will be taken. This is called—or was called when it was an accepted principle in political and other affairs—"the rule of the majority." Evidently, under the malign conditions supposed, it is the only practicable plan of getting anything done. A and B rule and overrule C, not because they ought, but because they can; not because they are wiser, but because they are stronger. In order to avoid a conflict in which he is sure to be worsted, C submits as soon as the vote is taken. C is as likely to be right as A and B; nay, that eminent ancient philosopher, Professor Richard A. Proctor (or Proroctor, as the learned now spell the name), has clearly shown by the law of probabilities that any one of the three, all being of the same intelligence, is far likelier to be right than the other two.

It is thus that the "rule of the majority" as a political system is established. It is in essence nothing but the discredited and discreditable principle that "might makes right"; but early in the life of a republic this essential character of government by majority is not seen. The habit of submitting all questions of policy to the arbitrament of counting noses and assenting without question to the result invests the ordeal with a seeming sanctity, and what was at first obeyed as the command of power comes to be revered as the oracle of wisdom. The innumerable instances—such as the famous ones of Galileo and Keeley—in which one man has been right and all the rest of the race wrong, are overlooked, or their significance missed, and "public opinion" is followed as a divine and infallible guide through every bog into which it blindly stumbles and over every precipice in its fortuitous path. Clearly, sooner or later will be encountered a bog that will smother or a precipice that will crush. Thoroughly to apprehend the absurdity of the ancient faith in the wisdom of majorities let the loyal reader try to fancy our gracious Sovereign by any possibility wrong, or his unanimous Ministry by any possibility right!

During the latter half of the "nineteenth century" there arose in the Connected States a political element opposed to all government, which frankly declared its object to be anarchy. This astonishing heresy was not of indigenous growth: its seeds were imported from Europe by the emigration or banishment thence of criminals congenitally incapable of understanding and valuing the blessings of monarchical institutions, and whose method of protest was murder. The governments against which they conspired in their native lands were too strong in authority and too enlightened in policy for them to overthrow. Hundreds of them were put to death, thousands imprisoned and sent into exile. But in America, whither those who escaped fled for safety, they found conditions entirely favorable to the prosecution of their designs.

A revered fetish of the Americans was "freedom of speech": it was believed that if bad men were permitted to proclaim their evil wishes they would go no further in the direction of executing them—that if they might say what they would like to do they would not care to do it. The close relation between speech and action was not understood. Because the Americans themselves had long been accustomed, in their own political debates and discussions, to the use of unmeaning declamations and threats which they had no intention of executing, they reasoned that others were like them, and attributed to the menaces of these desperate and earnest outcasts no greater importance than to their own. They thought also that the foreign anarchists, having exchanged the tyranny of kings for that of majorities, would be content with their new and better lot and become in time good and law-abiding citizens.

The anarchist of that far day (thanks to the firm hands of our gracious sovereigns the species is now extinct) was a very different person from what our infatuated ancestors imagined him. He struck at government, not because it was bad, but because it was government. He hated authority, not for its tyranny, but for its power. And in order to make this plain to observation he frequently chose his victim from amongst those whose rule was most conspicuously benign.

Of the seven early Presidents of the American republic who perished by assassination no fewer than four were slain by anarchists with no personal wrongs to impel them to the deed—nothing but an implacable hostility to law and authority. The fifth victim, indeed, was a notorious demagogue who had pardoned the assassin of the fourth.

The field of the anarchist's greatest activity was always a republic, not only to emphasize his impartial hatred of all government, but because of the inherent feebleness of that form of government, its inability to protect itself against any kind of aggression by any considerable number of its people having a common malevolent purpose. In a republic the crust that confined the fires of violence and sedition was thinnest.

No improvement in the fortunes of the original anarchists through immigration to what was then called the New World would have made them good citizens. From centuries of secret war against particular forms of authority in their own countries they had inherited a bitter antagonism to all authority, even the most beneficent. In their new home they were worse than in their old. In the sunshine of opportunity the rank and sickly growth of their perverted natures became hardy, vigorous, bore fruit. They surrounded themselves with proselytes from the ranks of the idle, the vicious, the unsuccessful. They stimulated and organized discontent. Every one of them became a center of moral and political contagion. To those as yet unprepared to accept anarchy was offered the milder dogma of Socialism, and to those even weaker in the faith something vaguely called Reform. Each was initiated into that degree to which the induration of his conscience and the character of his discontent made him eligible, and in which he could be most serviceable, the body of the people still cheating themselves with the false sense of security begotten of the belief that they were somehow exempt from the operation of all agencies inimical to their national welfare and integrity. Human nature, they thought, was different in the West from what it was in the East: in the New World the old causes would not have the old effects: a republic had some inherent vitality of its own, entirely independent of any action intended to keep it alive. They felt that words and phrases had some talismanic power, and charmed themselves asleep by repeating "liberty," "all men equal before the law," "dictates of conscience," "free speech" and all manner of such incantation to exorcise the spirits of the night. And when they could no longer close their eyes to the dangers environing them; when they saw at last that what they had mistaken for the magic power of their form of government and its assured security was really its radical weakness and subjective peril—they found their laws inadequate to repression of the enemy, the enemy too strong to permit the enactment of adequate laws. The belief that a malcontent armed with freedom of speech, a newspaper, a vote and a rifle is less dangerous than a malcontent with a still tongue in his head, empty hands and under police surveillance was abandoned, but all too late. From its fatuous dream the nation was awakened by the noise of arms, the shrieks of women and the red glare of burning cities.

Beginning with the slaughter at St. Louis on a night in the year 1920, when no fewer than twenty-two thousand citizens were slain in the streets and half the city destroyed, massacre followed massacre with frightful rapidity. New York fell in the month following, many thousands of its inhabitants escaping fire and sword only to be driven into the bay and drowned, "the roaring of the water in their ears," says Bardeal, "augmented by the hoarse clamor of their red-handed pursuers, whose blood-thirst was unsated by the sea." A week later Washington was destroyed, with all its public buildings and archives; the President and his Ministry were slain, Congress was dispersed, and an unknown number of officials and private citizens perished. Of all the principal cities only Chicago and San Francisco escaped. The people of the former were all anarchists and the latter was valorously and successfully defended by the Chinese.

The urban anarchists were eventually subdued and some semblance of order was restored, but greater woes and sharper shames awaited this unhappy nation, as we shall see.

In turning from this branch of our subject to consider the causes of the failure and bloody disruption of the great American republic other than those inherent in the form of government, it may not be altogether unprofitable to glance briefly at what seems to a superficial view the inconsistent phenomenon of great material prosperity. It is not to be denied that this unfortunate people was at one time singularly prosperous, in so far as national wealth is a measure and proof of prosperity. Among nations it was the richest nation. But at how great a sacrifice of better things was its wealth obtained! By the neglect of all education except that crude, elementary sort which fits men for the coarse delights of business and affairs but confers no capacity of rational enjoyment; by exalting the worth of wealth and making it the test and touchstone of merit; by ignoring art, scorning literature and despising science, except as these might contribute to the glutting of the purse; by setting up and maintaining an artificial standard of morals which condoned all offenses against the property and peace of every one but the condoner; by pitilessly crushing out of their natures every sentiment and aspiration unconnected with accumulation of property, these civilized savages and commercial barbarians attained their sordid end. Before they had rounded the first half-century of their existence as a nation they had sunk so low in the scale of morality that it was considered nothing discreditable to take the hand and even visit the house of a man who had grown rich by means notoriously corrupt and dishonorable; and Harley declares that even the editors and writers of newspapers, after fiercely assailing such men in their journals, would be seen "hobnobbing" with them in public places. (The nature of the social ceremony named the "hobnob" is not now understood, but it is known that it was a sign of amity and favor.) When men or nations devote all the powers of their minds and bodies to the heaping up of wealth, wealth is heaped up. But what avails it? It may not be amiss to quote here the words of one of the greatest of the ancients whose works—fragmentary, alas—have come down to us.

"Wealth has accumulated itself into masses; and poverty, also in accumulation enough, lies impassably separated from it; opposed, uncommunicating, like forces in positive and negative poles. The gods of this lower world sit aloft on glittering thrones, less happy than Epicurus's gods, but as indolent, as impotent; while the boundless living chaos of ignorance and hunger welters, terrific in its dark fury, under their feet. How much among us might be likened to a whited sepulcher: outwardly all pomp and strength, but inwardly full of horror and despair and dead men's bones! Iron highways, with their wains fire-winged, are uniting all the ends of the land; quays and moles, with their innumerable stately fleets, tame the ocean into one pliant bearer of burdens; labor's thousand arms, of sinew and of metal, all-conquering everywhere, from the tops of the mount down to the depths of the mine and the caverns of the sea, ply unweariedly for the service of man; yet man remains unserved. He has subdued this planet, his habitation and inheritance, yet reaps no profit from the victory. Sad to look upon: in the highest stage of civilization nine-tenths of mankind have to struggle in the lowest battle of savage or even animal man—the battle against famine. Countries are rich, prosperous in all manner of increase, beyond example; but the men of these countries are poor, needier than ever of all sustenance, outward and inward; of belief, of knowledge, of money, of food."

To this somber picture of American "prosperity" in the nineteenth century nothing of worth can be added by the most inspired artist. Let us simply inscribe upon the gloomy canvas the memorable words of an illustrious poet of the period:

That country speeds to an untoward fate,
Where men are trivial and gold is great.

One of the most "sacred" rights of the ancient American was the trial of an accused person by "a jury of his peers." This, in America, was a right secured to him by a written constitution. It was almost universally believed to have had its origin in Magna Carta, a famous document which certain rebellious noblemen of another country had compelled their sovereign to sign under a threat of death. That celebrated "bill of rights" has not all come down to us, but researches of the learned have made it certain that it contained no mention of trial by jury, which, indeed, was unknown to its authors. The words *judicium parium* meant to them something entirely different —the judgment of the entire community of freemen. The words and the practice they represented antedated Magna Carta by many centuries and were common to the Franks and other Germanic nations, amongst whom a trial "jury" consisted of persons having a knowledge of the matter to be determined— persons who in later times were called "witnesses" and rigorously excluded from the seats of judgment.

It is difficult to conceive a more clumsy and ineffective machinery for ascertaining truth and doing justice than a jury of twelve men of the average intelligence, even among ourselves. What, then, must this device have been among the half-civilized tribes of the Connected States of America! Nay, the case is worse than that, for it was the practice to prevent men of even the average intelligence from serving as jurors. Jurors had to be residents of the locality of the crime charged, and every crime was made a matter of public notoriety long before the accused was brought to trial; yet, as a rule, he who had read or talked about the trial was held disqualified to serve. This in a country where, when a man who could read was not reading about local crimes he was talking about them, or if doing neither was doing something worse!

To the twelve men so chosen the opposing lawyers addressed their disingenuous pleas and for their consideration the witnesses presented their carefully rehearsed testimony, most of it false. So unintelligent were these juries that a great part of the time in every trial was consumed in keeping from them certain kinds of evidence with which they could not be trusted; yet the lawyers were permitted to submit to them any kind of misleading argument that they pleased and fortify it with innuendoes without relevancy and logic without sense. Appeals to their passions, their sympathies, their prejudices, were regarded as legitimate influences and tolerated by the judges on the theory that each side's offenses would about offset those of the other. In a criminal case it was expected that the prosecutor would declare repeatedly and in the most solemn manner his belief in the guilt of the person accused, and that the attorney for the defense would affirm with equal gravity his conviction of his client's innocence. How could they impress the jury with a belief which they did not themselves venture to affirm? It is not recorded that any lawyer ever rebelled against the iron authority of these conditions and stood for truth and conscience. They were, indeed, the conditions of his existence as a lawyer, a fact which they easily persuaded themselves mitigated the baseness of their obedience to them, or justified it altogether.

The judges, as a rule, were no better, for before they could become judges they must have been advocates, with an advocate's fatal disabilities of judgment. Most of them depended for their office upon the favor of the people, which, also, was fatal to the independence, the dignity and the impartiality to which they laid so solemn claim. In their decisions they favored, so far as they dared, every interest, class or person powerful enough to help or hurt them in an election. Holding their high office by so precarious a tenure, they were under strong temptation to enrich themselves from the serviceable purses of wealthy litigants, and in disregard of justice to cultivate the favor of the attorneys practicing before them, and before whom they might soon be compelled themselves to practice.

In the higher courts of the land, where juries were unknown and appointed judges held their seats for life, these awful conditions did not obtain, and there Justice might have been content to dwell, and there she actually did sometimes set her foot. Unfortunately, the great judges had the consciences of their education. They had crept to place through the slime of the lower courts and their robes of office bore the damnatory evidence. Unfortunately, too, the attorneys, the jury habit strong upon them, brought into the superior tribunals the moral characteristics and professional methods acquired in the lower. Instead of assisting the judges to ascertain the truth and the law, they cheated in argument and took liberties with fact, deceiving the court whenever they deemed it to the interest of their cause to do so, and as willingly won by a technicality or a trick as by the justice of their contention and their ability in supporting it. Altogether, the entire judicial system of the Connected States of America was inefficient, disreputable, corrupt.

The result might easily have been foreseen and doubtless was predicted by patriots whose admonitions have not come down to us. Denied protection of the law, neither property nor life was safe. Greed filled his coffers from the meager hoards of Thrift, private vengeance took the place of legal redress, mad multitudes rioted and slew with virtual immunity from punishment or blame, and the land was red with crime.

A singular phenomenon of the time was the immunity of criminal women. Among the Americans woman held a place unique in the history of nations. If not actually worshiped as a deity, as some historians, among them the great Sagab-Joffoy, have affirmed, she was at least regarded with feelings of veneration which the modern mind has a difficulty in comprehending. Some degree of compassion for her mental inferiority, some degree of forbearance toward her infirmities of temper, some degree of immunity for the offenses which these peculiarities entail—these are common to all peoples above the grade of barbarians. In ancient America these chivalrous sentiments found open and lawful expression only in relieving woman of the burden of participation in political and military service; the laws gave her no express exemption from responsibility for crime. When she murdered, she was arrested; when arrested, brought to trial—though the origin and meaning of those observances are not now known. Gunkux, whose researches into the jurisprudence of antiquity enable him to speak with commanding authority of many things, gives us here nothing better than the conjecture that the trial of women for murder, in the nineteenth century and a part of the twentieth, was the survival of an earlier custom of actually convicting and punishing them, but it seems extremely improbable that a people that once put its female assassins to death would ever have relinquished the obvious advantages of the practice while retaining with purposeless tenacity some of its costly preliminary forms. Whatever may have been the reason, the custom was observed with all the gravity of a serious intention. Gunkux professes knowledge of one or two instances (he does not name his authorities) where matters went so far as conviction and sentence, and adds that the mischievous sentimentalists who had always lent themselves to the solemn jest by protestations of great *vraisemblance* against "the judicial killing of women," became really alarmed and filled the land with their lamentations. Among the phenomena of brazen effrontery he classes the fact that some of these loud protagonists of the right of women to assassinate unpunished were themselves women! Howbeit, the sentences, if ever pronounced, were never executed, and during the first quarter of the twentieth century the meaningless custom of bringing female assassins to trial was abandoned. What the effect was of their exemption from this considerable inconvenience we have not the data to conjecture, unless we understand as an allusion to it some otherwise obscure words of the famous Edward Bok, the only writer of the period whose work has survived. In his monumental essay on barbarous penology, entitled "Slapping the Wrist," he couples "woman's emancipation from the trammels of law" and "man's better prospect of death" in a way that some have construed as meaning that he regarded them as cause and effect. It must be said, however, that this interpretation finds no support in the general character of his writing, which is exceedingly humane, refined and womanly.

It has been said that the writings of this great man are the only surviving work of his period, but of that we are not altogether sure. There exists a fragment of an anonymous essay on woman's legal responsibility which many Americologists think belongs to the beginning of the twentieth century. Certainly it could not have been written later than the middle of it, for at that time woman had been definitely released from any responsibility to any law but that of her own will. The essay is an argument against even such imperfect exemption as she had in its author's time.

"It has been urged," the writer says, "that women, being less rational and more emotional than men, should not be held accountable in the same degree. To this it may be answered that punishment for crime is not intended to be retaliatory, but admonitory and deterrent. It is, therefore, peculiarly necessary to those not easily reached by other forms of warning and dissuasion. Control of the wayward is not to be sought in reduction of restraints, but in their multiplication. One who cannot be curbed by reason may be curbed by fear, a familiar truth which lies at the foundation of all penological systems. The argument for exemption of women is equally cogent for exemption of habitual criminals, for they too are abnormally inaccessible to reason, abnormally disposed to obedience to the suasion of their unregulated impulses and passions. To free them from the restraints of the fear of punishment would be a bold innovation which has as yet found no respectable proponent outside their own class.

"Very recently this dangerous enlargement of the meaning of the phrase 'emancipation of woman' has been fortified with a strange advocacy by the female 'champions of their sex.' Their argument runs this way: 'We are denied a voice in the making of the laws relating to infliction of the death penalty; it is unjust to hold us to an accountability to which we have not assented.' Of course this argument is as broad as the entire body of law; it amounts to nothing less than a demand for general immunity from all laws, for to none of them has woman's assent been asked or given. But let us consider this amazing claim with reference only to the proposal in the service and promotion of which it is now urged: exemption of women from the death penalty for murder. In the last analysis it is seen to be a simple demand for compensation. It says: 'You owe us a *solatium*. Since you deny us the right to vote, you should give us the right to assassinate. We do not appraise it at so high a valuation as the other franchise, but we do value it.'

"Apparently they do: without legal, but with virtual, immunity from punishment, the women of this country take an average of one thousand lives annually, nine in ten being the lives of men. Juries of men, incited and sustained by public opinion, have actually deprived every adult male American of the right to live. If the death of any man is desired by any woman for any reason he is without protection. She has only to kill him and say that he wronged or insulted her. Certain almost incredible recent instances prove that no woman is too base for immunity, no crime against life sufficiently rich in all the elements of depravity to compel a conviction of the assassin, or, if she is convicted and sentenced, her punishment by the public executioner."

In this interesting fragment, quoted by Bogul in his "History of an Extinct Civilization," we learn something of the shame and peril of American citizenship under institutions which, not having run their foreordained course to the unhappy end, were still in some degree supportable. What these institutions became afterward is a familiar story. It is true that the law of trial by jury was repealed. It had broken down, but not until it had sapped the whole nation's respect for all law, for all forms of authority, for order and private virtues. The people whose rude forefathers in another land it had served roughly to protect against their tyrants, it had lamentably failed to protect against themselves, and when in madness they swept it away, it was not as one renouncing an error, but as one impatient of the truth which the error is still believed to contain. They flung it away, not as an ineffectual restraint, but as a restraint; not because it was no longer an instrument of justice for the determination of truth, but because they feared that it might again become such. In brief, trial by jury was abolished only when it had provoked anarchy.

Before turning to another phase of this ancient civilization I cannot forbear to relate, after the learned and ingenious Gunkux, the only known instance of a public irony expressing itself in the sculptor's noble art. In the ancient city of Hohokus once stood a monument of colossal size and impressive dignity. It was erected by public subscription to the memory of a man whose only distinction consisted in a single term of service as a juror in a famous murder trial, the details of which have not come down to us. This occupied the court and held public attention for many weeks, being bitterly contested by both prosecution and defense. When at last it was given to the jury by the judge in the most celebrated charge that had ever been delivered from the bench, a ballot was taken at once. The jury stood eleven for acquittal to one for conviction. And so it stood at every ballot of the more than fifty that were taken during the fortnight that the jury was locked up for deliberation. Moreover, the dissenting juror would not argue the matter; he would listen with patient attention while his eleven indignant opponents thundered their opinions into his ears, even when they supported them with threats of personal violence; but not a word would he say. At last a disagreement was formally entered, the jury discharged and the obstinate juror chased from the city by the maddened populace. Despairing of success in another trial and privately admitting his belief in the prisoner's innocence, the public prosecutor moved for his release, which the judge ordered with remarks plainly implying his own belief that the wrong man had been tried.

Years afterward the accused person died confessing his guilt, and a little later one of the jurors who had been sworn to try the case admitted that he had attended the trial on the first day only, having been personated during the rest of the proceedings by a twin brother, the obstinate member, who was a deaf-mute.

The monument to this eminent public servant was overthrown and destroyed by an earthquake in the year 2342.

One of the causes of that popular discontent which brought about the stupendous events resulting in the disruption of the great republic, historians and archæologists are agreed in reckoning "insurance." Of the exact nature of that factor in the problem of the national life of that distant day we are imperfectly informed; many of its details have perished from the record, yet its outlines loom large through the mist of ages and can be traced with greater precision than is possible in many more important matters.

In the monumental work of Professor Golunk-Dorsto ("Some Account of the Insurance Delusion in Ancient America") we have its most considerable modern exposition; and Gakler's well-known volume, "The Follies of Antiquity," contains much interesting matter relating to it. From these and other sources the student of human unreason can reconstruct that astounding fallacy of insurance as, from three joints of its tail, the great naturalist Bogramus restored the ancient elephant, from hoof to horn.

The game of insurance, as practiced by the ancient Americans (and, as Gakler conjectures, by some of the tribesmen of Europe), was gambling, pure and simple, despite the sentimental character that its proponents sought to impress upon some forms of it for the greater prosperity of their dealings with its dupes. Essentially, it was a bet between the insurer and the insured. The number of ways in which the wager was made—all devised by the insurer—was almost infinite, but in none of them was there a departure from the intrinsic nature of the transaction as seen in its simplest, frankest form, which we shall here expound.

To those unlearned in the economical institutions of antiquity it is necessary to explain that in ancient America, long prior to the disastrous Japanese war, individual ownership of property was unrestricted; every person was permitted to get as much as he was able, and to hold it as his own without regard to his needs, or whether he made any good use of it or not. By some plan of distribution not now understood even the habitable surface of the earth, with the minerals beneath, was parceled out among the favored few, and there was really no place except at sea where children of the others could lawfully be born. Upon a part of the dry land that he had been able to acquire, or had leased from another for the purpose, a man would build a house worth, say, ten thousand *drusoes.* (The ancient unit of value was the "dollar," but nothing is now known as to its actual worth.) Long before the building was complete the owner was beset by "touts" and "cappers" of the insurance game, who poured into his ears the most ingenious expositions of the advantages of betting that it would burn down—for with incredible fatuity the people of that time continued, generation after generation, to build inflammable habitations. The persons whom the capper represented—they called themselves an "insurance company"—stood ready to accept the bet, a fact which seems to have generated no suspicion in the mind of the house-owner. Theoretically, of course, if the house did burn payment of the wager would partly or wholly recoup the winner of the bet for the loss of his house, but in fact the result of the transaction was commonly very different. For the privilege of betting that his property would be destroyed by fire the owner had to pay to the gentleman betting that it would not be, a certain percentage of its value every year, called a "premium." The amount of this was determined by the company, which employed statisticians and actuaries to fix it at such a sum that, according to the law of probabilities, long before the house was "due to burn," the company would have received more than the value of it in premiums. In other words, the owner of the house would himself supply the money to pay his bet, and a good deal more.

But how, it may be asked, could the company's actuary know that the man's house would last until he had paid in more than its insured value in premiums—more, that is to say, than the company would have to pay back? He could not, but from his statistics he could know how many houses in ten thousand of that kind burned in their first year, how many in their second, their third, and so on. That was all that he needed to know, the house-owners knowing nothing about it. He fixed his rates according to the facts, and the occasional loss of a bet in an individual instance did not affect the certainty of a general winning. Like other professional gamblers, the company expected to lose sometimes, yet knew that in the long run it *must* win; which meant that in any special case it would *probably* win. With a thousand gambling games open to him in which the chances were equal, the infatuated dupe chose to "sit into" one where they were against him! Deceived by the cappers' fairy tales, dazed by the complex and incomprehensible "calculations" put forth for his undoing, and having ever in the ear of his imagination the crackle and roar of the impoverishing flames, he grasped at the hope of beating—in an unwelcome way, it is true—"the man that kept the table." He must have known for a certainty that if the company could afford to insure him he could not afford to let it. He must have known that the whole body of the insured paid to the insurers more than the insurers paid to them; otherwise the business could not have been conducted. This they cheerfully admitted; indeed, they proudly affirmed it. In fact, insurance companies were the only professional gamblers that had the incredible hardihood to parade their enormous winnings as an inducement to play against their game. These winnings ("assets," they called them) proved their ability, they said, to pay when they lost; and that was indubitably true. What they did not prove, unfortunately, was the *will* to pay, which from the imperfect court records of the period that have come down to us, appears frequently to have been lacking. Gakler relates that in the instance of the city of San Francisco (somewhat doubtfully identified by Macronus as the modern fishing-village of Gharoo) the disinclination of the insurance companies to pay their bets had the most momentous consequences.

In the year 1906 San Francisco was totally destroyed by fire. The conflagration was caused by the friction of a pig scratching itself against an angle of a wooden building. More than one hundred thousand persons perished, and the loss of property is estimated by Kobo-Dogarque at one and a half million *drusoes*. On more than two-thirds of this enormous sum the insurance companies had laid bets, and the greater part of it they refused to pay. In justification they pointed out that the deed performed by the pig was "an act of God," who in the analogous instance of the express companies had been specifically forbidden to take any action affecting the interests of parties to a contract, or the result of an agreed undertaking.

In the ensuing litigation their attorneys cited two notable precedents. A few years before the San Francisco disaster, another American city had experienced a similar one through the upsetting of a lamp by the kick of a cow. In that case, also, the insurance companies had successfully denied their liability on the ground that the cow, manifestly incited by some supernatural power, had unlawfully influenced the result of a wager to which she was not a party. The companies defendant had contended that the recourse of the property-owners was against, not them, but the owner of the cow. In his decision sustaining that view and dismissing the case, a learned judge (afterward president of one of the defendant companies) had in the legal phraseology of the period pronounced the action of the cow an obvious and flagrant instance of unwarrantable intervention. Kobo-Dogarque believes that this decision was afterward reversed by an appellate court of contrary political complexion and the companies were compelled to compromise, but of this there is no record. It is certain that in the San Francisco case the precedent was urged.

Another precedent which the companies cited with particular emphasis related to an unfortunate occurrence at a famous millionaires' club in London, the capital of the renowned king, John Bul. A gentleman passing in the street fell in a fit and was carried into the club in convulsions. Two members promptly made a bet upon his life. A physician who chanced to be present set to work upon the patient, when one of the members who had laid the wager came forward and restrained him, saying: "Sir, I beg that you will attend to your own business. I have my money on that fit."

Doubtless these two notable precedents did not constitute the entire case of the defendants in the San Francisco insurance litigation, but the additional pleas are lost to us.

Of the many forms of gambling known as insurance that called life insurance appears to have been the most vicious. In essence it was the same as fire insurance, marine insurance, accident insurance and so forth, with an added offensiveness in that it was a betting on human lives—commonly by the policy-holder on lives that should have been held most sacred and altogether immune from the taint of traffic. In point of practical operation this ghastly business was characterized by a more fierce and flagrant dishonesty than any of its kindred pursuits. To such lengths of robbery did the managers go that at last the patience of the public was exhausted and a comparatively trivial occurrence fired the combustible elements of popular indignation to a white heat in which the entire insurance business of the country was burned out of existence, together with all the gamblers who had invented and conducted it. The president of one of the companies was walking one morning in a street of New York, when he had the bad luck to step on the tail of a dog and was bitten in retaliation. Frenzied by the pain of the wound, he gave the creature a savage kick and it ran howling toward a group of idlers in front of a grocery store. In ancient America the dog was a sacred animal, worshiped by all sorts and conditions of tribesmen. The idlers at once raised a great cry, and setting upon the offender beat him so that he died.

Their act was infectious: men, women and children trooped out of their dwellings by thousands to join them, brandishing whatever weapons they could snatch, and uttering wild cries of vengeance. This formidable mob overpowered the police, and marching from one insurance office to another, successively demolished them all, slew such officers as they could lay hands on, and chased the fugitive survivors into the sea, "where," says a quaint chronicle of the time, "they were eaten by their kindred, the sharks." This carnival of violence continued all the day, and at set of sun not one person connected with any form of insurance remained alive.

Ferocious and bloody as was the massacre, it was only the beginning. As the news of it went blazing and coruscating along the wires by which intelligence was then conveyed across the country, city after city caught the contagion. Everywhere, even in the small hamlets and the agricultural districts, the dupes rose against their dupers. The smoldering resentment of years burst into flame, and within a week all that was left of insurance in America was the record of a monstrous and cruel delusion written in the blood of its promoters.

A remarkable feature of the crude and primitive civilization of the Americans was their religion. This was polytheistic, as is that of all backward peoples, and among their minor deities were their own women. This has been disputed by respectable authorities, among them Gunkux and the younger Kekler, but the weight of archæological testimony is against them, for, as Sagab-Joffy ingeniously points out, none of less than divine rank would by even the lowest tribes be given unrestricted license to kill. Among the Americans woman, as already pointed out, indubitably had that freedom, and exercised it with terrible effect, a fact which makes the matter of their religion pertinent to the purpose of this monograph. If ever an American woman was punished by law for murder of a man no record of the fact is found; whereas, such American literature as we possess is full of the most enthusiastic adulation of the impossible virtues and imaginary graces of the human female. One writer even goes to the length of affirming that respect for the sex is the foundation of political stability, the cornerstone of civil and religious liberty! After the break-up of the republic and the savage inter-tribal wars that followed, Gyneolatry was an exhausted cult and woman was relegated to her old state of benign subjection.

Unfortunately, we know little of the means of travel in ancient America, other than the names. It seems to have been done mainly by what were called "railroads," upon which wealthy associations of men transported their fellow-citizens in some kind of vehicle at a low speed, seldom exceeding fifty or sixty miles an hour, as distance and time were then reckoned—about equal to seven *kaltabs* a *grillog*. Notwithstanding this slow movement of the vehicles, the number and fatality of accidents were incredible. In the Zopetroq Museum of Archæology is preserved an official report (found in the excavations made by Droyhors on the supposed site of Washington) of a Government Commission of the Connected States. From that document we learn that in the year 1907 of their era the rail-roads of the country killed 5,000 persons and wounded 72,286—a mortality which is said by the commissioners to be twice that of the battle of Gettysburg, concerning which we know nothing but the name. This was about the annual average of railroad casualties of the period, and if it provoked comment it at least led to no reform, for at a later period we find the mortality even greater. That it was preventable is shown by the fact that in the same year the railroads of Great Britain, where the speed was greater and the intervals between vehicles less, killed only one passenger. It was a difference of government: Great Britain had a government that governed; America had not. Happily for humanity, the kind of government that does not govern, self-government, "government of the people, by the people and for the people" (to use a meaningless paradox of that time) has perished from the face of the earth.

An inherent weakness in republican government was that it assumed the honesty and intelligence of the majority, "the masses," who were neither honest nor intelligent. It would doubtless have been an excellent government for a people so good and wise as to need none. In a country having such a system the leaders, the politicians, must necessarily all be demagogues, for they can attain to place and power by no other method than flattery of the people and subserviency to the will of the majority. In all the ancient American political literature we look in vain for a single utterance of truth and reason regarding these matters. In none of it is a hint that the multitude was ignorant and vicious, as we know it to have been, and as it must necessarily be in any country, to whatever high average of intelligence and morality the people attain; for "intelligence" and "morality" are comparative terms, the standard of comparison being the intelligence and morality of the wisest and best, who must always be the few. Whatever general advance is made, those not at the head are behind—are ignorant and immoral according to the new standard, and unfit to control in the higher and broader policies demanded by the progress made. Where there is true and general progress the philosopher of yesterday would be the ignoramus of to-day, the honorable of one generation the vicious of another. The peasant of our time is incomparably superior to the statesman of ancient America, yet he is unfit to govern, for there are others more fit.

That a body of men can be wiser than its wisest member seems to the modern understanding so obvious and puerile an error that it is inconceivable that any people, even the most primitive, could ever have entertained it; yet we know that in America it was a fixed and steadfast political faith. The people of that day did not, apparently, attempt to explain how the additional wisdom was acquired by merely assembling in council, as in their "legislatures"; they seem to have assumed that it was so, and to have based their entire governmental system upon that assumption, with never a suspicion of its fallacy. It is like assuming that a mountain range is higher than its highest peak. In the words of Golpek, "The early Americans believed that units of intelligence were addable quantities," or as Soseby more wittily puts it, "They thought that in a combination of idiocies they had the secret of sanity."

The Americans, as has been said, never learned that even among themselves majorities ruled, not because they ought, but because they could—not because they were wise, but because they were strong. The count of noses determined, not the better policy, but the more powerful party. The weaker submitted, as a rule, for it had to or risk a war in which it would be at a disadvantage. Yet in all the early years of the republic they seem honestly to have dignified their submission as "respect for the popular verdict." They even quoted from the Latin language the sentiment that "the voice of the people is the voice of God." And this hideous blasphemy was as glib upon the lips of those who, without change of mind, were defeated at the polls year after year as upon those of the victors.

Of course, their government was powerless to restrain any aggression or encroachment upon the general welfare as soon as a considerable body of voters had banded together to undertake it. A notable instance has been recorded by Bamscot in his great work, "Some Evil Civilizations." After the first of America's great intestinal wars the surviving victors formed themselves into an organization which seems at first to have been purely social and benevolent, but afterward fell into the hands of rapacious politicians who in order to preserve their power corrupted their followers by distributing among them enormous sums of money exacted from the government by threats of overturning it. In less than a half century after the war in which they had served, so great was the fear which they inspired in whatever party controlled the national treasury that the total sum of their exactions was no less annually than seventeen million *prastams*! As Dumbleshaw naïvely puts it, "having saved their country, these gallant gentlemen naturally took it for themselves." The eventual massacre of the remnant of this hardy and impenitent organization by the labor unions more accustomed to the use of arms is beyond the province of this monograph to relate. The matter is mentioned at all only because it is a typical example of the open robbery that marked that period of the republic's brief and inglorious existence; the Grand Army, as it called itself, was no worse and no better than scores of other organizations having no purpose but plunder and no method but menace. A little later nearly all classes and callings became organized conspiracies, each seeking an unfair advantage through laws which the party in power had not the firmness to withhold, nor the party hoping for power the courage to oppose. The climax of absurdity in this direction was reached in 1918, when an association of barbers, known as Noblemen of the Razor, procured from the parliament of the country a law giving it a representative in the President's Cabinet, and making it a misdemeanor to wear a beard.

In Soseby's "History of Popular Government" he mentions "a monstrous political practice known as 'Protection to American Industries.'" Modern research has not ascertained precisely what it was; it is known rather from its effects than in its true character, but from what we can learn of it to-day I am disposed to number it among those malefic agencies concerned in the destruction of the American republics, particularly the Connected States, although it appears not to have been peculiar to "popular government." Some of the contemporary monarchies of Europe were afflicted with it, but by the divine favor which ever guards a throne its disastrous effects were averted. "Protection" consisted in a number of extraordinary expedients, the purposes of which and their relations to one another cannot with certainty be determined in the present state of our knowledge. Debrethin and others agree that one feature of it was the support, by general taxation, of a few favored citizens in public palaces, where they passed their time in song and dance and all kinds of revelry. They were not, however, altogether idle, being required out of the sums bestowed upon them, to employ a certain number of men each in erecting great piles of stone and pulling them down again, digging holes in the ground and then filling them with earth, pouring water into casks and then drawing it off, and so forth. The unhappy laborers were subject to the most cruel oppressions, but the knowledge that their wages came from the pockets of those whom their work nowise benefited was so gratifying to them that nothing could induce them to leave the service of their heartless employers to engage in lighter and more useful labor.

Another characteristic of "Protection" was the maintenance at the principal seaports of "customs-houses," which were strong fortifications armed with heavy guns for the purpose of destroying or driving away the trading ships of foreign nations. It was this that caused the Connected States to be known abroad as the "Hermit Republic," a name of which its infatuated citizens were strangely proud, although they had themselves sent armed ships to open the ports of Japan and other Oriental countries to their own commerce. In their own case, if a foreign ship came empty and succeeded in evading the fire of the "customs-house," as sometimes occurred, she was permitted to take away a cargo.

It is obvious that such a system was distinctly evil, but it must be confessed our uncertainty regarding the whole matter of "Protection" does not justify us in assigning it a definite place among the causes of national decay. That in some way it produced an enormous revenue is certain, and that the method was dishonest is no less so; for this revenue—known as a "surplus" —was so abhorred while it lay in the treasury that all were agreed upon the expediency of getting rid of it, two great political parties existing for apparently no other purpose than the patriotic one of taking it out.

But how, it may be asked, could people so misgoverned get on, even as well as they did?

From the records that have come down to us it does not

appear that they got on very well. They were preyed upon by all sorts of political adventurers, whose power in most instances was limited only by the contemporaneous power of other political adventurers equally unscrupulous. A full half of the taxes wrung from them was stolen. Their public lands, millions of square miles, were parceled out among banded conspirators. Their roads and the streets of their cities were nearly impassable. Their public buildings, conceived in abominable taste and representing enormous sums of money, which never were used in their construction, began to tumble about the ears of the workmen before they were completed. The most delicate and important functions of government were intrusted to men with neither knowledge, heart nor experience, who by their corruption imperiled the public interest and by their blundering disgraced the national name. In short, all the train of evils inseparable from government of any kind beset this unhappy people with tenfold power, together with hundreds of worse ones peculiar to their own faulty and unnatural system. It was thought that their institutions would give them peace, yet in the first three-quarters of a century of their existence they fought three important wars: one of revenge, one of aggression and one—the bloodiest and most wasteful known up to that time—among themselves. And before a century and a half had passed they had the humiliation to see many of their seaport cities destroyed by the Emperor of Japan in a quarrel which they had themselves provoked by their greed of Oriental dominion.

By far the most important factor concerned in bringing about the dissolution of the republic and the incredible horrors that followed it was what was known as "the contest between capital and labor." This momentous struggle began in a rather singular way through an agitation set afoot by certain ambitious women who preached at first to inattentive and inhospitable ears, but with ever increasing acceptance, the doctrine of equality of the sexes, and demanded the "emancipation" of woman. True, woman was already an object of worship and had, as noted before, the right to kill. She was treated with profound and sincere deference, because of certain humble virtues, the product of her secluded life. Men of that time appear to have felt for women, in addition to religious reverence, a certain sentiment known as "love." The nature of this feeling is not clearly known to us, and has been for ages a matter of controversy evolving more heat than light. This much is plain: it was largely composed of good will, and had its root in woman's dependence. Perhaps it had something of the character of the benevolence with which we regard our slaves, our children and our domestic animals—everything, in fact, that is weak, helpless and inoffensive.

Woman was not satisfied; her superserviceable advocates taught her to demand the right to vote, to hold office, to own property, to enter into employment in competition with man. Whatever she demanded she eventually got. With the effect upon her we are not here concerned; the predicted gain to political purity did not ensue, nor did commercial integrity receive any stimulus from her participation in commercial pursuits. What indubitably did ensue was a more sharp and bitter competition in the industrial world through this increase of more than thirty per cent, in its wage-earning population. In no age nor country has there ever been sufficient employment for those requiring it. The effect of so enormously increasing the already disproportionate number of workers in a single generation could be no other than disastrous. Every woman employed displaced or excluded some man, who, compelled to seek a lower employment, displaced another, and so on, until the least capable or most unlucky of the series became a tramp—a nomadic mendicant criminal! The number of these dangerous vagrants in the beginning of the twentieth century of their era has been estimated by Holobom at no less than seven and a half *blukuks*! Of course, they were as tow to the fires of sedition, anarchy and insurrection. It does not very nearly relate to our present purpose, but it is impossible not to note in passing that this unhappy result, directly flowing from woman's invasion of the industrial field, was unaccompanied by any material advantage to herself. Individual women, here and there one, may themselves have earned the support that they would otherwise not have received, but the sex as a whole was not benefited. They provided for themselves no better than they had previously been provided for, and would still have been provided for, by the men whom they displaced. The whole somber incident is unrelieved by a single gleam of light.

Previously to this invasion of the industrial field by woman there had arisen conditions that were in themselves peculiarly menacing to the social fabric. Some of the philosophers of the period, rummaging amongst the dubious and misunderstood facts of commercial and industrial history, had discovered what they were pleased to term "the law of supply and demand"; and this they expounded with so ingenious a sophistry, and so copious a wealth of illustration and example that what is at best but a faulty and imperfectly applicable principle, limited and cut into by all manner of other considerations, came to be accepted as the sole explanation and basis of material prosperity and an infallible rule for the proper conduct of industrial affairs. In obedience to this "law"—for, interpreting it in its straitest sense they understood it to be mandatory—employers and employees alike regulated by its iron authority all their dealings with one another, throwing off the immemorial relations of mutual dependence and mutual esteem as tending to interfere with beneficent operation. The employer came to believe conscientiously that it was not only profitable and expedient, but under all circumstances his duty, to obtain his labor for as little money as possible, even as he sold its product for as much. Considerations of humanity were not banished from his heart, but most sternly excluded from his business. Many of these misguided men would give large sums to various charities; would found universities, hospitals, libraries; would even stop on their way to relieve beggars in the street; but for their own work-people they had no care. Straman relates in his "Memoirs" that a wealthy manufacturer once said to one of his mill-hands who had asked for an increase of his wages because unable to support his family on the pay that he was getting: "Your family is nothing to me. I cannot afford to mix benevolence with my business." Yet this man, the author adds, had just given a thousand *drusoes* to a "seaman's home." He could afford to care for other men's employees, but not for his own. He could not see that the act which he performed as truly, and to the same degree, cut down his margin of profit in his business as the act which he refused to perform would have done, and had not the advantage of securing him better service from a grateful workman.

On their part the laborers were no better. Their relations to their employers being "purely commercial," as it was called, they put no heart into their work, seeking ever to do as little as possible for their money, precisely as their employers sought to pay as little as possible for the work they got. The interests of the two classes being thus antagonized, they grew to distrust and hate each other, and each accession of ill feeling produced acts which tended to broaden the breach more and more. There was neither cheerful service on the one side nor un-grudging payment on the other.

The harder industrial conditions generated by woman's ir-ruption into a new domain of activity produced among labor-ing men a feeling of blind discontent and concern. Like all men in apprehension, they drew together for mutual protec-tion, they knew not clearly against what. They formed "labor unions," and believed them to be something new and effective in the betterment of their condition; whereas, from the earliest historical times, in Rome, in Greece, in Egypt, in Assyria, labor unions with their accepted methods of "striking" and rioting had been discredited by an almost unbroken record of failure. One of the oldest manuscripts then in existence, preserved in a museum at Turin, but now lost, related how the workmen employed in the necropolis at Thebes, dissatisfied with their allowance of corn and oil, had refused to work, broken out of their quarters and, after much rioting, been subdued by the arrows of the military. And such, despite the sympathies and assistance of brutal mobs of the populace, was sometimes the end of the American "strike."

Originally organized for self-protection, and for a time partly successful, these leagues became great tyrannies, so reasonless in their demands and so unscrupulous in their methods of en-forcing them that the laws were unable to deal with them, and frequently the military forces of the several States were ordered out for the protection of life and property; but in most cases the soldiers fraternized with the leagues, ran away, or were easily defeated. The cruel and mindless mobs had always the hypocritical sympathy and encouragement of the newspapers and the politicians, for both feared their power and courted their favor. The judges, dependent for their offices not only on "the labor vote," but, to obtain it, on the approval of the press and the politicians, boldly set aside the laws against conspiracy and strained to the utmost tension those relating to riot, arson and murder. To such a pass did all this come that in the year 1931 an inn-keeper's denial of a half-holiday to an under-cook resulted in the peremptory closing of half the factories in the country, the stoppage of all railroad travel and movement of freight by land and water and a general paralysis of the in-dustries of the land. Many thousands of families, including those of the "strikers" and their friends, suffered from famine; armed conflicts occurred in every State; hundreds were slain and incalculable amounts of property wrecked and destroyed.

Failure, however, was inherent in the method, for success depended upon unanimity, and the greater the membership of the unions and the more serious their menace to the industries of the country, the higher was the premium for defection; and at last strike-breaking became a regular employment, orga-nized, officered and equipped for the service required by the wealth and intelligence that directed it. From that moment the doom of labor unionism was decreed and inevitable. But labor unionism did not live long enough to die that way.

Naturally combinations of labor entailed combinations of capital. These were at first purely protective. They were brought into being by the necessity of resisting the aggressions of the others. But the trick of combination once learned, it was seen to have possibilities of profit in directions not dreamed of by its early promoters; its activities were not long confined to fighting the labor unions with their own weapons and with superior cunning and address. The shrewd and energetic men whose capacity and commercial experience had made them rich while the laborers remained poor were not slow to discern the advantages of coöperation over their own former method of competition among themselves. They continued to fight the labor unions, but ceased to fight one another. The result was that in the brief period of two generations almost the entire business of the country fell into the hands of a few gigantic corporations controlled by bold and unscrupulous men, who, by daring and ingenious methods, made the body of the people pay tribute to their greed.

In a country where money was all-powerful the power of money was used without stint and without scruple. Judges were bribed to do their duty, juries to convict, newspapers to support and legislators to betray their constituents and pass the most oppressive laws. By these corrupt means, and with the natural advantage of greater skill in affairs and larger experience in concerted action, the capitalists soon restored their ancient reign and the state of the laborer was worse than it had ever been before. Straman says that in his time two millions of unoffending workmen in the various industries were once discharged without warning and promptly arrested as vagrants and deprived of their ears because a sulking canal-boatman had kicked his captain's dog into the water. And the dog was a retriever.

Had the people been honest and intelligent, as the politicians affirmed them to be, the combination of capital could have worked no public injury—would, in truth, have been a great public benefit. It enormously reduced the expense of production and distribution, assured greater permanency of employment, opened better opportunities to general and special aptitude, gave an improved product, and at first supplied it at a reduced price. Its crowning merit was that the industries of the country, being controlled by a few men from a central source, could themselves be easily controlled by law if law had been honestly administered. Under the old order of scattered jurisdictions, requiring a multitude of actions at law, little could be done, and little was done, to put a check on commercial greed; under the new, much was possible, and at times something was accomplished. But not for long; the essential dishonesty of the American character enabled these capable and conscienceless managers—"captains of industry" and "kings of finance"—to buy with money advantages and immunities superior to those that the labor unions could obtain by menaces and the promise of votes. The legislatures, the courts, the executive officers, all the sources of authority and springs of control, were defiled and impested until right and justice fled affrighted from the land, and the name of the country became a stench in the nostrils of the world.

Let us pause in our narrative to say here that much of the abuse of the so-called "trusts" by their victims took no account of the folly, stupidity and greed of the victims themselves. A favorite method by which the great corporations crushed out the competition of the smaller ones and of the "individual dealers" was by underselling them—a method made possible by nothing but the selfishness of the purchasing consumers who loudly complained of it. These could have stood by their neighbor, the "small dealer," if they had wanted to, and no underselling could have been done. When the trust lowered the price of its product they eagerly took the advantage offered, then cursed the trust for ruining the small dealer. When it raised the price they cursed it for ruining themselves. It is not easy to see what the trust could have done that would have been acceptable, nor is it surprising that it soon learned to ignore their clamor altogether and impenitently plunder those whom it could not hope to appease.

Another of the many sins justly charged against the "kings of finance" was this: They would buy properties worth, say, ten millions of "dollars" (the value of the dollar is now unknown) and issue stock upon it to the face value of, say, fifty millions. This their clamorous critics called "creating" for themselves forty millions of dollars. They created nothing; the stock had no dishonest value unless sold, and even at the most corrupt period of the government nobody was compelled by law to buy. In nine cases in ten the person who bought did so in the hope and expectation of getting much for little and something for nothing. The buyer was no better than the seller. He was a gambler. He "played against the game of the man who kept the table" (as the phrase went), and naturally he lost. Naturally, too, he cried out, but his lamentations, though echoed shrilly by the demagogues, seem to have been unavailing. Even the rudimentary intelligence of that primitive people discerned the impracticability of laws forbidding the seller to set his own price on the thing he would sell and declare it worth that price. Then, as now, nobody had to believe him. Of the few who bought these "watered" stocks in good faith as an investment in the honest hope of dividends it seems sufficient to say, in the words of an ancient Roman, "Against stupidity the gods themselves are powerless." Laws that would adequately protect the foolish from the consequence of their folly would put an end to all commerce. The sin of "over-capitalization" differed in magnitude only, not in kind, from the daily practice of every salesman in every shop. Nevertheless, the popular fury that it aroused must be reckoned among the main causes contributory to the savage insurrections that accomplished the downfall of the republic.

With the formation of powerful and unscrupulous trusts of both labor and capital to subdue each other the possibilities of combination were not exhausted; there remained the daring plan of combining the two belligerents! And this was actually effected. The laborer's demand for an increased wage was always based upon an increased cost of living, which was itself chiefly due to increased cost of production from reluctant concessions of his former demands. But in the first years of the twentieth century observers noticed on the part of capital a lessening reluctance. More frequent and more extortionate and reasonless demands encountered a less bitter and stubborn resistance; capital was apparently weakening just at the time when, with its strong organizations of trained and willing strike-breakers, it was most secure. Not so; an ingenious malefactor, whose name has perished from history, had thought out a plan for bringing the belligerent forces together to plunder the rest of the population. In the accounts that have come down to us details are wanting, but we know that, little by little, this amazing project was accomplished. Wages rose to incredible rates. The cost of living rose with them, for employers— their new allies wielding in their service the weapons previously used against them, intimidation, the boycott, and so forth— more than recouped themselves from the general public. Their employees got rebates on the prices of products, but for consumers who were neither laborers nor capitalists there was no mercy. Strikes were a thing of the past; strike-breakers threw themselves gratefully into the arms of the unions; "industrial discontent" vanished, in the words of a contemporary poet, "as by the stroke of an enchanter's wand." All was peace, tranquillity and order! Then the storm broke.

A man in St. Louis purchased a sheep's kidney for seven-and-a-half dollars. In his rage at the price he exclaimed: "As a public man I have given twenty of the best years of my life to bringing about a friendly understanding between capital and labor. I have succeeded, and may God have mercy on my meddlesome soul!"

The remark was resented, a riot ensued, and when the sun

went down that evening his last beams fell upon a city reeking with the blood of a hundred millionaires and twenty thousand citizens and sons of toil!

Students of the history of those troublous times need not to be told what other and more awful events followed that bloody reprisal. Within forty-eight hours the country was ablaze with insurrection, followed by intestinal wars which lasted three hundred and seventy years and were marked by such hideous barbarities as the modern historian can hardly bring himself to relate. The entire stupendous edifice of popular government, temple and citadel of fallacies and abuses, had crashed to ruin. For centuries its fallen columns and scattered stones sheltered an ever diminishing number of skulking anarchists, succeeded by hordes of skin-clad savages subsisting on offal and raw flesh —the race-remnant of an extinct civilization. All finally vanished from history into a darkness impenetrable to conjecture.

In concluding this hasty and imperfect sketch I cannot forbear to relate an episode of the destructive and unnatural contest between labor and capital, which I find recorded in the almost forgotten work of Antrolius, who was an eye-witness to the incident.

At a time when the passions of both parties were most inflamed and scenes of violence most frequent it was somehow noised about that at a certain hour of a certain day some one —none could say who—would stand upon the steps of the Capitol and speak to the people, expounding a plan for reconciliation of all conflicting interests and pacification of the quarrel. At the appointed hour thousands had assembled to hear —glowering capitalists attended by hireling body-guards with firearms, sullen laborers with dynamite bombs concealed in their clothing. All eyes were directed to the specified spot, where suddenly appeared (none saw whence—it seemed as if he had been there all the time, such his tranquillity) a tall, pale man clad in a long robe, bare-headed, his hair falling lightly upon his shoulders, his eyes full of compassion, and with such majesty of face and mien that all were awed to silence ere he spoke. Stepping slowly forward toward the throng and raising his right hand from the elbow, the index finger extended upward, he said, in a voice ineffably sweet and serious:

"Whatsoever ye would that men should do unto you, even so do ye also unto them."

These strange words he repeated in the same solemn tones three times; then, as the expectant multitude waited breathless for his discourse, stepped quietly down into the midst of them, every one afterward declaring that he passed within a pace of where himself had stood. For a moment the crowd was speechless with surprise and disappointment, then broke into wild, fierce cries: "Lynch him, lynch him!" and some have testified that they heard the word "crucify." Struggling into looser order, the infuriated mob started in mad pursuit; but each man ran a different way and the stranger was seen again by none of them.

CHRONOLOGY

NOTE ON THE TEXTS

NOTES

Chronology

1842   Ambrose Gwinnett Bierce born June 24 in Meigs County, Ohio, the youngest of ten children of Marcus Aurelius and Laura (Sherwood) Bierce. (Both of Bierce's parents were descended from families who emigrated from England in the seventeenth century. Father worked at various times as farmer, shopkeeper, and property assessor. He maintained an extensive personal library of which Bierce later remarked: "All that I have I owe to his books." Bierce's older siblings were Abigail, Amelia, Ann, Addison, Aurelius, Augustus, Almeda, Andrew, and Albert.)

1846   Family moves to Kosciusko County, Indiana. Bierce attends school; meets Bernice ("Fatima") Wright and her sister Clara. Younger brother Arthur dies aged nine months.

1848   Twin sisters Adelia and Aurelia born; both die within a few years of their birth.

1857   Leaves family and moves to Warsaw, Indiana, where he works as printer's devil for abolitionist newspaper *The Northern Indianan*.

1859   Goes to live with uncle, Lucius Verus Bierce, in Akron, Ohio. In the fall, begins attending Kentucky Military Institute at Franklin Springs.

1860   Drops out of Kentucky Military Institute; moves to Elkhart, Indiana, and works at odd jobs.

1861   Confederates fire on Fort Sumter, April 12, beginning Civil War. Bierce enlists on April 19 for three months service in the 9th Indiana Infantry Regiment. Serves in western Virginia and sees action in the Union victories at Philippi, June 3; Laurel Hill, July 11, where his bravery in carrying a wounded soldier under enemy fire is commended in a newspaper report; and Carrick's Ford, July 13. Mustered out in late July, he reenlists in the 9th Indiana for three years and is promoted to sergeant major. Returns to Virginia and participates in actions at Cheat Mountain, October 3, and Buffalo Mountain, December 13.

1862   Bierce's regiment is sent to Nashville and becomes part of brigade led by Colonel William C. Hazen, an officer Bierce will come to admire. Confederates attack Union forces at Pittsburg Landing, Tennessee, on morning of April 6, beginning Battle of Shiloh. Bierce reaches battlefield with his regiment on night of April 6 and fights in successful Union counterattack the following day. Participates in Union advance on Corinth, Mississippi, April 29–May 30, that forces the Confederate evacuation of the town. Serves in Mississippi, northern Alabama, Tennessee, and Kentucky, June–November. Promoted to second lieutenant on December 1. Fights in Battle of Stones River, Tennessee, December 31–January 2, a Union victory.

1863   Goes into winter camp with his regiment near Readyville, Tennessee. Promoted to first lieutenant on April 24. Joins Hazen's brigade staff in May as topographical engineer, an assignment that will often require him to conduct terrain surveys close to forward Confederate positions. Fights in Battle of Chickamauga in northwestern Georgia, September 19–20, and retreats with defeated Union army to Chattanooga, which the Confederates place under siege. Helps open supply line to town in late October. Fights with Hazen's brigade during successful assaults on Orchard Knob, November 23, and Missionary Ridge, November 25, that break the siege. Receives furlough in December and visits family in Warsaw, Indiana.

1864   Becomes engaged to Bernice Wright before returning to his brigade in February. Takes part in Union offensive in northern Georgia under command of General William T. Sherman and fights in engagements at Mill Creek Gap, May 9, Resaca, May 14–15, and Pickett's Mill, May 27. While leading skirmishers at Kennesaw Mountain on June 23 Bierce is hit by a bullet that strikes his left temple and lodges behind his left ear (will later say his head had been "broken like a walnut"). Recovers in hospital at Chattanooga. Returns on furlough to Warsaw, where his engagement with Bernice Wright is broken off. Still suffering from the effects of his wound, returns in mid-September to his brigade in Georgia, now led by Colonel Sidney Post after Hazen is promoted to divisional command. Bierce is captured by Confederates while on a reconnaissance mission near Gaylesville, Alabama, in late October, but is able to escape before he is sent to prison camp. Observes Union victory at

Franklin, Tennessee, on November 30, although his brigade does not take part in the fighting. Serves on staff of division commander General Samuel Beatty during the Union victory at Nashville, December 15–16.

1865 Resigns from the army for medical reasons on January 10. Becomes Treasury Department agent charged with the collection of "captured and abandoned property," chiefly bales of cotton. Works in Selma, Alabama, under Captain Sherburne B. Eaton, a former member of Hazen's staff. Visits Panama in September.

1866 Resigns from Treasury Department and joins Hazen on inspection tour of western army forts; serves as map maker in the expectation of receiving a captain's commission in the postwar army. Inspection party leaves Omaha, Nebraska in July and travels up the Platte River and along the Bozeman Trail into Wyoming and Montana, then goes to San Francisco by way of Salt Lake City. Bierce receives commission as a second lieutenant, which he rejects.

1867 Settles in San Francisco, where he secures a job as night watchman at the U.S. Mint. Meets Bret Harte, who also works at the mint. Bierce's first published work, the poem "Basilica," appears in September in *The Californian*, followed by other poetry and prose, including his first signed essay, "Female Suffrage" (December), in which he advocates woman suffrage (a position he will reverse in later years).

1868 Writes for *Golden Era* and *San Francisco News Letter*. Publishes "Letters from a Hdkhoite" (April), a satirical fantasy set in an imaginary world. In December he becomes editor of the *News Letter* and columnist, writing 173 "Town Crier" pieces over the next three and a half years.

1869 In January publishes brief article, "Webster Revised," that represents his first attempt at satirical definitions in the manner of his later *Devil's Dictionary*. Literary acquaintances include Ina Coolbrith, Charles Warren Stoddard, and Joaquin Miller.

1871 Bierce contributes series of humorous sketches, "Grizzly Papers" (January–June), a story "The Haunted Valley" (July), and other pieces to *Overland Monthly*, edited by Bret Harte. George T. Russell, a journalist and printer, unsuccessfully sues for libel after Bierce describes him in print as a "vacant-headed simpleton" and "peripatetic liar." Bierce marries

Mary Ellen ("Mollie") Day, daughter of a prosperous mining engineer, on December 25.

1872   Resigns from *News Letter* in March; his farewell statement to readers concludes: "Cultivate a taste for distasteful truths. And, finally, most important of all, endeavor to see things as they are, not as they ought to be." Sails to England with Mollie and settles in London. Writes humorous stories for Tom Hood's *Fun*, columns ("The Town Crier," "The Passing Show") for *Figaro*, and letters on England for *Alta California*. Forms friendships with English literary figures, including George Augustus Sala, Henry Sampson, and Captain Mayne Reid. (Will later write: "I have not elsewhere heard such brilliant talk as among the artists and writers of London. I found these men agreeable, hospitable, intelligent, amusing.") Troubled by aggravation of his chronic asthma, moves with wife to Bristol in September. Son Day is born in December.

1873   *The Fiend's Delight* (John Camden Hotten) and, later in the year, *Nuggets and Dust* (Chatto & Windus) are published under the pseudonym "Dod Grile"; both consist largely of sketches and squibs reprinted from the *News Letter*. Visits Paris with wife and mother-in-law during the summer. Moves to Bath in November.

1874   *Cobwebs from an Empty Skull* published by Routledge under the name "Dod Grile"; it contains "The Fables of Zambri, the Parsee" along with other satirical stories and sketches from *Fun*. Son Leigh born April 29. Writes both issues of *The Lantern*, where he uses the title "Prattle" for a satirical column for the first time. Publishes "The Night-Doings at 'Deadman's'" (March) and first version of the essay "What I Saw of Shiloh" (April & May) in the *London Sketch-Book*. Moves in April to Leamington Spa. Has occasional meetings with Mark Twain. Tom Hood, Bierce's closest English friend, dies in November.

1875   Mollie, Day, and Leigh return to San Francisco in April; Bierce joins them in September. Resumes work at U.S. Mint. Daughter Helen born October 30. Moves family from San Francisco to San Rafael.

1876   Father dies in February. Publishes first version of "The Man Overboard" (as "Some Unusual Adventures") in *Tom*

Hood's Comic Annual for 1876. Serves as secretary of the Bohemian Club, 1876–77.

1877   Becomes associate editor of the *Argonaut*, founded by Frank Pixley. (In his first issue writes: "It is my intention to purify journalism in this town by instructing such writers as it is worthwhile to instruct, and assassinating those that it is not.") Writes ninety-two "Prattle" columns over the next two years. Begins association with writers W. C. Morrow, Emma Frances Dawson, and Richard Realf. Writes satire *The Dance of Death*, a purported condemnation of the lasciviousness of ballroom dancing, with Thomas A. Harcourt, published under the pseudonym "William Herman." (A response, *The Dance of Life*, issued shortly thereafter, is probably not by Bierce.) Publishes revised version of "The Night Doing's at 'Deadman's'" in the *Argonaut* (December).

1878   Mother dies in May. Bierce is attacked at the offices of the *Argonaut* by a reader to whose wife he had alluded in print; Bierce fends off attack with a loaded revolver, which he thereafter carries around with him. "The Famous Gilson Bequest" published in the *Argonaut* (October).

1879   "A Psychological Shipwreck" published in the *Argonaut* (May 24) as "My Shipwreck." Resigns from the *Argonaut* in June.

1880   In July becomes general agent for the Black Hills Placer Mining Company in Rockerville, Dakota Territory, whose owners include Sherburne B. Eaton. Mining operation fails and he resigns in October; spends several months in New York. Writes occasional articles for the *Californian* (including "On with the Dance!," a satirical discussion of dancing) and the *San Francisco Call*.

1881–85   Returns to San Francisco in January, and in March 1881 joins staff of *The Wasp* as columnist and associate editor; he will write 235 "Prattle" columns for the paper over the next five years. Begins publishing *The Devil's Dictionary* serially on March 5, along with fables, poems, editorials, stories, and miscellany, including "What I Saw of Shiloh" (*Wasp*, December 23–30, 1881); "A Holy Terror" (*Wasp*, December 23, 1882); "George Thurston" (*Wasp*, September 29, 1883), his first Civil War story; "A Cargo of Cat" (*Wasp*, January 3, 1885). Writes vigorous attacks on railroad barons, especially

Collis P. Huntington, Leland Stanford, and Charles Crocker. Lives largely apart from his wife and children.

1886   Publishes in *The Wasp* the stories "An Imperfect Conflagration" (March 27), "A Revolt of the Gods" (as "The Ancient City of Grimalquin," April 24), "'The Bubble Reputation'" (May 8). Resigns from *The Wasp* in May but continues writing occasional unsigned articles and editorials. "An Inhabitant of Carcosa" appears in *San Francisco News Letter* (December 25).

1887   Joins staff of William Randolph Hearst's *San Francisco Examiner* as chief editorial writer in February; on March 27 publishes first of 469 "Prattle" columns (will continue column to 1899). Writes many short stories for the paper including "Killed at Resaca" (June 5) and "The Man out of the Nose" (July 10); "Visions of the Night," an account of Bierce's weird dreams, appears July 24.

1888   Publishes stories in the *Examiner* including "A Bottomless Grave" (February 26), "One of the Missing" (March 11), "For the Ahkoond" (March 18), "The Fall of the Republic" (March 25, an early version of "Ashes of the Beacon"), "The Kingdom of Tortirra" (April 22, later incorporated into "The Land Beyond the Blow"), "A Son of the Gods" (July 29), "My Favorite Murder" (September 16), "A Tough Tussle" (September 30), "One of Twins" (October 28), along with "The Crime at Pickett's Mill" (May 27) and "Four Days in Dixie" (November 4), accounts of his Civil War experiences. Quarrels with son Day over his desire to be a journalist; Day leaves home to work on the Red Bluff (California) *Sentinel*.

1889   Bierce separates from Mollie during the winter after discovering what he believes to be love letters to her from another man, a "Danish gentleman." Remarks to a friend: "I don't take part in competitions—not even in love." Publishes stories in the *Examiner* including "Chickamauga" (January 20), "One Officer, One Man" (February 17), "A Horseman in the Sky" (April 14), "The Coup de Grâce" (June 30), "The Suitable Surroundings" (July 14), "The Affair at Coulter's Notch" (October 20), and "A Watcher by the Dead" (December 29). Day Bierce becomes engaged to Eva Atkins, a young cannery worker living in Chico, but she elopes with his best friend Neil Hubbs. When they return, Day shoots both of them, fatally wounding

Neil Hubbs, then commits suicide, dying on July 27. Bierce sees Mollie for the last time at Day's funeral.

1890 Publishes stories in the *Examiner*—"The Story of a Conscience" (June 1), "The Man and the Snake" (June 29), "An Occurrence at Owl Creek Bridge" (July 13), "The Realm of the Unreal" (July 20), "The Middle Toe of the Right Foot" (August 17)—and in the *Oakland Tribune*, "Oil of Dog" (October 11), along with the autobiographical reminiscences "A Sole Survivor" (October 18) and "Across the Plains" (November 8).

1891 Visited in January by the young California writer Gertrude Atherton. Publishes stories in the *Examiner*—"Parker Adderson, Philosopher" (February 22), "A Lady from Redhorse" (March 15), "The Boarded Window" (April 12), "The Secret of Macarger's Gulch" (April 25), "The Mocking-Bird" (May 31), "The Thing at Nolan" (August 2)—and *The Wave*: "The Widower Turmore" (January 10), "Haïta the Shepherd" (January 24), "A Baby Tramp" (August 29), and "The Death of Halpin Frayser" (December 19). *The Monk and the Hangman's Daughter*, Bierce's rewriting of a translation by Gustav Adolph Danziger of "Der Mönch von Berchtesgaden" by Richard Voss, is serialized in the *Examiner* (September 13–27); Bierce and Danziger will subsequently quarrel over literary rights to the book.

1892 *Tales of Soldiers and Civilians* published by E.L.G. Steele (dated 1891). Publishes "An Adventure at Brownville" (*Examiner*, April 3) and "The Applicant" (*The Wave*, December 25). Book publication of *The Monk and the Hangman's Daughter* (F. J. Schulte) and *Black Beetles in Amber* (Western Authors Publishing Co.), a collection of satirical verse; Chatto & Windus publishes *Tales of Soldiers and Civilians* in England under the title *In the Midst of Life*.

1893 Publishes stories "One Kind of Officer" (January 1), "John Bartine's Watch" (January 22), "The Hypnotist" (September 10), "A Jug of Sirup" (December 17) in the *Examiner*, as well as "The Damned Thing" (*Town Topics*, December 7). Story collection *Can Such Things Be?* is published by Cassell. Becomes acquainted with poet Herman Scheffauer and critic Percival Pollard.

1895 Becomes briefly acquainted with Lily Walsh, a young deaf woman whose poetry he admires; she dies later that year.

Begins association with Rachel ("Ray") Frank, who will become a leading lecturer and writer on Judaism and Jewish history. Begins correspondence with poet Edwin Markham. Feuds bitterly with fellow journalist Arthur McEwen.

1896   Travels to Washington, D.C., at Hearst's request, to lobby against funding bill postponing the repayment of debts owed by Southern Pacific Railroad magnate Collis P. Huntington. Between February and May Bierce writes more than sixty articles attacking Huntington for the *Examiner* and for the *New York Journal*, another Hearst newspaper. Funding bill is defeated in June. Bierce, exhausted and suffering from a severe recurrence of asthma, rests in New Jersey and elsewhere in the summer and early fall. Returns to San Francisco in November. Begins association with the poet George Sterling.

1897   Publishes stories "The Eyes of the Panther" (October 17) and "An Affair of Outposts" (December 19) in the *Examiner*.

1898   Writes commentary on the Spanish-American War in the *Examiner*, as well as satirical stories inspired by the conflict, "Marooned on Ug" (February 10) and "The War with Wug" (September 11), both later incorporated into "The Land Beyond the Blow." Publishes "A Little of Chickamauga," an account of the Civil War battle, in the *Examiner* (April 24). Augmented edition of *Tales of Soldiers and Civilians*, now definitively retitled *In the Midst of Life*, published by Putnam.

1899   Writes several columns (January–February) condemning Edwin Markham's poem "The Man with the Hoe" as political propaganda. Last "Prattle" column in the *Examiner* appears March 19; begins new column, "The Passing Show" on August 6; it will run until 1904. Publishes "Moxon's Master" (*Examiner*, April 16). Book publication of *Fantastic Fables* (Putnam). Leaves for Washington in December, to write simultaneously for the *New York Journal* (later *American*) and *San Francisco Examiner*. He is accompanied by Carrie J. Christiansen, a schoolteacher who becomes his secretary.

1901   Leigh Bierce dies in New York on March 31 of pneumonia after years of heavy drinking; Bierce is present at his deathbed. Publishes "At Old Man Eckert's" (*Examiner*, November 17) and "A Diagnosis of Death" (*New York Journal*,

December 8). Becomes acquainted with publisher Walter Neale.

1903   *Shapes of Clay*, a poetry collection funded by George Sterling, published by W. E. Wood. *Can Such Things Be?* reprinted by Neale Publishing Co.

1904   Writes many columns of "The Cynic's Dictionary" for *New York American* (later incorporated into *The Devil's Dictionary*). Mollie Bierce files for divorce in December.

1905   "Ashes of the Beacon" published in *New York American* (February 19) and *San Francisco Examiner* (February 26). Mollie dies in April before divorce proceedings are finalized. In May Bierce begins writing for new Hearst magazine *Cosmopolitan*.

1906   *Cosmopolitan* publishes stories "One Summer Night" and "Staley Fleming's Hallucination" (March). *The Devil's Dictionary* published in book form as *The Cynic's Word Book* (Doubleday, Page). Makes final contribution to the Hearst newspapers, an installment of "The Cynic's Word Book," on July 11.

1907   Publishes "The Moonlit Road" (January) and "Beyond the Wall" (December) in *Cosmopolitan*. *The Monk and the Hangman's Daughter* reprinted by Neale Publishing Co.; a limited edition of *A Son of the Gods and A Horseman in the Sky* published by Paul Elder. Bierce arranges publication of George Sterling's poem "A Wine of Wizardry" in *Cosmopolitan* (September) and praises it in an accompanying essay. Responds to critics of the poem and of his essay in "An Insurrection of the Peasantry" (*Cosmopolitan*, December). Visits his friend S. O. Howes in Galveston, Texas during the winter.

1908   In April, Walter Neale broaches plan to publish Bierce's *Collected Works* in ten volumes (later extended to twelve). Bierce begins the work of compilation. "A Resumed Identity" published in *Cosmopolitan* (September).

1909   "The Stranger" published in *Cosmopolitan* (February). Bierce resigns from the magazine in May, ending his association with Hearst. Writes a few articles for the *Washington Herald*. *Collected Works* begins to appear; first volume (February) includes "Ashes of the Beacon," "The Land Beyond the Blow," and other political satires, as well as "Bits of Autobiography." Second volume (October) contains revised version of *In the Midst of Life*. *The Shadow on the Dial*, essay collection assembled by S. O. Howes, published in July by A. M. Robertson. Neale publishes *Write It Right*, a book on grammatical usage.

1910　　　Third volume of *Collected Works* (April) contains revised version of *Can Such Things Be?*; fourth volume (December) contains revised version of *Shapes of Clay*. Bierce returns to California for an extended visit, May–October. Meets Jack London, Mary Austin, and other writers.

1911　　　Fifth volume (revised version of *Black Beetles in Amber*), sixth volume (*The Monk and the Hangman's Daughter* and revised version of *Fantastic Fables*), seventh volume (revised version of *The Devil's Dictionary*), eighth volume (humorous and satirical stories), and ninth and tenth volumes (literary, polemical, satirical, and miscellaneous essays) of the *Collected Works* appear, March–August. Spends a month in Sag Harbor, Long Island, during the summer with relatives of George Sterling. In December attends funeral of Percival Pollard, where he makes acquaintance of H. L. Mencken.

1912　　　Final volumes of *Collected Works* appear: eleventh volume (October) contains "Antepenultimata" (revised version of *The Shadow on the Dial*), twelfth (December) contains "Kings of Beasts" (humorous essays in dialect) and miscellaneous satires, stories, and sketches. Makes last visit to California, June–October.

1913　　　Leaves Washington in October. Visits Civil War battlefields at Chattanooga, Chickamauga, Stones River, Nashville, Franklin, and Shiloh before going to New Orleans and Texas; in New Orleans, tells a newspaper reporter: "I'm on my way to Mexico, because I like the game. I like the fighting; I want to see it," and adds, "there are so many things that might happen between now and when I come back." Makes trip into northern Mexico before returning to Texas, then crosses the border again. Writes letter from Chihuahua on December 26, concluding "I leave here tomorrow for an unknown destination"; he is not heard from again, and his fate remains unknown.

Note on the Texts

This volume contains four book-length collections by Ambrose Bierce—
In the Midst of Life (Tales of Soldiers and Civilians) (1909), *Can Such
Things Be?* (1910), *The Devil's Dictionary* (1911), and *Bits of Autobiog-
raphy* (1909)—along with a selection of eight additional stories. These
collections are presented in the order in which they were first published in book form—as *Tales of Soldiers and Civilians* in 1892, *Can
Such Things Be?* in 1893, *The Cynic's Word Book* (later expanded as *The
Devil's Dictionary*) in 1906, and *Bits of Autobiography* in 1909—but
Bierce substantially rearranged the contents and revised the texts of
all but *Bits of Autobiography* after they were first published. The texts in
the present edition follow Bierce's extensively revised, twelve-volume
Collected Works (New York & Washington, DC: Neale Publishing,
1909–12), with one exception: the story "Mrs. Dennison's Head," not
included in the *Collected Works*, is reprinted from the first edition of
Bierce's *Cobwebs from an Empty Skull* (London & New York: George
Routledge & Sons, 1884), where it was first published in book form.

The Collected Works of Ambrose Bierce.   In May 1908, the young publisher Walter Neale approached Bierce with a proposal that they produce an edition of his *Collected Works*, in ten volumes, over five years.
Bierce expressed his doubts that the proposal would prove a financial
success for Neale but quickly agreed to it; he signed a contract in
June, assisted Neale in the preparation of a prospectus, and within a
couple of months had planned and largely assembled a manuscript for
the first five volumes. Finished volumes began appearing in 1909, the
first in February and the second in October; two followed in 1910, six
in 1911, and two more in 1912, Neale having decided he was able to
expand his original scheme from ten to twelve volumes. Bierce was intensely involved in the preparation of each volume: he selected the
contents, revised the texts, and with his assistant, Carrie Christiansen,
carefully corrected two sets of proofs. Though its contents were
drawn mainly from previously published works, he took the new edition as an occasion for definitive revision, leaving little untouched.
Preparing his works for the typesetter, he significantly altered the arrangements of earlier collections and in some cases extensively rewrote
earlier versions. And though he found cause for concern in some exigent
circumstances as he prepared the new edition—he complained particularly about the incompetence of Neale's printer and proofreaders,

and he sometimes struggled to find ways of fitting previously published collections into volumes arbitrarily designed at the outset to run to about 400 pages each—he retained an unusual degree of control over the form in which his works finally appeared. The *Collected Works* was not reprinted during Bierce's lifetime, nor were the individual collections it contains. The text of the present volume follows that of the *Collected Works* (except for "Mrs. Dennison's Head"); the original publication history and the extent of Bierce's revisions to prior collections is discussed below.

In the Midst of Life (Tales of Soldiers and Civilians). This second volume of Bierce's *Collected Works*, published in October 1909, contains twenty-six stories: fifteen "Soldiers" and eleven "Civilians." All of these stories had appeared initially in periodicals, mainly the *San Francisco Examiner*, between 1878 and 1897. All had been published in book form as well: fifteen in *Tales of Soldiers and Civilians* (San Francisco: E.L.G. Steele, 1891 [February 1892]), later republished in England, under a title to which Bierce strenuously objected after the fact, as *In the Midst of Life* (London: Chatto & Windus, 1892, 1898, 1910); seventeen in an expanded edition of *In the Midst of Life* (New York & London: G.P. Putnam's Sons, 1898, 1901); and nine in *Can Such Things Be?* (New York: Cassell Publishing, 1893). Bierce chose not to include, in *In the Midst of Life (Tales of Soldiers and Civilians)*, four stories included in the 1892 and 1898 editions of *Tales of Soldiers and Civilians / In the Midst of Life*: "A Tough Tussle," "An Inhabitant of Carcosa," "The Middle Toe of the Right Foot," and "Haïta the Shepherd," gathering them instead, in the *Collected Works*, in *Can Such Things Be?*

The list that follows gives further details about the original periodical appearances of the stories in the *Collected Works* text of *In the Midst of Life (Tales of Soldiers and Civilians)*. Stories collected in the American and English first editions (*Tales of Soldiers and Civilians* [1892] and *In the Midst of Life* [1892]) are marked with an asterisk (*); stories first collected in the expanded 1898 *In the Midst of Life* are marked with a section sign (§); and stories first collected in the 1893 first edition of *Can Such Things Be?* are marked with a dagger (†):

SOLDIERS
   *A Horseman in the Sky: *San Francisco Examiner*, April 14, 1889.
   *An Occurrence at Owl Creek Bridge: *San Francisco Examiner*,
      July 13, 1890.
   *Chickamauga: *San Francisco Examiner*, January 20, 1889.
   *A Son of the Gods: *San Francisco Examiner*, July 29, 1888.
   *One of the Missing: *San Francisco Examiner*, March 11, 1888.

*Killed at Resaca: *San Francisco Examiner*, June 5, 1887.

*The Affair at Coulter's Notch: *San Francisco Examiner*, October 20, 1889.

*The Coup de Grâce: *San Francisco Examiner*, June 30, 1889.

*Parker Adderson, Philosopher: *San Francisco Examiner*, February 22, 1891.

§An Affair of Outposts: *San Francisco Examiner*, December 29, 1897.

†The Story of a Conscience: *San Francisco Examiner*, June 1, 1890.

†One Kind of Officer: *San Francisco Examiner*, January 1, 1893.

†One Officer, One Man: *San Francisco Examiner*, February 17, 1889.

†George Thurston: *The Wasp* (San Francisco), September 29, 1883.

†The Mocking-Bird: *San Francisco Examiner*, May 31, 1891.

CIVILIANS

†The Man Out of the Nose: *San Francisco Examiner*, July 10, 1887.

†An Adventure at Brownville: *San Francisco Examiner*, April 3, 1892.

†The Famous Gilson Bequest: *Argonaut* (San Francisco), October 26, 1878.

†The Applicant: *Wave* (San Francisco), December 17, 1892.

*A Watcher by the Dead: *San Francisco Examiner*, December 29, 1889.

*The Man and the Snake: *San Francisco Examiner*, June 29, 1890.

*A Holy Terror: *The Wasp* (San Francisco), December 23, 1882.

*The Suitable Surroundings: *San Francisco Examiner*, July 14, 1889.

*The Boarded Window: *San Francisco Examiner*, April 29, 1891.

*A Lady from Red Horse: *San Francisco Examiner*, March 15, 1891 (as "An Heiress from Redhorse").

§The Eyes of the Panther: *San Francisco Examiner*, October 17, 1897.

While the revisions Bierce introduced in the *Collected Works* text are demonstrably authoritative, it has been argued that by 1909 he had grown remote from the spirit in which he originally conceived his *Tales* and that in rearranging them he damaged their aesthetic integrity (see Donald T. Blume, *Ambrose Bierce's Civilians and Soldiers in Context: A Critical Study*, and Blume's eclectic text of *Tales of Soldiers and Civilians*, both published by Kent State University Press in 2004). Readers of the present volume, which accepts Bierce's revisions, may nevertheless obtain a sense of Bierce's 1892 collection by following its order of presentation of the stories: "A Horseman in the Sky" through

"The Affair at Coulter's Notch" (pages 3–60), "A Tough Tussle" (262–69), "The Coup de Grâce" through "Parker Adderson, Philosopher" (61–73), "A Watcher by the Dead" through "The Suitable Surroundings" (149–88), "An Inhabitant of Carcosa" (370–73), "The Boarded Window" (189–93), "The Middle Toe of the Right Foot" (331–39), "Haïta the Shepherd" (364–69), and "A Lady from Redhorse" (194–99). The text of *In the Midst of Life (Tales of Soldiers and Civilians)* in the present volume follows that of the *Collected Works*. A line of type inadvertently dropped from the *Collected Works* text—"road in the opposite direction at headlong" at 54.22–23 in the present volume —has been supplied from the 1891 Steele edition.

Can Such Things Be?   All of the supernatural tales Bierce gathered in *Can Such Things Be?*—the third volume of his *Collected Works*, published in April 1910—had appeared in print at least once before, but Bierce revised them, in some cases extensively, for the *Collected Works*. He had published a considerably different group of stories under the same title in 1893 (New York: Cassell Publishing), and again, with the addition of a new preface, in 1903 (Washington, DC: Neale Publishing). Of the thirty-three stories contained in both the 1893 and 1903 editions of *Can Such Things Be?*, Bierce selected fourteen for inclusion in the 1910 *Collected Works*; he omitted nineteen, and added twenty-eight from other sources. (Of the nineteen omitted stories, eleven are reprinted elsewhere in the present volume: nine in the 1909 text of *In the Midst of Life (Tales of Soldiers and Civilians)*, and two in "Selected Stories.") In the list that follows, which gives details about the original periodical publication of each story in the *Collected Works* text and their subsequent publication history during Bierce's lifetime, those stories that were collected in the 1893 and 1903 editions are marked with an asterisk (*); stories first collected in the 1892 first edition of *Tales of Soldiers and Civilians* are marked with a dagger (†); one story first collected in 1898 in *In the Midst of Life* is marked with a section mark (§):

CAN SUCH THINGS BE?
   *The Death of Halpin Frayser: *The Wave* (San Francisco), December 19, 1891.
   *The Secret of Macarger's Gulch: *The Wave* (San Francisco), April 25, 1891.
   One Summer Night: *Cosmopolitan*, March 1906.
   The Moonlit Road: *Cosmopolitan*, January 1907.
   A Diagnosis of Death: *New York Journal*, December 8, 1901.
   Moxon's Master: *San Francisco Examiner*, April 16, 1899.
   †A Tough Tussle: *San Francisco Examiner*, September 30, 1899.

"MYSTERIOUS DISAPPEARANCES"
> *The Difficulty of Crossing a Field: *San Francisco Examiner*, October 14, 1888.
> *An Unfinished Race: *San Francisco Examiner*, October 14, 1888.
> *Charles Ashmore's Trail: *San Francisco Examiner*, April 14, 1888.
> Science to the Front (coda to "Charles Ashmore's Trail"): *Oakland Daily Evening Tribune*, September 27, 1890.

The text of *Can Such Things Be?* in the present volume has been taken from the 1910 *Collected Works* edition.

The Devil's Dictionary. Bierce's *The Devil's Dictionary*, first published in its entirety in June 1911 as volume seven of his *Collected Works* and not subsequently reprinted during his lifetime, gathers a selection of his contrarian "dictionary" definitions originally written over a span of three decades, between 1881 and 1911. He had begun publishing such definitions even earlier: a group of forty-eight, titled "The Demon's Dictionary," appeared in the *San Francisco News Letter and California Advertiser* on December 11, 1875, though Bierce did not subsequently republish these. He first used the title "The Devil's Dictionary" in *The Wasp* (San Francisco) on March 5, 1881—beginning with a definition for "Accuracy"—and by 1886, when he ceased writing for *The Wasp*, he had proceeded through the alphabet to "Lickspittle." He published two more groups of definitions in the *San Francisco Examiner*—beginning with "Life"—on September 4, 1887 and April 29, 1888, under the title "The Cynic's Dictionary." His original title had probably been censored by his editors at the *Examiner* or its publisher William Randolph Hearst, though no particular evidence about the matter is known to be extant. A subsequent publisher—Doubleday, Page—also disliked it, as Bierce explained in a 1906 letter to the poet George Sterling: "They (the publishers) won't have 'The Devil's Dictionary.' Here in the East the Devil is a sacred personage (the Fourth Person of the Trinity, as an Irishman might say) and his name must not be taken in vain."

No further "dictionary" items appeared for another sixteen years, and Bierce is not known to have commented on this hiatus in his project. In July 1904, however, he revived "The Cynic's Dictionary" in the *New York American*, first with new "A" definitions, then beginning again in the alphabet where he had left his project in 1888, with "Ma." By January 1905, he had proceeded part-way through the letter "P." The reappearance of Bierce's dictionary items in print may have been prompted by some discussions in the previous year with his protégés Herman Scheffauer and George Sterling about collecting his "Devil's Dictionary" items in book form. In September 1903, he wrote Scheffauer that he lacked "enough 'epigrams and aphorisms' to make a published collection," but he hoped that "some publisher of the future" might be interested in "my 'Devil's Dictionary,' which I want to keep intact." In October 1903, Sterling proposed to arrange for the publication of *The Devil's Dictionary*. (Along with Scheffauer, he had similarly arranged and paid for Bierce's *Shapes of Clay*, a book of poems published earlier in the year). Bierce declined Sterling's offer, and another in March 1905 from Robert Mackay, editor of *Success*. Instead, he decided to publish with Doubleday, Page, and in November 1905 he reported he was compiling the collection for them. He finished a draft of the book in January 1906 and signed a contract in February. In March, writing to another correspondent—S. O. Howes of Galveston, Texas, then putting together a book of Bierce's newspaper work, *The Shadow on the Dial* (1909)—he complained that Doubleday, Page had, "in the manner of publishers," wanted "some alterations made— as if I had not made enough!" and protested a new title they had suggested: "'A Few Definitions.' The idea!" Eventually, Bierce and Doubleday, Page compromised on *The Cynic's Word Book* as a title (*The Cynic's Dictionary* having been used for a 1905 volume by Harry Arthur Thompson), and he accommodated their requests for other revisions. ("My dealings with them have been most pleasant," he went on to report to Sterling.) He began proofreading in May 1906, and *The Cynic's Word Book*, including definitions from A through L, was published in October. Bierce hoped to follow up with a second volume of definitions from M through Z, but sales of the first volume ultimately failed to support this aspiration. With a sequel in mind, however, he continued to publish new definitions for "The Cynic's Word Book" in newspapers (revising his earlier title to match that of the the new collection), while the first volume was at the press, working through the alphabet to "Reconciliation" before he once again set the project aside.

He resumed in 1911, when he added *The Devil's Dictionary* to his *Collected Works*. His setting copy for the new edition was assembled first from the pages of *The Cynic's Word Book*, which he lightly revised, without attempting in any systematic way to undo the changes he had made to his original newspaper columns at the request of Doubleday, Page. To these entries (A–L), he added those (M–R) he had published in the *San Francisco Examiner* and the *New York American* but not in book form, again lightly revising. To complete the alphabet, he added a typescript mainly consisting of newly composed definitions, with some interpolation of previously published material. Throughout, he occasionally cut, added, or rearranged entries. For further detail about the prior publication history of individual definitions in *The Devil's Dictionary*, see *The Unabridged Devil's Dictionary*, edited by David

E. Schultz and S. T. Joshi (Athens: University of Georgia Press, 2000), a collection that also contains dictionary items Bierce omitted from *The Devil's Dictionary* either deliberately or inadvertently.

As with other volumes in his *Collected Works*, Bierce complained about the typesetting of *The Devil's Dictionary*. However, with his assistant Carrie Christiansen, he saw the book through second proofs and retained considerable control over the form in which his work ultimately appeared. The present volume, in addition to correcting the typographical errors listed at the end of this note, has rearranged the sequence of entries in the text of the *Collected Works* so that it follows alphabetical order: GENEALOGY now comes after GARTER rather than GENEROUS; HOMŒOPATHIST AND HOMŒPATHY after HOMILETICS rather than HOG; IN'ARDS after INADMISSIBLE rather than INK; LOGANIMITY after LODGER rather than LOGOMACHY; POLITICIAN after POLITENESS rather than POLITICS; RADICALISM, RADIUM, RAILROAD and RAMSHACKLE after RACK not READING; SANDLOTTER after SALAMANDER not SACRED; and TRUST after TRUCE not TRUTHFUL. The text of *The Devil's Dictionary* in the present volume has otherwise been taken from the *Collected Works*.

Bits of Autobiography. Bierce's *Bits of Autobiography* was first published as a distinct work in February 1909, as volume one of his *Collected Works*, and it was not reprinted during his lifetime. In assembling the new work, Bierce drew on autobiographical essays he had published over a period of twenty-five years, beginning in 1881; he revised all eleven essays, in some cases extensively, for the *Collected Works*. In the case of two of the essays, "On a Mountain" and "'Way Down in Alabam'," original publication details are now obscure: Bierce's typesetting copy of the *Collected Works*, now at the Huntington Library, includes clippings of published versions of these essays, probably from 1887–88 issues of the *San Francisco Examiner* no longer known to be extant, but they are not definitively identifiable. The remaining essays were originally published as follows:

What I Saw of Shiloh: *The Wasp* (San Francisco), December 23 and 30, 1881.

A Little of Chickamauga: *San Francisco Examiner*, April 24, 1898.

The Crime at Pickett's Mill: *San Francisco Examiner*, May 27, 1888.

Four Days in Dixie: *San Francisco Examiner*, November 4, 1888.

What Occurred at Franklin: *Cosmopolitan*, December 1906.

Working for an Empress: *The Wasp* (San Francisco), December 23, 1882.

Across the Plains: *Oakland Daily Evening Tribune*, October 18, 1890.

The Mirage: *San Francisco Examiner*, August 14, 1887.
A Sole Survivor: *Oakland Daily Evening Tribune*, October 18, 1890.

The text of *Bits of Autobiography* in the present volume has been taken from *Collected Works*, vol. 1 (1909).

Selected Stories.   The eight "Selected Stories" with which this volume concludes are presented in chronological order of first complete publication. The texts of two, marked with an asterisk (*) in the list below, have been taken from Bierce's *Collected Works*, vol. 1 ([February] 1909), where they were published as independent items; the texts of five, marked with a dagger (†), follow *Collected Works*, vol. 8 ([July] 1911), where they were published, along with other stories, in the group "Negligible Tales." One story, "Mrs. Dennison's Head," does not appear in Bierce's *Collected Works*; the text presented here has been taken from the first book version in the absence of evidence of Bierce's involvement in its subsequent publication history. Bierce revised all of these stories apart from "Mrs. Dennison's Head," sometimes extensively, when he included them in his *Collected Works*. The following list gives details of their original appearances:

> Mrs. Dennison's Head: *Fun* (London), July 12, 1873; *Cobwebs from an Empty Skull* (London and New York: George Routledge & Sons, 1874, [1878]); *Cobwebs: Being the Fables of Zambri the Parsee* (London: Fun Office, [1884]).
> †The Man Overboard: *Tom Hood's Comic Annual for 1876* (London: Fun Office, [1876?]) (as "Some Unusual Adventures").
> †Jupiter Doke, Brigadier-General: *The Wasp* (San Francisco), December 26, 1885 (as "Materials for History"); *Can Such Things Be?* (1893/1903).
> †A Bottomless Grave: *San Francisco Examiner*, February 26, 1888.
> *For the Ahkoond: *San Francisco Examiner*, March 18, 1888.
> †My Favorite Murder: *San Francisco Examiner*, September 16, 1888 (drawing on the plot first presented in "Jo Dornan and the Ram," *Fun* [London], November 15, 1873); *Can Such Things Be?* (1893/1903).
> †Oil of Dog: *Oakland Daily Evening Tribune*, October 11, 1890.
> *Ashes of the Beacon: *Collected Works*, vol. 1 (1909). The 1909 version is essentially a new work, gathering and substantially revising previously published partial versions: "The Fall of the Republic: An Article from a 'Court Journal' of the Thirty-first Century," *San Francisco Examiner*, March 25, 1888; "The Ashes

of the Beacon: Written in 3940: An Historical Monograph,"
New York American, February 19, 1905, and *San Francisco Examiner*, February 26, 1905; "The Jury in Ancient America: An Historical Sketch Written in the Year of Grace 3687, translated by Ambrose Bierce," *Cosmopolitan*, August 1905; "Insurance in Ancient America: Translated from the Work of the Future Historian," *Cosmopolitan*, September 1906.

This volume presents the texts of the editions chosen for inclusion here but does not attempt to reproduce every feature of their typographic design. The texts are reprinted without change, except for the correction of typographical errors. Spelling, punctuation, and capitalization are often expressive features, and they are not altered, even when inconsistent or irregular. The following is a list of typographical errors corrected, cited by page and line number: 467.24, glackguard; 494.31, "What!'; 496.24, Israelities; 506.5, HABEAS CORPUS. A; 506.18, "Αιδης"; 513.31, homocide; 541.19, your have; 543.23, Potter; 622.39, *pâtès*; 636.33, *celebre*; 676.20, *apres*; 715.2, cooperation; 761.32, abroad; 778.14, wordly; 784.8, betwen; 793.4, gentleman; 800.29, nightclothes.

Notes

In the notes below, the reference numbers denote page and line of the present volume; the line count includes titles and headings but not blank lines. No note is made for material found in standard desk-reference works. Biblical references are keyed to the King James Version. Quotations from Shakespeare are keyed to *The Riverside Shakespeare*, ed. G. Blakemore Evans (Boston: Houghton, Mifflin, 1974). For additional information and references to other studies, see Ambrose Bierce, *A Sole Survivor: Bits of Autobiography*, ed. S. T. Joshi and David E. Schultz (Knoxville: University of Tennessee Press, 1998), Ambrose Bierce, *The Unabridged Devil's Dictionary*, ed. David E. Schultz and S. T. Joshi (Athens & London: University of Georgia Press, 2000), S. T. Joshi and David E. Schultz, *Ambrose Bierce: An Annotated Bibliography of Primary Sources* (Westport, CT & London: Greenwood Press, 1999), and Roy Morris, Jr., *Ambrose Bierce: Alone in Bad Company* (New York: Crown Publishers, 1996).

IN THE MIDST OF LIFE: TALES OF SOLDIERS AND CIVILIANS

1.1–2 *In the Midst . . . Soldiers and Civilians*)] When he published *In the Midst of Life* (*Tales of Soldiers and Civilians*) in his *Collected Works* in 1909, Bierce restored the "Preface to the First Edition," dated San Francisco, September 4, 1891: "Denied existence by the chief publishing houses of the country, this book owes itself to Mr. E.L.G. Steele, merchant, of this city. In attesting Mr. Steele's faith in his judgment and his friend, it will serve its authors main and best ambition." No evidence is known to be extant about Bierce's attempts to publish his book before the 1891 first edition. A new edition in 1898 bore a revised preface, subsequently omitted: "In reissuing this book, with considerable alterations and additions, it has been thought expedient, for uniformity, to give it the title under which it was published in London and Leipzig. The merely descriptive name of the original American edition (published by the late E.L.G. Steele) is retained as a sub-title in order to prevent misunderstandings by purchasers—if the book be so fortunate as to have any." Steele (d. 1894), a wealthy businessman, was the head of C. Adolphe Low & Co., importers.

4.29 Grafton] A town (now in West Virginia) that was occupied by Union troops on May 30, 1861; Bierce participated in the operation.

7.20 "Peace, be still."] Mark 4:31.

10.3 A man] In the first appearance of the story (*San Francisco Examiner*, July 13, 1890), the sentence began: "One morning in the summer of 1862 a man . . ."

11.34 "unsteadfast footing,"] Shakespeare, *1 Henry IV*, I.iii.193.

12.35 Corinth] A town in northern Mississippi occupied by Union troops on May 30, 1862. See "What I Saw of Shiloh" in this volume.

21.4–5 curb . . . star] Byron, *Childe Harold's Pilgrimage* (1812), canto 3, stanza 38; the reference is to Napoleon.

24.20–21 "the thunder . . . shouting."] Job 39:25.

34.3–4 Kennesaw Mountain, Georgia] Bierce was seriously wounded at Kennesaw Mountain on June 23, 1864, and a major battle was fought there on June 27.

40.5 Missionary Ridge] A ridge overlooking Chattanooga, Tennessee, and the site of a Union victory on November 24–25, 1863.

40.33 "green and salad days"] A paraphrase of Shakespeare, *Antony and Cleopatra*, I.v.73–74.

46.1 *Resaca*] A town in Georgia and the site of a battle on May 14–15, 1864.

46.15–16 "the speaking trump of fame"] Byron, *English Bards and Scotch Reviewers* (1809), l. 400.

46.28 Stone's River] Stones River, the site in central Tennessee of one of the bloodiest battles of the Civil War, December 31, 1862–January 2, 1863.

47.24 "not a happy one,"] See W. S. Gilbert and Arthur Sullivan, *The Pirates of Penzance* (1879): "A policeman's lot is not a happy one."

61.28 "bivouac of the dead,"] The title of a poem (1847) by Theodore O'Hara (1820–1867), commemorating the Americans slain in the battle of Buena Vista, February 22–23, 1847; the phrase also occurs in line 4. Bierce used it as the title of a memoir of his Civil War experiences (*New York American*, November 22, 1903).

64.9 a herd of swine] See "On a Mountain" in this volume.

75.19 'the unwritten law'] The supposed right of an individual to avenge moral offenses committed against members of his family; here, the right of a husband to kill his wife's lover.

76.6–7 battle at Pittsburg Landing] Also known as the battle of Shiloh, April 6–7, 1862. See "What I Saw of Shiloh" in this volume.

76.17–18 "excursions and alarums,"] The sounds of war and battle, used as a stage direction in Elizabethan plays for moving soldiers across the stage.

77.3–4 unstrained quality . . . heaven] See Shakespeare, *The Merchant of Venice*, IV.i.184–86: "The quality of mercy is not strained; / It droppeth as the gentle rain from heaven / Upon the place beneath."

107.16–17   topographical engineer] Bierce began serving as a topographical engineer in May 1863.

118.5   North Beach] The waterfront region in the northernmost part of San Francisco, home at this time to much of the city's immigrant population.

118.11   "from the foundation of the city."] An English rendering of the Latin phrase *ab urbe condita*, the title of Livy's history of Rome.

124.9   that other law] Exodus 20:14: "Thou shalt not commit adultery."

124.31   Stockton asylum for the insane] The Insane Asylum of California (now Stockton State Hospital) was established in 1853.

124.36   Mission Dolores] Properly, the Mission San Francisco de Asís, founded in 1776 by Father Junipero Serra.

125.1–2   Goat Hill] Apparently a reference to Billy Goat Hill, in the Noe Valley district south of Market Street.

126.36   Ina Lillian Peterson] Niece of the poet Ina Donna Coolbrith and one of Bierce's friends and correspondents.

128.22–23   "in her habit as she lived."] See Shakespeare, *Hamlet*, III. iv.135: "in his habit as he lived."

128.25–26   mute inglorious hero] See Gray's *Elegy* (1751), l. 59: "mute inglorious Milton."

136.21   short and simple annals] See Gray's *Elegy*, l. 32: "the short and simple annals of the poor."

137.17   copper the queen] "To copper" is a term in faro, in which a player bets that a given card will lose.

146.4   toil not, neither spin] See Matthew 6:28.

146.33   goodness and joy] Bierce wrote in a letter to C. W. Doyle on December 26, 1897: "How I hate Christmas! I'm one of the curmudgeons that the truly good Mr. Dickens found it profitable to hold up to the scorn of those who take such satisfaction in being decent and generous one day in 365."

147.30–31   "read his title clear"] "When I Can Read My Title Clear" is the title of a hymn (1707) by Isaac Watts (1674–1748).

151.29   'confederate season'] Shakespeare, *Hamlet*, III.ii.256.

152.9–10   not of woman . . . Caesarean section.] See Shakespeare, *Macbeth*, V.viii.13–17.

159.37   Bloomingdale Asylum] The New York Lunatic Asylum, established in 1808 at Morningside Heights on the Upper West Side of Manhattan; renamed the Bloomingdale Insane Asylum in 1821; moved in 1894 to the Westchester division of the New York Hospital in White Plains.

160.9 Morryster's *Marvells of Science*] A fictitious author and work. Cf. "Prattle" (*San Francisco Examiner*, July 6, 1890): "*Morryster's Marvells of Science* can certainly not be obtained in the 'book market.'"

161.34 "dragons of the prime"] Alfred Tennyson, *In Memoriam*, LVI, 22–23.

162.38 "matter out of place"] "Dirt is only matter out of place; and what is a blot on the escutcheon of the Common Law may be a jewel in the crown of the Social Republic."—John Chipman Gray (1839–1915), *Restraints on the Alienation of Property* (Boston: Soule & Bugbee, 1883).

164.17 Memnon's statue] An immense statue of Memnon near Thebes, in Egypt, when broken, emitted sounds upon the rising of the sun.

169.23 sere and yellow leaf] Shakespeare, *Macbeth*, V.iii.22–23: "my way of life / Is fall'n into the sere, the yellow leaf."

173.22 Messalina] Empress Messalina Valeria (d. 48 C.E.), wife of the Roman emperor Claudius (r. 41–54 C.E.), who gained notoriety for her promiscuity.

183.14–15 phonograph] Thomas Edison invented the phonograph in 1877, but phonograph records were not sold until 1892.

194.2 CORONADO] An island near San Diego and the site of a resort hotel for the wealthy.

194.35 Blavatsky people in Northern India] Helena Petrovska Blavatsky (1831–1891), Russian mystic and founder of theosophy, lived near Madras (in southeastern, not northern, India) from 1878 to 1885.

195.13 Sepoy] The Sepoy Mutiny in 1857–58 was a large uprising of Indian soldiers (sepoys) serving in the British army.

195.20 Thugs] Members of the Thuggee cult, a group of Indian criminal gangs. They were suppressed by the British, who executed the last Thug in 1882.

196.19 Garrick] David Garrick (1717–1779), British actor and playwright.

CAN SUCH THINGS BE?

213.13 *Hali*] A fictitious prophet first mentioned in "An Inhabitant of Carcosa" (p. 370).

213.19 St. Helena] A town in Napa county. Bierce lived there and in nearby Angwin in the 1880s, as his worsening asthma compelled him to give up residence in San Francisco.

214.20–21 his sleep was no longer dreamless] The following dream is based on one that Bierce recorded in his essay "Visions of the Night," *San Francisco Examiner*, July 24, 1887.

217.14–15   thunder . . . shouting]   See note 24.20–21.

217.39–218.1   gift and faculty divine]   See William Wordsworth, *The Excursion* (1814), I.79: "the vision and the faculty divine."

221.33   Calistoga]   A town nine miles northwest of Saint Helena.

222.8   Napa]   A town about twenty miles southeast of Saint Helena; the seat of Napa county.

222.18   heeled]   Armed.

226.20–227.3   "Enthralled . . . viewless—"]   The poem is adapted from one published in "Prattle," *San Francisco Examiner*, June 12, 1887. The final stanza reads: "At last, praise God! I broke the viewless chain, / And, flying breathless to the sunny plain, / Met Dr. Josselyn. He smiled. I sought / The lesser horror of the wood again." Dr. Charles Josselyn, the fire commissioner in San Francisco, was evidently indicted on a charge of conspiracy to murder.

229.2   Indian Hill]   There were two mining towns in California named Indian Hill, one in El Dorado County north of Placerville, and another in Sierra County, five miles southwest of Goodyears Bar; given Bierce's subsequent mention of the foothills of the Sierra Nevada, he is probably referring to the latter town.

231.20–21   a more . . . of man—]   Byron, *Manfred* (1817), 3.4.4–5.

240.24   Unacquainted with grief]   See Isaiah 53:3: "He is despised and rejected of men; a man of sorrows, and acquainted with grief."

242.25   Remote . . . slow.]   Oliver Goldsmith (1728–1774), *The Traveller* (1764), l. 1.

244.26–27   "the captain of my soul."]   William Ernest Henley, "Invictus" (1875), l. 16.

244.36   THE MEDIUM BAYROLLES]   First cited in "An Inhabitant of Carcosa" (p. 370).

251.7   Chopin's funeral march]   Originally a composition for solo piano and later incorporated into Chopin's Piano Sonata No. 2 in B-flat minor, Opus 35 (1839).

255.16–18   "Life . . . sequences."]   From *The Principles of Biology* (1864–67), part I, chaps. 4–5, by British philosopher Herbert Spencer (1820–1903).

255.21   Mill]   Bierce alludes to British philosopher John Stuart Mill (1806–1873), *A System of Logic, Ratiocinative and Inductive* (1843).

257.11–12   Saul of Tarsus]   St. Paul was known as Saul prior to his conversion. See Acts 9:3–4.

257.13–14   "The endless . . . thought."]   From *The History of Philosophy from Thales to Comte* (London: Longmans, Green, 1867), I:51, by British historian and critic George Henry Lewes (1817–1878).

263.12   Philippi, Rich Mountain, Carrick's Ford and Greenbrier]   Battles occurring on June 3, July 11, July 13, and October 3, 1861, all in western Virginia. Bierce participated in all four engagements.

264.36   without form and void]   See Genesis 1:2: "And the earth was without form, and void."

282.7   Celestials]   A derisive term for the Chinese, taken from the common nickname of China, the Celestial Empire.

283.11–12   laid down . . . serpent]   An allusion to chapter 7 of Exodus.

296.30   Denneker's "Meditations."]   A fictitious author and work first cited in "A Psychological Shipwreck" (p. 326).

299.7   Gaines's Mill]   One of the Seven Days Battles, fought near Richmond, Virginia, on June 27, 1862.

299.11   bombardment of Port Royal]   On November 7, 1861, the Union navy gained control of Port Royal sound in South Carolina by bombarding the two Confederate forts that guarded the harbor.

299.13–16   A few days . . . his own line]   General Philip Henry Sheridan (1831–1888) and General George Edward Pickett (1825–1875), who fought in the battle of Sayler's Creek, Virginia, April 6, 1865. The battle was a devastating defeat for the Confederates and helped force the surrender of the Army of Northern Virginia at Appomattox Court House on April 9, 1865.

300.28–29   Stone's River battlefield]   See note 46.28.

301.3   General Hazen]   General William Babcock Hazen (1830–1887); Bierce joined his brigade staff as a topographical engineer in 1863.

302.7–8   loquacious barber of the Arabian Nights]   In the *Arabian Nights* (nights 29–30), a tailor tells the story of a barber who relentlessly pesters him with questions when all he wants is a haircut.

302.35   a square, solid monument]   See note 46.28; General Hazen had caused this memorial to be erected at his own expense while the war was still in progress.

303.3   "one with Nineveh and Tyre."]   Rudyard Kipling, "Recessional: June 22, 1897," l. 16.

306.19   Winnemucca]   The seat of Humboldt County in northwestern Nevada; founded as a trading post in 1850.

306.26   Piute Indians]   A Shoshonean tribe chiefly occupying portions of Utah and Nevada. They were the subject of an essay, "The Pi-Ute Indians of Nevada," that Bierce published in the *Golden Era*, July 4, 1868.

310.13   Sonora]   The seat of Tuolumne County in east-central California.

313.30   Modoc]   An American Indian tribe inhabiting an area of the Cascade Range in south-central Oregon and northern California.

318.31   *non sum qualis eram*] "Non sum qualis eram bonae / sub regno Cinarae" (I am not the same as I was under the rule of Cynara). Horace, *Odes* 4.13–4; used as the title of a poem by Ernest Dowson (1867–1900).

324.36   'blown by the viewless winds'] Cf. Shakespeare, *Measure for Measure*, III.i.123–125: "To be imprison'd in the viewless winds / And blown with restless violence round about / The pendant world."

327.25   "Denneker's Meditations,"] See note 296.30.

340.2   "the tragedy, 'Man'"] Edgar Allan Poe, "The Conqueror Worm" (1843), l. 39.

340.33–35   *Rough notes . . . transcription.] Leigh Bierce (1874–1901) was Bierce's second child; he died of pneumonia. Bierce wrote to George Sterling on March 12, 1906: "Yes, the 'Cosmopolitan' cat-story is Leigh's and is to be credited to him if ever published in covers. I fathered it as the only way to get it published at all. Of course I had to rewrite it; it was very crude and too horrible. A story may be terrible, but must not be horrible—there is a difference. I found the manuscript among his papers."

342.3   Auburn and Newcastle] Towns in Placer County, about four miles apart. In 1884–85 Bierce lived in Auburn, about which he wrote the satirical poem "The Perverted Village" (*Wasp*, July 5, 1884).

343.11   Putnam House] A hotel on Lincoln Way in Auburn, built in 1880. In 1900 it became the Conroy House; in 1912 it burned down, and another hotel was built on the site.

343.20–21   Bohemian Club] A prestigious social club founded by the journalist James F. Bowman, with the assistance of Bierce and others, in 1872; Bierce served as its secretary in 1876–77 but later resigned to protest what he felt was its flattery of royal and noble visitors.

346.5   "sentences letters"] Byron, *English Bards and Scotch Reviewers* (1809), l. 443.

346.10–11   veils . . . expires,] Alexander Pope, *The Dunciad* (1742), 4.649–50.

356.30   manifold paper] An early type of carbon paper.

363.20   'actinic' rays] Ultraviolet rays.

364.6   Hastur] An invention of Bierce's; later borrowed by Robert W. Chambers in *The King in Yellow* (1895) and by H. P. Lovecraft in "The Whisperer in Darkness" (1930), although their usages do not conform with Bierce's.

374.30   Big Bend] An archaic term for the wide southward curve of the Gila River southwest of Phoenix, as it skirts the Gila Bend Mountains.

382.4   Franklin, Tennessee]   Site of a battle during the Civil War, November 30, 1864, in which Bierce fought. See "What Occurred at Franklin" in this volume.

382.27   Palace Hotel]   A lavish hotel built by William C. Ralston in 1875; destroyed by the earthquake and fire of 1906.

385.3   "a still and awful red"]   Coleridge, *The Rime of the Ancient Mariner* (1798), l. 271.

389.9   Fort Phil Kearney]   Army post in north-central Wyoming.

389.9   Colonel Carrington]   Colonel (later General) Henry Beebee Carrington (1824–1912).

389.14   Captain Fetterman]   Captain William J. Fetterman of the 18th Infantry left Fort Phil Kearny on December 21, 1866 with seventy-nine soldiers and two civilians to rescue a wagon train that was being attacked by Sioux Indians; Fetterman and his entire command were killed in an ambush.

389.15   Fort C. F. Smith]   The first army post in Montana, just across the border from Wyoming.

389.19   Henry rifle]   A lever-action repeating rifle patented in 1860 and manufactured, 1862–66, by the New Haven Arms Company; the forerunner of the Winchester rifle.

392.3–4   Carthage, Tennessee]   The county seat of Smith County in north-central Tennessee; the site of a skirmish between Union and Confederate troops on January 23, 1863.

395.2–5   Readyville . . . Tullahoma]   Murfreesboro, in Rutherford county in central Tennessee, was the site of the battle of Stones River (see note 46.28). Readyville is a village about ten miles east of Murfreesboro, on the Woodbury Road; Woodbury is a town four miles east of Readyville. Tullahoma is a city in Coffee county, thirty miles south of Murfreesboro.

398.14   "green and salad days"]   See note 40.33.

398.18–19   Sir Andrew Aguecheek . . . first.]   See Shakespeare's *Twelfth Night*, III.iv.284–285: "I'd have seen him damn'd ere I'd have challeng'd him."

399.33   Society for Psychical Research]   An organization founded in England in 1882 to investigate psychic phenomena; an American branch was established in 1885.

401.2   *The Isle of Pines*]   The Isla de Pinos, an island in the Caribbean Sea, sixty miles south of Cuba; discovered by Columbus in 1494, and for the next 300 years occupied by pirates and runaway slaves, until formal colonization began in 1827.

401.3–4   Gallipolis, Ohio]   The seat of Gallia County in southern Ohio, directly south of Meigs County, where Bierce was born.

405.3–4   Cincinnati *Commercial*] A newspaper published between 1843 and 1883.

408.3   Maysville] County seat of De Kalb county in northwestern Missouri.

421.11   "In September . . . siege."] The siege of Atlanta began on July 22, 1864, and lasted until September 2, when Union troops captured the city.

428.2–3   Leamington, Warwickshire, England] Bierce lived in Leamington from April 1874 to June 1875.

430.34   Dr. Hern] Dr. Hern and his book are fictitious.

THE DEVIL'S DICTIONARY

437.9   Poor Isabella . . . abdication] Isabella II (1830–1904) abdicated the Spanish throne in 1870 following the revolution of 1868.

439.22–24   Dr. Samuel Johnson . . . abruption."] See Johnson, "Life of Cowley," *Lives of the English Poets* (1779–81).

439.25   "move in a mysterious way,"] William Cowper, "Olney Hymns" (1774), 35.1.

441.18   de Joinville] Jean de Joinville (c. 1225–1317), author of *The Life of Saint Louis*, containing an account of the Seventh Crusade led by Louis IX, in which Joinville participated.

444.6   Herodotus says] See Herodotus, *Histories* 4.45.

447.37   the ass that carried Balaam] Numbers 22:21–35.

448.1   dog of the Seven Sleepers] The Seven Sleepers of Ephesus were Christian youths said to have fled into a cave to escape the persecutions of Emperor Decius, and who awoke some two centuries later during the reign of Theodosiuis II. In Islamic tradition they were guarded by a dog keeping watching outside the cave (Qu'ran, surah 18, verses 9–26).

448.24   *facilis descensus Averni*] Virgil, *Aeneid* 6.126: "The descent to Avernus is easy." Avernus was a lake believed to be an entrance to the underworld.

455.11   *Henry Ward Beecher*] Congregationalist clergyman, social reformer, and abolitionist (1813–1887); Bierce frequently attacked him.

456.27   Zeno] Zeno of Citium (335?–263? B.C.E.), founder of the Stoic school of philosophy.

459.34–35   scripture story . . . John the Baptist on a charger] See Mark 6:24–28 and Matthew 14:6–11.

471.5–6   "men . . . days,"]   From Alexander Pope's translation of Homer's *Iliad* 5.372 and 12.540.

474.8   Senator Depew]   Chauncey M. Depew (1834–1928), U.S. senator (Republican) from New York (1899–1911).

475.27–28   Pliny . . . Cæsar]   Druids are mentioned throughout Pliny the Elder's *Natural History*. For Caesar on Druids, see *Gallic War* 6.13–16.

477.23   Brillat-Savarin]   Anthelme Brillat-Savarin (1755–1826), French jurist and author of *Physiologie du goût* (1825), a celebrated treatise on gastronomy.

478.13   Minos, Rhadamanthus, and Æacus]   Legendary Greek kings who became judges of the dead in Hades.

480.23–26   The cur . . . key.]   A parody of the first stanza of Gray's *Elegy* (1751).

482.9–10   Byron . . . "entuzy-muzy,"]   Byron uses the expression "entusimusy" (attributing it to John Braham) in a letter dated April 26, 1817.

486.12–13   "The Exile of Erin,"]   A poem by Thomas Campbell (1777–1844).

492.16–17   "how . . . refines"]   A loose quotation from Alexander Pope's *Essay on Criticism* (1711), l. 420.

492.19   "gift and faculty divine"]   See note 217.39–218.1.

492.35   Dick Watson Gilder]   Richard Watson Gilder (1844–1909), American poet and editor.

494.1–2   Gibbons . . . Potter]   James Gibbons (1834–1921), Roman Catholic bishop, archbishop, and cardinal; Henry Codman Potter (1834–1908), Episcopal bishop of New York.

496.18   Homer's narrative]   *Batrachomyomachia* (*The Battle of Frogs and Mice*), parodistic mini-epic attributed to Homer by some ancient authorities.

496.21   Dr. Schliemann]   Heinrich Schliemann (1822–1890), archeologist who discovered the site of Troy in 1871.

500.5   "in his habit as he lived."]   See note 128.22–23.

505.12   Hon. James Wilson]   Wilson (1836–1920) was secretary of agriculture under McKinley, Roosevelt, and Taft (1897–1913).

507.36   Dr. Mary Walker]   Walker (1831–1899) was a social reformer, suffragist, and a nurse and physician during the Civil War.

510.36–37   *Delectatio Daemonorum*]   A rough translation of *The Fiend's Delight* (London: John Camden Hotten, 1873), Bierce's first book.

511.1   Professor Dam]   Henry J. Dam (d. 1906), briefly a co-owner of *The Wasp* when Bierce was writing for it.

511.4   Professor Tyndall] John Tyndall (1820–1893), British physicist best known for his work on the absorption of gases by radiant heat.

511.9   *Crede expertum*] Incorrect Latin for *crede experto* ("believe one who has experienced it"), from Virgil's *Aeneid*, 11.283.

511.12–13   Professor Howison] George Holmes Howison (1834–1917), professor of philosophy at the University of California and author of several works on religion and philosophy.

513.3   Bishop Kip] William Ingraham Kip (1811–1893), first bishop of the Episcopal Church of California.

513.15   Niebuhr] Barthold Georg Niebuhr (1776–1831), German historian who revolutionized the study of ancient history.

523.7   Dr. Gunsaulus] Frank W. Gunsaulus (1856–1921), prolific writer on religion, education, and other subjects.

523.10   Professor Garret P. Serviss] Garret Putnam Serviss (1851–1929), journalist, astronomer, and novelist. He was not a professor.

525.30   Victor Hugo] Hugo conducted séances when living in political exile on the isle of Jersey.

527.4   "Heaven lies about us."] Wordsworth, "Ode: Intimations of Immortality from Recollections of Early Childhood" (1807), l. 60.

537.20   "the most pious Edward"] Shakespeare, *Macbeth*, III.vi.27, referring to Edward the Confessor (r. 1042–66). The three other quotations from *Macbeth* are from IV.iii.141–145, IV.iii.154–56, and IV.iii.150–52.

540.32   Dr. Meir Witchell] A parody of S. Weir Mitchell (1829–1914), American physician, novelist, and poet who wrote on scientific and medical subjects.

542.17   Muhlenberg, "care not to stay."] See William Augustus Muhlenberg, "I Would Not Live Alway" (1823): "I would not live alway, I ask not to stay / Where storm after storm rises dark o'er the way."

542.27–28   Bella Peeler Silcox] A parody of Ella Wheeler Wilcox (1850–1919), popular poet whose work often appeared adjacent to Bierce's in the Hearst papers. He held her work in low esteem.

543.19   Dr. Jordan] David Starr Jordan (1851–1931), professor of biology and later president of Stanford University (1891–1913).

543.23   Jane Porter] Jane Porter (1776–1850), British novelist and author of a popular historical novel, *Thaddeus of Warsaw* (1803), about Thaddeus Kosciusko.

547.9–10   Harry Thurston Peck] Peck (1856–1914) was a professor of Latin at Columbia and a literary critic and editor with whom Bierce occasionally engaged in journalistic battles.

550.15–16   Baring-Gould's *Curious Myths of the Middle Ages*] Collection
of folk legends (1866) by British writer S. Baring-Gould (1834–1924).

550.19–21   "Teddy . . . Brisbane"] "Teddy" refers to Theodore Roosevelt; John Sharp Williams (1854–1932) was a U.S. representative from Mississippi; Arthur Brisbane (1864–1936) was one of Hearst's leading writers.

550.30   the poet Gilder] See note 494.14.

550.33   Huntington] Collis P. Huntington (1821–1900), one of the "Big
Four" railroad barons whom Bierce relentlessly attacked in 1896 when Huntington was lobbying Congress to gain a lengthy extension on his repayment
of government loans for the building of the Southern Pacific Railroad.

551.13–15   Lucian, Locke . . . Newcomb] Lucian of Samosata (second
century C.E.), Greek satirist and author of the *True History*, about a voyage to
the moon; Richard Adams Locke (1800–1871), American journalist and the re-
puted author of a hoax about the inhabitants of the moon, published in the
New York Sun in 1835; Simon Newcomb (1835–1909), Canadian-born professor of mathematics and prolific writer on astronomy.

560.10   *"Mens conscia recti,"*] The proper quotation is *mens sibi conscia
recti* (Virgil, *Aeneid* 1.604): "A mind aware of the right."

563.13–14   The bones . . . monument,] From Andrew Lang's sonnet
"Homeric Unity" (1893).

567.25–26   Lewes . . . thought."] See note 257.13–14.

570.12   Disraeli . . . Wilberforce] The source of the Disraeli quotation
has not been ascertained. Disraeli would have been referring to Bishop Samuel
Wilberforce (1805–1873), a leading Anglican theologian of his day.

580.1–2   "There is . . . face."] A loose quotation from *Macbeth*, I.
iv.11–12.

584.4   "The Matter with Kansas."] See "What's the Matter with Kansas?,"
editorial by William Allen White published in the *Emporia Gazette*, August 15,
1896.

588.20   "Stone . . . make,"] Richard Lovelace, "To Althea: From Prison"
(1649), l. 25.

588.30   Jo. Miller] Joaquin Miller (1837–1913), California poet and long-
time friend of Bierce.

589.2–3   Mr. Edward Bok] Bok (1863–1930) edited the *Ladies' Home
Journal* from 1899 until his death.

595.33   Mr. Debs] Eugene V. Debs (1855–1926), labor leader and Socialist
candidate for president.

599.31   Leonard Wood] General Leonard Wood (1860–1927), military governor of Cuba (1899–1902) whose promotion to brigadier general in 1901 had been opposed by Bierce.

600.21   Altgeld] John Peter Altgeld (1847–1902), governor of Illinois (1893–97) whose political career was largely finished by his 1893 pardon of a group of anarchists convicted of murder during the Haymarket riots in Chicago on May 4, 1886.

611.20   Denis Kearney] Kearney (1847–1907) was a leader of the Workingmen's Party in San Francisco.

618.23   James F. Bowman] Bowman (d. 1882) contributed to the *Argonaut* when Bierce was writing for that weekly paper (1877–80).

623.11–12   William D. Howells] Bierce refers to Howells's two collections of ghost stories, *Questionable Shapes* (1903) and *Between the Dark and the Daylight* (1907).

623.20–21   Rudolph Block . . . Percival Pollard] Block (1870–1940), journalist and fiction writer whose work frequently appeared in *Cosmopolitan* during Bierce's tenure with that magazine (1905–09); Percival Pollard (1869–1911), editor, critic, and friend of Bierce, who wrote about Bierce in *Their Day in Court* (1909).

623.31   W. C. Morrow] Morrow (1854–1923), fiction writer and friend of Bierce. Bierce highly praised his collection of horror stories, *The Ape, the Idiot and Other People* (1897).

624.4   J. J. Owen] Owen (1827–1895), author of a column in *Better Times*, a religious magazine in San Jose, and several books on religion.

624.15   Rear-Admiral Schley . . . Charles F. Joy] Admiral Winfield Scott Schley (1839–1911), American naval commander at the Battle of Santiago, Cuba (July 3, 1898); Charles Frederick Joy (1849–1921), U.S. representative from Missouri (1893–94, 1895–1903).

624.22–23   General Miles] General Nelson Appleton Miles (1839–1925), who led the force that occupied Puerto Rico during the Spanish-American War.

624.35   Champ Clark] James Beauchamp "Champ" Clark (1850–1921), U.S. representative from Missouri (1893–95, 1897–1905).

625.32   H. H. Wotherspoon] General Harold Herbert Wotherspoon (1855–1940), president of the Army War College.

626.6   General Barry] Edmund Chaffee Barry (1854–1915), who succeeded Wotherspoon at the Army War College.

626.23   "John A. Joyce."] John Alexander Joyce (1842–1915), American poet and biographer whose work Bierce disdained.

632.31   Madame Blavatsky] See note 194.35.

632.35–37   Lillian Russell . . . Pauline Hall] Russell (1861–1922) and Hall (1860–1919) were popular singers of the day.

638.25   Sir Boyle Roche] Roche (1743–1807), Irish politician known for the flamboyance of his speeches.

642.6–7   "the glory . . . Rome."] See Edgar Allan Poe's "To Helen" (1831), ll. 9–10.

651.15–17   Buffon . . . *Nature*] Georges-Louis Leclerc, comte de Buffon (1707–1788), *L'Histoire générale des animaux* (1788–1804; completed by E. de Lacépède); Oliver Goldsmith (1730?–1774), *An History of the Earth and Animated Nature* (1774).

BITS OF AUTOBIOGRAPHY

655.11   "in which . . . afternoon."] Tennyson, "The Lotos-Eaters" (1832), l. 4.

655.15   "most immemorial year,"] Poe, "Ulalume" (1847), l. 5.

656.13   the opening lines of "The Pleasures of Hope,"] Thomas Campbell published *The Pleasures of Hope* (1799) when he was twenty-two. Its opening lines describe a mountain seen from a distance.

657.24   "the mast . . . admiral"] Milton, *Paradise Lost* (1667), 1.293–94.

657.25   "made the pile complete"] Tennyson, *In Memoriam: A. H. H.* (1850), 54.8.

658.3–4   Pursuit . . . possession.] A misquotation of "Possession" (1866), by Robert Kelley Weeks (1840–1876): "And love may be, so it seems to me, / Complete without possession."

661.19–20   "telling of the sound,"] Coleridge, *The Rime of the Ancient Mariner* (1798), l. 559.

661.33   General Johnston . . . Beauregard's army] General Albert Sidney Johnston (1803–1862), was fatally wounded during the first day of fighting at Shiloh; General Pierre Gustave Toutant Beauregard (1818–1893) was Johnston's second in command at Shiloh.

673.21   "cloud by day"] Deuteronomy 1:33.

679.18   Rosecrans] General William Starke Rosecrans (1819–1898), commander of the Army of the Cumberland.

679.23–24   Crittenden . . . McCook] General Thomas Leonidas Crittenden (1819–1893), commander of the XXI Corps; General George Henry Thomas (1816–1870), Rosecrans's second in command and commander of the XIV Corps; Alexander McDowell McCook (1831–1903), commander of the XX Corps.

680.12   "day of danger" . . . "night of waking."] See Sir Walter Scott, *The Lady of the Lake* (1810), 1.31: "Days of danger, nights of waking."

680.33   Wood's division] General Thomas John Wood (1823–1906), commander of the 1st Division, XXI Corps.

681.14   General Garfield] General James A. Garfield (1831–1881), Rosecrans's chief of staff. He later became the twentieth president of the United States (1881).

681.22   General Negley] General James Scott Neagley (1826–1901), commander of the 2nd Division, XIV Corps.

684.14   General Howard] General Oliver Otis Howard (1830–1909), commander of the IV Corps of the Army of the Cumberland.

684.31   Schofield] General John McAllister Schofield (1831–1906), commander of the XXIII Corps (also called the Army of the Ohio) in the Atlanta campaign.

684.32   (Polk)] General Leonidas Polk (1806–1864), commander of a corps in the Army of Tennessee. He was killed by an artillery shell at Pine Mountain on June 14, 1864.

685.18   Stanley] General David Sloane Stanley (1828–1902), commander of the 1st Division, IV Corps of the Army of the Cumberland.

685.28   Chancellorsville . . . Stonewall Jackson] The Battle of Chancellorsville was a Confederate victory in Virginia, May 1–4, 1863. On May 2 General Thomas Jonathan "Stonewall" Jackson led a flank attack that routed the Union XI Corps, led by Oliver Otis Howard.

685.34   Hood] General John Bell Hood (1831–1879), commander of a corps in Johnston's army.

686.22   Sheridan] General Philip Henry "Phil" Sheridan (1831–1888).

687.2   General Johnston] General Joseph Eggleston Johnston (1807–1891), commander of the Army of Tennessee during the first part of the Atlanta campaign. The quotation is from his *Narrative of Military Operations* (New York: Appleton, 1874), 328–29.

687.5   Cleburne's division . . . Hardee's corps] General Patrick Ronayne Cleburne (1828–1864), commander of one of the best fighting divisions in the Confederate Army; General William Joseph Hardee (1815–1873), commander of a corps in the Army of Tennessee in the Atlanta campaign.

687.7   General Hood . . . says:] The passage is quoted in Johnston's *Narrative of Military Operations*, 587.

687.12   Major-General Wheeler] General Joseph Wheeler (1836–1906), commander of the cavalry corps of the Confederate Army of Tennessee.

689.13–28 "The Fourth Corps . . . devotion."] Johnston, *Narrative*, 329–31.

691.20–21 General Lowry] General Mark Perrin Lowrey (1828–1885), commander of a brigade in Hardee's corps.

691.21 Colonel Baucum] George Franklin Baucum (1837–1905), commander of the 8th Arkansas Infantry Regiment.

692.7–10 "I witnessed . . . minute."] William B. Hazen, *A Narrative of Military Service* (Boston: Ticknor, 1885), 261.

692.17–19 "The Federal . . . them."] Johnston, *Narrative*, 331.

693.5 the fall of Atlanta] The Union army occupied Atlanta on September 2, 1864.

693.12 Colonel McConnell] Colonel Henry Kumler McConnell (d. 1898), acting brigade commander in the 2nd Division, XV Corps of the Army of the Tennessee, now commanded by General William B. Hazen.

696.4 Andersonville] Confederate prison camp in south-central Georgia where 13,000 Union prisoners died from disease and malnutrition, 1864–65.

697.3 O'Hara's . . . dead,"] See note 61.28.

699.22 Jeff Gatewood] John P. Gatewood led a small band of guerrillas in eastern Tennessee and northern Georgia and Alabama who killed Union soldiers, southern unionists, and Confederate deserts, while sometime robbing and terrorizing local civilians. Gatewood survived the war and moved to Texas.

702.17 Forrest's cavalry] General Nathan Bedford Forrest (1821–1877), commander of a cavalry corps that fought with the Army of Tennessee at Franklin.

702.25 Colonel P. Sidney Post] Colonel Philip Sidney Post (1833–1895) commanded the Second Brigade, Third Division of the IV Corps at Spring Hill.

703.25 Cheatham] General Benjamin Franklin Cheatham (1820–1886), commander of a Confederate corps at Spring Hill.

705.10 General Wagner] General George Day Wagner (1829–1869), commander of the Second Division of the IV Corps.

706.20 Opdycke] Colonel Emerson Opdycke (1830–1884), commander of the First Brigade, Second Division, IV Corps.

706.29 "more . . . desire."] A paraphrase of Edward FitzGerald's translation of the *Rubáiyát of Omar Khayyám* (1859), 99.4.

711.11–12 had . . . see.] Alfred Tennyson, "Lady Clara Vere de Vere" (1842), II. 31–32.

713.36–37   "enterprises . . . moment"]   See Shakespeare, *Hamlet*, III.i.84.

720.7   Scott's incomparable romance.]   Sir Walter Scott, *Kenilworth* (1821).

720.13   James Mortimer]   Mortimer (1833–1911) founded the London *Figaro* in 1870 as the official newspaper of Napoleon III's government-in-exile. The emperor was captured in 1870 during the Franco-Prussian War and, after his release, lived at Chislehurst, in Kent, until his death. He had married Eugénie de Montijo (1826–1920) in 1853.

721.2–3   M. Rochefort's famous journal, *La Lanterne.*]   Henri Rochefort (Victor Henri, Marquis de Rochefort-Luçay, 1831–1913), French periodical writer and editor of *La Lanterne* (1868–69).

722.25   escaped from New Caledonia]   Rochefort, who had publicly supported the Paris Commune, was arrested following its collapse in 1871 and deported to New Caledonia; he escaped to San Francisco on an American ship in 1874 and subsequently made his way to England.

726.2   John Bidwell]   Bidwell (1819–1900) was the author of *A Journey to California* (1842), published six years before John W. Marshall discovered gold on the estate of John August Sutter in 1848.

726.29–30   Hardee's tactics]   *Rifle and Light Infantry Tactics* (1855), the standard military manual of the period, written by William Joseph Hardee (see note 691.5).

727.11   "ancient solitary reign"]   Gray *Elegy* (1751), l. 12.

727.17–18   "reverend pile"]   Wordsworth, *The Excursion* (1814), 8.461.

727.27–28   Mayne Reid's romances]   Thomas Mayne Reid (1818–1883), Irish-American author of *The Rifle Rangers* (1850), *The Scalp Hunters* (1851), and many other adventure novels. See "A Sole Survivor" in this volume.

727.32   "great rock in a weary land."]   Isaiah 32:2.

729.14–39   "The most . . . scalp."]   Cyrus Townsend Brady, *Indian Fights and Fighters* (New York: McClure, Phillips, 1904), 14–15.

731.9   Hans Breitmann]   Hero of a series of ballads in German-American dialect written by Charles Godfrey Leland (1824–1903), collected in *The Breitmann Ballads* (1871) and other volumes.

735.27   "could not . . . were,"]   See Shakespeare, *Macbeth*, IV.iii.222.

735.34–35   "vast . . . stone."]   Shelley, "Ozymandias" (1818), l. 2.

736.10–13   like stout . . . Darien,]   Keats, "On First Looking into Chapman's Homer" (1816), ll. 11–14.

736.31   "I've done, i' faith."]   See Shakespeare, *1 Henry IV*, I.iii.259.

740.20   Jim Beckwourth]   James Pierson Beckwourth (1798–1866),

African American explorer of the American West. Bierce wrote a number of semi-fictional sketches about him in *Fun*, 1873–74.

740.21   "beated . . . antiquity."] Shakespeare, sonnet 62, l. 10.

740.29–31   our . . . order,] Byron, *Manfred* (1817) III.iv.43–45.

741.1   "we . . . company"] Byron, *The Siege of Corinth* (1816), Prologue, l. 3.

741.33   John Camden Hotten] Hotten (1832–1873) published Bierce's first book, *The Fiend's Delight*; upon his death, his publishing firm became Chatto & Windus, which published Bierce's second book, *Nuggets and Dust* (1873).

743.4–5   George Augustus Sala . . . Tom Hood, the younger] George Augustus Sala (1828–1896), British journalist; Henry Sampson (1841–1891), owner of *Fun* (1874–78); Thomas Hood the Younger (1835–1874), son of the poet Thomas Hood and editor of *Fun* and *Tom Hood's Comic Annual*.

743.8   Sir Boyle Roche] See note 643.19.

743.21   Lord Brougham] Henry, Lord Brougham (1778–1868), British politician and man of letters.

743.38   Boone May] Daniel Boone May (1852–1878), American gunfighter and a shotgun messenger for several Western express companies.

SELECTED STORIES

754.6   Macaulay's "Naseby Fight"] "The Battle of Naseby" (1824) by Thomas Babington Macaulay (1800–1859), a poem about the English Civil War.

754.21   Kinglake's "Crimean War,"] *The Invasion of the Crimea* (8 volumes, 1863–87) by Alexander William Kinglake (1809–1891).

754.22   trial of Warren Hastings] Warren Hastings (1732–1818), governor-general of India, was impeached and tried (1788–95) on grounds of corruption and cruelty; he was ultimately acquitted. The *Minutes of Evidence* of the trial were published in eleven volumes (1788). Macaulay wrote a lengthy biographical essay on him (1841).

762.15   in a story before that] Bierce refers to an earlier story of his, "The Captain of the *Camel*," first published as "A Nautical Novelty" in *Tom Hood's Comic Annual for 1875* (1875).

762.26   the *Mudlark*] "A Shipwreckollection" (first published as "The Cruise of the Mudlark," *Fun*, July 4, 1874).

764.2   *the Secretary of War*] Simon Cameron (1799–1889) served as secretary of war from March 11, 1861 to January 15, 1862, when he was replaced by Edwin M. Stanton (1814–1869).

768.35–36   "moving . . . field"]   Shakespeare, *Othello*, I.iii.135.

770.20–21   *the Confederate Secretary of War*]   Judah P. Benjamin (1811–84) served as Confederate secretary of war from September 17, 1861 to March 23, 1862.

781.3   Ahkoond of Citrusia]   The title "Ahkoond" became popular when in 1878 American poet George Thomas Lanigan (1845–86) wrote a comic poem, "A Threnody" (1878), on the "Akhoond of Swat" i.e., Abdul Ghafur (1794–1877), the Akhund (or Akhond) of Swat, a region in northwestern India (now Pakistan). "Citrusia" refers to California, with its abundant crops of citrus fruits.

782.37–38   dragons . . . in their slime.]   See note 161.34.

786.24   Smugwumps]   A play on "mugwump," a term coined in the 1830s from an Algonquin word, *mugquomp*, meaning "great man, chief, captain, leader"; used in 1884 for Republicans who refused to support their presidential candidate, James G. Blaine.

791.10   Nigger Head]   Fictitious; but in the first publication (*San Francisco Examiner*, September 16, 1888), the reading was "Nigger Tent," a way station in the Sierra Turnpike in Sierra County in central California.

791.11   road agency]   A "road agent" is a slang term for a highway robber.

792.21   Knights of Murder]   A parody of the Knights of Labor, a union initially organized by garment workers in Philadelphia. Bierce was generally hostile to labor unions.

797.10–11   fond . . . view]   See Samuel Woodworth, "The Old Oaken Bucket" (1817), ll. 1–2: "How dear to this heart are the scenes of my childhood, / When fond recollection presents them to view!"

797.21–22   Professor Davidson]   George Davidson (1825–1911), professor of geology at the University of California and author of many papers on the history and geology of California and on astronomy.

798.19   Ol. can.]   Not *oleum cannabis* (oil of hemp; a greenish oil used as a demulcent and protective), but *oleum canis*.

803.1–2   lets . . . all!]   Alexander Pope, *The Dunciad* (rev. ed. 1742–43), 4.655–56.

806.40   Richard A. Proctor]   Richard Anthony Proctor (1837–1888), British writer on mathematics, astronomy, and other subjects. Bierce may be referring to his book, *Chance and Luck: A Discussion of the Laws of Luck, Coincidences, Wagers, Lotteries, and the Fallacies of Gambling* (1887).

807.14   Keeley]   Apparently a reference to a charlatan named John Ernst Worrell Keely (1827–1898), who proposed to build a motor powered "from intermolecular vibrations of ether" and fraudulently sold many shares of stock to fund the Keely Motor Company.

811.10–33   "Wealth . . . food."]   From Thomas Carlyle's "Characteristics" (1831); quoted by Bierce in "Prattle" (*San Francisco Examiner*, July 6, 1890).

811.38–39   That . . . great.]   The lines are by Bierce.

817.25   Hohokus]   Actually Ho-Ho-Kus, a town in northeastern New Jersey.

825.29–30   "the voice . . . God."]   *Vox populi vox Dei*. The earliest recorded expression of the utterance occurs in Alcuin's letter to Charlemagne (c. 800 C.E.).

834.33–34   "Against . . . powerless."]   "Mit die Dummheit kämpfen Götter selbst vergebens." From *Die Jungfrau von Orleans* (1801), act 3, scene 6, by Friedrich von Schiller (1759–1805).

THE LIBRARY OF AMERICA SERIES

The Library of America fosters appreciation and pride in America's literary heritage by publishing, and keeping permanently in print, authoritative editions of America's best and most significant writing. An independent nonprofit organization, it was founded in 1979 with seed funding from the National Endowment for the Humanities and the Ford Foundation.

To subscribe to the series or to order individual copies, please visit www.loa.org or call (800) 964.5778.

*This book is set in 10 point Linotron Galliard,
a face designed for photocomposition by Matthew Carter
and based on the sixteenth-century face Granjon. The paper
is acid-free lightweight opaque and meets the requirements
for permanence of the American National Standards Institute.
The binding material is Brillianta, a woven rayon cloth made
by Van Heek-Scholco Textielfabrieken, Holland. Composition by Dedicated Book Services. Printing by
Malloy Incorporated. Binding by Dekker Book-
binding. Designed by Bruce Campbell.*

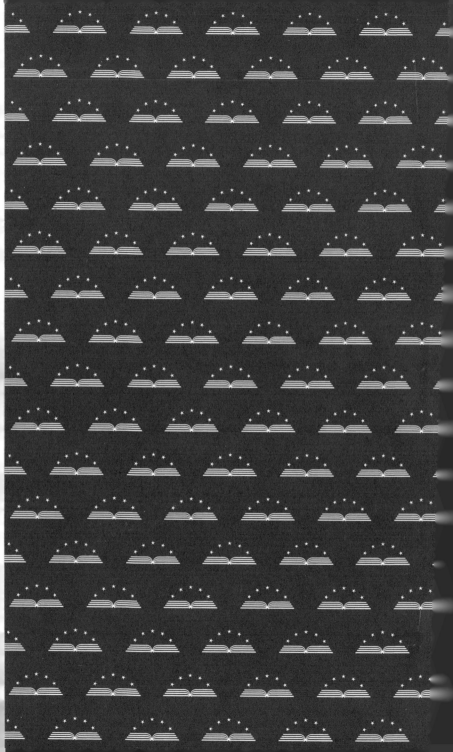